Planet of the Orange-red Sun

Series Volume 10

Guilds, Genetics, and Gods

Planet of the Orange-red Sun Series

Volume 10 Guilds, Genetics, and Gods

by Vic Broquard

http://www.Broquard-ebooks.com
Broquard eBooks
103 Timberlane
East Peoria, IL 61611
author@Broquard-eBooks.com

Artwork by Crooked Willow Studios.

For Morgan and L. Ron Hubbard

Table of Contents

Part III The Return of Order

Part I The Rise

Chapter 1 The Beginnings

Jacques the Contortionist cautiously unzipped the suitcase shipping crate in which he had folded his lean, flexible body. He'd carefully counted the computerized drone signals, marking his crate's passage into the bowels of the baggage system of the spaceport on Aquila Prime. Timing was critical for this theft. Jacques accepted this mission, primarily because of its challenge, but also for the credits. An hour from now, if all went well, he could retire to the pleasure planet of Vegas-3. For a moment, images of the many enticements offered by this planet flooded his mind. Quickly, he forced himself back to the job at hand.

All shipping crates entering or leaving on one of the many spaceships were effectively handled by the ususal Imperium Baggage Systems. Like nearly everything else in the vast Imperium, the handling of baggage was fully automated, controlled by the many computers of the spaceport. Giant connecting conveyors transported one's crates from the check-in counter to the baggage compartment of the destination ship or vice versa. Tons of crates passed through this system daily, countless billions, if one considered all the many Imperium spaceports. A computer-readable tag on each crate controlled its path through the gigantic underground maze of the baggage system. Additionally, when the crate was checked in, its weight was added to the tag, allowing the computer system an infallible way to track each specific crate, and thus guaranteeing that the right crate arrived at the right destination. Along the way, the crate's ID tag and its weight were checked at each junction, avoiding any chance of mis-routing or substitution. No human intervention was needed. That is, unless a mechanical breakdown occurred.

At the tenth drone signal, indicating the passage through another junction and indicating that again, the crate's tag was read and its weight calculated, Jacques had acted. He climbed out of the crate and carefully stepped off the horizontal conveyor and began walking. He soon spotted the substitute crates precisely where he had been told they would be waiting for him. Now, he took out his hand-held scanner, preprogrammed with the ID tag of the crate that he was to steal. As the nearly uniform crates came moving along the conveyor, he scanned them. Quite why this particular crate was worth ten million credits to his unnamed benefactor was unknown to Jacques. He'd not asked and was not told, only that this last theft would allow him to retire.

This section was chosen because it was the longest haul between junctions. At last, he spotted the innocuous crate, double-checking its ID tag. He lifted the twenty pound crate off the conveyor and opened it up. Carefully, he removed the secondary, sealed container crate. His orders had been very explicit. If he opened this secondary crate, he would be killed. Hastily, he swapped the replacement secondary crate back into the original one, noticing that it too weighed an identical twenty pounds. After resealing it, he lifted it back onto the conveyor. The computer would take this one dutifully to its destination. Now came the hard part. He quickly put on the maintenance worker's uniform that was in the other crate stored here for him. Then, he placed the remainder of the contents back into his original suitcase, zipping it up and storing it into the shipping container. A minute later, the crate in which he'd arrived continued merrily on its way to the baggage claim center, taking the stolen twenty-pound crate and enough sand to match his weight. As instructed, he placed everything else into the remaining container crate and sent it on its way as well.

Quietly, he began to follow the map of how to get out of the Baggage System. According to the instructions, at the maintenance bay, he would find yet another change of clothes. Once he'd donned the suit, he would make his way to the baggage claim center, pick up his crate that contained the stolen crate, and head out to the shuttle taxi area. There the exchange would be made, and he would be on his way to retirement, a luxury retirement at that!

The map led him to a maintenance building. As he stepped inside, he spotted the crate that contained his new suit. Hastily, he changed clothes once again. As he was tied up doing so, a man dressed in black stepped out of the shadows. He held an ancient handgun. The silencer guaranteed that the only noise was a soft popping sound. Three rapid pops and Jacques was officially "retired." The man in black stuffed the body into another shipping crate, piled all manner of equipment and junk over the crate, hiding it from view, and then stepped quietly out of the building. The man in black made sure that no one was around before he moved silently on down the corridor, entering the maintenance worker's restroom. Here, he changed clothes. Two minutes later, he stepped out, dressed in a business suit and carrying a small, aluminum briefcase, in which his black clothing and sneakers were now stored.

Ten minutes later, he picked up his "shipping crate" at the baggage claim center, flashing the proper ID card, which he'd taken from Jacques. Ten more minutes passed before he entered the shuttle transport or taxi center. Here, he climbed into a shuttle, swiped his ID card, and punched in the destination coordinates. The door shut, and the automated shuttle craft lifted gently off of the ground. An hour later, it settled down at the arrival entrance of the Ritz Hotel in Central City of Aquila Prime. He walked into the giant lobby, amid the fountains and shining lights. Dozens of well-dressed men and women were lounging around the lobby. Some were playing cards; some were watching the holo-screens, and others were chatting.

As he entered, another man in a business suit spotted him, rose, and picked up an identical silver briefcase. The two men soon reached each other, seemingly not noticing the other. Each put their briefcase down and consulted their cell phones. Then, each picked up their briefcase. However, they took each other's case. The original man in black now headed back out of the fancy hotel and took another shuttle back to the spaceport. Later, the Central City News carried a report of a shuttle explosion that occurred, killing one unknown businessman.

Farid Hamal smiled. He'd taken the briefcase up to his room and checked its contents. Sure enough, the small twenty pound shipping crate was intact. Its seal had not been broken.

The label said Aquila Prime Genetics Research Laboratory. The thirty year old Farid smiled again. The network of contacts had been nicely eliminated. His role was to deliver this package to his boss, the Holy Father Janos of the True Believers, a splinter sect of the Holy Lords, one of the more wide spread religious orders among the planets of the vast Imperium.

He stowed the precious crate into his own luggage crates and checked out of the Ritz Hotel. Two hours later, Farid was safely on his way back to his home base on Echo-4 and his Holy Father Janos. Upon arrival, he bowed respectfully and entered the elder man's private room in the Church of the Holy Lords. "I trust it all went well, Prelate Farid?" the sixty year old man asked solemnly.

"As planned, Your Eminence. Will that be all?" Farid asked, noting his new, elevated position within the church. It was and he left. Father Janos opened the crate, inspected its contents. Satisfied, he placed a secure call to Jan Rumani on Zon-2.

Jan was the grandson of the late Bindaz Rumani, founder of Mal Dynamics and a member of the Consortium some years ago. After the mysterious death of Bindaz, for a decade, Mal Dynamics remained a splintered corporation. Now, Jan had once more united the separate units and reinstated the original company logo, Mal Dynamics. This giant corporation made motors for everything from spaceships to giant earthmoving equipment. Jan's father had overseen the diverse smaller corporations, but upon his death three years ago, Jan had once more reformed the original giant industry into one unified whole, just as it had been in the years of his grandfather. Credits, it's said, can buy you anything. Jan was a living testimonial to that saying and in more ways than one.

Rare earth elements were needed in the EM engines that Mal Dynamics manufactured. These represented the most costly portion of engine construction and one that Jan had been working to eliminate. Last year, he'd found the answer that he needed. The answer lay on Aquila Prime, a highly developed world of some ten billion.

Vast new deposits of all the rare elements that were

needed for EM motor constructions had recently been discovered in the Atlas Mountains. The President of Aquila Prime had already made overtures to Mal Dynamics, hoping to market their newfound deposits. However, he was asking far too high a price. If Jan didn't pay the exorbitant rates, their President threatened to sell them to his competitors. That was a risk Jan could not accept and which had led to this very day.

Jan looked at the labeling on the cylinder. In large block, red letters, it read: Dangerous Genetic Biological Agent. Jan smiled. He held one of the half-full cylinders of the bio weapon that had been invented many years ago during the ill-fated war with the Federation of Planets. This very nasty biological weapon was widely known throughout the Imperium here in 1325. Many years ago, terrorists had first used it on the Imperium Senate on Proxima Prime, followed shortly after that on the President and other very wealthy men and women who were attending an opera performance. Since that time, various other terrorists had also used it on other groups on other planets. Further, the Imperium Senate had and was still using it on all the hardened criminals, drastically reducing the cost of incarceration of Imperium criminals.

This was a very nasty genetic weapon, which, within a week of exposure, drastically re-engineered the human body. It turned men and women into hermaphrodites. Yes, each had fully working male and female organs, and any individual could even breed themselves. But this was the least of the bio agent's effects. The victims developed massive breasts, the size of basketballs. Their waists reduced to barely a foot around, while their pelvis regions enlarged and now held displaced organs. They were forced to wear severe pipe corsets to help their backs support the massive weight of their enormous breasts. The victim's lips were split forcing them to have to wear a pair of foot in diameter lip plates, severely impacting their speech. Only Imperium Standard could be partially understood when spoken by these victims, to say nothing of eating and drinking difficulties. Their hair thickened and grew to about five feet in length and could not be cut shorter. Any such attempt caused massive pain to the victims, plus their cut hair regrew rapidly to its original length.

Even more debilitating, their feet became malformed into a super-high arch. Only their toes were able to lie flat on the floor. Their heels were high above them, forcing them to wear toe shoes in which their tall spiked heels were barely behind their toes on the floor, making walking exceptionally difficult. However, the worst genetic modification of this bio agent was the victim's loss of arms. Within a week of exposure, their arms withered and dropped off as dried-out husks, turning the victims into helpless men and women. While this was intentional in the case of criminals, whose lives of crime were ended, with the other victims, the effects of this nasty biological-genetic agent were horrific.

In the case of the senators and other wealthy nobles, a genetic modification had been discovered that re-grew their lost arms. That breakthrough in genetics was attributed to Doctors Alex and Ruth Hammil, living on Ashford-5, who had also been victims of the bio agent. Even so, the re-growth process was an expensive one, costing ten thousand credits per person. While the original groups of victims had their arms regrown, the exorbitant cost had precluded many other victims during the past two decades.

After the initial bio attacks on the Senate and the opera house, extreme measures were put in place to keep the remaining samples of this horrific biological weapon secure. However, in the ensuing two plus decades, many other genetic research facilities demanded access to the bio agent. Everyone wanted in on the genetic research and genetic studies of this revolutionary bio agent. Although in general human experimentation had been forbidden, slowing down all further attempts to devise a cure for the many victims, the Imperium Senate did allow a few criminal volunteers, who were sentenced to life, to volunteer to become human guinea pigs. However, after many died horribly during the genetic experiments, not even these desperate men volunteered these days, preferring to accept the bio agent modifications. At least they were alive.

Still, many geneticists throughout the Imperium wanted samples to study. This was the arena of security breaches. Originally, a sample of this bio agent weapon had been stolen from one of the research labs. Using the Fabrication Machine, that lone cylinder was duplicated many times over these past many years. Various enforcement agencies had very nearly stamped out all of these, though that had not stopped various terrorist organizations from duplicating and using the bio agent in their attacks. Security was gargantuan around these many genetic research labs. For two decades, no samples had been stolen from any of these research labs. They were impossible to break into these days.

Jan, however, had found their weak link: transportation. Samples had to be sent to the research facilities. He'd carefully worked out the theft of one such shipment to the Aquila Prime Genetics Research Laboratory. His plan had worked to perfection. True, by now the authorities would have discovered the sand that had replaced the cylinder. Their investigations would lead nowhere. The contortionist was dead, as was his immediate contact. Nothing would lead them to suspect him. Jan smiled, and personally carried the crate into his own research laboratory.

Here, Jan made good use of his corporation's Fabrication Machine. It was Sunday, and only his security guards were onsite, making this an easy process. After stacking up one hundred of the duplicate cylinders, he made another couple of dozen and stashed them away in his personal safe. Next, he carefully covered all of the bio hazard warning labels on the cylinders. Using a cart, he ferried them into his experimental aviation laboratory. His new drone was sleek and constructed from the latest polymers, making the stealth ship invisible to conventional spaceship detection methods, such as radar. All RFI ID tags had been removed as well. Nothing on the ship could be traced back to him or to his corporation.

Hours later, his hands aching from manual labor, Jan had the hundred cylinders hooked into the delivery lines and mounted securely to the stealth drone. Next, he rolled the heavy drone over to his personal transport ship and attached it to tether lines beneath it. Then, he rolled a second drone, a duplicate of the first, out of its hiding place, positioning it where the original had sat. Sweat poured down his face; his synthetic unisex cat suit was soaking. *I'm really out of shape,* he thought to himself, catching his breath while leaning against the second drone. *Still, I dare not trust this to any of my regular employees. The fewer who know, the safer I'll be.*

Some minutes later, he double-checked everything. Satisfied, he changed his soiled cat suit and tossed the old one into the recycling bin. He then checked on the time. He still had an hour before he was scheduled to lift off in his transport for Winno-3 and a meeting of one of his subsidiary companies there. Jan boarded his deep space transport and fired up the electronic controls of his drone CPU. After verifying all was working properly, he turned it off and made his preparations for departure. A heavy conveyor hauled his deep space transport out of his laboratory and positioned it for takeoff from his private spaceport. Right on schedule, he punched in the first set of coordinates and contacted the Zon-2 Spaceport.

"Jan Rumani requesting flight clearance for Transport 14598," he spoke clearly.

A moment later, the tower replied, "Transport 14598 is cleared for takeoff to Winno-3." Jan smiled; this was just too darn easy! A moment later, he was airborne and jumped into hyperspace. There, he entered a second set of coordinates and activated them. His scheduled flight to Winno-3 would take nearly twenty-four hours. Zon-2 was located in the hub of the galaxy, while Winno-3, part of the Ataro Empire, was about halfway down the spiral arm. To get there so quickly, he would have to burn his entire load of fuel, but such was expected for the head of Mal Dynamics. His intermediate target, Aquila Prime, was also in this mid-section. Satisfied all was going according to his plan, he took a shower and changed into his business suit. After dining, he took a nap.

As the ship dropped out of hyperspace, the computer signaled the resting corporate executive. Jan smiled and headed for the control center. After verifying his location, many miles above Aquila Prime, a blue-white globe, he fired up the drone's control system. He triple checked the drone's program. Then, he activated it. The tether lines dropped, and gas thrusters pushed the drone away from the transport ship. Once clear, it fired its main engines. Jan monitored its flight for several more minutes. At last, he received confirmation the drone was not only in a high orbit above Aquila Prime, but also its programming opened the valves, releasing the bio agent into the atmosphere of the planet. Jan activated his nav system and jumped back into hyperspace. Thus far, he had stayed sufficiently distant from Aquila Prime that he had not been detected. Hours later, he landed on Winno-3 and was met by Mal Dynamics personnel, who were pleased to welcome this unusual visit by their CEO.

Meanwhile, the drone continued to circle Aquila Prime in an ever-changing orbit, ensuring an even spread of the bio agent over the entire planet's surface. An hour later, the cylinders were exhausted. The drone's programming terminated the flight by purposely flying into the side of a mountainside. Simultaneously, an explosion triggered a massive fire, melting the remains of the ship. If others investigated the crash site, there would be little they could learn about the drone's origins.

That ten billion men, women, and children were about to suffer a horrific biological-genetic attack, which would likely result in their deaths, was of little concern to Jan Rumani. True, he was sacrificing a Mal Dynamics plant on Aquila Prime, but plants could easily be restaffed. Besides, he didn't know many people from this world. Overpopulation was a major problem on many of the hub worlds. Once the indigenous population died off and the danger of contagion passed, the world could easily be resettled, handling the overpopulation situation on many other worlds. The Imperium Senate would certainly work to that end. Jan's conscience was clear, as he met with the executives at his plant on Winno-3. He was ready for the next step in his grand plan to acquire the vital rare earth resources his enterprise needed and at very little cost. That this was the first planetary test of the effectiveness of this bio-genetic weapon was also not lost on Jan. For his part, he was content to let others stake their claim to this test.

The invisible airborne attack struck the planet uniformly, but the consequences varied widely between the day and night portions of the world. Initial symptoms were mostly those of a great fatigue. An hour after that, one by one, the population dropped into coma, lasting for three to five days, on the average. Those who were lucky were in bed. On the daylight side, all manner of secondary catastrophes followed, because the victims dropped into comas wherever they were. The thousands of shuttles and spaceships in the air were all under computer control and eventually reached their destinations, landing automatically, though their comatose passengers remained onboard.

Rather other disasters occurred on the daylight side. Many were caused by kitchen fires that blazed up, when those manning them dropped to the floor. Sporadic fires broke out, but there were no firemen to put them out. Whole sections of towns and cities burned. Construction crews dropped into comas, while their machines continued on their way, plowing through houses and businesses, like vicious wild beasts on a chaotic rampage. Elevators stopped at their last entered floors. Conveyor systems, in such wide spread usage, piled up their cargos forming mountains of people, shipping crates, supplies, and materials. Men and women dropped onto the floors of the buildings they were in; children slumped over their school desks. Worse, those undergoing operations in the many hospitals were left partially handled, when doctors and nurses drifted into their own forms of unconsciousness. Those on foot merely dropped where they walked, some falling down stairs to a merciful death.

Those who were safely in bed on the dark side of Aquila Prime fared the best, at least initially. Besides being in bed when they entered their comas, they were not wearing much clothing. For those fully dressed on the daylight side, the genetic effects on their bodies were particularly bad. As their massive breasts grew and their feet deformed, their clothing and shoes began to interfere with the process. At least with their tops, the fabrics soon burst, but their shoes merely crushed their altering feet, snapping bones, as their bodies tried to follow the new genetic blueprints for their feet, rendering them wholly unable to stand or walk.

Newscasts credited Captain Hans Jurgens with the initial discovery of the attack. Piloting his freighter, the Lone Star, he dropped out of hyperspace and contacted the tower for automatic docking permissions and controls. Silence. "I tried to contact the tower a dozen times!" he exclaimed to the reporter on the nightly news some days later. "Then I headed to my secondary landing site. No one answered there either." He related how he had tried to contact any of the dozen other spaceports scattered across the three continents of Aquila Prime. Only then did he attempt a blind landing. "Mind you, I just descended carefully, knowing something was wrong. That's when I saw them. Dead men lying everywhere on the tarmac. I lifted back off and contacted Winno-3 for help."

Later, an Imperium Space Fleet from Winno-3 arrived and discovered the planet had suffered a worldwide bio agent attack. The fleet estimated their arrival was on the fourth day of the victims' comas. It was these men who discovered the deadly bio agent was responsible and quarantined the world. Days later, news crews arrived, filming the disaster, but staying well above the surface. Thus, the Imperium at large learned of this most deadly attack in Imperium history. Ten billion were infected. Those still alive awoke utterly helpless.

Because of the sporadic terrorist attacks of the past two decades, most major worlds had some HasMat prepared units ready to deal with such bio attacks. However, no one was prepared to have an entire world infected. Even as the victims were beginning to regain consciousness, the Imperium began acting. Imperium President Len Digmar and his six Legates held a combined meeting with the Imperium Senate, with Senate President Elato Plat presiding over the several thousand senators.

"How do we handle ten billion infected people?" President Len asked. He'd outlined briefly what little was known about the disaster, now hoping and praying the Senate would be able to answer what he could not. A near riotous hour followed with many venting their dismay and anger that something of this magnitude could have ever been allowed to happen. Many wanted to know the current state of counter-genetic experiments. Was there any hope that a full cure was at hand? This President Len could answer. "I'm sorry. To date, there is no cure beyond re-growth of arms at ten thousand credits per person."

Senator Ames spoke up. "The solution is clear. We must have every known world accept their fair share of the victims. The only way they can live is in assisted living facilities. Hence, we should have each world accept their share. Ten billion divided by a thousand or so leaves about ten million per world. Surely, we can handle this many."

"But who will pay for the care of ten billion?" another senator protested.

Legate Marhildt Chyldt spoke up. He was in charge of the Imperium Financial Affairs. Although he was eighty-one, he looked fifty years younger, compliments of the Rejuvenation Machine. "I've been in touch with several major corporate heads. We agree. The assets of the entire world can be calculated. Aquila Prime can be resettled by reducing the overpopulation on other worlds, and they can donate more credits to the fund. The infrastructure, the buildings — all these are fundamentally intact. Mal Dynamics, for example, has already offered to take over mining operations, donating profits to the fund. I'm sure other corporations will follow suit. In short, senators, I believe each survivor will have sufficient funds available to pay for their long term assisted living."

"But how do we move ten billion people?" another senator asked.

Legate II-cubed, or rather Helyeon H. Hoon of Broom-5, replied to this one. He was a victim of the second attack well over twenty years ago. He'd had his arms regrown, accepting his fate. As always, he coveted being in the nightly news as frequently as possible. These days, he often voiced rather radical views towards the terrorists. "We must send in mass transport ships, along with volunteer care givers. I propose each batch of transport ships stops at the recipient planet first and load up on temporary care givers. Then, they arrive on Aquila Prime and go door-to-door acquiring their quota of victims. Once they have rescued them, the mass transports return to the designated world, letting the officials of that world take over from there. Simple. However, we'll need an on-site Fabrication Machine. Each victim will need apparel and shoes. I've discussed this with our Resource Minister, Legate Dalag Mulack. Such a ship can be in orbit over Aquila

Prime within three days, assuming Senate approval."

By the end of the day, the President and the Senate were in agreement on the rescue operation details and passed the required legislation to implement it. However, days would pass before the first of these mass transport ships could make landfall. In the meantime, beyond extinguishing the fires, rescue operations were simply not carried out. Anyone still living was in dire need of assistance. The several hundred Imperium soldiers and fire fighters could do nothing of consequence. After all, what was a hundred versus ten billion? They had no choice but to ignore the wailing and pleading of those victims, whom they encountered, as they secured the critical complexes, such as the spaceport control towers.

While a human being can survive many days without food, lack of water became the mass killer of the population of Aquila Prime. By the time the first mass transport ship arrived to take the first thousand to another world, where the victims could receive the care they needed, many days had passed. Dead bodies were more frequently found than the living! The soldiers organized a systematic, but massive, door-to-door plan of action, one that would eventually visit each and every building on the world. Still, in the end, the would-be rescuers found dead corpses predominating. When the mammoth search was finished, the official tally consisted of barely a hundred thousand rescued men, women, and children. Mass cremations became the major operation, thankfully carried out primarily by the military.

The lack of survivors allowed the Senate to revise drastically the number of victims per planet in the Imperium. Many planets were already overpopulated; these were not asked to accept any. A limit of one thousand per planet was enforced, so none would become overburdened. Only one hundred fifty worlds ended up taking in some of the Aquila Prime victims. Most were mid-arm and rim planets, avoiding the overpopulated hub planets.

Aria and Backus Acronis were twenty-two year old Academy students. Married for the last year, she was a history major, while he was studying to become a civil engineer. Like all those on Aquila Prime, their skin was yellowish; their hair was flaming red, and their eyes, hazel. They lived in the married dorms of Heirdonus Academy along with many other young couples. In another year, they would both graduate. Already they had made plans to move to Athena Way, where Aria was born, and to search for employment there. Aria expected to become a teacher. They snuggled together that fateful night, when the bio agent attack occurred. Both slipped into comas while they slept.

Five days later, both awoke, screaming at the top of their lungs. Dried husks of their arms lay beside their genetically modified bodies, as they struggled to sit up, stricken with utter panic. They'd heard of similar bio agent attacks on other worlds, seen images of the other victims on the nightly newscasts. Both knew analytically they'd become victims of yet another attack, but reactively, neither could stem their sheer panic. No one ever expected the peaceful world of Aquila Prime to be targeted.

One can scream only so long before either passing out from fright or from sinking further down the emotional tones. Their unanswered screams of terror gave way to intense grief. Sobbing, both struggled with their malformed bodies just to sit up in their bed. Aria cried out, "I have to go to the bathroom!" Unfortunately, neither could understand what she was saying. Their lip loops prevented the sound formation of most words of their native language.

Backus remembered something from the newscasts. "We have to use Imperial Standard. Remember? That's what they said on the news — the only way the victims could be understood."

Aria repeated her plea in IS. Quickly, the two found by helping each other they were able to remove each other's undergarments. Trying to stand with only their toes on the floor was so wild, that by the time they reached their bathroom, both broke into hysterical laughter. "This is almost impossible!" she exclaimed, sitting down on the toilet. "You look like one of those penguins in the zoo, Backus."

"Not funny! Hurry up. I have to go too!"

After he used the toilet, Aria nervously proclaimed,

"Backus, I don't want to die — not like this!"

"Dear, we won't die. Help will come. We should press the emergency button in the comm center. Help will come to us, just like it did for the Imperium senators," Backus suggested. "Come on; let's get to the comm center and call for help." Together, wobbling wildly, the two made it into their study, where their textbooks and notes were scattered. Both had been cramming for final exams before they'd gone to bed. Backus finally used his nose to depress the emergency button, which glowed red, signaling that it was activated. They lived in the married couples' dorms and expected help would soon arrive. After all, hundreds of married couples were housed here. Both sat naked on their couch waiting patiently for aid to come. It didn't.

For a time, both looked at each other's malformed bodies. Their flaming red hair had both thickened, filled out substantially, and greatly lengthened, reaching to their ankles, much to his dismay. Both had basketball-sized breasts, shocking both, though he more than she. Their backs ached from trying to support the unfamiliar weight. Their lips were slit forming two giant, dangling loops. Their feet were malformed, but that they already had experienced. Rather, both were staring in total disbelief at their new sexual organs. "I've got yours," Aria whispered. Backus had never been so embarrassed in his entire life and couldn't say anything.

Meanwhile, both experienced a ravenous hunger and intense thirst. At last, Backus suggested, "We've got to get something to drink and eat. Come on; maybe if we work together, we can do this."

"But how, Backus? We're helpless," Aria wailed. Her stomach knotted, realizing no help was coming quickly.

Somehow, the two managed to get to their small kitchen. Using their feet, they were able to move the cold water, lever-controlled faucet. Only with difficulty were they able to twist and turn to get their mouths beneath the running water and thus quench their thirst. After that tiny success, they began to work together to get something they could eat. Their pantry was well stocked, if only they had hands with which to cook. Their electric can opener saved the day, and Aria swore

16

never to be without one ever again.

With their large lip loops, eating was challenging. Soon, they worked out a way to feed each other using their feet and a fork or spoon. Hours passed before they were full of cold soups. They headed back to their study and comm center. Again, using their noses and feet, they managed to get the viewer activated and sat back to listen to the news. Of course, by now the off-world networks were covering nothing but the bio attack on Aquila Prime. The news the pair heard was disheartening. Their whole world was infected, ten billion people.

"Backus, no one is going to come to rescue us! There's no one who can!" Aria wailed, breaking down yet again.

"We must be patient and survive until help comes, Aria my love. They said the Imperium Senate will be sending mass transport ships and rescue personnel," he tried to console her, but failed utterly.

"Ten billion, Backus. They'll never get to us."

"We are going to survive, my love; we have to, somehow," Backus countered, trying to keep his own terror at bay. "We have a lot of food and water. We can wait. Help will come."

They had no way of contacting their other married friends in the adjoining complexes. Try as they might, they could not figure out how to unlock and open their front door. Still, these two were very lucky. They were youthful and with the good sense to help each other. Of the hundred thousand who survived until help came to them, most were young married couples. Most all these survivors had strong wills to live, a factor that cannot be emphasized enough.

Days stretched into weeks. With each day, the pair grew stronger and continued to invent more ways to accomplish simple tasks, primarily dealing with food preparation, feeding each other, and handling hygienic needs. They kept the news monitor on continually. After all, that took no effort on their part. A month after they regained consciousness help finally arrived. Someone knocked on their front door.

"Help! We're inside. Bust it down! We can't unlock it," Backus yelled in Imperium Standard. After a crashing noise,

Aria and Backus saw the welcome faces of two men and a woman peering inside their front door. Help had finally come.

"Are you two all right? Any others in here besides you?" one man asked.

"No, just us. We need help," Backus pleaded.

"That's what we are here for," the woman explained. "We've brought you clothing and shoes. We've got helpers at the mass transport to assist you with everything. You will be taken to an assisted living center right away. Relax, you are now in good hands. Come on; let's get you bathed and clothed properly."

Two hours later, they were finally dressed properly. Both wore panties and a rigid pipe corset, which finally relieved their back aches caused by the sheer weight of their massive breasts. They didn't even comment on how hard breathing now was, so relieved from the constant back pain. They wore a satin gown that was more like a sack without sleeves. Walking was easier in their new toe shoes, though only slightly. Both now wore the giant lip plates, which prevented their lip loops from catching on things. At Aria's request, their flaming red hair was tied into ponytails, though their hair still nearly touched their ankles. Both found this was far more manageable.

With a helper supporting them, they finally walked slowly out of their dorm complex into the sunshine of a new day. They were assisted into a waiting shuttle and taken to the giant mass transport ship. There, they spotted some of their married friends who had also survived.

Fifty couples were brought onboard before the ship's captain spoke to everyone. "Okay, it's time to get going. You are being transported to new assisted living accommodations on Ashford-5. Per the Senate and Legate's orders, the total assets of Aquila Prime will be divided up among the survivors. I assure you that you will have more than enough credits to help you get by without any monetary worries. Sit back and relax. The trip will take about thirty-six hours."

Aria insisted they sit next to their dearest friends, Alexia and Hermes Anias. He was studying to become a computer technician, while she was a mathematician. Both were the same age as Aria and Backus and had lived in the next-door dorm complex. Alexia gushed, "Have you heard the news estimates? They are guessing that only a hundred thousand of us survived the attack! Out of ten billion! My god, Aria, that's staggering!"

Hermes interjected, "Hey, the good news is all of us in the married dorms made it out alive! That's what I call a miracle. Glad you both made it!"

"I've never been so scared in all my life, but we had to live," Aria admitted.

"Same with all of us, I expect," Hermes replied. He added, "But the Holy Lords proved the bio-genetic weapon of mass destruction does work. Too bad it was on us and not some Federation planet years ago during the war."

"Still, Hermes, ten billion people dead. That's genocide, not war," Aria countered.

"I hope they kill every one of those damned Holy Lords people. They are worse than animals," Alexia declared.

"Say, does anyone know anything about where they're taking us? Where is Ashford-5 anyway? I've never heard of that star system," Backus asked.

All three shrugged their shoulders. However, one of their many assistants called out, "It's in the far outer rim. I think it must be a rather primitive world since it is a Closed World, but it's part of the Ataro Empire of the Twelve Sacred Planets of the Wasp. So it can't be all that bad. They are limiting each welcoming planet to taking in only a thousand refugees. This way, you won't be overloading their assisted living complexes. Ashford-5 is only being given you fifty though, since it is a more primitive world. But don't worry. I'm told this is where Doctors Ruth and Alex Hammil live and work. They are famous for developing the arm regrowth process."

"Wow! Sounds like we are going to the right place," Hermes declared, very much relieved. Until that last bit, he was growing more and more worried about being sent to a primitive, Closed World. At last, he and the others began to relax. From the newscasts, they knew about this famous pair of geneticists.

After chatting with their friends for an hour, Aria finally asked, "Does anyone know why the Holy Lords wanted to wipe out all of us on Aquila Prime? We've never done anything to them that I've ever heard of. Why us? Why kill ten billion men, women, and children? Does anyone know why they did this to us?" Blank stares greeted her eyes.

Alexia volunteered, "A better question to ask is how did the Imperium authorities allow these mass murders to get their hands on this terrible biological weapon? It must have taken a whole lot of it to have wiped out our world."

Aria replied, "According to all I know, Alexia, is that, after the attacks on the Imperium Senate and opera house on Proxima Prime, they surrounded all that stuff with the tightest security imaginable! So I suppose your question is a good one."

Hermes added, "Hey, you all know there've been quite a few random biological attacks throughout the Imperium during the two decades since those first two. It's just this time, they went after a whole planet. I want to know why. I agree with Aria. Why were we attacked? I can see no point to it at all."

"Unless the overpopulated planets of the hub were behind it," Alexia countered. "I wouldn't be surprised to discover they banded together to wipe us out, so they could resettle their excess populations on what's left of our world. Hell, they've got a whole world that's fully developed — everything is fine, except where the fires damaged a few buildings. All they have to do is move in. Even our spring crops have already been planted." She sounded quite bitter.

"Well, we can move back once we get our arms regrown," Hermes countered. "Then we can set things to right."

Backus pointed out soberly, "I heard on the news they are not planning to regrow our arms. Too expensive. Ten thousand credits per person. Times a hundred thousand of us — oh hell, Alexia, what does that come too?"

"A billion credits," Alexia replied with a sigh. "Who could afford that much?"

"Well maybe we can," Backus suggested. "If we truly do

get compensation from what's left of our world, we each can afford the price." Aria flashed him a relieved smile.

"Don't count on seeing any of that money anytime soon. You know bureaucracies. It may be years and years before we see any of those supposed credits," Hermes added in a hostile manner, gritting his teeth and frowning.

"But we can't live like this," Aria protested.

"Do we have a choice?" Alexia put in very antagonistically. All fifty knew they didn't and that they were at the mercy of the bureaucracy and their assisted living helpers — now and into the foreseeable future! Quite sobering.

"Damn everyone!" Hermes declared. His sentiments were echoed among all the others. However, Aria had a new thought. She recalled how she had been feeling emotionally this past month. From stark terror, she'd dropped into a profound grief. But necessity had forced her and Backus to fight back. She'd risen to anger and pain. Now she felt positively antagonistic, bitchy even, though she dare not show that to her much needed assistants just now. *In a way,* she thought, *I do feel better. Helpless still, but I feel better. Life is about to become one of complete and utter boredom. All I can do is sit around and do nothing. If we could just get our arms back. . .*

Chapter 2 Arrivals

May of 1325 became a pivotal time around the Imperial Castle in Exchange City on Tierra or Ashford-5. Things were complicated, growing more so with each passing year. Tierra had entered this new century as the thirty-seventh planet in the Ataro Empire of the Twelve Sacred Planets of the Wasp. It had been the only way that Queen Amy Valen Gervasi Bellweather was able to keep Ashford-5 as a Closed World. The Imperium had been hellbent on opening up the world and putting the many telepaths to work throughout the vast Imperium. Only with the clever manipulations of Amy and Emperor Kino Sango had they been able to retain their Closed World status. Both the emperor and Amy knew this was absolutely vital. The Imperium would only exploit their telepaths. Yet, this meant Amy had to become an official Ataro Queen with all the physical restraints that accompanied her exalted status and abilities.

The armless Queen Amy presided over Tierra's Supreme Court. Her task was somehow to maintain peace and prosperity among the many kingdoms, rulers, and fractions. Yearly, this was becoming more and more problematical. Why? Nearly thirty years ago, the many guilds of Tierra banded together and overthrew all the ruling kings in all the kingdoms. They supplanted the rulers, but kept the many Senates and local courts of justice. They placed severe restrictions on the many towers and Circles, effectively forcing them to do their bidding and not those of their own or their kings. Further, the standing armies were now under Guild control. The Supreme Guild Masters, a totally secret band of men and women, ran what had been the major towns and cities and countries. Other than the local Guild Master, the identity of all higher leaders continued to be a closely guarded secret. Even when they chose to hold annual meetings at the Imperial Castle with Queen Amy overseeing them, they used fake names and wore masks. Worse, all were *mentales* gifted, of that Amy was certain.

The lords, nobles, and ex-kings hated what the guilds had done to them. From the beginning, most all these men and women held vast estates. By 1325, they all had declared their independence from the original kingdoms, which were now ruled by the many guilds. Worse, they took many tower trained *mentales* gifted men and women with them, denuding the many ancient towers. Most towers now were able to field two or three full Circles at best. Only Amy's Imperial Tower still had five complete Circles in full operation. Friction between the two opposing forces continued to grow year by year. However, Queen Amy was thankful for one aspect of this change. The towers had ended their re-invention of terrible weapons of mass destruction, which had nearly destroyed Tierra in past centuries. That had been her greatest fear — a return to the Age of Chaos.

It had taken nearly three centuries for Tierra to get a superb Governor in charge. For nearly thirty years, Governor Katrina Lutgard and her staff had done an admirable job. In fact, she, her wife, and assistants were counted among Queen Amy's closest friends. Katrina had married her amazing Doctor Whitney Jones. Her computer technician, Carla Childa, had married her archaeologist, Elfe Heilwig. These four were nearly constant companions with Amy and her group for many reasons, not the least being they were all given the *mentales* gift in the distant past.

In fact, ten were bound together by much more than mental abilities. They had been through terrible biological-genetic agent attacks. First, Amy and her mate, Jan, along with Katrina, Whitney, Carla, and Elfe had suffered the accidental bio attack that began the entire genetic modification mess, which the Imperium had been facing for nearly thirty years now. Indeed, everyone on Tierra had been altered by that first attack. The massive genetic alterations included all becoming hermaphrodites, with thick hair that fell to their ankles, split lips requiring the massive foot in diameter lip plates, and the massive basket ball sized breasts, which required they wear pipe corsets for back support and which outlined their twelve inch waist line. Their fingernails had grown to a foot long, while their feet became deformed and required wearing the toe shoes. Even worse, initially neither their hair nor nails could be cut. Doing so caused the person intense pain! Thankfully, the Goddesses Ariana and Lysandra undid the genetic modifications across Tierra. They knew if they didn't, their humans would be destroyed.

Of course, the Goddess Lysandra required a sacrifice for her intervention. As a result, while everyone on Tierra woke from a seeming nightmare dream, Amy, Jan, Katrina, Whitney, Carla, and Elfe paid the price. Their bodies did not return to normal.

Shortly after that, Doctors Ruth and Alex Hammil, a pair of young geneticists, were brought to Ashford-5. They had been the victim of a nasty biological genetic agent attack. Their leader had used them as guinea pigs to verify the invented bio agent worked. This was the very agent, which later on was so widely used within the Imperium. In addition to the other effects, they also lost their arms, making them completely helpless.

Then came the bio agent attack on the Imperium Senate. Senator Zarita Valen, her wife Senator Celenia Agahve, along with their close friend Senator Ari Laag, were stricken, along with over two thousand other senators. If that wasn't bad enough, a mad bomber later struck, killing Zarita's mate and Ari's too. Not long after that, Zarita and Ari married and retired from political life, returning to Tierra to create a life for themselves.

Thus, the ten became the closest of friends, bound together by their physical deformities. All ten were hermaphrodites and that, more than anything else, kept them extremely close. As of 1325, each of the ten had had three children. Their unique genetic traits carried forward into their offspring. Ruth and Alex's first born, May and Andy, had to have their arms regrown. However, after that, all children were normal as far as having arms went. Ruth and Alex's children did not have the enormously long fingernails that the others had, likewise with Zarita and Ari's children.

In time, Doctor Whitney, in conjunction with Ruth and Alex, had been able to reduce the genetic demands for foot long fingernails. Plus, time aided. Here in 1325, their nails were only six inches long. If any tried to file them shorter, intense pain resulted, and their nails quickly regrew to the genetically determined length. Still, this was a vast improvement.

Their children numbered thirty, all hermaphrodites with all the other modifications as well. The eldest were twenty-nine, while Ari's youngest was twenty. As the children grew up, Emperor Kino gave Queen Amy and Governor Katrina orders to send their children off to the Academy on Winno-3 to become properly educated. Six had just graduated and were heading home any day now. Six others were still in their last years at the academy and were coming home for the summer with the others.

However, there were even more complications. Wisely, the thirty hermaphrodite children of the ten dear friends decided to marry among themselves and not to others who were normal. Grandchildren abounded around the Imperial Castle. The older eight had already had two children of their own, now eight and six years old. Six others had six year old children. Four others had five year olds. Six others had four year olds. That tallied thirty-two grandchildren — all hermaphrodites with the many other body modifications as well. If that wasn't enough, all thirty were pregnant again, expecting at various times during 1325. Yes, the men also bore children, which helped account for the prolific proliferation of children — a wholly unexpected side effect of the bio-genetic agent. By the end of the year, the ten parents anticipated having sixty-two grandchildren dashing about the castle! On top of all this, each was also *mentales* gifted!

Although Amy never spoke about her astute observation with anyone besides Doctor Whitney, the two realized the ultimate social impact of the hermaphrodites on their society. It was twofold. First, these ten had thirty children. In contrast, the dozen normal couples in the Underground had but fourteen. Because the male hermaphrodites also bore children, the birthrate of hermaphrodites was double that of normal humans. Second, since there were so few men among the ten, their children consisted of nine males and twenty-one females, far out of balance from the normal birthrates. Usually, the ratio was fifty-fifty between the sexes. Of course, that imbalance stemmed from so many female-female marriages, born from personal desires, as well as the scarcity of available hermaphrodite men.

Now that their thirty children were grown up, married, and beginning their own families, the grandchildren were approaching a more normal distribution between the sexes. Nineteen of the grandchildren were female, while twelve were male. Both Doctor Whitney and Amy were most relieved at these promising numbers. They were well aware most women were attracted to men, not other women, as they were. Still, both were relieved the birth balance was being restored, but the double birthrate continued to bother both, though they seldom spoke of it to others.

This fall, the eight eight-year olds were planning to start their schooling this fall. Now, Queen Amy realized why Emperor Kino had been so insistent about sending their children to the Academy on Winno-3. Thirty were professionally trained and well educated, the first batch of natives from Tierra to be so educated. Most had already agreed to spend at least part of their time teaching in the ever-expanding school system in Exchange City. Knowledge was vital, and Emperor Kino had given them a route to the future!

Queen Amy's twin brother, Bernardo and his wife, Lena Squire, the ex-Sector ID minister, was in charge of the Imperial Castle Security and operations. Her younger sister, Gabriela had married Herm Smith, and they had two children. She handled the castle comm system for Amy. Other members of her original Gang of Ten held vital positions as well. Henry Valen Frank was the venerado for the Imperial Tower, while Adrianna was a capa, a leader of one of the five Circles. Ben and Drina took over the Underground operations.

The Underground had been founded to do everything possible to keep the peace on Tierra and to prevent wars. They had a super-sophisticated spy system setup in their underground base of operations below the northern city of Brom. Drina was also a katalyein telepath, as was one of her children, Marisol. Each of these had three children as of 1325.

Their children as well as those of the other Underground members tended to intermarry among themselves, similar to the hermaphrodites. However, compare their twenty children to the sixty-some of the hermaphrodites and you can get a sense of just how much the hermaphrodites were dominating.

With all the children growing into adulthood and considering how close the ten were, Queen Amy and Governor Katrina decided to build an extension to the Imperial Castle. Just north of the outer castle walls and on leased spaceport land, a walled complex was constructed housing twenty small manor houses. Each of their fifteen young couples was allowed to design the layout of their new manor house. Additionally, Zarita and Ari took one for themselves. Likewise, the four spaceport couples took four more, their home away from the sterile apartments in the space complex. Further, Queen Amy had her tower construct underground passages from each manor house to her castle. Governor Katrina had her people construct an underground tunnel connecting the spaceport Admin Building to this tunnel as well. She also installed one of the Imperium conveyor systems for rapid transport across the twenty miles. Small electric cars were positioned at either end, and the trip could be made in just twenty minutes. For the past few years, Governor Katrina and her group spent nights and weekends in their new manor houses.

However, another factor was at work. Queen Amy and most all the others had been born during the Great Baby Boom and were now forty-nine. Governor Katrina and her staff were somewhat older, in their fifties. Enter the next complexity. Queen Amy and Governor Katrina had just received a direct order from Emperor Kino to make use of the Rejuvenation Machine. He wanted them and their associates to appear twenty-one. He even suggested that Nadja and Diego Baldo also make use of the machine. They were the founders of the school here in Exchange City. She was also a top Imperium linguist, though she no longer traveled to other planets to do fieldwork.

The fifth of May, the ten plus Nadja and Diego were sitting around Amy's living room discussing the orders just received from Emperor Kino. "Well, we're almost fifty," Amy commented.

"Yes, we are," Jan pointed out a bit sardonically. "I remember when we married, Amy. You were going to have a daughter, and as soon as she was fourteen, you were going to send her off to Winno-3 to be trained as a queen and have her take your place. And here we are, almost fifty and still you are the queen. Not one of your three daughters has yet to get Ataro queen training."

Amy sighed. She recalled how she had longed to get her arms back and not be so helpless, dependent upon her *mentales* gifts. She remembered that original plan to be as normal as possible by her thirtieth birthday at the latest. "I just couldn't do it to Sandy or Rafaela or Linda. It's a bitch living like this." Hearing her mate admit this, Jan was mollified.

"Why? That's what I want to know," Katrina asked. "Why does he want us all to keep our positions far longer?"

"Perhaps he wants us to have many more children," Doctor Whitney suggested. "The proliferation of children among us hermaphrodites is staggering. Double the norm. I wonder if that has anything to do with his request."

"Well, I admit I won't protest too much," Nadja spoke up. "I'm getting a touch of arthritis. I assure you that I won't miss it. Still. . ."

Zarita spoke up, "There must be some other reason. I'm sure he must want you all to retain your current positions for many more years. He's always been highly politically motivated, as is Queen Altha. I heard they both are now twenty-one again. That means they can rule for at least another fifty years."

"You might be right," Governor Katrina replied. "But why? Is something brewing? Trouble?"

"I admit Ari and I have totally ignored Imperium politics for the last thirty years," Zarita sighed, reflecting her admission.

"And we don't regret it either!" Ari added sternly, then broke into a smile, though it wasn't visible because of her lip plates. However, everyone sensed it.

Carla spoke up. "Well, if we become twenty-one again,

Elfe and I'll certainly have more children. We love sex too much to avoid it, and besides, we don't believe in abortions. A human life is precious, even if it is a hermaphrodite. Amy, you are just going to have to build more manor houses!" Everyone laughed.

"But I can't keep track of all our grandchildren as it is!" Amy jested. "How can I possibly keep track of a hundred plus?" Everyone roared again. Indeed, this was becoming somewhat of a problem.

Ari added, "In that case, we'll have lots of children to look after us when we finally do get old and infirm." More laughter followed. "Speaking of children, two of mine and ten others are due back from the Academy in a couple of days. I've rather missed my Lissi and Dari. Thank goodness for summer vacations. They've still got another year to go."

Just then, Amy's eldest, Sandy, and her mate Rae Lutgard came bustling into the room, as fast as they could manage in their toe shoes. Holding onto each other for balance, they were able to walk significantly more swiftly. "Mom! Turn on the news! It's terrible! A whole world has been bio attacked, just like Tierra was years ago!"

"What?" exclaimed Amy. "To the comm center everyone!" Wearing toe shoes, one had to be extremely careful rising. Balance was everything with only toes on the floor. The tiny heel right behind the toes helped a little, but only a little. For Amy, this was even more of a challenge. As always, Jan rose first and then helped her rise. Like a dozen penguins, they all headed out and down the hallway. Soon, they entered the large comm center, where Gabriella already had the giant monitors on. After adjusting their extremely long hair, the dozen sat down on the comfortable sofas to watch and listen.

"Where is Aquila Prime?" Amy asked. No one knew for sure. Later, the newscaster answered her question. It was in the middle of the spiral arm, not too far from the Ataro Empire. Now Amy began to worry. What if they attacked some of the emperor's planets?

"Ten billion people are affected? Mind-blowing," Jan gushed.

"My god! How can anyone possibly get to these people

in time?" asked Katrina.

Her face turning white, Doctor Whitney replied, "They can't dear. You're looking at a mass extinction on Aquila Prima. It's a weapon of mass destruction after all."

"My god. Those poor people!" Ruth declared.

"So what's so vitally important about Aquila Prime that someone wanted to exterminate all of its population?" asked Zarita. Her long-buried hatred of men surfaced again. Although she had her Basic Therapy, still this reeked of a male-sponsored atrocity.

"Maybe if they can get there fast enough, they can save some of them," Elfe suggested, ever hopeful.

Carla pointed out, "Even if they can rescue all of them by some unimaginable miracle, where will they get ten billion care givers to look after their needs? It'll take months to regrow their arms."

"I hate to point out the obvious, Carla," Alex said solemnly, "but it'll be impossible for that many arms to be regrown. There isn't enough genetic material available in the entire Imperium to handle that many people." His touch of rationality sobered the whole group even further, as they continued to watch the news.

Just then, the comm center received a secure video call from Emperor Kino. Gabriella quickly suggested, "You stay put, sis. I'll set the video camera on you. We can all listen, unless he wants to speak to you privately." Hastily, she set about making the slight adjustments.

"Queen Amy here, along with Governor Katrina and our companions. Over."

"Amy, have you seen the news about Aquila Prime? It's okay if the others listen. Over." His face looked quite young. Zarita was right. He was twenty-one once more.

"Yes, we're all watching the awful news right now. Why? Who? This is a disaster. Over."

"Indeed. As I have always said, this is really nothing more than a weapon of mass destruction. Now, it's been put to its intended use. Ten billion people, Amy, ten billion! The Holy Lords are taking responsibility for it, but it's way too soon to know for sure if they are behind it. Something of this magnitude, I believe, is far beyond their technical skills. As to why, I can only speculate at this time. I'll insist on a full, complete investigation, Ataro style. Meanwhile, I've heard from the Senate on Proxima Prime. They are going to send as many mass transport ships there as possible. The plan is to rescue the people and take them to assisted living complexes on other planets. They have ordered every Open World to take in at least a thousand victims. However, I cannot believe all ten billion will survive this. It'll be many weeks before this rescue process can be fully implemented. Is Ruth or Alex with you? Over."

"Yes, they are right here too. Over."

"Ah, Ruth, Alex. You have been through this. Is it possible you could have somehow survived on your own for several weeks when you first woke up from your attack? Over."

Alex laughed. "Hardly, Emperor Kino. We were utterly helpless. Without help, we couldn't even go to the bathroom. Besides, when we awoke, we were dehydrated and starving. We needed very good food and vitamins immediately to make up for what had been consumed during the genetic modifications our bodies underwent while we were in a coma. Over."

"As I anticipated, but I wanted to make sure. In that case, we cannot expect many of the ten billion to survive long enough to even be rescued. I'll do all that I can to expedite the operations. I'll get back to you later when I have more information. Over."

"Emperor, we could take some victims here on Tierra as well. We want to help too. Over." Queen Amy suggested.

"Excellent. I'll see what I can do. As the Senate Ruling stands, they were only going to send them to Open Worlds. Time will tell. More later. Over and out."

"You should have asked him why he wants us all to use the Rejuvenation Machine," Jan broke in. "Ah well, you can ask him that the next time he calls."

Just then, Jane Bolivar of the Underground called Amy. Her sister, Gabriella, answered and relayed the message to the large group. She was Queen Amy's Communication Minister, handling her rather large Imperium comm center here in the

Imperial Castle. "Hey all, that was Jane calling. She wants to remind you of your rejuvenation center appointments. Jan, mom, you two are up on Wednesday. Katrina, Doctor Whitney, you are scheduled for Thursday. Carla, Elfe, you are up on Friday. Zarita, Ari, Saturday. Doctor Ruth, Doctor Alex, Sunday. Nadja, Diego, Monday next. She said don't forget."

Several grumbled. "Okay, sis. We won't. Twenty-one again! Whee, isn't this fun?" Amy replied. Many grinned, but with their lip plates stretching their mouths and lips, they weren't visible, though Gabriella's teasing smile was. Her body was one of the few normal ones around the castle.

"So when do all my aunts and uncles get here, Katrina? Have you heard?" Gabriella asked.

"Tomorrow around ten," Governor Katrina replied. Satisfied, Gabriella waltzed out of the room, whistling a tune of Diego's.

Already eight of the children had their degrees from the Academy on Winno-3. Sandy (Amy's) and Rae (Katrina's) Lutgard were both botanists. Sandy specialized in plants, while Rae dealt also dealt with animals. Both were already knee deep in preparing the first complete species analysis of indigenous plant and animal life on Tierra. Additionally, Rae had gotten far more paca herds established in the foothills. They were being raised for both their superlative fleece and their beast of burden capabilities in the grasslands, ideally suited for these lovable animals.

Mindy (Carla's) and Andy (Alex's) Hammil were both doctors, specializing in genetic research. Both were rather driven, naturally, and following in the footsteps of Ruth and Alex. Many here secretly hoped these four would finally come up with a genetic cure for them all. May (Ruth's) and Lelos (Elfe's) Heilwig had their degrees in linguistics and archaeology, respectively, taking after his parents and Nadja. Janet (Jan's) and Hank (Whitney's) Bellweather specialized in communications and computer programming, not surprising in Janet's case.

Amy was excited about the returning children for another reason. Eight more had just graduated from the Academy with their degrees. Eight more highly trained individuals would certainly benefit all Tierra, especially if she could get some of them to teach others in their budding schools. Jan had already planned another party celebration for tomorrow night. Indeed, the mood would have been quite festive around the castle had it not been for this most disturbing genocide on Aquila Prime.

While most of the women continued to wear the typical long, satin gowns so popular on Tierra, the men had long ago fought against them. Although they first had no choice but to wear women's clothing, Nita and Lilly brought the design facilities of Elegant Fashions Inc to bear on their unique situation. Years ago, they invented a men's shirt that would accommodate their basketball-sized bosoms, along with a tailored dress jacket. Combined with matching pants, the men were able to look somewhat like normal men, if one discounted their impossibly long nails, hair, and monstrous bosoms. Still, the clothes did much to help the men gain back some of their self-respect. These days, all the men wore these new-style men's suits, particularly so, when they were off-world at the Academy.

The many adults stood together just outside the main entrance of the spaceport, straining their heads upwards watching the large deep space shuttle gently descend from the blue skies. Even though they'd seen many shuttles landing, excitement tingled their senses. Besides, their children or siblings were on this one, coming home after the long nine month school term.

In pairs of helping hands, they stepped out of the large transport. The seven men wore suits that had been tailored by Elegant Fashions Inc. That is, the men looked much like the other few hermaphrodite men here. They wore their long hair in a tight bun, but there was no disguising their enormous bosoms beneath their jackets. Their six inch nails didn't help either. Queen Amy knew that, until there were vastly more genetic breakthroughs, they had done as much as they could to look like normal men. The young women all wore conservative, black skirts, hemmed at their knees, displaying their black nylons-clad lower legs and striking toe boots in patent leather. White silk blouses contrasted, typical of the other Academy female students. All wore their enormously long, thick hair draped across their backs, held in place by traditional bluebird clasps. The orange-red sunlight reflected off their giant lip plates, which drooped down to their chests, but sent blinding rays at those anxiously waiting to welcome them home.

Both groups could scarcely contain their enthusiasm, but their toe shoes prevented them from rushing into their parent's arms or those of their siblings. Like two groups of penguins, they shuffled towards each other, before welcoming hugs turned the large group into one giant mass of moms, dads, brothers, sisters, aunts, uncles, cousins, and dear friends. Meanwhile, the ground crew began unloading the student's many crates.

"Now!" Bernardo whispered. Suddenly, a large banner unfurled from the top floor of the ten story housing building. It read, "Congratulations Graduates!" Jan and Bernardo yelled, "Surprise!" The ten new Academy graduates flushed and grinned invisibly, though they could not hide their pride.

"Just you wait, Bernardo, Jan," Rafe called out. "We're here to stay now, so you two had best watch your backsides. Quite a few laughed. The old Gang of Ten was still at it, even after all these years. Still, Rafaela was pleased with this minor prank. As she hugged her mother, Queen Amy, she added, "Mom, we need to talk privately and soon."

"We can do it, after you and Rupert get settled in, dear. How are my two new grandchildren to be doing?" Amy asked. Her wry grin wasn't visible though. Rafe and Rupert were both seven months along now.

"You are going to have another pair of grandchildren running underfoot this summer," Rafe teased her mother. "Seriously, mom, we're all fine, all of us. We've all been checked up by the doctors before we left Winno-3. Nothing to worry about in that department, except that there are so many of us now." She grinned back; Amy picked it up as well.

"I always worry about that, dear. Childbirth is the leading cause of women's deaths here on Tierra," Amy replied, though Rafaela already knew that.

An hour later amid constant chatting among the ten pleased parents, thirty siblings, the thirty-one grandchildren, and the others of the Gang of Ten and their children, the combined welcome home and graduation party was in full swing. Rafaela (Amy's) had her degree in Sociology, while her husband, Rupert (Whitney's) Gervasi-Jones had his in general medicine. Delia (Katrina's) and Frank (Alex's) Hammil had their degree in Green Technology, which they hoped they could put to good use here on Tierra. Lela (Whitney's) had hers in history and her mate Ruthy (Zarita's) Agahve-Jones held a degree in political science. Both wanted to become teachers here at Nadja's school. Misty (Jan's) and Karl (Carla's) Childa-Bellweather had their degrees in electronics and hoped to put their skills to work for Amy and the Underground, improving their many systems. Sandy (Elfe's) had hers in math, while her husband Theo Hammil (Ruth's) had his in physics. Like Lela and Ruthy, both wanted to teach here.

The younger dozen children had not totally decided on their majors yet. These included Maggie (Katrina's) and Len (Carla's) Childa, Ann (Ruth's) and Diego (Zarita's) Valen, Mary Beth (Elfe's) and Bethi (Ari's) Laag, Linda (Amy's) and Rael (Zarita's) Valen Gervasi, Lisa (Alex's) and Lissi (Ari's) Laag-Hammil, and Melisa (Jan's) and Dari (Ari's) Bellweather.

Gabriella interrupted Queen Amy and Governor Katrina during the mad partying. Emperor Kino was calling for her and Governor Katrina. "It's urgent, mom, Kat! Sounds important," she gushed, pleased with her awesome responsibility of monitoring Amy's giant Imperium comm center.

A bit later, the three sat in front of the video camera, and Gabriella pressed the Send button. "We're here, Emperor Kino. Over," Amy said solemnly.

After the usual five minute delay, the youthful emperor's face appeared on their large monitor. "Ah, good. Queen Amy, Governor Katrina," he used their formal titles. Hence, both women knew this was an official call of some importance. He went on, "I have acquired fifty young married couples from Aquila Prime to be resettled on Ashford-5. These are all Academy students who are or were in their third or fourth year. Some were close to graduation before the biological attack. Expect their arrival around noon tomorrow. They are all quite bright young men and women. More importantly, they are all survivors. I can't impress how significant these poor survivors are. Barely a hundred thousand survived out of ten billion people! These that made it represent a thousandth of a percent of the population of Aquila Prime! So yes, these people have a vicious tenacity to live, but I can't begin to tell you how terrible their emotional and physical states are at this point in time."

He went on, quite sober, "Genocide. I'll get to the bottom of this. I'll not rest until I've done so. Meanwhile, I picked the most promising of these hundred thousand survivors and am sending them to you. I trust you'll be able to handle them. Brilliant minds, all of them and survivors too. Over."

"This is almost unimaginable. Yes, we'll care for them and do all we can to help them recover," Amy replied.

Katrina added, "If there is anything more that we can do, let us know. My god! Nearly ten billion dead. Unthinkable! Over." That was all the emperor had, and they signed off. "We best see to the accommodations today. We've got less than twenty-four hours to prepare," she added.

"We'll house them here with us in the manor extensions. Our kids can put a couple up with each of their families," Amy suggested. "There are nineteen of us families of hermaphrodites between us, so we house say about two of these new arriving families each."

Katrina interrupted, "Even that's not going to do it, Amy. How can we go about our business with four or more who will need constant care? Perhaps, we should hire some women to take care of them during the daytime hours. How about one per family? That would be fifty to hire. Can we get that many women on such short notice?"

A few minutes later, the two interrupted the graduation-welcome home party. Amy explained and added, "So we have fifty junior and senior Academy married couples from Aquila Prime arriving here around noon tomorrow. We

36

need to hire fifty women care givers and get fifty bedrooms prepared for them quickly."

Rafe spoke up, "Mom, these are really well educated people, but they're going to have to have Basic Therapy almost at once. My god, the trauma these people have is staggering. But only a hundred thousand survived? Out of ten billion people?"

"Yes, I can't imagine how awful that must have been," Amy replied with a deep sigh. "Still, we have to salvage them. If we can, their education can be invaluable for us. Although they probably don't think so, they do have something valuable to give back to us. I'll alert Nita and Lilly. Hopefully, Elegant Fashions Inc can help us with them."

The party mood evaporated. The many families headed off to begin making arrangements to take in the fifty. Meanwhile, Rafaela decided to corner her mother. "Mom, now is as good a time as any for us to chat. More so, what with this news." She and Amy remained in the party room, as the others headed out, still talking among themselves.

"Okay, Rafe, what's so important?" Amy asked.

"Mom, I've got a confession to make, about who I really am. There's no easy way to say this, so I'll just tell you, and we can go from there. I used to be Benjamina Blackwater."

"What?" Amy asked confused by her daughter's pronouncement. "The creator of Basic Therapy? But I don't understand."

"Yes, that's me. I know, everyone thought I was over in the Easterlings, but I goofed that whole project up. Long story, but I saw where things were headed. Back then, we could literally 'make' anyone we chose into a *mentales* gifted person. Our greatest fear was giving such powers to the wrong person, creating other Damiano conquerors. Plus back then, there were almost none with the gifts over in the Easterlings, so when my old body died, I headed there to spread my therapy to them, as well as working on developing a way to remove the evil impulses that men and women sometimes have. If I could have done that, we'd no longer run the monumental risk of creating another evil tyrant with *mentales* gifts."

Rafe sighed, "I failed on both counts. I just couldn't get

enough people willing to learn how to deliver my Basic Therapy. I never got what I'm calling a critical mass of therapy givers. True, hundreds of Easterlings have been helped, but unlike the mermaids of Brom, I couldn't get any significant numbers of volunteer therapy givers. Plus, everything over there is so far apart and isolated. When my Easterlings body grew too old, I decided to come back to the Midlands and try again. I chose you and Jan to be my parents this time, partly because of what all you and Katrina have gotten established for all Tierra here."

She went on, "I also wanted to see what else is known out there in the vast Imperium that might help shed light on Basic Therapy. Besides, I thought that given the thousands of other worlds, *surely* someone else has already discovered methods for a person to achieve the freedom that beckons us all, becoming as able as the goddesses Lysandra and Ariana. That's why Rupert and I went to the Academy. He's really my longtime companion, Tim. Anyway, we've really spent our school years searching the Imperium for clues. Alas, among all the planets and societies of the entire Imperium, Amy, only *we* have Basic Therapy, and a real way for a person to discover that they are not a body and that they are an immortal spiritual being. No one has any way for us to recover what we once must have been as powerful beings, who do not need or want to have these fleshly bodies in order to live and operate. None, mom, nada."

Quite seriously, Rafe continued, "Rupert and I are shocked. This makes what I've developed unique and so vitally important that there are no words for it. I've just got to get it further developed and spread throughout all Tierra, before those with the power crystals destroy us forever," Rafe finished up.

Amy looked at her second daughter in a whole new light. She had thick, brown hair, slightly wavy. Like most Midlands women, she had it pulled to her back. A bluebird clasp held much of it behind her, though her tresses fell to her ankles, just as her own did. Rafe's face was roundish with the thin cheeks of Jan, but her own thicker eyebrows. Her yellow eyes seemed to sparkle, indicating that Rafaela was very much present and alive. She wasn't a beauty model, only fairly attractive, but then Amy knew that neither she nor Jan was either, for that matter. Having to wear the giant lip plates didn't help their looks, rather distorting their mouths. Amy realized she'd never really known Benjamina, only as that old, bed-ridden woman there in the Underground. Still, Amy held her Basic Therapy creation as something of immense value, utterly valuable, which is why she stared at her daughter somewhat in awe.

A moment of silence caught Amy off guard. She realized Rafe had finished and was waiting on her reply. "Incredible Rafe. I can still call you my Rafe, can't I?"

Rafaela grinned invisibly. "Mom, don't be silly. Of course, you can. I'm not going to go changing my name."

"Good. It's just I had no idea of this." Amy's mind finally registered the full impact of what Rafe had told her. Her ruling instincts kicked in. "Okay, so what do you need so you can get Basic Therapy delivered to everyone on Tierra? What do you need to advance us into, well I don't know what to call it, but godhood? Who else knows this? Oh, does Rafaela and Andres know about this? She's worked so damned hard on all this stuff, these many years. Oh, this is going to be confusing. Two Rafaela's."

"Yes, she and Andres knows. She's very perceptive and spotted me when I was three years old, but I asked her to remain quiet about it. I told her about my needing to go off-world to see if others out there in the Imperium had developed anything like this that we could use to further our own selves here on Tierra. She agreed with me. We had to find out. To avoid confusion, mom, I'm going to use my usual nickname, Rafe. That way, everyone can tell us apart easily."

"Well, that's a relief. Things are confusing enough around here with so many children and grandchildren. That's a side effect that Kat and I've observed. We hermaphrodites tend to have twice as many children as normal," Amy admitted.

Rafe laughed. "We know, Rupert and me." She patted her bulging abdomen lovingly. She and he were due in a few more months. "Anyway, mom, Rupert and I have our official

Sociology Degrees from the Academy. More importantly, we've kept abreast of this whole genetic biological weapon scene. As you probably know, there have been a rather alarming number of such terrorist attacks during the last quarter of a century or more. Until Aquila Prime, most were rather small in their impact — that is, if you consider wiping out several thousand people at one time as small. Well, compared to this planetary genocide, they have been. Still, over these many years, it has become more and more of an Imperium problem."

"How so?" Amy asked.

"That's a long story. Let me just say that these hundred thousand survivors from Aquila Prime are likely the straw that breaks the donkey's back, as we say here on Tierra. Rupert and I have been thinking about this situation since the news broke about the bio attack on that world. Mom, I want us to take in a thousand more of these refugees. I'm going to work with Alpha and Beta. I think with their bots and the Madiera artificial city, these survivors will be able to have some kind of workable life. I want to train them up to be my Basic Therapy givers. This way, we'll have a large force, able to deliver it in volume. Perhaps, with them, we can gain a critical mass, enough to push it forward to all who live on Tierra. That's my plan, anyway. After I get it worked out with Alpha, can you see if Emperor Kino can get us another thousand of these survivors?"

"Sure thing, dear. I hadn't thought about using Madiera's facilities. Again, you are ahead of me," Amy agreed and admitted. "I've not had much to do with those robots and Madiera."

"Of course not. Most all the old mermaids have died of old age. Thank god that Alpha and Beta were able to repair their genes so their children didn't have the same Calder-given deformities. What we've got now is bad enough," Rafe admitted. "By the way, I fully agree. All of you should use the Rejuvenation Machine. I think it's going to be very critical that all of you, Katrina and her group as well, remain in power for at least another half century. I feel it in my bones. Something awful is going to happen. These genetic biological attacks are escalating, big time, what with Aquila Prime."

40

"You think we're going to be attacked again?" Amy asked, rather shocked by Rafe's suggestion.

Rafe answered slowly, choosing her words carefully. "Tierra? Not so likely. The refinery on the moon, perhaps. Down here, I doubt it. Rupert thinks the Imperium as a ruling body might be doomed. Time will tell."

"Well, that's a relief. What did you mean about the Imperium Problem?" Amy asked. She'd not forgotten what Rafe had said a moment ago. She was curious. After all, she and so many of her closest friends were hermaphrodites now.

Rafe sighed. "Well, as you know, all of the major criminals of the Imperium were subjected to these genetic modifications. During the last quarter of a century, they've had quite a large number of children, just as we have here on Tierra. Everyone now knows that essentially, the hermaphrodite birthrates are nearly double that of so called normal humans, because men also have babies was well. Add to the sheer number of criminals, all those victims of terrorist biological attacks, and you have quite a huge hermaphrodite population. Admittedly, they are spread out across a large number of planets, so no one planet has an exorbitant number of them."

Rafe went on, "You see, back in 1297, they modified some two thousand criminals, who then had children the following year. By 1298, they'd converted another ten thousand criminals, closing down most all prisons. These soon added another ten thousand babies the following year. Add to that all those victims of bio terrorist attacks, such as Zarita and Ari, and you can add another ten thousand babies before the turn of the century. All those are now in their twenties and have been having babies as well. Plus, add in another twenty more years of terrorist attacks and another twenty thousand victims. They too have now have had a number of children. Carla can probably work out a computer program that models the population explosion of us hermaphrodites, but suffice it to say, we number in the millions now, mom."

"The worst part of it all, mom, is that it costs around ten thousand credits to modify a given person to regenerate their arms so they can live a reasonable life. Thanks to the

Imperium Senate appropriations, while that's been done to most all of the actual terrorist's victims until now, that leaves an alarming number of offspring from the criminals who are still armless, unable to afford the medical cost, and wholly dependent upon their respective planetary societies for their support. There just isn't funds available for that many arm restorations and genetic modifications. Hence, every year, thousands more are born, just as helpless and dependent as their parents are. Can you see where this is leading, mom?" Rafe asked.

"A huge monetary drain on those worlds who are providing for them. Are they beginning to protest against this?" Amy asked.

"Precisely so mom. Discrimination and bigotry are springing up on all those worlds that have taken in these men and women. Right wing groups are calling for the mass extermination of their hermaphrodite populations! On several worlds, it's getting downright ugly, though so far most governments are hushing it up. I think this backlash is only going to get worse as time goes on and their populations continue their explosive growth. Already, they've begun to implement birth control methods on all of the hermaphrodite prisoners. The current Imperium law is allowing each criminal to have one child before they are medically prevented from further procreation, mom."

"Well, I can see how such feelings arise. Still, this isn't good. I don't see how Tierra could take in more than the thousand you are wanting, Rafe. Madiera can only hold so many. I haven't asked Doctor Whitney or Doctors Ruth and Alex yet, but I suspect they will want to regrown the arms of our fifty new arrivals. Still, I don't think we could possibly regrow them on the additional one thousand you want to rescue," Amy replied, thinking about the entire situation. "Yet, if we don't, they'll certainly have children, and the problem will only escalate here too, rapidly beyond our ability to provide for them."

"I know, mom. I've taken that into consideration before I made my suggestion. I hope and pray our doctors can get to all these thousand men and women as well, in time, that is,"

Rafe added hopefully. "I'll talk to them about it tomorrow," she promised.

"Okay, if our doctors think that in time they can alter the genes of these thousand so we don't have a population explosion of helpless children, then I give my consent to your proposal," Amy proclaimed in her official voice. "Besides, not all of the thousand, which Emperor Kino can manage to get for us, will be armless. We best have a long chat with our doctors tomorrow morning, first thing. After that, I'll give the emperor a call."

"You realize it costs about ten thousand credits per person?" Doctor Whitney exclaimed. She and Doctors Ruth, Alex, and their children, doctors Mindy and Andy Hammil had come to Amy's throne room at nine the following morning. Queen Amy and Rafe had explained Rafe's plan to bring another thousand here to Tierra. Of course, Amy had then asked if they were going to be able to regrow the fifty new arrivals, due here around noon, as well as these others that Rafe planned to bring to Tierra.

"I've an idea about that," Amy countered. "As I understood Emperor Kino, the Imperium is planning to sell the resources of Aquila Prime and divide up the proceeds with the surviving hundred thousand victims. We could have him use a portion of those funds to purchase whatever you will need, doctors."

While their faces showed no visible reactions due to the huge lip plates, their eyes did. "Well, that's acceptable then," Doctor Whitney replied. "Still, we haven't facilities here to do more than a few at a time. It takes two weeks per person, before we dare let them out of our intensive care facilities. Another two to three months are needed before their new arms are truly ready for action, during which time they do need to be carefully monitored. So we're looking at needing about two years to get these fifty fully recovered, right Ruth?"

"Precisely. So, Rafe, you are talking about nearly forty years for us to regrow a thousand people's arms," Doctor Ruth explained, calculating the figures in her head. Both she and Alex were very skilled in using their minds; they had had to, having spent so long without their arms, after their attack on Ashford-4.

Rafe frowned. "Can we get more equipment or something to speed it up some? Use more of the Aquila Prime funds to pay for the stuff? Forty years will bring at least another two generations of children who'll also need arms regrown."

Doctor Alex countered, "But that's Ruth's point, Rafe. We could not possibly hope to keep up with it. More children will be born who'll need theirs regrown. It would be a losing battle. We'd never finish that project, especially if terrorists keep on striking." He sounded a bitter note, shared by all present.

Doctor Andy added his thoughts. "Look, mom and dad have one medical bay where this work can be done. Doctor Whitney has a second one on the base. If you could add three more fully equipped medical bays, one for each of us, then we could handle five patients per two weeks. We'd need until the end of the year to get your fifty new Aquila Prime victims back to battery. We'd need about eight years to get your one thousand more fixed up. Even allowing for some children to be born, the project is doable then."

Doctor Whitney stated, "Ah, there's the problem. What with this explosion in terrorist victims these past twenty-five years, the needed medical machines are very hard to acquire. Every planet wants more than can be manufactured and supplied. It takes so damn many stem cells to charge fully a unit. We might not be able to get three more units anytime soon, unless the Emperor can pull some strings for us. Perhaps, Amy, you could ask on our behalf."

"Okay, I'll do my part," Queen Amy declared, using her official voice. "Say, how has your genetic research been coming along? I've not checked in some time. I know the others are pleased that you've been able to get their twelve inch talons reduced to six inches. Any other progress?"

Glancing at the other four doctors, Doctor Alex decided to speak for them all. All five had been engaged in genetic research, going over all the records and experiments that had been done at the secret research base on Ashford-4, the experiments that had resulted in the nasty biological genetics weapon used by the terrorists for a quarter of a century. "Well, we are definitely making progress and without using humans as test subjects, I might add. We are getting close, Amy, to being able to undo the fingernail and hair modifications. In non-geneticist's terms, nerve cells are added to each hair follicle and to the fingernails, neither of which have such cells in normal humans. Of course, the dilemma is we now actually need to try the undo process on someone to see if it actually will work. Genetic testing on humans is wholly illegal and unethical, so we are rather boxed in on this one."

Doctor Mindy broke in, "However, we are going to try it on ourselves fairly soon. We don't want to try it on someone else, in case we're wrong. This way, it's our own lives that we are risking. If it is successful, we'll then ask the others if they want this much of a cure. I know, it's not really solving the worst of the genetically altered body problems we all face, but it's a start."

Doctor Ruth added, "Plus, we believe we are also close to a total foot repair process. Of course, some women might still desire to remain fashionable and wear the toe shoes," she added hastily.

"Some of us don't," Doctor Andy quickly added. Alex and Mindy nodded their agreement with that point.

"Well, that's something. If everyone could at least walk properly again, that would go quite a long way! Keep up the good work," Queen Amy praised her five doctors. "Thanks for coming. I suppose we'd best head over to the spaceport to greet our fifty new arrivals. My god, I can't imagine their emotional states." That was a sobering thought, but it steeled the wills of the five doctors to continue their research.

Amy could not help but sense the terrible emotional states of the fifty new arrivals! Neither could the other forty who were with her. They were telepaths. Sensing the state of others was as normal and common as breathing. All forty had to take a moment to dampen down their sensitivity to the newcomers, even before the lengthy disembarkment began. Emotionally, none of the fifty was in remotely good shape, but then Amy didn't expect they would be. Physically, they appeared much as she did, but without her *mentales* gifts, she knew they felt and were utterly helpless human beings, terrified beyond description. Still, they attempted to suppress it all, frantically trying to grasp the present, strange planet with the dim orange-red sun and its unusual smells.

Their clothing, or sack gowns to be more accurate, were ill-fitting. Amy guessed someone had just slipped anything that could possibly fit over their bodies. At least, they all wore toe shoes and thus could barely walk on their own. "I'll get them properly attired," Nita whispered to Amy. She grimaced at the sight of their abysmal their dress.

Being greeted by others who looked just like themselves, but with arms, did much to alleviate their current fright and apprehensions. Further, the steadying arms of all these welcoming people gave them a small bit of security, while they walked into the spaceport. From there, they were taken via electric cars to the Imperial Castle and into Queen Amy's Throne Room. Here, she and Governor Katrina gave them their welcoming speeches. The governor spoke first.

Once everyone had been seated, Katrina welcomed them. "Hello. I'm Governor Katrina Lutgard. On behalf of my entire staff, we welcome you to Ashford-5 or Tierra as we call our world. It is part of the Ataro Empire and possibly the safest planet in the Imperium on which to live at this time. Let me also express our deepest sorrow for what has happened to your home world of Aquila Prime. Emperor Kino Sango had promised me he will find the terrorists who did this to you and your people, and see they are punished. As you probably have heard, in time, reparation funds will become available to all of you."

"My mate, Doctor Whitney, and her colleagues, the geneticists Doctors Ruth and Alex Hammil are here and are still actively working on genetic cures for us all. They are planning to use the existing technology to regrow your arms. However, our medical facilities here can only handle two of you at one time. More are on order. She assures me she will be able to meet her goal of having all your arms restored by the end of the year. So that is the best news I can give you at the moment."

"You'll be staying here at the Imperial Castle and Manor, home to Queen Amy Valen-Gervasi and all of us. Yes, everyone you've seen here today are like yourselves, victims of the same or similar genetic terrorism. I'll let Amy tell you more, Amy?" she motioned to her and sat down.

Purposely, Jan helped her rise gracefully, knowing these fifty men and women saw the queen as being like themselves, physically helpless. Queen Amy looked out on to a veritable sea of flaming red hair, some curly, some wavy, some fairly straight. Their skin tones were somewhat yellowish, but again their ill-fitting apparel and lip plates caught her attention. "Welcome one and all. As long as we speak Imperium Standard, we can understand each other, though do speak slowly." She then explained their living arrangements. After that, she continued, "As soon as we can, we'll get each one of you properly outfitted in good quality and properly fitting clothing. Men, I'm sure you'd rather wear suits similar to those you see around us." More than a few heads nodded. She knew that was very much appreciated by the men. After outlining some additional details, she asked if anyone had any questions.

One young woman spoke up, "Yes, please. I'm Aria Acronis; Backus is my husband. What about all of our relatives? Our parents, siblings, aunts, uncles? No one seems to know anything about them. Same with all of us. We know most everyone has died, but there are survivors. How can we find out if any of our families survived? Are they being transported to many other worlds? If any survived, can't we be brought back together? We all want to know, and no one has told us anything or answered us." Her frustrations were obvious, and Amy sensed all fifty had the same concerns and worries. Were any of their relations still alive and if so, where?

"I'll let Emperor Kino know about this mess. I'm sure he will track down any of your relations that have survived. If some have, I'll see that he brings them here too. We ought to get full names of everyone soon. and I'll relay them to the emperor. Okay then, let's get everyone to your new homes. Today, we'll take each couple over to Elegant Fashions Inc and get you properly outfitted. Aria, Backus, how about let's get you two fixed up first?" she suggested. Amy had already sensed these two were the defacto leaders of the small group.

As the group filed out, Jan and Carla stayed behind to escort Aria and Backus over to visit Elegant Fashions Inc. There, Nita and Lilly were waiting for them, having put all else aside in anticipation of handling the fifty arrivals during the long afternoon. Both were waiting. "Hello, I'm Nita, my older sister Lilly. Welcome to our fashion store."

"Aria. My husband, Backus. Can you really fix him up with a men's suit? This has been a nightmare for him and for all our husbands," the fiery red headed woman volunteered. Lilly smiled; she'd anticipated this.

Nita answered, "Of course. Lilly's going to get him fixed up, while I get you fancied up. Come on in. First, let's leaf through our catalogue of styles that will fit you." Jan and Carla relaxed; the two were in competent hands. Lilly and Nita were famous across all Tierra for having only the best and finest made apparel. Plus, both had excellent tastes.

An hour later, Backus exclaimed, "Dear, look at me now! This is more like it. I sort of look like a man, even though I obviously am not anymore."

"Wow. Yes, you look like my handsome Backus again," Aria gushed, trying hard to reconcile his new look with what it had been before the biological attack. Having his flaming hair tied up in a tight bun helped considerably, but his massive bosom simply could not be hidden, although he wore what was obviously a men's suit, cut to fit. That the shirt and jacket had no sleeves was also more than visible. She fought back hard to keep from breaking down again. This was all so utterly impossible; still she wanted to live.

"You look sexy yourself," Backus countered. "I won't be able to keep my hands off of you!" Instantly, he realized that he had no hands now. A surge of intense grief swept over him, but he fought hard to keep himself under control. *Can't cry. She needs me strong. Can't cry. Not in front of all these women. Just can't. Just can't. Strong. Be strong.*

"Yes, you both look as good as possible. If only the circumstances were otherwise. We all sure do love your flaming red hair. We've got a few red heads around the Midlands, but they are very few. Well, let's get you back to your new home. We need to outfit your friends too," Lilly replied soothing their frayed nerves. She also spotted Jan and Carla attempting to send out calming energies over the young couple.

After the four left, Nita commented, "They are right on the edge, aren't they?"

"Yes, sis, they certainly are, but they are very strong-willed. I think everyone believes that's why they actually survived the bio attack, when so many others didn't. Can you believe nearly ten billion died, but only these two and some hundred thousand others made it? Alone, no help, locked inside your own home for a month? I surely don't know how they all managed to do that. I don't think I have the strength, Nita. Still, we have given them back a wee bit of self-pride in their appearances, a little anyway. Oh, here come two more." Lilly and Nita had a very long day!

Chapter 3 Therapy and Recovery

The next day, four Basic Therapies were begun there at the Imperial Manor. Meanwhile, the first of many rejuvenations began. Initially, Rafe wanted to give these survivors the very best therapy sessions. In part, these were aliens from another world. Would her therapy work without needing any alterations? While it had for Katrina and her group, these were from another civilization entirely. Further, they'd never had any contact with Tierra and its people. Hence, Rafe's concern.

She and Rupert began working with Aria and Backus Acronis. Her idea was that Backus would respond better to a male than a female, especially so considering the genetic changes along the sexual line. Rupert's body was just like his, except he had his arms. Kinship in deformity. She also pulled in Rafaela and Andres to work on the Acronis' best friends, Alexia and Hermes Anias. Again, these two were the best therapy givers in Brom. That they also did have their arms added to the moral rapport for the young couple. If all went as expected and with no surprises, then Rafe would press everyone here at the Imperial Castle who knew how to deliver Basic Therapy into service, along with as many as she could pull down from Brom.

By the end of a week, Rafe realized that people were people, no matter from what society they came or what planet. All were spiritual beings, and all responded identically to her Basic Therapy. True, the specific traumatic incidents were varied, but still similar. Horrendous physical loss from the bio attack was uniform. Rape was rape. Beatings were beatings. Killings were killings, whether from a sword, poison, or d-gun. Pain and unconsciousness was always there.

Buckets of tears. That's how Aria described her first session to Backus. She'd cried more in that one day than she had in her life, or so she claimed. The emotional loss associated with the biological attack on her was positively enormous. Rafe had expected this. Aria had undergone horrific genetic mutations of her body, leaving her barely a shell of her former self, utterly ruining her life and that of everyone she knew, including the death of every other family member. The losses she and the other forty-nine had endured were almost unimaginable. She'd lost what she considered most of own body's livability, her parents and relatives, many of her friends, her possessions, her entire world, and her own imagined future. All she had left was her husband and her innate will to survive somehow. Now, the four therapy givers realized why it was that nearly ten billion had died. Their very will to live had been completely crushed.

Two weeks later, these first four patients were finally finished with their Basic Therapy. Rafe had already given the go-ahead for others to begin work on the remaining forty-six survivors. Aria exclaimed, "I've never felt so wholly alive, so present, so enthusiastic! I feel I can touch the clouds! Everything is so vibrant, so clear. How can I ever possibly thank you, Rafe? You've given me back my whole life!"

Rafe had officially ended her Basic Therapy. "Well, Aria, Doctor Ruth is ready to begin the regrowth of your arms. Once that's finished, you and Backus and your other friends have something of immense value to all of us on Tierra. Knowledge and education. There is so much that you could teach our children. Only Queen Amy and Governor Katina and their relations are allowed to travel to the Ataro System and attend the Academy. Ashford-5 is still officially a Closed World. We've begun to establish schools. As you know, Nadja and Diego have a school here in Exchange City."

"Hey, could we teach there?" Aria asked, realizing just how important an education actually was.

"I am sure Nadja and Diego would love to have you. Perhaps, Backus could help others invent useful technology. We're all spoiled by the little things of more modern worlds, like central heating in the winter and electric lights," Rafe replied. "But first, let's get your arms back."

That evening, Aria, Alexia, Backus, and Hermes discussed their future plans. Tomorrow, all four were going to begin the long process of having their arms regrown. "I am going to teach at Nadja's school, just as soon as my arms are back," Aria declared.

"I am good at math. She's going to let me teach mathematics there too, Aria. Isn't this fabulous?" Alexia gushed.

Backus added, "You bet. I'm going to put my civil engineering to good use. It's going to be a challenge seeing what all can be done here to improve the infrastructure, considering it's a Closed World. But geothermal energy can be harnessed. I'm going to see what can be done, working with what is available. Quite a challenge."

Hermes sighed, "Well, not much use for a computer programmer here, but I do have a good applied math background, so I'm going into business with Backus here. I can work out the calculations behind his plans. Several other natives have CE degrees too, from Winno-3's Academy. I think we can make a huge difference for Tierra. After all, it is our home now. Besides, we all have dual citizenship, and that means that we can import some technology for our own use, where the locals are prohibited from doing so. Closed World status and all that. Plus, we're hopeful some of our other friends will want to help too, once they've gotten their therapy and arms restored."

Aria summed up, "Well, a month ago, I thought there was no hope for us all. Now, the whole world has suddenly opened up for me. Still, the lighting is so dim. That's going to take some getting used to." They all laughed. The dim orange-red sun was a far cry from their yellow dwarf Aquila.

Later June and after the many rejuvenations were complete and many were "twenty-one" once more, Doctor Ruth assembled her team of geneticists. Doctors Alex, Whitney, Mindy, and Andy gathered around her big monitor. "Thanks for coming. I believe we've finally worked out another genetic modification in its entirety. I've highlighted the appropriate DNA sequences in red. They affect five specific genes. We're convinced these are the ones, which caused hair and nails to have neuron cells with their axons and axon terminals to transmit pain. As you can see in the second image of one of my hairs, the long strand is filled with axon terminals that sense pain, transmitting that impulse through the long connecting axons to the neuron. The image just below that one on the left is from one of my nails. As you can clearly see, the same terminals are present along with the axons and neurons. This is the physical mechanism that causes us pain when we try to cut our nails or trim our hair shorter."

She continued, "The highlighted red sequences, we believe, are the genes that lay behind the creation of these structures. Doctor Alex has created a sequence that can be used to undo the red mutations, reversing them."

Doctor Andy declared, "Incredible! Damn, if only experimentation on humans wasn't illegal and unethical, we could run a simple test of dad's sequencer and see if it works. If so, we could lose these impossible nails and finally cut our hair."

"It's a small step, dear," Doctor Mindy countered, "but a step nevertheless. "Speaking of which, as long as we are all here, I have something I wanted to share and get everyone's opinion on. I believe I've a way to actually restore fused and twisted foot bones in our feet." She gave a half hour presentation of her latest work. She ended with, "I believe it might be possible to reprogram the existing medical machines to do this. However, I've not the skill to touch the computer controls."

Doctor Whitney volunteered, "How about Karl or Hank or Carla? They might be able to do it. However, we again are on experimental grounds here too. We can't prove it will work, and there is a chance the person's feet will be in even worse condition."

Both Alex and Ruth laughed. Ruth commented, "Such a position! We've all been subjected to a genetic mutation attack. Of necessity, the cure must involve a genetic reprogramming of our bodies. Yet, our ethics, to say nothing of Imperium Laws, prevents us from conducting the requisite tests — tests that could prove both will work and restore victims' bodies. However, the geneticists who created this horrific mutation weapon were not bound or limited by this sense of ethics. Nothing prevented them from what must have been many hideous failures on their own victims. Yet, here we sit, constrained. Frustrating." None disagreed with her.

Later, Doctor Mindy decided to see if Hank could reprogram her own medical machine on the quiet. For a week, the two spent evenings working on this project. Unknown to the others, the husband and wife team of geneticists, Doctors Ruth and Alex, decided to see if they could formulate a genetic mutation cure for the neurons that now inhabited their hair follicles and whose attached axon terminals prevented cutting their hair and nails. "What's to prevent taking our own formula, eh?" Alex hinted snidely. "This is my body. I ought to be able to do whatever I desire with it, as long as I'm not endangering others." Ruth agreed, and they set about making their attempt at reverse engineering this part of the genetic mutations.

One morning in early July, Doctor Mindy reported for work wearing the old fashioned six inch oxfords, found so commonly among some of the nobles of Tierra. "What? What happened to your feet? Your toe shoes?" exclaimed Doctor Whitney. Always before, when anyone attempted to use the medical machines to repair their feet at least partway so that they could at least wear the more comfortable heels, within a day their feet reformed back into their previous distorted arch, forcing them to go back to wearing the toe shoes.

"These sure make walking vastly easier. We'll see how long the change lasts this time," Doctor Mindy replied. She didn't mention she was keeping her fingers crossed on this one. A week later, her feet still had not reformed. Now, everyone began watching her every day. Before long, the doctors decided her feet were not going to revert. After that, everyone wanted her new "cure." A month later, Hank had reprogrammed all the many medical machines, implementing Doctor Mindy's cure. After that, nearly everyone who had been genetically modified underwent the hour long procedure. Finally, they could wear much better footwear. Walking became drastically easier for these hermaphrodites. Still walking in such heels was challenging, but everyone agreed it was so much better than the awful toe shoes.

A week after Doctor Mindy shocked everyone, Doctor Alex added his bombshell. He walked into the dining room for breakfast, sporting quite short hair, a proper men's cut! Many cringed when they saw him. "God, that must have hurt like the devil!" Carla commented when she saw him. Many others nodded. Hardly anyone hadn't experienced the sharp, intense pain when they tried to cut their extremely long hair.

Although smiling like a cat, his broad grin wasn't visible. "Not in the slightest, Carla. Our formula works. Ruth's formula actually works. At least on our hair. We think it will also work on your claws too, Carla," he suggested. While Doctor Whitney encouraged everyone to use extreme caution, the desire among the many victims to no longer deal with six inch nails and, among the men, dealing with hair that fell to their ankles won out. Everyone wanted the cure at the same time.

Still cautious, the two doctors worked their magic on Sandy first, since she was one of the many who also had the long nails, compliments of the original biological accident that affected all of Ashford-5. A week later, she was able to trim her nails short as well as trim her hair. It now fell to the middle of her back. Once she appeared stable, again, everyone wanted this cure post haste. By August, all of the original hermaphrodite victims were able to cut their hair to their own personal preferences. All trimmed their nails short. Only Queen Amy and Governor Katrina continued to wear the debilitating toe shoes. They still felt they needed to wear them, since most all of the nobles did. Plus, Amy needed to maintain the traditional Ataro queen profile of physical limitations. She was not about to press Emperor Kino on this point.

During the summer months, Emperor Kino found smaller groups of terrorist victims who were willing to resettle on Ashford-5. By July, these, the first of the promised one thousand, began trickling into the spaceport, ferried here on various transports. All were in pretty bad shape; their living conditions in their assisted living accommodations had been quite dismal. Still, his agents were carefully selecting these victims, based upon previous skills, jobs, education, and/or previous IQ levels. Soon, Governor Katrina realized that he was bringing Rafe one thousand of the brighter minds in the Imperium, who had been a victim of various terrorist bio attacks. She discovered this while she processed their personal data upon their arrival at her spaceport. Katrina grinned, "That old bird sure knows what he is doing!"

August also brought a very strange visitor to Ashford-5. A sleek, silver light cruiser bearing Imperium markings radioed the control tower for permission to land. Once granted, the tower controller contacted Governor Katrina. "Boss, an Imperium light cruiser is landing in about thirty minutes."

Well, that's strange. What's a light battle cruiser doing here? "Boss, it's not registered to the fleet. Thought you ought to know," he added. At her request, he relayed the ship's identification numbers, which she entered into her computer system. Shortly, the ships basic statistics appeared on her monitor along with a red flag, stating: Top level Security Code required. The ship certainly wasn't from the Ataro Empire nor was it part of the Imperium fleet. *How very strange!* She headed out to personally meet this ship, wondering just who was onboard!

Governor Katrina arrived in time to see the large ship land. She noted it was one of the newer models. Already, it had requested a full refueling. She suspected the ship had probably traveled at top speed in order to use up all its fuel just getting here, either that or it had come a very long way. As she watched, a door opened. An elevator lowered a group of five men and a woman to the tarmac. At once, she detected that the woman was in charge; the men looked to be ship's security. The woman was young, perhaps thirty at most, with fairly short, blonde hair. Her eyes were a rich, deep blue eyes. More important from Katrina's point of view, the woman was extremely attractive, and she had to work to keep the arousal of her male organ in check.

"Welcome to Ashford-5. I'm Governor Katrina. How can we assist you?" she said formally in Imperium Standard, not trusting to the ULAT boxes to translate her highly modified speech. Lip plates were a definite liability beyond the confines of Tierra.

The woman had an alto voice, brisk and business-like. "Commander Torres. I need to meet privately with ex-senator Zarita Valen. I'm told she lives not far from the spaceport.

Please bring her to me. I'll await her arrival in my quarters. That will be all."

"Of course," Katrina replied to the back of the woman's head. Already, she'd turned around and headed back to the ship's elevator! *Bitch!* She thought; her arousal gone.

Well, I suppose it can't hurt to meet with this woman, Zarita replied to Katrina's message. *Be there in, say, a half hour.*

"I don't like this, not one little bit," Ari exclaimed. "She could well kidnap you or something. Please be careful, my love." After giving her mate a loving hug, Zarita headed off to the spaceport, using one of the electric cars in the fancy tunnel that ran from the Imperial Castle to the spaceport Admin Building.

She now wore the six inch oxfords, thankful for even this much relief from her body's genetic modifications. At the spaceport, Governor Katrina volunteered, "I don't trust that woman. If she tries something, let me know. I'll not grant them permission to take off."

"Thanks. I'm wearing my many crystals, so I don't think they can do anything to me that I don't want. Still, be prepared. I don't trust the Imperium," Zarita replied. Slowly, she walked across the tarmac to the sleek cruiser. At the elevator, two men stood, obviously waiting for her. One merely said her name. After she nodded, he asked her to follow them, which she did, riding the elevator up into the bowels of the large ship, quite unlike the much smaller deep space transport that she owned.

She soon became lost in the myriad corridors, but the men led her unerringly to a small room. At least one was courteous and opened the door for her, announcing, "Zarita Valen, as ordered." He did not follow her into the room. As she entered, she instantly recognized the woman: Torres of the Bops!

"My, you are looking quite young," Commander Torres said pleasantly, but without emotion. "Have a seat, please."

"You've not aged either. Marvels of the rejuvenation machines," Zarita replied, taking a seat. There were only two chairs and one small table. They sat facing one another.

"This room is secure. Nothing is being recorded, and nothing we say can be heard beyond this room. We will not be interrupted, senator," Torres began. Old memories of Torres returned to Zarita. Well over twenty-five years ago, she'd asked, no begged, Zarita to join her organization, the Bops or Black Operations. The Bops was a super secret organization whose supposed purpose was to protect the Imperium and its leaders. Well, they did that and more, much of which Zarita considered wholly illegal and unethical. She wasn't about to subscribe to their use of means to achieve an end. She'd turned her down back then.

"What do you want this time, Commander Torres?" Zarita asked, ready to probe the woman's mind, if needed, or if she suspected she wasn't being told the truth or all the details.

"Let's not be two cocks fighting," Torres replied calmly. "I know we've had our differences in the past. I've come today to beg you to lend us a hand. Let me explain."

"Not likely this time, but go ahead," Zarita countered. It was her subtle way of letting Torres know she'd best present her finest arguments.

"Since you left the Senate and as you know, there have been many terrorist genetic biological attacks," Torres began.

"Yes, each has been in the newscasts. I thought your organization retrieved all of the stolen bio agent cylinders," Zarita zinged her where she knew it would hurt. The Commander flinched slightly, but only ever so slightly.

"Yes, we retrieved all of the known ones at that time. It seems we missed some cylinders," Torres justified.

"Missed quite a few, if you ask me," Zarita bandied with her. Again, she noticed a slight rise in the woman's blood pressure, and knew that she'd scored.

Unplussed, Commander Torres continued. "Damned Fabrication Machines. They will duplicate anything! A few eluded our seizures. The unscrupulous duplicated them. We've been tracking them down, but always a few more slip through our net. For each one of the terrorist attacks that have occurred, three others have been prevented by our work. Three, Zarita, three!"

"I will accept that," Zarita gave her that point. The

58

Commander didn't seem to be lying to her about this detail.

"Still, there should be no terrorist attacks. My god, Zarita, every one of those attacks totally ruins the lives of the victims. We can't afford to miss even one; yet, I am sad to say that we have. The newscasts highlight our failures."

"Then, Aquila Prime must have been a monster failure," Zarita countered. Commander Torres definitely reacted to that point, in spite of her efforts to remain wholly emotionless.

"Genocide, Zarita, simple genocide. That's not even remotely classified as a terrorist attack. Genocide. Ten billion men, women, and children — dead, most horribly too. That's why I am here. You see, we had no clue that anyone was going after an entire planet. We monitor all the underground chatter. Until the attack, there was not the slightest clue that such a monumental plot was in the works. Nada. Nothing."

Zarita asked, "Is that unusual?"

"You bet it is. With all the other terrorist attacks, we had some hints that something big was in the works. Criminals always do something to get themselves caught somehow. This time, nothing at all. The genocide took everyone in the entire Imperium by total surprise."

"Well not everyone," Zarita retorted. "At least one person knew about it and carried it out."

"True. But you know what I mean. That a whole planet can be wiped out has now become common knowledge."

"Well, that was the purpose of this bio weapon when it was invented by the geneticists on Ashford-4," Zarita replied.

"Of course, a weapon of last resort, should the war with the Federation be lost. Still, every criminal organization now knows this bio weapon can be used to wipe out a whole planet. While we have developed reasonable methods to deal with a simple terrorist bio attack and get those victims assisted, this one caught everyone with their pants down. Worse, Zarita, no matter what policies the Imperium Senate passes, the Imperium is wholly unable to deal with ten billion victims at one time. It's physically impossible. Handling perhaps a few thousand is max."

"I believe you. So now you need my help preventing other planets from being attacked?" Zarita probed.

"Not exactly, but yes, that would be helpful if you would do it. No, I've come to ask your help with this Aquila Prime mess," Commander Torres paused a moment, reflecting on just the proper way to present this to Zarita. *She is no dummy, in spite of her appearance.*

"Let's go over what we do know for a fact about the attack on Aquila Prime." Zarita perked up. If nothing else, she knew she was about to hear very inside information about the genocide attack.

"First, we found a destroyed drone vehicle, along with a hundred of the bio agent cylinders. We know the drone was the delivery system. Unfortunately, going over Aquila Prime's security system logs, we could find no trace of that drone. It is as if it was wholly undetected while in flight. Some kind of new stealth technology — had to be. We tried to trace the origins of the drone, but that led nowhere. All of its RFI tags and other ID markings had been removed or were destroyed in the crash. Mostly a dead end."

"Much after the fact, other organizations claimed to have been behind the attack. We've been able to prove that none are factual, mere bragging. If nothing else, a Bops investigation is thorough. We found there was one cylinder of the bio agent stolen just a day before the massive attack. The cylinder was being shipped to a qualified genetic research facility. They'd had ten previous shipments, all above boards. This shipment was also beyond suspicion; we triple checked that detail. Somehow, a contortionist twisted his body inside a suitcase and shipped himself. Partway down the baggage conveyor system, he climbed out, found the shipping crate containing the bio agent, stole it, and replaced it with precisely the same weight in sand. Only when the crate arrived at the research facility was the theft discovered, which was only a few hours before the attack on Aquila Prime."

"The man's body was found in a maintenance storage room. He'd been shot with a old style projectile gun. Later on, another man was killed in a shuttle bombing, which we suspect is linked to the contortionist. We believe the contortionist handed off the bio agent to this other man, who then killed the flexible man, and who, in turn, was killed by whoever set this whole thing up. Trail dead ends there, naturally."

"So we explored other avenues. Obviously, someone wanted all the people on Aquila Prime dead. Why? What is to be gained? Did someone have a long, bitter dispute with that world? We've found no such animosity towards that world. Rather the opposite is more the case. So who is benefitting from the genocide? Well, certainly the Senate jumped at the chance to ship excess populations from many other hub worlds there, selling off the real estate of that world. However, from all that we can tell, the sudden genocide took the entire Senate by total surprise. In order to deal with the population resettlement, the Senate was in a particularly confused mess for several weeks. That alone tells us they were not expecting any such thing to happen."

"So who else has gained from it?" Zarita asked, growing curious with this line of inquiry.

"Mal Dynamics has. They've already begun opening up ten new mines. Needed rare earth elements are just now coming onto the market from their mines. Incidentally, that company purchased up large tracts that just happen to hold these valuable ores. We find that highly suspicious. Obviously, Mal Dynamics already knew where the ore deposits were located. They've not purchased anything else. Our attention is now focusing on that corporation. Incidentally, it's back into one giant corporation once more. When Bindaz Rumani, one of the Consortium members that you killed, passed away, Mal Dynamics splintered into twenty separate companies. Under their new head, one Jan Rumani of Zon-2, his grandson, the smaller companies have once more united into a giant corporation."

"Considering the price Mal Dynamics has paid for these new mines, they can expect to make almost unheard of profits from the rare earths they are now mining. We find that highly suspicious. In fact, Zarita, that's why I've come here today. We have nothing concrete on Jan Rumani, nothing to link him to the genocide attack, other than at the time of the attack; he was on a flight to a meeting on Winno-3. He could have taken a slight detour, but we can't prove it. At this point in time, he is our best guess for the perpetrator of this genocide. So I've come to beg you to at least lend us a hand. You have your unique talents. You can get into his mind and see if he has done this incredible mass murder or if he knows who did it for him. Please, Zarita, the Imperium needs your help. Ten billion men, women, and children need justice. Will you help us? If you agree, I will brief your Emperor Kino and get his permission for your assistance. I know the Bops has not done right by you in the past, but the times we are facing demand we put that in our past. Please, Zarita, please." *There, I've begged. Told her all I know. I don't know how I can put this any better. She's just got to help us or we are going to have to do some very illegal things.*

"Okay, I'll do what you wish, just this once. I wholly agree; the ten billion need justice, as well as those who survived. They deserve to know why this happened to their world and themselves. But you are right; my participation should be authorized via Emperor Kino. Get his ok, and I'll go with you," Zarita replied. For once, Torres displayed a slight emotional reaction. She briefly smiled. Zarita sensed the woman's tensions lifting.

A half hour later, Zarita listened to Torres outlining all she had told her to Emperor Kino. After the usual long distance hyperspace delay, he replied, "Excellent Commander Torres. Your investigation is following the same path as ours. We, too, believe this Jan Rumani of Zon-2 needs to be thoroughly investigated. He is the only one who is greatly benefitting from the genocide, though many other planets are resettling excess populations on Aquila Prime. If Zarita is willing to help you in your investigation, then I officially back her. However, if Jan should be found guilty of this heinous crime, he is not to be killed. Rather, he should be treated as a hardened criminal. I insist on this detail, Commander. He must not be killed. That would be giving him an easy way out and will not satisfy many of his victims. Over."

"Agreed, Emperor Kino. I'll keep you abreast of developments. Over and out. Okay, Zarita, how soon can you be ready to lift off?" she asked.

"Give me two hours, please."

A short while later, Zarita explained all she'd learned to Ari, Amy, and Katrina. After that, Ari helped her pack a small bag and accompanied her to the spaceport to see her mate off. Ari also agreed with Zarita's decision to help this top secret organization. Everyone wanted to see justice done for those of Aquila Prime. Right on time, the light cruiser lifted off.

After getting Zarita settled in her quarters, Torres took her to the galley for coffee and tea. "So Zarita, I've just heard your doctors have come up with some more revolutionary breakthroughs on these genetic modifications?"

"Well, yes, in fact, they have. Of course, the long fingernails mutation only affected a few of us on Tierra, er I mean Ashford-5 — from the original biological attack. However, they've solved the inability for any of us victims to cut our hair. I don't quite understand it all, something about the genetic modification putting neurons into our hair and nails. Anyway, the men love this repair. Now they can get finally get men's haircuts and look more like men," Zarita chatted.

Torres flashed a pleasant smile. "I couldn't help noticing you aren't wearing toe shoes any longer."

"Right, they were able to finally repair our feet. Well at least partially."

"Couldn't the medical machines repair them before?" Torres asked, wishing she'd paid more attention to her own doctor, when he explained the results of the genetic mutations caused by the bio agent.

"Oh sure, from the start, the medical machines could repair them as much as they are now. But you see, within a couple of days, our bodies rejected the modifications, and we were right back having to wear the toe shoes again. It never took, so to speak. Now another genetic change was made, making it permanent. We all really appreciate this one. I can walk so much better now, though these tall heels are still challenging. I think our doctors are making these procedures available to the rest of the Imperium doctors," Zarita replied, pleased she could report such good news.

"I have to commend your doctors. Honestly, who would ever have thought that it would be doctors on a primitive

Closed World that would have developed such cures. It amazes me that, with all these highly advanced, civilized worlds and their many top geneticists, they have not come up with anything in the way of a cure yet. Instead, they continually demand more of the bio agent samples, which provides terrorists with more and more opportunities to steal this horrific biological weapon of mass destruction," Torres commented.

"How come? What could they possibly be doing all this time?" Zarita asked. That Torres was making less of Tierra didn't bother her. Most others always had this opinion. She'd heard such things a million times during her stints as President and as Tierra's senator.

Torres laughed. "It's not for lack of trying. Of that, I am certain. You see, human genetic experimentation is illegal, except on volunteer criminals. After most of those original volunteers died rather horribly, few volunteer. Besides, those planets, who are legally allowed samples for their private research, have cut off all knowledge of their research, classifying it top secret. That bothers me, Zarita. What if some of them are building up a stockpile of the cylinders to use as a weapon later on?"

"Oh dear god!" Zarita exclaimed. She'd never consider this aspect.

"I agree. I've placed five deep cover operatives onto five of those worlds. Their mission is to infiltrate and discover just what is truly going on behind the scenes. You would be ideally suited for such planetary espionage, Zarita. A woman with your skills would be invaluable in ferreting out what is really happening behind closed doors, so to speak. However, right now, we need to focus on Jan Rumani."

"Sure."

"Okay. We know he is going to attend a fundraiser for terrorist victims to be held on B'lag-3 in one week. We'll outfit you with an elegant gown and see that you get the chance to meet Jan in person. After that, it's up to you to use your skills to find out what we need to know. If he is the person responsible, then we can use what you find out to help obtain positive proof of his guilt. If Emperor Kino had not been so insistent and if he was guilty, I would have suggested you do what you do to melt his brain. However, somehow, we'll have to obtain hard evidence based upon what you can find out for us."

"Makes sense. I only need to meet him once, but I'll have to be on the same planet with him after that in order to work my magic," Zarita explained.

Thirty-six hours later, they approached the yellow sun of B'lag-3. Zarita watched as the blue-green world appeared on the viewer. Here comes justice, she thought as she watched. Several hours later, she along with Torres and her Strike Team 1, ST1, were heading to Alsa, the sprawling city, where in just a few more days Jan Rumani was scheduled to address the APVFR, the Aquila Prime Victims Fund Raiser.

"Testing, testing, testing," Zarita whispered. One of Torres' men put a trans-dermal transmitter by her left ear. A male voice replied, indicating he could hear her. She had her hair up in a fancy, curly pile, the latest in B'lag-3 fashion. Her sleek gown revealed much of her legs, far more than she was accustomed to displaying. Still, she knew she looked good in this new red dress and black nylons, old style with back seams. Confident, she began her short walk into the enormous Grand Hall, a stately old building sporting a dozen giant marble columns that held up the arched roof over the enormously wide entrance doors. As she slowly approached, dozens of well-dressed men and women in equally provocative gowns stood waiting to gain entrance, invitations at the ready. Dozens of reporters were on hand calling out questions and recording the entrance of these most wealthy men and women. A few wore military uniforms, generals, she thought. At last, she was able to hand the white gloved doorman her invitation. He motioned for her to enter, and she followed an older couple into the spacious hall.

For a moment, she gagged from the combined perfumes and colognes of some two thousand women and men. Unaccustomed to such odors and in such volume, the mixture was overpowering to her senses. For a minute, she had to focus on regaining control of her body. Then, she was able to dampen the sense down. Zarita was prepared. She had all of her compacted germanium crystals on her person, from her tiara down to her belt around her waist. Confident, she moved out among the throng.

As she expected, a number of young men gyrated towards her, striking up conversations. Most were just angling to find a way to get into her pants. *Honestly, if I hear 'don't I know you from somewhere' just one more time, I am going to scream!* Then, she smiled, though it was invisible because of her golden lip plates, which were also attracting attention, as well as her incredible shape. *If they got into my pants, I'm sure that they would wish they hadn't! Thank god for telepathy.*

To avoid the younger men, she took a seat at one of the fancier tables, where an older couple was sitting, striking up a conversation with them. "It's just awful, you know, those poor victims. Sarita Val," she used a fake name.

"Oh yes, dearier, so awful. So tragic. We're here to do what little that we can do." The woman was very eager to chat. Time passed quickly.

"Oh! Here he comes now. That's the man himself. Jan Rumani of Zon-2. He's about the wealthiest man in the Imperium, now that he's got control of all the Mal Dynamics companies," the woman explained.

Her husband grumbled, "I don't think it's right for one man to control a whole industry like this. Monopolies are never good." Zarita agreed with him and then hushed, as the lights dimmed slightly, and the man moved before the microphone and video cameras.

Jan had short, black hair and a perfect moustache to go along with his bushy eye brows and angular face. His tuxedo was immaculate, and he spoke in Imperium Standard, so everyone here could understand without the noisy ULAT boxes. Zarita paid little attention to his actual speech. As the Imperium President and as a senator, she'd heard enough pontificating to last her a lifetime. Using a sympathetic and propitiative tone, he played the assemblage like an Aeolian harp to the tune of over five million credits before the evening was finished. Zarita was one of the few who did not succumb to his pleading message. However, she got what she needed, familiarization with him.

Around eleven that night, she finally was once more aboard the light cruiser. "Well, how did it go? Have you got what you need so you can do what it is that you do?" Torres asked. Zarita sensed the ex-Interrogator's absolute frustration. Here was this seemingly nobody whose skills at interrogation so far exceeded hers that she could scarcely contain her jealousy and envy.

"Yes, if you'll permit me to retire to my cabin, I'll see what he is hiding," she replied. A half hour later and after changing into her own clothes, Zarita laid down on her bed, closed her eyes, and focused. Her many powerful amplifying crystals began to glow, filling her small, metallic and plastic room with a soft pale blue luminance. *Ah, he is going to bed as well. She waited, sensing his physical body.* Time drifted. *He's asleep. Good. Now let's see what we have here.*

An hour later, Zarita smiled. *One of my trifecta. Sex, money, power, though fame sometimes plays an alternate role. Money. Greed.* She placed a thought in Torres' mind and rose. As anticipated, Torres was waiting for her in the communications-secure room. "Well?" Torres asked.

"We have found the guilty man. He masterminded the theft of the bio agent cylinder using that contortionist, but had him killed, as well as the other intermediate man. He used one of his company's new stealth drones, substituting a second prototype for the missing drone. He used the company's Fabrication Machine to make a hundred duplicate cylinders, and he attached them to the drone. He carried the drone attached to his deep space transport. He altered course while in hyperspace, launched the drone attack on Aquila Prime, and then jumped back into hyperspace, heading for his destination. Why did he do this? His companies desperately need more of the rare earths found in abundance on Aquila Prime, but he didn't want to pay them the going rates and came up with this plan to acquire the ores dirt cheap. His plan has worked to perfection." Zarita outlined what she'd seen in his mind.

"Damn! Damn! Bastard!" Torres cursed, a rare show of emotion for the Commander of the Bops. Then, she grimaced.

"You didn't kill him, did you?" She recalled the men whose brains had been liquefied by Zarita.

"No. Emperor Kino wants him brought to justice. Death would be too sweet for this man. He has no sense of guilt over what he's done. Appalling. Men!" Zarita swore.

"Ok. Let me get this to my people. We'll use what you've discovered to find hard evidence. We know precisely what to look for. Thank you, Zarita. On behalf of all the ten billion, thank you."

"Survivors too," Zarita added. In her mind, the dead were dead and could care less. Rather, the poor victims who lived needed this man brought to justice and the attack's reasons illuminated for all to see.

A week later, the Bops ST1 had acquired or put together the "hard evidence." However, in doing so, they had not counted on the many spies that Mal Dynamics had working for them.

"Shit! How the hell did the Imperium forces find out about my attack?" Jan Rumani angrily cursed. He'd just received word from one of his agents that the Imperium was filing official terrorist charges against him, naming him as the person responsible for the genocide of Aquila Prime! Jan had not gotten to his position by losing his cool in tight situations. Hastily, he packed a few essentials and headed for his private deep space shuttle. *In an hour, I'll have totally disappeared. I can still run Mal Dynamics from hiding. They won't catch this fox!* Walking briskly, he got to his company shuttle taxi depot. Here, he boarded one of the four man shuttles, a fully automated craft identical to the millions on use on Proxima Prime. He selected the menu item for the company's spaceport here on Zon-2. Then, his hand reached over to punch the Execute button.

Torres had wisely followed Zarita's suggestion. She'd said, "Look, if he gets wind of your investigation, he's going to flee, just like the Consortium trio did, just like Legate Emeryk did. Keep me close to Zon-2, where he's at now. I can monitor him and keep him from fleeing." Hence, Torres kept her light cruiser docked at Zon-2's spaceport and oversaw her Bops investigation from here.

Meanwhile, Zarita maintained a light telepathic contact with Jan. His sudden reactions caught her attention. Soon, she realized he was indeed fleeing, just before the ST1 team was about to apprehend him. She watched through his eyes, as he brought up the shuttle's menu. That brought back memories of her own many trips in similar shuttles, years ago during her stint as Ashford-5's senator on Proxima Prime. She recognized what he was seeing. Zarita acted.

When ST1 raided his office, Jan was not there. The men raced through the building and out onto the taxi ground. Wildly running from shuttle to shuttle, the six men frantically looked for Jan. At last, they found him. He was sitting rigidly in its seat, his right index finger poised to press the Execute button. He looked to them as though he were somehow frozen mid-action. Only after the ST1 members arrested him and physically lifted his body out of the shuttle did Zarita finally release her control over his body.

A day later, the news of the arrest of Jan Rumani hit all of the news outlets of the Imperium! All stations carried the Chief Imperium Prosecutor's detailed public speech. The immaculately dressed man spoke clearly, outlining in detail what Jan Rumani had done. He cited proof. The two damning pieces of evidence were the missing stealth drone prototype and the money trail. The recovered materials from the destroyed drone matched those of the existing prototype. The financial authorities were able to trace funds drawn from Jan's private account and deposited into the two dead men's accounts, payment for services rendered. The prosecutor spelled out in no uncertain terms what he felt Jan's motive behind the genocide had been — simple corporate greed.

As Torres and Zarita watched the news presentation, she cleverly asked, "So, Zarita, how does it feel to have been instrumental in bringing this criminal to justice? Good, eh?"

"Well, yes, as a matter of fact, it does," Zarita had to admit.

"So how about considering coming to work for us?" Torres tried once more to recruit her. "Someone with your talents would be invaluable."

"Well, I don't know. I guess you can call upon me later

on when you have another situation where I could help," Zarita gave her this much ground.

Wisely, Torres realized this was about as much as she could hope for and agreed. "Okay then. Let's get you home. Don't be surprise if I come calling upon you again."

Unknown to all, Sven Bartold, Jan's Vice-president of Operations, had also been monitoring their field agent's reports. He'd realized at once, what was going on. At first, he was shocked that his boss might well have been behind the genocide on Aquila Prime. *Fallout will be horrific. I have to protect myself, but how? Surely, they'll break up the company, and I'll be out of this cushy job.* He then began doing some of his own investigation. By chance, he found the original bio agent cylinder and accompanying crate of clothing stored in Jan's private safe. As soon as he saw the cylinder, everything fell into place — the terrorist attack on Aquila Prime, the sudden purchases of fifty mines on that world, and the instant acquisition of the expensive rare earths the company needed.

Hiding this in his own safe — my god, this is the first place they will search! Without any further thought, Sven took the crate and cylinder from the safe, taking it home with him that very afternoon. Once safely home, Sven began thinking hard about his own future. "I'll be out of a job. There's not a chance in Hell of any other company ever hiring me, not when they discover I worked for Jan Rumani. He'll be the most hated man in the Imperium. I'll be blacklisted on every world. Hell, I'll be broke in a year. That's not fair! Damn, I never knew about it. I had no part in Jan's dealings, but I'll be drawn and quartered right along with him! Jan's a fool. I sure as hell am not! Think, Sven, think!"

Slowly, he realized the immense value the single crate represented. First, he thought about just turning it in to the authorities. He might be able to regain some respect, perhaps, but he'd still be out of a job. What new boss would ever trust him, once they knew he'd stolen the crate from his boss' safe? None. In the business world, he'd be seen as a traitor and never trusted again. No, while turning the bio weapon in might gain him some respect, it would end his career. "Hell, I'm only twenty-five!"

"I need to sell this on the Black Market. I ought to get enough to get by for a while," he declared to his walls. "Wait, if I duplicate it, say twenty times, I'll get twenty times that amount." Slowly, his mind developed a workable scheme. "How long do I have? Two days, at most," he concluded. At midnight, he put his plan into operation. With the crate concealed in a suitcase, he returned to Mal Dynamics Corporate Headquarters. His ID card allowed him entry. Hastily, he made his way to the Fabrication Machine. The place was deserted, except for the night guards. Perfect.

An hour later, he'd fabricated two dozen more complete crates along with twenty-five shipping containers. Carefully, he packaged the crates into the shipping containers and carefully addressed each one. Then, he sent them into the automated mailing system of Mal Dynamics, confident the system would route them all safely to their destination. He'd carefully chosen a little used Mal Dynamics storage depot on Proxima Prime for their arrival. That done, with his now empty suitcase, he left headquarters. It was two in the morning. Once home, he fired off six emails from his home computer network. Finally, he took a d-gun to the computer, destroying the machine completely. Now, his only contacts would be via his small, hand-held PA, Personal Assistant. Next, he packed a few things into his suitcase and finally took a brief nap.

At dawn, he first went to the bank and withdrew most of his funds. After stuffing the credit notes into his suitcase, he then took a shuttle into the seedier part of the city. Here, he knew anything could be had for the right price. He needed two things, well three actually. It took him an hour and a hundred credits to find just the right place to have the two actions done.

"You sure this is what you want done?" the ruff-looking man asked. He'd explained what he wanted done.

"Yes, there is an additional five hundred in it for you, but only if you get it done today."

"'K. It's your money. Need it up front."

"Agreed. I'll return with the funds in about a half hour.

Will you be ready by then?"

"Sure thing. I'll send someone out to get some things you'll be needing."

Sven then headed to the Public Shuttle Depot. There, he removed the needed funds from his suitcase. Then, he stuffed the case into a private locker and put the key into his pocket. Hastily, he headed back.

Three hours later, Sven awoke from the medical machine's operations. Not fully trusting the man, he sat up and inspected his body — well, her body now. Sven had just had a complete sex change operation. His hair had been lengthened to shoulder length. His voice was in the alto range. She had respectable breasts and all the right "plumbing," as he considered it.

"Ah, you're awake. Good. Here, see if these fit." The man pointed to a woman's outfit that his wife had just purchased — a white silk blouse, conservative black skirt, purse, hose, and flats.

"Perfect. Give me a few minutes to dress," she said. The man smirked, and left her in the room with her new clothes and the medical machine. She fumbled about getting herself dressed for the first time. Satisfied, she retrieved her old ID card and the locker key, leaving behind the old clothes. A half hour later, the man handed her a new ID card. Officially, she was now Savina Ruckhard, twenty-five. Her card was marked "Ambassador," giving her official rights to travel under diplomatic immunity to any Open World in the Imperium.

She headed back to the locker. She retrieved more credits, putting them into her purse. Savina then took a shuttle to the spaceport. An hour later, her deep space transport lifted off, bound for Proxima Prime. Of course, everyone onboard was now talking about the arrest of Jan Rumani of Mal Dynamics and that he had caused the genocide on Aquila Prime. As Savina listened to the conversations around her, most wanted him to be executed for it. She could only smile. She was safe and soon to be independently wealthy.

Chapter 4 The Gypsies

"The damned gypsies have got to go. They's as bad as 'dem freaks of nature, I tells' ya," swore a spacer guard. He and a dozen others were drinking it up at Jonah's Tavern in Halcion City, Beltar-3. Their President had just made a public announcement that they would be taking in another fifteen hundred victims of the genetic mutation terrorist attacks.

"Hell, all those damned gypsies do is eat up our food and tells our fortunes. Anyone can tell fortunes. Just give 'em a crystal ball. Whoo, I see many credits in your future, Alzog. Oh, and a sexy woman will soon enter your life. There, how's that?" Dozens roared and poured him another mug. Suds overflowed, white froth slipping down the sides and onto the table, mingling with the shells of peanuts.

A third man concurred, "Yeh, I agree. My woman works at Brenner's Assisted Living. Those pathetic victims are completely helpless. All they do is consume all of our valuable tax credits. Someone really ought to put them out of their misery. Hell, everyone knows they can't live on their own. Besides, she tells me they have more babies than rabitons or mice, for that matter. Their baby creatures are just as pathetic as they are. Someone ought to sterilize 'em all, that's what I think."

"Oh just put them down, like we do for any animal that breaks its legs. That's the only sensible thing to do. Solves the baby problem wholly," a fourth commented.

The first man added, "Hey, my wife — she's a math teacher — she says that the freaks birthrate is double ours. She claims that in a century, we'll be in the tiny minority. All Beltar-3 will be filled with the freaks. Hell, we all will end up being nursemaids to 'em. Don't know what the damned President is thinking, bringing more of 'em here. We should vote him out! Still, the gypsies are just as bad. They rape our women, you know. Everybody says so. Hell, they steal anything that's not tied down. It's not just fortunes they tell; no they take fortunes. They have to go too."

The second responded, "He's right. I heard yesterday down at the docks that them gypsies are demanding rights now. They ain't got none. Hell, they ain't from Beltar-3. Send them on their way or kill 'em too."

"He's got a point," the fourth guard pointed out. "I knows for a fact that they don't have a home planet. They're from nowhere. Some say they were born in space. Spacers, the lot of them. Send them back into space where they belong."

"Nah, get rid of them all. I'm tired of my taxes going to waste on the gypsies. They get free health care, and we hardworking stiffs are paying for that. Hell, we're paying through the nose to support the freaks as well. I say kill them all and be done with the whole project," the third man replied.

Unknown to the guards, several other men were listening carefully to their boisterous conversation, taking their sentiments to heart. One was a Holy Disciples' priest. Later that night, he reported to his bishop, relating what he'd heard. Then, he added, "You are right. Public sentiments are running very high against the Devil's Spawn and these infernal gypsies."

"Ah my son. The Lord has spoken to us. Verily, tis time we acted. The Devil's Spawn must be sent to the Negative Afterlife that they're due. Plus, we need to teach these gypsies that they are not wanted here on Beltar-3. We must convince them to leave and stop consuming the staff of life our own faithful deserve, created by their own sweat and blood. Yes, it is time we take the action our politically correct leaders refuse to do. They'll support these Devil's Spawn until the freaks overrun our whole society, leading us all into the Negative Afterlife! Well, it is our Holy Duty to put our leaders back on the Righteous Path, the path to the Positive Afterlife. Come. We have some planning to do, father."

That night, a dozen masked men broke into Brenner's Assisted Living complex. One pasted up a sign that read: Get rid of all the freaks or we'll do it for you. Armed with d-guns, the others raced through the complex, opening doors, and shooting the genetically modified terrorist attack victims in their sleep. Over a hundred helpless men, women, and children were executed that first night.

Across town and just beyond the spaceport, a dozen deep space transports sat in a giant U-shape, parked on the rolling grasslands within walking distance of the city. These ships were painted in gay colors. Reds, yellows, greens, and blues predominated, though here and there some of the silver metal did show through, adding to the colors. These were the ships of the gypsy Braith Clan.

The gypsies of the Imperium were a strange people, space nomads. No one now knew their original planet of origin, including themselves. Born in space or on the various planets they visited for brief times, these people had no home world. Indeed, their ID cards, when they actually had them, were merely stamped "Gypsy" in large red letters. Only rarely did they use such cards, mostly to pay for refueling their ships at the spaceports they visited.

The gypsies were organized into various clans, which often were at odds with each other. Fighting sometimes broke out when two clans attempted to land on the same planet. Beltar-3 was technically a rim planet, though just barely beyond the middle sectors, in contrast to Ashford-5, which was on the outer rim, quite distant from it. At this time, the Braith Clan had spent some six months parked on the grasslands beyond the spaceport, just outside Halcion City. Some of their men had taken on odd jobs around the city, bringing in much needed funds for their resupply. Additionally, some of the women "told fortunes" to bring in a little extra.

The clans were matriarchal in nature. Each clan leader was the elder woman, who carried the clan's name. Their word was law in all things. Thus, these women commanded and demanded the highest respect from other clan members. Their numbers ranged from a hundred to two hundred. Often when a clan's population became too large, an amicable arrangement was made, splitting into two separate clans.

However, once each year, the Rendezvous was held. All of the various clans, who were in that general area of space, met, docking with the host transport ship or landing on an uninhabited planet. At the meeting, the leaders worked out which clan was going to which planet next, solving a centuries-old problem of having two or more clans on the same world and thereby avoiding the usual blood baths. This also prevented having too many gypsies on one specific world. Further, at the annual Rendezvous, some men and women were exchanged between the clans. Inter-clan marriages were accepted, though frowned upon.

The Braith Clan was led by Matriarch Blodwen Braith. She was forty-five and widowed last year. Like nearly all gypsies, her skin tone was a pale yellowish, tending towards brownish. She had brown eyes and dark brown hair, distinctive of the Braith lineage. Like most gypsy women, her wavy hair just touched her shoulders, falling evenly at the sides of her face that was perfectly round and quite stern. Brushed upwards to give her hair a fuller drape, her hair also made her head look several inches larger than it was.

Blodwen seldom smiled. A gypsy's life was a hard one, particularly so for the matriarch. One wrong move could well spell starvation or running adrift in deep space. Having to be rescued by another clan meant an instant loss of respect and very likely her position. Her face was also somewhat flat, not helped by her thin lips.

The sternness of the gypsy women was partially compensated by their use of bright, gay colors in their dresses. Even their men wore colorful sash-like belts, usually three inches wide. In contrast to the other gypsy women, the Braith matriarch and her two daughters wore matching very dark red cotton dresses. Two petticoats gave a bit of flair to the bottoms of their dresses, but their matching dark red corsets worn over their dresses added to their striking appearance. The subdued red of their dress combined with the yellow-brown, stern faces gave the matriarch and her two daughters their commanding look.

Blodwen had two daughters, who closely resembled their mother. Anwyn, twenty-two, was her heir; Ceri, twenty, was second in line. Neither was married as yet, though it was high time that Anwyn chose a mate. While not mandatory, the matriarch ought to be married and subsequently to be proven fertile, yielding a daughter who would eventually take over the rulership of the clan from her mother. However, it was also perfectly acceptable for the matriarch to take any man of her choosing into her bed, particularly so if she continued to bring forth male children. If she had no daughters to inherit her throne, then the clan met and chose a new matriarch. Most all matriarchs did everything possible to avoid this, naturally.

One skill any matriarch must have is the ability to foresee the future. The better she was at this, the better the chances for survival of her clan. This evening, Blodwen and her daughters sat stiffly on their cushioned chairs before the Summoning Table in the matriarch's Official Chambers, a small room filled with cushions, tapestries, and hanging, semi-transparent curtains. When needed, fortunes of guests would be told in this room. Otherwise, the matriarch conducted all her formal clan sessions here.

Blodwen frowned. "I don't like what I've been seeing. I wish the visions would be clearer." Anwyn knew just what she meant. Visions could be quite tricky to comprehend. Only last week, she'd seen a guest's future for him. Holding his left hand over a bloody gut wound while his right hand held a d-gun, the guest man was looking at a finely dressed young woman. A dead body lay a few feet from him. So what did the vision mean? Was the guest supposed to shoot this man? Was the woman to be his? Had he become involved in a love triangle? Had he intervened where he should not have? Confusing. In the end, she had only told the guest just what she'd seen, leaving the interpretation of the vision up to the man. He left quite pale, though he paid her the fifty credits. She still didn't know the significance of her vision. Hence, Anwyn could sympathize with her mother's frustration. So much depended upon her getting it right.

In contrast, Ceri's visions had yet to mature or even materialize to any significant extent. Of course, this frustrated Ceri no end. Unless she got visions, she knew she'd never be able to take her mother's place as the Braith Matriarch, assuming something bad happened to her older sister. Still, Ceri clung to the hope her visions would one day begin. It was not uncommon for visions to begin to appear later in life. Ceri prayed this would be so.

Trying to be helpful, Anwyn suggested, "Ivarr ought to be back soon. Perhaps, he's heard something that would be helpful, mom."

"I suppose you are right, child. It is so confusing this time. I hadn't planned to leave this world for another month, just in time to make the next Rendezvous. The visions are so dark, my daughters, so utterly dark. A grey veil covers the Universe. So hard to pierce through the swirling clouds. I only get glimpses. Perhaps Ivarr will bring news," Blodwen sighed. She'd been the matriarch for some twenty years, since the untimely death of her mother, who had been stabbed by an ungrateful guest upset over the dark future she'd seen for him. In turn, before he could leave, Blodwen had stabbed the guest. His body washed up on a desolate seacoast. Yes, obtaining justice also was the responsibility of the clan's matriarch. Certainly, no gypsy would ever get justice from the authorities of the world on which they were currently staying.

Just then, someone knocked on the door. Reflexively, all three women reached for their druga, a short dagger strapped to their waists. Ivarr stuck his head in the door and the three relaxed. "Come in Ivarr. What news?" Blodwen asked.

The twenty-three year old Ivarr entered, pushing aside some veil curtains, taking a seat across from the three stern faced women. He was tall and thin, but keen eyed, probably the best of their observers. Each clan had several "observers," who had the uncanny skill to be able to see and understand the motives of the local population of the various worlds upon which they parked for a time.

Ivarr spoke in a hushed, serious tone. "Blodwen, I don't like what I'm hearing. Bad talk. Mostly, they grow more intolerant of the poor terrorist attack victims — those victims of the genetic mutations. It's true; the hermaphrodites breed true and at an alarming rate, twice the rate of the rest of us. Already here in Halcion City, the assisted living centers are overflowing with these helpless victims and their many offspring, who are just as helpless as their parents are. Common folk are complaining bitterly about the financial drain these victims are creating here. It's overflowing onto us now. We're being lumped together with these victims. I don't like the sound of it. There's always some who take matters into their own hands."

"Those poor victims!" Anwyn spat, her emotions rising. "It's not enough their whole lives have been ruined. Now, they are being blamed for their own helplessness. Honestly, I sometimes think we ought to abandon all these damned worlds. There isn't a sane world anywhere in the whole universe!"

"Aye, Miss Anwyn. But you have to see their point. Each of these terrorist victims has lost everything. They are only barely able to walk by themselves and need someone to assist them with nearly all things. The care giver profession has grown exponentially during the past twenty years, but those are low wage jobs. The assisted living complexes are busting at their seams from overcrowding. There are just so darn many of them. Add to that their many children, and you can see the mess that they are in. I do sympathize with them. Caring for all these victims really is draining funds like mad. Surely, I don't know what the solution is. The talk I hear is that they ought to all be killed, put out of their misery."

"But they are people, Ivarr, just like the rest of us," Anwyn countered. "If they'd just get going and spend the funds to regrow their arms, then they could live on their own."

Ivarr nodded. "True, Miss Anwyn, quite true. Ten thousand credits per person. That's what they say it costs to rehabilitate one of the victims. Sure, the wealthy can afford to have it done right away, but those are in the minority. Worst, they let the criminals breed. Half of these young adults in these centers are children of the mutated criminals. Who is going to pay for their rehabilitation? No one. So the problem only escalates. Rhys worked out that in a century these helpless hermaphrodites will vastly outnumber the rest of the population here on Beltar-3. Probably, it's going to be similar on the other worlds that have taken in these victims and the children of the criminals."

"God! That bad?" Blodwen gushed. "Hell, maybe Anwyn's right. We should just head off to some nebula where star systems are being born, find us an uninhabited planet, and settle down."

Ivarr, Anwyn, and Ceri laughed. "A gypsy settle down?"

he added mirthfully. Blodwen finally cracked a smile. No, that would be the absolute last thing any gypsy would ever do!

"I should contact some of the other clans and see what their situation is on the worlds they're on. It may be wise to do this before the coming Rendezvous," Blodwen decided. "Get Madoc for me, will you Ivarr? Tell him I wish to contact Morwen and Siana of the Glaw and Rhian Clans. Yes, tonight." She saw his eyebrows rise and added that last. She knew that such contact was highly unusual, especially since the Rendezvous was only about a month away.

An hour later, Blodwen returned from her late night off-world calls. Her face was grimmer than before she'd left, Anwyn observed. "Mom?" she asked. Both she and Ceri were both concerned and curious about what their mother had learned.

"Despicable. The backlash against the poor victims is spilling out onto all worlds. It's as Ivarr told us. Rhys may well be right. In a century, there'll be more of these helpless victims than any world can possibly support. No government is willing to spend the ten grand needed to regrow their arms. Utter fools! They spend more than that in armaments. What good are all their guns and battleships if they wind up having to support millions and millions of helpless victims? Tell me that! Grim, dears, simply grim. I've got to get some sleep. Perhaps tomorrow will be a better day."

The two helped their mother prepare for bed. After that, they too turned in. Their rooms, which they shared with five other close relatives and their husbands, were in the mother ship. Also, Ivarr, Rhys, and Madoc had rooms in this ship, along with their pilot, Wyn, and their navigator Mostyn. These five were unmarried as yet. One of the other husbands, Tudyr, was in charge of their security. Young Ivarr had hopes of one day marrying Anwyn, while Rhys had set his sights on winning over Ceri.

While the others turned in, Ivarr was worried, more than he'd said before his matriarch. He'd heard such vile talk before on other worlds. Thrice, it had escalated into violence against other clans, who made hasty exits from the confrontations. Would it happen here? He decided he needed to take a late night walk to clear his head and ponder the significance of what he'd overheard in the tavern earlier. Would some of the disgruntled take matters into their own hands? If so, he pitied the poor, defenseless terrorist victims. But what other possible solution was there? Would the rulers finally see sense and open their treasuries, performing the regrowth operation for the many thousands who needed it? At least, they could then become somewhat productive members of these worlds, instead of being a total leech. As he walked, he was more than proud to be a gypsy and not a citizen of any of these crazy worlds.

His walk did clear his mind. As he started to head back, he heard some explosions in the distance! Boom! Thrice. "What the hell?" he whispered. It was coming from the edge of the city, about a mile from him. Hastily, he began jogging back to the gypsy encampment. If someone was sabotaging something, he didn't want them blaming the gypsies just because he was out for a walk. As he approached the dozen ships, he spotted three men wearing red bio containment suits! "What the Hell?" he whispered, ducking behind a tree. From his vantage point, he couldn't tell just what they were doing. Their flashlights illuminated small areas of the ships only. He felt for his knife at his side. Reassured he wasn't entirely defenseless, he crept closer. The men were doing something to the air intake system, but what? Were they planting more bombs? Then, it struck him. They were executing a biological terrorist attack! Why else would they be wearing such heavy protection suits! He panicked. He had to do something, but what? There were three of them that he could see.

Ivarr drew his knife. He calculated that he could take one of them, before the others jumped him. But would they? *No, they move cumbersomely in those suits. Have to protect Anwyn!* He stole silently up to the closest man, who was moving away from the ships. One quick upwards thrust. His knife cut through the plastic suit, plunging into the man's upper back. He felt the blade slip through ribs. Instinctively, he pivoted the blade, causing the edge to cut downwards. He'd severed the man's heart and aorta.

81

His cries were partially muffled by the suit and helmet. Still, the other two men turned. Seeing their compatriot fall, both moved as quickly as they could in their suits. Now, Ivarr spotted two small shuttles parked not far from them. Ivarr broke into an all-out dash. Although he gained on them, they reached one of the shuttles before he did. Still, he was able to come up behind the second man. He stabbed him, just as he'd done the first. The third men activated the shuttle. As it took off with its door open, Ivarr was knocked to the ground.

He got back to his feet. "Anwyn!" He ran as fast as he could to the matriarch's ship. "What did they do? Perhaps, it's not too late. Look, look!" he told himself. A half hour later, he spotted the cylinder, the biological attack agent. His heart sank! A slight hissing sound told him the damage was already done. The gas was being released into the ship's air system!

His memories of all the many newscasts flooded into his mind. He sunk to the ground. *Shutting it off now is too late. The cylinder is about empty. If I go in there, I'm going to be infected too. I've failed her! The others!* Suddenly, he realized the other ships might also be infected! He picked up the flashlight that one had dropped and began inspecting the other ships. One by one. His heart sank even further with each ship he checked. These terrorists were thorough. Every ship was infected. By now, all the cylinders were empty, their hideous contents spread throughout the many ships. There was nothing he could do now. From the news reports, he knew they would all be in a coma for probably four days, before waking to find themselves helpless victims. He sat down, pulled his legs up to his chin, and began sobbing.

Time passed. At last, he roused. "Got to dispose of the two men." Mechanically, he dragged each corpse to the remaining shuttle and deposited it into the back seat. Then, he hopped in and powered up the ship, noticing it was registered to the Holy Disciples, the fanatical religious group. He piloted the ship over to the river. There, he landed, but not before resetting the controls. He watched as the shuttle moved out over the water and set down, sinking slowly from sight. That done, he made his solemn way back to the gypsy encampment, arriving near dawn. "What do I do now?" he asked himself.

He sat down, leaning against a nearby tree. He imagined his girlfriend lying in her bed, but now in a coma. All were in a coma. "The whole clan is wiped out, but me. Good god, what do I do now? I can't even call for help. I don't dare go inside to use the comm center." He knew he had to stay outside for at least three days, if he were to remain uninfected. "I must be here to help Anwyn when she wakes. That much I can do for her. No, I can always be with her and help her with everything. Ceri too. I have to." His stomach growled. He rose and headed off into the waking city to get some breakfast, counting the few credits he had on his person. "It'll have to do," he said.

When he returned later that afternoon, he found the authorities had been alerted to the bio agent attack. Security Guards in full armor ringed their small settlement. Six men in red containment suits were walking slowly back to the armada of shuttle craft. "Halt. You can't go in there. Biological attack," one guard forcibly stopped him. He waited. Soon, the suited men began removing their helmets.

"Okay, it's verified. Another bio attack. Spread the warning tape all around this entire gypsy camp. Post guards," one man ordered the Security Guards. He then noticed the lone gypsy and nodded to him, making his cumbersome way over to Ivarr. "Sorry son. Your camp is now quarantined for the next three days. Another terrorist bio agent attack. They're all going to be victims and in need of assisted living. We'll be back in three days to help them out and get them to assisted living quarters, such as we can find."

Ivarr said nothing, but nodded he understood. While eating lunch, he'd heard the news. One of the assisted living complexes had been attacked last night. Men with d-guns had raided the place, shooting many victims while they slept. Then, they'd set some explosives and blown up a third of the facilities, killing another two hundred. The scene there was ghastly, but the newscasters insisted on showing video of the site, while rescue workers were combing the wreckage. Again, he sat down, resting his back against a tree, watching the men string the bright yellow warning tape around the whole area. Later on, all left but two guards.

As the days passed slowly, Ivarr continue to figure out just what he could do to rescue them all. There were a hundred or so in the clan and a dozen deep space transport ships. Normally, there were about eight per ship, though the matriarch's ship held more like twenty. He knew he could fly one ship, but not the eleven others or could he? A plan formed. He could manually set up an automated sequence and course. When activated, the ship's computers would take over, safely flying them to the destination. But then what? He imagined he could dock with each ship, board it, and reset the controls. Yet, how would the victims manage to survive? They would be helpless, just like all the other terrorist victims. He knew he could not kidnap others to become their care givers.

"Maybe they'll all want to be moved into assisted living homes," he reasoned. "No, they are like me, gypsies. We'd rather die in space than be confined for the rest of our lives on some dump of a world. No, I have to get us off this planet and into space before the authorities haul them off to assisted living homes. Somehow, I must."

The more he thought, the more he believed he could pull this one off. He knew the precise time the bio agent would no longer be active, around one in the morning. The authorities would not likely show up until the following morning, giving him some nine hours before they could interfere. He had to save the clan, somehow.

He tried to imagine just what he would need to do, once they were awake. They would be starving, in dire need of food and water. They'd need to use the bathroom. Once that was done, he could then program the dozen shuttles, lifting off before the authorities intervened. How long would it take to program a shuttle's computer? He guessed twenty minutes. Times twelve, that would use up four of the possible nine hours he had to pull this off. Then, he realized all just had to have new clothes, shoes, and the strange lip ornaments. Without them, they would be naked, since their current clothing would scarcely fit their vastly modified bodies any longer.

Try as he might, he could think of no way to acquire them for the victims. That would have to come later. As one o'clock approached, his nerves began to fray. So many things could go wrong. Surely, they all would be hysterical at the very best. They'd be waking up to a hideous nightmare without end. Again, he thought about just allowing them to go into assisted living quarters here in Halcion City, but he just as quickly rejected it. After all, one of them had already been bombed and hundreds killed. No, this had to work.

As soon as his watch displayed one o'clock, Ivarr braced himself for the hysterical screaming. He had to work fast, if they had any chance at all. He dashed into the matriarch's ship, ran past his own quarters, on up to the pilot's seat, and powered the ship up. Then, he slipped over to the navigator's chair and brought up the coordinates. Thank god, the Rendezvous coordinates were already entered. He activated them and set automatic takeoff for six in the morning, giving him five hours. As he dashed back down the hallway, he began to hear moaning, signs at least one woman was coming around. While he desperately wanted to be there for Anwyn, he had the responsibility of the whole clan on his shoulders now. He ran over to the next shuttle.

He heard a woman screaming, but he had to ignore her for now. Fifteen minutes later, he had this shuttle programmed, but the screams from men and women were deafening. Once more he didn't respond to them, but made a mad dash for the next shuttle. By now, screams came from all dozen of the Braith Clan's deep space transports. Steeling himself, he continued setting and activating the ships' navigation and automatic pilot systems.

After finished the last one, he glanced at his watch. He'd used up three of the hours; he was ahead of schedule. It was 4 a.m. Two hours to go. He raced into his own shuttle; the hysterical screaming had subsided. Now, he faced hysterical sobbing. He headed straight for Blodwen's room. He knocked and then entered. The sight was grizzly. She was lying at a crazy angle on the floor. Blood oozed from her head, angling at a crazy position. A trained observer, he instantly grasped what had happened. She's gotten up and taken a bad fall, breaking her neck. Stunned, he stood and stared for a minute, before he heard the sobbing of Anwyn coming from her room next door.

Ceri's voice was recognizable as well. He rushed over to her door, knocked, and, opened it.

Anwyn was sitting up, sobbing loudly. If there was any doubts about the nature of the bio agent attack, they were dispelled the instant his eyes fell upon her. He went to her side. Anwyn looked up at him, recognizing him. "Anwyn, I'm here for you. Be brave. You are our matriarch now. Blodwen is dead. Took a bad fall and broke her neck. Anwyn, please focus. I need your okay. We've only minutes."

Between sobs, she managed to bury her head in his chest. His arms went around her, pulling her tight. "We're all dead now," she cried.

"Not yet. Anwyn, if we do nothing, the authorities will try to put all our clan into one of their assisted living homes forever. We have to get off-world. I've arranged it. I need your okay to do this. Please, focus. You don't want all our clan to end up caged in one of those homes here do you?"

"No, no, we can't live like that. We can't live like this, Anwyn. Kill us all; please, kill us all. I have to pee. Oh god! We're all helpless," she wailed. "I'm starving."

"Okay, let's get you to the bathroom. I'll hold you. Come on; you have to do this," he forced her up, noticing just how badly deformed her feet now were. Slowly, they made their way to the bathroom. He left her sitting on the toilet and headed off to bring Ceri. By the time that he had her sister calmed down and in the room, Anwyn had relieved herself and also calmed down a little.

"Ivarr, how come you weren't infected? Is everyone else a freak now? How bad is it?" she asked, fighting from breaking down again.

"I was out walking and killed two of the men who did this. The third man got away and brought the containment men here. They quarantined all our ships. I think everyone but me has been genetically modified, but I'm not sure. I've got all the ships programmed to take off at six, barely two hours from now. All will head to the Rendezvous. There, we can get help. But Anwyn, you are now our matriarch. I need your okay to allow this exodus to happen."

"Do it, Ivarr, do it. None of us wants to spend the rest of

our lives here. We're helpless, Ivarr. I think you should kill us all. Put us out of our misery. You can't possibly care for a hundred of us," Anwyn pleaded with him.

"Okay. At six, our ships will depart. I've still got two hours. I'm going to try to make some food and feed as many as I can get to before then. See if you and Ceri can get back to your rooms. He headed to the galley. A half hour later, he'd whipped up a huge batch of stew. He filled a baby bottle with water and jammed a straw in it. Then, he headed to find Anwyn and Ceri. Both had made it back to Anywn's bedroom and were sitting helplessly on her bed, sobbing quietly to themselves.

"Ivarr to the rescue, my matriarch. Open up." He inserted the straw and began to pour a little water into her mouth, ignoring the huge, dangling pair of lip loops. She drank half the bottle. After giving the rest to Ceri, he alternated giving them spoonfuls of the stew. Once they were full, he began to do the same to the others in their ship. By the time he finished with all those on his ship, it was too close to six for him to try to get to the many others. They would have to wait longer.

Holding onto Anwyn, he led her to their comm center. Hastily, he patched into all the dozen ship's intercom systems. "Attention everyone. This is Ivarr. I'm the only one of us who wasn't genetically modified. I was outside when the attack came, and I killed two of those who did this to you. The local authorities quarantined our ships, and soon they are coming to take you all away to their assisted living houses. We are gypsies. We can't live cooped up like that. I've programmed our shuttles to take off at six, about ten minutes from now. Each ship will travel on automatic to the Rendezvous location. That should take about a day. Once there, I'll dock our ship with each other ship in turn and come aboard to feed everyone and do what I can for you. Until then, do your best to survive."

He sighed, "More bad news. Matriarch Blodwen is dead. She fell and broke her neck. Anwyn is now our matriarch. Long live Matriarch Anwyn Braith. Anwyn, tell them that you are ordering this evacuation." He nodded to her.

Amid brief spells of crying, she said, "It's true. Mom is

dead. We have to leave and try to get help from the other clans. We can't go into their assisted living homes. I'd rather Ivarr use his knife and put me out of my misery."

He cut her off. "Don't be silly, a Braith never gives up! Everyone, hang in there for twenty-four hours. I'll get to you then. We can make it; we have to. Best get ready for takeoff now. I'll contact you this way in a little while. Out."

"Come on; let's get you back to your room, my dear Anwyn." He gently helped her up and, with an arm around her, assisted her back to her bedroom.

Ceri spoke up. "Ivarr, I'm ready. Stab me now. We can't live like this. You can't take care of a hundred of us. I'm ready to die like mom."

After he helped Anwyn sit back down beside her sister, she said, "Look at us, Ivarr. We're total freaks now, just like all the other victims. I can't even see over my boobs, but I can see Ceri has male organs now. Our lips are sliced open and our feet barely work. We can't live like this. You have to kill us. I order you to."

"Anwyn, I love you. There's no way I'm going to kill you or any other Braith Clan member! I know it's hideous, but we'll find a way. See, the ship is taking off. I've gotten us all this far. Trust me. You must be brave and lead us now. Everyone will be looking to you for guidance. Use your visions, Anwyn. Guide us," he pleaded, and then kissed her gently. She lowered her head onto his chest once more. For a time, he sat between the two, holding them both lovingly.

Sometime later, Ivarr realized more order was needed. Everyone was mostly naked or wearing very little, having been in bed when the attack came. "Let's get you two dressed, shall we?" He tried his best to dress them. While their panties mostly still fit, though a bit tight since their pelvis region had enlarged some, their dark red dresses didn't remotely fit them. Their waists were drastically reduced, ignoring their basketball-sized bosoms. However, he did his best, loosely tying the backs of their dresses together using shoelaces. Then, he put their matching corsets around them, but even those were vastly too loose. Still, they felt much more human. He could do nothing about their shoes.

88

"Thanks, Ivarr. Look at our hair! It's down to our ankles. See if you can tie it up or something," Anwyn suggested. He tied it into a ponytail and then wrapped it up, securing it with a clasp that Ceri suggested he try. That worked well, so he did the same for Ceri.

"Okay, you two stay put. I ought to dress everyone else, if I can." Ivarr left them. The moment that he did, both women began to panic again. He was their sole lifeline now!

Two hours later, Ivarr had all the men, women, and children dressed as best he could manage. Anwyn then suggested they all meet in the commons. One by one, he helped each to safely negotiate the halls and get seated. Anwyn then tried to officiate as her mother had done. "We must give mom her proper burial. Since we can't walk to the air lock, let us pray for her here. Ivarr can send her off into the space that she loved." For a few minutes, only the low vibrations of the ship could be heard. Prayers said silently, Ivarr rose and solemnly left them. Fifteen minutes later, he returned. Anwyn spotted his red eyes and knew he'd also felt her loss, just as every Braith Clan member did.

Wyn, their pilot, spoke up. "Ivarr, you ought to help me to the pilot's seat. I would like to check over what you did to make sure everything is right."

"Me too," Mostyn, their navigator hastily spoke up. "I'd feel better if I can verify the coordinates are laid in properly."

One of the four children, a ten year old girl, spoke up. "You don't have to hold on to me anymore, Ivarr. I can walk, as long as I lean on the side of the halls. Can't we, Maddi?" she nodded to her girlfriend.

Anwyn took heart. "Perhaps, we all should learn how to walk ourselves. We can't have Ivarr tied up walking us around all the time. Come on; while they check on our course, let's see if we can emulate Morgan here and manage at least to walk. We can't do much else, but this would help Ivarr some." He smiled. *That's the spirit, Anwyn. You are our leader.*

A half hour later, both Wyn and Mostyn were satisfied Ivarr had setup the course properly. Further, following Mostyn's commands, Ivarr was able to verify that all dozen ships were close together in hyperspace and on the proper course. He had no idea of the conditions onboard the other eleven ships, though. Probably dreadful, he imagined. On their way back, Ivarr allowed the two men to see if they could not manage to walk without his steadying arms. They did so. That alone gave Ivarr some hope that the many others on the other ships would be able somehow to get by. At least, he'd left them all naked so they could go to the bathroom when they needed to. If they could at least walk to the bathroom, that would go a long way with them, or so he hoped.

Later, he found Anwyn back in her own bedroom. "I can sort of do it, walk myself, Ivarr. Leave it to the children to show us bravery. Come. Sit beside me. I have some decisions to make." He did as asked.

"Ivarr, Ceri and Rhys want to be married. I'm going to allow it and perform the ceremony in a few hours. Ivarr, I care deeply for you, and I think that you care for me."

"I sure do. I've had my eye on you for ages, but I was too afraid to ask Blodwen for your hand. I didn't think she approved of me," he replied.

"Then, Ivarr, I want you to marry me today too. I love you too. While I know that some of the others will think I'm marrying you because you are the only man left who isn't a freak like the rest of us, that I will be monopolizing you, but for the sake of the clan, I must do this. If something should happen to me, Ceri will be the matriarch. She and I must have a daughter soon, just in case."

"I would be honored to be your husband, Anwyn. You would make me the happiest man in the universe. I don't care what others might think."

She smiled for the first time, but both suddenly realized her smile was invisible. Her huge lip loops just draped down below her chin. He leaned over and kissed her as best he could. Suddenly, she gasped. "What's it doing down there? Oh!" Her face flushed crimson.

"We'll just have to get used to it doing that. I assure you mine is too, my love," he whispered.

An hour later, the group was again gathered in the commons. Looking regal in their dark red dresses with stern faces, the two faced their clan members. Anwyn spoke formally, but using Imperium Standard, since everyone had already discovered this was the only way that they could understand their speech any longer. "We are gathered here today to bear witness to two unions. Because of the circumstances, I'll keep this short. Ceri Braith, do you of your own free will accept Rhys Owain to be your lifelong mate, until death do you part?"

"I do," Ceri replied, just as formally.

"Do you, Rhys Owain, of your own free will accept Ceri Braith to be your lifelong mate until death do you part?" Anwyn asked.

"I do," Rhys replied.

"Then, I, Matriarch Anwyn Braith, pronounce you wed. Rhys, from this day forward, you shall be called Rhys Braith. You may kiss your bride." Everyone watched as the two did their best to kiss.

Ceri then spoke in her stern, official tone, "Anwyn Braith. . ." She repeated the simple ceremony for her sister.

That done, Anwyn apologized. "I'm sorry none of us can clap; nor can we play dances and celebrate the weddings."

"Hey, we can still sing and cheer," Wyn suggested. "Hip, hip, hurray!" At once, the others joined in. After that, his tenor voice broke into a traditional gypsy wedding song. Everyone added their voices, bringing unseen smiles to everyone's faces, a touch of happiness amid their nightmare of horrors.

Later, Ivarr helped Anwyn undress for bed. Bit by bit, Anwyn began to look beyond her own situation to that of her clan. Sitting on her bed, she asked, "Do you think the other clans will really help us?"

Ivarr chuckled. "Not that's not for me to guess. That's your responsibility. You are our matriarch, Anwyn. I can help you with things, but I've no idea about such things."

She sighed, knowing he spoke truthfully. Matriarchs ran the clans, not the men. It had been that way always, as far as anyone knew. For that matter, no one knew if the gypsies even had a planet of origin in their distant past. For all that anyone knew, they could have all been born of spacer families. Certainly, most everyone in her clan had been born in space or on one of the worlds on which they occasionally stopped for supplies and plied their fortune telling trade.

"I heard your report to mom — about how the locals back there hated us. Do you suppose other worlds hate we gypsies as much as they do? Do you suppose some of the other clans have been attacked too?" Anwyn asked, growing quite serious.

Ivarr knew she was now speaking as his matriarch. For a moment, he was silent. She and all his clan were now victims as well, so a very sensitive touch was needed. Slowly and choosing his words carefully, he expressed his best conclusions, based upon his unique skills as an observer. "Matriarch, the sheer number of victims that have been accepted on some worlds is definitely causing a population explosion. Twenty plus years of the high birthrates has exceeded their ability to pay for arm regrowth. Their assisted living facilities must be stretched to their limits. Normal people are bearing the taxation brunt to support them and with no return on their investment. I would expect hostile sentiments to be present on most of those worlds."

"Yes, that is reasonable, but do you think other clans have been attacked like we were?" she insisted on his opinion.

"I can't say, but it is possible. I would urge caution. We should not resupply on another world that has accepted a large number of terrorist victims."

"Agreed. I never want to set foot on such a world again! But will the other clans help us?"

Ivarr shrugged his shoulders and didn't answer. "We need men and women to help us, Ivarr. You can't be the arms and hands of a hundred of us. We should get clothes and shoes that fit us, as the other victims were given. I suppose we'll have to wear those strange lip disks too. Where will we get all that?"

"You must ask the other matriarchs at the Rendezvous," Ivarr stated the obvious.

"Yes, I must ask them to find a way to get us clothes, shoes, and those lip things. We must have more able bodied helpers, Ivarr. I can see they might possibly help us with the clothing, but lending us men and women — I doubt it. Only by cross marriages are clan members ever exchanged. There are a few Braith men and women who are single, but what other clan member is going to even deign to look at us, as we are, Ivarr? We're helpless freaks — at least in their eyes. I know, I had that notion too, before our attack. Worse, some clans might decide we are no longer a proper clan and confiscate our possessions. Maybe even toss us all out an air lock. Perhaps, that would be merciful, Ivarr."

"Anwyn!"

"Well, let's be practical, Ivarr. We're as helpless as all the other victims are. Deadweight. Albatrosses to all. Useless, but consuming much. Perhaps a merciful death is better."

"Please, no such notions. We've come this far. Surely a vision will help you guide us, my matriarch," Ivarr pleaded.

"Visions? We should have had a vision that would have saved us from this nightmare without end, Ivarr. We didn't," she retorted angrily. She saw her harsh words bit deep. Hastily, she backed off. "Okay, I'll see if visions come to direct us, my Ivarr. We best get some sleep. We should be at the Rendezvous tomorrow."

The next morning, Ivarr spent two hours getting everyone dressed and fed. By then, the ship dropped out of hyperspace at the Rendezvous location, nearly a month ahead of the scheduled meeting. Everyone made their precarious way to the view ports. All around them, glowing nebulosity shimmered and glowed. The nighttime, star-filled sky was replaced by gossamers and filaments of reds, yellows, blues, and greens. They had arrived in a giant gaseous nebula, the birthplace of new suns and planets. Spectacular did not even begin to describe what they saw; yet all were familiar with the sight.

Unlike nearly all space travelers who journeyed from place to place through hyperspace, just as they had done to get here, the gypsies usually cruised among the stars, basking in the visible sights this arm of the galaxy had to offer. At least half of each year, the clans ambled among the stars, avoiding hyperspace. One might say that the gypsies were the last of the true explorers of the Imperium.

Below them was Rendezvous, a relatively newly formed, uncharted, and unknown planet circling a star that wasn't even unknown to the Imperium. While it had sufficient oxygen and water vapor in its atmosphere, life had barely begun on this new world. Strange plants covered the land continent. Some were quite tall; most had leaves that looked more like ferns than leaves. There was no known animal life, but the water was pure. Once each year, the clans descended here for their meeting. While some inter-clan marriages were consummated, normally the matriarchs met to pick out resupply planets for the next year. A cardinal rule going back beyond memory dictated that no two clans resupply on the same world, and certainly not at the same time. Some speculated this was an attempt to bypass any possibility of inter-clan fights. Others suggested that it was more practical — not taking too much of any one world's resources and goodwill.

For Ivarr, the immediate question was how to land the dozen ships safely. He had no idea how this was done. He helped his pilot and navigator, Wyn and Mostyn, to their places up front. "Tell me what must be done, and I'll try to do it," Ivarr said, growing quite worried. His grand plan was to get them here. How to land was beyond his skill.

"We can use last year's landing site," Mostyn suggested. "It should still be programmed into the nav system. Bring up the menu." Ivarr did. Following Mostyn's orders, he got the sequence ready to be activated, but halted.

"Wait. If I press Execute, we'll land, right?"

"That's the idea," Mostyn replied, wondering why the delay.

"Well, how do I get the other ships to land? I mean, if we land, then how do I get back up here to land the others? We can't just leave them in orbit. My god, they've not had any food or water since the attack," Ivarr pointed out.

"Good point," Mostyn admitted.

After a pause, Wyn suggested, "All of the ships should have their last landing coordinates in their nav system. If somehow their navigators could press the menus and the Execute button, they could all automatically land beside ours."

Mostyn laughed rather sickly. He retorted sarcastically, "Yeh, fine, if I had fingers, Wyn. I seem to have misplaced mine!"

Ivarr jumped in. "Look Mostyn, we have to find a way

94

for you to press the menu sequences. If you can, then we can call up the other navigators and walk them through it."

A half hour later, the three men worked out a way for Mostyn to activate successfully the landing sequence. Biting down on a pen, he was able to use it to press the touch screen menus properly. Ivarr then opened a channel to the other eleven ships. When all the other pilots and navigators were at their stations, he relayed what they needed to do. It took over a half hour before all the other navigators managed to get the five touch screen items selected and the Execute button pressed. One by one, the dozen ships began their gentle descent to the planet named Rendezvous. Never was anyone so thankful that their last landing locations were still in their nav systems than Ivarr!

Now, he could finally get to all the other victims. The dozen ships were in their familiar U-shape, centered around their matriarch's ship. Ivarr kissed Anwyn and headed outside. His plan was simple. Go from ship to ship, helping the other hundred clan members. For twelve hours, Ivarr was kept busy. He used his makeshift baby bottle to get a bottle of water into each victim. He cooked up a dozen large pots of stew and fed everyone. He crudely dressed everyone in women's dresses, but left all underpants and panties off. "Look, this way you can squat over the toilet. I can't help a hundred go to the bathroom whenever they need it." He also crudely tied up everyone's hair to keep it from getting in their way. He also dragged five corpses out of the shuttles. Like Blodwen, they had taken a nasty fall and died, though he wondered if they had done so intentionally.

The one thing that helped him was the simple fact these other victims had at least begun somehow to walk a little on their own. Of necessity, they'd worked together to get what little clothing they had been wearing off each other and to get themselves to the bathrooms. Further, most had worked out a way to get themselves much needed drinks of water. For this, Anwyn was later greatly relieved, when Ivarr told her about it.

Exhausted, Ivarr finally fixed more stew for his own ship and fed them. He then fell into a deep sleep. Meanwhile, embolden by what Ivarr had told her about the rest of her clan,

Anwyn and Madoc made their way to the ship's comm system. After some struggles, Madoc managed to get the ship to ship intercom active. "This is Matriarch Anwyn. We've arrived on Rendezvous. In a month, the other clans will gather here. I hope to get us some help from the other clans, but we'll have to see. Tomorrow, let's all see if we can get outside and hold a clan meeting. Gather at our usual places, the center of the U." She was referring to the grassy area just outside her own ship.

The next day, Ivarr had to stand back and allow the hundred plus men, women, and children make their precarious way down the shuttle ramps and onto the grassy knoll on their own. He simply could not put his arms around each one. Instead, he came to the assistance of those who fell down, some ten. He did, however, escort Matriarch Anwyn and Ceri down.

The children were only too glad to wander off to try to play some games, if they could. Hence, it was the adults who officially met. Matriarch Anwyn, with Ceri on her right, sat on the ground facing the assembled clan members. Ivarr and Rhys sat behind their wives.

More stone-faced than ever before, thanks to their drooping lip loops, the two leaders gazed out on the hundred like victims. Anwyn spoke slowly. "Thanks to Ivarr, we have made it this far. That alone is a miracle. He has gotten us all fed and rather dressed. Finally, we, as a clan, can meet. We face a terrible and unknown future. At first, I wanted only for Ivarr to use his knife and put me out of my misery."

Several yelled their agreement. "Yes, he should have put us all down!" But not everyone felt that way.

She continued, "We of the Braith Clan are fighters, survivors. We always have been. We are true gypsies. We don't go down without a fight, not ever. I agree with Ivarr's actions. If he had done nothing, the local authorities would have dragged us all off to one of their assisted living places, stuffing us in little cells for the rest of our lives!" Many cried out bitterly, and she knew she's hit a raw nerve. Death would have been welcomed by all over that.

"Ivarr made the right choice. We're here; we're alive; we're not caged birds. I give you my word; we never will be caged birds, not ever! We are Braith gypsies." Everyone cheered, much to her relief.

"We are survivors. Look, here we are at Rendezvous, safe and sound. Even our pilots and navigators managed to get our ships landed. Ivarr allowed Wyn and Madoc to land mine. We are not wholly helpless yet. Just mostly. The question before us today is what do we do now?"

She paused and then continued, "We can get by for a month with Ivarr making our meals for us. I would suggest some of us women instruct him on cooking. I don't think I want to eat his stew for a month!" That brought several chuckles from the many women.

"At the Rendezvous, I'll ask for help from the other matriarchs. How that will be received and what they'll agree to do has me worried. Hence, this meeting. It is possible they'll send us a number of men and women to be our assistants."

"Matriarch, is that likely? Surely, they won't actually do that, will they?" one man asked.

"I don't think that's likely, Urien. That would reduce their clan numbers. Still, I must ask. As we all know from the Imperium newscasts, terrorist victims are supposed to get clothing, shoes, and those weird lip things. I'll ask the other matriarchs if they can somehow get us these things. Again, I'm not hopeful they can."

"So what are we to do, matriarch? Have you visions for us?"

Anwyn sighed. "Not as yet, but they'll come when we need them. One thing we can do is to settle down here on Rendezvous. We can send Ivarr off to get more supplies when we run low."

"But we're gypsies. We don't stay long in one place."

"I know. I know. If we are in a dozen ships soaring among the stars, Ivarr can't possibly cook and feed us all. If we stay here, he can possibly do this, though I don't think he can do much else; there are so many of us."

Urien spoke up, "What I fear is the other matriarchs will declare us dead and confiscate our things and ships, perhaps even killing us."

"True, I have considered this, Urien. I'll have Ivarr

enter some escape coordinates into all our ships' nav systems. If they try to take us over, we will lift off into space, where we belong. If the matriarchs don't assist us, what I don't know is where we can go for help."

An older woman, Gwyneth, spoke up. "If we could get our arms regrown, like the wealthier victims have, we could manage the rest of it. We'd not be helpless, matriarch."

Urien countered, "Aye, Gwyneth is right, we could. But we all heard the newscasts. It costs ten thousand credits to get one person's arms back. Rhys, do the calculation. We're a hundred plus."

Rhys spoke up, "A little over a million credits." That sobered everyone.

"Aye, now where would we get a million credits?" Urien commented hostilely. "What world is going to give us gypsies a million credits? Answer me that one." No one could. A hush fell. Unspoken, all knew they desperately needed their arms regrown, but they all also knew virtually no one respected them or would offer gypsies such aid.

"It's up to me to find a way," Anwyn declared. Only a few actually believed her. They discussed the issues for some time. In the end, Anwyn had to accept the wishes of her clan. If they could not find some way to get their arms back and if the other clans didn't provide men and women to assist them, they all wished to end their lives while up in space where they were born. "We're star-stuff," Urien claimed, echoing the sentiments of many.

During the many days that followed, the best that Ivarr could do was to prepare one meal a day and feeding it to everyone. Slowly, he was being dragged down with the rest of them, or so Anwyn thought. He always fell asleep the moment he lay down on their bed.

As the day of the Rendezvous approached, Anwyn finally had visions! She saw the assembled five other clan leaders, their stern faces staring at her. While it was a still image that she saw, she got the feeling they were unable or unwilling to help the Braith Clan. A second image suggested to her that the other clans were going to take over her clan, stealing their ships and possessions, such as they were. A third image showed their dozen ships lifting off this primitive world, escaping their clutches. The fourth and last image was of a welcoming world, a strange world with a dim, orange-red sun.

As Ivarr fed her and Ceri their solitary meal for the day, she confided her visions with him. "Ivarr, you must program all of our ships to liftoff and go to this strange new world."

"I will, but where is it? What coordinates? What's its name?" he asked. Without coordinates, he was lost. "I can get us into hyperspace, that much I can do without the exact coordinates."

"See if you can find it. Use the computer system," she suggested.

Later on, he sat down and began searching the Imperium Net. He typed in the keywords "orange-red sun." The screen soon filled up with a dozen links. One by one, he went through each one. Then, he spied something interesting and went to bring Anwyn to see it.

A few minutes later, he had her sitting before the monitor. "See, this strange place is the home of the famous geneticist Doctors Ruth and Alex Hammil. They discovered how to regrow the arms of the many original terrorist victims. Perhaps, this is what you saw in your vision."

"Ivarr! This must be it! It cannot be a coincidence. This strange planet has the very doctors that can save us. It has to be what I saw; it just has to be. I'll tell the clan we will go to the very doctors who invented the cures. Surely, they will help us, Ivarr. You go program the coordinates into our ships. Prepare the way."

"Love, it is a Closed World. They won't let us land," Ivarr pointed out.

"First, get us there, Ivarr. Then, we'll worry about landing. When has landing on a world ever been a problem for we gypsies?" Both chuckled.

Several days later, hundreds of gaily painted gypsy deep space transport ships began slowly descending on Rendezvous. Later at the appointed time, Ivarr, an arm around both Anwyn and Ceri, led them to the grassy knoll where the five other matriarchs had gathered for their annual council. Of course, the topic of nearly all other gypsies was the terrorist attack on the entire Braith Clan.

Anwyn gazed at the circle of equally stern faces of the five other matriarchs. She was asked to give an account of what had happened to her clan. This she did, though Ivarr was called upon for specifics that had happened while they were in a coma for those days. After that, Morwen of the Glaw Clan spoke up. "We were assaulted and lost five men. Hostilities have never been greater."

"Aye," Siana of the Rhian Clan added, "someone tried to bomb us. We lost one ship and ten gypsies." Next, Brang of the Wen Clan, Mared of the Bron Clan, and Lynn of the Hafren Clan all spoke of increasing hostilities to all gypsies in general.

That business done, Anwyn made her pitch. "The Braith Clan needs your help. Only Ivarr here has been unaffected. He cannot care for the needs of a hundred of us. We have none of the special clothes and shoes that we victims are supposed to get. We need your help."

"Yes, that is more than apparent, Anwyn," Morwen replied. "You must know you are now freaks. You are helpless and always will be so. What reason can you give for us not disbanding the Braith Clan and dividing up your people among the five remaining clans?"

Lynn added, "Tis true, some victims have had their arms regrown, but that's a most expensive operation, done only for the wealthy of the Imperium, who can afford it. Are you suggesting some of us steal the clothing and shoes that you need?"

"Anwyn, you must face the facts," Mared spoke up, "your clan is finished. You are now nothing but a giant liability for us all. To care for you, we'd each have to donate over twenty of our members, seriously weakening our clans. Everyone knows you freaks breed like mice. In no time at all, there would be two hundred of you, then three, then four. Soon, your kind would outnumber the rest of us gypsies, and we'd all die. Surely you can see, if we take you on, that would sign the death warrant for all of us."

Siana stated solemnly, "Anwyn, you should tell your people we promise to give all a painless, quick death, and burial in space, like the spacers we all are. I vote we give the

Braith Clan a day to prepare." The other four concurred. Seeing that the meeting was over, Anwyn nodded to Ivarr, who helped her and Ceri get precariously to their feet. The trio made their slow, careful way across the strange looking grass to their ship. Once inside their commons, both women broke down and cried a little.

Within minutes, the others of their ship made their way to the commons, using the hall walls for support. All were intensely curious about what had happened at the matriarchal meeting. Between sobs, all that Anwyn could say was, "They are going to kill us tomorrow."

As dusk fell and the shimmering, multi-colored sheets of glowing gas appeared across the sky; the gay sounds of gypsy music filtered into all of the dozen shuttles. Outside, small groups were dancing. A few went a'courting in other clans. The Rendezvous was, after all, a festive occasion, but not for the doomed Braith Clan. At last, Anwyn whispered one word to Ivarr, "Liftoff." He left the others and headed to the comm center. After making the connections, he spoke that same word to the other eleven ships.

When he finished, he headed to the front of the ship. Already, Wyn and Madoc were making their own precarious way to their stations there as well. Around midnight, the dozen Braith Clan ships lifted off from Rendezvous, quickly jumping into hyperspace. The sole decision Ivarr made was upon the duration of their flight. They could get there in one day, but that would require burning most of their fuel. On the other hand, if they took two days to get to this strange world, they would still have somewhat less than half of their fuel reserves. In case this planet did not pan out, they could still travel elsewhere. He chose this longer trip duration, calculating the others would not starve to death in two days' time. He wanted some options, should this Ashford-5 not work out.

Chapter 5 Disparate Deals

"Damned. Another one. This one, I can't handle," Governor Katrina swore. She'd just received a communication from a small fleet of gypsy deep space transports. She focused and telepathically send to Queen Amy, *Got a new problem here. Some gypsies have been subjected to a bio terrorist attack. There are twelve incoming ships and only one man who still has his arms. He's not a pilot. They are asking for our help. Bring Lena with you; I need her expertise. I know virtually nothing about these gypsies. How the hell are they going to land the ship?*

Coming. Be there as soon as possible, Amy replied. *Have they got clothes and shoes?*

Nope, nothing, just makeshift. Bare feet. They want to have their arms regrown somehow. Good lord, Amy, is this never going to end?

Okay, I'll bring Lilly and Nita as well as the doctors. I can use the Imperial Circles to land the ships if there's no other way.

Shortly, Doctor Whitney joined Katrina, along with Carla and Elfe. Elfe commented, "Wow, real gypsies. Now there is something that you don't see every day! We could learn a lot from them, anthropologically that is. Read a little about them at the Academy."

Katrina, however, did not share her enthusiasm, grumbling, "Look, without pilots, these dozen ships are very likely to crash land. I can't have half this base wiped out."

Carla spoke up, "Boss, look, they've obviously gotten this far on their own. They must have some way to control their ships."

"Hum, I suppose you are right. Let's hope so. They said there is about a hundred men, women, and children on board," Katrina related.

"We ought to be able to handle that many," Doctor Whitney suggested. "We're geared up to take double that each week, part of the thousand that Rafe wants. Maybe we can just add them to the thousand."

"Ah, here comes Amy and Lena," Katrina pointed out the obvious. Jan had her arm around Amy, Lena and Bernardo ambled behind the two, followed by Doctors Ruth and Alex Hammil. In the distance, another electric car came speeding up, carrying Lilly and Nita.

When everyone was gathered together just outside the main entrance of the Admin building, Katrina explained the situation once more. "We've got several problems here. Getting the dozen ships landed safely is of paramount importance."

"Why not see if they are able to land themselves safely," Amy asked.

Katrina pressed the Talk button and spoke to her Control Tower. "Patch me through to the spokesman for these gypsies." A moment later, she had her connection. "This is Governor Katrina Lutgard of Ashford-5. Permission to land granted. How can you land the dozen ships safely? If you cannot, let me know now. I can't have a bunch of crash landings here. Over."

"If we can get specific coordinates, it'll take the navigators about a half hour to enter them. The automated guidance can then land us safely. Thank you! Over."

A half hour later, the dozen gaily painted deep space transports began descending from the sky. All landed safely. One of the side doors opened and a man stepped out, waving to them, though he also looked around at the strange sights. When he joined the group, he explained. "I'm Ivarr Braith, the spokesman for Matriarch Anwyn Braith. This is the Braith Clan. We need help. I've not been able to feed most of them for two days. Matriarch Anwyn would like to meet with you and begs for your compassion. We don't want to die, but gosh, it's cold here. Oh, according to the newscasts, none has any of the special clothes or shoes they are supposed to have. I suppose I can carry her to meet with you."

"Okay, you are safely down. That was my primary worry, Ivarr. How many victims are there? Nothing to eat for two days?" Katrina asked.

"Just over one hundred. Six didn't make it. Right.

Before, I was able to cook up enough and feed them one meal a day for the last month," Ivarr answered, then begged, "Please, we need your help. There's no one else we can turn to."

"Okay, first things first. Carla, Elfe, you to see to getting all properly fed. Doctors, check on their current health. Doctor Whitney, send two nurses up here with wheel chairs. We can't have them trying to walk across this cold tarmac in their bare toes. Ivarr, bring your matriarch and one other. We'll discuss just what can be done, but first, I want my doctors to make sure everyone is healthy," Governor Katrina ordered. "Lilly, Nita, see what their apparel needs are going to be."

After leaving orders for the small party to be brought into her formal meeting room, she, Amy, Jan, Lena, and Bernardo headed there. The others headed into the dozen ships to check on the others. Once the five were seated, Katrina asked, "Okay, Lena. I need your advice. Gypsies. I know practically nothing about them. As our resident ex-Sector ID Minister. . ."

Lena interrupted her. "I know. You want to know what I know about them. I'm acquainted with them somewhat. They are true nomads, wandering this spiral arm of the galaxy. They have no known planet of origin. They are clan oriented. Apparently, this one is called the Braith Clan. The clans are matriarchal in nature. The matriarch runs the clan, much like you and Amy run the spaceport and Tierra. Their usual pattern is to land on some planet where they do odd jobs to earn credits to pay for refueling and re-supplying their small fleet. No two clans are ever on the same world at the same time. Their women also tell fortunes, but who knows if this isn't just a sham. Anyway, they often stay on a world for three or four months before leaving."

"They know an awful lot about the galaxy, that's for sure. They prefer to travel at normal speed and rarely drop into hyperspace. There is also a strong distrust of the gypsies. Some believe they kidnap and/or rape women, to say nothing of stealing what they can sell. Mind you, those are just hearsay reports. Very few gypsies have ever been actually arrested," Lena finished up.

"So they are not really a threat?" Katrina asked.

"No, but they like to park their ships on the outskirts of a city and work from there. In this case, they are all victims and helpless. So, no, you don't have security worries, if that's what you are worried about," Lena answered.

Relieved, Katrina then asked, "So what can we offer them?"

Amy replied, "Certainly, we can partially repair their feet and fix their hair so the men can cut theirs. I'm sure Elegant Fashions Inc can get them descent clothing. Of course, the real question is can we regrow their arms? We're tackling the one thousand that Rafe requested now."

Lena spoke up. "Well, they won't take kindly to being housed in Madiera, at least not for long. These are a wandering people. Unless I'm terribly misinformed, if we leave them in Madiera for a long time, they will feel like caged birds."

Bernardo pointed out, "In Madiera, they could learn to use the bots. But if they do get their arms back, they'll certainly want to leave here. We can't have them spreading the word about Madiera and the bots. If we don't regrow their arms, we're going to need many care givers soon. How long will they be content to remain helpless victims? Shouldn't they get some Basic Therapy too?"

Queen Amy volunteered, "Well, we can put them up in the Imperial Castle for now. I can hire some temporary helpers. I've enough funds to handle their apparel needs and feed them, so that's not a problem. The doctors can put them through the medical machines fairly rapidly. So the real question boils down to whether or not we attempt to regrow their arms. If we don't, honestly, they are a doomed people."

Katrina pointed out, "Regrowing their arms runs about a million credits. We'll have to put our heads together to see where we can come up with the funds to purchase the supplies the doctors will be needing. We've got a thousand people already allocated in our budgets."

"True, but fortunately, the thousand are just trickling in here and there, and not all at one time. So we can just stretch our budgets," Amy countered.

Jan grinned. "Hey, I can always siphon off a million

credits from the wealthy of Proxima Prime. They'll never miss it." Katrina gave her a dirty look, but everyone laughed.

Before long, the two nurses wheeled the two women into the meeting room, Ivarr followed behind them, along with the rest of the group. The group got their first look at the gypsy women; both were in their early twenties, that much was obvious. All three gypsies' skin tones were a pale yellowish, tending towards brownish. The women had brown eyes and dark brown hair. Since the genetic modifications, their hair had become twice as thick, but still was wavy. Ivarr had the women's hair tied up in a very crude bun at the top of their heads. The group suspected their hair would otherwise reach their ankles, assuming the genetic modification affected them as it had others. The women's faces were perfectly round, but somewhat flat, not helped by their thin lips, now thickened and split, drooping far below their chins. They had quite a stern appearance. The two wore very ill-fitting, matching very dark red cotton dresses. Two petticoats gave a bit of flair to the bottoms of their dresses, but their matching dark red corsets worn over their dresses added to their striking appearance. Yet even these no longer properly fit their drastically smaller waists.

In fairness, the gypsy trio saw a number of women who were also barely in their twenties. Queen Amy looked much as they did, an armless victim too. However, the tall, black-skinned, armless woman, Lena, didn't. She appeared to be wearing men's clothing, certainly not a dress. The others wore tall heels, fancy gowns, and had the same massive bosoms. However, Amy and Katrina also wore the giant lip plates they'd seen on some newscasts.

After some introductions, Governor Katrina said, "Matriarch Anwyn, why don't you tell us what happened to you and your clan?" She thought this would be a good way to break the ice between the two groups.

Anwyn was only too eager to do so. She outlined all that had happened, including her visions and what the matriarchs of the other clans had decided. "So my visions were correct. Ivarr was able to get us all safely off that world and got us here, where my vision led us."

She sighed, *Now comes the hard part!* "We know we are now a terrible burden. We are mostly helpless and can barely walk. We also know the local people of the various worlds that have taken many of the other victims are now quite antagonistic towards us freaks. Rightly so, Rhys, our mathematician, claims within a century, these helpless freaks will likely outnumber the normal people of those worlds. Back in Halcion City, Beltar-3, where we were attacked, the freaks have multiplied so much that they are swamping all of the assisted living quarters there. In fact, some terrorists bombed one of them the same night they attacked us, killing some three hundred freaks. So we know we are an awful liability to you. Yet, we have nowhere else to turn."

She went on, "If we can somehow get our arms regrown, we can leave and go our way. We can survive somehow. Yet, we know it will take a million credits or more to get all of us healed. I'm so sorry we cannot pay such a fee. Ceri tells me we might be able to get ten thousand credits together, if everyone chipped in. We don't want to be a burden on you, and yet we are just that, unless we can somehow get our arms regrown. We are gypsies. We cannot stand being cooped up in an assisted living place for very long. We all would rather be dead than that. So if you cannot help us, please allow us to leave. Ivarr will give us a painless death and cast our bodies into space, from which we have come. We come from star dust and to star dust we must all go one day." *There, I've said it all. I don't think I could have said it any better. At least I've been honest with these people.*

Queen Amy spoke up, "Well, on behalf of everyone, let me welcome you to Tierra, or Ashford-5 as our world is known in the Imperium. You've come to the right world. Let me tell you what we can offer you immediately, okay?" Anwyn nodded, holding her breath.

"First, just weeks ago, our geneticist doctors have just developed a couple more genetic cures. We will get everyone's feet partially restored. Unfortunately, you will be forced to wear heels such as the others here are wearing, but I assure you, those are infinitely better than these darn toe shoes. Second, we can repair your hair so it can be cut. They've somehow removed the pain sensors in the hair that prevent cutting it. This much we can do for all of your people within a few days."

"Second, we are blessed with a fabulous clothing company, Elegant Fashions Inc, owned by Lilly and Nita here. They'll soon be making several complete outfits for each of you. Your men will still have their massive bosoms, but their suits look more masculine. Our men do love them."

"Amy," Lilly interrupted her. Amy nodded and she continued, "We will be making clothes to emulate your styles and colors. So Nita and I will need to visit with each person and find out just how they'd like their new apparel to look and feel. Your choices of colors are quite remarkable and cheerful. It'll take a little time to make so many outfits. Also, we'll hold off on your footwear until your feet are partially repaired."

"Thank you. How much will this cost? We only have maybe ten thousand credits," Anwyn asked, growing rather worried. All this sounded rather expensive.

"No charge," Queen Amy answered. "You see, we on Tierra have compassion for our fellow man, especially for fellow terrorist victims. At this point, we're in the process of bringing another thousand victims here. So your clothes and minor healing is already in our respective budgets. No charge. Meanwhile, we'll put you all up at my Imperial Castle. I'll try to have an assistant for each of your people to help out during the daytime."

"Third, I'd like to offer all of your people our Basic Therapy, which will wholly erase the horrible emotional trauma you've all suffered because of this attack. You'll feel much happier and relieved as a result. Again, no charge. One of my daughters, Rafe, will see that this gets done. She's a hermaphrodite too and knows precisely what you have all been through."

Amy sighed. Now came the hard part. "All of these will only make your lives a little easier, not wholly restore your independence. I know, and I make no suggestion otherwise. Everything comes down to regrowing your arms, doesn't it? Without that, you are doomed."

She sensed Anwyn fighting back tears. "We don't want

you doomed. I know the process is a costly one, but somehow we must work together to make it happen for your hundred clan members. Perhaps, you and your people have something to trade that our people would consider of comparable value."

Anwyn's hopes raised and then fell. "What do we have that you could possibly want?" *This is hopeless. We're mere gypsies, not rich planet dwellers.*

"Tierra is a Closed World, Anwyn. Elfe, our resident anthropologist, tells me our world is classified as Bronze-Iron Age. Still, looks can be deceiving. Some of us have progressed far beyond that. A few of us are just beginning to venture out there among the stars of the galaxy. I know; we are dependent upon the Imperium and its hyperspace travels. Yet as I am told, your people shun hyperspace, traveling among the wonders and splendors of the stars. If we can regrow all of your people's arms, in return, would you and your people educate some of ours? Take them to see the wondrous sights that are never seen on the hyperspace travels. We have so much to learn about the stars."

"Yes, we certainly can do that, but it seems so valueless compared to regrowing our arms," Anwyn protested slightly.

"Of course it would to those who have traveled among the stars as you and your people have. But our people have not. A few of us have traveled a bit, but only through the black of hyperspace. We are desperate for knowledge. What do you say? Fair trade?" Amy asked.

"It's not a fair trade, but I'll gladly accept it! With our arms back, we can easily take your people on as long a tour as they desire. There is so much to see out there, wholly lost on all those who travel via hyperspace," Anwyn replied. "Frankly, I'm amazed to see others who share what we gypsies hold dear to us — the incredible splendor of the universe out there."

Queen Amy declared with finality, "Then, we have a deal. Right now, Governor Katrina's people are feeding your people. Tonight, when it's dark, some of her people will fly your ships the very short distance over to my castle's courtyard. I think we can squeeze them all in there. That way, you and your people won't be disconnected from your homes, while you are staying with us inside the castle. I'm afraid from what you are used to, our home will seem very crude. It certainly is chilly, and this is our late summer. Tomorrow, we'll get started on all the minor repairs. As some finish that up, we'll get you next door to Elegant Fashions Inc and into Lilly and Nita's capable hands. Regrowing arms is going to take some time. Months, actually, before you can really use them. So plan to winter over here on Tierra, okay?"

Anwyn gushed, "I don't know how to thank you all enough. You are saving all our lives."

Governor Katrina replied, "You are most welcome, Anwyn. Others have done the same for all of us as well. Perhaps, one day you can help others who are in desperate need. I'd best let you return and tell your people the good news. I think they're quite worried about all this." She didn't tell her that she sensed them with her *mentales* gifts. Further, Amy hadn't yet mentioned telepathy. It wasn't her place to do it.

That night around midnight, the dozen ships were moved over into the courtyard of the Imperial Castle. It was a tight squeeze, but now their guests would have access to their homes and possessions, while still remaining within the castle, where others could help them as needed. The doctors used all four of their medical machines simultaneously, handling one person per hour. They worked twelve hour shifts, handling the entire group in just over two days.

The best that Lilly and Nita could do on such short notice was provide them with proper heels. Now they could at least walk more readily and not have to negotiate the cold stone floors of the castle and grounds in their bare feet. It took Elegant Fashions Inc many weeks to get each person properly attired — double that to also make them a second outfit.

As soon as the gypsies had their feet repaired and new heels, Amy had them dining with her large group. Anwyn was amazed to see so many hermaphrodites, all related to those whom she'd met so far. Plus, her heart went out to the fifty young couples from Aquila Prime, who were living the same nightmare as she was. Company in misery. Still, the gypsies found comradery and began to relax. Their lives were rebounding beyond their wildest imaginations.

Rebounding was definitely not what had or was happening to those lords and nobles who had declared themselves independent of the kingdoms now being run by the many Supreme Guild Masters! Over a quarter of a century ago, the many guilds had wrestled control of the kingdoms away from the kings and lords. Even the many towers were now fully under their control as well. Several of these nobles, such as Lord Alano Valen, owned vast tracts of land. Hence, they were unwilling to relinquish control to these upstart guild masters, who waged an economic war against them.

Five kings separated from their guild-controlled kingdoms and formed their own new kingdoms. They also took most of the skilled tower technicians with them, including some venerados and capos. Their initial plan was to build up strength, an army, and powerful new weapons, based upon the many giant crystals of power in their possession. They miscalculated just how strong the guild system actual was around the turn of the century!

Steadily, the guild-run kingdoms flourished and prospered, while their new autocratic kingdoms did not. Year by year, these lords and nobles saw their vast fortunes slowly being consumed in the maintenance and support of their new kingdoms. The tenant farmers, who worked their lands, demanded higher pay and better working conditions. When they didn't get them because the hard pressed lords couldn't afford it, family by family, they moved away, finding new lands in the neighboring guild-run kingdoms. Even threat of force had not stemmed the outflowing tide of common laborers.

The situation only grew worse. During the last six years, many of their craftsmen and women also fled for greener pastures. A weapons maker, for example, found he could get a fifty percent raise just by moving into a guild-controlled kingdom. The same thing happened to the armies they were forming up. Originally, they raised their armies so one day they could retake the guild-controlled lands back. While they might have succeeded during the early formative years, once past the turn of the century, even that was denied them. Conscripting local farm lads into their army resulted in poor quality soldiers and escalating hatred by the families, who lost their sons. At this time, desertions were commonplace. Bit by bit, these once prosperous lands of the nobles were crumbling, and few had sufficient farmers to till their land.

With steadily falling crop production, all else slumped as well, despite the lords and nobles doling out their own personal wealth, in an attempt to prop up these new kingdoms. Many began to regret deeply having followed their lord or king in seceding from the guild kingdoms, and sought for ways to rejoin them without starting a war.

Old King Alano Valen and his group had passed away, leaving his new kingdom to his sons. Prior to the turn of the century, he had worked long and hard to get one of his women married to Governor Konrad. For a time, he had attempted to manipulate the aliens according to his wishes or at least know precisely what they were doing. His goal was to get Tierra reclassified as an Open World and then to get all that incredible alien technology brought to Tierra, d-guns included. All that had failed utterly, when the war with the Federation of Planets took a turn for the worst and the aliens abandoned Ashford-5.

Upon their return, Tierra now had a new governor and worse, they were part of the Ataro Empire, under the control of Emperor Kino Sango. Queen Amy's rule was fully backed up, leaving no wiggle room to get out or around her decisions. Worse, the new governor and her staff were close friends with Queen Amy and her group, thick as bees, his wife had declared. For years, King Alano looked in vain for some way to get back the control over the aliens that he once had had, all to no avail whatsoever! His only consolation in all this was that Brom Castle and Tower now seemed also to have lost their influence and importance with Queen Amy and Governor Katrina.

Lord Alano then contented himself with trying to build up his new kingdom, in hopes of soon attacking and retaking his old kingdom, ruled by the guild masters. Even that had failed to bear fruit. He'd finally retired, giving control to his sons. Lord Carlos Valen now ruled, with his brothers controlling the tower. Rodrigo Valen was its venerado, while

Francisco Valen was capo of their First Circle. Lord Carlos still attempted to achieve what his father had failed to do. As of the summer of 1325, he had not remotely achieved it. He griped and bellowed, "We're still a Closed World, but now Amy and her gang are importing all the alien technology that they desire! It's not fair at all."

In fact, the situation had grown far worse, from his point of view. The alien terrorist attack had left Amy, Katrina, and several of their associates genetically mutated, freaks of nature. The Imperial Castle seemed to be filled with their vile offspring, mutated freaks as well. At least at this point in time, Lord Valen had given up all desires of trying to insert one of his people into either Amy's court or Governor Katrina's spaceport group.

Today, word reached him that Queen Amy was accepting another thousand of these freaks of nature! That was the last straw. Well, second to last. Word also reached him that Amy and Katrina and their families suddenly looked twenty-one again, not in their late middle ages! That could only mean they had used the alien's rejuvenation machines! "That bitch will outlive us all now! She has to go!" He was thirty-two; his brothers, two years younger.

"I wholly agree, brother, but how can we stop them? They are all in cahoots with the governor," Venerado Rodrigo complained.

"I say we attack the Imperial Castle! Yes, we drop some of our acid bombs on them. Fly three of our flying ships over them and bomb them, dissolve their freakish bodies once and for all," King Carlos declared. "Nuevo Castillo Valen will triumph!" His new kingdom was barely twenty miles further west of old Castle Valen and Valen Tower.

All three men laughed. "I can make that happen!" Venerado Rodrigo declared in no uncertain terms. The trio began making plans. The attack would commence in two days.

Unknown to them, the Supreme Guild Masters had infiltrated their kingdom. Late that same afternoon, Diego Ramirez focused on his crystal. *Queen Amy. Supreme Guild Master Diego Ramirez here. I want to warn you of an impending acid bombing attack on your Imperial Castle. In two days, Nuevo Castillo Valen is planning to destroy you and your people. King Carlos and Venerado Rodrigo are making their preparations as I speak. Thought you ought to know.*

Damn! Once more, I'm in your debt, Supreme Guild Master. I'll see that the attack does not happen. Thank you.

You are welcome, as always. Keep the peace. He broke his connection, his obligation and duty completed.

"As if we don't have enough to do with these Aquila Prime victims, groups of the promised thousands of other victims arriving weekly, and now this gypsy clan. Bernardo, Lena, Jan, front and center. We're about to be attacked by King Carlos Valen and his tower!"

After briefing the three, Bernardo suggested, "We could use our Circles to pull their flying ships down, smashing them into the Goza."

Lena countered, "True, but then what about all of the acid bombs. They could well damage the spaceport or even Exchange City. We need a better plan."

While the three discussed other possibilities, including a preemptive strike, Queen Amy began to have a kernel of an idea. "Preemptive strike, gang. That's what we need. No, not the way you are thinking," she interrupted their destructive ideas, some of which might well reduce the small kingdom to rubble. "Our senator has been suggesting we need an official ambassador in residence on Proxima Prime. True, it is basically a powerless figurehead, but the post should be filled. How long has the Valens been trying to weasel their way into the Imperium? Centuries. Why not appoint one of the as Tierra's ambassador? They would be powerless to make any real deals. Emperor Kino is strictly enforcing the Closed World status."

Lena grinned, "Brilliant. Preemptive strike. Appoint one of them to the post in return for not bombing the Imperium Castle. Best not let them know this is giving in to an extortion plot, though. Otherwise, many others will try the same thing."

"Point taken. I'll have Venerado Henry contact King Carlos Valen right now. Nip this in the bud," Amy both replied and suggested.

An hour later, both King Carlos and Venerado Rodrigo teleported to the Imperial Tower, compliments of Capo Francesco. Jan and Bernardo met them. "So what is so vitally important that Amy wanted us here right now? We're busy men," King Carlos gripped rather loudly.

"Can't say," Bernardo lied. "She just said it was very important and to bring you to her private study immediately. This way. Wonder what she wants?" He and Jan led the way, opening the study door for them and quietly leaving them alone with Amy. Jan had protested this, but Amy had been most insistent.

"Ah, good to see you both. Please have a seat. Something has come up, and I have to make a decision." She waited until they sat down before continuing. "Senator Franco Hermanes had been begging me to appoint a Tierra Ambassador to the Imperium for months now. I agree; he has his hands full with Senate meetings and no time for ambassadorial duties. Gentlemen, I have to appoint our ambassador soon. The next shuttle to Proxima Prime leaves in about a week."

She paused to allow the topic to sink into their minds. Amy sensed both had strong mental blocks raised. No way were they going to allow her to sense they were planning to bomb her and the castle. "I have been thinking about whom would best fill that position, Tierra's Imperium Ambassador. I know Valen, or rather Nuevo Castillo Valen, has long wanted to establish stronger relations with the Imperium. The other kingdoms have traditionally been opposed to such. I'd rather appoint someone who is not so closed minded about the Imperium. Those would only create bad public opinion of us all. So gentlemen, I would like to appoint someone from your kingdom to be Tierra's Ambassador. I first thought of you, King Carlos, but then you might not want to give up your ruling position or be away from your kingdom for some years. The duration of the posting can be as long as you want it, just like our senator."

"So I asked you both here today to see if Valen is still interested in forming better ties with the Imperium," Amy finished. Already, she'd seen their visible reactions. The two looked at each other for a moment.

King Carlos said, "Well, this does change things, rather significantly, Queen Amy. Until now, we figured you were going to perpetually block us Valens from any participation with the Imperium."

"I've had to pacify the many other kings and rulers, which is why Franco was appointed our senator. Just between us, I do think Valen deserves a chance to prove to all the other rulers that they can fairly represent Tierra's interests with the Imperium, don't you?" Amy cleverly hinted.

"Why yes, perhaps even long overdue," King Carlos replied with a hint of antagonism. "If I take this post, am I free to choose whoever I desire to temporarily hold my throne during my absence? Will I have a way to communicate from this Proxima Prime to here? To my kingdom?"

"Of course. You'll be staying with Senator Franco, who will introduce you to the other ambassadors and lend you all the help you need to get started. He has an official comm center in his apartment. With it, you can contact the Imperial Comm Center here. My sister can then put you in direct contact with whomever you wish at your castle, via one of your Circles. Will that be acceptable? I'm afraid I've got the only Imperium Comm Center, outside the spaceport, that is. Technically, I'm part of the Ataro Empire and am allowed it, you see."

"Of course. Can we have a day to discuss this? I'll need to make some arrangements."

"Certainly, take all the time you need to discuss this opportunity. The shuttle will leave in a week. If that isn't enough time, I can find out when the next one will be arriving," Amy suggested, once more emphasizing the time factor. "If you accept the post as our ambassador, you can expect to be landing on Proxima Prime eleven days from now. I'll alert Senator Franco, and he will meet you at the spaceport. Of course, before you leave, Governor Katrina will also issue you an official ambassador's ID card."

"Excellent. This is indeed a momentous day for Nuevo Valen. I'm sure we'll be able to accept this incredible posting. We'll do our very best to represent all Tierra. But how will you sell our appointment to the others?" he asked, rather pointedly.

"Easy. Nuevo Valen has minded its own business for what? Thirty or more years. You've proven to me and the other rulers that you are not out to destroy me or them. I will go to bat for you. I'm sure I can sell them on your appointment. After all, none of them are likely to accept. It's hard enough trying to find a senator."

"Excellent. We will discuss this and let you know soon. I have many preparations to make and so little time. Eleven days, eh? Well, you certainly do move fast," King Carlos suggested.

"Blame it on Senator Franco. He's been hounding me weekly to appoint someone. I think you or one of your associates is ideally suited for this post, if not long overdue. I will be looking forward to hearing from you soon. My brother can show you the way back to the teleport pad. If I'm not being too presumptuous, congratulations Ambassador Valen."

He smiled, rose, bowed, and left, followed by Venerado Rodrigo. When Jan stuck her head back in, she asked, "Well? How did it go?"

"Perfect. Such a deal. I believe I've done a preemptive strike. I'm certain one of the two will accept the post and call off the attack on us. They were drooling over the appointment. Bombing us will cost them the appointment. However, once again, this incident has shown me just how ignorant we are of the Supreme Guild Masters and their organization! I think we're going to have to find out more about them, somehow, someway."

Later that evening, King Carlos sent Queen Amy his reply. He accepted, but Venerado Rodrigo would temporarily hold his throne. Again, a Venerado was in charge of a kingdom, but there was little Amy could do about that. While the ambassador post was darn near a useless one, preventing the brazen attack on the Imperium Castle was not. Peace was vital just now.

Part II A Race Against Time

Chapter 6 Bigotry and Preparations

30 August 1325. Juno-3, the bluish planet just barely in the outer rim of the Imperium Arm of the galaxy, was an ocean planet with only two large land masses, one located in the north temperate hemisphere, one located on the opposite side in the south temperate hemisphere — North Juno and South Juno respectively. President Fishwaters II paced his oval office there in the capital city of North Waters, North Juno. He had a serious problem. Well, he'd seen it coming for the last ten years, but their senators had been utterly unable to get the Imperium Senate to tackle the issue.

Juno-3's problem was simple. Vast overpopulation. No, not of the normals — the name now being used to refer to the original human population of this world. Their population was a respectable two billion. Under normal circumstances, their numbers were perfect for this world, where ninety percent of the planet was ocean. In fact, with their incredibly mild weather, balmy days, Juno-3 had become a magnet for retirement aged couples, who flocked to this nearly perfect-weather planet. According to their last census figure, these older men and women accounted for one quarter of their normal population. And this was good for the economy. These retired folks supplied nearly a third of the Gross Income of Juno-3!

Because of their unique normals population, Juno-3 had developed extensive assisted living complexes scattered across both hemispheres. These facilities used to provide stable employment for a flotilla of CNAs, that is, Certified Nurse's Assistants, usually younger men and women, who cared for the needs of these wealthy elderly.

Over thirty years ago, because of their unique standing in the Imperium in the assisted living arena, Juno-3 had been appointed the official Terrorist Victim's Assisted Living Center. Initially, Juno-3 welcomed this designation. Many ex-senators and their families and wealthy nobles of Proxima Prime, who were the initial victims of the bio genetic terrorist attacks on the Senate and Opera House, ended up here for their long term care and recovery. This only added to their prestige and, of course, income, since these men and women were quite rich by any standard.

However, Juno-3 was also asked to take in the newly converted prisoners. The hardened criminals sentenced to life in prison on the penal planet Xeros-1 had been subjected to the same bio genetic modifications that the terrorists used on the senators and those in the opera house. "We have to take the good with the bad." That was the universal slogan used to sell this program to the normals of Juno-3. Thirty years ago, that slogan was acceptable. About three thousand wealthy easily offset three thousand criminals, the latter of which were completely helpless in their new freakish physical state.

Freaks. That was the common designation, although derogatory, the locals used for these victims. True, all new arrivals came properly clothed. That is, these mutated freaks had no arms and horribly distorted feet. They looked just like all the other victims of the bio genetic agent attacks, wholly helpless. Yet as wild as all these physical changes were, these alone had not given rise to the derogatory term: freaks.

No, that arose because all had mutated into being hermaphrodites! The male organs lay below their female ones. This unusual arrangement allowed for self-breeding as well. Until this genetic bio agent was developed, hermaphrodites were extremely rare throughout the vast Imperium. History books pointed to five known cases in some two thousand years. The last known hermaphrodite had mysteriously vanished near the beginning of the long war with the Federation of Planets.

In her extensive study of the computer records she'd gotten from the secret research facility on Ashford-4, where this horrid bio attack agent had been created, Doctor Ruth discovered that the he-she had been abducted and brought to Ashford-4 for study. Finally, she and her companion geneticists knew where those original geneticists had gotten their ideas from and where they'd gotten the needed hermaphrodite DNA to study. True, the geneticists on Ashford-5 knew quite a bit about just how and why those scientists had created this extremely nasty genetic modification now being used to terrorize the Imperium.

On Juno-3, the former President had placed the criminals into the assisted living facilities in South Juno. Many original inhabitants there complained about being forced to move to North Juno facilities. It was less than a year later that the "complications" were first recognized. Babies. The prisoner-freaks all had babies within that first year, both men and women. True, one could still tell males from females, but only by watching them urinate. None of the prisoners could speak. By law, their voices had been removed before they had been sent to prison.

The Senate acted quickly, issuing laws that these "innocent" children of the prisoners were to be given assisted living quarters, and both raised and educated. The idea bandied about back then was to give them a chance to become productive members of society. Although protesting and asking for monetary resources to carry out these new laws, Juno-3 complied, but still housed these children in South Juno facilities.

Within a few years, the true nature of the "problem" became apparent. These freaks bred like field mice! Baby freak after baby freak was born. Even attempting to force them to sleep in separate beds failed. They merely impregnated themselves! Their many senators raised bill after bill in the Senate, begging to have a law passed requiring them to be neutered. Always, these bills failed. Too many were worried about false imprisonment lawsuits. Just one person incarcerated, who was later found to be innocent, could bring a devastating lawsuit against the Imperium.

Instead, the Senate appropriated more credits to Juno-3 for their care. At first, this mostly appeased those on Juno-3. In the thirty some years since the establishment of these prisoners on South Juno, they had some ninety thousand children. Worse, in the last fourteen years, those children had some six hundred thirty thousand children. All that was just counting those original prisoners, ignoring the three thousand wealthier patients.

For the most part, the wealthier hermaphrodites

eventually had their arms regrown and then moved back to their own worlds. In the meantime, they too gave birth to children at an alarming rate. Often, though, they did not provide for their own malformed freaks of nature, abandoning them to their fate on Juno-3. One must then add in another three hundred thousand more into the totals.

However, it didn't stop here. As more and more bio terrorist attacks occurred, such as the one on the exotic Space Paradise, an elegant space station in orbit above Proxima Prime, many of the terrorist victims were also sent to Juno-3 for assisted living care. That the Senate also appropriated more funds for their care helped smooth the acceptance of the new freaks on Juno-3. As the years rolled by, more and more terrorist victims came to this world. Often the victims were given their choice of what world they wished to be sent to for long term care. Naturally, many chose the highly respected Juno-3. These, too, bred like mice. Thus, by 1325, one must add in another six hundred thousand freaks, bringing the total freak population of South Juno to a whopping one million six hundred twenty thousand, with each year bringing roughly another million freak babies into the world!

This was the massive problem facing President Fishwaters II here in late August. Vast, vast over population of freaks. In order to care for the nearly constant needs of nearly two million helpless people, nearly that many CNAs were needed, not to mention the flotilla of doctors and nurses. Even the support staff was enormous. So many mouths to feed, beds to change, laundry to do — mind boggling. Plus, the millions of babies and small infants, who required loving attention, gave rise to a new industry of Baby Care Givers.

The problem had become almost un-confrontable. All large buildings in South Juno were purchased by the government, and turned into makeshift assisted living centers. Workers were transferred from all types of jobs and hastily pressed into service in some form to assist the freaks. Finding a doctor on North Juno was darn near impossible, except for dire emergencies, when one would be flown up from South Juno. Most all commerce came to a near standstill. Only food production continued, but at an escalating rate. The quiet, laid-back population had finally had enough. Riots and protests broke out all over North Juno. Some were actually calling for North Juno to secede from the government and form their own country, abandoning South Juno to its fate.

"Kill the bloody freaks!" Those words and similar ones were heard quite openly, wherever normals gathered. Everywhere, the President was besieged with admonitions to "solve" this monstrous problem and soon! Hence, President Fishwaters II paced his oval office, wearing the carpet thin from his constant circling, while praying for a solution to enter his blank mind.

Already someone had bombed one of the assisted living complexes, killing some thousand criminals. Well, he could care less about them, but his advisors cautioned him to expect more such bombings. While he had to go on record condemning such violence against the utterly helpless, in fact, he did nothing to investigate, ordering the police to stand down. "Keep order" was his official statement to the head of South Juno Security.

"Keep order" was also the secret byword on five other populous hub worlds. These big five were often considered as the most important, most powerful worlds of the Imperium. Fully a quarter of all senators came from these worlds. Zelan-3, Beta Carnae-4, Zeta-3, Longditch-4, and Bailey-3, together boasted a combined population approaching two hundred billion. Wealthy and powerful, these big five attempted to control the direction the Imperium took. The current problem was taxation. The wealthy ought to contribute more — that was the popular opinion running rampant in the Senate. Although these five constantly lobbied against such measures and vetoed them at every opportunity, still the excessive taxation continued, fueled in part by the rapidly escalating costs related to the explosion in the number of "freaks," who had to be cared for on a continuous basis for the rest of their lives, unless they could get the prohibitively expensive arm regrowth process. Of course, those who could afford it, one way or another, had it done.

These big five had originally lobbied hard to obtain

samples of the bio agent that caused the horrific genetic mutations. Guised in promises of putting their extensive medical facilities and geneticists to work on finding a cure for the mutations, these five obtained the samples and kept them at extremely secure facilities. From the get go, whatever went on at these top security facilities became a very closely guarded secret.

To understand what did go on behind these closed doors, one must understand something of ancient Imperium history. Some two thousand years ago, these five worlds along with Proxima Prime were independent confederations. Bitter fighting among them was the normal, each vying with the others for ultimate supremacy of the hub worlds of the galaxy. It was at that time that the Emperor of the Ataro Empire of the Twelve Sacred Planets of the Wasps stepped in to put an end to the centuries of warfare. He negotiated a lasting peace between the six worlds, forming the Imperium, which, by agreement, was to be located on the then most powerful world of Proxima Prime.

Although two thousand years had passed, the five other worlds still held ancient grudges against each other. At least, now they no longer hated Proxima Prime. That world and its people had literally vanished from sight, buried miles beneath a shell of concrete and steel. Not a trace of that original world was visible on its surface. Its current hundred plus billion people were primarily dedicated to running the vast Imperium. The vast majority on Proxima Prime were part of the bureaucracy that oversaw the Imperium. The few who were still considered native to the planet were confined to working beneath the surface, providing the life support for the giant bureaucracy. A few lucky ones attended the Academy.

Having gotten their hands on this incredibly powerful bio weapon, theoretically a weapon of mass destruction, the leaders of these five worlds instructed their research scientists and geneticists to work on effective methods of delivery to other hostile worlds. In effect, they were continuing the secret research begun on Ashford-4 during the war with the Federation. Using the samples to find a cure for the mass mutations was an extremely low priority mission, especially since the revolutionary discovery of Doctors Ruth and Alex Hammil of Ashford-5, a discovery that regrew lost arms, undoing that part of the genetic mutations.

Delivery systems became their primary research topic. Ordinary means, such as flying a transport ship around an enemy world enough times to fully saturate the atmosphere with the bio agent, allowing it to descend and infect that world's population, were out. With all of the sophisticated detection satellites and ships, such an attack would be spotted almost instantly, resulting in the destruction of said ship. Statistical studies suggested that such a ship would be destroyed before it completed even one pass around the world to be attacked.

Then came the shocking terrorist attack on Aquila Prime. An entire world was wiped out by this bio genetic weapon. Finally, it became a proven weapon of mass destruction, the likes of which were unknown in the Imperium. Needless to say, these five worlds suddenly paid extremely close attention to the ensuing investigation, gleaning clues about how it had been executed. Unmanned, preprogrammed stealth drones suddenly cornered the focus of these world's top scientists. It was imperative they develop the means to deliver a crushing blow to their enemies before their enemies crushed them! Of course, all these frantic efforts were hidden beneath the guises of Imperium sociality, a cold covertness.

All five worlds strained their spy networks on these other worlds, prying out clues about just how far along their enemies were to developing such a drone capable of executing the attack. Uncertainty and paranoia ran rampant within the upper levels of leadership on these five worlds. They saw the continued development of the bio agent as their only protection, their only safeguard from inhalation by their enemy worlds. "Of course, we'd never use it," more than one president proclaimed officially. "Mutual deterrent. They know, if they should attack us, we'd counterattack them with our bio weapon. Stalemate, but only if we can get our delivery systems ready in time."

During the years leading up to 1325, concerning their

geneticists' lack of progress in finding a cure for the genetic mutations, their senators reported to the Senate, "This is a most difficult problem, considering we cannot experiment on human test subjects. After all, we've not heard about more breakthroughs from the eminent Doctors Ruth and Alex Hammil of Ashford-5 either."

Late summer, 1325, spies reported seeing successful test flights of unmanned stealth drones on their enemy planets. Stakes rose higher; paranoia escalated. Adding further fuel to the unrest, the normals of their worlds were protesting the explosive growth among the freaks their governments had accepted from other worlds, providing them with assisted living accommodations and a lifetime of support. Not one evening newscasts didn't have another expose on this humanitarian crisis. At least, the newscasters didn't call them freaks, but still referred to them as terrorist victims and physically challenged offspring. Despite their politically correct references, the average person knew what they meant: freaks of nature. Unrest only grew. If something wasn't done about this situation soon, violence was sure to erupt, something the newscasters suggested constantly over the airwaves.

"Something needs to be done soon," declared Amalie Hadwig, a twenty year old Air Recycler First Class. She and her three close friends had just watched the latest newscast here on Proxima Prime.

"I can't believe it! A whole damned world — gone! Billions! God damn this 'acursed Imperium bureaucracy!" Elke Traud, a twenty-one year old Water Purifier First Class.

Their long time boyfriends were with them. It was seven at night, and they had been having pizza and beer. Adolf Brecht, also a Water Purifier First Class, added, "Elke's right. The damned Imperium bureaucracy has no right to exist anymore!"

"Amalie's right, something needs to be done soon," Askel Rabendorf, another Air Recycler First Class broke in, adding his bass voice to the mix. Often, the four sang together as a quartet, Amalie taking the soprano lines. "It wasn't like this two millennia ago. Not when we true Proxima Prime inhabitants ruled the Imperium. How did we lose control of our own world? That's what I'd like to know."

"Hell, Askel," Amalie answered, "we true Proxima Prime people are now delegated to lower than subservient slaves — slaves to all these billions of ignorant, pompous foreign pigs. Do we even have a senator anymore? Hell no. We work and slave here in the bowels of our own planet and never even see the light of day."

"Who would want to be topside these days, Amalie?" Askel retorted. "They've totally modified everything up there. Nothing of our own world is left topside. At least down here, we can see the bedrock of our world — if we look hard enough, that is. She's right, someone has to do something. A whole bloody world — gone — what? Ten billion dead? And what have these Imperium pigs done to prevent it? Nada."

"Hell, Askel, this time they can't save any of the victims," Amalie added. "Someone has to put this Imperium bureaucracy out of its misery!"

"Why not us? Hell, there's no way we true Proxima Prime people can ever regain our world. Hell, who'd want to, not as destroyed as it is?" Adolf suggested. "We ought to do it for all we true people. I say get revenge on the Imperium for having totally destroyed our world and our race, for turning us into fifth-class citizen-slaves. We four should do something about it. Who else will? Eh? No one. Our own people have become willing slaves."

"Not us, we're not slaves, not really, are we?" asked a slightly confused Elke. The other three gave the alto voiced woman a cold stare. She shut up.

"So how do we do it? We need to take them all down," Amalie asked.

"Hey, give them a taste of what was done to those innocents on Aquila Prime," Adolf suggested.

"Cool! I like that, Adolf," Amalie gushed, a big smile appearing on her roundish face, still grimy from her ten hour shift in the bowels of the Air Recycling System.

"How? How do we get that stuff? Isn't it illegal?" asked Elke.

The others stared hard at her. Adolf finally replied, "Obviously, it's illegal, Elke. Haven't you a brain?" She pouted, and he quickly apologized. "Sorry, Elke. I just got carried away. Yes, it's illegal, but has that stopped the zillion terrorists from getting their hands on the stuff? Not in the slightest. We should see about getting one of those cylinders ourselves."

The four put their heads together. A search of the Net yielded results, far quicker than either had anticipated. Adolf spotted a notice posted by a Sven Bartold. "Hey, gang. Look at this. It sounds like what we need. Ten thousand credits. Where can we get that much money?"

"Leave that to me," Askel replied. "I know where I can filch that much. You place the order tomorrow. I'll have the funds by then. This is going to be the greatest achievement ever done by us true Proxima Prime people!"

The next night, the four met once more. "It's all done," Adolf reported. "Askel filched the funds, and I sent them to this Sven Bartold. He claims our package is being sent. It should come to me in a week. I hope we aren't being taken. Could be a hoax. Still, we aren't out a single credit. Good going, Askel."

The four had a long, nervous wait. However, right on time, the automated computer-controlled delivery system routed the package from the spaceport right to Adolf's door, where he had a small hovel some two miles below ground. "Let's see it! This is *so* great!" Amalie gushed, unable to contain her excitement. Carefully, Adolf opened the package, revealing the single cylinder and the strange clothing, disks, and shoes. They discarded the apparel and focused on the cylinder and its dire warning markings.

"Now we have to duplicate this cylinder. I wonder how many it's going to take to get everyone?" Amalie asked. None knew. For days, they discussed ways and means of delivering it planet-wide. The newscasts suggested a drone had done the deed on Aquila Prime. They had nothing like this available to them.

"Hey, we have access to the air and water systems," Adolf suggested.

"Cool. We can put into the master lines. The air vents

will circulate it everywhere," Amalie built upon his suggestion.

"And we can put it into the water system too," Elke added, not wanting to be left out. "Then, everyone will get it when they drink."

"Great. I wonder how many cylinders we're going to need?" Askel asked.

"We should see about how we can hook them into the two systems. We want planet-wide coverage," Adolf suggested. They agreed. The next day, the four examined their respective systems. As First Class personnel, they had access to the whole system. Further, they knew the overall design and just where to insert their revenge. They decided to dump the contents of two hundred cylinders into the air and water. By choosing the insertion points carefully, the agents would be sucked into the master lines that fanned out chaos-fashion to serve the entire world. That is, from the master lines, the lines branched into pairs, then each into smaller pairs, and so on until the small lines wound up serving a specific room, in the case of air, and various bathrooms, kitchens, and water fountains, in the case of the water supply.

Since they worked in these two critical areas, each department had their own Fabrication Machine. This way, failing components could be replaced with newly made parts. One only had to enter the broken part's id number, and the machine then retrieved the master sample from the warehouse behind the Fabrication Room, and duplicated it, all on automatic. For two weeks, the four spent several of their off-duty hours here, making exact copies of the precious cylinder. When they finally had their two hundred cylinders, Adolf's single room dwelling was totally filled. They then put them into bags and loaded them onto two hover carts, designed to allow a person to move heavy objects easily.

They waited until midnight when most of the workers were off. Only a skeletal night crew was watching over the control systems. They paired up. Adolf and Elke took one hover cart, heading for the master water intake line, while Askel and Amalie took the other to the main air intake line. Each of the four also wore a two-way head set, tuned to a normally unused frequency. They could chat without fear of anyone hearing them. Timing was critical; at least they thought so.

When the four were in their respective locations, Adolf pressed the intercom. "Hey, got a slight breakdown on the main water intake line."

The night watchman responded, "Shit. Adolf, is that you?"

"Yeh, it's me. Out for a walk, and I spotted the leak. I can handle it, if you like."

"Sure go ahead. Beats having to wake up the top bosses. Thanks, Adolf. I owe you one. Beer on Saturday morning?"

"Sure thing, but you have to buy the pitcher." Both men chuckled. Now Adolf and Elke could work freely.

A mile away, Askel and Amalie did the same thing, reporting a small breakdown and volunteering to fix it, much to the relief of that watchman. They too set to work. It took them an hour to make all the connections. One hundred cylinders had to be inserted into the main intake lines. Finally, Amalie called out, "Adolf. We're ready here. How about you and Elke?"

"One minute. There, Elke's got the last one hooked up. Are we all set?" Adolf asked.

"Yes," Amalie replied. "Okay, on the count of three. One. Two. Three." Simultaneously, all four began opening the valves of the two hundred cylinders. A faint hissing sound could be heard as the bio agent left the pressurized cylinders, forcing their deadly bio agents out and into both the water supply and the air. Of course, it would take hours for the agent to reach the furthest points from these master intake lines.

When they finished, Amalie declared over their intercom, "Congratulations. We've struck a blow for all us oppressed Proxima Prime slaves. We are putting the incompetent, pig headed, ineffectual bureaucrats out of business. We strike a blow of freedom from the oppressive Imperium! Back to base everyone. Beer time!"

A half hour later, the four gathered around Amalie's dining room. A giant keg of beer sat on the table. "A toast," Amalie declared. "Here's to us taking down the whole damned Imperium in one blow."

"Here's to finally getting long overdue revenge for our ancestors!" Adolf added. The four clicked their beer mugs together and drank deeply.

After more victory toasts, Elke finally said, "We best get to it. I'm feeling a little tired. I don't want to go into that coma and wake up like the hundred billion bureaucrats are about to."

Amalie poured a dark liquid into their pitcher, then refilled their mugs. Again, the four toasted their incredible victory. Then, they split into pairs. Amalie and Askel went into her bedroom, while Elke and Adolf used her couch. "One last pleasure, Askel," Amalie whispered seductively. He grinned and did so.

An hour later, Amalie's place finally became totally quiet. Whether she was sleeping, dying, or in a coma, Amalie could not tell. She only felt a great sense of accomplishment and pleasureful satisfaction.

Chapter 7 Horrors Begin

On the twentieth of September 1325, Sven Bartold, or rather now Savina Ruckhard, woke up. She was twenty-five and, thanks to her advance planning, extremely wealthy. She'd sold all of her bio agent cylinders, had transferred all the funds into her new account, had a new apartment on Proxima Prime, and was finally getting used to her recent gender change. Now, no one could possible tie her back to the Mal Dynamics corporate Vice-president, Sven Bartold. She was free and with a whole new life opening before her. She woke up and tried to scratch an itch on her face. She felt funny, had to pee badly, and felt incredibly thirsty and hungry. Her hands didn't manage to find her itch. Still foggy, she tried reaching her forehead once more. Nothing. She became more alert. Then, she screamed, louder than she imagined a person could scream, way off the decibel charts!

Terror screams woke Commander Torres from her deep sleep. She was in her bedroom, miles beneath the surface of Proxima Prime in the super-secure Bops headquarters, living quarters floor. Screams. She heard screams of men and women, muffled somewhat by the concrete walls, but terror screams no doubt. She felt foggy, like she'd been drugged. She knew that wasn't possible. She was the Commander after all. She had to pee in the worst way, and felt hungrier and thirstier than she could ever recall. What's all the screaming about? Her mind began to work once more. Are we being attacked? She tried to sit up, but her arms didn't push her body up. How strange, her mind registered. She became less foggy and looked down at herself. For a minute, she just stared in disbelief, all the while the screaming continued, providing a chaotic background to her senses, which were reeling over what her eyes were registering. Then, her own terror-filled screams added to the cacophony.

King Carlos woke to billions of terrified screams swamping his mental senses. He tried to sit up but couldn't.

His own germanium crystal glowed a brilliant blue, and then his mental blocks were once more in place. The terror-filled panic was silent. No, now he heard muffled screams from apartment suites above his that he shared with the elder Senator Franco Hermanes. As he took stock of his own self, slowly the realization of what must have happened to him hit him like a sledgehammer! His bass screams added to the din.

In the next bedroom, Senator Franco was roused by the screams of his new ambassador. As he tried to get up, he became acutely aware of his own body's terrible genetic mutations. "Well, I was rather expecting this to happen one day, but not before I could retire. So it has come to this. I wonder how bad it is this time? Crap, I'm darn near helpless." He focused. His crystal glowed, while he sent calming waves over King Carlos' body. Then, he used a bit of his energies to push his body into a sitting position. Now, he could survey the many changes, none good. Carefully, he rose, standing only on his toes, wobbling a bit while trying to get his balance. His new lip loops drooped almost to his chest. His new giant breasts obstructed his view of his feet. As he stood, his now thickened hair had changed from grey back to the black of his youth, but dropped on down nearly to his ankles. Slowly, he began walking carefully to King Carlos, his new ambassador.

He found him sitting on his bed now, trying to come to grips with what had happened to him. "If you stand carefully, you can make it. We need to use the bathroom, and then see what we can drink and eat. I was afraid this would happen. Come on, ambassador; we need to see if we can find out how bad this attack has been. Oh, speak in Imperium Standard. We won't be able to be understood otherwise. Nasty business, this genetic warfare." Slowly, he turned and headed for their bathroom.

"But I'm a helpless freak now too!" Carlos bellowed.

"Well so am I, Carlos, and so are many others, if my ears don't deceive me. Come on, young fellow. Unlike the others, we've still got our *mentales* gifts. Time to put them to good use, I say," Senator Franco countered. Even if he'd wanted to help Carlos, he physically could not.

A half hour later, the two naked men had relieved

themselves and somehow quenched their thirst, using the push lever control of their sink. They looked hopelessly at their kitchen, wondering where their Academy student helpers kept their food. Both managed to sit down, but grimaced as they sat on their long hair.

"Hadn't we ought to contact someone?" Carlos grumbled, wondering if he'd ever eat again.

"I suppose the authorities already know about this attack. No sense wasting our energies on that. We should try to contact Queen Amy and let her know. She can send a deep space transport for us and get us some help in perhaps four days. We can't starve in that time," Senator Franco suggested, rather bored with the whole situation. "On the bright side, we'll be going home soon, I hope."

Carlos grumbled again. "I'm a bloody freak, that's what I am!"

"No, we both are terrorist victims, Carlos. Just like thousands before us, we too are now victims. Still, once we get back to Tierra, I'm sure the good doctors there will regrow our arms. After that, it ought not be too awfully hard for us."

"But we'll be freaks for the rest of our lives," Carlos growled, still unwilling to accept his miserable fate.

"True, but we are alive. I suspect that if this attack is wide spread, many will die, just like on Aquila Prime. Come on; let's see if together we can somehow get the comm center powered up and get us a rescue."

Over near the Presidential Office skyscraper, in his secure Legate's Compound, Legate H-cubed, that is, Helyeon H. Hoon, once a victim of the terrorist attack on the opera house, woke to the terror-filled screams of others. He struggled to sit up. Then, he grumbled, "Oh no. Not again!" He sat patiently, knowing a rescue was sure to come, just as it had before. Surely, they would rescue the Legates first, perhaps after the President.

Of the millions of inhabitants that could still trace their lineage back through the millennia to the original people of Proxima Prime, only a handful were chosen to attend the

Academy. Only the apt and brightest students were selected. All others were farmed out to the many needed service groups, such as the Air and Water Recycler Divisions, based primarily on the needs of the Imperium bureaucracy at the time. These few Academy students would not necessarily have to follow the abject slavery of their parents.

The Academy often had married couples attending, especially since many disciplines required advanced graduate studies. Located in the southern hemisphere of Proxima Prime, the Academy classrooms and laboratories sprawled over a dozen skyscrapers. Nearby skyscrapers housed the many students. South-123 was the address of the married student's dorms, yet another skyscraper. #42 was the giant suite designed to house three married couples, providing each family with their own private spaces, but also a common living room, dining room, and kitchen. This was a cost-cutting measure. Why spend more on student housing than necessary?

#42 was the residence of three married couples, who had lived together, sharing living costs for the past four years. All were twenty-two; all were beginning their graduate studies; all had blue eyes; all had brown hair, typical of the original inhabitants of Proxima Prime. Dietmar Eldric was a budding geothermal engineer. His wife, Ilsa, was a green engineer, applying various energy saving technologies to civilizations. He had a round face with bowl-cut hairstyle, claiming it made him look distinguished. She was rather tall and slender, but physically strong, able to handle the heavier equipment that was needed in her fieldwork. She kept her hair wavy and trimmed rather short, preferring not to be bothered with it getting in her way while she worked on a project.

Hagan Kyler sported a thick moustache, claiming it made him look professional. He was studying astrophysics and navigation. His wife, Karla, was several inches shorter. She was an observational astronomer and a keen observer. Of the six, she was always the first to notice small things, often pointing them out to the others, whether they so desired or not. Sometimes, Karla was accused of being rather abrasive, but she always had a smile on her face. Why? The shape of her mouth gave the impression of a smile, even if she was frowning. She also had wavy hair, but kept hers trimmed around the middle of her back. She always wore a clasp behind her head to keep her tresses from interfering with her work.

Hans Lambrecht was tall and thin, with a smart looking goatee and moustache. He was becoming a hydroelectric engineer, and one day hoped to design power plants on other worlds. His wife, Kathe, was short and somewhat pudgy. Her hair was rather curly, and she kept it trimmed just barely touching her shoulders. Always friendly, she was into the design of electronic circuitry, a rather strange interest, as she always told others.

These six all had high IQs and were already into their second year of graduate studies. The fall term had just begun, and the six were already pounding their books. Actually, the books were all electronic books. No one had real books. They were too heavy and took up too much space. Their laptops contained hundreds of books and articles pertinent to their fields, along with some light reading, that is, novels. Naturally, they had numerous photographs pertaining to their fields. Hagan and Karla had numerous images of fantastic stellar gaseous clouds and galaxies on their computers, for example.

The night of the attack, the six were lounging around their living room, laptops at hand, studying for the morrow's classes. Dietmar commented, "You know, geothermal energy is really the answer for many worlds. Vastly cheaper in the long run. No mining needed."

"Oh I don't know, love, solar energy is abundant on every world. After all, every world has a sun, and you don't have to dig those deep holes in the ground," Ilsa countered.

Hagan looked up, "You know, Ilsa has a point. The stars emit an enormous amount of energy. If we could learn to tap into that, energy resources would be unlimited. Now if we could learn to make use of all that hydrogen floating around out there, we wouldn't need all that fuel from psi crystals. Mishaps in mining them are common."

Hans stopped his calculations and added his opinion, "No, you are both wrong. The cheapest source of unlimited energy is from flowing water. Every world had rivers. A simple dam and you have unlimited, steady hydroelectric power — all you could want."

Kathe laughed. "Men. No matter which source you choose, you still need to have the proper electronics hooked up to harness all that power. Now that *is* what is truly interesting. Power grids. Computer controlled, naturally. Neural networks are fascinating things, almost alive."

"Say," Karla broke in, desirous of changing the topic, "do you suppose that one day we'll be able to make computers smart enough to control robotic bodies? I know, we have dumb robotic arms in factories, but how about a robot in human form, one that can think and act? Now that would be something. We could use them to perform dangerous jobs and avoid having humans harmed."

"Oh, the technology is light years away from all that, Karla," Kathe explained. "I'm afraid we have to do our own thinking for the foreseeable future. And that means we all have to study like mad. My courses are definitely going to be tough ones this semester. Of course, the crowning glory will be the class trip into space to observe the stars from the orbiting observatory. Won't that be something!"

"No thank you. I want to keep my feet planted firmly on the ground," Kathe teased.

"Ah, my dearest, the ground is miles below us," Hans teased his wife back. All laughed and returned to their readings. Like typical Academy students, they finally headed to bed around midnight.

The next morning, Karla and Kathe woke around seven. Wearing their house robes, they shuffled to the kitchen to whip up some strong coffee first and breakfast, second. Ilsa joined them when the pungent odor of freshly made coffee filtered into her bedroom. She shuffled out to the kitchen, tossing her short hair with her fingers. "Morning. Coffee, coffee, coffee," she moaned mischievously. The other two women chuckled, while Ilsa took a large sip from her mug, before setting the table for the three couples. By the time breakfast was ready, the three men staggered out, heading for the coffee as well.

Once breakfast was done, the six disappeared into their

private rooms to get dressed and ready for the day's interesting classes. However, as the group rendezvoused in their living room, packing their laptops, notebooks, and pens into small backpacks, Ilsa began to feel quite tired, most unusual. She was a morning person. This was her time of day, unlike the two astronomy students, who were, by their natures, night owls. Kathe and Hans were also morning birds.

"Gang, I feel incredibly tired. How very strange! Kathe?" She looked at her close friend, who was uncharacteristically yawning heavily. Even Hans looked dull and sleepy as well.

"You're right. I feel so tired. Don't know why," Kathe mumbled, her speech slightly slurred.

Worry struck Ilsa. This was totally unlike her friends and herself, for that matter. "Gang, something is wrong with us. Could something we just ate have been bad? Food poisoning?"

Dietmar yawned himself. "I'm really tired, like I've run a mile or something. No, dear. If we had food poisoning, we should have bellyaches, nausea, or something like that. I'm just really, really tired for some reason."

"Same here. This is really strange for us," Hagan added. "Really so for you, Ilsa, and Hans and Kathe, too. You three are the morning birds around here."

"I don't like this. I've had more than my share of coffee," Kathe exclaimed. "I should be more than wide awake, but I think I could sleep for days. What's going on?"

"Hold up a minute. I'm going to splash some cold water on my face. See if that wakes me up," Ilsa requested. She dashed into her bathroom and did just that. Suddenly, she called out, "Hey, the water smells really strange. Come look!"

The six took turns smelling the water. It did have a strange odor. "Is that sulfur?" Karla asked.

"No, sulfur would smell like rotten eggs. I've never smelled anything quite like this before. Rather a strong odor," Karla pointed out.

Ilsa, who had backed away slightly, began to get very nervous. "Gang, something that Kathe just said a minute ago. Sleep for days. Remember. When the terrorists struck, releasing their bio weapon, the poor victims slept for days. They fell asleep or rather went into a coma."

"She's right. I remember the news reports," Kathe added. "Three days. They were unconscious for three days. They fell asleep and woke up three days later, their bodies horribly disfigured."

Now Hans began to worry. "I don't like this. We're all about to fall asleep on our feet. That's not like us, not with full stomachs and our strong morning coffee. We should be at the top of our game, not dragging out of bed. You don't suppose we're somehow infected with that hideous bio weapon, do you?"

Now all six stomachs knotted. After a bit more discussion, Karla, the observational astronomer, spoke up. "Gang, look at us. We should be panicking or at least really, really nervous even thinking about being the latest victims of some terrorist attack. But look at us! Look. We are all falling asleep on our feet. This isn't right. It's *very* wrong. I think maybe we are ill or something."

The two practical engineers, Hans and Dietmar, took charge. Hans suggested, "Look. We might all be ill. On the other hand, we might be suffering another terrorist bio attack. No matter which, we all should go back to bed and wait this thing out."

Dietmar added, "Wait, if we are being attacked, we could be out for days."

"Right," Hans continued his line of reasoning. "If we end up like all the other terrorist victims. . ." His wife gave him an awful look and he didn't finish his sentence.

"He's right," Ilsa stuck up for Hans. "If we are being subjected to that same kind of attack and if we all pass out and if our bodies get all mutated like all those other victims, dressed like we are now, there will be hell to pay. We ought to strip naked before we fall asleep — just to be on the safe side, don't you think?"

Dietmar nodded, "I agree. At least, we ought to be prepared. We're in no condition to go to class today. So, we skip classes, go back to bed, and get well. But if this is another terrorist attack, we should be prepared for the worst. Sleep in the buff. Ilsa will like that."

"We should have some food easily within reach if the unthinkable does happen. I'm short as it is," Kathe added. "God, I'm so darn tired. I'm falling asleep just standing here."

Karla spoke up, "Okay, let's get some easy to fix things out on the cabinet, just in case. Fill some water bottles and have them there too. Damn, I'm so tired. I can barely function."

The six moved slowly back to the kitchen. With great effort, the six pulled various boxes and containers down from the shelves, putting them within easy reach on the counter top. They filled six water bottles, putting them on the table. All six stumbled back to their own private three bedrooms. With great efforts, they managed to get themselves undressed and back into their beds. Ilsa snuggled up to Dietmar, whispering, "I have a very bad feeling about this. God, Dietmar, what happens to us if we *are* being attacked? Those poor victims, they are completely helpless. Their lives are ruined. I don't want that to happen to us."

"I don't know dear. Just remember, I love you more than anything else in the world. I'll always be here for you," Dietmar whispered back.

Ilsa tried to say, "But you'll be just as helpless as I," but she could no longer force her mouth to work properly. She drifted into a deep sleep and coma, just as the hundred billion others on Proxima Prime were doing about the same time. At some longitudes, people were just rising as the Academy students were. At other longitudes, the day was in full progress with activities abounding. At others, people were asleep. Those who fell into their comas during the day while at work were in big trouble, to say the very least.

The next thing Ilsa was aware of was the distant sound of men and women screaming. Groggy, her mind barely registered the muffled sounds coming from the apartments above and below theirs here in the Academy married student housing complex. Her face began to tickle. Vaguely, she realized her hair was the source of it. *How strange,* she thought. *It's always so short just so it doesn't get in my way.* She raised an arm to push her hair back. Nothing happened.

How strange, she thought once again. Slowly, the fog in her mind began clearing. She tried once again to brush her short hair out of her face. Nothing. Now, she did wake up and tried once more. Nothing. A sheet covered her and Dietmar. She tried to pull the sheet back. Nothing. At last, she began kicking with her feet and pushed the sheet off them. Seeing parts of her body and all of Dietmar's, Ilsa shrieked. Her stomach knotted in utter panic!

Dietmar's cries of terror joined hers, along with those of their four friends. Ilsa fought against it, but her efforts were futile. This wasn't some hideous nightmare, but really real! Wiggling and jerking wildly, she managed to sit up. Her now very long hair fell over the front of her body, but she now noticed her massive basketball-sized breasts. Beside her, Dietmar was lunging his own body into a sitting position. She shrieked again. He too had the same sized breasts, just as all the terrorist victims had. Now she noticed his lips were split. Two large lip loops dangled from his mouth, his white teeth were quite visible. His hair also dropped down over his massive bosom. Still involuntarily shrieking, both looked at each other's lower body, their cries crescendoing. He had female organs above of his male ones, while she had male organs below her female ones. At last, their eyes found their feet. Both pair were horribly malformed, with terrifically high, bent arches. Only their toes could rest flat on the floor. Their heels were parallel to the floor but at least seven inches above the floor!

Finally, Ilsa managed to say something coherent. "Dietmar, we're helpless freaks! Just like all the other terrorist victims on the news." Unfortunately, she couldn't understand her own speech.

Dietmar said, "Huh? I can't understand you. Oh, I can't even understand myself!" Ilsa couldn't understand what he was saying and panicked even more so. "Wait. I remember. We have to speak in IS," he said slowly in Imperium Standard. "Can you understand me now?"

"Oh! Yes, oh Dietmar! We're helpless freaks now, just like all the others!" Ilsa said again. "Oh god! I got to pee! What do I do now?"

"I have to pee too. We must have been out for days. We have somehow to get ourselves to the bathroom. Come on; maybe we can do it. We have to try, Ilsa," Dietmar urged her. When they rose and wiggled around wildly trying to keep their balance with just their toes on the carpet, their hair, now more than double its previous thickness, fell down, almost touching the floor, like some kind of thick blanket, scaring them even further. Both tried using their non-existent hands to pull their hair back and out of the way, all to no avail. Then nature called. Both began taking tiny steps to the bathroom.

A half hour later, the pair began making their slow, careful way out to the kitchen. Both were craving water and food. As they neared the kitchen, their four close friends were also making their slow way to the kitchen. All six were naked, which they realized later had probably saved their lives. For a moment, the six stopped and stared at the others. Their own monster breasts prevented them from having a good view of their own lower bodies, but this way, they could see the others, who obviously were like themselves. All six had a pair of enormous, drooping lip loops, quite thick; all had overly thick, lush hair that fell down to their ankles; all had nearly identical massive bosoms; all had the same malformed feet, and most important, all had both sexual organs. That they were now like the other hermaphrodite victims was quite real to the six.

After pausing for a moment, their thirst took hold. After struggling to sit down, each faced the challenge of trying to drink from their water bottles. They stared at the screw tops. Ilsa began laughing hysterically. "We should have left the tops unscrewed!"

After a minute of thinking, Dietmar suggested, "Hey, Hans, we're the engineers here. We ought to be able to undo a screw top. I'll try to hold the bottle with my feet. You try to open it with your feet." While the others watched desperate for a drink, the two did just that. Once opened, they faced their next hurdle: how to drink from the bottle. Again, Hans used his feet to lift one up to Kathe's mouth. She wiggled into position and was finally able to get a drink, though at least half of it spilled. Plus, she no longer had lips to help hold it in her mouth.

Emboldened, the other men followed suit. Then, the women emulated the men, giving them a much needed drink. With their thirst satisfied, the six turned their attention to eating something, anything. They felt like they hadn't eaten in days, which was factual, though they didn't know that fact yet. Once more, Dietmar used his feet to hold a piece of bread dosed with a glob of peanut butter up to Ilsa's mouth. In turn, she wiggled her mouth into position to be able to bite into it. So it went for the six friends. An hour later, all felt full for now.

"We have to get help," Ilsa stated the obvious. "How can we even open our front door? We have to let the campus security men know we are in big trouble, that there has been a terrorist attack."

"I think they probably already know, Ilsa," Karla advised, speaking slowly in IS. "I heard everyone else in the surrounding apartments screaming. So it isn't just us. There must be a whole lot of us victims. We should see if we can get our laptops going. Maybe we can catch the news, see how bad it is, and how soon they'll come and rescue us."

"God, I hate long hair!" Ilsa complained. Again, hers was in her face, and she stepped on it while trying to get to her feet, nearly falling over as she wobbled about trying to not fall down while getting off her thick, long hair.

"What about me? This is absurd. How can any woman deal with it this long?" Dietmar complained.

A half hour later, the six used their feet to get their laptops up and running. "My god, none of the news channels are working," Karla exclaimed.

"Hey, none of the channels are working, not even the sports channels," Hagan added.

"Try the emergency channel," Kathe suggested.

"What's its number?" Ilsa asked.

Shortly, all six watched a repeating emergency broadcast loop that was just minutes long before starting over. "This is Legate Mary Smith and acting Hub Sector ID Minister. Three days ago, Proxima Prime was attacked by unknown terrorists, who released the same biological weapon of mass destruction. I was fortunate to be inspecting one of our new battle cruisers when the attack was launched. I'll speak quite frankly. All of Proxima Prime has been infected. By now, everyone ought to be waking from their three-day comas. As far as we have been able to determine, the entire planet has been affected. Yes, over a hundred billion are victims, much like what happened on Aquila Prime. I've been pulling in all the resources of the Imperium. Soon, we'll have thousands of rescue ships in orbit around Proxima Prime, but we can do nothing to help until the scientists tell us it's finally safe for us to do so. Apparently, the attack was delivered both via the air supply and in the water. It will take us a while to cleanse the water system. Hang in there as best you can, but realize even with a thousand ships, it may be months before we can reach every person. We'll do our best, as I know you will. Stay tuned to this channel for further updates. The next one will be at six tonight. This message loop will be repeated continuously until then. Out."

The six listened to the message four times before anyone said a word. Karla broke the silence. "Well, a hundred billion divided by one thousand ships is a hundred million. So each ship will have to handle a hundred million people. Considering most large ships can handle maybe a hundred people at a time, that's a million trips to get to us all. Gang, at a week per trip per rescue ship, that's a million weeks. We'll be long dead by then."

For a moment, no one said anything. Her figures shocked them all. At last, Ilsa spoke up, "Well, we could be lucky. Someone has to be on that first rescue ship. Could be us."

"Probability is against that, dear," Dietmar countered. "They'll get the President, other Legates, and the senators first for sure. After that, they'll probably focus on the really important government people. I don't think we can expect to be rescued anytime soon. Maybe a month, if we're lucky."

"But how can we survive that long? We're helpless now?" Karla asked, fighting to keep from breaking down again.

"We work together, just as we did a bit ago," Hagan suggested. "First thing we should do is figure on not being rescued for a while. We should take stock of our food and implement some kind of rationing."

Hans added, "That's assuming we can even open some of the containers."

"Well, we have our feet still," Ilsa admitted. "Can someone please get my hair out of my face, please?" Several sat back and attempted to do so using their feet. "Thanks. Say, look at this! My own leg can go way up now. I never used to be this flexible before. Damn, I can use my own foot to push my hair out of the way. That's something at least. Come on. You fellows don't know the first thing about cooking. How are we going to get the cans opened?"

"I think from now on, we're going to have to work together," Hagan suggested. From this point on, that became their operating principle: work together to accomplish any given task. A couple hours later, they had a good idea of their food supply. It wasn't that good, perhaps a normal week's worth. By mutual agreement, strict rationing was begun, aided by their inability to do much of anything in the kitchen in any reasonable amount of time.

As six o'clock approached, the six were back with their laptops, eager for any further news. The Legate appeared once more, but had little more to say, other than it wasn't yet safe for anyone to land on Proxima Prime. After that, they headed for their bedrooms. After mostly falling into bed, Ilsa twisted and wiggled onto her side. "I can't make this without you, Dietmar."

"I know. I can't do this by myself either. It's like Hagan said, we have to help each other. I'm here, and I love you still." He struggled a bit to get into a position where he could give her a passionate kiss.

"Oh god, Dietmar! My other thing — it works! This is *so* weird!" Ilsa whispered, quite shocked. An hour later, both were very satisfied and fell into a relaxed and much needed sleep. This had been the strangest day of their lives, in more ways than one. Still, Ilsa felt secure in that somehow they had all survived one day as helpless freaks, all on their own.

Chapter 8 Detection and Salvage

The twentieth of September 1325, Legate Mary Smith checked her appearance in her mirror, gazing at her relatively new youthful self, twenty-five. She was actually seventy-eight, but had undergone the rejuvenation process a few years back. As always, her appearance was very businesslike and yet feminine. She wore a white silk blouse, a simple black skirt hemmed just below her knees, black stockings and matching patent leather low heels. A trim blazer with a light purple scarf rounded out her apparel. Her hair was fairly short, a wavy blonde, but her blue eyes were quite sharp. Her nose, angular. Her face, rather narrow with a pointed chin, though her skin had a distinct hint of light grey in it. In fact, her appearance was very much as it had been when she was a Hub Sector ID Minister and had been promoted to Legate in charge of the Intelligence Division. Mary Smith was in fact not her original name. She was from Descartes-3. Her native language was one of those in the click linguistic family. In fact, she was born ^Markarita ^Ya^maita^motia, but had change it to Mary Smith because her original name was too hard for most people to pronounce.

Legate Mary was on board the battleship Star Cruiser, for its christening ceremony. This was the Imperium's newest and finest yet, equipped with a cloaking device, the first battleship ever to have this new technology. Satisfied she looked her role as Legate, she marched out of her quarters. Just outside her door, a guard jerked to attention. "I'm to escort you to the ceremony, Legate Smith."

"Very good, at ease soldier. Lead on," she said in her firm, alto voice.

Entering the large war room, Legate Smith instantly sized up the situation. The new General Stalock and his staff, wearing their finest formal uniforms, stood at stiff attention before a temporary platform. A wall of reporters, cameras, and microphones pointed towards them. As she entered, the hushed chatting died down. Quite erect, Legate Smith began walking towards the podium. She'd not gone five feet, when a breathless ensign came running into the room. "Wait!" he whispered to her, and she halted. The general, obviously disturbed that this ceremony was being interrupted, walked briskly to the pair.

"This had better be good, ensign!" he barked, but softly so the reporters couldn't hear him.

The ensign held up a note. Both read the single sentence: Huge bio agent attack on Proxima Prime. "Just came in a minute ago," the ensign whispered.

"I need this war room cleared!" General Stalock barked to Legate Smith.

"I'll handle this quickly, general," Legate Smith whispered back. She took his arm and walked formally to the podium. The reporters sensed something was quite wrong here, but ceased their speculating, as soon as the two moved before them.

Speaking formally, Legate Smith said, "Thank you for coming to witness this dedication of the newest and finest battleship of our great Imperium. I hereby dedicate the Star Cruiser. Now then, this meeting is over. We need this war room vacated ASAP. We've just received word that Proxima Prime has had another terrorist attack. As soon as we know more, I'll hold a press conference with you. The Security Guards will escort you to another room. I urge you to get setup there. I'll address you formally, as soon as possible. Now move out," she barked. The general cracked a smile. He liked the attitude and cool of his new boss, Legate Smith. He sensed she was a no-nonsense type person with whom he could work.

Fifteen minutes later, crewmen rushed to their posts. Messages began streaming in from many ships hovering over the various spaceports on Proxima Prime. All reported pretty much the same sights. Bodies of workers lay on the various tarmacs. No shuttles were moving, completely unheard of for this world. On the dayside, there ought to be millions in flight. Proxima Prime was always a bustling world. Even the night side should have had a good deal of surface activity.

"No reply," barked one communications officer. "Can't reach the President's Office." Similar reports were called out, as the war room became a hive of activity. Legate Smith and General Stalock stood at his post, absorbing the reports, as they began flooding into the war room. Aides began putting red pins indicating affected areas on a giant map of Proxima Prime.

"Nothing from the Senate. They should be in session at this hour." "Controller Alpha is down." "Nothing from the Backup Tower." "Security Base One isn't responding." On and on came the awful news. Legate Smith began to feel sick at her stomach. The red pins began to give her a feeling this attack was planet-wide, similar to Aquila Prime.

His frustrations mounting, the general barked, "Isn't anyone responding?" Several comm officers glanced his way, shaking their heads.

"Okay, let me at the controls, son," Legate Smith barked. He moved over, giving her room. She switched to a secure frequency. "Don't look, son, or I'll have to have you shot." He quickly turned aside. "Legate Smith calling Commander Torres. Come in please." She waited and tried three more times. Silence. "Damn! This is bad, general, really bad."

"General, I'm declaring Martial Law on Proxima Prime. Everyone will now follow my orders. Send out spy drones; circle Proxima Prime. We're looking for a crash site, similar to the drone that wiped out Aquila Prime. Tap into the geo-sats, and review the last twenty-four hours. Find me the source of the attack. Radio our entire fleet. Have them make for Proxima Prime at top speed. Have them maintain radio silence. We could be under attack from the Federation of Planets. Take no chances. Establish a public communications blackout. I don't want any of the onboard reporters to broadcast anything until further notice."

"Aye sir!" General Stalock barked. "You heard her. Snap to it!" Never had Legate Smith seen so many men go into such action. For a half hour, she could scarcely hear herself in the war room over the din of barking orders and messages being sent to the entire fleet. At this point, the map was pretty well filled with red pins.

She left the war room and entered the smaller room

where the reporters had reassembled and setup their recording gear. As she walked solemnly into the room, the loud chatter instantly died. She could hear the tapping of her low heels on the steel floor, as she moved before the wall of microphones and video camera. "At this time, I have some very bad news to relay. Proxima Prime has suffered a wide spread terrorist attack. We believe it's similar to the one on Aquila Prime. People are down across the entire planet. We've been unable to make contact with any facility on the ground. I've declared Martial Law and have taken all necessary steps. Until we have established that we are not under an attack by the Federation of Planets, I'm blocking all transmissions, including those of the press. That is all for now. I'll address you when we know more. You can thank your lucky stars that you are up here and not planet-side." She made a hasty exit, before the stunned reporters could call out questions or protest the blackout of their news.

An hour later, more subsequent reports began returning from their drone surveillance. For the first time ever, the entire planet was quiet. Nothing stirred anywhere visible from the air. Some scattered fires had broken out where unattended machinery had smashed into structures and ships. All was an eerie silence in the streaming video being returned to the war room. Legate Smith noticed many soldiers had very pale faces.

"No immediate sighting of any crashed ship, Legate," General Stalock reported. "On Aquila Prime, the remains of the stealth drone were visible, smoke tendrils. Nothing here as yet. A quick glance at the geo-sat images hasn't shown any Federation ships, and none of the orbital stations has reported seeing any unauthorized ships arriving period. I don't get it. How was this devastating attack carried out?"

"There are other ways, general. I need a secure line again," she commanded. A few minutes later, she sat alone at a secure comm center. She knew she had to make the calls, but the news she had to relate would be devastating at best. First, she called up the Secondary Bops. "Commander, I've bad news." She explained what was currently known. "Make preparations to extract Proxima Prime's Bops center."

"On it as soon as it's safe. Martial Law is the correct procedure. Over and out."

She sighed and called Emperor Kino Sango. With the entire population of Proxima Prime wiped out, there was a humongous power vacuum. The Ataro System was now the largest intact power base. "Emperor Kino, Legate Mary Smith here. I have the worst possible news." She began to outline what had happened thus far.

After the usual time delay, Emperor Kino appeared on her monitor. Were those tears on his face? "Legate Smith. I've been expecting something bad would happen ever since the discovery of the bio genetic mutation weapon was discovered and used. You are right. Martial Law for now. If this attack follows the previous ones, you have three days, well perhaps two now, to get prepared. It will not be safe for anyone to land on the surface until then. Check the air supply and the water supply. Those are the next most likely sources for such an attack. The humanitarian problem will be enormous. There's no way a hundred billion people can be saved. Physical impossibility. First action, arrange for the key personnel to be located and recovered, where possible, just as soon as it's safe to put feet on the ground. President, Senators, Legates. I leave those for you to work out. Next, secure the key facilities, bases, weapons, labs, and warheads. Prevent them from looters and falling into the wrong hands."

"I'll head up the rescue efforts of the civilians. We should attempt to extract the most valuable people. I know that sounds harsh beyond belief, but as you well know, on Aquila Prime, only a thousandth of a percent of its population survived during the month that rescuers took to get to each residence. This time, it's a factor of twenty or more worse. Over."

"Excellent. Thank you for your coordination of the civilians. I'll place the entire military vessels at your disposal on the civilian rescue efforts, once I have the planet secured. I now have to notify the other worlds' leaders. Will we even be able to survive this catastrophic loss? Over."

"We must. Anarchy will follow if we do not. I do fear we've not seen the last of this. Biological weapons of mass destruction should never have been created in the first place. Over and out."

Legate Smith sighed. For now, she was leading the entire Imperium; the weight of it, the enormity of what she had to face hit her hard. She took a minute to compose herself and steel her mind to what she had to do. Then, she began making the hundreds of secure calls to many other worlds' leaders.

Queen Amy and Governor Katrina were silent for a minute. Emperor Kino had just signed off from his conference call to both of them. He'd related the awful news and asked for their help. Both women were stunned. At last, Governor Katrina found her voice, "My god! The whole world — a hundred billion people — the entire governing bureaucracy of the Imperium! How can the Imperium survive this?"

"Mind blowing, Katrina. I can't imagine the suffering. A hundred billion people. They were only able to rescue a hundred thousand from Aquila Prime — what did he say, a thousand of one percent of those people? Good god. Well, we can take more here. Rafe can still take another five hundred in Madiera. I can house another five hundred here at the castle."

"We could put maybe fifty more on the base. We do not have rooms for more than that. I'll prepare my deep space shuttle now," Katrina replied. "Time is not on our side."

"I'll send Jan with our shuttle. They can fly together. Over and out." Amy signed off. Her crystals glowed briefly, as she sent a telepathic message to many others. A half hour, her Gang and many others flocked into her throne room.

Queen Amy relayed the awful news, and then added, "So I've promised Emperor Kino we would do our part. We'll try to take on another thousand survivors. Rafe can handle another five hundred in Madiera. We'll put another five hundred up here in the castle. Jan, you'll take our deep space transport and travel there with Katrina's transport. Coordinate with Emperor Kino. Doctors Mindy and Andy will go with you, in case their medical skills are needed. Bernardo, Lena, you go with them, providing security and logistics. How many can you bring back on our transport, Jan?"

"Well, if it's just the five of us going and if we pack them in, we can bring around twenty back with us, maybe more. Katrina's ship will hold about as many too. Between us, we can bring perhaps fifty back at most. Several trips?" Jan answered and asked. For once, Amy was glad that she refrained from making any comments.

"Don't know. Probably. Half of the transports of the entire Imperium will be there. Maybe they will drop some off here. Too soon to know the details. I need you five on your way in an hour," Amy replied. "Meantime, the rest of us will have to get things arranged here for the incredible flood of victims. Expect their arrival in about a week or two at most. Let's get cracking."

Bernardo whispered to Lena, "Can the Imperium even survive this disaster? Wasn't the entire Imperium run from Proxima Prime?"

Lena looked a bit pale, if one could really tell. "The bureaucracy there ran everything. If that's been wiped utterly out, I surely don't see how, Bernardo. We could be witnessing the collapse of the entire Imperium. Scary. Come on; we need to pack a few things. We're in a race against time. These victims can't survive long on their own."

An hour later, Jan's ship landed at the spaceport. Katrina met them. "Carla, Elfe, and Doctor Whitney are going in my transport, along with a pilot and security guard. Our orders are to use top speed to Winno-3 and refuel. Expect further orders when you get there. Good luck." She gave her mate, Whitney, a farewell hug. A bit later, she watched the two ships slowly receding from view and then vanish, as they slipped into hyperspace. She knew in twenty-four hours, they'd be on Winno-3, having used every drop of fuel to make it at top speed. Still, would they be able to get there in time? How could so many be saved? Analytically, she knew at the very best only a minuscule number of the victims on Proxima Prime would be ultimately rescued. The others — billions were doomed to die, probably from starvation and in stark terror. Her heart went out to them, but she could do little more.

Three hours after she placed the first of her calls, Legate

Smith finished the last one. She headed back to the war room for an update. The general filled her in. "Still no sign of any Federation ships. I have six bio containment crews planet-side now. It's confirmed; it's the same bio genetic agent used on Aquila Prime and many other earlier attacks. It's in the air and also in the water. Whoever did this certainly knew our vulnerability. Must have had inside help. They're taking samples now, but all indications suggest it'll be days before it's safe to send anyone down there, except in bio containment suits."

"Thanks for the update. I've let the many other worlds' leaders know and asked them to send transports to help rescue civilians. Emperor Kino will coordinate that aspect. We'll handle the critical ones. We ought to begin making a list and prioritizing the rescues," Legate Smith suggested.

"I like your style, Legate. I have some military priorities to handle as well. Let's get started. It's going to be a whopping list. Glad Emperor Kino is taking over the civilian side. Don't envy him though," he sighed in a rare show of emotion, she noticed.

A day later, the two transports landed on Winno-3. Queen Altha was there to greet them. "No, stay put," she said, as they attempted to disembark. "You'll be leaving as soon as you are refueled. A tanker will refuel you when you get to Proxima Prime. You are to be there in two more days. Now then, I'm to relay specific orders to both of your groups." Her assistant handed them sealed papers. She continued, "When you get clearance that it's safe for you to land and begin rescue operations, these are the people you are to first try to rescue. I'm told the papers have their names and addresses. Winno-3 has already sent off a flotilla of transports. We're going to try to rescue a thousand ourselves. This is a monumental disaster. Some of us are wondering if the Imperium can even survive. Well, enough of my worries. You best stretch; you'll be off in about a half hour."

Lena chatted a bit longer with Queen Altha. Meanwhile, Whitney and Jan opened their sealed envelopes. Jan commented, "Coordinates even. Well, this ought to be more like a snatch and grab, don't you think?"

"Sorry, Jan. Not familiar with that expression, snatch and grab," Whitney admitted.

"We go in fast and snatch up these survivors, if they are alive. Get out quick. I think the get out quick is going to be important. It says we're to ignore any and all pleading from others who want to also be rescued by us. God, how can we do that? It's inhumane," Jan protested her orders.

"Well, I suspect Emperor Kino is prioritizing the rescue operations, trying to salvage those who are more important than the others. As terrible as that sounds, it makes sense. It is like a plague, Jan. One doctor and thousands of sick patients. Some will die no matter what treatment you give them. Others, the survivor types, will respond with minimal treatment. We doctors do what we can, but handing the survivor types yields the maximum survival rates from plague. It's the worst part of being a doctor — knowing you cannot save everyone, that some are going to die no matter what you do for them. All I can say is that we should follow his orders as best we can, Jan. We know countless other rescue transports from other worlds will be landing and rescuing people. He's coordinating thousands of rescue ships, maybe more."

"I suppose you're right, but it's going to be hard to turn down those who beg us to help them," Jan admitted, thankful she was not a doctor. She reread her orders. "Have you got a script to follow too?"

Doctor Whitney replied, "Yes, I can see what lies behind the emperor's orders, Jan. He's selecting educated men and women who could make a difference on our world. Clever man. With our limited resources, he's trying to select victims who could ultimately bring a higher state of civilization to Tierra. Devious, but smart. What would we do with a thousand chefs, eh?"

"I see. One of mine is supposed to be a geothermal engineer. From what I know about this field, it could be useful on Tierra. We don't really have electricity outside the castle and Underground. So no central heating. Geothermal energy could possibly work. Still, I feel guilty rescuing only these people, leaving the rest. But we couldn't support a hundred billion on Tierra anyway," Jan concluded.

Forty-eight hours later, the two deep space transports dropped out of hyperspace at the coordinates supplied by the Star Cruiser. "Oh my god!" Jan exclaimed, staring out her pilot's view port. Never in her life had she seen so many spaceships in orbit around a planet. Dozens of giant battleships and heavy cruisers dwarfed the countless other ships. Even the light cruisers were so numerous she gave up trying to count them. The sheer number of transport ships boggled her mind. She and Whitney's ships were mere pebbles in a sea of ships!

Doctor Whitney's voice came over the comm system. "Jan, are you seeing this? Unbelievable! So many ships!"

Just then, their ship to ship conversation was cut off. "This is Legate Mary Smith. Maintain your current position. The surface is still contagious. The bio agent is out of the atmosphere mostly, but it's also in the water supplies. Engineers are working on that problem. The people are rousing now. It's bad, but we can't land until it's safe to do so. We anticipate that in a day or so operations can begin. Over and out." Jan sensed what she'd just heard was a recorded message. She could not believe as busy as Legate Smith was, that she'd call them personally. Jan was right. Legate Smith had made quite a number of pre-recorded messages.

Bored, Jan took some videos out of her view port and transmitted them back to Amy and Katrina. After that, true boredom set in, just as it was across the thousands of other transports. However, that all changed the next day. "Legate Smith here. The surface of Proxima Prime is now cleared of the bio agent except in the below ground levels. Whatever you do, do not go below the surface yet. You may commence your civilian rescue operations now. However, Martial Law is being strictly enforced. Any looters will be executed on the spot. All secure facilities are totally off limits to all civilian fleets until further notice. Please, let's have an orderly rescue. Over and out."

"Okay, you heard the lady, action time," Bernardo exclaimed. "Let's do this, Jan. Fire her up."

"One second. I'm videoing our descent. Look at them

all. Wow, there are a dozen news crews going down first. Idiots. Who are they going to rescue?" Jan grumbled, firing up the engines and laying in the first set of coordinates. A half hour later, she turned off the video and focused on setting the shuttle down beside the tall skyscraper at South-123. As her group stepped out onto the concrete ground, they stared up at the hundred story building. A large sign read Academy Dorm. "Okay, let's hope the elevators still work. Our destination is #42, halfway up this monster."

As they entered, the first floor was filled with shops. They spotted several shop owners. Doctors Mindy and Andy insisted on stopping to check on them. Several were dead. They had either taken a bad fall when the coma struck them or their tight clothing had caused internal ruptures, as their bodies attempted to follow the genetic modifications. One woman was still alive, and Doctor Mindy removed her clothing, much to the woman's relief. Unfortunately, she could do no more for her.

The elevators still functioned, and soon, the group of five stepped off. To their right was #42 and to their left was #43. They headed to the correct apartment suite. Bernardo knocked on the door.

"Help! Help! Bust it open! We're trapped," a muddle of several voices yelled loudly. Bernardo did just that, smashing his shoulder into the door. It didn't give.

"Allow an expert, silly," Jan teased him. Lena smiled. Hastily, Jan picked the electronic locks and calmly opened the door. "See, haven't met a lock yet that can stop Sly Dog." Lena laughed, more than thankful Jan was on their side. They entered, and found the six naked men and women sitting in their living room on their couches, laptops opened, and playing Legate Smith's announcements over the emergency channel.

"We're looking for the Eldric, Kyler, and Lambrecht families," Jan said in IS, but slowly. She, Andy, and Mindy wore the giant lip plates. Jan wanted to make sure these people could understand her. Six heads nodded.

"Dietmar, my wife Ilsa. Please, we need some help. Can you even understand me? I can sort of understand you."

"Yes, we can. Use IS and speak slowly, like we do," Jan answered, noticing the great relief on all six faces.

Dietmar continued, "Hagan and his wife, Karla. Hans and his wife, Kathe. Are we really being rescued? We're mostly helpless, but we've managed to get by on our own for several days."

"Yes, as the news has probably explained, there's a massive rescue operation in progress right now. There are probably a thousand transport ships landing right now. Each of us are to rescue specific people," Jan explained.

"But where will we go? We all want to be together. We're best friends. We have been helping each other survive this," Karla spoke up, pleading with Jan.

"Okay, obviously, no matter how successful this whole rescue operation will ultimately be, only a tiny fraction of the people on Proxima Prime can be rescued. We can't get to a hundred billion in time. Even if we could, there's no place where we could take that many people," Jan explained.

"But where are you taking us? Please don't split us up," Ilsa begged.

Hans added, "Some of the worlds that have taken in other victims are now killing them. Please, don't take us there. We heard that on the news."

"I better follow the script. We are to take you to Ashford-5. We won't be separating you," Jan began again.

Hagan interrupted her. "But isn't that clear across the galaxy, on the very rim?"

Karla added, "Say, isn't that where the famous geneticists live? Doctor Ruth and Alex Hammil?"

Doctor Andy replied before Jan could. "You bet. They're my parents. I'm Doctor Andy. My wife, Doctor Mindy. We both are also geneticists and working on more cures to these hideous genetic mutations. We've only recently come up with a cure for a bit more. You see, Mindy, Jan, and I have had our feet partially repaired now. Believe me; walking in these six inch heels is vastly easier than those toe shoes. Plus, as you can see, we've been able to undo the genetic modifications to our hair, allowing us to cut our hair finally. Yes, ours used to be as long and thick as yours is. The neurons, axons, and axon terminals were behind both the added thickness and the pain sensors in our hair. So now I can at least look more like a man." He sported a crew cut, while Jan and Mindy's hair fell to the middle of their backs, a vast improvement over their previous ankle length hair.

He went on, "We've got excellent clothing manufacturers who designed my suit, so I look more like a man should. Of course, we have had our arms regrown. We'll be taking you to Queen Amy's Imperial Castle; she's Jan's mate. There's over fifty of us there now, so you'll fit right in. Rafe, Amy's daughter, is taking in another thousand victims too. In time, we'll get everyone's arms back, but that's a very long process, what with a thousand to do."

Jan was a bit flustered; they were deviating from her script. "Anyway, I'm supposed to tell you a bit about Ashford-5. It is a Closed World, because technically our people are in a sort of Bronze-Iron Age. We're part of the Ataro Empire, so we've got all manner of technology at our Imperial Castle and at the spaceport, of course. Oh heck with this silly script," Jan declared. "We're to offer you a new life on our world, if you are willing to lend your knowledge to helping us build a better world. Of course, we'll get you well cared for until you have your arms back and all that. We hermaphrodites are well respected on Tierra, that's our name for our world. Other worlds are not so tolerant, but you already know that. So are you six willing to come to Ashford-5 and lend us a hand? If so, we'll be lending you a hand as well."

"Hey, that would suit us fine, right Ilsa?" Dietmar replied. "I'm almost a geothermal engineer. She's big on green energy, like solar power. Hans is big on hydroelectric power. But what about our parents and our brothers and sisters? They are native to Proxima Prime and live below the artificial surface."

"Right now, no one can go down there. It's still actively contaminated by this nasty bio agent. Probably be days before anyone can go down there to search for survivors," Jan explained what Legate Smith had said earlier. "I'm sure that in time they will be found and helped too." She doubted that very much, but didn't say so.

Ilsa spoke up, "Dear, it's just like they did on Aquila Prime. Remember, it was in the newscasts. They put every survivor's name in a database so everyone could check up on their friends and relatives and see if they survived and where they were now staying."

Hagan commented, "Hey, on Aquila Prime, they were able to rescue barely a thousandth of one percent of the people. Proxima Prime has over a hundred billion people. Despite good intentions, there's no way they can rescue this many of us. Jan's right. Where could they take that many of us? We're all so darn helpless. Say, we heard that it costs around ten thousand credits to get the medical procedure to recover a victim's arms. We don't have that kind of money. We're just Academy students."

"You don't have to worry about the credits, at least not on Ashford-5," Doctor Andy answered. "We'll manage to do it somehow, at least as long as we can keep on getting the chemicals that we need."

"Okay, so are you all in agreement with us?" Jan asked, tossing the script aside completely. All six said so.

"Now, the problem is how to get them to our shuttle," Doctor Mindy spoke up. "They can't go around naked. We should have brought along clothes and shoes."

"We couldn't. Don't know their sizes," Lena pointed out. "Let's get them covered in some sheets. We've blankets on the ship."

"We have to take our laptops with us," Hagan declared. "Can we take other things too?"

"Sure. Okay, let's split up and go with them and gather up their things," Jan suggested.

Ilsa made an awkward lunge up off the couch, wobbling wildly until she had her balance. Jan hastily moved to her side, a bit slow in her heels. "I'm supposed to help you, Ilsa. My wife's an Ataro queen. I'm used to helping her with everything."

"We can do this much ourselves. We have to. Besides, we've got things sort of worked out, don't we gang?" Ilsa replied, trying to sound as independent as possible, in spite of feeling entirely the opposite. Jan helped Karla rise, while

Mindy assisted Kathe. Bernardo and Andy made sure the three men made it to their feet as well. Jan sensed the six wanted to show them that they were not completely helpless, and wisely let Ilsa tentatively lead the way to their bedroom. Lena took up a guarding position at the door.

The six sighed, as they looked at their old clothes. "No use taking any of them. We'll never be able to wear them again," Ilsa commented. "My family pictures, please."

Bernardo was with Dietmar, as he looked through his drawers. Dietmar whispered, "Do we men actually have babies, like women do?"

He replied softly, "You bet. Lots of the men at the base and castle have had children. I think you have something very special that normal men can never have." Bernardo sensed this was what Dietmar desperately wanted to know. By making him feel special, Bernardo felt the man's apprehensions vanish, at least for the moment. In fact, the six ended up taking very little possessions with them, mostly pictures and their laptops. Lena noted these were poor students, typical of those in the Academy, but she kept that observation to herself.

Wrapped in sheets and with a steadying arm around them, the group made their slow, careful way back to their ship. The three families were quartered in three separate cabins, adjacent to each other. Now both doctors began their examinations of their six patients, while Jan, Bernardo, and Lena punched in the coordinates for their next stop. All six were healthy, but low on vitamins and more than a little hungry. They'd not eaten a balanced meal for days. Hence, Mindy headed for the small galley to whip up a nourishing meal, figuring everyone they rescued would be in dire need of a good, square meal. She was not wrong.

Six hours later and four stops, Jan had finished off her list. She'd picked up a total of twenty-one young men and women. However, one young man refused to come unless he could bring his girlfriend with him. She'd been sleeping with him when the attack came. "If she can't come, I won't go and leave her. How can I? We love each other and want to get married," he'd protested. Jan's heart went out to them and agreed to bring her along. She wasn't about to leave the young woman behind, helpless all by herself.

Much later, when their guests were all asleep, Jan pointed out, "These all managed to survive by helping each other. Alone, they are completely helpless, but each can do something to help the other, especially the first six. We need to put that knowledge to good use when we get home. Let them do what they can for each other. That'll take the heavy burden off of us."

A burden it was. Once they had gotten all of their passengers aboard, Mindy had the food ready, having been stopped in her cooking four times. Now the five had to go about feeding twenty-one. Lena used her feet, unwilling to put her telekinetic skills to work in front of these strangers. No sense giving them any kind of false hopes, she thought.

As they headed for home, Jan decided to experiment and see if each of their passengers could somehow help feed their spouses and friends. If so, that would help the five immensely. They all needed baths, but that would have to wait until they arrived home.

While she and Bernardo checked over their instruments, he volunteered, "Sad really, Jan. We've picked up twenty-one very grateful people. But what's twenty-one against a hundred billion? Hell, I can't even count that high!"

Jan laughed; she couldn't either. "Well, silly, it *is* a weapon of mass destruction — people destruction, that is. I wonder what's going to happen to all the rest of the buildings and objects? Maybe we can get a bunch of the four-person automated shuttles for Tierra. We could zip around in style."

Bernardo chuckled. "I prefer my horse, thank you ma'am." She laughed.

Lena joined them and overheard their brief exchange. "Glad I'm not in Legate Mary Smith's shoes. She came up from the ID ranks, you know. She was a Hub Sector ID Minister, like my old post. Now, she's effectively the whole darn Imperium. No President, no Senate, no Courts, and no bureaucracy to run things. It's almost as if we lost the war with the Federation of Planets. There's going to be hell to pay over this terrorist attack; mark my words."

"Will the Imperium collapse?" Jan asked. Bernardo

could care less, but she'd spent many years out here among the planets as Sly Dog.

"As you well know, Jan, the entire financial system of credits runs off of the massive computer systems at the Imperium Bank on Proxima Prime. Right now, they are on automatic. Someone has to watch over them. If that bank should fail, the Imperium Credit, our universal means of exchange, will be worthless. That alone will collapse the entire Imperium. On the other hand, it's a great time to immigrate to Proxima Prime. There'll be no shortage of jobs. If the Senate were still active, I'd bet that they would off load large numbers of people from the overpopulated worlds of the hub. Maybe Legate Smith is already working on that. Someone's got to step in there and swiftly. However, what the devil do you do with a hundred billion dead bodies? My god, what she must be facing right now!"

"Hadn't thought of that. Sobering," Bernardo commented.

"Another thing that is really bothering me — Sector ID Ministers don't really retire, you see — this makes the second planet that has been completely wiped out by these bio agent weapons of mass destruction," Lena pointed out. "If I were a betting woman, which I'm not — Bernardo, except when we're playing cards and the pot is really big — I'd be planning for more attacks on other worlds just like these two."

"Ouch. That hurts," Bernardo teased her about her winning the large pots. "Why so? Isn't the devastation here enough to deter any rational person from ever even thinking of doing such a thing?"

"Sociopaths are never rational. If they were, they wouldn't be sociopaths. Worse, far too many other worlds have sociopaths in powerful positions. Mark my words, my love; we've not seen the last of these mass planetary genocides. I probably should have a chat with Emperor Kino about this. Best wait until this mess is over. He has his hands full right now. Oh, he hasn't any hands either." Bernardo chuckled at her tease and gave her a loving kiss.

The next few days found the five extremely busy handling their twenty-one victims. From countless trips to the bathroom, to feedings, they were kept on their feet nearly constantly, until they turned in for the night. Even the refueling stopover on Winno-3 didn't give them any respite. They were very pleased to see Tierra looming ahead of them, when they dropped out of hyperspace.

The usual afternoon thunderstorm was raging over Plateau Grado and Exchange City. Into the inferno of lightning and deafening thunder, Jan drove the shuttle, enjoying the buffeting and the excitement. Bernardo, Lena, Mindy, and Andy did their best to keep their guests calm. "It's just an afternoon thunderstorm. We have them every day, except in the winters," Bernardo explained.

"Dear, these people have never seen a thunderstorm or any real weather at all," Lena chided him. "Kids, Tierra has real weather, the kind that you've probably read about. Harmless and necessary to water all the grass, crops, and trees. You are coming to a real world, not the artificial one on Proxima Prime. I know, back in your ancient history, your world had forests, grasslands, and weather too. I spent most of my life living out of spaceships. Until I came here, I had no idea what I was missing. The odors of the world just after the rains are breathtaking. You'll soon see for yourselves."

Jan halted their descent a few feet above the tarmac at the spaceport. After getting tower clearance, she drove it a few more miles across the station to the southeastern corner. Exchange City rose up before her along with the Imperial Castle and Manors. The storm was easing slightly, as she calmly sat the transport down in the largest open space still left in the courtyard. The dozen gypsy transports were still there, taking up most of the space.

Once down, a number of castle servants rushed out to the bay doors that Bernardo opened. Already, Lena had sent word to Queen Amy. These twenty-one were in dire need of baths and had no clothes. They were wrapped in sheets and blankets. One by one, the servants lifted up one of the new arrivals and carried them into the castle's throne room, placing them carefully on chairs. Amy and Katrina had all their extended clan here to help out, as well as the hundred gypsies. Amy's thought was to allow these new traumatized victims to see many others, who were in similar straits as they now were, and to let them see firsthand some of the possibilities for dress.

"Hello everyone. I'm Queen Amy Valen Gervasi. Governor Katrina Lutgard. Welcome to Tierra or Ashford-5 as the Imperium out there calls our world. You are in the Imperial Castle and Manor here in Exchange City, just southeast of the spaceport. Between Katrina's group and ours, we've got over fifty children and grandchildren, who are just like us and yourselves. So we hope you'll fit right in with us. Also, a few weeks ago, a gypsy clan was attacked, and we've given them sanctuary here too. They are over on that side. Yes, we've not had time to regrow their arms as yet, but we're working on it. Our doctors will soon at least get a couple of modifications from your attacks undone. Specifically, your hair and feet take about an hour to be repaired as much as possible. These two here, Lilly and Nita, own Elegant Fashions Inc. Once we get you all settled into your new quarters and cleaned up, they will visit you and provide new clothing for you. Each of you will get to pick your own styles and colors. Later today, you will all dine with us, and we can chat more."

"My staff will now take you to your new quarters. Our guest rooms here are arranged in large suites. Each suite has a number of private bedrooms that share a common living area. To help ease you into your new quarters, the gypsies have volunteered to share suites with you. Okay, let's get you all cleaned up, fixed up, and into some descent clothes. Supper will be around six. See you all then."

A short while later, Dietmar, Ilsa, Hagan, Karla, Hans, and Kathe found themselves in a large suite. Tapestries hung on some of the grey stone walls. A resinous pine fire crackled against one wall. Sofas and couches lay at convenient locations around the carpeted room. Five bedrooms angled off this main room, along with a huge bath. Four gypsies joined them.

"Hello. I'm Matriarch Anwyn Braith, leader of the Braith Clan. My husband, Ivarr. He's the only one of our clan who wasn't infected, and he saved us all. My sister, Ceri, and her husband, Rhys. We're in those two rooms," she pointed with her head. "They're going to get you bathed first, so we can chat while they do that."

Ilsa introduced her group of six. While the staff began to prepare their baths, Anwyn chatted away. "You see, we were staying just outside the spaceport at Halcion City, Beltar-3, when the locals attacked us while we slept. They hate us for some reason. Ivarr was able to rescue us and got us here. Queen Amy has been unbelievably compassionate and helpful to us. We would have perished, if she had not given us sanctuary, and all the help she and her people have, you see."

"They've already cured whatever was done to our hair. All of ours used to be as long as yours is. Of course, we learned on this world, most women prefer long hair, so we've had ours trimmed so it falls to the middle of our backs — tons better than having it go down to your ankles, you see. Then, they were able partially to fix up our feet. Honestly, it is so hard to walk in those toe shoes. We can only wiggle to keep our balance, but you already know that. Anyway, the doctors told us they'll be partially repairing your feet real soon. I know; we still have to wear these impossibly high heels, but it's a whole lot better than the toe shoes. Everyone around here has to wear them, excepting Queen Amy; she has to, since she's an official Ataro Empire queen. Anyway, you fellows can then get your hair cut short, as Ivarr and Rhys have, if you like. You just have to tell the hairdresser how you want yours cut, you see. They're very good at it. Rhys is wearing Lilly and Nita's specially designed men's suits. Pants, shirt, jacket. So our gypsy men do look a bit more like men."

Rhys flushed. He spoke up, "It's awful looking like we did. Now, we sort of look like men again, but not really. Hey, you don't have to wear those huge, golden lip disks if you don't want too."

"Oh, he's right," Anwyn continued, having forgotten this detail. "You see, we thought they looked really ugly. Without arms, we can't deal with them. But on this world, all the nobles wear them. They are the height of fashion for men and women. That's why you see so many wearing them, but I suppose they would be manageable if we had our arms. Anyway, we can help each other so much better if we aren't wearing them. So we don't. Of course, it's your choice."

Ceri interrupted her, "Tell them about their incredible Basic Therapy, Anwyn!" The six were preoccupied with all their chatting, barely noticing as the staff bathed them and washed and pat-dried their hair before combing out the tangles. By then, the medical staff arrived and began the repair of their hair and feet. This time, the six got to chat with the very famous Doctors Ruth and Alex Hammil. Of course, Doctors Mindy and Andy were also there along with several nurses and six portable medical machines.

Doctor Ruth explained, "So we've got nearly a thousand of you to handle. In time, we'll do our best to get your arms regrown. Meantime, with your feet fixed up like ours and your hair manageable, you'll be able to at least be a bit more independent. Just be patient. It takes several months for arms to be developed sufficiently for you to use them. Usually, it's a year before they are really strong. Right now, we're facing a severe shortage of the organic compounds we need for the process. Still, we won't rest until we can get everyone's arms back."

"But what about all the other changes?" Dietmar asked his face flushing quite red.

Doctor Alex handled his query. He knew just what he was asking. "Oh, that. Well, we four geneticists and Doctor Whitney are still researching for more cures. We're rather hindered by the inability to experiment on human patients. But that's certainly preferable to having patients die on us because we were not right. We just need time. Obviously, we're all able to get by just fine as we are. Plus, some of us men find it rather beautiful to be able to have babies as well. Quite an experience that men virtually never get to experience. In my professional opinion, you are extremely blessed in having such an opportunity. I've had three children of ours. Just between you and me, that's brought Ruth and me closer than we've ever been before."

"But we don't look like men anymore," Hans countered.

"No, these knockers interfere, no getting around that. The steel corsets do help keep our backaches in check," Doctor Andy added. "But short hair and these suits rather help. I just wish they would stop all these senseless bio agent attacks. It's genocide actually. First, it was genocide on Aquila Prime. We've got quite a few of those survivors here. They are all Academy grads or students. Oh, most all of the adults you just saw there in Amy's Throne Room — we're all grads or finishing up at the Academy on Winno-3. So you'll have lots of company. We have fifty Academy students from Aquila Prime. Aria and Backus Acronis are twenty-two years olds. She is a history major and he's a civil engineer. Then, there are their close friends, Alexia and Hermes Anias. He's a computer technician, and she is a mathematician. All four are planning to teach at our local Exchange City school. So what are your fields?" he asked, slipping the conversation over onto the six.

Dietmar answered for the group. Doctor Andy then explained, "Wow. You six have a golden opportunity here on Tierra. Beyond this spaceport and Imperial Castle, the world is really primitive by Imperium standards. You have an excellent opportunity to put your skills, education, and training to incredibly valuable use here. You can make a huge difference to the people of this world. That's what Mindy and I are doing, putting out genetics training to the best use imaginable, healing what we can and working on new cures for all the rest of the many victim's genetic mutations." He wanted to instill some real hope for the future in these six new victims.

"Okay, all done," Doctor Alex interrupted their chats. "Lilly, Nita, and their staff are on their way. They will get you new clothes and deal with your hair. We have to go fix up another six of you. Queen Amy wants all twenty-one of you ready to go by suppertime. A doctor's life is a busy one. See you all at dinner." The six thanked them profusely, and they left, pushing the medical machines along with them.

Lilly and Nita entered after they left. Each had four assistants with them. After introducing themselves, Lilly explained, "First, we'll go over our catalog of choices. Today, you need to pick out one outfit and decide how you want your hair done. We're going to get you fixed up with one right set right now. Then, in the next few days, we'll meet again, and let you choose another half dozen." She and Nita sat between the six, flipping through the pages, while their assistants took notes of the individual choices that were made.

Hagan protested, "Look, even in these pants and jackets, we are still going to look like women, not men. Even the short haircuts look positively strange with these monster boobs. Only our voices sound right."

Karla came to his defense. "He's right. Even with all that and having to wear those really tall women's heels, he's still going to look really weird. Maybe he should keep his hair longer and wear dresses like us. I think he might be less embarrassed that way."

The six discussed this further. Ilsa had the final word. "Honestly, the way the other men around here now look, it's so utterly weird. I think they should look like we are going to look. I think they'll be far less embarrassed in public this way. Besides, if they change their minds, they can get their hair cut short and try the pants and suits, right?"

Nita cleverly replied, "Certainly. I agree, Ilsa. You can always cut your hair short. It takes years to grow it back out. So perhaps this is the wisest path to follow for now. Later on, if they wish, they can easily switch." She was acutely aware of their huge emotional trauma that lay just barely partially suppressed at the moment. Their mental health was exceedingly fragile, and would be until they had their Basic Therapy. After that was finished, the six would be more rational about their choices.

Lilly again took charge. "Okay, that's settled. We'll get your hair trimmed to fall just to your waists. No lip plates for now. The remaining question that affects your choices is whether or not you wish to wear the pipe corsets. From much experience, they do help to reduce our back pain from trying to support these massive knockers of ours. However, the consequences of wearing them are three-fold. You will find breathing more challenging at first, but you'll soon get used to it. Plus, you'll eat smaller amounts. You will lose a good deal of flexibility. Still, the benefits far outweigh the drawbacks of back pain." The six decided to try them, at least with this first outfit. Already, they'd all been having rather severe back pain from the weight of their bosoms. Without hands to massage their backs, they were willing to try anything for a bit of relief, especially since this wasn't a permanent change.

An hour later, the six were finally properly dressed. "I can't breathe, but my back feels better, and I can actually walk!" Dietmar exclaimed, taking a short walk around the commons room.

Ilsa thanked them repeatedly. Nita graciously accepted and rose, "Okay, we best go take care of the next six of your group. See you all at supper. Practice walking, sitting, and rising." As she and her group left, the six began doing as she asked.

Once they were gone, Dietmar whispered, "Ilsa, as long as I don't open my mouth, I look just like you, Kathe, and Karla. I don't feel constantly embarrassed. You do most of the talking, please!"

Anwyn and Ceri, who had been hovering in the background all this time, now joined them, along with Rhys and Ivarr. Anwyn began chatting away once more. "I like your choices. I'm glad you didn't go with those lip disk things. We can help each other when we need to use the bathroom or commode thing. One of us can use our teeth to pull your dress up, while you sit down. It works pretty well. Still, the hardest part is sitting down and standing up."

"No, Anwyn," Rhys countered. "Handling steps is much harder. Hell, we can't see our feet over these monsters of ours." The small group began to chat, and the six new arrivals soon felt far more at ease.

A week later, Jan and her crew was back on Proxima Prime, rescuing another twenty Academy students. They never made a fourth trip, though. Their third trip was quite unusual.

Chapter 9 Martial Law

Legate Mary Smith had her hands full. The situation facing her on Proxima Prime was wholly unprecedented and potentially explosive, to say the very least. Down there lay some of the most important men and women of the Imperium. Military weapons were stored in depots. The financial heart of the Imperium operated from the Banking Center Skyscraper. Untold billions of credits worth of equipment and supplies covered the planet. Then, there were over a hundred billion men, women, and children, whose lives were horribly ruined. No matter what she did, she knew most of them would die, probably of slow starvation or from lack of water.

That she was now elevated to a position of a goddess over Proxima Prime was not lost on her. Never in her wildest dreams did she ever imagine she'd have such an enormous responsibility resting on her shoulders. Yet, by a twist of fate, she did. Somehow, of the many in the executive branch, she alone was not a victim of the terrorist attack! *And now I am playing god. Who dies — who lives.* She sighed, and continued making her lists of people to be rescued, coordinating the many ships under her command. Still, she was grateful the Emperor Kino stepped in to deal with the vast majority of the people down below.

One set of military shuttles was sent to locate and retrieve the President, the Legates, and a number of their top support staff and families. Another batch was sent to find and retrieve the Imperial Court justices and personnel. The vast majority of the military shuttles went after the over two thousand senators and their families. However, other military craft dealt with securing the most vital infrastructure, along with potentially deadly supplies, such as the Nuclears. Military personnel went down to secure the spaceport control towers, and get them back online, so they could then control and direct the flotilla of smaller transports, descending on their varied rescue missions. All this, she had to organize and oversee. Legate Smith worked far into the night, barely sleeping at all for three days. Only when the all-clear signal came from the red-suited containment crews, who handled the contaminated water supplies, did she finally relax and issue the Execute orders. Now, all she could do was sit back, and deal with the inevitable chaos that would soon arise.

Ambassador Carlos cursed and swore, unwilling to accept the fact that he too had become one of the freaks. Senator Franco continued to attempt to calm King Carlos, "Hey, we still have our *mentales* gifts. We're getting by okay. Relax. I'm sure they'll send a rescue for us first. After all, we senators and ambassadors are some of the most important people on Proxima Prime, along with the President and Legates. I suspect someone will be here for us very soon, just as soon as it's safe. Calm down. There's nothing we can do about it now."

"How can you be so damned calm, Franco? We've been turned into utterly helpless freaks," Carlos countered.

"Oh, well in time, I'm sure they'll quickly regrow our arms. Plus, when we get back to Tierra, our doctors there can partially repair our feet and fix our hair so we can cut it short again. After that, we ought to be able to get by just fine, though I don't like the damned lip plates we're going to have to wear. I wish they'd solve that one soon," Franco countered.

"Hell, we'll still be complete freaks!" Carlos fumed. He wanted to storm around the living room! He wanted to pound something into dust! Anything to relieve the intense frustration and hatred he felt, but he could only just barely stand up, let alone do much of anything for himself. He knew that his own *mentales* gifts were pretty well useless at the moment. He was a master of Dominate Others and had many mental attack and defense forms. He was even able to Create Light, albeit a faint one. He had an uncanny sense of direction and was a superb swordsman, the latter of which was gone, probably forever. Even if his arms were regrown, it would be many years of strenuous practice before he had his skill back.

Just then, someone knocked on their door. Carlos bellowed, "Help! We're trapped inside! Bust the damned door down." He lunged forward, trying to get to his feet. He tripped on his hair and nearly fell. Only his wild wobbling kept him from falling. Senator Franco remained seated. Shortly, their door opened and a pair of soldiers entered.

"Senator Franco Hermanes? Ambassador Carlos Valen?" one asked.

"That's us. Senator Hermanes," Franco replied. "We need rescuing."

"Understatement, sir. We have orders to rescue you and your families."

"Just us. Our families are back on Ashford-5, thank god," Franco replied.

"Okay then. We're to wrap you in some blankets and take you onboard our transport. Once we have picked up our group of you senators, we're taking you to the light cruiser Defiant. From there, you are scheduled to be taken to Beta Carnae-4, where you will be fully taken care of. Doctors there are awaiting your arrival to begin the regrowth of your arms and properly clothe you."

"See, Carlos. I told you we'd be promptly taken good care of," Franco replied. "Thank you soldier." Swiftly, the two men were wrapped in some blankets and carried out to their waiting military transport. Carlos wanted to complain about being carried about like a sack of flour, but wisely kept his mouth shut. He knew he probably couldn't have walked this far on his own. Besides, he was horribly embarrassed about his naked body, which in his mind now looked more like that of a woman's than a real man's.

Already several other senators and their wives were onboard, all wrapped in blankets just as they were. From Carlos' point of view, thankfully no one said anything. The men were just too embarrassed and traumatized. Some time passed before the soldiers filled the cargo bay of the shuttle and lifted off Proxima Prime. Franco counted thirty-one victims. One solider returned to the cargo bay to watch over them.

"It's planet-wide, isn't it?" Franco said slowly in IS.

"Yes sir. Planet-wide. Scary. At least you are the lucky ones. The military is going after you senators right away. Emperor Kino is handling the rescue operations for everyone else. Grim. Still, we'll have you on the cruiser in just a few minutes."

True to his estimate, within ten minutes the transport docked with the Defiant. Once more, the victims were physically carried onto the much larger ship and deposited in cabins, four to a room. A young soldier then took his position by the door. "I am assigned to help you with whatever you need. The major said we'll have you on Beta Carnae-4 in twenty-four hours." Franco laid back, attempted to relax, and get some sleep, ignoring his hunger, confident that food would come sometime. Even more embarrassed, Carlos did the same. He couldn't tell if the other two sharing their room were male or female. He was totally humiliated.

Hours passed before another pair of soldiers arrived, carrying a pot of what appeared to be stew. Awkwardly, the three men fed the four victims and got some coffee into their mouths, using spoons. Again, none of the victims said anything. All were encased in their own personal grief and trauma, embarrassment of their physical forms not being the least. Later, Franco felt the gentle tug, as the light cruiser shifted into hyperspace. For a time, he wondered where in the galaxy Beta Carnae-4 was located. He rightly reasoned that it must be in the hub since travel time was relatively short.

Precisely on schedule, the Defiant landed at the military spaceport on Beta Carnae-4. Yellow sunlight entered the cargo bay, and Franco correctly guessed their sun was a yellow dwarf. Once more, strong arms of soldiers carried the victims out of the cruiser, placing them into waiting air shuttles. Their shuttle driver explained, "We're taking you to the Genetics Hospital in Rush City. They are expecting a hundred of you. Be there in an hour. Sit back and relax." With that, the shuttle took off, ferrying twenty of the victims to Rush City. From a side glance out of the port side viewport, Franco could see another four shuttles being loaded with the rest of his fellow senators, ambassadors, wives, and a very few children. Again, he relaxed. Soon, the nightmare would be over, and they'd be on their way back to Tierra.

An hour later, the tall, imposing Genetics Hospital came into view. Massive was all Franco could tell. Built of shining metal and glass, the facility shone brilliantly in the noonday sun. Once the shuttle landed, aides were waiting for them. One by one, they were lifted out, placed on gurneys, and wheeled inside the building. After an elevator ride, they found themselves in a spacious waiting area. Soon, a hundred gurneys were parked side by side.

A doctor and an aide began visiting each person. "Your name, position, and home planet, please?" he asked politely.

"Franco Hermanes. Senator. Ashford-5."

"Ambassador Carlos Valen. Ashford-5. How long will this take?"

"We've got five regrowth facilities here, ambassador, but there are a hundred of you. Just be patient with us. We'll get to all of you in due time. First, we're going to get you to your rooms, cleaned up, and into hospital gowns." He moved on to the next victim, not giving Carlos an opportunity to say anything further.

Later, the pair was moved into one room. A pair of women entered and proceeded to give both men a bath, washing their hair as well. Then, they tied the flimsy hospital gowns on them and helped them into the two narrow beds. Neither woman said anything, for which Carlos was eternally grateful. He was too embarrassed even to say a word to these women. Franco sensed their minds. They too were embarrassed, not knowing whether these were women or men that they were bathing. Sometime later, two volunteer helpers arrived with trays of food and proceeded to feed them both.

Days passed by the two, with one day running into the next. The only variety was the changing menu of meals. "I wish they would hurry up and get to us," Carlos grumbled. Both men remained rather quiet. What was there to say or do? At least, the aides often turned on the newscasts for them to watch. Thus, the two were kept abreast of the rescue operations on Proxima Prime, that is, what was allowed to be released to the general public.

The one aspect Franco found key was that Legate Mary Smith was now in charge of the Imperium. "She's a good person to have in charge of the Imperium, Carlos. I've met her. Very level headed woman. Sure is better than some egomaniac general." Carlos chuckled. Days drifted by.

Doctor Larnia entered with his clipboard. "Okay, senator, ambassador. It's your turn to have your arms — blood hell! Where are they? Nurse! Nurse!" A young woman came running into the room. "Where are these two victims?"

"They are supposed to be right here!" She checked the adjoining bathroom. It was empty. "I'll get security to scour the floor. Perhaps they went for a walk or something."

An hour later, the entire wing had been searched. There was no sign of either man. No one had a clue what had happened to the pair. Hence, Doctor Larnia moved on to the next pair of victims. Meanwhile, the entire hospital security staff conducted a full investigation into the disappearance of the pair from Ashford-5.

"Hello senator, ambassador. I am Doctor Larnia. You both are from Ashford-5, is that correct?"

"Yes," Senator Franco replied.

"Excellent. Let me check your vital signs." He flashed a bright light into each man's eyes. "Follow the light, please. Excellent." He verified both had yellow eyes with brown speckles. Satisfied, he said, "It's your turn to get your arms regrown. My aides will wheel you to the room now."

"About time," Carlos griped. Two men in white gowns entered and lifted both men onto a pair of gurneys. Soon, the three men were wheeling them down the aisle and into an elevator. A bit later, they were both lifted onto large medical machines. "You will be unconscious for a little while. When you wake, your arms will have already begun to form. In about three months, you'll have full use of them. So lie back and relax." Both men did so and soon were knocked out.

"Okay, make haste. Remove their voices," a fourth man whispered. He'd been hiding behind a screen. The man pretending to be the doctor did as ordered. It was a very quick operation. "Good. Now into the body bags. Be quick about it." The three slipped both unconscious men into the black bags and zipped them up. Next, the three changed clothes, stuffing their previous apparel into a bag, and then stuffing that into one of the body bags as well. Both bags were then lifted onto gurneys. The two men now wore funeral attendant's uniforms. The "doctor" appeared to be some form of priest. The hidden man stepped out, dressed as a funeral director. With the priest holding a Holy Book between his hands, he led the director out of the room, followed by the two men wheeling the gurneys.

Down the elevators and through a maze of halls, the four walked quite solemnly. In the sub-basement, they lifted the body bags into a waiting hearse shuttle, painted all black. Money changed hands, and the two helpers left. The director and priest boarded the shuttle and departed the hospital. Hours later, they landed on the vast estate of a very wealthy businessman. A fifty year old man, dressed in an expensive, grey tweed suit stepped out of his mansion to greet their arrival. "No problems?" he asked.

"None. Verified. Voiceless. Delivered as requested, boss," the "funeral director" replied. More money changed hands. Meanwhile, Alan Arkoldt partially unzipped the bags and checked on the color of the two sets of eyes. Satisfied, he snapped his fingers. Two servants came rushing out to transport the body bags inside his vast mansion. He paused briefly, until the black shuttle departed, then re-entered his security codes, reactivating his force shield around his large estate and grounds. He turned and followed the bags.

The bags were deposited on tables in a side room. Two servant women entered, carrying crates of clothing. "Okay, they're all yours. Get them prepared, please," Alan ordered. Both women nodded. They too had no voices, but were well paid. They unzipped the bags, got the pair of naked bodies out, and on the tables. Then, they set to work, under the watchful eyes of Alan, who sat quietly on a chair against the back wall. "Will you look at the size of those knockers!" he exclaimed, very much impressed with their sheer size.

"Damn, they are old-looking. Okay, first, let's get them into the Rejuvenation Machine. I think they would look best at say twenty-one, don't you?" Both women had no choice but to nod in agreement. He summoned his doctor. Several hours later, the doctor removed the second of the unconscious telepaths from the machine. "Ah, now that's better. Can't have old telepaths, can we? Excellent, doctor. That'll be all." The man nodded and left. "Sonia, Sofia, front and center." Both women re-entered the room. "Go ahead, ladies. Get them dressed nicely."

The two struggled to get the severely restrictive, metal re-enforced pipe corsets on the two and fully closed. That last took all of their combined strength to manage. After slipping black nylons on their legs, they slid panties up, covering their strange sexual anatomy. Then, they got the women into slips and finally into curve fitting, red satin gowns, rolling them onto their sides to zip up their backs. The design of the gowns gave no trace of sleeves, as if they never had arms. The gowns fell to about six inches below their knees, but had only a tiny walking slit. Next, they tied on pairs of black patent toe shoes, double knotting them so there was no way for the bow ties to come undone. Finally, they carefully inserted the mouth forms that would hold the giant lip disks. That done, they fastened the foot in diameter disks into place, slipping the thick lip loops into place around the circumference of the plates.

Now fully dressed, in turn, each was raised into a sitting position and held there by one woman, while the other gently brushed out her hair, draping it across the woman's front. Then, they did the same to the other. They stood back and waited. Alan said, "Well done, Sonia, Sofia. You may go to your rooms now. They'll sleep for some time yet. I'll send for you when they awake." Both women bowed slightly and retired, leaving Alan looking over their handiwork. "Well, now I have two new, youthful telepaths. You'll work out perfectly. Not the slightest chance in hell you can ever escape this estate." He turned, turned out the lights, and left the room.

It wasn't until October that the hospital officials finally sent word to Queen Amy Valen Gervasi that somehow Senator Franco and Ambassador Carlos had become "lost." Emperor Kino vowed to launch a full-scale investigation, but even his resources were stretched to the breaking point by this time.

"Legate Smith," General Stalock reported, "the President and two aides were found dead. The other Legates have been rescued and are on their way to Bailey-3 for recovery. The many senators are accounted for, though fully one hundred-six didn't make it. They've been taken to various other facilities."

"Excellent. What about the other military operations?" she asked quietly. *The President is dead. Damn. How unfortunate. I'm going to be stuck with this job, until and if the Senate ever meets again to elect a temporary President.*

"The bank is secure and now heavily guarded. A team of computer specialists is monitoring the servers. We've secured all the military installations. You can relax about Nuclears being stolen. The many spaceports are back in limited operations. Two-man patrols are on every street now. There'll be no looting. I believe we have the situation well contained."

And the other Bops have recovered the bio agent stocks being held here as well. Thank god for that. She replied, "Excellent. Excellent work, general. Please convey my deepest thanks to all the other generals and commanders."

"Will do, Legate Smith. We're ready to lend a hand on the civilian situation. Where does Emperor Kino stand on the massive rescue operations?" he asked.

"He has obtained commitments from thirty worlds, each of which has agreed to accept another thousand survivors. Half of that number has already been picked up and are on their way to their new locations," she relayed the depressing news.

"So few? Thirty thousand? Out of a hundred billion?" he asked, dumbfounded.

"Yes, so many worlds are already overtaxed with all those they'd accepted from previous attacks. He's making a broad appeal to the other worlds. Hopefully, he'll obtain further commitments from many additional planets. If so, I'd like to use your men to rescue those."

"God. I hope so." He left, mulling over what was left unsaid, the fate of nearly a hundred billion people.

The next day, Emperor Kino called Legate Smith. "I had to beg, but I was able to obtain commitments from fifty more worlds, which will accept another thousand each. Here's the list." His assistant uploaded the file, while a soldier retrieved them from the computer for the Legate.

"Thank you, Emperor, thank you. I'll make use of the military forces to fill that batch. Is there any chance we can rescue more? Over."

"Not likely, Legate Smith. Still, we must try. Over and out."

The military quickly retrieved fifty thousand more survivors and sent them on their way to their new assisted living homes. Finally, more worlds came forward to accept a thousand each. Three weeks after the first person was rescued, close to one hundred twenty thousand men, women, and children were plucked from Proxima Prime and given new assisted living homes on some hundred sixty other worlds.

However, during that third week, the soldiers doing the rescue work had increasingly difficult times trying to find living survivors, what with the stench of decomposing bodies becoming almost unbearable without masks. The flotilla of doctors reported the majority had died of thirst, while some slowly starved to death. A relatively small number had died from other causes. Now, Legate Smith faced the very problems her general had long ago thought about: how to dispose of nearly a hundred billion dead and how mercifully to kill those who were still suffering and hoping to be rescued.

Legate Smith had already worked out a solution to the disposal problem. The dead could be taken to the abandoned penal colony on Xeros-1, where the daytime temperatures would dispose of the remains. Just how to transport the bodies there was her prime concern she needed to solve before issuing her orders. However, what to do about the still living gnawed at her.

There was no place else to take them. By themselves, they were completely helpless, utterly dependent on others to survive, at least that was the going opinion. They were dying even as she wrestled with the problem. At last, she worked out the best approach to take and summoned the general.

"Okay, we're ready for the next phase of this grizzly business. We bring in as many ore wagons as we can. Issue proper protection for all those soldiers who go planet-side. Have them go building by building, clearing them out. Put the dead in the ore wagons. If they find some still living, they are to report that location back to us, and we'll come back later. However, on the off chance they find some still living and if those people are doing very well, healthy and all that, don't ask me how that could be, then they are to bring those people back here. They'll become my responsibility to resettle. Pick a designated ship for those survivors. Somehow, I'll find a place for them. I doubt we will find many. Oh yes, when an ore train is filled up, it is to go to the old penal planet of Xeros-1 and dump the bodies. Let the scorching heat take care of the remains for us. What do you think of these plans? Are they doable? Have I overlooked anything?" she asked.

The general cracked the briefest of smiles. "No, commendable. Ore wagons. I would never have thought of that. Yes, we are equipped with gas masks. Some have already requested them. I'll see to it right away. I'll use the Destitute as the temporary quarters for those who're still surviving well. You see about finding the ore wagons. They'll be civilian owned."

Three days later, the first of the ore trains left for Xeros-1. Essentially, the engine was a powerful spaceship. It had living quarters for four people. The rest was all engines and fuel tanks. It carried a dozen ore wagons, essentially floating boxes, each of which was able to contain fifty tons of cargo, in this case corpses, around seven hundred. As Legate Smith expected, in a skyscraper apartment complex that once was home to around two thousand people, ninety percent of the occupants were deceased. A few were still marginally alive, but there were the very rare occurrences of healthy survivors. Always, these were youthful, ranging from ten to twenty-five. Always, there was at least a pair living together, though usually four were found. Somehow, these people had a fierce will to live, and had worked out ways and means of taking care of themselves. Quite how, Legate Smith could not imagine, but she was determined somehow to find a place for these survivors.

With all of the military ships hovering in orbits above Proxima Prime, the general had sufficient troops to quickly surpass the capacities of the ore trains, though each day more arrived from more distant worlds. Once into high gear, a dozen skyscrapers were cleared per day. True, many other locations had to be cleared other than living quarters, especially the areas that were in the middle of their workday when the attack came. After the first few days, Legate Smith was finally able to get an estimated completion date: 15 November 1325.

Armed with the date, she then made yet another Imperium-wide broadcast. After describing the situation and the anticipated date, she explained, "The repopulation of Proxima Prime can then begin. Here's how it is going to work. I know many companies had offices and factories and such here. After you work out whom you are going to send here, contact me for your clearance codes. All worlds are encouraged to appoint new senators and ambassadors. Forward their names to me, again for clearance. Once I have okayed them, they can come and take over whichever apartment suite they desire, first come first served, but only in those buildings which used to house the senators. Additionally, all worlds are to submit names of replacement judicial personnel. I will pick the best candidates and present them to the Senate for confirmation. All those who wish to work for the Executive Branch are encouraged to forward your credentials to me. Once the Senate elects a new President, I'll present them to him. Should the Senate not reconvene, I'll go ahead and make the needed temporary appointments."

"Finally, I know there are many worlds that are somewhat overpopulated. Once I have the Imperium government functioning, I'll entertain resettlement proposals. Obviously, the homes and infrastructure are in perfect working order. In fact, one could just move in. To facilitate this, I'll not be charging any settler relocation fees. Once accepted, they can choose their new homes and move in, free and clear. This is a one time, golden opportunity to alleviate the overcrowding of many of our worlds. Please take advantage of it. More to follow. Thank you."

There, I've gone and done it. I'm playing god over the entire Imperium. Will they even send enough new senators to begin to recover? Will settlers actually come to this concrete and steel world? Legate Smith was filled with doubts and second guesses, but she'd done what had to be done. "General,

I'll need to keep Martial Law enforced for the foreseeable future. Until the world is resettled and they have their local government working and a new police force, it will be up to us to fulfill those duties."

"Legate Smith, I'll be frank. Do you really think the Imperium government will survive this catastrophe?"

"I have to think so, general. Look, the property and possessions left down there are worth fortunes. Surely, some will come to claim a share. We just have to prevent widespread looting and theft. I didn't ask to be god, but god I am. We will see. If a year from now, the situation hasn't improved, we'll abandon this mess. There has to be a time limit. God help us if the Federation of Planets decides to break the treaty about now."

"Amen to that, Legate." The two headed off to grab something for lunch.

Amen was what Commander Torres thought when quiet finally returned to the underground Bops center. Days ago, she'd awakened to the terrified screams of her people, the best fighting force in the Imperium, par none. She had added her own terrified screams to the others. For a time, she thought she was drowning in her own, thick, long blonde hair. Her short cut was replaced with ankle length hair, nearly twice as thick as it had been when she went to bed.

She finally calmed down. Everyone here in the Bops center was in the same mess as she. She struggled valiantly and finally got to her toes, wiggling wildly. Her hair fell down over her body, tickling her, as it slipped over her naked form. Try as she might, she could not lean over enough to see over her now massive bosom. Her back began aching from supporting its unexpected, heavy weight. Keeping her balance was challenging. She felt as though she was continually falling forward. At last, she managed a few hesitant steps and stood before mirror. She gasped at what she saw she'd become.

At this point, nature took over. Wiggling madly, she maneuvered to her bathroom. That done, she used her nose to turn on the water. She found a new use for her bosom. Leaning over her sink, they kept her from falling while she drank heavily. That done, she was starving. She looked out of the bathroom towards her door. No way could she open it. As she began making her way back to her bed, she remembered she still had some leftover MREs left. She found the backpack. After more or less collapsing onto her floor, she used her teeth to get the bag opened. Soon, she had one stick out. She ate it paper covering and all. Soon, she felt the carbohydrates kicking in and knew the protein was right behind it. "Well, I won't starve before help comes."

She then struggled up and over to her bed, falling down on it. As she lay there, her mind began racing down the protocols. *If an agent is no longer able to fulfill his or her duties, they are to be summarily cancelled.* That meant executed. "I don't want to die," she called out, as she remembered that protocol. Then, she realized that sooner or later other Bop units from other planets would soon come to secure these facilities, particularly all the bio agent cylinders they'd so arduously confiscated. She knew when they came, they would summarily execute everyone here! She also knew there was no hope whatsoever that rescue teams would find this super-secret installation. However, the President and Legate Smith knew its location. Surely, one of them would contact the secondary Bops units, and they would fulfill their sworn duties. She'd be executed as soon as they arrived. "But I want to live!" she called out to her walls.

She was thirsty again and made another trip to the bathroom. Then, she was hungry and ate a second MRE. She then fell asleep; it must be nighttime, at least her clock suggested it was, though she wondered what day it was. *How long have I been out?* She drifted into an ill sleep.

Noise. Her keen hearing roused her. Again it came. Gunfire. D-guns. Panic swept over her. She strained her ears. She heard heavy footsteps. A Bops Strike Team was here. They were doing their duty, securing the complex and canceling the personnel. Torres acted. She rolled off her bed, wiggled, and rolled underneath it. She stored some long unworn clothes beneath her bed on the off chance she might one day want to wear them again. Pushing and shoving with her feet and head, she got them around her, effectively hiding her strange body from view. Now, she waited. Before long, someone burst into her room. She heard the heavy boots moving rapidly from room to room, even checking her shower. A male voice called, "Clear!" The boots stamped out of the room, leaving the door open. She strained her senses. More d-gun fire. More voices. At last, someone reported, "All cleared. All canceled."

Another voice, again male and emotionless, barked, "Okay. Retrieve the bio weapons and all the other weapons. We need to clear this place out. Thirty minutes. Go." She heard the sounds of many men running, imagining what they must be doing. After an eternity, she finally heard them departing, sealing their main exit behind them. Then silence, an eerie, total silence. *Amen,* she thought. *I've made it! I'm alive!*

She wiggled her way out from under her bed and struggled to sit up. Still worried they might return, she decided to remain where she was for a time. Hours passed. Torres again had to use the bathroom. That done, she took another long drink and ate another MRE. Still all was silent. Now, she decided to venture out of her room. The man had conveniently left her door open. Wiggling and wobbling precariously on her toes, she made her way slowly out of her bedroom into the long hallway. Other sleeping quarters lined the hall. Hers was the last one, so she had only one direction to travel.

Carefully, she looked into each bedroom. She grimaced each time she saw another dead person. These were her people, her lifelong peers, all dead. Slowly, Torres began to realize for the first and only time in her long life, she was truly and totally alone, helpless to boot! Her stomach tensed. *I have to live! I just have to, somehow.*

She arrived at the elevator, having traversed the long hall and finding nothing but dead men and women. *The comm center. I have to get to the comm center and call someone for help.* Fortunately, the elevators were controlled by simple buttons, which she could press with her nose. She rode it up two floors and exited. Ahead lay the large comm center, normally a veritable hive of activity. From here, her workers monitored all interplanetary and planetary communications that they could get their hands on, legally or otherwise. It took a team of Intel agents, pouring over the volumes of data, synthesizing, sifting, sorting, prioritizing, and analyzing the significance of potential threats to the Imperium. Memories of her head of the Intel Studies Department, Lela, came to mind. Of all the base personnel, Lela was the closest person she could honestly call a friend. One didn't have friends in the Bops. Agents routinely died on missions, and others were canceled. It didn't pay to have friends, but Lela was the closest thing to a friend that Torres ever had. This comm center was Lela's arena.

In fact, both she and Lela had undergone the rejuvenation process at the same time. Both were once more twenty-five years old, in appearance, at least before this horrific mutation. Torres smiled at her vivid memory of the short black haired woman who always wore thick, black framed glasses perched on her nose. "Wow, it's all still working," Torres spoke aloud to the room. "Incredible. They didn't shut it down. Well, it is too much trouble to have to restart everything."

Just then, a faint voice called out, "Torres? Is that you? Are we safe?"

She recognized Lela's voice! "Lela? Is that you? It's me, Torres. Everyone's been canceled, but I hid from them. Where are you?"

"Me too. Behind the computers. Help me; please help me," Lela answered. From her weak voice, Torres suspected she was injured. Slowly, she moved around behind the wall of computers and desks. There lay Lela on the floor, totally out of sight. Her glasses were broken, but her short black hair literally covered her body.

"Can you get up?" Torres asked. "I can't really help you do it. Your glasses are broke."

"My eyes are better now, but nothing else is." Lela began using her legs and head to rather push herself along and out from behind the barrier that had saved her life. "I'm starving and so thirsty. I haven't had anything to eat since it all happened."

"If you can get to your feet, I've got stuff in my room. You can lean on me, if you can get up. Please, Lela, you have to get up," Torres pleaded. With a great effort, Lela managed to get onto her feet, but needed to lean on Torres. She was quite weak. Torres led her down the hall to the elevator, keeping Lela's right side against the walls when possible, while pressing her own body into Lela's left side for support.

After what seemed an eternity, she had Lela leaning over her bathroom sink, drinking madly. That alone brought Lela more back into the land of the living. A bit later, Lela chewed one of the MREs and soon felt the rush of much needed carbohydrates in her system.

Only then did Lela felt like talking. "I was on duty when it happened. Because we're so isolated from the other planetary systems, it took longer to get to us. I knew an attack was happening, but I was too tired to do anything about it. The only thing I remember is frantically stripping. I awoke to all that screaming. I guess I screamed too. No one came to help me, but then I didn't figure anyone could. So I waited for a rescue. It didn't come."

She grimaced as more vivid memories returned. "I saw the Bops team coming over the monitors. Then, I saw them shooting everyone. I rather fell behind there. Torres, I don't want to die either. What are we going to do?"

"I want to live too, Lela. We have to help each other. There's no one else alive here. It's just us two," Torres replied. "We have to think this through. Surely, they will be sending rescue crews down now that it's safe."

"But no one knows about this place," Lela pointed out. "Except other Bops. If they come back, they'll execute us too."

"I know. I know. Think, Torres, think."

"We have the comm center," Lela suggested. "We could call someone."

"Right, but who can we trust? Who can come here and who would be willing to risk all to rescue us and take us in?" Torres countered.

Lela's head sank. She muttered, "No one, Torres. We're freaks too now. Helpless freaks."

"No we aren't, Lela. We've gotten this far on our own. We can make it. I just need to think."

There was only one person who Torres could think of who just might think kindly enough of her to risk all on a rescue mission. "Zarita! She just might be able to get to us. Come on; we have to see if we can somehow use the comm center to call her."

A long half hour later, they arrived back in the comm center. What ought to have been a couple minute walk took excruciatingly long, filled with many near falls. Both quickly plopped down into chairs with rollers. Now, they could scoot around easily, as long as they avoided running over their own hair. Lela stared at the controls. "How can we do this?"

"We use our feet. Come on; lend me your feet. We have to do this somehow," Torres pushed her. An hour later, the two had the connection made. "Torres calling for ex-Senator Zarita. This is an emergency. Over." She waited what seemed an eternity. The time delay through hyperspace from the hub of the galaxy out to near the very edge was close to fifteen minutes. Both women watched the clock nervously. Fifteen minutes passed and then some.

"Hi, Gabriella here at the Imperial Castle. I've sent word to Zarita. She'll be along in a few minutes. It's a miracle that anyone's alive on Proxima Prime!" She chatted a bit before ending.

"She talks a lot, doesn't she?" Lela commented.

"If Zarita will only come," Torres whispered.

"Hi Torres. Zarita here. Are you okay? Rescue operations are nearly over on Proxima Prime. Over."

"Zarita! Thank god you took my call! Lela and I are alive, but in our secret Bops base. The other Bops agents came and killed everyone else. Security risks and all that. Lela and I want to live; we hid from them. Please, can you come rescue us somehow? We don't want to die. Please, Zarita. We've got no one else in the universe we can ask. We are desperate. Please. Over."

"Do you think she will come? After all, we did murder her first wife and tried to brainwash her," Lela asked.

"I hope that is all in the past. If not, we're as good as dead, only we don't know it yet," Torres replied. Both women could scarcely endure the lengthy comm delay.

At last, Zarita reappeared on their monitor. "Okay. We are supposed to be officially finished with our rescue runs, but

I talked Jan into making one more run. We need the coordinates of where you're at. We'll have to land cloaked, because she says she can't get permission to make another trip. Marshal Law is in effect, you see. Over."

She rattled off the coordinates. "We can't stay here. They might come back at any moment. We'll be topside around this location, hiding. How long will it take for you to get here? Over."

"Jan says it'll be four days, maybe five. Fuel is the problem. She's working out a way now. We'll land cloaked and call out your name. If you hear us, come out from hiding. Okay? Over."

"Perfect. I think we can survive five days out there. Somehow, we must. Zarita, you are saving our lives. Thank you, thank you! Over and out." Torres let out a huge sigh of relief.

"But how are we going to survive topside?" Lela asked. "We are naked. Nothing fits us now."

"I've still got that pack of MREs. Water will be the big thing. Maybe we can take some blankets with us. We have to try, Lela. We have to. Come on; we have to get out of here as soon as we can. They could return at any time," Torres advised. Back in her bedroom, Torres looked around for some way to carry things. Lela pointed out an old backpack. Together, using their feet, they began clumsily stuffing all the remaining MREs into the pack. With Lela's feet helping, Torres managed to get one strap over her head. "Now I can carry it. Water. We need water and blankets. Come on; we can drag the blankets with our teeth, I hope."

"We got bottles of water in the fridge," Lela suggested. Each bit down on a blanket and dragged it along between their feet. A half hour later, they arrived at the fridge. Lela sat down and used her feet to open it, and then began knocking plastic bottles off the shelf. Together, they used their feet to push the bottles into the pack. Finally satisfied that they had all they dared take, they struggled to their feet once more. Torres very nearly didn't make it because of the added weight of the pack. A half hour later, they entered the elevator and maneuvered their blankets inside as well. Torres used her nose to push the

Top button. Both held their breaths. What would they find when they reached the surface and the concealed exit point of the Bops center? Any number of things could now go wrong, very wrong. Soldiers were likely topside, as well as possibly returning Bops agents. Stress ran high.

Luck was with them. It was nighttime, though distant lights provided reasonable illumination. No one was in the immediate vicinity. "Look for a good hiding place," Torres whispered.

"How about behind that dumpster?" Lela whispered back. They made their cautious way across the cold concrete. Lela managed to wedge her body between a wall and the back of the dumpster, pushing it out from the wall. Each woman then entered from opposite sides, dragging their blankets with them. Once centrally positioned, they slumped to the ground. Again using their feet, they got their blankets mostly over themselves. Lela then used her feet to get the pack over Torres' head, sitting it on the ground between them. Thirsty and dry-mouthed from holding their blankets, the two faced figuring out how to open the twist top of a water bottle. While one held it securely between her feet, the other used her feet to twist the top loose. In order to drink it, one woman used her feet to lift the bottle up, while the other wiggled and got her head beneath the top. While some spilled, both were able to get a good drink. Now, they relaxed, counting the days. Could they remain undiscovered for five days? Could Jan actually sneak her transport down to the surface? Much could go wrong, but they'd made it this far on their own. That gave them some comfort.

"I know it's illegal," Jan complained to Amy. "But Zarita and I are going anyway. She gave her word to Torres and this Lela woman. Whether or not we agree with the ethics and actions Torres has done in the past, she's treated Zarita right that last time. Besides, Zarita says both women have so far shown a really powerful will to live. It's the least we can do."

"Okay, okay. But what about the refueling problem?" Amy asked. That was her real concern. Certainly, there was no problem stopping on Winno-3 for a refuel. It was halfway there. The problem would be that Jan would arrive with almost no fuel left. How could she refuel enough to get back to Winno-3?

"Emperor Kino's got a refueling tanker in orbit there. You make the arrangements to have our ship refueled there five days from now. Okay?" Jan suggested. Amy grumbled but consented to make the call.

Bernardo and Lena insisted on tagging along with Zarita and Jan. "Hey, we are your security guards," he teased.

Jan grinned, invisibly of course. "Bring along some cards. It's going to be a boring five days." Lena laughed.

The second leg of their journey, Jan traveled slower than normal, conserving fuel. As expected, she arrived near Proxima Prime with a quarter in reserve, more than enough. Cloaked, she very, very carefully manually maneuvered her sleek, relatively new transport between the hundreds of ships in low orbit. Finally clear of the traffic jam, Bernardo punched in the landing coordinates. Cautiously, Jan allowed the autopilot to make their descent. Twice, she had to override, when their ship came too close to another. She had the three watching out of the view ports in all directions, looking for incoming ships. At last, she felt the ship touching the ground, a slight lurching sensation.

"Okay, now for the dicey part. We have to call out for Torres, while not attracting any attention to us. We can't be seen, period," Jan cautioned.

"Couldn't we wait for night?" Lena asked.

"Not parked here. Some vehicle might come by. Some soldiers might wander by. With they run into the invisible ship, the jig is up. Snatch and grab, and get the hell out of here. Besides, we have to keep the refueling appointment on time or more questions will be asked," Jan countered.

Bernardo opened the bay doors. Zarita called out, "Torres! Torres, it's us. Zarita. You here?" Meanwhile, the others kept watch, looking in all directions, praying that no one would spot them.

"Behind the dumpster. Help," Torres answered at once.

Bernardo raced across the alley and moved the dumpster out farther from the wall. "I got them. You get ready to take them from me when I bring them to the bay." He lifted Torres up and carried her over to the bay, sitting her down just inside the ship. Jan and Zarita took over, helping her up and moving her to a nearby seat. Lena continued to keep watch. A minute later, Bernardo ran up the ramp and inside the bay. Lena was right behind him, closing the doors by using a bit of her telekinetic skills to operate the controls.

Jan explained, "No time to talk. We have to get out of here. I need everyone watching for collisions. Come on; time's our enemy." Within a minute, Torres felt the ship lifting off and began to relax.

A half hour later, Jan breathed a huge sigh of relief. She'd just pulled up to the tanker and requested a refueling. The controller acknowledged her and gave her docking instructions. As soon as the refueling lines attached, Jan finally relaxed. Just a half hour more, she thought.

She was never so glad a refueling was completed, and received departing orders. Slowly, the ship responded, moving gracefully away from the tanker. Once clear, she dropped into hyperspace, setting a course for Winno-3. She and Bernardo headed down to the bay to join Lena and Zarita. Jan commented, "Well, we made it. In and out. No one is the wiser. Four days and we'll be back home."

"Thank you, thank you," Torres replied. "I know Lela and I are mostly helpless mutants now, but we both want to live, somehow. Maybe if we can somehow get access to our bank accounts, we can withdraw our funds."

"We best not," Lela countered. "The second we do that, the Bops will know we escaped, and they will hunt us down and kill us. We're security risks in their eyes. We know too much."

"Crap. She's right. How can we possibly pay for our care? I don't want to be a leech for the rest of my life," Torres replied.

"Well, there is a way. If you give me your accounts, I can retrieve your funds, and it can't be traced," Jan suggested.

"But how?" Lela replied. She was in charge of Intel and wise to just about every trick in the book. Then, she remembered how Senator Carlos had somehow lost his entire

191

fortune to Isabella, Amy, and Jan, after he had kidnaped and tortured them. She's spent many long days trying to track where those billions of credits had gone, but she'd never found out.

On the other hand, Torres knew. Jan was Sly Dog, the most wanted Underground Hacker in the Imperium. Without a reservation, she rattled off her account number and password, which Jan jotted down. Lela divulged hers.

"Okay, ladies, your funds will be waiting for you on Tierra when we arrive," Jan teased them, winking at Torres. A while later, she launched her Bank Bomb, effectively wiping out both women's accounts, but leaving a single credit in each. When investigators checked on what had happened, if they ever should, they would see that the funds went into several other accounts and from there the credits simply seemed to vanish into cyberspace.

With Lena and Bernardo watching the controls, Zarita and Jan proceeded to take care of the two women's immediate needs. First came a good, long, hot, soaking bath, including a thorough washing of their hair. Both women were quite grimy after spending so much time outside lying behind the filthy dumpster. Zarita had brought along a fair selection of apparel, in several sizes, one of which she hoped would be a descent fit.

Torres pointed out, "Look, we were able to do some things on our own. If we wear those tight corsets, we might not be able to do some of it."

"For now, let's get you all fixed up, and let us handle your needs. Later on, once you are back and fixed up some, we can re-evaluate. This is just temporary. Believe us, back pain is nothing to take lightly," Zarita advised.

Jan concurred, "Much as I hate to admit it, she's right. I have to give up some too. Without it, my boobs really give me a back ache by nighttime."

An hour later, the two had their guests laced up securely and into really elegant, tight-fitting satin gowns, complete with black hose and toe shoes. Next, they did their hair, fastening a bluebird clasp back of their heads to help hold their hair from coming over their faces. Both complained about having to wear the giant lip disks, but again, Jan insisted. "There are too many things in the ship that your lip loops could get caught on. It's an awful, bloody mess if they get ripped off. I don't have a medical machine with me. They are all being used back home."

At last, Zarita held up mirrors so the two young women could see their new look. "See, you look just like me and hundreds of others at the Imperial Castle. I'm going to have you both move in with me and Ari. She's already got your room all fixed up for you. It will be great, you'll see. You both will fit right in. It's the men who have the hardest time adapting to these changes, but that's to be expected. They're men." Torres again detected the hatred that Zarita still held for men, but perhaps it had mellowed to a mere contempt for men.

Jan had Bernardo and Lena join them, proudly showing off Torres and Lela. "Well, you both look stunning," Bernardo replied.

"Keep your hands to yourself, buster," Lena teased her husband. Both laughed soundly. "So do either of you play cards?"

Later, Lela asked her burning question. "Zarita, will we ever be able to have our arms regrown, like yours? If we get access to our credits, we could pay the ten thousand credits the operation costs."

"I am sure that in time you can. Right now, though, you are going to have to wait your turn. We've taken on more than a thousand victims, some from the Aquila Prime attack, the Proxima Prime attack, and recently some gypsies who were attacked. I'm sure it will happen, just not how soon. Don't worry, with all of us around and with Lena to show you how to do some things, we'll get by nicely. As you can see, lots of us have recently used the Rejuvenation Machine. Ari and I each had three daughters, but now that we're young again, we want more children. We discovered we love raising children, though we're now grandmothers too. What about you two? Are you going to become a couple too, like Ari and I or even Amy and Jan? There's quite a few of us. Katrina and Whitney, Carla and Elfe."

Both Torres and Lela flushed. During their long years in

the Bops, such things were never, ever considered. Becoming pregnant was tantamount to being canceled! There was no room for close, intimate personal relationships. Now, both were entirely free from those constraints. A completely new life was opening up before them. Torres merely shrugged her shoulders, and Zarita left it at that, having planted the idea in their minds that such relationships were acceptable and even commonplace, at least in her large circle of friends.

Chapter 10 Adjustments

The Imperial Castle and Manor were swamped with all the nearly helpless new arrivals. Each had to be given the two quick cures, namely their feet and hair, bathed, clothed, and fed — all before Rafe could arrange for their Basic Therapy sessions. Many were also resettled in Madiera, where they could make use of Alpha and Beta's many bots and thus live somewhat independently.

Behind the scenes, Amy and Rafe were, in fact, sorting them out into two categories. Into the first category went all those who had an Academy education or training or significant experience that Amy felt could be of immense value to Tierra. Rafe took all of the others, sending them to Madiera, where she planned to turn them into her army of Basic Therapy givers. Ignoring their own native children, by the fifteenth of November 1325, Amy had the original fifty from Aquila Prime, a hundred-six from Proxima Prime, including Torres and Lela, another thirty-three from various other worlds that Emperor Kino had "rescued" for her, and the hundred gypsies who she promised to handle. All these were being housed at the Imperial Castle and Manor. Rafe counted nine hundred-ten men, women, and children housed in Madiera.

Into the middle of all this confusion, Queen Amy received notice that the Supreme Guild Masters demanded a meeting with her. They gave her a half hour to prepare for their arrival. "Darn, how inconvenient. Okay, Jan, get as many of our Gang here as possible. We'll need at least fifty chairs in the Throne Room," Amy suggested.

Lena moved to her side. "So what's this all about? Did they give you any hints? Another load of victims is due today as well. I think it's the last one. By the way, have you heard anything about our missing Senator Franco and King Carlos?"

"No hints. Yes, it's the last of the victims who could be saved. As I understand it, Legate Smith rescued these herself. They are supposed to be real survivors. I guess they must be, since somehow they survived well for over a month on their own. I'm inclined to keep them here with the others, but we'll evaluate them when they arrive. No, nothing on Franco. Emperor Kino believes someone kidnaped them. I'm inclined to believe him, after all that Jan and I've been through out there. Here they come now," Amy answered.

Lena made sure Amy was able to get to her throne chair, just as Bernardo led other members of her Gang of Ten into the room, followed by the mask-wearing fifty Supreme Guild Members. As they filed in, Amy noted with some curiosity many of the women were wearing fancy satin gowns from Elegant Fashions Inc and the popular six inch oxfords. More than half of the men and women also sported the giant lip disks, protruding beneath their quaint, expressionless facemasks. They marched in and took the seats. Bernardo and the others moved up behind Queen Amy.

"Queen Amy, Diego here," one man spoke up. She recognized his voice and knew he was often their spokesperson. "Is it true that in the past few months, you have brought a large number of helpless, alien mutants to Tierra? If so, will they be staying on our world?"

"Yes, I've granted sanctuary to around a thousand men, women, and children. Yes, they are aliens to our world. Yes, they have all been victims of hideous biological and genetic attacks and at the moment are practically helpless, dependent upon others for their immediate survival. Yes, their bodies have been mutated by these vicious attacks," Queen Amy answered him, sensing their discomfort at her blatant admissions.

"We are concerned you are using our hard-earned taxes we give to you and the Imperial Court to support these aliens," he declared, relatively tactfully.

"I assure you I have done nothing of the kind. We keep very accurate records here at the Imperial Court. Not one silver we received from the people of Tierra has been spent on these terrorist attack victims. I have been using my own personal funds to pay for their needs," Queen Amy replied formally.

A woman spoke up. "When they have recovered, is it your intention to send these alien mutants back to where they came from?"

"Good question," Amy played for time and setting them up. She guessed what was really on their minds and the reason for this visit. "I'll never keep any of them here against their wishes. That said, I have offered them all sanctuary for life here on Tierra." She kept her senses aware to detect how the group accepted her rather blunt statement. She felt many protests arising.

Amy quickly continued before they could vent their protests. "First, this is the only compassionate route. They, like us, are human beings. Unlike yourselves, their entire lives have been wiped out by senseless terrorist attacks, leaving them nearly helpless, until our doctors can work their miracles on them. So we are showing the entire Imperium that we on Tierra do have compassion for our fellow man. Second, many of these men and women are very highly educated and, once rehabilitated, I expect they'll be applying their knowledge and skills to help our world."

She went on, "Several have already asked if they could become teachers at our new school here in Exchange City. I've accepted them. By spring, they will join Nadja, Diego, and the others, teaching our young many things, such as mathematics. Most, however, will be offering us their expertise in many other areas. I've been discussing our urgent need for many more schoolbooks for the ever growing number of children and parents who want schooling. This means we have a desperate need for large quantities of paper and a way to print the books. Copying by hand is way too slow. I've talked with some of these young engineers about this. By spring, I hope to come to you with their proposals for the establishment of several new guilds. They'll be inventing some new devices to both cut lumber very efficiently, to make paper from the sawdust, and a thing called a printing press. As I understand them, they'll be making use of our many rivers to power them."

"When they have their designs ready, we hope by spring, I intended to summon you here and make some proposals. Certainly, we'll need new guilds to oversee these new crafts. This is just a hint of what I believe we can expect from these highly educated men and women. Already, some are discussing ways to heat our buildings without using wood burning stoves. None of this includes any form of weapons or anything that could be used as such. These developments will be made available to everyone on Tierra, just as swiftly as the guilds can build them."

She ended with a disclaimer. "However, if all this should not come to pass and they wish to leave Tierra, returning to their own worlds, then Tierra is not out the cost of their upkeep. I alone will suffer the financial loss. However, I seriously doubt they will desire to leave. These are intelligent, bright, and educated men and women. Given time to adjust and recover from their nightmare traumas, I fully expect they will give back tremendous benefits to the average person of Tierra."

Several whispered among themselves. Amy sensed they were all conferring telepathically. *Well, I'd be doing the same thing, if I were in their shoes.* Finally, "Diego" spoke up. "We will accept your explanation for now. In the spring, we will listen to these aliens and make our decisions then. Frankly, many are worried that you are supporting these aliens with our taxes. You have been wise not to do that. As you know, the aliens have always been distrusted by most of us on Tierra. We are rightly concerned about the alarming numbers being taken in, especially since they seem to be utterly helpless and dependent upon us. It is good that they do not bring weapons with them. Tierra does not need better weapons."

Queen Amy chuckled. "You can say that again. The Imperium out there has weapons of great mass destruction. Already, sociopaths have used these terrible weapons to kill nearly every person on two planets. Some of these are the few survivors. No, we certainly do not want such terrible weapons on Tierra. We already have had such things. Acid bomb, fire bombs."

"We agree on that. Okay. We will await your summons in the spring," Diego summarized. "We thank you for hearing us today." With that, the group arose and quietly walked out of the Throne Room, leaving the Gang and some others watching.

Lena spoke first, "Well, that was interesting. I think you

allied their fears for now. Best have a good plan by spring, though."

"A lot depends on getting their arms regrown. Until that happens, they are mostly helpless, just as he says," Amy replied.

Meanwhile, Rafe and Rafaela began Basic Therapy on Torres and Lela personally. Why? From discussions with Zarita, she knew that these two women had suppressed their emotions entirely for at least a half-century or more, and that they had been responsible for espionage and killings, though on behalf of preserving the peace. Still, as far as Rafe was concerned, she didn't know if her Basic Therapy would actually work on the two, or if their own "crimes" would interfere. Certainly, they had been a part of having Zarita's wife, Senator Celenia, and others murdered in a failed attempt to coerce Zarita into using her *mentales* gifts for them, though admittedly in an effort to help the Imperium and stop the spread of these weapons of mass destruction.

They began by having the two women return and re-experience their recent terror trauma from the bio attack. This was very real to both Torres and Lela, very real. For the first time in their lives, they'd experienced real emotions. However, after slugging through it all day, this recent trauma was not easing up. If anything, it seemed to be strengthening. The next day, following Rafe's suggestion, she and Rafaela asked Torres and Lela for any earlier emotional trauma. Suddenly, the dam broke. Fifty years of suppressed emotions swept over the two women!

Never had Rafe or Rafaela seen such volume of tears. Torres and Lela bawled and bawled. A seemingly never-ending flood of grief, loss, regrets, and guilt swept over the two women, threatening to extinguish their very life force. That second day was one wild ride for the two therapy givers, as one flood of tears was followed by yet another, then followed by suppressed guilt over many of the actions they'd done. True, had they objected, they would have been "canceled." Still, that was only justifications, and the two knew it, bawling all the harder.

This tidal flow of suppressed emotions continued on into the third day, an unrelenting flood. However, it was releasing, which was the whole point. Already, Rafe could see enormous changes in Torres' face, which was lightening up, as if by magic. Lela's complexion and rash vanished from view, right before Rafaela's eyes.

The fourth day, both women begged to be slain for their crime of having Zarita's wife and others murdered by the bomber they'd brainwashed into doing the deed for them. Their crime seemed magnified a thousandfold, because it was Zarita who had risked all to rescue them from Proxima Prime. Another ten more passes over the whole incident did not produce significant relief. Thus, Rafe and Rafaela followed procedure and began asking for earlier material that was similar. Soon they got it, accompanied by more grief, blame, shame, and regret — accompanied by all manner of justifications as well.

The fifth day, both women were now running similar incidents when they were first recruited into the Bops. During training, they had been forced to fight others, frequently injuring their sparing partners, as well as suffering many beatings themselves. However, the severe intensity of the grief and pains began to lessen. Near the end of that day, the two finally had run dry, having released enormous volumes of suppressed grief, loss, and trauma.

The sixth day, Rafe and Rafaela pushed them further, looking for even earlier incidents, which were similar. Now childhood incidents came up and desensitized after a few recountings. Then, birth appeared, shocking both women, who never suspected anyone could recall such things. Still, this enormous chain of trauma didn't fully erase. The two were pressed for even earlier similar incidents.

Each discovered a past life traumatic incident. After six long days, both Torres and Lela began laughing, true laughter, not the fake chuckles they had done all their lives, particularly while they were in the Bops. The giant chain had finally erased. Both women laughed and laughed. Periodically, they stopped and were given a drink, but simple things mentioned brought on more rounds of laughter. It was as if huge quantities of memories were suddenly being re-filed in their minds. Never had Rafe or Rafaela seen such continuous laugher, such an enormous relief from Basic Therapy. They could not continue their therapy that seventh day, for the two were still laughing at seemingly nothing at all. Only by the eight day were they able to continue.

"You mean there's more?" asked an incredulous Torres.

There was, naturally. From this point on, Basic Therapy ran textbook style. After fourteen days, both Torres and Lela finished their Basic Therapy. "My God, Rafe," Torres exclaimed, "I feel like ten tons have been lifted off of me! I'm so light, that I'm about to float away!" Then, the significance of it all hit her and Lela. "Oh my God! I have lived before! I am me, not this body. Oh God! That changes everything, doesn't it?" Rafe could only nod her head in agreement.

Torres and Lela insisted on meeting with Amy and Katrina, as well as Rafe and Rafaela. Torres took point, as she always had, only now she recognized why. She was protecting Lela, of whom she was very fond. In fact, Lela was the only person she had ever felt so strongly about. "Look, Queen Amy, Governor Katrina. I know you've got no reason to trust us, but after what Rafe and Rafaela have done for us, Lela and I simply *must* contribute to everyone. I'm not talking about credits. Lela is the best damn interpreter of Intel in the galaxy. Somehow, we want to help you protect this world from the ravages of the Imperium out there. If you don't trust us with such things, we understand. We can never make up the damage we've done to Zarita, but we intend to devote our lives to making amends. Lord, we have a lot to make amends for! If we can't help you, then we want to learn how to do what Rafe and Rafaela do, this Basic Therapy. We can at least deliver it to as many others as we can find. Please, we have to help you all. We know you're all telepaths. You have the yellow eyes. So if you doubt us, probe our minds or whatever it is that you do, please."

Queen Amy made a snap decision, based primarily on what she'd observed about the two during the last two weeks and from Rafe's reports. "Your help is most welcome, Torres, Lela. Why not do both? I'll introduce you to our Intel group, and let you see what you can do to help them. I'm sure Rafe and Rafaela would dearly love the help delivering Basic Therapy. Just remember, there's always Advanced Therapy available, once we get the thousand other victims handled."

"Thank you, thank you, thank you," Torres gushed.

"You are most welcome. Oh, Zarita and Ari want to see you now that you're finished with your Basic Therapy. Go chat with them, and then this afternoon, we'll get you introduced to the others," Amy replied. Governor Katrina merely smiled, knowing they now had two of the very best Intel experts of the Imperium working for them.

Thus, it was that Torres and Lela finally discovered the Underground that Sly Dog and Eager Beaver had long ago setup here on Tierra. Those were the two most wanted fugitives in the entire Imperium for the last two centuries. The two Intel agents soon proved their worth.

The day after the visit of the Supreme Guild Masters, Gabriella summoned Amy to the Comm Center. "It's Emperor Kino! Sounds important. He's making a big conference call. Come on!" Jan's steadying arm allowed Amy to move a bit more quickly than normal in her toe shoes. Bernardo and Lena were already there waiting for Amy.

"I wonder what's up?" Lena asked, though more in the way of a comment.

Amy sat down and her sister activated the controls. "Queen Amy here. Over."

After the usual five minute delay, suddenly her monitor seemed to split into pieces, thirty-seven to be exact. Actually, it was a split-screen conference call. Amy saw thirty-six queens, just like herself. Some were rather young looking, others in their fifties or so she guessed. Emperor Kino appeared in the center. "Hello. I now have all thirty-seven of you queens connected together. There is a five minute delay with Queen Amy, so let's bear that in mind. Now then, I must explain some things to all of you at the same time."

He continued. Amy noted he seemed terribly serious. Further, she'd never seen these other queens, other than Queen Altha, of course. *To have us altogether like this, it must be really be bad.* Amy listened intently. "The genocide on Proxima Prime is of monumental proportions for the Imperium. Legate Mary Smith has done an admirable job with the rescue operations. However, the final numbers are beyond belief. Around a hundred thirty thousand survived. A hundred billion did not. Staggering loss. Yet, it goes vastly deeper. Proxima Prime was, in many ways, the Imperium. The huge bureaucracy there ran the Imperium. True, Legate Smith has the critical systems well-guarded, and the automated systems are functioning normally. Banking transactions are all normal."

"As you may have heard on the newscasts, Legate Smith has asked the worlds to send new senators to Proxima Prime. She's asked companies to send replacement teams to recover their companies and continue their operations. She's asked the other worlds to send replacement bureaucrats to begin to rebuild the governing structure."

"So far, she has only gotten a few token senatorial commitments. Companies are sending personnel as we speak. The many major businesses will likely be back in some kind of operation within a few months. Rather, it's the reluctance of the other world to send new bureaucrats and senators that is the serious problem. Many fear a repeat terrorist attack. However, Legate Smith is doing her best to alleviate those fears. She's been able to trace the origin of the attack. Four local inhabitants sabotaged the air and water intake lines. As far as the ID Ministers are concerned, these four acted alone and have no known terrorist ties. Lord knows what those four were thinking or trying to do. We've only pure speculation. One theory is they were seeking revenge for the Imperium making their ancestors, the original inhabitants of Proxima Prime, fourth-class citizens, relegated to the bowels of the planet. But it's anyone's guess as to the motives of those four."

"So the really significant detail is that the other worlds are not responding to the Legate's repopulation pleas. Specifically, my own analysis suggests most worlds are waiting to hear from the big five — the most populous and prestigious worlds. Those are Zelan-3, Beta Carnae-4, Zeta-3, Longditch-4, and Bailey-3. All are within the hub sector. History lesson. It was these very five planets, along with Proxima Prime, which Emperor Lian convinced to unite together forming the core of the Imperium, well over two millennia ago. I've chatted a bit with their presidents, but gotten the brush off."

"I fear we've not seen the end of these genocide attacks. Hence, I am planning for the future. Since we now have an enormous number of rescued victims on each of your worlds and since any one of the women meet our physical limitations requirement, I would like each of you queens to select the very best female candidate from among the survivors on your worlds and train them to become a queen in her own right. I've no idea if it will be possible for you to do so. Queen Altha alone has the experience of training off-world queens, but then, Isabella and Amy both desired to become an Ataro queen."

"Queens, please error on the side of caution, just like Queen Altha has done. Drill them extremely well. Much may rest on their ability to put their training to practical use. Then again, I could well be completely wrong. Yet, I feel it in my bones that we are in a deadly race against time. Queen Amy, I know you are not prepared to train a queen. In part, that is my fault for not providing you with the necessary training and materials to do so. Until this year, I didn't think such was needed. Thus, if you can find a potential candidate, send her to Queen Altha for training. Amy, I'm still looking for a few more survivors for you. Questions? Over."

Amy had none and so replied, "Thank you. Will do. Over."

After the time delay, a volley of chat came all at once from the thirty-six others, but nothing new came from them. The conference call then ended. "Well, that's interesting," Lena commented. "I'm going to chat with Lela and Torres about these five worlds. See what they know."

"I'll tell everyone else about this at supper, when we're altogether," Amy decided.

Lena got an earful from Torres and Lela. She'd related what Emperor Kino had to say about the Big Five. Lela commented, "Well, it makes sense. What has always troubled me about those five worlds is that they have the five largest genetic research labs in the Imperium. They received quite a number of samples of the bio agent, promising to help develop cures. Yet, all existing cures are coming from your doctors here on Tierra. Those five haven't produced a single new cure. True, they continue to take in their share of terrorist victims and provide assisted living housing for them, but no cures. I've always found that to be a red flag, warranting further investigation."

Torres added, "Some good news for a change. I just listened to the latest newscast. Good old H-cubed." She was referring to Helyeon H. Hoon, Legate of State Planning. "He's back before the cameras once more. I swear nothing stops him from appearing in the news. His arms are growing. He promised he will be back at work within three months, once he is released by his doctors on Broom-5. As soon as he made his announcement, the other Legates finally decided to resume their positions as well. I suspect they were waiting to see if he would return. Since he has, they probably felt obligated to do so as well. So at least Legate Smith has all the Legates onboard with her recovery plans. That's the best news yet. Perhaps, that'll spur others to send new replacement workers."

She continued, "However, Lela is right. We should do all we can to monitor those Big Five worlds. Say, is there always this much snow around here?" Lena laughed, and explained more about the weather to the two newcomers.

After supper, Amy discussed Emperor Kino's request to send someone off to be trained as another queen, along with why. Many agreed to keep an eye out for likely candidates, especially Rafe, who had hundreds in Madiera, but she, like many others, were reluctant to toss aside all of their Academy training just to become an Ataro queen with only vague possibilities of actually ruling a planet. Besides, no one wanted to leave Tierra.

That night, Amy also received her weekly call from her youngest daughter, Linda and her mate, Rael. After their usual chatting, Amy filled them in on the Emperor's request.

"Mom, we know about it. Word has spread throughout the Academy. Rael and I've been thinking about it. We'd like to volunteer. The way we figure it, since we are both keenly interested in sociology and politics, we'd like to get the training that you have. We both will apply, if you agree. That way, we figure that with two of us doing it together, we stand a fifty percent better chance of one of us making it. If we don't, we can always have Doctor Alex regrow our arms and repair our feet again. What do you say? Can we?"

"Dear, what if you pass and then get sent to some distant world?" Amy tried to talk sense into her youngest daughter.

"Mom, we can always request that we become your heirs. He'll have to agree to that," Linda countered. "Besides, Doctor Alex can always fix us back up if we bomb out at it. Wouldn't it be great for you to have some help?"

Amy sighed, "Of course it would be of immense help. But it's so awful living like this."

"You've managed just fine. So can we," Linda argued. In the end, Amy agreed, but only if Rael got Zarita's permission. An hour later, Linda called back and told her they had gotten her permission too. "Wish us luck!" Amy did so, but with many, many reservations.

Chapter 11 Captivity

Senator Franco finally awakened. His body felt strange, somehow different. His breathing was quite shallow. A slight surge of panic swept over him, as he remembered he'd been kidnaped from the hospital. He was sitting up. Two young, well-dressed women were sitting on a pair of sofas across from them. A strange man was waving a vial of something in front of Carlos' nose. Franco tried to speak and found he could make no sound at all. His voice was gone!

Beside him on the couch, Carlos jerked awake and also tried to say something, probably a curse, Franco decided. The well-dressed man stepped back, facing the two. "Well, awake at last. Don't try to speak, ladies. You can't. I've had your voices removed, just like my Sonia and Sofia here. They will be your servants from now on. You ladies are now my personal telepaths. You work for me. As long as you do what I ask of you, you will be very well treated indeed. Cross me, and I'll remove more of your bodies, though you've scarcely got much of them left to remove."

Carlos sent, *I'm going to kill him right now!*

Don't for God's sake. We've lost our crystals. Let's find out what's been done to us. We're damned near helpless. Wait a while before you kill him or you may end up killing us! He felt Carlos grumbling, though no sounds were heard from him.

Oblivious to their brief exchange and just how close he had come to having his brains fired, the man went on. "I am Alan Arkoldt, one of the richest men on Beta Carnae-4, and an aide to our illustrious President. You are here on my vast estate. Escape is impossible for you. I'm told you are barely able to walk by yourselves on level surfaces. Sonia and Sofia here will care for your personal needs and assist you in walking, as long as you behave. Your bodies are now a youthful twenty-one and you look like very attractive young women, if I do say so myself. So you need appropriate names. You," pointing to Franco, "shall be called Sasha. You," pointing to Carlos, "shall be Suse. From now on, you answer to those names, Sasha, Suse. Nod your heads for yes. Good girls."

"Now your duties are to use your telepathic skills during my business meetings. I need to know what they are thinking. Are they cheating me? What is it that they want from me and aren't necessarily saying? Call it corporate espionage if you like. So do you understand me? Use your telepathy to let me know."

We understand. Please, our skills are very limited if we aren't wearing our crystals. Those stones we had around our necks. We can't be of much use to you without them, Franco or Sasha sent him. Carlos was quietly fuming.

"Oh, those stones? Well, okay. Sonia, Sofia, what did you do with those stones they had around their necks? Go fetch them and put them around their necks, please." The two women rose and left the room, walking rather slowly. Franco noticed they both wore very tall, spiked heels, quite similar to those that were so popular on Tierra. Meanwhile, Alan chatted more about what he wanted from them.

Franco continued making his own observations. The two women were attractive with a brownish hue to their skin. Both had wavy, light brown hair, trimmed at their waists. They were trim and fit. Alan, on the other hand, was at least thirty pounds overweight. He looked to be perhaps forty and sported a black moustache and sideburns. What struck Franco as more significant was his skin tone: yellowish. He began to wonder if Sonia and Sofia were also captured prisoners, slaves as well.

A short while later, after getting the right stone around the right woman's head, Alan then ordered, "Sonia, Sofia, will you please help Sasha and Suse rise? Walk them over to the full-length mirrors so they can see their beautiful womanly shapes?" His voice had a hint of a sneer in it, Franco observed, concluding Alan was a control-freak, a psychopath, not a sociopath. Alan wasn't out to destroy the world.

Carlos, or Suse as he was now being called, very nearly lost it. *I'm a bloody woman! I'll kill him! I swear it!* Indeed, looking into the mirror, Franco barely recognized himself. He saw what appeared to be an attractive young woman staring back at him, one with monster breasts, a tiny waist, and an elegant, red satin, form-fitting gown with almost no walking slit. Well, he could only take very tiny, hesitant, shuffling steps anyway. Stairs were out, as well as rough ground and the grassy lawns he spotted just beyond the window. He also knew they were utterly dependent upon Sonia and Sofia for nearly everything.

Poor Franco. It wasn't enough he had to deal with his own physical helplessness, but he had to keep Carlos' anger and brashness in check. He sent, *Calm down. We're trapped for now. Bide our time. We'll get out of here in time, Carlos. Meantime, we best do what we can to please Sonia and Sofia. We're going to be wholly dependent on their care. Best not to cross them. Observe, Carlos. Find things we can use to get out of here. Maybe even find some of those alien things you've always wanted. There are bound to be plenty of the gadgets around this place. Alan's quite rich. Observe, observe.*

I'm a bloody woman! He repeated himself. *I can't live like this!*

Of course, you and I can. Sonia and Sofia are here to help us with everything. Stay alert and learn where things are. It's going to take some doing for us to get out of this one. We have to work together and with Sonia and Sofia. I think they are prisoners too. If so, they may help us to escape, if we take them with us. Observe, Carlos, observe.

Alan broke in on them. "Okay, that's enough admiring your beautiful womanhood. Walk them back to the couch, please. Tomorrow, I have a business meeting. I need you two to work your telepathic magic. I need to get the best of this coming deal. Sonia, Sofia, you get to watch them. You can show them around the estate and your rooms, if you like. Oh, yes, if you need to go to the bathroom, nod your head to the right. That will signal your keeper. Supper is at six. Pheasant under glass tonight, if I am not mistaken. Enjoy your afternoon, ladies."

I can't even walk! Carlos sent. Sofia put a steadying arm around her and gently nudged Carlos forward. Sonia did the same for Sasha. When they finally reached the couch, both women carefully repositioned their hair to their front and then helped them sit down, though it was more like falling down onto the couch. They took their previous seats on the two sofas opposite them.

Utter silence, though four sets of eyes alternatively look at each other. The complete lack of sounds was unnerving to say the least. Then, Sonia put her hands up to her eyes, cupping them, as if looking through tubes. She moved her head and hands this way and that, indicating they wanted to show them around. She and Sofia rose and moved over to Sasha and Suse. Neither could do much to protest, as they were helped to their feet once more. Sasha sent, *We best practice walking a lot, if we're ever to escape.*

They found the two women were quite observant of their inabilities, steadying them all the way. Down one long hall, they were shown a very fancy dining room. Further on down, they were shown two adjacent bedrooms. With some gesturing, Sasha realized she and Sonia would be sleeping in this room, while Suse and Sofia would be in the next one. The bathroom was enormous, equipped with gold fixtures. Suse indicated he had to use it and Sofia quickly assisted her, much to Carlos' embarrassment.

After that, they entered an entertainment room, filled with various games and tables. Along one wall was a giant screen. Sonia indicated they should sit facing it. Soon, she had turned on the newscasts. Again, she cupped her hands over her eyes, indicating she wanted to watch the news. *Good. Now we can find out what's been going on and what date this is,* Sasha sent to Suse. After watching for some time until they began to repeat their lead stories for the second time, Sonia held up a box and then did something. Now a movie began, taking both men by surprise. They found this quite interesting indeed.

Supper went surprisingly well. The two women had apparently been instructed in how to operate the lip plates. They secured them in the horizontal positions and used overly long forks and spoons to feed them. Their after dinner coffee took forever to spoon, though. After that, Alan chatted about what to expect tomorrow at his business meeting and told them what they were to do for him. After that, they were taken back to the entertainment room where they watched another movie. When it finished, the two servants led them to the adjacent bedrooms.

Sonia helped Sasha sit down on the edge of the bed. Gently, she undressed her, except for the corset. She pointed to it and shook her head no. Franco knew the women back on Tierra never took theirs off except when bathing, so this wasn't a surprise. Naked except for the corset, Sonia carefully brushed out her hair for her and then helped Sasha gracefully lie down, keeping her ankle length hair on her front side. Then, Sonia undressed herself and slipped in beside Sasha. The sheets were a fine quality satin, plush by any standards. Sonia leaned on her side and looked Sasha's body over carefully. Then she gently ran a finger over one of her monster breasts. Franco became aroused, catching the attention of Sonia, who smiled. She leaned over and gave Sasha a loving kiss, then mounted her.

Sometime later, two satisfied people lay on their backs. Sasha sent, *Thank you, Sonia. You are being very good to us.*

Startled, Sonia pointed to her head, making a quizative gesture. *Yes, I can talk into your head. If you think your thoughts, I can hear you too, Sonia.*

Oh! Sasha, you are a woman, right? But with a man's thing?

No, we both are men, but we were victims of that terrorist attack on Proxima Prime. Have you heard about that in the news?

Yes, so horrible. I'm sorry I took advantage of you. Perhaps I shouldn't have.

No, that was very good for me, Sonia. Next time, I'll make it better for you.

But it was good for me, Sasha. A bit later, he slipped into a deep rapport with Sonia, filling her with an intimacy she'd never known existed. After that first time, Sonia looked forward to their romantic nights, the only pleasure she'd known.

During the ensuing days, Sasha learned the story of Sonia and Sofia. They were sisters. Alan's men had raided their home, killing their family, while kidnaping them. They'd been forced to be his house slaves for the last six years. Both were twenty-one now, though not identical twins. Taken when they were just fifteen, they were terrified of being raped. However, that had never happened. Alan wanted nothing to do with them sexually. He wanted pretty flowers around his estate when he was here. During their six years of captivity, not once had they been away from the estate. However, they had explored every inch of it and knew all its secrets.

Sonia put it succinctly. *We can escape whenever we want, but we have no credits and don't have anywhere to go.* Both Sasha and Suse promised to take them with them when they escaped. However, they had as yet not figured out how they could do that.

Alan had them prying into the minds of his business associates, effectively robbing them blind. However, the two couldn't do much about that yet. *Bide our time,* Sasha continually sent Suse. Suse began to relax. Besides truly enjoying Sofia's love, he was enamored with the movies. He began to work out some way to take them with him when they escaped.

Months passed before Alan varied their routine. Over supper, he announced, "Tomorrow, there is a very important meeting with the President. As I once told you, I am his top advisor. We are meeting with the Presidents of four other worlds. You four will accompany me to this meeting. You'll be allowed to sit in the observation level, but you can see and hear everything. I need you to tell me what the other four Presidents are actually thinking during the meeting. This is vitally important. Don't screw it up. Got it?" Both nodded.

The next day, Alan led the four out of the estate building. Although Sonia had a good grip on Sasha's waist, both were barely able to move across the grassy knoll to the waiting shuttle. More than once, Sasha lost her balance, nearly pulling Sonia down with her. Sonia wasn't doing all that much better though. Behind them, Suse and Sofia were having even more difficulty negotiating the terrain. Never were four women so glad to sit down, even if it was inside a rather cramped shuttle.

Now, both Sasha and Suse began to pay very close attention. If nothing else, they planned to use this trip to get themselves oriented to their location on this world. From the air, they could see they were about thirty miles from a sprawling city. Alan told them it was the capital and that there were ten million people living there. "It's one of our smaller cities," he commented. "That's the Presidential Estate there, where our President sometimes hosts foreign dignitaries."

Shortly, they entered the city proper. A huge domed structure appeared to be their destination. Alan confirmed it, "That's the Presidential Palace. We'll be meeting there. Mind you, be on your best behavior. If you screw this up, I'll remove more of your bodies, perhaps your feet or legs."

Sonia looked fearfully at Sasha. He quickly touched her mind. *Please, don't let him do that to us. We'll be helpless too and won't be able to help you.* He reassured her they wouldn't let that happen.

Once across a small patch of grass, treacherous in their heels, they reached concrete and stability once more. An aide met the party. Alan ordered, "My guests. They can't speak. Take them to the guest gallery so they can watch this historic meeting, please." Alan was always polite, if nothing else. A half hour later, the four were seated behind a glass shield of some kind. Below them, they saw a dozen chairs. Soon, a number of well-dressed men entered, amicably shaking hands with one another. Alan had forgotten to tell them who was who, or even who his President was. The two guessed it was the man sitting next to Alan and occasionally leaning over, whispering in his ear.

Both the senator and ambassador found the verbal discussion much the same as any other Senate meeting. A lot of talk, blustering, but of little substance, each assuring the other that they were on the same page. All were resisting Legate Smith's endeavors to restart the Imperium Senate. Franco probed the surface thoughts of the other Presidents, not knowing who was who. Carlos did likewise.

What do we do? They all hate each other. I think they are about to come to blows, Carlos sent to Franco, deferring to the more knowledgeable senator.

Right. I sense they are feeling each other out. Each wants to be running the Imperium themselves, but each is jockeying for some leverage over the others. If we aren't careful with what we tell Alan, we could well start a war. That's the last thing we need. We'd never get out of here. Wisely, he then sent to Alan, *They are all jockeying for better positions. I don't think any of them like the others.*

A bit later, he began picking up innuendoes and hints each president had something over the other. Without delving deeper, he couldn't tell what that might be. If he did, then the men would know that a telepath was into their minds. That would surely cause more strife. He decided to send to Alan, *They each have something to back up their threats, but I can't dig deeper without alerting them. You don't want them to know about us spying on their thoughts. Can't your presidents agree on anything?*

The meeting lasted two hours, but produced no real results, save a significant increase in hostilities. For a time, Franco thought they might come to blows over the table. When the five Presidents left the room, they were substantially more hostile towards each other than upon their arrival. He also relayed that to Alan. Again, the two took note of the locations of landmarks on the ground as they were flown back to the estate.

Later that night, Franco pondered what he'd seen and learned about these five Presidents. He knew these five had a disproportionate number of senators, compared to other worlds. That meant they had larger populations, prestige, and importance. He also knew that, while their senators tried to push through certain pieces of legislation, the other senators effectively blocked them. Conversely, the senators from these big five also sometimes blocked other legislation, in turn, forcing behind the scenes compromises, usually over the lunch hour. Yet, what did all this mean? Certainly, these Presidents were quite hostile towards each other. If he used the kings of Tierra as a parallel, he was sure the kings would join in battle one day soon. Yet, these were the cream of the Imperium worlds. Surely, they would not war with each other, or would they?

The more that Franco thought about it, the more worried he became. Were he and Carlos about to be on a planet that was about to be attacked? It seemed more and more likely to him. Worse, he knew the Imperium had monstrous weapons. Whole populations could be killed in an instant. Sasha became quite worried. He also knew the date: 25 December 1325. He'd been a prisoner for nearly four months now, with no hope of rescue in sight. Here on Beta Carnae-4, it was midsummer. If it were only winter, he thought, they might not go to war; at least those on his own world would never fight during the heavy snows.

The next day, Alan seemed quite excited. Finally, when breakfast was finished and Sonia and Sofia were spooning coffee into Sasha and Suse, Alan broke the news. "Amazing break. Looks like Legate Smith is going to pay our President a visit on January first. They will be staying at the Presidential Estate, not far from here. Of course, I'll attend too. You four will have to stay here. I can't risk you contacting the Legate. I trust you'll stay out of mischief while I am gone for a few days. If you don't, I will remove your entire legs — of all four of you." He glared quite seriously at the group. Sonia and Sofia flinched and lowered their heads, terrified he might just do that to them.

He left, and Sasha sent Sonia, *Don't worry. We'll kill him if he even tries to harm you, Sonia.* She flashed him a smile, but he also sensed she didn't believe him.

Later while sitting on the living room couch, Franco decided to confide his observations in Carlos. He explained just why he feared these five worlds might just go to war. *If they do, we have to get off this world somehow.* Carlos was mostly in apathy with his long confinement. Franco got no help from him. *Just as well. It has always been up to me. Observe, Sasha, observe.* Even he was often confused on his name these days.

"Damn those Presidents anyway. What the devil are they thinking?" Legate Smith cursed. She'd just learned of their meeting on Beta Carnae-4 and its outcome. Nada. No agreement to provide new senators. Most other worlds were holding back committing new senators, waiting to see what the Big Five did, and they were doing precisely nothing. "How dare they hold up the re-establishing of the Imperium. I've a mind to just go ahead without the Senate."

General Stalock rubbed his face, equally disgusted. It had been nearly four months since the attack and still there seemed no end in sight for re-establishing law and order. "Well, you could go pay one of the Presidents a personal visit. It might be harder for him to refuse you in person."

"I believe you are right about that. I won't take no for an answer. No more stalling. I'll need a ship," she replied.

"I'll take you in this battleship, Legate. No way am I allowing the leader of the Imperium out of my sight. If anything happens to you, we are in deep trouble. It'll be months before the other Legates will be returning to their posts. I'll get another general to take temporary command over Proxima Prime. We'll leave today. Call up that President and make the arrangements." She smiled and did just that. In a half hour, the huge battleship pulled out of orbit and jumped into hyperspace, headed for Beta Carnae-4.

They arrived in orbit in the wee hours of the first. As arranged, Legate Mary Smith, accompanied by six Security Guards, boarded a deep space transport and headed down to the Presidential Estate. She entered the coordinates the President had given her, sat back, and allowed the automated computer to take her safely down. The transport was fully loaded with fuel. During the short flight, Legate Smith considered the approach she intended to use on the recalcitrant President. If she could just get one of these five to send new senators, she felt certain the other four would follow suit.

The transport landed on the perfectly manicured lawn, close to the giant, glass double doors that led into the conservatory. The President and his assistant Alan stood just outside, waving to her as she stepped down. As always, she wore a white silk blouse, fine hose, a black skirt hemmed at her knees, and low heels — a professional appearance that matched her personality. She walked up to the two men and exchanged greetings. They led her into the conservatory, and the President took this opportunity to point out all of the flowers in full bloom. *He's trying to distract me. Well, it won't work!*

A bit later, the three seated themselves in his Formal Office and the serious discussions began. Legate Smith was not about to leave until she had his formal agreement to send new senators from Beta Carnae-4 and soon. For some unknown reason, the President seemed to be in a most agreeable mood this morning, she noted. She'd anticipated very serious resistance from him.

"Oh yes. We certainly should send new senators to Proxima Prime, and soon. I have already picked them out. I can have them on the next shuttle out of here. Would that be satisfactory?" the President asked.

Legate Smith was a bit taken aback. "Well, yes, yes, of course. I don't quite understand. Earlier, I felt you were stalling me. Pardon me if I speak frankly. Have you had a change of heart?"

His face looked positively jolly, most unusual, she thought. "Let's just say that today, I feel you are precisely correct. We have been dragging our heels, so to speak. But today, we must step forward and set an example for the Imperium. We Beta Carnaeians must be seen as Imperium leaders. I assure you our new senators will be leaving later today. It's a short hop to Proxima Prime. They'll be ready to resume Senate work on Monday."

"That is most admirable of you, Mr. President. Thank you. Yes, Monday will be perfect," she replied, still in awe over his sudden, dramatic change of position on this matter. She wondered what had caused it? Surely, it wasn't anything that she'd said.

"Since you are here, why don't we give you a tour of the Presidential Estate? While our world is over populated, we still have great spaces of grasslands and even some trees, unlike the sterile Proxima Prime that you are accustomed to. Walk with us; enjoy the fresh air, and the smell of real grass," he suggested. She dare not refuse, but saw no harm in a guided tour. Indeed, she hadn't smelled real grass in many, many years. Arm in arm with the two men, she headed out onto the lawn. Soon, she felt very tired, uncommonly so. She started to say something to the President, but slumped to the ground instead. From the corner of her eyes, she saw a drone passing low overhead, a yellowish gas trailing behind it. Her mind registered, and her stomach knotted, but then relaxed as she passed out on the lawn.

What she didn't know but would find out much later was that very morning, the President had issued the Launch Command. Already flights of unmanned, stealth drones were heading to Zelan-3, Zeta-3, Longditch-4, and Bailey-3. The President planned to take total control of the Imperium within just a few days. No one would have any clues about who had launched the drones. They were classified with the highest level of security on Beta Carnae-4. Already, those men, who knew about or helped develop the drones, were being rounded up and soon executed. Only his assistant, Alan, knew what was happening.

Just as the three began their stroll on the lawn, the other four worlds detected the attack on their worlds. Each in turn launched a counter-strike. None of the four could tell for certain just which of their enemies had launched this sneak attack on them. Hence, each of the four launched counter-strikes against the other four. The only positive aspect was their total supplies of the bio agent were being used, except for one cylinder kept as a master, should more need to be fabricated.

At the same time, Sasha saw their chance. Alan had left his transport sitting on his lawn. She smiled invisibly and made contact with the other three. *Time for us to escape. We'll take his transport ship.*

Sonia raised her hands, protesting. *How? We don't know how to fly it and you can't.*

I know how to fly it. I'll be telling you, Sonia, everything to do. Once we enter the coordinates, the ship pretty much flies itself. Trust me, Sonia. It's now or never.

Hey, I want to take some of these alien things with me, Suse interrupted her. *The movie things.*

Okay. Suse, you and Sofia pack what you want to take. Sonia and I will get the ship ready to fly. We are not in a rush. Alan is supposed to be gone for two days. Take it easy and don't fall down.

Sonia entered the field deactivation codes she'd seen

Alan use on many occasions. With her arm around Sasha, she led the way out of the estate, across the grassy lawn to the waiting transport ship. Sasha directed her, showing her just what to do. Soon, the bay doors opened. Both struggled mightily to get up the ramp and inside. Presently, they entered the pilot-navigator section up front. *You sit there; I sit here. Okay, thanks, Sonia. You are doing great. Push that button.* Sasha directed her carefully. *Good. See, it is fully fueled. Now, I have to think. There's not enough fuel to get home. We'll have to stop over on Winno-3. Okay. Now, we have to enter its coordinates.* Sasha took a half hour to carefully direct Sonia. Getting the coordinates entered accurately was imperative. If they were off even slightly, they'd drop out of hyperspace far from Winno-3 and probably drift forever. *When we're ready to take off, we press that button. Let's see how they are doing.*

Suse and Sofia were both breathing rapidly and shallowly. They'd been hauling out the video system and stacks of movies, piling them into the shuttle's cargo bay. Also, Sofia insisted on bringing along all of their clothes and heels. In a flash, Sasha realized these clothes were the only real possessions the two young women actually could call their own. She was rather shocked and appalled. She swore to rectify that, if she could ever get back to Tierra. *We'll help,* she sent to the others.

An hour later, they had most all the women's things also in the shuttle. That's when everything changed! Sasha glanced up at the sky. Something caught her attention. *My god! That's a drone. Yellow vapors are coming out behind it! Dear god, it's another bio attack!* She sent, *Suse, Sofia, Sonia, get into the shuttle immediately. There's another bio agent attack! Hurry. Push that button when we get inside!* The four fairly fell into the cargo bay. Sonia did as asked. The doors shut. Sasha listened intently and heard the sealing hiss, which meant they were hermetically sealed inside.

The two women had no idea why Sasha was so spooked, but even Suse looked scared. Sasha explained, *Someone is attacking all of Beta Carnae-4 with the same biological agent that did this to our bodies. We used to look something like*

Alan before that agent mutated our bodies. She then took her time and explained what was likely going to happen to all the people on this world. *We are safe inside this ship. The chemicals cannot get in here. You both will be safe.*

Then, Sasha thought of Legate Smith. *Suse, we have to rescue the Legate.*

Suse had been mostly silent, but now spoke up. *Look, for the Legate to have gotten here, there must be one of those big Imperium battleships up there. The newscasts always had her in that big one. If they know this world is being attacked and we try to lift off, they'll think we are responsible and blow us to kingdom come. We have to stay put.*

Good point. You are quite right. There has to be a big Imperium ship in orbit. Still, it's too late to get to Legate Smith right now. The bio agent is all over the place. I know, we can fly the shuttle to the Presidential Estate where she's supposed to be located. As soon as it's safe, we can hop out and get her, Sasha suggested.

Suse countered. *Don't be hasty. If they are not yet in a coma, they might shoot us or try to capture this shuttle. The girls will be doomed if the doors are opened while the bio agent is still active. We wait it out, and go once we're sure the people are in a coma.*

Sonia made eating motions with her hands. Sasha smiled invisibly and directed everyone to the galley. An hour later, the two women had figured out how to use the equipment and had fixed the four a nice lunch. Suse commented, *We have to figure out how to get this coffee stuff on Tierra. It's vastly better than our tea.* Sasha didn't think so, but nodded anyway. They spent the afternoon organizing the chaos in the cargo bay.

The next morning, Sasha figured everyone would be in a coma. Thus, it would be safe to attempt to take the shuttle over to the Presidential Estate. Chances were not good they would find them outside. Still, after three days, they could then head inside and look for her. No one would be able to stop them. After giving Sonia constant instructions, the transport landed on the grassy knoll near the transport that had brought Legate Smith to the meeting. More importantly, they spotted all three of them lying on the grass where they'd fallen into a coma.

Staring out of the view port at the unconscious Legate Smith, Sasha realized another critical detail. She still had her shoes on and her blouse was buttoned. When her body began mutating, her feet would be crushed. From the newscasts, she also knew many on Proxima Prime had died, because they wore tight fitting tops so that when their breasts had expanded so enormously, the constricting pressure ruptured their hearts. At least, they had a merciful death and never knew what had happened to them, she thought. This was likely to happen to Legate Smith as well.

Suse commented, *I promised I would one day kill Alan for what he did to us. I think I'm going to change my mind. Let him live as we have to live. Let him mutate too.*

I agree with you, Suse, but we need to figure out how to get the Legate's shoes off her and her blouse unbuttoned, Sasha replied.

Well, we can't open the bay and do it ourselves. I don't want Sofia to be harmed. Find another way, Sasha.

After some thought, she sent, *Suse, can you join with me, like a Circle technician? Flow your energies to me. I have some weak telekinetic skills. With your added power boost, I might be able to free her.*

A few minutes later, Suse and Sasha joined, much like a capo and a technician. While watching from the view port, Sasha focused on the Legate's shoes. Shortly, they slipped off her nylon-clad feet. She also knew that was the easy part. Straining to the utmost, she was able to get one button undone, then the next, and the next. Finally, her blouse was free. She gently moved the two sides apart, revealing her exposed, small breasts. Done, she broke the rapport.

Suse looked for herself. *We did it,* she sent to all. She then had to explain what they'd done, how they'd done it, and why. Both young women seemed to understand. *Now, we have to wait probably two more days until it's safe to go out there. Come on, Sofia; let's slip into the bed for a while.*

The third day, all four took turns watching for any signs of the three stirring out there on the lawn. From everything the two knew about the bio attacks, the agent itself was short lived and was gone or became inert by the time the victims awoke from their comas. Only then was Sasha willing to gamble with the lives of Sonia and Sofia. She was dependent upon the two and their arms. Without them, she knew she very likely was doomed.

Around noon, Sasha spotted movement. Legate Smith was coming around. Shortly, they heard her terrified screams. Now, the four acted. Once the cargo bay was opened, Sasha knew she and Suse would be useless trying to walk across the grass. They would only hinder Sonia and Sofia. *Go out there and carry her back inside, please, please,* she sent. Both women nodded. Holding onto the sides of the doors, they carefully made their way down the ramp. Their tall heels made this exceedingly treacherous. Going up the ramp was easy; going down, something else entirely.

Legate Smith was still screaming, terrified, as were all the victims. Sasha touched her mind, sending calming waves. *Relax. We're rescuing you now. Just relax, and let the women carry you into the shuttle. Relax.* The words appeared in Mary's mind. Her body began to relax, but not from anything that had to do with her, Mary was certain of that. She was panicking utterly. She saw the two young women coming towards her. She thought only one word, Help!

The women bent down and raised the stricken woman into a sitting position. Then, they gently lifted her up to her feet, well toes actually. Each had an arm around her, and they began walking slowly back to the transport. Mary's feet more or less began to work. Sonia smiled, as she came up the ramp. Going up was much easier, she thought to herself.

To her credit, Legate Smith had calmed down, especially, when she saw they were taking her into a transport. They sat her down and shut the door. Just then, the two men roused and began screaming, just as she had done minutes before. She remembered the victims had to speak only Imperium Standard. "Thank you. I'm Legate Mary Smith. I need to contact my battleship. It's in orbit above us. Can you do this for me?" Silence.

Sasha sent, *Alan Arkoldt kidnaped us and removed our*

voices. I'm Sasha er no, that's what he was calling me. I'm Senator Franco Hermanes. This is Suse or Ambassador Carlos Valen. We were about to escape when the terrorist attack came. We knew you were here, so we stuck around to rescue you. I can tell Sonia what to do, but none of us can speak. Can you talk to your ship?

"You don't look like Senator Franco."

He must have used a Rejuvenation Machine on us. Our bodies are quite young now. He wanted slave telepaths for a long time.

"Well, okay then. Help me to the comm system." *I have to be brave, even if I'm not! They are worse off than I am.*

A half hour later, with Sonia pressing the proper controls, Legate Smith attempted to contact General Stalock. Nothing but static could be heard. After ten minutes, she slumped and gave up. Was the battleship destroyed too? *What is happening? I need data but how?*

We are escaping now. We'll take you to Tierra with us. Our doctor can help fix you up, Sasha explained. They left her sitting at the comm controls. A few minutes later, a very proud Sonia pressed the Execute button. The ship lifted off Beta Carnae-4. They were on their way to Winno-3 and a refueling.

While Sonia and Sasha were getting them airborne, Suse and Sofia began helping Mary. Suse could not do anything, but relay Sofia's questions and orders to Mary. Sofia first helped her remove all her clothes, noticing Mary's body had the same physical characteristics as Suse's. She then helped her to use the bathroom. That done, she insisted on giving Mary a bath and washing her hair.

Suse or Carlos, already in a deep apathy over his destroyed physical body and confused mental state, grew more and more depressed. *My life is over. I'm just a useless piece of freakish trash. Whom am I kidding with those movies? We don't have the power thing even to make the machines I stole work. Look at her, Legate Smith. She's acting as if nothing much has happened, as if she's going right back to running the Imperium. Well, crap, she's a woman anyway. How can I ever return home looking like this womanly mutant? I can't. I just can't.*

Just then, Sonia and Sasha joined them. From their pale faces, Suse could see that something was very wrong. Sasha focused and sent to them all, *We have a serious problem. Alan has sabotaged his own ship. If we try to jump into hyperspace, a bomb will go off unless we enter his secret code.*

"Oh dear god," Legate Smith cried out in surprise, and then controlled her reactions. "Where is this bomb? Can we defuse it? Push it out the air lock? Come, think. We are not totally helpless."

In the rear somewhere. Sofia, you keep on fixing the Legate up. We'll go find the bomb, Sasha ordered.

Sonia didn't know what to look for, but she began rummaging into the several rooms off the main hallway. Sasha and Suse moved slowly on towards the very rear, where the docking bay was located. *Ah, follow that humming sound, Suse!*

What dopes we are, Suse! It's right here in plain sight. Duh. Wait, it's armed. Think, old man, think!

Carlos grasped the situation in a rare flash of insight. Here was his way out! If only. . . He sent, *Do you know how to open the air lock?*

Sure, but why? Oh, I see. We push it out. Great thinking. Wait.

I know. Someone's got to go with it and push it on out. I'll do that. I have to save the Legate. He lied. *Promise me you'll take care of Sofia for me.*

Yes, of course, but you can't do this. You'll be killed.

A king's valiant death. Tell my brother I died a king's death. Now do it. Do it for all our sakes!

With as deep a sigh as possible, Sasha complied, pushing the keypad entries with her nose. When the door opened, Carlos, now in full control of his mind, used his body and all the psi power he could muster tried to push the ticking explosive bomb on out into the narrow bay, wobbling wildly, but somehow managing to keep from falling. His efforts yielded nothing. Then, he had a bright idea. He sat down and began pushing it along with his feet. That worked. He stopped near the final hatch. *Do it now. Do it now.*

There must be some other way.

There isn't. Do it now. Save everyone else. The Legate is the one who is truly important. Do it.

Sasha did it. Again, she used her nose to push the keypad entries. The other hatch opened. The air rushed out into the near vacuum of space, carrying Carlos and the bomb with him. She pushed another entry and the hatch sealed. Air came hissing back into the corridor; the pressure equalizing. Slowly and with tears swelling, Sasha made her slow way back to the still frantically searching Sonia. *It's over. Suse died saving our lives. She got rid of it. We're safe.*

Sonia began silently crying, but put her arms around Sasha, leading them back to the other two. "What's wrong? Something happened. I heard the air lock. Oh!" Legate Smith asked, but stopped short, seeing their tears.

Sasha explained what Carlos had done. *He died a king's death to save us all, Legate Smith.*

"Ambassador Carlos Valen will long be remembered. I shall see to that," Legate Smith swore.

While Sofia continued to finish cleaning her up, Sonia and Sasha headed to the pilot's seat to make the jump into hyperspace. This time, they were successful. After returning and reporting they were officially in hyperspace and on their way to Winno-3, Sofia was finished with Mary, who next needed clothes. Sofia and Sonia headed off to see what could fix from among the clothes they'd brought onboard.

An hour later, they had Legate Smith dressed reasonably well. While Sofia continued working on her hair, Sonia began spooning her a drink of berry juice. When she finished that, Sonia headed off to cook something substantial for the four. Three hours after her miraculous rescue, Legate Smith was stuffed, cleaned up, and dressed much like Sasha.

"Thank you all. I would have died had you not thought to rescue me. Thank you all. I've had half the galaxy out looking for the both of you, Senator Franco, and for Ambassador Carlos. If you don't mind, I'd like to hear what happened to you. The last we knew, you both were in the hospital room waiting your turn to get your arms regrown."

Still somewhat confused by his or her identity, Sasha-

Franco began to relate all that had happened to them, sparing no details. After that long tale, she asked about the other two silent women. This time, Franco told her what little they had told him.

Just then, Sonia gestured to him. He made contact with her. *What's going to happen to us? We want to be with you, always. We're scared.*

Franco made a decision. He sent, *Sonia, Sofia, will you marry me? On my world, some men have more than one wife. Then, we can be together always.* Their faces burst into a pair of giant smiles.

The request took the Legate by total surprise. Here, she was a victim herself, totally helpless, dependent upon this highly unlikely group, and they wanted her to marry them! The incongruity of it all caused her to burst out laughing. "Yes, yes, I can marry you. That's a rarely used power of Legate, but I've a problem. I can't sign the proper documents just now. Doesn't matter. I can get someone to sign for me later. Do you want to do it now?" All three nodded vigorously. Thus, Legate Mary Smith did the least likely thing any terrorist victim ever did just hours after regaining consciousness. She officially married the three.

However, during the rest of their trip to Winno-3, Sofia stayed with Legate Smith, just as she had done for Suse. Their first night in bed, Sofia taught Mary a few unsuspected "features" of her new genetically mutated body.

Two days later, they dropped out of hyperspace above Winno-3. Of course, the control tower immediately challenged them. Anticipating this, all four were crammed into the front section of the transport. With Sasha telling Sonia what to press, Legate Mary Smith did the talking. "This is Legate Mary Smith on this transport. I've been a terrorist victim too. We need help. I have three others with me, and we're all pretty darn helpless. Can someone dock with us and land the transport? I need to contact General Stalock on the battleship Star Cruiser immediately!"

Chapter 12 Frantic Moves

General Stalock paced his deck rather bored. Legate Smith had been gone barely an hour, but it seemed like an endless eternity. Until she returned, he had absolutely nothing to do. A man of action, this infernal inactivity was maddening. What was going on back on Proxima Prime? For the second time, he checked with the general whom he'd left in charge. All quiet. He checked with his ship reporting stations. At least, that gave him something to do. Nothing at all. Well, that was to be expected; this was a mere diplomatic meeting.

Just when he wondered if anyone had ever died from boredom, several comm officers barked into the intercom, nearly simultaneous. "General. You should see this." He didn't quite get all of the messages; they barked out of the speaker overlapping each other. Ah, this is more like it, he thought, racing down to the comm center. Red warning lights flashed at five stations. Five officers tried to speak at the same time!

"One at a time!" he brought instant order with his bark.

"Sir, we're detecting a bio agent attack on Beta-Carnae-4!"

"Sir, we are hearing reports of a bio attack on Zelan-3!"

"Looks like one on Zeta-3!"

"One on Longditch-4. They are asking for help."

"Got reports of one on Bailey-3."

"Slow down. Beta-Carnae-4. Where's it coming from?" the general barked, trying to comprehend what was going on. "The Legate's down there. Any word from her? How bad is it?"

"Sir, we've not detected anything on radar, but forward observation posts are reporting seeing unmanned drones. Lots of them."

"What's lots? Any markings on them? Get all gun crews to battery. Battle stations. Shoot those bastards down. Route everything to the war room!" He raced to the large room, where his junior officers were already responding at a run. Gongs echoed throughout the gigantic ship.

Already, he heard gunfire and headed to the video feed

from the firing stations. He punched a fist into the air, as he watched one of the stealth drones disintegrating. Then, he saw it was useless. There were waves upon waves of the damned drones. "Where did they all come from? Someone find their origin points! Take us out of orbit, clear of the atmosphere entirely."

In a war, field generals have to make key decisions, often based on incomplete or confusing data and aligned with their current mission. Seeing the sheer number of drones, he knew there was no chance to rescue Legate Smith. None whatsoever. This ship and the Imperium instantly became his prime concern. Five of the most populated planets and powerful ones too were being attacked simultaneously from source or sources unknown. He ordered, "Take us to Proxima Prime at top speed!" He'd made one of those instant decisions for which he'd trained all his life. For good or ill, the Imperium had to be protected. This could well be a deception for the real strike on what remained on Proxima Prime. If the automated computer systems were destroyed, the Imperium would be instantly thrown into utter chaos, likely ceasing to exist.

An hour later, hovering above Proxima Prime and with every military ship in the entire Imperium on highest alert and at battle stations, General Stalock finally was able to hold a comprehensive meeting in which all available data was presented. The picture began to clear, as many other cruisers and light cruisers reported their findings, sightings, and received transmissions from ground bases to the war room on the Star Cruiser. As the officers relayed their reports to him, the general finally began to relax. The clouds cleared.

He summed up, "Okay. As I see it, the Big Five worlds each launched an unmanned, stealth drone attack on the other four worlds, releasing the bio agent on them. So each of the Big Five worlds have essentially suffered four such attacks each. Hell, one would wipe them out. No other attacks have been reported. Estimated casualties?"

An aide, anticipating this tally, spoke up, "Sir, roughly two hundred billion, all added together."

The general sighed and then sat up straight. "Okay then, issue the following orders to the fleets. Maintain High

Alert. Look for incoming stealth drones, unmanned. Quarantine the Big Five worlds until further notice. Dismissed. I have some calls to make."

In his private quarters, General Stalock sighed. With the Legate out of action and presumed dead, her last orders of Martial Law still held. He was now in charge of the entire Imperium! That was the very last thing he wanted. He was a military man. He detested politicians and their ways. The other Legates, though rescued, would not be able to resume control for at least another two months. "Hell, the whole damn thing can be gone by then!" He did the only thing that he could think of — he placed a secure call to Emperor Kino Sango of the Ataro Empire, the sole remaining power broker of the Imperium. He hated the five minute comm delay, but it could not be avoided.

After reaching the man, he slowly explained what had happened and the actions he'd taken. "I'm afraid Legate Mary Smith is lost to us, likely dead, or so wishing in a few days. What the hell are we going to do to save the Imperium from a total collapse? Over." He didn't expect much from a helpless, armless man. He was about as useless as all the other terrorist victims were, perhaps more so. Well, there was no one else who commanded as much power as this man did. "What has the mighty Imperium come to?" he muttered to himself.

After the delay, the image of the emperor appeared on his monitor. God, the man's crying. Pathetic, he thought. The emperor began, "It's a very sad day indeed. All those innocent lives are lost. General Stalock, you're still the man in charge for now. I will back you, if you meet any resistance. I agree with all the actions you've taken so far. Excellent military protocol."

He sighed and continued, "Personally, I've been expecting something like this, but not on such a large scale. Ancient hatreds still smolder. Those five worlds have been antagonists for at least three millennia, maybe more. Obviously, they were never having their geneticists working on cures for the terrorist victims. Rather, they were improving these weapons of mass destruction for just such a day. Such bio weapons are really not a weapon at all. They've deceived only themselves by so thinking and acting. It's genocide, pure and simple. Well, they've certainly done that."

He sighed again. "At this time, all available worlds, who have sufficient assisted living housing, are at or near their capacity. I regret to say this, general, but I seriously doubt many at all can be rescued this time. By your time estimates, we have perhaps two and a half days yet before their genetic mutations will be complete, and the billions will come out of their comas. Once more, I'll make calls to the many other worlds, and see if they can accept any more victims. We might be able to rescue a few, but that will be a drop in the sea."

He went on, "If and after any possible few rescue attempts are made, the real question we face is what do we do about the two hundred billion on those five worlds. Do we drop weapons on them and kill them mercifully or do we sit back and let nature do her thing? Ideas? Over."

The general sighed this time. "With all due respect, Emperor, I can't have my men killing two hundred billion humans, just to put them out of their misery. I say let them live with what their rulers wanted. It will take months to haul off the dead. We are still clearing out Proxima Prime. It will probably be another couple of months before all the dead there are disposed of on that world. We're still finding dead bodies. Over."

"Agreed. We'll let nature run her course. My suggestion is, once it is safe, let the few rescue ships down. Then, quarantine the five worlds for say a month. After that, allow representatives of the various Imperium companies go down and salvage what equipment and records they desire. Once that's done, setup a permanent quarantine. When you have the time and manpower, begin clearing the dead. It will probably take years to finish that process. We can't keep on using all the civilian mining trains. They are needed for commercial runs. Over."

"Excellent strategy. I will see to it. Perhaps one rescue ship ought to search for Legate Smith. Here is her last known position. We can put up permanent quarantine beacons, though that isn't likely to stop thieves. Over."

Emperor Kino suggested wryly, "Then, let it be

publically known that, because of the sheer volume of the bio agent used in the attacks, the surface will be contaminated for many years. Anyone going there will become another mutated victim. That ought to scare thieves away for a while, giving us more time to deal with the situation. Over."

Politicians! He thought, deceptive to the end. "Yes, that's a brilliant idea. I'll see to it. Next question. Do you want to handle breaking the news to the reporters? I sure as hell don't want to do that. Over."

"You are probably right. It would not look good to see a military man running the Imperium at this most pivotal point in time. I'll do it from here shortly. Keep me fully informed, and I will do the same. Excellent work, general, excellent. Over and out."

General Stalock breathed a huge sigh of relief. He didn't have to go before those cameras and face those biting questions! He set about carrying out his new orders.

Emperor Kino had his Personal Assistant wipe his face. It was rather wet. Then, he placed a secure call to Governor Katrina and Queen Amy. The news he had to share was dismal. After relaying what had just happened, he then asked, "We need to send a transport ship to see if we can locate and rescue Legate Mary Smith. However, I also need to know how many more victims Tierra can take? Based on your answer, I will have my staff again search out the best candidates for your world. Over."

"My God, the Big Five? Gone? Two hundred billion? Is the Imperium collapsing?" Governor Katrina exclaimed, utterly shocked by this surprise and horrific news.

Queen Amy added, "I'm checking with Rafe now."

After the long delay, he replied, "I am afraid it's so, governor. Admittedly, I suspected something like this might happen. Ancient history has always stated those five worlds were frequently warring with each other, before they were brought into the Imperium, some two millennia ago. Hindsight is good. If only the Senate had been wise enough to investigate just why these worlds had not produced any cures for the terrorist victims in over thirty years of research, they might have been able to prevent this massive genocide, for genocide it is. I doubt very much I'll be able to find new assisted living homes for many of these victims. Over."

Amy replied, "We can take another seventy-five victims here. A hundred, if there's no other place for them. We're almost at capacity. We need far more supplies, if we are to regrow all their arms. That's imperative, unless we also become overrun with helpless victims and their children. If only it wasn't genetically inherited. How soon do we need to get a transport to you? Over."

"This time, I'll handle the transports, Queen Amy. Thank you for opening your world for these victims. If only more worlds would display the compassion that Ashford-5 has. Okay then, I best prepare to make the dreaded newscast. We will talk more about the survival of the Imperium later. Over and out."

Later, Katrina, Amy, and their whole gang watched the Emperor's newscast. He looked somewhat shaken, Amy thought. "I am Emperor Kino Sango of the Ataro System. Legate Mary Smith is temporarily unavailable. I have to tell you all perhaps the saddest news that has ever been reported. Ancient hostilities have once more come to the forefront of modern history. The worlds collectively known as the Big Five have gone to war with each other. Zelan-3, Beta Carnae-4, Zeta-3, Longditch-4, and Bailey-3, have each launched massive attacks against the others. Using unmanned, stealth drones, they've saturated each world four times over with the same deadly bio agent that we've seen terrorists use on many other worlds, including Proxima Prime several months ago. Rough estimates suggest somewhere near two hundred billion people are infected with the horrible genetic mutation that so many other victims have faced."

"Each world received attacks from the other four. The result is four times more deadly than what happened on Proxima Prime. The contamination from such a massive overdose of the biological agents will prevent even landing on those worlds for months to come, perhaps even longer. Soon, I will be contacting all worlds to see if any still are able to accept survivors. I know that most worlds with available assisted living quarters have already filled those to capacity. Hence, I do not hold out much hope for a massive rescue operation at this time."

"The Imperium military has issued a total quarantine of these five worlds effective for the foreseeable future. The Imperium is still vital and strong. There is no danger of a collapse. I would like to reiterate Legate Smith's plea for all worlds quickly to send replacement senators to Proxima Prime, as well as new bureaucrats. We need to get daily operations back to normal as soon as we possibly can. I'm sure Legate Smith will have more for you later on. Together, we can flourish and prosper. Before I sign off, I would like us all to take a private moment and say prayers for the uncounted billions who are suffering and dying. Thank you." He stood silent with his head down for about a minute. Then, as the reporters shouted questions at him, he calmly made his slow walk out of the room.

Lena commented, "Even if they send new Senators, I don't see how they'll be able to hold the Imperium together!"

"If we don't, anarchy is going to run rampant," Katrina replied, quite sober.

Anarchy. That was precisely what Emperor Kino was trying desperately to avoid. For all practical purposes, the Imperium had just broken down, though most probably didn't quite realize it had happened. There was no working government. Legate Smith was the very last one left, and now she was missing or dead. Sooner or later, the news reporters would get wind of her situation. After that, there was no government left!

As he met with his advisors, his real concern was just how many more worlds had their hands on this damnable bio agent? That was his uppermost concern. If more worlds used it, there would be no stopping the total collapse of the Imperium! Time was now his worst enemy. He put his many local queens on the task of making the hundreds of calls to other worlds, asking if they could accept any more victims. Meanwhile, he and his aides culled every scrap of intelligence they had accumulated over the last thirty years that related in any way to this bio agent and the cylinders. How many more worlds could possibly launch such genocides?

233

"Let's not consider the individual terrorist organizations that might or might not have any of these bio agent cylinders," he spoke to his army of aides. "Look for worlds that have legally been given duplicates of these cylinders. We want to prevent any more genocide attacks. It will take a world-organization to fabricate the quantity of cylinders needed, along with the methods of delivery. Yes, it includes those who got them for research purposes. I want them all identified."

He took one aide aside. "I have another special project for you. Go over all the Academy records that you can on these Big Five worlds. Identify the top two hundred students for me. We might be able to rescue those. Yes, just like you did for Proxima Prime." The aide nodded and left the room.

Thirty-six hours after the attack was discovered, Emperor Kino placed another secure call to General Stalock. The general had little news to report, other than the quarantine was now in full force. He'd given the battleships and cruisers orders to shoot down any arriving ship that was not authorized by him.

Emperor Kino explained, "Okay, we've identified a hundred six worlds who, in the past, have been given at least one duplicate cylinder of the bio agent in question. Reputedly, they were supposed to use them for their genetic research into cures for the victims. We both know the Big Five used them for entirely different purposes. So we need to prevent more such genocide attacks. Over."

"What do you propose that we do? More attacks? Is that likely? It's bloody suicide. Over." Damned communications lag, he cursed silently.

"I can vouch for thirty-seven of these worlds. That leaves sixty-nine that must be investigated immediately. Send troops to each of these and have them execute a strict accounting of all the cylinders and all those that the world has subsequently made by use of the Fabrication Machines. Verify that all are being used in genetic research. If your men find any who have stockpiled some for eventual wars, confiscate the lot, every last cylinder on that world. We want to prevent more planetary genocides, if we can. Let's ignore for now the lone terrorist, who can infect a few thousand. We have to stop further planetary-wide disasters, if we can. Over."

"Well, I do have Martial Law backing me. I assure you the politicians of those worlds won't like this, but I do! I'll get on it yet today. Send me the list of worlds. Brilliant move, Emperor. I wish Legate Smith had thought of that a month ago. Over."

"Even if she had, there would not have been the precedent established for such a drastic action. She would have met violent protests. No, the timing would have been off, if she had thought of that. Keep me posted. Over and out."

"Damn, he's on the ball," the general commented to himself. He sprang into action once more. He loved action.

A transport landed on the Presidential Estate's grassy lawn. A soldier stepped out and looked towards the two screaming victims. One looked vaguely like the photograph he held of the President of Beta Carnae-4. "Help us please, help, I beg you. I'm the President."

"Where is Legate Mary Smith?" the soldier asked.

"She was with us. She's not here. Help us please. I'll give you a fortune," the man pleaded. The soldier turned and walked back to the transport, ignoring the screams from the two men and offers of millions of credits. The transport lifted off.

"Damn. No sign of her at the Presidential Estate," Emperor Kino swore. "Where could she have gone? Ask them to continue their search and rescue operation, but stay alert for the Legate."

After two more days, he'd given up hope of ever finding the Legate. He didn't know how much longer he could withhold the information that she too was lost. However, another hundred bright young Academy students were on their way to Ashford-5 and a new life. That was something. They were the only people he was able to rescue this time. The sentiments of the other worlds were simply: let them stew in their own mess. All compassion was gone from the leaders of the other worlds of the Imperium.

Suddenly, he got an emergency call from Winno-3. He was patched through at once. "Emperor, this is the control tower supervisor here. Our controllers picked up an unauthorized transport ship on approach to Winno-3 a half hour ago. I'll replay the recording made there." He listened intently, then breathed a huge sigh of relief, at least as huge as his overly tight corset would allow.

"This is Legate Mary Smith on this transport. I've been a terrorist victim too. We need help. I've got three others with me, and we're all pretty darn helpless. Can someone dock with us and land the transport? I need to contact General Stalock on the battleship Star Cruiser immediately!"

"Has she landed safely?" the Emperor asked.

"Yes. She's with the medical staff now. I'll put you through to her, as soon as the doctors will allow. Over and out."

Legate Smith held her breath. Would they send someone up to help land the transport? Or would Sasha-Franco have to try to tell Sonia how to land it? That latter made her extremely nervous, and Sasha sensed it.

"Legate Smith. Stay in your stationary position. A crew will board you directly. Over and out."

"Thank god for that. I do think we have made it, Sasha, Sonia, Sofia. I can't thank you enough," Legate Smith said formally, doing her best to be understood, since her lips no longer worked. Rather she had long, thick dangling lip loops. At least, I don't have those giant lip disks on me, she thought, looking at Sasha or rather Franco.

An hour later, their transport was safely on the ground. A shuttle docked with them, two men came aboard, and landed it for them. After the bay door was lowered, they kindly lifted the four apparent women down onto the tarmac, where a squad of soldiers were waiting, taking no chances. From there, they were loaded onto an electric car and driven to the local hospital, despite Legate Smith's protests that she had to contact the general.

Finally, a team of doctors arrived. "Okay, Legate Smith. We are going to get you as fixed up as we can. The geneticist doctors on Ashford-5 have sent us their latest cures. We'll be able partially to repair your feet so you can walk far better.

We'll be able to remove the neurons in your hair so that it can be cut as short as you prefer. The process takes about an hour. Then, we'll have someone come to see about apparel for you. After that, I'm told Emperor Kino wishes to speak with you. We will wait a bit before starting your arm regrowth. Now just lie back."

"But I need — oh there is on use arguing with a doctor. Go ahead. But make haste. I must speak to the Emperor as soon as possible," Legate Smith replied.

Nearby, other doctors began using their medical machines to examine what had been done to the other three, particularly their lack of voice. At last, the doctors conferred and one spoke to the three, who were lying on adjacent beds. "Well, I have bad news for you. It seems your voice boxes were actually removed. I'm afraid we can't restore your ability to speak. I'm so sorry."

He went on, "Sonia, you are perfectly healthy, but I've good news for you. You are pregnant. Your due date is around next July. Sofia, you are perfectly healthy as well. Sasha or Franco, we have the Asford-5 doctors' latest cures. We'll be able partially to restore your feet, though you will have to wear heels similar to your charming wives. The pain sensors in your hair will also be removed. You can then get your hair cut as short as you desire. The process will take an hour or so. After that, we can discuss your arm regrowth process or if you prefer, you can have your own doctors do that for you when you get back to Ashford-5. Nod, if this is okay with you." He did so. "Good. I'll be with you in a few minutes, after we get the Legate going."

Incredible, Sonia. We're going to have a baby! Don't worry, Sofia, we'll have one soon too.

I'm so happy, Sasha. I was scared you would be unhappy about that.

How can I be unhappy about our having a baby? Children are precious.

She smiled and pointed to her head. He picked up her next thought. *Do you have to cut your hair? Sofia and I love it this long.*

For you two, I won't have it cut, but you'll have to help

me with it, until I get my arms back. Okay? Both women smiled and also nodded just to make sure he understood.

Sonia then pointed to her belly. He made contact. *You can have a baby too. Then, we all will have one.*

Sasha smiled invisibly and nodded. *I guess I'm more woman than man now, so why not?*

An hour later, Legate Smith was finished with the medical machines. "Okay, Legate Smith, let's get you to the hair dresser and get you attired as you wish. Then, we'll put the call through to the Emperor and go from there."

As he wheeled her out in a wheel chair, she commented. "Thanks for everything, but let's be quick about this. I've work to do." As she left, Sasha could sense the Legate was totally suppressing her emotions and trauma, fighting hard to keep them at bay.

"Now then, Sasha, let's get you to the hair dresser and then attired as you desire. Sonia, Sofia, please come with us," the aide said, pushing Sasha in another wheel chair. They were done very quickly and waiting on Legate Smith in a lounge. Sasha only wanted new heels; she was content with the rest of her clothing and hair. As she and her wives walked out of that room and to the waiting lounge, she discovered walking was now much easier. The three women wore identical height heels. Sasha felt far more relaxed being able to walk without needing support.

Finally, Legate Smith walked out. She had her hair cut short, just the way it had been before the genetic modifications altered it. She too wore similar heels to the three. However, she'd discarded the gown that Sofia had put on her, back in the transport. She wore a white blouse and a black skirt that fell just to her knees, about as professional as she could now look. She also refused to have the giant lip plates inserted. Hence, her two lip loops draped and dangled as she walked. "Well, I see you are done too. This is much better. Come, he's going to take us to their comm center." The three rose and followed her.

"Yes, Emperor Kino, I'm perfectly fine." She outlined what had happened to her and the details of her miraculous rescue, including the discovery of Senator Franco Hermanes and the heroic death of Ambassador Carlos Valen. "I need to be updated on what's happened. I need to get back to the hub as soon as possible. I ought to talk to General Stalock as well. And yes, thank you for stepping in."

Emperor Kino did as ordered, launching into a detailed explanation of what happened and in chronological order. He outlined his reasoning behind the orders he'd had to give in her absence. When he finished up, Legate Smith was rather pale. "My god. It's worse than I imagined! Thank you, Emperor. You've probably saved the Imperium! Two hundred billion? It's almost unimaginable. Still, I concur, there's no way really to launch a rescue operation this time. We are simply out of options. I agree quarantining those worlds is the best route. In the future, the Senate can decide what to do with them. Over."

"I am so glad that you are safe. As soon as you feel up to it, you should hold a news conference. I have sent a transport to bring you to my place. We can hold it together and discuss in depth the next actions to take. As far as I can tell, only you and I stand between the survival of the Imperium or its destruction. We are on a perilous precipice. It can go either way, and time is not on our side. Oh, I will have a Personal Assistant for you when you get here. See you at dinner. Put Senator Franco on next please. Over."

That chat went swiftly. All he wanted was for the three to be flown to Tierra as soon as possible. The three found themselves on a flight to Ashford-5 within the hour. Emperor Kino also promised to let Queen Amy know of the death of King Carlos Valen for him.

"I feel like such a helpless baby," Legate Smith commented to Helene, her new Personal Assistant. She'd arrived at the Emperor's Royal Palace an hour ago, been introduced to Helene, and shown to her temporary quarters.

Helene replied, "I understand. You and I will need a bit of time to make adjustments. I assure you I learn swiftly. Before long, I'll be able to anticipate your needs so you will not be embarrassed by having to ask. I'm fluent in many languages. I do like your choice of dress, so very businesslike.

I've ordered some additional blouses and skirts to match. They should be ready by the time we're ready to leave for the hub."

"Excellent. I suppose it's time to eat and discuss this horrid mess. Plus, I'll have to face those cameras and the reporters sometime very soon. Be brave, Mary, be brave. Okay, let's get started. At least in these heels, I can get myself up from chairs now. Stairs are going to be a nightmare. I can't see my feet at all."

Helene grinned. "Leave that to me."

As she dined with the Emperor, she didn't feel out of place. His own Personal Assistant was feeding him, just as Helene was doing for her. She relaxed a bit more, but still kept everything suppressed. She had to be seen as a strong leader. The stakes were far too high for her to feel pity for herself.

The two held her first news conference right after dinner. As she and he walked by themselves across the room to stand before the wall of microphones and video cameras, to say nothing of the many reporters, she noticed she had a vastly easier time walking than he did. She felt a bit more embolden by such a tiny thing.

She began, "Welcome. I'll speak more slowly and hope I can be understood well enough. Yes, I've obviously had a run in with this genetic mutation bio agent. It happened during my visit to Beta Carnae-4. Thanks to Senator Franco Hermanes and Ambassador Carlos Valen of Ashford-5, I'm safe and well. As you know, the Big Five worlds have been withholding sending replacement senators and bureaucrats to Proxima Prime. I went there in a last ditch attempt to get them to see reason. Instead, the Big Five chose to use their bio weapons of mass destruction on themselves. Well, I do hope they are happy now."

"The Imperium is still strong and vital. We can't let this push us off course. I urge all the many Imperium worlds to hurry up and send your new senators, justices, and bureaucrats to Proxima Prime, so we can get the show on the road. Look where stalling has led us. Two hundred billion plus are now dead. We simply cannot afford to wait. As you already know, General Stalock and Emperor Kino have been acting on my behalf. Just so the record is quite clear, I would have issued the exact same orders. We three work together and think alike. We aren't about to allow other worlds to commit planetary genocide. Period. End of discussion."

"As far as the quarantine period goes, we just don't know how long these worlds will have to be isolated. Unlike Proxima Prime's attack, each of these worlds received, we estimate, four to five times the dosage of the bio genetic agent. It may be many weeks or months before it is truly safe for others to land there, without wearing bio containment suits. However, we'll make some attempts to accommodate companies who need to land to recover business assets."

"In summary then, we, the many united worlds of the Imperium, must move swiftly to rebuild our executive, legislative, and justice branches on Proxima Prime. Thank you for your attention." Legate Smith backed away.

Naturally, reporters, being reporters, began shouting questions at her. Among them, was: "Legate Smith, do you think you can still lead the Imperium with your mutated body? Aren't you severely limited now?"

She decided to field that one. She stepped forward to the microphones. "Only a darn fool cannot see I now have very severe physical limitations. Yes, I need help eating and dressing. I can't open doors. If that isn't obvious, then perhaps you should see your optometrist. My mind isn't in my arms. I checked." Several reporters chuckled. "We need great thinkers, great planners, and great leaders. None of these requires athletic, normal bodies, but rather sound, intelligent minds. Those are my qualifications, as they always have been. If you think you can do better than me, for heaven's sake, put your name in for the new bureaucratic pool and get yourself elected President or senator. I'll gladly step aside, when the newly reconstituted Senate elects a new temporary President." She stepped back.

More questions were shouted out. One bothered her. "How can we just let over two hundred billion people die? Can't they be saved?"

She moved back up. "Two hundred billion. It's got a name. Planetary genocide. Rescue them you suggest? Look, a deep space transport can carry say twenty-five victims, plus rescuers. That will require eight billion transport trips. Sorry, we don't have a fraction of that number of transports in the entire Imperium. Each victim is much like myself, in need of another normal person to assist them just to live. Most would have to reside in assisted living complexes. Those are already full beyond capacity with all the other terrorist attack victims that have been rescued. Where would we put them, ignoring the eight billion transport ships? Don't think that my heart doesn't goes out to all those people. It does. If you have some ideas of just how we could save them, please contact me immediately, because none of us who are running this show has." She stepped back again, noticing their stunned reaction to the sheer magnitude of such a rescue operation.

None of the other questions troubled her, and shortly after that, she and the Emperor made their way out of the room. "Well, Legate, that was a brilliant performance. Well done. I thought you handled it very well indeed," Emperor Kino complimented her. He added, "Just for your information, Ashford-5 stepped forward and accepted another hundred fifty victims from these five worlds. I know, it's hardly a grain of sand on a beach, but for a Closed World, I think this is commendable."

"Yes, you know, one day, I should visit this thirty-seventh world of your empire. It hasn't escaped me that the only known cures for any portion of this awful genetic mutation have come from their few doctors."

"I hope to one day arrange that visit for you. I think it would do you some good. Well, we've done about all we can for one day. I'm exhausted, and I assume you are too. Let's call it a day and get back at it first thing in the morning. I think a cruiser will be arriving later tomorrow to take you back to your battleship in orbit around Proxima Prime," he advised. She agreed, feeling more tired than she'd ever been. It had been a most stressful day indeed.

In her quarters, Helene undressed her, brushed her teeth for her, and helped her into bed, covering her up. "If you need anything during the night, just holler. I'll be right next door."

"Thank you, Helene. I should be fine. Good night."

Helene turned out the lights and left the room, though leaving her door open. Mary lay on her back staring at the ceiling. All of her suppressed grief seeped to the surface. Tears welled up in her eyes, and she couldn't even wipe them, which only made her feel even worse. For the first time in her life, Mary cried herself to sleep.

In the morning, she was hammered by her own physical helplessness once more. Helene cheerfully helped her up and prepare to face the day, though while dining with the Empress and Emperor, she felt slightly more comfortable. Sympathy in kind, she thought while looking at the pair across from her, being fed by their helpers. No human should have to live like this.

Later her frustrations only rose, as she had to have Helene operate her laptop for her so she could check her incoming mails. Five more worlds had notified her they were sending their replacements to Proxima Prime within few days. That cheered her slightly, but the cheer was lost when she was unable to hit reply and answer them, forced to dictate them to Helene.

As they finished their preparatory work, Helene suggested, "When we get a chance, I'm going to see about getting a voice activated program for your laptop. Once you learn the commands for it, you can operate it just by speaking, though with your lips, I'm not sure how good it will actually be. It's worth a try, don't you think?"

"I should have thought of that myself. Yes, please, let's give it a try. That would be a big help. We ought to hurry up and not keep the Emperor waiting."

A bit later, the two met in private. He said, "There are a few things you and I should discuss before you head back. Even with your speech yesterday, the results are not promising. I think we should have a backup plan, if not enough worlds respond to lend legitimacy to the reforming Imperium government."

"You mean what the devil are we to do if the Imperium continues to collapse, don't you?"

"I was trying to not be so blunt, but yes. The two most critical operations are the Central Bank Servers, which handle almost all the interplanetary financial transactions, as well as many others. The second is the Central Flight Control, which handles all the interplanetary flights via automated pilot controls built into all larger ships. I'm ignoring the military for the moment, since they are under your direct control."

She replied, "Well, those two have built in redundancy features. One that few know about is the parallel servers. Every banking transaction is duplicated on a set of backup servers, in case the main ones should totally fail. That's ignoring the massive data backups. Unfortunately, that duplicate set of servers is also on Proxima Prime. The CFC that you mentioned also has a parallel backup set of servers, but again they are also on Proxima Prime. Perhaps, it would be prudent of us to move the two backup server systems to another, more stable world."

Emperor Kino smiled, but Mary suddenly realized she could no longer smile. She fought hard to keep her emotions from being visible to him. "We think alike, Legate Smith. Any ideas where these backup servers could be located in case the Imperium crumbles on Proxima Prime?"

"Your Ataro System. Is it still quite stable?"

"Of course. They could be moved here on the quiet. Then, if Proxima Prime ends up being abandoned, the backups could take over from here."

"Excellent. I will have General Stalock get in touch with you about making that move, as we say, on the quiet and soon. The military is quite another problem. Should the unthinkable happen and the Imperium fail, who will end up with the many battleships, heavy cruisers, light cruisers, to say nothing of the weapons and men? If the Imperium fleet gets disbanded and the ships divided up among the member worlds, isn't that likely to lead to more anarchy and interstellar wars?" she asked.

"That is what frightens me the most. By constitutional rights, the member worlds are entitled to their share of the monetary value of Imperium property and the fleet. It's the fleet divided up that fair scares me the most. I haven't worked out any possible way to avoid that, should the worst happen. I only fear our time is rapidly running out. Please, exercise extreme caution and keep me posted on events, as I will you. I believe he's coming to tell us that your transportation has touched down, Legate. Just between you and me, I believe you are the best person to be handling the Imperium at the moment. You are doing a splendid job, in spite of everything. We must be brave and work for a lasting peace and prosperity. I best let you get going. Don't forget, you'll have to visit my Ashford-5 one day." He smiled and bowed to her.

Helene followed the messenger into the private meeting. As the Legate rose, she said, "I've everything packed. A shuttle is awaiting us now. I'm told we should be back by this time tomorrow."

"Thanks, Helene. Let's do it." She steeled herself for the trip out among normal people, hoping to keep her humiliation disguised for now.

An hour later, the light cruiser was in hyperspace, on its way back to the main fleet. However, Legate Smith was called to the radio room for a secure call. "It's H-cubed, Legate," the operator whispered, as she took her seat in front of the equipment, wholly unable to operate even the simple comm system. Helene worked the controls for her, but she didn't activate them until they were left alone and the door closed.

"This is Legate Mary Smith. Over."

Shortly, the image of Helyeon H. Hoon appeared on the screen. He was wearing a hospital gown-like top that didn't disguise his massive bosom. He wiggled his tiny, baby-like arms. "See, I've got baby arms for the third time. Looks like I'll have the doctor's permission to get back to work around April. You have been doing an admirable job of running the entire Imperium. Please accept my deepest sympathies for your current situation. How is the restructuring of the bureaucracy and Senate going? How are you holding up? Over."

She briefed him on the basics. "So as you can see, it's not going at all well. I can't afford to take time off to get my arms regrown. If I do that, you won't have an Imperium to come back to in April. Over."

His face looked serious, though his own dangling lip loops made it more difficult to read him from his face. Still, he was jovial, but that was just H-cubed, she thought. "My sources suggested as much. Look, I know I'm officially on sick leave and all that, but I still have quite a few connections I can contact. Let me see what little I can do from my hospital bed here on Broom-5 to help. It's in my interests to see that you are successful. It is, after all, as you just said. If you don't succeed, I won't have an Imperium to come back to. Over."

"Fine with me. Only don't go against any of the rulings I've made. That would undermine my authority. Any help you can give will be most appreciated. Over."

"Excellent Legate Smith. I'll do what I can. Pull some strings. You've done an amazing job thus far. Keep up the good work. Stay in touch. Over and out."

She sat back. "Well, I wonder if he really does have that kind of pull? Guess we'll see. Let's get back to our cabin. I need to do some thinking."

At that point in time, there were a great many people throughout this spiral arm who were doing just that, some serious thinking.

Chapter 13 From Thinking to Action

Doctor Alex Hammil looked over the chart of his current Aquila Prime young woman, whose arms he was regrowing. "Yes, you are going to be just fine. Let's check your new reflexes, shall we?" He tapped gently on her new elbows and then wrists. "Yes, perfect. You are officially allowed to use them. Just remember, they're still relatively weak. Think of them as being a three year old child's arms, and you'll do well. By summer, they should be very much stronger. From that point onward, you can exercise them as much as you want."

"Thanks, Doctor Hammil. Truly, you've salvaged my life — all our lives. We just can't thank you and the others enough. I'm going to be a teacher at Nadja's school."

"Well, teaching our children is all the thanks that I or any of us doctors need. Here on Tierra, education is our hope for the future. We need hundreds of schools, if we are to ever develop to our true potential as a people." She smiled invisibly and left.

He then consulted the master list on his computer, joined shortly by his wife. Doctor Ruth said, "I've released mine too. If Mindy and Andy releases theirs, then we've finished the last of the Aquila Prime fifty. Amazing. They've all got terrifically useful educations, are young, and wanting to contribute."

"I know, my last one is going to be a teacher for Nadja. You have to hand it to old Kino. He brought us the cream of the crop. I've been looking over the nearly thousand more that Rafe's added. I don't think there is a looser in the lot. Many are young and well educated, apparently with high IQs to boot," Doctor Alex replied.

She smiled invisibly. "I know. I've been scanning their records as they arrive in batches. But the real problem, love, lies with us. Even using Whitney's setup, we can only handle five patients every two weeks, though we have to watch them carefully for another six weeks. It is going to take us nearly eight years to get all thousand handled. I guess Rafe's plan to house them in Madiera is a very wise one. I just wish it could go faster. Are you going to Amy's Party tonight?"

"Sure. Our kids will be expecting us to come. Say, did you hear they've found Legate Mary Smith and Senator Franco?" he asked.

"Yes, Mindy just told me about it. Two more victims. When will it ever end? What I find appalling is, this time, they are not even going to try to rescue any of the over two hundred billion victims," Ruth replied. Alex shrugged. She added, "I know dear. Where could we possibly put more victims here on Tierra? We're booked up for the next eight years. Even if we did take another thousand, we'd be sixteen years handling them, but by then, we'd have a large bunch of children also to handle. Still, my heart aches just thinking about them. Five whole worlds, six with Aquila Prime, completely wiped out. I don't think Proxima Prime counts."

"Five whole worlds wiped out," Alex repeated. "Say, if they aren't going to rescue anyone there, quarantining the worlds, if we could get our hands on some more of these special medical machines for arm regrowth. . ." He didn't finish his sentence; he was lost in thought. "Dear, excuse me. I've got to talk to Amy and Katrina right away!" She smiled invisibly, having picked up his unfinished idea.

While Doctor Ruth finished both their record keeping, Doctor Alex sent a quick telepathic message to both Amy and Katrina, asking to meet with them in Amy's study. Twenty minutes later, Katrina arrived, sitting down beside Amy and Jan, and across from Doctor Alex. "Thanks for dropping everything. I've just had a bright idea. As you know, we have only five machines to regrow arms. We estimate we'll need close to eight years to handle the thousand more victims that Rafe has in Madiera right now."

"I know; it's dismal. That's why Rafe is putting them up in Madiera," Amy replied, not knowing what he was asking for. Perhaps more of the machines. So she added, "We've tried to get more, but they are almost impossible to get right now. So many other worlds are taking all that get made just to handle the thousands of victims they've accepted."

"Right. We doctors thank you for making the effort to

try to get them for us. But something Ruth told me just now got me to thinking. Legate Smith has ruled out all rescues of any people on the Big Five worlds and has them quarantined indefinitely, right?"

Katrina verified, "Right."

"I know for a fact that on Bailey-3, they have ten such machines. Two months ago, one of their doctors was emailing me about our latest procedures on hair and feet. Look, if Bailey-3 is quarantined and basically abandoned, why can't we get permission to go there and confiscate their ten machines and all the supplies we can find. With an additional ten machines, we can handle triple the number of patients we're now handling. That would cut the eight years down to under two years. I don't know if the other four worlds have any of these machines, but if they did, those should be retrieved and used as well."

"Brilliant idea. Why didn't I think of that one," Katrina replied, quite enthusiastically. "Let me contact Legate Smith and see if she'll allow it. Of course, I don't know how soon it would be safe to land and go exploring. Still, this could really help us here. Brilliant idea, doctor, keep them coming."

Later, she placed the call to Legate Smith, outlining Doctor Hammil's great idea. As harried as Legate Smith was just now, she replied, "Yes, your request is quite warranted. Other worlds that have accepted thousands of victims also have the technology to manufacture more of the medical machines. Ashford-5 obviously doesn't have that luxury. I will so order the retrieval of the equipment just as soon as it is deemed safe to do so. Again, on behalf of the Imperium, thank you for having the compassion to accept so many of these terrorist victims. Over and out."

Doctor Alex was quite pleased to hear his idea was accepted. He and Amy set to work planning a new hospital wing for the Imperial Castle. Although it was the dead of winter, they decided to place the hospital next to the castle compound, but just across the road that ran east-west across the southern edge of Plateau Grado and the spaceport. Amy didn't want to take more land from the spaceport nor did she want to purchase existing homes and businesses nearby.

Across the road, a jagged mountain rose up. Its peak was four thousand feet higher than the plateau, and Governor Katrina volunteered the use of her Imperium machines to prepare the ground.

During early January while most of Exchange City was mostly snow bound beneath some fifteen feet of snow, the giant machines carved out a niche in the side of the mountain, ending with a granite stone bed five hundred feet square. Queen Amy had Venerado Henry and his five Circles begin construction of the large, stone building. Additionally, Katrina had her drilling machines carve out a tunnel between the Imperial Castle's extensive tunnel system and the new hospital. By spring, the expansive, single story, grey stone hospital was built, though the interior was just stone walls. During the spring, the Wood Workers Guild would then install doorframes and doors. The Furniture Maker's Guild was contracted to provide the furnishings.

Doctor Alex's plans called for two genetics research rooms, fifteen medical treatment rooms, where patients could be kept during the crucial first two weeks of arm regrowth, and fifty recovery rooms, where they could be kept for many more weeks. Additionally, he added two emergency rooms and ten long-term care rooms. Thus, in 1326, Exchange City boasted two hospitals. The one in the city proper housed a pair of normal medical machines, six nurses trained to use them, ten bed rooms, and six Basic Therapy rooms, in addition to living quarters for the two therapy givers and the nurses, along with two domestic staff.

On the eighth of January, Senator Franco and his two wives arrived back on Tierra. Originally from the city of Valen, in the Kingdom of Valen, the one that was run by the guilds, and not the renegade Neuve Valen kingdom, he had left there as a young, unmarried man. Now, he was returning as a married man, but twenty-one and not in his old age. Further, having been forced to be "Sasha" for so many months on top of his own trauma from the terrorist attack on Proxima Prime, he arrived a very confused man of two personae.

In fact, Governor Katrina hardly recognized him, when

he, Sonia, and Sofia, made their careful way down the ramp from the transport ship. She saw a young woman, obviously a terrorist victim, with ankle length, wavy black hair, wearing a tight fitting, sleeveless blue satin gown, and tall heels like her own. Beside him and with an arm around him were two equally young, rather attractive women, with waist length, wavy brown hair and round faces, but definitely alien to Tierra. She also knew all three had their voice boxes removed by the man who had kidnaped them.

"Welcome home Senator Franco. On behalf of all Tierra, we thank you for your many years of service as our senator. We're all deeply saddened by both your kidnaping and for having suffered the terrorist attack. I'm told the doctors will get your arm regrowth process started yet today. Queen Amy will be providing a place for you to stay. It's my honor to accompany you to the Imperial Castle. We've an underground tunnel between here and the castle now, complete with electric cars. It's good to have you back home."

Sasha please, I'm Sasha now. Franco is long gone, he sent to her. *My wives, Sonia and Sofia. I could not abandon them. Oh, King Carlos died a hero, saving us all from a bomb. Let his brother know, will you?*

"Yes, I've already taken care of that notification. Welcome Sonia, Sofia. The first stop is to get you three your new ID cards. You three will have dual citizenship, Tierra and your home world, Sonia. Forgive me, but we don't know Sonia and Sofia's home world."

Bailey-3, but that doesn't matter any longer. It's now a dead world, he replied for them.

An hour later and with their new ID cards dangling from their necks, they were led into Amy's Throne Room. After welcoming them, she had Jan show them to their own private suite. When they arrived, their few possessions were already there waiting for them. The two women quickly unpacked their things, while Sasha sat on a bed watching them.

Doctor Alex arrived shortly, taking them to his medical bay. "Okay, here's how it works, senator, ladies. For the next two weeks, he'll have to lie here on this bed while his arms begin regrowing. They will be very delicate and tiny at first.

After two weeks, you will be moved to a suite nearby and can have limited mobility, as the arm growth progresses. In three months, you'll be able to use them normally, though their full strength will not appear for about a year. During this time, your wives will be right here with you. Okay?" All three nodded. He began the process.

Two weeks passed quickly for the three. Each day, a few of the many hermaphrodite adult children came by to introduce themselves to the three and chat. Slowly, the three learned the names of the thirty other children of the adults Franco had known before he left for the Senate so many years ago. Rafe also saw she had a particularly challenging Basic Therapy with him, or her as she continually insisted.

Once the two-week period was done, life became far easier for the three, because Sasha was able to dress and move around, though in limited amounts. At this point, Rafe began his/her Basic Therapy. That took the better part of a week, made more difficult because Franco could not speak. Instead, Rafe had to maintain constant telepathic contact with him.

I'm so alive now. I can see how I had to suppress that trauma. It was necessary to do so, and it paid off. Thank you, Rafe.

You're most welcome, Franco. It's the least I could do for you after all the service you've given us as our senator.

Sasha please. I'm just going to be Sasha Hermanes now. I look like a woman in all ways, and it's not going to change, unless our doctors have some new giant breakthrough. My wives love me as I am. Who could possibly ask for more? So it's Sasha from now on.

Sasha it is! Now with the good doctor's permission, let's get you next door to Elegant Fashions Inc and get you three the wardrobe of your choice. Lilly and Nita want to see you three have at least a dozen outfits.

Four hours later, the three had picked out their new dresses. At first, Nita was rather surprise that Sasha wanted to keep her very long hair and to dress as a woman. But then, she soon realized why and catered to their desires. After all, this genetic mutation was hardest on the men, she knew from past experiences.

Once their apparel was handled, Queen Amy visited the three to discuss where they would live once the doctors released Sasha later in the early spring. "I've transferred your bank account to Tierra, well to the spaceport at least. You have about a half million credits, though more may be coming if the Senate ever meets and doles out the funds for the Proxima Prime survivors. You can live anywhere you desire."

A small home at the edge of Exchange City where we can see the grasslands and the valley is all we desire.

"I'll see to it. Your new home will be waiting for you just as soon as the doctors release you, Sasha," Amy promised and later delivered.

After she left, Rafaela came by. *Sasha, I would like to give your two wives a very special gift. Would you object if I gave them the mentales gifts? Then, they would have a way to communicate with you and others.*

Sasha looked up, quite startled. *Is that even possible? Yes, yes, that would be a Holy Miracle. Please, if you can do such a thing, do it!*

When Doctor Alex finally released Sasha, both Sonia and Sofia had received their *mentales* gifts, their tower training, and their own personal germanium crystals. Both women had telekinesis as their major skill, due in part to having seen so many other victims of the genetic mutations. Further, both were pregnant. Sonia was due the middle of July, Sofia, the middle of September. Doctor Ruth was particularly interested in these two pregnancies. Until now, most all the hermaphrodites had interbred. In this case, the two women were normal. How would the genes work in the mixed marriages? She hoped to learn more about how the awful genetic mutations worked.

On Winno-3, Linda and Rael were pleased to hear they were accepted into Queen Altha's queen training pool, along with one other young woman from Winno-3. Gladly, they finished their semester's work and took a Leave of Absence from the Academy there. Early December 1325, they underwent their body modifications. While both were used to wearing toe shoes, neither really desired to have to go back to wearing them. Walking was so treacherous. However, the loss of their arms gave them both quite a shock. They awoke from their surgery as helpless as all the many victims they'd seen around Tierra. Now, walking was more than a little scary, but they were determined to see this through.

Each was assigned a Personal Assistant, who was unable to speak, but was able to handle their physical needs, and to write and take notes for them. After the frightening first few days, they both threw themselves into learning the Ataro judicial technology. Quickly, they both progressed rapidly, having seen firsthand Amy using many of these techniques. The pair also discovered that being so completely helpless allowed them to focus all their attention onto their studies, without any distractions.

"No more late night pizza parties for us," Linda commented. "I can't even use the comm system to call them up."

"And I can't get any credits out of my purse to pay the delivery man. I think all we really can do now is study," Rael replied. "Let's dive into this stuff." That the two did, progressing rapidly.

Three of the flaming red haired men from Aquila Prime tackled the most pressing problems facing Nadja's school: a lack of textbooks. Backus Acronis was a civil engineer; Nikola Stratos was a general engineer, and Priamos Leukos was a mechanical engineer. Well, they were almost engineers, and would have been, had they graduated this year instead of becoming terrorist victims, like everyone else on Aquila Prime. With their arms restored, they set to work on this pressing problem. It was a bit more complicated than just textbooks. First, there were no paper plants on Tierra. Paper sheets were made by hand primarily from sawdust and wooden presses, far too slow a process to meet the perceived demand for pages. Second, there were no printing presses, and no electricity to run modern ones, if they could be imported, which they couldn't. Third, all books were hand copied and bound by hand. While these were usually of top quality, they could not be made in sufficient quantities and had the liability of transcription errors. Fourth, inks were also made by hand.

"Look fellows, we need to approach this from the very beginning. We need mechanical sawmills that can produce sawdust in quantity and swiftly," Nikola re-oriented them.

"He's right. That will also allow them to make boards far more rapidly and smoother cuts as well. Kill two birds with one stone," Backus pointed out.

Priamos added, "We can't use electricity to power the saw, but we can use water — rivers specifically. So we're going to have to invent sawmills powered by streams. That's got to come first."

Nikola continued, "Right. Then, we need to develop a paper manufacturing machine. Only then can we move onto the actual printing presses and type setting. So let's get cracking. Design us a water powered sawmill." The three set to work.

An hour later, Nikola commented, "Say, this is challenging and a whole lot of fun — trying to build a sawmill out of primitive methods. Cool, guys!"

"I think we need to build a working model to use to demonstrate to the guild masters how it'll work," Backus pointed out.

"We can't use metal gears in this thing. Iron is too expensive. We have to substitute wood where possible. Back to the designing boards," Priamos corrected one of their assumptions.

So it went with the three. By February, they had the designs finished and set to work on building their small scale model. By March, that was finished to their satisfaction, but would it work? After extensive testing consisting of pouring water over the water wheel that then drove the gearing mechanisms that spun the saw blade rapidly, they knew some modifications were needed. By May, they had perfected their model and were ready to sell it to those who would build it.

In Madiera, the nearly one thousand refuges quickly learned to use the many bots. Alpha reprogrammed the door bots and others to respond to the Imperium Standard, as modified by their lack of lips. None of these wore the lip plates.

255

Rafe had decided it was far too dangerous and complicated to have them wear the disks, since there were almost no assistants around with hands, and the bots could not insert nor remove them. These men, women, and children adapted nicely to the mechanical arms, operated by their feet, allowing them to feed themselves, to pick up things, and to carry them from place to place. That the women could even manage to cook a meal in the automated kitchens brought a sense of hope to everyone. However, with everyone having long hair, the hair dressing bots and electrostatic hair bots were particularly prized.

Rafe allowed them to have three weeks to learn to adapt and make use of the bots before embarking on her massive therapy project. After the learning period was over, she assembled everyone in the town square. "Okay everyone, as it currently stands, our doctors will be regrowing everyone's arms. However, due to their limited facilities, they tell me that it'll take about eight years to get everyone here finished up. In the meantime, I want to start giving you my Basic Therapy sessions. After you have had yours, I would like you to consider learning how to deliver it, and then lend me a hand in delivering it to everyone else."

"I'm bringing in twenty others who know how to do it. Between them, Rafaela, and me, we'll get to twenty-two of you at one time. We anticipate roughly a week per person. Some take longer; some, less. Time is of no importance; we have all the time in the world. Still, if no one who has had it wants to learn how to deliver it and to help us, we expect to have everyone done in less than a year. However, as soon as the doctors are ready for some of you, we'll let you get that process started."

"Basic Therapy handles any and all painful emotional trauma that a person has suffered, as well as any painful and unconscious incidents, such as breaking an arm or leg or even getting knocked out. It is very easy for you, as patients, to do. You'll remember everything that's done to you in therapy. It's not hypnosis, not remotely. We've used it on thousands here on Tierra already. Everyone who has had it simply raves about its benefits. Okay then, let's get going. I've a list of everyone's

256

names. When your name is called, waggle your head, and your therapy giver will come to you."

As the weeks passed, Rafe was not far off on her time estimates. Roughly, a week of intensive sessions usually handled each of them. Why? These were all young people, generally between about fifteen and twenty-five. Beyond this horrible genetic mutation, few had any real disasters befall them, other than the occasional broken limb as a child. Yes, all had rather terrific amounts of emotional charge and trauma surrounding their terrorist attack and subsequent days. Most of the first few days of therapy ended up being a slug-slug through the attack period. After that, a few childhood experiences arose, and then uniformly birth appeared and was run. Prenatal injuries were rather easily found after that. Of course, the real revelations were the past life incidents that invariably arose, as the person neared completion of their Basic Therapy.

The final products were all the advertisement that Rafe needed. The first twenty-two who finished up simply raved about Basic Therapy. Over half wanted to learn how to do it, much to Rafe's pleasure. As the days passed, those, who hadn't at first, now volunteered to learn as well. Week by week, the process began to mushroom, just as it had so long ago with all the mermaids, the Daughters of the Sea. By late spring, all one thousand plus had received their Basic Therapy, nearly three-quarters of a year ahead of Rafe's original pessimistic projection.

Now, she and Amy had further decisions to make. Most of these victims were quite bright and well educated. Many had just the skills that, if utilized, could well make a huge difference in the modernization of Tierra. Yet, Rafe wanted them to continue to deliver her Basic Therapy broadly to all the inhabitants of Tierra. The two goals were basically in opposition to each other. These new people could be used to push therapy forward or they could be used to push technological improvement across Tierra forward. Both were equally valid and worthwhile goals. This would be a tough choice. However, Queen Amy's primary concern was that these hermaphrodites simply had to be seen as making a very valuable contribution to Tierra. The Supreme Guild Masters had to see proof positive that these men and women were valuable additions to Tierra and not helpless aliens to be shunned because of their strange physical forms.

In April, Amy and Rafe reached a compromise. As each person had their arms regrown, they were given a choice: apply their education to Tierra or continue to deliver Basic Therapy to the people of Tierra. As one by one they made their choices, the results were about fifty-fifty. However at this time, only thirty of the one thousand had their arms regrown and had made their choices. That was about to change too.

During January 1326, Legate Smith had the two critical backup server farms moved to Winno-3. By March, they were back up and running in parallel with the main servers on Proxima Prime. Both the Legate and the Emperor breathed a huge sigh of relief once they became operational. Why? Things were not looking up on Proxima Prime.

During January, some worlds did send new senators and some bureaucratic replacement men and women, along with their families. Two hundred senators did not a quorum make, much to everyone's displeasure. Still Legate Smith had them studying the existing laws and procedures, preparing them for the future.

Even more troublesome, a general from Alpha Zepheus-3 deserted from the Imperium fleet, taking his battleship, two heavy cruisers, and five light cruisers with him. He did allow those crewmembers not from Alpha Zepheus-3 to disembark on other worlds. Alpha Zepheus-3 then declared itself independent of the Imperium. This world was located within the middle of the spiral arm, but quite some distance from the Ataro System. Still, Emperor Kino grew worried.

General Stalock was furious, demanding to be allowed to go there and retake the Imperium ships by force if necessary. Legate Smith found herself plopped into the middle of a potentially explosive situation. If she did nothing, that would encourage other defections, which could well rapidly spread to many worlds, resulting in the total collapse of the

Imperium. If she allowed the use of military force in an attempt to retake the ships, she would be starting a war with Alpha Zepheus-3, and in all likelihood, the stolen ships would be destroyed along with others of the Imperium. Perhaps, such would bring other worlds that saw themselves as allies to join in. She was in one of the proverbial catch-22 situations. No matter what route she took, disaster was likely to follow. That the press continued to exploit this story hourly didn't help in the slightest. She had half a notion to start censoring the press, but rejected doing so.

She and the Emperor had a lengthy discussion about this potentially explosive situation. "Look, I don't see any way to not avoid going there and directly discussing this with their rulers," Legate Smith concluded.

"As much as I regret it, I don't see any other way either. It will be quite risky for you, Legate. I'll send along one of my queens as well. Between the two of you, perhaps you can talk some sense into their rulers, before it's too late."

"Okay, I'll send them word of our arrival and bring my battleship to Winno-3. We can meet up there and go over our strategies, before making landfall on Alpha Zepheus-3," she replied.

The next day, she made the call and talked to their President Zargnoot III. He insisted they arrive by transport. "Bring your battleship, and we'll open fire, taking that as an act of war," he declared quite belligerently. The Legate had no choice but to agree to his terms, knowing she was placing herself in dire jeopardy.

General Stalock fumed, but made arrangements to have his battleship and five others standing by in hyperspace, mere seconds from being in position to attack Alpha Zepheus-3. "Look, if you don't check in with me every hour on the hour, I'll take that as trouble. My fleet will drop out of hyperspace, all guns blazing. Take my offer or you don't go." She took it.

The two worked out how she could provide the periodic signal. One of the ship's computer programmers wrote a simple program, and put it on her laptop. She was currently controlling her laptop via voice commands in her own native language of Descartes-3, not IS. Her dangling lips prevented making a number of sounds, specifically the bilabial sound made by the lips. Her own language was one of the rare click languages. A number of women on her world also wore lip plates, though smaller than these foot-in-diameter monsters. Her real name was actually ^Markarita ^Ya^maita^motia, where the ^ represented a type of clicking sound. Hence, her computer vocal program was programmed to respond to her click language commands. The special program was sensitive to a simple double clicking sound, ^^. Whenever she made that sound, the laptop sent a signal that a receiver in the battleship's comm center received. Since the laptop also had the time displayed in one corner, all she had to do was watch the clock and make the ^^ sound periodically, indicating all was well. The signal would be relayed to the transport, and from there to the battleship in hyperspace. If she failed to make the notification, then she was in trouble, and the general would react at once.

A day later, her transport set down at the spaceport of Kronos City, the capital of Alpha Zepheus-3. She and Helene had been joined by Queen Pepper and her assistant, Sali. The two hashed over tactics during the flight. Each of their assistants carried their laptops for them. Legate Smith thought this was a doomed meeting. Two helpless women were about to confront the rulers, who had just more or less seceded from the Imperium. Talk about pathetic, Mary thought, but didn't say anything. *I must focus on the facts,* she told herself, as she felt the transport touch down.

A dozen soldiers wearing full battle armor met them. It was all the Legate could do partially to suppress a laugh at the incongruity of it all. Perhaps, the leaders wanted to cow her, what with her being so helpless now. Trying hard to keep from laughing, Legate Mary Smith followed the men, though purposely going slow enough for Queen Pepper to keep up. The poor woman was forced to wear the awful toe shoes. She involuntarily recalled how next to impossible it had been for her to walk in them, and she felt a pang of pity for this queen.

Queen Pepper was probably in her mid-thirties, Mary guessed. It wasn't polite to make such an inquiry of a woman. Her hair was golden and quite wavy and full, draped over her shoulders and the sides of her oval face. Mary wouldn't call Pepper particularly attractive; certainly, a face full of freckles didn't help. She wondered why Pepper had not undergone the medical procedure to have them removed. She remembered to say, "^^."

Before long, they were ushered into an underground bunker that the Legate presumed was a bombproof facility. At least, they took an elevator down, saving her and Pepper from having to take a stairs, which was always now an utter nightmare. Mary couldn't see her feet over her massive bosom. They entered a sterile, white room. The walls were concrete and steel. A pair of tables and chairs faced each other, but one table and chairs were raised about a foot above the other. Legate Smith moved immediately to the lower table, knowing what the differing heights meant, a not so subtle hint of one's place at the meeting.

Helene helped her sit, while Sali arranged Pepper's hair and helped her sit gracefully. Both assistants then opened up the laptops. While Sali needed to operate Pepper's, Legate Smith ran hers herself. She expected the leaders would make them wait a bit, again a hint as to just who held the power at this meeting. She was not disappointed.

Fifteen minutes later, four men entered. One was clearly a general from his uniform. Two looked like advisors. President Zargnoot III was obvious; he led the small procession. In a way, Legate Smith thought he was rather comical. He was short by all Imperium standards for men. She estimated perhaps five-five at most. He wore a tall, black stovepipe hat, greatly exaggerating his physical height. A black man, he had overly oiled black hair and a large moustache. His eyes were a striking blue, as were many of the men of Alpha Zepheus-3. After sitting across from her table, the President appeared somewhat taller than she and Pepper did. An aide announced, "President Zargnoot III."

"Legate Mary Smith, Queen Pepper. Our Personal Assistants. Shall we begin, Mr. President?"

"Yes, though I don't see any reason for this visit. I've already made our position quite explicitly clear. It's obvious the Imperium is no more, gone in the wind, as is our saying here on Alpha Zepheus-3. Our world has pumped untold credits into the Imperium coffers all these centuries. Now that it's gone, I owe it to our people at least to salvage something from all their hard-earned tax credits. My general here did just that. Now, we can protect ourselves from our neighbors, if need be. Let me caution you, if you should try to take back the ships that are rightfully ours, we'll fight to the death. Plus, we have several allied worlds who will not hesitate to send their ships into the fray, just as we would if they were attacked." He seemed finished and overly proud of his definitive statements.

Legate Smith began to unravel his basic assumptions. "First, Mr. President, the Imperium is not dead. Far from it. Already many worlds are sending replacement senators and new bureaucrats to Proxima Prime. Everyone understands just how difficult it has been for most worlds to have suddenly to elect new senators to represent their worlds. No one will suggest these are not trying times, however. Certainly not I. As you can see, I too am a victim of the latest round of planetary genocides."

"I assure you the Imperium is far from gone in the wind. Second, Mr. President, you are absolutely correct about Alpha Zepheus-3 having a legal claim. It is clearly pointed out in every world's formal recognition papers, duly signed and sworn to, when that world officially joined the Imperium."

President Zargnoot III interrupted her. "So, I can see no point in holding this meeting. Obviously, we have the right to secede and to retrieve something to recompense us for our centuries of taxation."

"Mr. President, you are perfectly within your rights as a member world of the Imperium to do just that. However, I've come here today to discuss this with you."

"What's the point," he again interrupted her. "You've just confirmed what we already know. We are within our rights."

"Of course you are, Mr. President. However, as acting head of the Imperium until the newly reconstituted Senate exercises their obligation to elect a new temporary President, it is my responsibility to attempt to prevent you from making a terribly blunder, one that will cost your people dearly."

"Idle threats, Legate Smith. Like I said, we have a lot of allies who will help us fight to defend what's ours," he spat out argumentatively.

"On the contrary, Mr. President. I don't mean to suggest the Imperium will attack you or the ships that you've confiscated. Hardly. No, I am here to keep you from making a huge financial blunder. Will you allow me to explain more fully?" she said politely, adding a "^^."

"Financial blunder? What are you talking about, Legate," he spat, but with a hint of curiosity. She knew she had him now.

"You see, one of the first actions that the Senate must address, once it has done its constitutional duties to elect a new President and Senate President, is to address the equitable division of property and possessions that have been lost on Proxima Prime, Zelan-3, Beta Carnae-4, Zeta-3, Longditch-4, and Bailey-3. All six worlds, as you know, have lost almost all their populations. All their real estate, treasury funds, and possessions will have to be equitably divided among the remaining worlds, though some of those credits will have to go to the surviving victims to provide for their long-term care at assisted living quarters. At this time, I don't have an accurate estimate of the total monetary value of those six worlds, but as soon as Legate Marhildt Chyldt, the Minister of Finance, returns to active duty that will be his first action. He'll then see to an equitable disbursement of said property and funds."

"While I don't have such an estimate at this time, surely you can see that the sum total is an enormous amount, considering these six worlds were perhaps the most populous within the Imperium. You see, the legal share that Alpha Zepheus-3 would be entitled to, if you were still a member of the Imperium, vastly exceeds the value of the few ships that you've tentatively taken as your share. My guess is between ten and a hundred thousand fold difference, but again, we must wait for Legate Marhildt's accurate accounting to know precisely. In all honesty, Mr. President, I simply would not be doing my job properly if I failed to come here and discuss this with you. The press would certainly insinuate that I was cheating Alpha Zepheus-3 out of hundreds of billions of credits that should rightfully be yours."

She finished up by adding, "So before I leave, I must have a video of you formally stating that you are giving up your world's legal rights to the untold billions of credits due you, in return for the few spaceships that you've taken. That way, I'll be able to prove to everyone that just because I'm a helpless woman now, I've not failed in my duties and obligations to the member worlds of the Imperium. You can understand my position, I'm sure."

President Zargnoot III looked completely shocked. She'd hit him where it hurt, financially. "But we had no idea of this distribution of the six world's property and funds."

"No, of course, you didn't. I have first to get the Senate reconstituted; Legate Marhildt needs time to properly assess the assets, and only then can the Senate see to the equitable distribution of said assets. Considering the unprecedented magnitude of the problem, considerable time will be needed for a thorough, accurate, and fair job to be done. Honestly, it's enormous. I don't envy Legate Marhildt's task!"

She went on, "You see, for the moment, it's my obligation to protect all the assets of these six destroyed worlds. I'm also responsible for protecting every member world's constitutional rights to said assets. I simply couldn't sit there on Proxima Prime, Mr. President, and see Alpha Zepheus-3 make such a gigantic blunder. I know other worlds are cheering you onwards. But look, they have a vested interest in seeing you secede. That will ultimately give them your giant share of the assets, when they can finally be divided up. I'm sure you don't want your neighboring worlds to legally take your huge share of the assets." She had played him perfectly, though she could no longer smile. At least, she didn't have to conceal her facial expressions any longer. Her lip loops just dangled below her chin, hiding all such expressions.

"I see. We were not aware of this aspect. Perhaps, a small mistake has occurred that could be put right?" he hinted, probing for a way to undo what they'd done.

"Oh yes, most definitely. I've not signed your secession papers, not without getting your agreement to forgo your billions of credits later on. The press would have been all over me for gypping Alpha Zephus-3 out of its due inheritance, you see. So really, unless you've destroyed the ships, nothing has really happened, has it?"

"I see. No, the ships are fine. Just here to give the men from our world a needed shore leave," the President wiggled for position.

"Precisely," Legate Smith followed up on his hint. "What with all the nasty work of removing so many dead from Proxima Prime, the valiant soldiers do need some shore leave. I should have seen that for myself and so ordered it for all the fleet." She added another, "^^," as though it was a nervous habit of hers.

The President smiled and visibly relaxed. Now, it was Queen Pepper's turn. "Mr. President, I'm here on behalf of Emperor Kino Sango. He feels a certain kinship with all the other worlds out here in the middle of the spiral arm. We need to stick together against the large block of hub worlds, which, as you know, try to dominate the policies of the Imperium. Anyway, he was most concerned that someone was working in an underhanded way to gyp your world out of its legal inheritance or to even get the Imperium to go to war with you."

"Well, of course, we mid-arm worlds do need to stick together. Everyone knows that the hub worlds always try to dominate everything," he generalized.

"Exactly. Might I ask who first suggested to you the Imperium had collapsed, and that you should attempt to take some of the fleet which is commanded by your soldiers as your rightful inheritance?" Pepper asked demurely.

"Well, the destruction of the Big Five was all over the news," he responded. "Pretty obvious that something was collapsing."

"True, but surely someone suggested secession to you," Pepper persisted.

"Well, I guess it was my aide here, Mr. Jackson. Didn't you present this to us in a special session?" the President turned to the man on his right.

"Well, yes I certainly did, but. . ." His flustered face

shown crimson.

Queen Pepper deftly added, "But someone so informed you?"

"Why yes, yes, he did. James Bertolini sent me a complete dossier on the whole situation. The document showed the relevant sections of our Imperium Contract — how we're entitled to our share if and when the Imperium dissolved. In it, he also pointed out that our general here was commanding a battleship and that our crews manned several other cruisers. Mr. President, you remember me showing you that document at that emergency meeting, right?"

"Well, I believe so, Mr. Jackson," the President sounded a bit confused, not at all certain where all this was heading.

"Ah, James Bertolini. Give us a moment, please." Queen Pepper nodded to her silent assistant who typed away on her laptop. Shortly thereafter, she had to enter Queen Pepper's top secret clearance code. Finally, the data appeared on her screen, but only after an awkward silence. There was a thirty second comm delay between here and her world and the Ataro System servers there.

"Oh my goodness," Queen Pepper looked extremely worried, as if she'd just discovered some deep dark secret, which, in fact, she just had. That she knew someone had to be behind this whole mess was a certainty, but until the data appeared on her screen, she didn't know who.

"What is it?" the President asked, growing even more worried simply because Queen Pepper looked so taken aback and startled. Legate Smith stifled a grin; Pepper was playing him brilliantly.

"Could you please turn my laptop so they can see the screen?" Queen Pepper asked her assistant. "Gentlemen, I've tapped into the Ataro Empire's database of — well, see for yourselves."

The four men read: James Bertolini, an alias for Jan Becktold, is a known spy for the Treggor-4 system. He is suspected of infiltrating the command structure of five arm worlds. He is tied to the theft of a bio agent cylinder, but his involvement has not yet been proven. Considered to be an extremely dangerous spy. Current location: unknown.

"Damn!" President Zargnoot III exclaimed. "General, have this James Bertolini or whoever he claims to be arrested immediately. How could this happen?"

"Yes, Mr. President!" the general barked. He rose and barked some orders into his handheld device, then returned to his seat.

"I am sorry. It looks like we were victims of that spy! Treggor-4 is one of our enemies, you see. We've been betrayed!" President Zargnoot III exclaimed rather vociferously.

Legate Smith interceded, smoothing this development over. "No one else besides us needs to know about this, Mr. President. As far as I am concerned, Alpha Zepheus-3 has never seceded from the Imperium. People have merely misunderstood the reason the battleship and cruisers are here — that is, the simple fact our brave soldiers needed shore leave after cleaning up the terrible, ghastly mess on Proxima Prime. I should take some of the blame for not having ordered shore leave for all those who did the work on Proxima Prime."

The relief on all four men's faces was quite clear. "Yes, of course. We should perhaps hold a news conference and explain this misunderstanding about the shore leave, Legate Smith. If you are willing, I will arrange it at once."

"Yes, that would be ideal, Mr. President," she replied.

Less than an hour later, Legate Smith, President Zargnoot III, and Queen Pepper stood before another wall of video cameras and reporters. Legate Smith spoke first, "Thank you all for coming to our news conference on such short notice. President Zargnoot III and I would like to clear up a widespread misunderstanding or misinterpretation of some recent actions. As you know, I have used many of our brave soldiers in the large Imperium fleet to remove the deceased from Proxima Prime. Honestly, it was a ghastly operation. I failed to see that our men needed some shore leave after having dealt with that awful situation. Fortunately, President Zargnoot III realized the soldiers from Alpha Zepheus-3 were in dire need of shore leave. Consequently, he asked them here for just that purpose."

She went on, "Somehow shore leave for our brave

soldiers of the fleet has been twisted into all manner of wild speculations, such as Alpha Zepheus-3 was seceding from the Imperium. I know. That sounds utterly crazy. For centuries, Alpha Zepheus-3 has been an integral part of the Imperium. And rightly so, this is a fine, brave, honest world. In this matter, I must accept some of the blame for not realizing just how badly these men needed shore leave after dealing with the grizzliest scene in our history, that is, until now and the Big Five worlds, which are still under quarantine. The bio agents are still active there, making it wholly unsafe for anyone to touch down without wearing a bio containment suit. As soon as I get back to Proxima Prime, thanks to President Zargnoot III's lead, I will endeavor to instigate fleet-wide shore leaves for our brave men in uniform. Mr. President, would you like to add anything?" she turned the conference over to him.

Smiling broadly, he spoke firmly. "Yes, Legate Mary Smith is precisely correct. The work that our soldiers performed on Proxima Prime was just hideous. I can't imagine how awful that was for them. I asked General Hanks here if his men needed a break. He concurred, especially since his ships were finished with that assignment and merely standing by indefinitely. Somehow, all this has been blown all out of proportion. I assure you Alpha Zepheus-3 has always and will continue to be an active member of our great Imperium. Further, I would like to take this opportunity to nudge our Senate to hurry up and elect our ten new senators and get them off to the Imperium Senate pronto. We have an enormous amount of work that must be done, and none of it can begin until the Senate acts." He rattled on for a few more minutes, before taking questions.

"What is Queen Pepper of the Ataro System doing here? What is her role in all this?" one reported shouted above the others.

She stepped forward. "This is rather embarrassing for Legate Smith. As you know, she was a recent victim of the massive bio attacks on the Big Five. She is unused to her physical handicaps. So I volunteered to come along with her for moral support. Please, you must understand just how hard this is for her. She's graciously agreed to continue working until the other five Legates have recovered their arms and abilities to work more easily."

Legate Smith wanted to laugh. Since when has any leader had public sympathy for their physical handicaps, she thought. Another reporter shouted, "But we had a press release stating the Alpha Zepheus-3 had seceded from the Imperium. That the Imperium was dead or dying."

"More misunderstandings by our junior staff who jumped to the wrong conclusions about the shore leaves," the President fielded that one. "I'll see that he's trounced upon."

Another shouted, "Legate Smith, isn't the Imperium collapsing? Hasn't it crumbled already?"

"Oh don't be so silly and sensational. Of course, it isn't dead. Look, no one will deny we've had the worst possible tragedy on Proxima Prime. A hundred billion men, women, and children perished. Of course, that's quite a blow. No one in their right mind would say differently. Yes, it takes time to replace over two thousand senators and a billion executive and legislative support personnel. But with the dedication of your President here and a thousand others, the task of rebuilding the executive and legislative offices on Proxima Prime is being done. Please, give us time to grieve for the loss of so many people and to rebuild. Personally, I'm thankful this didn't happen during the war years. Then, we could well be facing extinction, but not now in this time of peace and growing prosperity," Legate Smith finished and stepped back.

The President fielded several more rather insignificant questions and ended the conference. He thanked the Legate and queen profusely, and personally escorted them to their transport, promising the battleship would return to service within two days.

Shortly after that, they were again on board their battleship. As Queen Pepper prepared to depart in her shuttle, she commented, "Well, that was sure easy. He handed me the third party, who incited the whole affair, on a silver platter."

"So you knew about the spy beforehand?" Legate Smith asked.

"Not specifically, no. You see, for any conflict to come to blows, like this one very nearly did, there simply must be a hidden from view, third person, who, working behind the scenes, is actively promoting and creating the hostility that the President displayed. Such is irrevocably always the case. It is a Natural Human Interaction Law, as natural as the fact that we have to breathe in order to live. You know, you were brilliant too. When you retire from your position, you are welcome to come to the Ataro System and study to become a queen yourself, if you are interested. We have much that we can teach you."

Legate Smith laughed. "No thanks. I truly want my arms back. I could only just barely walk in those toe shoes you have to wear. Thanks for offering. I'll think about it."

"Excellent. That's all I ask; think about it. Honestly, once you get used to the physical limitations, it's not so bad. We always have our Personal Assistants at our sides. Well, goodbye for now and thanks." Legate Smith watched Queen Pepper and her assistant making their slow way down the hall and into the air lock that led to her transport. She shook her head and thought, no way!

A half hour later and while in hyperspace heading for home, Emperor Kino called to congratulate her. He also commented, "Legate Smith, I suspect we'll see many more such incidents before this is all over. Be prepared. Over and out."

God, I hope not! She thought to herself. *I'm too helpless to do this much longer.*

Chapter 14 Reaction and Action

Early February 1326, the heavy cruiser Dauntless hovered over Bailey-3. Earlier, it had been enforcing the quarantine, as other cruisers were doing on the other four worlds of the Big Five. Weekly, drones were sent down, sampling the air and reporting on the levels of the terrible bio genetic agent. These worlds had received a massive dose of the genetic mutation aerosol. While the active ingredients had become inert after a week, the chemical bindings took far longer to dissipate fully. Legate Smith demanded all safety protocols be strictly enforced. She didn't want more accidental victims. Play it safe, she had said repeatedly. Beside, everyone knew there would be no rescue operations on these five worlds as there had been on Proxima Prime. All available assisted living complexes on the many other worlds of the Imperium were at or beyond capacity. There was simply no place to put any of these victims. Cruel as it seemed, there wasn't any other option available, but to allow them to die, one way or another.

Sometime ago, Major Smythe had received top level orders from the Legate herself to confiscate the dozen special medical machines located on Bailey-3, the ones that regrew arms. Once recovered, they were to be shipped to Ashford-5. While the thirty-five year old major had no idea why they were to be sent to the end of the universe, he would obey his orders.

During their many weeks in orbit over the once populous Bailey-3, he'd begun using the new IR Imaging Camera. Essentially, from orbit, it took infrared images of the world below. Anything emitting infrared energies appeared in red on his giant monitor. Nuclear power plants were brilliantly illuminated, as were other facilities. Even water heaters within skyscrapers were visible. None of these concerned the major and his staff, who were also keenly interesting in this new technology. Why? It allowed them to see people and watch their movements while the ship was in a high orbit above the planet below.

In warfare, the IR Imaging Camera would be invaluable

for coordinating ground attacks. Although he didn't know it, the camera was developed on a much smaller scale by research scientists working within the Bops on Proxima Prime. They, of course, used it for coordinating their own raids on criminals, allowing them to monitor continually the positions of the enemy men.

Major Smythe and his staff were testing it out, sort of a field test, here on Bailey-3. They could either playback the single images as a sort of movie of what was happening at one location or they could superimpose one image over another. Either way, they could detect the deaths of the people on the ground far below them. That is, yesterday a red form was visible, and today's overlay was dark where the person had been. The video-like images worked better, showing the limited motion of the people down there, along with their "winking out," as they died.

When they first arrived a day after the massive attack, their monitors were filled with red images, so many that they were uncountable. As the days turned into weeks, the mass of red forms receded dramatically. As February came, there were only a very few red forms still visible that were human bodies.

He had the rough initial numbers of Bailey-3: thirty-six billion, five hundred ten million, sixty-three thousand, four hundred ten people. This world was somewhat unusual in that it had six continents, all about the same total area. As Bailey-3's population grew over the centuries, five of the six continents slowly merged into five continent-wide cities, somewhat akin to Proxima Prime. It was in these five giant cities that the vast majority of the nearly thirty-seven billion had lived in tall skyscrapers, modeled like all other Imperium standard buildings. In a way, Bailey-3 saw itself as a miniature Proxima Prime. By early February, the IR Imaging Camera showed very few red human forms over these five continent-cities. It was in these cities that the dozen medical machines were located.

With the final all clear signals from the drones, Major Smythe began making preparations for landing parties to go down, locate, and retrieve the many medical machines and associated supplies. However, the sixth continent continued to attract his keen interest. He knew this lone continent was still primarily farmland. Down there in giant commercial farms, great automated machinery handled the growing and preparation of food that supplied the billions, along with the seafood refineries along the coasts of the five metal continents. So essentially, this sixth continent was comparatively sparsely populated and by farmers and mechanics, all located in small settlements of a few thousand each. Perhaps as many as two million lived here when the attacks came.

With their fancy new IR Imaging Camera, this continent was monitored, but initially nowhere near as much as the other five. However, in February, that changed. "This can't be. Something must be going wrong with the new IR system. Run complete diagnostics immediately," Major Smythe ordered. He was seeing large numbers of red human forms down there. This had to be a gross malfunction of their new technology. There were perhaps a few hundred red forms on the other five continents combined, precisely what high command had expected. These victims were completely helpless and would soon perish, either by taking a bad fall, by lack of water, or lack of food, if they didn't die during the mutation process. On the daytime side, over half had died before even waking from their comas. Why? They were fully dressed and going about their jobs when the attack came. Their clothes prevented their bodies from fully mutating according to the genetic codes. Unable to expand normally, the ever-swelling breasts often compressed the rib cage, killing the person while they were still in the coma.

The IR camera proved the working theories on the five populous continents. Barely a few hundred survived, but were likely to succumb, given a few more days. However, the sixth continent was somehow anomalous. There were simply too many red human forms to count. Obviously, something was very wrong with the equipment. He hovered over the two technicians, who literally tore the device apart looking for the trouble. "Sir, we've found nothing wrong with it, but maybe we fixed it by taking it apart. You know; loose connections are common," one suggested. The major doubted that, but allowed them to fire it up.

Soon, they were once more staring at the images on the big screen. "Crap. Red forms all over the place. You can see the small towns clearly. Something is obviously wrong here," Major Smythe barked. He had no choice but to send down an unmanned drone that would send back streaming video of what it saw. An hour later, Major Smythe put in a secure call to Legate Mary Smith.

"Major Smythe of the heavy cruiser Dauntless here, in orbit over Bailey-3. Sample drones have finally given us the all clear signals. The five heavily populated continents are showing a few hundred or so humans still alive, widely scattered across those continents. However, we are also observing a wild anomaly on the sixth one. That's their agricultural continent, originally with maybe two million scattered across about two thousand small settlements. As I understand it, these people are the farmers and mechanics who tend the giant agricultural fields. The anomaly is that there are still at least half of them still alive! Millions! We are detecting a small amount of movement as well. Please advise on the proper course of action that we're to take. Over."

"Oh Hell! This isn't supposed to be happening. How can they possibly still be alive after a month? Okay, schedule a video drone fly over during their mid-day. Let's see if we can find out what's going on down there without actually landing. Once someone sets foot among the survivors, they're going to be swamped with pleas for help that we can't give them. Route the video to me as well. Over and out," Legate Smith finished, sat back, and sighed, feeling the biting restriction of her pipe corset. At least her backaches were gone, but she couldn't breathe but shallowly, which annoyed her. Many things were annoying her now. Far too many. She refused to consider she was completely helpless, dependent wholly on Helene. If she did, she knew she'd breakdown utterly. Then, she would need one of those head shrinkers, the psych men.

"What in god's name do we do if they are alive and healthy after more than a month?" she asked.

"I surely don't know, Legate," Helene replied. "I don't see how. . ." She hesitated.

"Go ahead and say it, Helene. My feelings won't be hurt.

You don't see how they could possibly be surviving on their own, as helpless as I am."

Helene flushed. "Well, yes. It seems utterly fantastic, so perhaps there is another explanation, like equipment failure or something."

"Ah, another reason. I wonder if the bio agent wasn't spread uniformly over Bailey-3, sparing this sixth continent. It is in the temperate region. Bailey-3's axis of rotation is perpendicular to the plane of its orbit, I see." Legate Smith had brought up the planetary details on her laptop. "That means there are no wild swings in seasonal weather, like on some worlds. It says temperate, constant growing seasons, perfect for continuous agriculture. I'll have to keep that in mind. We can always use excellent agricultural plots. Some of us like to eat real food, not the synthetic stuff. Anyway, Helene, that must be it. The bio agent didn't cover and infect that continent. Well, we shall soon see."

An hour later, both Legate Smith and Helene watched as the streaming video was beamed to her laptop via the comm center on the battleship across hyperspace via the heavy cruiser from the drone flying patterns over the sixth continent of Bailey-3. Both women stared in utter disbelief at what they saw. "My god! Now what in the name of all that's holy do I do now?" Legate Smith whispered, too shocked to say anything louder.

Frog Pond, Demesne Continent, Bailey-3, population: one thousand. The day before the attack. Lord Jim Weathers, twenty-one, felt like he was flying! He'd just proposed to his longtime girlfriend, Ramona Potters, a year younger than he, and she'd accepted his newly purchased ring.

The Demesne Continent was the agricultural breadbasket of Bailey-3 — had been since the dawn of time, by virtue of its continental location, absolutely perfect for farming. Its constant temperate climate was ideal, seldom rising about eighty degrees and never below seventy at night. Rains were constantly periodic, so much so, that one could set one's clock by the thunderstorms, which came every third day, always bringing just the right amount of moisture to the extremely fertile grounds.

Since antiquity, these lands had been divided up into two thousand individual plantations. The ownership of each was hereditary, always passing to the eldest son or nephew if the owner had no sons, something highly frowned upon by all. Take another wife was the solution to too many daughters. Jim's parents, like nearly all other older adults, had taken early retirement into the giant cities, escaping the continual sameness of demesne life. They'd passed the torch, so to speak, to Jim only last year, and now it was past time he marry and begat a son, so one day he too could retire and enjoy the many perks of city life.

Lord Jim controlled all aspects of his plantation known as Frog Pond. No one knew how it got its name, unless it referred to the cattle pond. Each plantation was about two hundred acres, laid out in squares exactly eight miles on a side. The manor or town always sat in the center of the plantation. A single road ran north-south through each town and another ran east-west, thus forming a connecting network of tightly organized plantations, covering all of Demesne Continent, though there were still some stretches of forested hills that had never been turned into farmland, and by legal decree two millennia ago, would never be. Unlike those on Proxima Prime, the rulers of Bailey-3 swore they would never completely cover their world in concrete and steel, though at this time, five of their continents actually were.

Each town or plantation was independent, fiercely so. It's Lord controlled its operation, which these days was a very highly profitable one indeed. A Lord or even a farmhand could easily retire by age forty at the latest. Those in the city paid handsomely for their agricultural products, though much had to be imported from off-world. Either that or eat the synthetic goo that many Imperium worlds ate.

All these farmers had light brown hair and matching skin tones. Likewise, they all had pale blue eyes, always had, as far back as anyone could remember. Each plantation housed around a thousand men, women, and children. Most were less than thirty years old, since by age forty, everyone retired to enjoy the city life. Honestly, there was little to do on these

276

plantations in the way of entertainment, mostly the daily work schedule, of which there was plenty to go around. The older folks taught their younger the needed skills, passing along the knowledge to smoothly run the plantation.

Frog Pond had some chickens and milk cows, though a few plantation folks had pet dogs. The plantation had head lettuce plots, barley fields, wheat, pinto beans, and peas. They alternated the crops, returning to the original one on a specific plot every four years. The animals provided extra fertilizer. Each year, a plantation yielded four crops per plot, on the average.

Great automated machines did most of the work. Essentially constrained to great metal tracks, these mechanical devices plowed a plot, planted it, and cultivated it. Later, the machines harvested the crops, packaging the produce for shipment, while mulching the rest into the soils. Part of the workers of a plantation were skilled maintenance workers, while others were old hands at the actual farming chores. The Lord had to oversee all the plantation work, but also had to be quite skilled at dealing with the various plants and animal's needs and diseases.

Each Lord had four close associates: a Lead Maintenance Engineer, a Crop Specialist, a Secretary, and a Treasurer. Jim's Lead Maintenance Engineer was Jason Bills, twenty-five, though his wife, Rene was nearly as qualified to work on any piece of equipment on the plantation. His fiancé Ramona was his Crop Specialist. Jim's Treasurer, who kept accurate records of the plantation income and each worker's shares, was Betty Fry, twenty-six. She was still single and rather a portly young woman, unafraid openly to speak her mind. She had a hook nose and, as a child, was teased about being bird-like. Keeping track of the plantation's records was Jim's Secretary, Leslie Patterson, twenty-five. She was rather tall and somewhat skinny, a late bloomer many said. She was also shy. The combination had yet to yield her a steady boyfriend. Leslie wasn't too worried about that, since she was only fifteen years from retirement. As a wealthy retiree, she often thought her prospects in the big cities would be much better than the rather slim pickings on the plantation.

Electric cars provided transportation whenever one wished to visit a nearby plantation. Seldom did plantation folk mix, though, because there was just too much work to be done to go gallivanting off to a neighboring plantation. These nearly two million had a strong work ethic.

After proposing, Jim said, "Ramona, next week, we can motor over to Lord Langly's and get married." Another duty of the Lord of a plantation was officially to marry couples.

"Yes, I can't wait," Ramona gushed, giving him another loving kiss. She'd finally snatched Jim. She'd been in love with him since they were children, and at thirteen had set her sights on him. Now, it was coming true at long last.

"Well, it's about time!" Jason teased the two. "She's been making goo goo eyes at you for as long as I can remember." Ramona flushed.

"Seriously, congratulations. Don't let Jason here embarrass you," Rene said, poking him under the table.

"I think it's wonderful you two are finally going to get married. I've predicted you would for nearly three years now. How come it took you so long anyway?" Betty spoke her mind.

Leslie saw their embarrassment and said softly, "I think we should call it a night and go to bed. Give them some private time to enjoy themselves, don't you think?" She was never too confident of her decisions, however. Thankfully, that didn't interfere with her duties as Secretary. Often Betty would tease her. She was never satisfied with locking her ledgers up in her desk. She'd lock it, then test it just to be sure, then test it again, and then once more, just to be sure it really was locked.

Tonight, Betty took Leslie's hint and rose. "Come on you two; let's give them private time. Perhaps you two need it too. I've not seen you have any children yet. Why is that?" she asked of Jason and Rene. Again, speaking what she thought often got her in trouble. Jason glared at her, and she knew she shouldn't have been so blunt about that touchy subject.

Jason bandied, "Like you have a leg to stand on, Betty."

"Oh knock it off you two. I'd rather have a party to celebrate Ramona saying yes. Come, let's pop in a pizza," Jim defused the two.

"I've never said no to a pizza," Betty replied, having

forgotten about Jason's dig. Food always had that effect on her. "I'll get it going. Leslie, you set the table."

Leslie grinned. "Okay. Wait, do we need the white plates with the simple silver edges or should we use the fancy ones with the floral designs, since we are celebrating? What do you think, Ramona?"

"I don't care; you decide," she answered, still clinging lovingly to Jim, while the two walked over to the dining room. As soon as she said that, she wished she hadn't.

"Oh dear, the floral ones would be appropriate, but then they are the really good ones. Maybe we should just use the everyday ones," Leslie replied, unable to decide.

Jim merely said, "Floral, Leslie." She brightened up and set to work.

As they sat around the table waiting on the pizza to get done, Jim commented, "You know, I saw on the news this morning that the Imperium Legate Mary Smith is supposed to come out here to Beta Carnae-4. I wonder why she's going there?"

"Probably to get them to send new senators, I should think," Ramona answered. "I got a call from mom yesterday. Everyone in the city is talking about the senator problem. I agree with her; who would want to risk going to Proxima Prime now? That's just too horrible to even imagine."

Leslie spoke up, "It's like a whole world up and died. At least I think so. So terrible. Did you see pictures of those poor people? I'm glad Bailey's taken some of them. I don't see how they can even live, do you?"

"They have to live in the assisted living complexes. That's what I heard. I suppose that's so. How else could they live?" Rene pointed out. "After all, without their arms and with their feet so malformed, they are so helpless."

"Shoot, even Imperium prosthetic arms are next to useless," Jason added. "Now, if they'd only lost a hand, our fancy mechanical-electrical hands work well or so I heard. But whole arm devices are mostly just a cosmetic add on. They don't do much for the person. Dad once knew a farm hand that lost his arm in an accident. Pulled it right off his shoulder."

Rene attempted to shut him up, "Oh Jason! Do we have

to have such grizzly images now? We're supposed to be celebrating their engagement."

"Oh, I don't mind, Rene," Ramona replied. "My heart goes out to those poor people. But why is the Legate visiting the rats on Beta Carnae-4? You can never trust a Carnae. Everyone knows that."

"Well, I think we have it pretty darn good here in Frog Pond," Betty declared. "Quiet, laid back. Such awful things could never happen here."

Jason added quickly, "And all the real food that you can eat."

Instead of flushing as he'd expected, she agreed, "You bet. Real food, not the synth slime that they call food on the Continents. Ugh, if I had to eat that, I'd be skinnier than Leslie." Everyone laughed.

Just then, a call came in on the community intercom system. Each building had a comm center in one corner of the large living room. The Lord's unit was the main receiver and transmitter to and from the other continents and the other worlds. His unit sent signals out to the other homes, who were dependent upon his set working. "Hey Jim. Lots of satellites in the evening skies over head. Must be twenty of them. Come out and take a look."

The six dashed outside, where hundreds of others were already standing, gazing up into the growing twilight. Indeed, dozens of fast moving lights arced across the skies. "Cool," Leslie exclaimed very much impressed.

"I wonder what those are? Never seen so many at one time. Maybe they are spaceships and not satellites," Rene commented.

"Hey, pizza is up. Come on inside," Betty hollered. They headed back to the dining room. The two pizzas didn't last long. Once done, Leslie put the dirty dishes into the dishwasher and checked the soap levels three times, just to make sure it was set right, before pressing the Start button. Of course, she stuck around a minute longer just to make certain it was going to work, before she headed to her private quarters.

The Lord's manor was often squarely in the center of

the town. The home's shape was that of a small plus sign. The communal living room was shared by four families: the Lord, his Lead Engineer, his Crop Specialist, his Treasurer, and his Secretary, and their families, of course. Each of the four families had their own private quarters in each corner of the building. In the center was also the kitchen and dining room, again shared by the four families that ran the plantation. Frequently, the wives took turns cooking for the group, but normally it was the responsibility of the Lord's wife to cook for the group. In this case, the four women took turns, but Ramona knew once married, that activity would fall on her shoulders.

The other homes in the town were also constructed similarly, allowing four families to more efficiently handle both their work and domestic chores. It had been this way since the founding of the plantations, millennia ago. It had proven to be a most successful decision, and still was, and would be, though no one knew that this fateful evening.

Ramona woke lying next to Jim, fond memories of his proposal drifting through her mind from the night before. Jim's last words still echoed in her mind, "I'll always be here for you." Such comfort had she felt. Now her face itched. No, somehow her face was smothered in her hair. Slowly, her mind changed focus, far slower than normal, as if she were doped up somehow. Like all the other farmers, she kept her hair trimmed short, not touching her shoulders. Around all the machinery, long hair was too dangerous. Its care took too much time away from work. How can my hair be in my face like this? She used her arms to push it out of the way. Her hair didn't move. She tried again. Still nothing. She remembered to open her eyes on the next try. She couldn't see well at all; hair was covering her face. How strange. She tried to push it way. Nothing. Using her arms, she tried to sit up. Her arms weren't there. Her eyes opened wide, and she got her first look at part of her body and all of Jim's. Involuntarily, she shrieked, yelling at the top of her lungs.

Startled by her screams, Jim roused, tried to sit up and push the mat of hair from his face. Nothing happened. As his eyes finally focused, he too screamed loudly. The unthinkable had happened. He heard but didn't register the screams coming from the other three private sections of the home. Vaguely, the sounds of others screaming from nearby homes filtered in through the windows. Jim just screamed, venting his sudden terror.

These were practical people: farmers and engineers. Their screaming quickly died down, turning into fits of sobbing and depression. At last, the calls of nature overrode their shock. "Jim! Help me. I have to pee so bad I can hardly hold it any longer," Ramona cried out pleadingly.

"Me too, but I'm just as helpless as you are. Come on; let's see if we can lean on each other and get to the bathroom. It's just next door," Jim suggested, trying hard to be supportive, knowing it fell far short.

"My feet are so twisted. I can hardly stand," Ramona complained bitterly, all the while wobbling her head and torso in extreme positions trying not to fall. Beside her, Jim was faring no better, perhaps worse. "Maybe if I lean against the wall," she said more to herself than Jim. He saw she was moving a little that way and carefully emulated her motions.

"Look at us; we're helpless freaks! No, I'm a helpless woman now. Oh dear god, I've become a woman," Jim exclaimed. The reality of his physical shape hit him hard. Both more or less ignored that their lips were slit, and their upper and lower lips formed giant loops falling below their chins, leaving their teeth quite visible. No, what finally struck Jim so hard was their hair and breasts.

Their light brown hair hadn't changed color; rather its thickness had doubled and uniformly fell nearly to their ankles. Neither could actually see over their enormous bosoms, unless they leaned their heads over almost as far down as they could bend their heads. What Jim then saw shocked him, but as Ramona finally sat down on the toilet, she too was just as shocked. "Jim! I've got one too. Oh! You've. . ." She flushed and didn't finish her declaration.

"I know. I'm a woman too," he moaned.

"Your voice is still the same," Ramona tried desperately to find something that was still right and unaffected. She hurried up, awkwardly changing places. "What's happened to us? A terrorist attack on Demesne? Why? It makes no sense. Why us? We've never harmed anyone. We're just farmers or were. Are we going to get rescued and taken to one of the continent's assisted living homes? Jim, I need you. I don't want us to get separated. How can we get married now?"

Jim looked morose. "How can you still want me? I'm not a man anymore? I'm a woman now, just like you." He broke down again, sobbing and unable to wipe himself.

"You are still my Jim, no matter what you look like," Ramona said, desperately trying to think of something to calm him down, to comfort him. While her own situation was awful, she realized this genetic mutation was much harder on the men.

"Hey, can someone help me, please!" The voice of Betty broke in on them. "My arms seem to have fallen off. I think I'm just having a very bad nightmare. Someone, anyone, little help here. I'm in my bathroom. I'm sort of stuck here. Help, someone, anyone."

Jim realized as the Lord of Frog Pond, he was responsible for everyone. "Coming Betty. Hold on." Together and hugging the walls for support, Jim and Ramona made their way out of their bathroom, through their bedroom, out into the common areas, and over to Betty's private suite.

Ramona followed along behind him, emulating his every move. She realized she was more afraid of being left alone than of falling down or being seen naked. *How silly. We're all probably naked right now. We just woke up.*

"I need help too," Leslie called out from her room. "Is anyone really okay? Is it just me? Probably not. Is anyone else still even alive? Help."

Jason's grief-stricken voice yelled from his suite, "Hang on; we're sort of coming. We're totally screwed too."

"Lean against the walls when walking," Jim yelled. He wasn't sure why he said that. Perhaps, it was the simple fact he was their Lord and responsible for all of them.

"I was trying to get a drink and my lip things got stuck," Betty explained. She was leaning over her sink with her head beneath the spigot. Her lip loops were around the spigot, and she couldn't raise her head up. "Sorry, got stuck."

"How the hell am I supposed to get you unstuck?" Jim cursed his helplessness.

"Try using your foot," Ramona suggested, trying hard to be helpful.

"Thanks. We're screwed aren't we?" Betty replied. Using a foot, he got her lip loops undone, and she stood up once more, leaning against the sink. "We better get to the comm center and call for help, don't you think? Gee, Jim, you look just like us now." Jim turned red as a beet, and Betty knew she shouldn't have said that.

Ramona began to lead the way back out of Betty's bathroom, making for the comm center in their commons. The other two followed. As they finally made it, Jason, Rene, and Leslie joined them, also leaning on the walls, going in single file like the other three. All six were naked.

"Gosh, Jason, you look like us too," Betty exclaimed, when she saw him coming, having already forgotten that she'd just embarrassed Jim with the same observation.

"Oh, you don't say!" Jason barked argumentatively. "Well, Betty, the change has done you good."

Betty looked startled by his comment. "How so? What do you mean?"

Rene decided now was not the time to banter. "You've become a lot thinner."

She looked surprised. "Oh. I thought he meant my boobs. They're something else, aren't they? But then, ours are so big. My back hurts. They make me feel like I am about to fall over all the time. Does yours do that too?"

Rene replied, "No kidding. It's terrible. We have to call for help."

Jason grumbled, "Obviously, dear, but how are we to do that?"

Trying to be helpful, Leslie suggested, "Maybe if we use our feet or noses we can get it going. I suppose. Don't you think so, maybe, possibly?"

The comm center was Jason's responsibility, and he knew it. He grumbled, "Okay, okay. Let's get the news on, and I'll try to see if I can get a video call going. I don't care if they see me naked. Hope you ladies don't mind that either."

Using his nose, he got the large monitor on, and then sat down to work the controls with his feet and toes to place a call for help. Meanwhile, Leslie picked up the controller pad between her teeth and took it to the large couch, where the others had finally arrived. Ramona advised, "We best swing our heads like this to get our hair out from behind us so we don't sit on it." The others emulated her head swings and plopped down on the couch beside each other. Leslie was the last to sit, dropping the controller onto the floor.

After sitting beside Betty, she used her toes to start switching channels. "Reruns. Reruns. Static. Reruns," she announced the obvious to the others. None said anything, however. At long last, she got to the local news channels. Static and more static. Finally, she got up to the Emergency Imperium Channel, the EIC as it was called. Now, they finally got news.

Jim called out to Jason, who was still trying to make the video connection. "Forget it, Jason. Come watch. It's beyond belief! War."

Ramona whispered, "Planetary genocide. We're doomed."

Betty whispered, "Two hundred billion? No rescues this time. I can't count to a billion. It's a large number, isn't it?"

Leslie whispered, "A really big number, Betty, really big. We're all going to die now, but I'm not dead, am I? Betty, am I dead? I don't feel dead, but then I've never been dead, so I really can't say for certain, one way or the other."

"Maybe it's just a dream, Leslie," Betty answered, "and soon, we're all going to wake up."

"We're not dead yet, Leslie," Ramona actually answered the now slender woman. "It's not a dream, though I surely wish it were."

"But I don't want to die," Leslie complained. "They are saying we'll all die. I don't want to die."

"I don't either," Betty added. "I don't suppose any guy will want to marry me now, though. I mean I've slimmed down a whole lot, but with no arms and these boobs, who's going to ask me now? Plus, I got this man's thing now too."

"Don't complain, Betty!" Jason grumbled. "I've got your

things now! And that's a whole lot worse. I'm not even a man anymore."

"Well, yes you are, Jason," Betty argued. "You've still got your thing. Oh!" She shut up, realizing she and the other women also had his thing. "Oh, we're all the same now. How very strange!" That brought silence among the six; the only sounds came from the newscast.

After a time, Jason grumbled again. "Okay, Lord Jim, what the hell do we do now? He just said there isn't going to be any rescues this time. Everyone on Bailey-3 is infected and as helpless as we are. So what are we going to do? Just sit here until we all die? You're the boss, so boss."

"I'm hungry," Betty interrupted him. "So are we supposed to sit here and starve to death or what?"

Jason retorted, "Well, that'd be something — to see Betty starving."

Rene admonished him, "Oh stuff it, Jason. None of us can cook now. We're all in the same boat, if you haven't noticed. Betty, I'm starving too, but what can we do about it?"

Jim took charge. "Hey look, the only way we are ever going to be able to do anything at all is if we all help each other. Use our feet, what else have we got? Come on; we're all starving. Let's all see if somehow we can fix something and then feed each other. Leslie, Betty, you two are now joined at the hips. Help each other. Come on; to the kitchen, but don't fall down. Ouch. Cow's bottom!" he swore, rising, and stepping on his hair, resulting in a sharp pain in his head. He nearly fell, as he wiggled to get off it. "This is darn near impossible!"

"Hey, try it this way," Jason offered a suggestion. With great care and forethought, the six began their first attempt at fixing some kind of meal. Jason also suggested they sit on the floor to eat. "Now, I can at least hold the spoon between my toes. Rene, you've got to move a little so I can get it in your mouth." Two hours passed before the six were quite full. Another half hour and Leslie used her foot to start the dishwasher. Then, they headed back to the comm center.

"Look, I have to tell everyone else in Frog Pond how to do what we just did. It's my responsibility," Jim said. Jason opened up a town-wide comm connection, usually used only for emergencies. Well, Jim thought, this certainly classifies as an emergency.

"Lord Jim here. If anyone still has their arms, please come to my place. I'm assuming we're all in the same mess. Here's what we have all worked out. To do anything, everyone in the house has to work together on it. We six took two hours to fix us something to eat. Best to sit on the floor. One person feeds the other. Looks like we here in Frog Pond are on our own. I freely admit to all of you, my friends, I need your help and ideas, if we're to live and not die, as the newscasters have predicted. We don't want to die, surrounded by all this food and our farms, but I don't know how we can continue to run the farm only that somehow we must. Let me know your ideas, as you come up with them. Frog Pond has been here for two and a half millennia, and I'm not about to abandon it now. Good luck everyone."

"That was inspiring, Jim," Betty commented as soon as he finished. "We need to find a way to carry things now. Milk, eggs, flour. The machines really do all the work. We just have to find a way to carry the final packages from the production lines to our houses. I think this ought to be Jason and Rene's project. Leslie and I'll worry about how to cook, won't we, Leslie?"

"Sure thing, I think. Maybe we can do it. Do you suppose that we can, Betty?" Leslie first agreed, but then became far more uncertain.

"We have to, Leslie. I like to eat and that hasn't changed one little bit," Betty declared. "Besides, I've got to regain all I've lost to this infection thing." Everyone chuckled a little; she did weigh at least thirty pounds less than she had before.

Rene added, "Betty, you don't want to overeat and lose your new perfect figure do you?" Betty grinned, but it wasn't visible, and chuckled some. Jason and Jim, however, both grimaced. They too had new "perfect figures," perfect for a super-shapely woman, that is.

Betty, Leslie, and Ramona headed for the kitchen to see what they could invent. Jason, Jim, and Rene began tossing out ideas for how they could invent someway to carry things. Finally, the two engineers had something they could deal with.

Their usual wheelbarrows were out. Rene pointed out they had many baskets used to collect apple-pears when they ripened on their two trees. Ramona also had smaller baskets she used to collect strawberries and similar items from their small garden patches. They also had duffle-like bags with long straps. Thus began numerous experiments.

Within a week, the engineers had managed to shut down most of the agricultural equipment, yet keeping just enough production to supply Frog Pond with what they needed to live well. There was still a massive pile of produce ready to ship to the now non-existent markets on the other continents. Jim estimated they wouldn't need to plant more wheat for a year, unless the bags somehow spoiled.

Lord Jim instigated a new policy that at least six adults should work together on a single project. Yes, that meant he, Jason, and Rene had to help out in the kitchen too. Everything took an exorbitant amount of time to accomplish. Hence, he also setup a whole new schedule for when farming actions had to be done, based heavily on many suggestions of his hands.

Perhaps more interesting, he decided to devote one day each week for a community gathering. The idea was to openly discuss ideas and share methods that worked with others. Clothing finally became an issue. "We can't keep going around naked," one woman stated flatly. "We need something to wear but we can't sew anything anymore."

That led to a number of related ideas. One man reported, "When Proxima Prime was attacked, the newscasts said the survivors were getting special clothes and shoes. That's what we need, don't you think?" Everyone agreed with him wholeheartedly.

"But where do we get them?" Jim asked, recalling a similar newscast he'd seen. At the time, he thought the victims looked like utter freaks. Now, he'd give anything to have something to wear.

"Hey, at one of those assisted living complexes on the other continents — they took in thousands of Proxima Prime victims. Surely, they have what we need there," a man called Wolf suggested. Many nodded.

"Great. How do we possibly get there?" Jim asked.

"Hey, I heard they also got special medical machines that can regrow arms. That's far more important," Wolf bypassed his question. That pronouncement got everyone's agreement.

"Great, but just how do we all get there? We don't have a clue how to perform that medical procedure, so we?" Jim asked.

Doctor Jenny White spoke up. She was the lone doctor for Frog Pond. "Well, if I could study the directions, I might be able to learn how to do it."

"Great. We need to launch an expedition to one of the continents," Jim replied, disgustedly. "Just how do we do that?"

"Take the shuttle, of course," Wolf replied without thinking. Then, he realized what he'd said and added, "Oh." They could no longer operate the shuttle.

"Hey, listen to the newscast," Jason called out. "They are saying Bailey-3 launched bio agent attacks by unmanned, stealth drones on the other Big Five worlds, and they launched them against us. It was a five-way war. The bastards!"

Wolf asked, "Why? Why would our leaders attack the other worlds? Why genocide?"

"We elected fools," Jim cursed. "So, back to the problem. Is it possible for us to travel to the other continents and get the things we need or even get our arms regrown?"

Doctor Jenny advised, "I just don't know if it is even possible for me to run the machine with only my toes, Jim. Clothes and shoes come in all sorts of sizes. There are a thousand of us. How would you even know what sizes to bring back? How could you carry that many things? I can say this much, though. I was paying some attention to the reports on how the victims we took in here on Bailey-3 were doing. Medical curiosity. By all reports, with those special shoes, they were able to walk better. Not great, mind you, but better than we're managing. Still, I don't see how we can possibly do this. Best we find other means. Let me show you why I say this."

She sat down at Jim's comm center. Using her toes, she finally brought up the images she'd studied, photos taken of some of the victims that had been given sanctuary on Bailey-3 months ago. "See, the clothes you're talking about are these very nice looking dresses, wholly impractical for us farmers. Plus, if we're wearing those pipe corsets and other undergarments, we'd not be able use the bathroom by ourselves. I doubt even eight of us working together could get someone out of that or into it, for that matter."

"Good god. They all look like women," Jim commented.

"Well, we are mostly women now," Jason again fumed. It was a sore point with him.

Jim added, "Doctor, I can see your point. No way could we deal with those clothes. Okay, let's forget about trying to get to the continents. We still need some kind of clothing. Going around totally naked is embarrassing for everyone, but at least we can go to the bathroom by ourselves."

Doctor Jenny suggested, "It would have to be something simple we could possibly put on ourselves or nearly so. I've been thinking about it for several days. I know; you men are taking the brunt of all this, but so are we women. We're embarrassed because we have male organs now. Don't think you guys have a monopoly on humiliation."

"What is your idea, doctor?" Jim asked. She was hitting too close to home for his liking. He wanted the topic changed before his face got any hotter.

"Actually, I've two related ideas. First, we gather up everyone's pants. I know, no one's pants now fits them. All of our hips have widened substantially. Because our waists are so reduced, some of the organs were moved down into the widened pelvis region. So what we do is pool all the pants together and then go through them one by one, fining a pair that mostly fits. Here comes the hard part that I've not yet worked out. Somehow, we fasten suspenders or ropes to the pant's top. With the help of others, we can probably get them pulled up and slip the suspenders over our shoulders to keep them up. That might work."

"I like that idea. I wonder if there are enough larger sized pants to go around?" Jim asked.

"Won't know until we pool them altogether and have at it. The second idea is to make use of the many bolts of cotton we women have. Some of us used to sew. My idea is to cut off a four-foot long section. It would be mostly square in shape. Then somehow, we cut a hole in the center. With help, we can slip it over our heads. The four sides would then drape over out tops somewhat."

"We'd at least be covered. I like the idea, but how do we do the cutting? Can anyone use scissors with their feet?" Jim asked.

"I certainly can't, but maybe someone else can come up with a bright idea how to do it," the doctor answered.

"Okay. Let's announce the pants part first, and see if we can possibly find even one pair for everyone, including the children," Jim decided.

As slow as everyone was, it took a week for everyone to retrieve all of their pants and to bring them into Jim's living room, the designated drop off point. Ramona, Rene, Leslie, and Betty arranged them into size groups. Another week passed before everyone finally had a pair that more or less fit them. With four working together, another two hours passed before one pair of pants had two ropes tied securely to the pants to serve as suspenders of sorts. However, with three others helping him, Jim was able to don pants. After that, he ordered everyone to take a day off from whatever they were doing and to work together to tie ropes to everyone's new pants.

Meanwhile, some of those women, who used to sew, attempted to make a poncho, as they called Doctor Jenny's design. With six women working together, they were able to make a pair of scissors make the first cut from the bolt of cotton cloth. One used her feet to steady the scissors from one side, a second kept them steady from the other side. Two others operated the pair of finger holes, while two more did their best to keep the cloth spread out smoothly. It was slow, tedious work, but they were successful at it. Cutting the center hole was even more difficult to manage, but after a day at it, they had a head hole cut.

They then worked together to get it over Jim's head and his long hair pulled outside of it. "It works!" he exclaimed, looking at himself in a mirror. "You six are geniuses!" They were kept busy making another thousand ponchos for everyone else.

Embolden by their designs, Lord Jim began contacting the other nearly two thousand Lords, outlining what his people had done to make crude clothing for everyone. It wasn't a one-way street. Many shared the ways and means that their people had devised, primarily for dealing with the animals and the farming machinery.

Although they didn't know the fate of those on the other five continents, here on Demesne, not a single person had died. Further, each plantation was beginning to get by fairly well. No one was starving, but nearly everything took many hours to complete, instead of a couple of minutes. The pace of life slowed to that of an earthworm, of which their fields were filled.

Then, in the middle of February, one of Jim's farm hands spotted a silver, unmanned drone flying overhead. The sighting caused widespread panic and nervousness with many predicting another bombing was coming.

"My god! Now what in the name of all that's holy do I do now?" Legate Smith whispered, too shocked to say anything louder. She and Helene were watching the streaming video being beamed to her laptop via the comm center on the battleship from across hyperspace via the heavy cruiser from the drone flying patterns over the sixth continent of Bailey-3. Both women stared in utter disbelief at what they saw. Legate Smith put in an emergency, secure call to Emperor Kino.

"Emperor, I have some startling video that you must see. Helene, replay it for me, please. This was taken minutes ago over the sixth continent of Bailey-3," she said hastily. "Brace yourself; this is most startling, but maybe in a good way." The five minute video played back. She added, "What the devil do we do now? Over."

Emperor Kino looked a bit pale, she thought. "Shocking. A testament to just how hardy we humans are. If you had not shown me this video, I would not have believed you. You were right in getting this to me. My assistant has captured the video here. Give me a few hours to check on some possibilities. In the meantime, belay the confiscation of the special medical machines from Bailey-3. Have them taken instead from Zelan-3. Over and out."

She went ahead and canceled the orders of confiscation for Major Smythe onboard the heavy cruiser Dauntless, circling Bailey-3. Then, she reissued similar orders for the heavy cruiser orbiting Zelan-3, but also asked for an IR Imaging report before executing the confiscation orders. Now, she could only wait and wonder what could possibly be done here on Bailey-3. She reconnected to Major Smythe. "Do you have IR images of that continent from shortly after the attack? If so, can you have the computer estimate the number of people both then and from today's scans? Over."

"On it, Legate. Will have the results in about an hour, I'm told. Over and out," the major replied. From the visible relief on his face, she knew he was very glad that she was taking over this operation and not he.

"Wow! Look at them!" Lena exclaimed. She, Bernardo, Jan, Amy, and Katrina were watching the same video. Emperor Kino placed a secure call to Queen Amy and asked her to summon Governor Katrina, before playing the Bailey-3 video for them. "Amazing, Bernardo."

When the video finished, Emperor Kino spoke, "We have a real problem. This continent is called the Demesne or their agricultural continent. The other five continents are filled with skyscrapers, much like Proxima Prime. The cruiser watching over Bailey-3 reports most everyone has died on the heavily populated five continents. But on this sixth one, their agricultural continent, they seem to be thriving and doing well. I've no idea how they could have survived, but they certainly have. It's been over a month since the attack, and they seem to be thriving and active. We have a real problem. What do we do to help them? We must take some action and immediately. Legate Smith is overseeing the Bailey-3 operations. Suggestions? Over."

"We should send in some of our people to assess their needs and doctors to check on their health. They need clothing and shoes," Amy suggested.

Lena added, "I should go. I can give them hope. Can a

293

Fabrication Machine be located? With it, clothing and shoes can be duplicated in volume."

Governor Katrina suggested, "Look, if there are a whole lot of survivors there, it's going to take a really long time to get all of their arms regrown. Perhaps, Bailey-3 could become another world in the Ataro Empire."

Amy added, "I like that idea. We could keep them insulated from the scavengers who'll likely denude the other continents. Do you have a new queen in training who is ready or about ready to graduate? Over."

Emperor Kino grinned broadly. "I was so hoping you would take the lead in this one. Yes, we have several who are about finished with their training. I can arrange to take Bailey-3 into the Ataro Empire. There are five Fabrication Machines on Bailey-3, that we know about. Can you put together a team and leave soon? Coordinate with Legate Smith. Over."

"Excellent. We can leave later today. Top speed?" Amy replied. He agreed and promised to have a queen waiting for them when they stopped on Winno-3 for refueling.

Lena suggested, "Bernardo, myself, and Doctors Mindy and Andy should go for sure."

Amy and Katrina agreed. They sent for the two doctors, while Lena and Bernardo headed off to pack. After watching the video replayed by Jan and Gabriella, Doctor Andy declared, "Okay, simply amazing. We ought to be able to get access to any number of medical machines on Bailey-3. So we can go light. We best get packing. Say, who's driving the transport?"

Doctor Ruth laughed. "You and Bernardo can fight it out over who drives, dear. Just be glad that Jan's not going."

Jan laughed. "You bet, cause I'd be driving." Everyone knew how she always hogged being the pilot.

Two hours later, Bernardo lifted the deep space transport off the tarmac at the spaceport. Doctor Andy sat in the navigator's seat, entering the coordinates for Winno-3, and they were off at top speed, burning an excessive amount of fuel. Time, everyone figured, was critical. Once in hyperspace, Bernardo opened a secure channel to Legate Smith.

"Bernardo Valen-Gervaise calling Legate Smith. We are

on our way from Ashford-5. Over."

After the usual delay, Legate Smith appeared on his monitor. "Legate Smith here. Emperor Kino has told me you are coming. Terrific. I agree with his assessment. I'll be issuing a formal declaration that Bailey-3 is now a member of the Ataro Empire. I have some more news about the situation. Major Smythe has done some studies using their new IR Imaging Camera. While nearly everyone has died on the densely populated five main continents, there have been an undetectable number of deaths on the agricultural continent. If any have died there, their numbers are too small to be detected. The population estimates for this continent lie around two million. Over."

"My god! How can we deal with that many people?" Doctor Andy replied, somewhat staggered by their numbers.

Bernardo added, "We should land on Winno-3 in twenty-four hours for refueling, and we'll pick up their new queen at that time. We should be at Bailey-3 two hours later. Over."

Legate Smith replied, "I've been doing some digging for information on this Demesne Continent of theirs. It seems this continent is the agricultural breadbasket of Bailey-3. The continental location is absolutely perfect for farming. Its constant temperate climate is ideal, seldom rising about eighty degrees and never below seventy at night. Rains are constantly periodic, coming every third day. They have no seasons, but their year has four growing seasons in it.

"Of importance to us, since antiquity, these lands have been divided up into two thousand individual plantations. The ownership of each is hereditary, always passing to the eldest son. The ruler of the plantation is called a Lord. All plantations have a population of around a thousand. So two thousand plantations times a thousand yields about two million people. Further, these farmers are all young. Apparently, they make so much money that the farmers retire by age forty, moving to the densely populated other continents. Hence, you ought to be seeing two million younger men, women, and children. Certainly, somehow they have adapted and are thriving. Over."

"Well, that makes it easier to handle. A thousand at a

time is a doable amount," Doctor Andy replied. "Still, it's going to take years to regrow two million people's arms, ignoring the new babies that will surely arrive during those years. Quite a challenge facing us. Over."

"Yes, we are catching a sorely needed break. When you arrive, contact Major Smythe on the heavy cruiser Dauntless. He'll be in charge of initial landings. He had pinpointed the locations of medical machines, Fabrication Machines, and other vitally important facilities. Over and out."

Chapter 15 Salvation

Ever since the drone was spotted over Frog Pond, Jim had Jason keep his comm system turned on. Many predicted yet another attack would soon be coming. Jim hoped that wasn't going to happen. Still, as their Lord, it was his responsibility to protect them, though he knew even if they'd never been attacked, he could do little to protect them. He didn't even own a d-gun, let alone anything that could harm a spaceship. His only thought was to attempt to contact the incoming attackers and plead for their mercy. Either that or a quick death.

Doctor Jenny's voice came over the town intercom. "Lord Jim. It's time for the annual health checkups for your house. Have everyone come over to my office please. No begging off this time. It's my job to see that everyone is healthy."

Jim lunged to his feet, wobbled a little to catch his balance, tossed his head several times to get his hair behind him, and made his way to the comm center. Using his nose, he activated the intercom. "Okay, doctor. We'll all be there in a while. Obviously, we're not okay, but that goes without saying," he grumbled, taking after Jason.

"Everyone, you heard the good doctor. Health exams for us all. Let's go. It's going to take us some time to walk to her place," Jim ordered.

"I don't see the sense in it," Betty countered. "We aren't okay, not by any stretch of imagination. I've lost thirty pounds! How can that be okay?"

Rene commented, "Betty, you haven't gained any of that back yet. You slipping?" She teased the short woman.

"Not for want of trying," Betty playfully countered. "Blame it on Leslie here. She doesn't feed me enough."

"Me? I do too, don't I? May be I don't feed her enough. I feel awful, Betty. I'll do better today. I hope so, anyway," Leslie replied, rather taken aback by her supposed failure to help Betty.

Ramona broke in, "Leslie, Betty's just teasing you. You are doing an excellent job of feeding Betty, and you know it. None of us is gaining any weight. Maybe that's a good thing. Let's ask the doctor about it. Come on; let's make this long walk. Be careful everyone. We don't want to take a spill."

There were only around a hundred homes in Frog Pond, laid out in a square, ten houses on a side. Lord Jim's was centrally located. The doctor's home and office was just three doors down, barely two hundred feet away. However, what used to take a minute at most to walk now took them far longer. Jason likened their walking to that of some imported penguins he'd once seen in Bailey's Zoo. They took a two inch step at most, wobbling to keep their balance as they did so, much like penguins, or so Jason claimed. No one else had been to the zoo, but one night, he showed them a video of the penguins at the zoo, compliments of the Net, which was still up and running without human intervention.

Some twelve hundred tiny steps and a half hour later, they entered Doctor Jenny's office. She, like everyone else, now left her doors wide open, held that way with a heavy box she'd slid there. "We're here, doc," Jim called out, waddling into her office.

"Have a seat. I'll need all of you to help me get each of you into the medical machine. Let's do Jim first. Have a seat and lay on your back." She need not have told him. He'd done this once each year since he could remember. Still, he mostly fell backwards. The others helped the doctor push the sides of the machine up to his body. Finally, she began to run her diagnosis. She had her clipboard on the floor, and she awkwardly sat down so she could use her toes to write Jim's data on it.

When she finished, the group helped her push the sides away so that Jim could get up. "Well doc, am I alive?" Jim asked.

Doctor Jenny gave him a strange look. "Alive? Of course. Healthy? Yes, even better than your last check up, Jim. However, well, I don't know how to say this, but I must. Everyone will know it in a few months anyway."

"What? Am I dying or something? I thought you just

said I was fine," Jim asked, getting rather annoyed. He just had not been feeling all that well in the mornings of late.

"Well, Jim, there is no easy way to say this," she replied hesitantly.

"Out with it. I'm a grown man, sort of. I can take it. Am I dying or something?" Jim asked again.

"No, you are perfectly healthy. So is your baby. You are pregnant, Jim." *There, I've just come right out and said it,* she thought defensively.

"What? Pregnant? That's impossible! I'm a . . ." He didn't finish his sentence.

"Have you been feeling a little queasy in the mornings of late?" Doctor Jenny asked.

"Well, yea, I guess so."

"Morning sickness."

He turned rather red. "But, but, but."

"We are all hermaphrodites now. That's one of the genetic mutations we've all got, Jim. Unfortunately, I can't tell if you are having a daughter or a son. The way I've got it all figured out is that if a woman gets impregnated by a man or a man gets impregnated by a woman, it is still fifty-fifty on the baby's sex. If a woman impregnates another woman, then their child will be female. If a male impregnates another male, I'm not sure, but I think the chances are high that they'll have a son. I guess in time, we'll see. Congratulations, Jim, Ramona. Now let's get Ramona checked out.

A half hour later, Doctor Jenny announced that Ramona was also pregnant. Unlike Jim, she was rather pleased, but hoped for a boy who would one day become Frog Pond's new Lord, when Jim and she retired.

No one noticed Jason's nearly continually red face, until it was his turn. To his further embarrassment, he too was pregnant, as was his wife, Rene. Next, Betty and Leslie had their checkups. If Jason was embarrassed, his was nothing compared to Betty and Leslie's. Doctor Jenny announced that each was also pregnant. Jason could not help get in a dig, "So now we know what little Betty and Leslie have been doing at night." Both women flushed beet red.

Doctor Jenny defused the tense situation. "It's perfectly

natural, Jason. Look, most of the people of Bailey-3 have died. How else can we ever hope to rebuild our population, unless everyone does their part? I think it's admirable of these two women to do their part. Look, I'm pregnant too, so is my friend, May. We've decided we need to do our part as well. Now, all six of you, let's talk about proper diets and regular checkups, shall we?"

"But how are we going to care for babies?" Ramona voiced what had been increasingly bothering her, ever since Doctor Jenny made her pronouncement.

Doctor Jenny replied, "Lord knows on that one, Ramona. I guess we all just have to keep on inventing ways and means. Your due dates are all going to be spread out during November or perhaps late October." She proceeded to lecture them on proper nutrition during their pregnancies. Jason only continued to grumble.

The next morning as they were preparing their breakfast, they heard a voice coming over their comm center. "Calling any of the Lords on the Demesne Continent of Bailey-3. This is Major Smythe of the Imperium cruiser Dauntless. Any of you Lord's got your ears on? Over." He repeated the message four times before Jim and Jason could make their way to the comm center. Jason pushed the button for Jim.

"Yes, Lord Jim Weathers of Frog Pond here. Are we being rescued at last? We need lots of help. We spotted another of those drones the other day. We might be getting attacked again. Over."

Bernardo had picked up the new twenty-five year old blonde Queen Anne Frankles and her Personal Assistant Beth Arvis, who had black hair and was a year younger. Queen Anne appeared much as Queen Amy, though with respectable, small breasts of a normal human. Her assistant also wore toe shoes and the tiny pipe corset as did her charge. Queen Anne had just graduated only two days before meeting Bernardo's transport. Full of youth and excitement, she felt ready for her new challenge, though Lena thought their choice of dress — tight fitting satin gowns — would not be practical on Bailey-3 farms.

A few hours after picking them up, they'd arrived at

Bailey-3, docking with the Dauntless. Major Smythe was there to meet them. After a lengthy briefing, he had opened a channel to all the comm centers on the agricultural continent, in hopes that one would respond. If so, Bernardo planned to take the transport down to visit and gain firsthand knowledge of just what the situation actually was. Meantime, Major Smythe was sending forces down to the five other continents.

"Greetings Lord Weathers. I'm sending a transport down to your location now. They will meet with you and ascertain the situation there. They are here to help. That was probably our drone that you saw. We have Bailey-3 secured at this time. There will be no further attacks. You are safe from that at least. Expect the transport within the hour. Good to hear some of you are alive. Over and out." Major Smythe breathed a sigh of relief. "I sure am glad you're making contact with them and not me or my men. I don't envy you one bit. Still, our task will be grizzlier. The dead will be everywhere. We'll have to all wear masks. Good luck then. Keep me posted, and I will do the same."

Bernardo agreed and led his group back to the air lock and their transport. After undocking, he had Doctor Andy enter the coordinates of the transmission from Frog Pond, while he gracefully arced the ship away from the mammoth cruiser, falling planet-side. Within minutes, they soared over the sixth continent. Though still at ten thousand feet, they could see the patchwork quilt of plantations, some two thousand of them. As they homed in on Frog Pond, they saw it was centrally located on the continent. A few minutes later, the small town appeared with its plus-sign style homes that served four families each. Bernardo spotted the small landing field and set the transport down there. He and Andy guessed here was where the cargo ships always landed to pick up the agricultural produce. There was quite a bit of produce stacked up, ready for deliveries, but their pickups had never come.

As they came down the cargo bay ramp onto the concrete pad, they spotted several out doing some chores in the fields or rather operating the giant machines that did the work. Ahead in the town of Frog Pond, they spotted a group out in the street, towards the center, and headed that way.

Vic Broquard

Only ten large houses square, this was barely a village, Lena thought. However, the short distance took them some time to traverse. They had to go at Queen Anne and Beth's pace in their toe shoes. Well, this must be the speed of these survivors, Lena thought, but didn't say anything. Eventually, they saw the six waiting for them, wobbling to keep their balance as they stood.

One could hardly tell them apart, save for size. One was strikingly shorter than the others were; one was somewhat taller. All wore ill-fitting pants and a square of cloth over their top, the edges of which were unraveling both around the neck holes and two outer edges. Lena correctly guessed they'd been simply cut from a bolt of cloth. Inventive, she thought.

In turn, Jim and his group saw a normal young man, the only one normal of the six. He was wearing a leather outfit and could well pass as a farmer. The black skinned woman, similarly dressed, obviously had no arms, but her boots were similar to the man's, quite practical, Jim thought. Then, there were two whose tall spiked heels clicked in unison with each step they took. Both had similar massive bosoms as Jim and everyone else in Frog Pond, obviously victims too. She wore a white cotton blouse and black skirt, very professional looking, while he wore what appeared to be a man's suit, greatly modified, but again professional in appearance. Both wore the giant golden lip plates, just as Jim and the others had seen on the newscasts. Even with their arms, they were obviously fellow terrorist attack victims. His hair was cut short, like that of a man. The other two wore tight fitting, satin gowns, one in red, one in blue. The woman in red had no arms, but wavy blonde hair, waist length. The other had a arm around her, stabilizing her as they walked. She had waist length black, curly hair. Neither wore lip plates, and their breasts were unremarkable in all ways. Hence, Jim and his group couldn't guess who she was, or the black woman, for that matter.

By the time that the six reached Jim's group, many others stuck their heads outside their homes to see what was going on. Lena and Bernardo sensed their many unspoken questions. "Hello. I am Doctor Andy Hammil, my wife, Doctor Mindy Hammil. We are both geneticists, specializing in these

302

genetic mutations that have afflicted us and yourselves. We are from Ashford-5. This is Bernardo and Lena, also from Ashford-5. This is Queen Anne Frankles and her Personal Assistant Beth Arvis. She's just come from the Ataro System. Shall we go inside and chat?"

"Oh! Sure. I am Lord Jim Weathers, my wife, Ramona. My Lead Engineer Jason Bills and his wife, Engineer Rene. My Secretary, Leslie Patterson-Fry, my Treasure, Betty Fry-Patterson. Please, we have so many questions. We need so much help." He led the way inside their home to the central living room. Bernard noticed the comm center was at one far corner of the room, while in the opposite corner, it opened into the dining room and kitchen. Both he and Lena quickly grasped how it was that these victims had survived! From their point of view, all of the homes were nearly identically shaped, much like a cross, supporting four separate families, who shared communal rooms. Hence, the four families could work together to help each other after the bio attack had left them like this.

"Let me speak first," Queen Anne began, after sitting down and facing the six. "As of now, Bailey-3 is officially the thirty-eight planet in the Ataro Empire. We've adopted you so we can protect you from off-worlders, who are likely soon to swarm here, stealing anything of value. I'm your queen, and I'll be your new top ruler. Emperor Kino and I guarantee you, from now on, you'll be very safe, and that we're going to make every possible effort to help all of you who have survived this vicious genocidal war. These two doctors from Ashford-5 have been helping other attack victims for years now. They are competent at arm regrowth and many other things. Let me have them speak next. Doctors?"

Doctor Andy spoke first, "Yes, we've been regrowing arms nearly every day for many months. Ashford-5 has taken in over a thousand victims, such as yourselves. We are doing our best to improve their quality of life. Yes, we too were attack victims, as you can see. I'm afraid I appear about as masculine as is possible at this time. From the initial survey done from space, we're told that perhaps two million of you here on this continent survived the attack, whereas only a handful may have on the other five continents."

Doctor Mindy picked up. "We were not expecting to find so many of you. First, we want to ascertain your general state of health."

"Oh we're all healthy," Jason grumbled, interrupting her. "Yeh, and we're all pregnant too. We men have become women, as you can see." Lena and Bernardo sensed his deep disgust and revulsion at what he'd become. His surface hostility was its manifestation.

Jim quickly added, "Yes, we have our own Frog Pond Doctor Jenny, who gave us our yearly health checkup only yesterday. We're all healthy. I think she knows the health status of everyone in Frog Pond, just ask her. She's got all the records."

"Well, that is good to hear!" Doctor Mindy replied, being as upbeat as possible. "You see, so many of the attack victims in the past were in very poor health, just barely alive when help finally came to them. That makes it vastly easier for us to help you right away. The first thing we must do is to get everyone far better clothing and shoes, items that are functional for the work that you do here and that are easy for you to put on. I can see what you've invented for yourselves is very ingenious and workable. If you will permit us, we'll see if we can improve on them, unless you would like some other type of dress."

"We're all farmers here, engineers too. We always wear pants," Lord Jim explained. "True, our women used to wear dresses on occasion. We really do need work pants. We couldn't do our chores wearing what Queen Anne or you are wearing."

"Good. I presumed as much. Lena here uses her feet as her hands. She's going to show you all the tricks she knows. However, her feet are normal, not malformed like yours and Queen Anne's and Beth's. The big question is what to do for shoes for you. We can repair your feet, at least partially. Andy and mine have been repaired, partially anyway. However, we still have to wear these tall heels. Walking is a whole lot easier in them, at least on solid surfaces, not so much on soils. But there is a shoe variation that might work well. I brought some along for me to try out. I know for the foreseeable future, you are still going to have to do your farming work with your feet. So let me experiment a little. Whatever we do for your footwear, you have to be able to put them on and take them off by yourself, not tied like ours are."

"If one of you can sort of lead me through a typical work day, I can try out different heels and see if any will work for you. The repair of feet takes about an hour per person. We have also worked out how to remove the pain sensors in your hair so it can be cut. That takes about an hour too. Some men like to cut theirs short again to look more like before."

"I can't see bothering with our hair," Jason complained. "We men are really women now. No sense in hiding it or pretending not to be. No offense, Doctor Hammil, but you still look like a woman to me. Now, if you can fix it so we can walk better, that would be most helpful. But best of all, we need our arms back. That's what we really need done."

Doctor Mindy replied, "I fully understand, Jason. We were victims too, we know. We want to be up front with all of you. Regrowing arms is both costly and time-consuming, but we're going to get it done somehow. Let me explain, since this is the most critical aspect."

"The cost is mostly in the complex chemicals that are required for the process. They are relatively scarce, which is why they cost so much. The going rates are about ten thousand credits per person, but you need not worry about the cost. As a member of the Ataro Empire, the empire will be assuming the cost for you. The time factor is our real barrier. The first two weeks of the process, the person is completely bedridden and has to be attended too at all times by us doctors and our nurses. After that period, they have to remain relatively inactive for three months, as the tiny arms grow rapidly. After three months, they look much like a small child's arms, and you can use them, just not for heavy work. By one year, they are back to as normal as they are going to get."

"We are limited in just how many patents we can do at one time, assuming we can find others to care for them during the longer three month period. It's the constant care for two weeks that slows us way down. Multiply that by the two million of you and you see what we are facing. That's about four million doctor-patient weeks or about eighty thousand doctor years with just one doctor." She watched as their faces reacted to the bind boggling numbers, knowing they simply had to understand the harsh reality they were facing here.

Doctor Andy then took over. "We've got to find a way to reduce the overall years this is going to take. With Queen Anne's approval, we've decided to try something else. As we understand your plantations each has their own doctor. Is this correct?"

A downcast Jim answered, "Yes, we have to — accidents happen, and we're too far from the other continents in an emergency. We've got Doctor Jenny."

"Excellent. If we can train each doctor in each of the two thousand plantations, then they can work their magic on everyone at their plantation. That will reduce the doctor-patient time down to around thirty-eight years. Still too long, but it's getting more workable, assuming we can acquire enough of the chemicals to keep the doctors all going at once. If they can handle two patients at the same time, the time is halved to get to everyone. If somehow they can manage three at once, we're down to about a dozen years to get to everyone. Now that's more like it."

"We need this more than anything else. Life has mostly come to a standstill," Lord Jim stated. "It takes all six of us about a quarter of each day handling meals, another quarter dressing and such. We get just enough actual farming done to keep food on the table."

"We understand," Queen Anne took over. "The real problem we are facing is where to get the two thousand special medical machines that are going to be needed. Right now, Major Smythe and his men are scrounging up all they can find on the other continents. They'll bring them here. We think there are perhaps a dozen on Bailey-3, far short of the two thousand we need. Emperor Kino is working on getting the manufacturers to jack up production. We just need time."

Lord Jim nodded. "It's like I feared. We are too many. Okay, look, we need to handle the most critical people first. That's Jason here and Rene. Every plantation simply must have their Lead Engineer fixed up first. If the equipment breaks down, we all starve. Then, we need our doctor fixed up. I can make a list of the really critical personnel that must be helped first before the rest of us. We Lords can go last; we're the least important people for the daily operations that keep us all alive. I just have to run things; I do very little actual farming." Jason mouthed a big thank you in his direction.

Queen Anne smiled. "Excellent. I was hoping there would be key personnel we could get to first. We'll schedule Jason and Doctor Jenny as the first two to get the arm regrowth process. Hopefully, Major Smythe will have rounded up some machines yet today. There is one more thing I need to ask, Lord Jim. I'm going to need a place for Beth and me to stay. If it's not too much trouble for you, I would like to share your home here. Make this my official residence."

"Sure, actually, that works out good for us," Jim replied. "You see, Leslie and Betty used to have their own suites, but since the attack, they've had to room together. None of us can do much for ourselves; we have to help each other. For most things, Queen Anne, we six work together to get it done. You'll see that everywhere now. I've made it a rule. No one does anything alone."

"Thank you. I'll attempt to do my part as well, but I'm afraid you'll need to show me how. We queens were never taught to do much except officiate. Beth can lend us her hands as well. Is there any way we could contact all the other plantations to let them know what's happening?" she asked.

"Sure, Jason can connect you to the broadcast system. It goes to all of the other Lord's systems. Before you do, can I ask you a question, Queen Anne?" Jim asked politely. She nodded and he asked, "Does anyone know why the other worlds attacked us? Why did they do this to us? We are in a big mystery about why they attacked us."

"Right now, we don't know for sure. Perhaps, when the major finishes securing all the facilities, he'll find some records that will tell us. All we know for sure is that while Legate Mary Smith was on Beta Carnae-4 trying to get them to hurry up and send new senators and bureaucrats to Proxima Prime, within minutes, each of the Big Five worlds sent squadrons of the drones loaded with the bio agent to each of the other four worlds. Each one of the Big Five worlds received a quadruple dosage. We just don't know why it happened. However, we find it highly suspicious that these worlds had made such a large amount of this terrible genetic mutation agent. They were supposed to be developing a cure for all this, not mass producing it and using it as a genocide weapon."

A short while later, Queen Anne began a lengthy one-way talk over the emergency line to nearly two thousand plantation Lords. She outlined what had happened, was now happening, and would soon be occurring. She then spent the rest of the day fielding many return calls.

While she was doing that, Lord Jim held a town meeting, outlining what had just happened. After that, Lena, Bernardo, and the two doctors paid a visit to Doctor Jenny. The doctor showed them her carefully maintained heath records of the village and was extremely pleased to learn how to regrow the arms of her fellow villagers. Now, it was all in the hands of Major Smythe and his men. They had to find the equipment.

As the sun descended, Bernardo, Lena, and the doctors were called back to the cruiser, but Queen Anne and Beth remained. As the four left them, Queen Anne explained to her new hosts, "Since I'm going to be your queen, I best learn how you do things. I should lend my assistance to you as well, instead of relying totally on Beth here. So how do I help feed someone? You'll have to show me."

Once back in their transport, Lena commented, "Queen Anne is going native. That's a very wise more on her part. Live among them and do her share of the work, just as these victims are having to cope."

"I agree, dear. But I wonder why the major is recalling us tonight?" Bernardo replied, activating the controls.

Back on the cruiser, Major Smythe summoned them directly into his small war room. "I can't begin to tell you how grim it is down there. Dead bodies everywhere. The stench is awful. But we have found three of their genetic research buildings where some of the machines are located. One of my men took some video. Brace yourselves. This is the most inhumane, sadistic thing I've ever seen." He started the edited video.

The opening scene focused on a document labeled, "Genetic Research Project III. From there, it focused in on a specific paragraph. It read: The Proxima Prime victims will be told, if they want their arms regrown, then they would need to first become willing, volunteer test subjects to additional genetic experiments, designed to test possible additional cures to all their genetic mutations. After the test is done, they will then have their arms regrown. They will be told that this research carries some risk, but without live testing, a full cure could never be found. We believe that most will volunteer.

The video then displayed an official register of results. Part of it read:

Test 143: Test subject's intestines dissolved. Subject deceased.

Test 144: Test subject's feet withered and fell off.

Test 145: Test subject went deaf and blind before dying from internal bleeding.

Finally, the video showed a special living quarters where a dozen men and women were still alive after all these weeks! "Oh my god! What did they do to them?" Lena whispered, completely aghast.

Major Smythe interpreted. "From what we've gathered, they developed a partial arm restoration process. Unfortunately, it only regenerated their upper arms, while removing their lower legs. The test subjects survived and are apparently somewhat mobile and able to do more things since they at least have their upper arms. We talked with them and got an earful. I've left three nurses with them this evening. Tomorrow, I need you to deal with them. I believe we will find others. They were showing up as some of the red forms on our IR images — survivors. Grim beyond words. Now go get some supper, if you have the stomach for it."

The next day, while Major Smythe's men began hauling the much needed special medical machines from Genetics Research Station 3, Doctor Mindy began going through the massive chemical supplies, sorting out what they really needed, leaving the rest. Doctor Andy, Bernardo, and Lena first conferred with one of the nurses, who had spent the night with the dozen research subjects who were living in Facility #5. The nurse explained their preliminary findings.

"What we have here are three families. Each of the parents has given birth to one child. They are between three and five years old. Everyone is perfectly healthy. They are rather happy and pleased to have part of their arms back and claim that with the loss of their malformed feet, they are now able to get around better without the constant fear of falling they used to have. They've been given a number of strange bronze tools that they slip onto their arms to feed each other, brush their hair and similar things."

The nurse continued. "We've correlated their experiment number with the computer records. The geneticists modified some recessive genes taken from a primitive world, where all women there are born without hands. It's called Karlson-3. A Doctor Voit was the first doctor who visited them and discovered the recessive genes and a cure, for that matter. The bronze tools come from that world, as far as we can tell."

"We have also uncovered some additional experiments that were conducted on others like them. They knew their genes are recessive. They artificially inseminated a normal victim with sperm from one of these males to prove its recessive nature. That child was born as a normal victim, that is, similar to her mother. They've kept these three families around for further testing and study. Part of the studies is to determine their long-term viability. Can they actually live long, contented lives? Apparently so, they've been living like this for seven years now. During recent years, they've continued to have babies, but were told that their pregnancies would be terminated at some point so that the doctors could harvest more of their stem cells. Once they had collected enough stem cells, the doctors promised them they would undergo further experimentation in an attempt to regrow the rest of their arms. Several are asking how soon that is going to be done."

Lena spoke up. "How were they able to survive for over a month on their own?"

The nurse answered quickly. "We wondered that too.

Their food supply is the nutritious synthetics found on every world. The supply cylinders were about empty. We've replaced those last night. Another few weeks and they would have starved to death as well. Follow me, I'll take you to the one way mirror where you can see them, but they can't see you."

A few minutes later, the trio watched along with the nurse. "You see, their Facility #5 is all set up just for them. Everything is low to the ground, and they have adapted quite well, in our opinion. So if you are going to move them, we'd recommend you take most of their strange furniture and things with them. Obviously, they're not going to be able to survive in a normal environment."

Doctor Andy had seen enough. "What have they been told about the war and genocide here on Bailey-3?"

"They know all about it. It seems they've been able to turn their entertainment center to the Emergency Imperium channel and have been watching it ever since. They are most concerned about what is going to happen to them. We told them that help is coming," the nurse replied. She added, "As you can see, the five year olds, Stefanie and Benji are just as active as any five year old. The two were waddling around on their leather leg cylinder pads, kicking a soccer ball around one area of their home.

"Oh, one more thing," the nurse added, "these six adults are not dummies. Al and Rae Gulock, twenty-six and twenty-five, the two older ones — they were banking vice-presidents on Proxima Prime. The two younger ones are Ron and Kelly Brokes, hydroponic specialists in growing food. They are twenty. Sal and May Rousch, twenty-two and twenty-one, were a pilot-navigator team when they were struck down. Their two children are four, Bethi and Donni. The three year olds are Seth and Mary. They are Ron and Kelly's."

Bernardo asked, "Don't they have any clothes?"

"No. As far as we can tell, they don't have enough motor skills to put anything on or take anything off themselves. As you can see, they are terribly limited in what they can do. However, from the many other terrorist victims that we've seen, they are doing a whole lot more, so I guess that's something positive."

Just then, Major Smythe's voice came over the handheld communicator that Bernardo carried. "Bernardo. We've found something far worse. Bring your team of doctors. Facility #8, sub-floor two." His tone sounded both annoyed and scared at the same time, rather confusing.

"You three head down there. I'll go bring Doctor Mindy," the nurse volunteered.

A few minutes later, Bernardo grumbled, "This is a bloody maze!"

"Yes, dear. We're on sub-floor two now. Look for this #8 place. No, the numbers are going up. We need to go the other direction," Lena quickly pointed out, turning around.

A few minutes later, they spotted Major Smythe and a group of soldiers standing before another one-way window. "Ah good. Found four more victims. These are all yours. We've cleared the dead bodies out of this corridor. Decomp smell is dissipating rapidly. All yours. Come on, soldiers; we've got more to clear out and another medical machine to locate." He added, "Data is on that clipboard."

Doctor Andy picked up the clipboard, standard Imperium medical issue. He read a bit before cursing. "This is discrimination if I ever heard of it. Inside are Jenni and Martha Cragston, twenty-six and nurses. They are lesbians and were picked on for this experiment because of their sexual orientations! Damn. Those are their children, Melinda and Sammi, each five."

"My god, Andy, they've only got one leg, the right one," Lena gasped. Other than that detail, they looked like the other terrorist attack victims. Bernardo unleashed a stream of cuss words.

"Hey, wait a second! Their foot is perfectly normal! The genetic research has been able to completely restore one of their malformed feet," Doctor Andy exclaimed, suddenly enthused.

"But all they can do is hop," Lena protested, but avoided the stream of explicatives her husband was gushing. "They did this just to torture them because of their sexual preferences? Wait. Are you saying the bastards discovered something here?"

312

"Yes, I think so, but I'll need to carefully study their work. They may have accidentally stumbled upon something that we can use to restore everyone's feet back to normal," Doctor Andy suggested, sounding as positive a note as he dared. Just then, the nurse brought an out of breath Doctor Mindy up to them.

"Oh dear god," she whispered, as she got her first look at these four. Doctor Andy quickly filled her in on what he'd discovered so far. "Well, let me and Lena make first contact with them." The others agreed and Doctor Mindy and Lena entered the women's suite.

"Hello. Who are you? We've never seen you before. Any word on when they will begin reconstructing our other leg?" Jenni asked, hopping over to greet them.

Her mate, Martha, hopped over behind her, adding, "What news? We've heard all sorts of awful things on the newscasts. What's happening? Why haven't we seen anyone for weeks?" She saw Lena and added, "Oh! Is she one of us who has been mostly cured?"

"Hello. I'm Doctor Mindy Hammil. We're from Ashford-5. Can we sit down? I've much to tell you."

"Sure. Sorry, where are our manners. Ignore the girls. This way," Jenni said a little embarrassed by her unrestrained outburst. Hopping over to a sofa, she added, "We're so surprised to see someone, anyone really. Come, sit."

After sitting down, Doctor Mindy asked, "So how are you both and your darling girls? I understand that you are both nurses."

"We are all fine. Yes, we are. Naturally, we keep close tabs on ourselves and the girls. We are doing very well," Jenni answered.

Doctor Mindy then outlined briefly what all had happened. All of those who were experimenting on them and their care givers were now dead.

Lena took point, "It must be awful with only your one leg."

Martha answered, "Oh no, Lena. Rather the opposite. We're from Proxima Prime. Somehow, we managed to keep each other alive until we were rescued, but trying to walk or do anything with our feet so badly mangled up, well, we jumped at this chance to have a good foot. Honestly, we were so terrified of falling every time we took a step. Thanks to the good doctors here, we now have a really good foot. We have ever so much better balance and can do so very much more with our new foot. It's been a real blessing for us. Getting around is more challenging, but we don't ever fall now. We've got our whole foot on the ground, not just our toes. But we're hoping they'd get the serum perfected soon so that we can get our other leg back in perfect working order. They kept saying any day now, but it never happened. I guess it never will now. What's going to happen to us and our daughters?"

"You are safe. We will do all that we can to assist you. I'm sure in time we'll be able to regrow your arms. That should help immensely," Doctor Mindy replied.

"You're kidding? The doctors have figured out how to do that?" asked Jenni. "Incredible. Yes, that would be fantastic! Then, we could return to our nursing duties. We both really miss helping others; that's why we went into the nursing field."

Meanwhile, Doctor Andy hunted around for a medical terminal. After finding one, he punched in their case number and brought up their files. "Well, this makes more sense. They were not trying to heal feet; that was an accidental side effect. They wanted to study whether or not people could survive with only a foot. Sociopaths! Hey, there's a reference to another case."

While typing in the reference case, he added, "It seems that these two were doing far too well to satisfy their sadistic tastes. Ah, here we are." He skimmed down the document. "Dear god, it only gets worse. They finally perfected the Ultimate Genetic Mutation Solution — their words. Come on; we need to get to Facility #12 pronto. Let Mindy and Lena know where we're going," he ordered Bernardo. He focused and sent the two a telepathic message, before scampering after the clicking heels of Doctor Andy.

After numerous twists and turns of the long hallway, they arrived at Facility #12 and gazed in through the one-way mirrors. Bernardo gasped, while Doctor Andy picked up their chart and skimmed it. "Doc, they don't have any arms or legs either! They are just head and torso!"

Andy added, "They are supposed to be able to get around on those flat, low to the ground electrical scooters. I don't see how though. Come on; we need to get in there. They don't look well at all." The two entered the small suite. The smell was awful, the two were barely alive. "Alfie is the blonde; Miranda is the brunette. Let's get them onto those sloped cushions. Gently, they are not in good shape at all." Carefully, he lifted Alfie up. Avoiding stepping on her long hair, which dragged along some three feet beyond the end of her torso, he sat her on the sloped cushion-like seat. The entire room was one giant padded cell. He draped her hair above her head and she came to.

"Help us," her faint voice whispered. "We want to die. We can't live like this. Please, help us." After making sure she was comfortable, Doctor Andy hastily explained who he was, and that they were being rescued.

He sent, *Bernardo, go find a normal medical machine so we can diagnose what's wrong with these women. Hurry, please.* They had no arms for him to use to check pulses, let alone insert an IV solution. He finally took their pulses using their necks. While Bernardo dashed around looking for a machine, Doctor Andy wrestled with her request. He was sworn to save lives, to help people get well, never to harm them or do what was not in their best interests, health-wise. These two were just barely alive. They wanted to die and were nearly there. Euthanasia. Here were to candidates exemplifying the cause of euthanasia.

They were so completely helpless, he thought, mere living torsos, unable to do the slightest thing for themselves. They wanted death. Should he give them what they desired? What kind of a life could they possibly have if he could cure them? Yet, he was a doctor. He'd sworn an oath to save lives. In time, he could regrow their arms. Surely then, they could live a much better life than the one they were facing now. Vets routinely put down larger animals that had broken a leg and could not stand. Surely, allowing these two women to die was even more justified. Who could possibly care for them until and if they got their arms back? His mind in turmoil, he stepped back outside to look at their charts again. He discovered Alfie was a senator from Bailey-3, while her wife, Miranda, was an ambassador. They'd been caught in the attack on Proxima Prime and sent home to be healed. Instead, they'd become test subjects, case #211.

Bernardo came back pushing along an ordinary medical machine. He held the door open while Bernardo pushed it inside. *I have to attempt to save them, Bernardo.* His friend nodded and helped him lift Alfie onto the machine. A few minutes later, he announced, "Severe dehydration, small lack of food. Okay, dehydration first. See if you can find some synth food around here." He activated the menus. The machine responded, injecting the proper amount of liquids into her blood stream through a vein in her neck. A few minutes after that, he lifted her out and placed her back on the slanted couch-like pad. Doctor Andy then handled Miranda. By the time he finished her and had her resting beside Alfie, Bernardo came running back with a bowl of the green goo, as he called the nourishing synth food fond on most spaceports. He handed Andy a spoon and the two began feeding the two women, who were coming out of their near coma.

While feeding Miranda, Bernardo sent Andy, *I let the others know about these two. They are on their way to see them now. Looks like you've got them stabilized. Good going, doc.*

Saved them, yes; that was the easy part. But have I done the right thing for them? Honestly, look at them. My god, Andy replied, feeding Alfie. He then sensed the presence of his wife and Lena just outside, watching them. He also felt their astonishment and compassion for these two women.

With their strength returning from their close touch with death, Alfie said softly, "I'm Senator Alfie Feliz, my wife, Ambassador Miranda. We were supposed to get our arms regrown, but ended up like this. They said something went terribly wrong, and that they were working to fix it, but it never happened. We rather got by in here using the scooters to get around. They did make us as comfortable as possible while we waited for another cure. It's not coming, is it? We're doomed to be like this forever, aren't we?"

"My wife and I are doctors and geneticists from Ashford-5. We can and will get your arms regrown, but I've no idea about your legs. We've not encountered this genetic mutation. Now relax, and let us see what we can do," he replied, rising. He and Bernardo stepped out of their room.

"They need a bath. They are covered in their own excrement. Their bedding must be washed too," he announced.

"Well done, dear. Look what I found out while you were feeding them," Lena interrupted them. She'd been using her toes to do some digging on their medical computer system. "We really, really lucked out on this one. Their case is #211. See the summary here," she pointed with her head to the monitor. "They've adopted their mutation as the model to follow for their biological agent weapons. They were putting this one into mass production. Thank god, the war came when it did. Another week or so and this mutation would have been sent to the other four Big Five worlds! What I don't understand about all these bio genetic warfare agents is why do they want to so mutate human bodies? Why not just fabricate a toxic gas that kills everyone, a viral agent like was developed on Ashford-4? Kills everyone outright. Why go in for all these horrific genetic mutations that kill slowly, if at all in some cases? I don't get it." Lena allowed her frustrations to surface.

"Dear, I don't get it either," Bernardo replied. "It seems to me if you want to wipe out a whole world and leave the infrastructure intact, why not use a chemical weapon that kills humans? Why go to all this trouble to genetically mutate them?"

Doctor Andy answered them both. "A chemical agent does kill, but it also kills other plants and animals, perhaps ruining the environment for a long time. A genetic mutation such as was done to Alfie and Miranda would target only the human life, rendering them incapable of surviving for any length of time. We've seen the one unleashed on us, on Proxima Prime, and now here on these five worlds, does not result in a total annihilation of the human populations. Some survive. Two million on Bailey-3, for example. Plus, there is the rescue factor to consider. Obviously, other worlds come to the rescue of the attacked world. Some lives can be saved. I suspect if they had gotten the one that they used on Alfie and Miranda into production and used it on the other four worlds, everyone there would have been dead within just a few days with no survivors and no potential for survivors."

Doctor Mindy commented, "Men certainly can do very evil things!"

Lena countered, "Women too. The research doctor behind this mutation here was a woman, Doctor Mindy. This time, we can't blame it on the fellows. I just can't understand the mentality behind such evil."

"That's what Rafe's studying with her Advanced Therapy," Doctor Andy explained. "We must make arrangements to get all these people back to Tierra. Some good might come from this, if we can figure out how they managed to repair completely their feet. We'll need to confiscate all their records as well."

Just then, Major Smythe walked up. "Ah here you are. What have we here?" He looked into the one-way mirror. Paled, he cursed. "Well, now it's making some sense. I've just had some reports relayed to me from the majors who are dealing with the other four worlds. They are reporting that one in five dead had no legs in addition. Now I understand. They've made a new bio weapon, haven't they?"

No sense in hiding it, Doctor Andy thought. "Precisely, major. Senator Alfie and mate, Ambassador Miranda, were their test subjects. We need to confiscate all this new agent that we can find. It's batch #211. Some good may well come from this, major. The one legged victims have a normal foot. We believe that somehow the researchers stumbled on a full cure for the malformed feet. If so, here's a bit more that we may be able to undo in all the survivors."

"Okay, but I have to report this to Legate Smith. What are you going to do about these new victims?" Major Smythe asked. "I'll relay that to her as well."

The group headed for a comm center. An hour later, fully briefed, Queen Amy gave her consent to bring them all to her Imperial Castle. Later, when Legate Smith was fully briefed by the major, she agreed and ordered him to confiscate everything the doctors wanted and sent it all to Ashford-5. She also insisted they keep this new genetic modification bio agent top secret for now. She didn't want any of it to fall into unscrupulous hands, as had the original bio agent developed on Ashford-4, some thirty years ago.

Things began moving swiftly. Within two days, a light cruiser arrived to transport the new victims and all their life-support items to Ashford-5, along with a volume of computer records and many samples. "We can drive ourselves," Alfie insisted, "but it will speed things along if you can put us on our scooters. We can do it ourselves, but it takes us about a half hour to do it." The two women were lifted and placed onto the scooters. Their massive bosoms kept their heads elevated enough so they could operate the joystick controller with their mouths. Soon, the pair was scooting along the hallway at a good clip.

The group joined up with Jenni and Martha and their two daughters, who insisted on making their own way by hopping on their foot. Finally, the slowly enlarging group met the dozen others, who also insisted on waddling along on their own steam. These eighteen survivors still had a bit of self-pride remaining, and they were determined individuals, especially the children who knew nothing else. Meanwhile, workers began dismantling the three facilities, crating it up for shipment.

Finally, at the surface where transports were waiting for them, the group from Ashford-5 said their farewells. "Look, we'll be back home and see you all in just a few weeks," Doctor Mindy explained. That satisfied them; they'd already formed bonds with the two doctors.

Once the transports lifted off, the group headed to their own transport, heavily loaded with a dozen special medical machines and all the supplies for arm regrowth that they had been able to find. First stop, Frog Pond. They put one machine and one-twelfth of the supplies into Doctor Jenny's office. Lena and Doctor Mindy remained behind, while the others took a machine to a nearby plantation. There, Doctor Andy remained with another machine and supplies. Bernardo headed off to drop off the other ten machines at other plantations.

Meantime, Doctor Mindy began teaching Doctor Jenny how the process was done, performing the regrowth process on Jason. Once he was started, she had Doctor Jenny use the machine to do Rene. Satisfied that Doctor Jenny knew what to do, she then performed the operation on her as well. Now, she could only sit back and care for the daily needs of her three patients during the first critical two weeks.

At Worm Crossing, Doctor Andy did the same thing to their Lead Engineer, his wife, and their doctor. Thankfully, Bernardo soon returned to lend him a hand caring for them for this first two weeks. On the fifth day of the process, ten other doctors from neighboring planets arrived. Bernardo ferried them to the other ten plantations where he'd dropped off the machines and supplies. Thus, ten other plantations had the arm regrowth process begun on their plantation doctor and Lead Engineers.

After the two-week period ended, they headed back to Ashford-5. However, during this time, others were found alive on Bailey-3. All of these were young folks who were fortunate to have been living in small groups. One was an orphanage, for example. All told, Major Smythe and his men rescued another thousand and five victims. These were transported to the plantations, where they were given new homes. No single plantation received more than one family, however.

On the other four planets of the Big Five, rescue operations there fared poorly. Around a thousand men, women, and children, all young, were found still alive on each of those worlds. Fortunately, four other nearby worlds agreed to take them into their assisted living housing.

A dozen more special medical machines and supplies were sent back to Ashford-5. Another thirty-five were subsequently sent over to the plantations on Bailey-3. During the next two months, various doctors from other worlds came for two-week stays, educating more local doctors on how to perform the procedure, as well as performing it on the doctor and two Lead Engineers. After three months, around fifty plantations had the machines and a doctor who knew how to use it to begin the long process. Still, that left one thousand nine hundred fifty plantations out of the healing process. Far more had to be done and soon.

To that end, Emperor Kino made a deal with Legate Smith. Soon, companies would want to begin the lucrative salvage operations on the Big Five worlds. To gain salvage rights, each company had to deliver a new modified medical machine per each anticipated hundred million credits worth of salvage or an equivalent in chemical supplies. Emperor Kino wanted each group of a thousand or so victims to have their arms back in three to four years' time. That meant there had to be around a dozen such machines and supplies for each large group. At least Ashford-5 had their new dozen, added to their existing five, thus anticipating the process there would be completed in three years.

Chapter 16 Dealing with the Guilds

Late winter while Bernardo and Lena were off dealing with the ever-expanding crisis on Bailey-3, Queen Amy and Jan turned their attention onto the guilds once more. For more than thirty years, the Supreme Guild Masters, a secret organization, continued to run the many kingdoms. They were in possession of a large number of the very dangerous giant germanium crystals. In Tierra's distant past, the towers had gotten a hold of only a tiny fraction of similar giant crystals and used them to create terrible weapons of destruction that very nearly wiped out civilization on Tierra. Now, not only did the towers have them, but also these secretive guilds. Amy had no way of knowing the precise quantities anyone had, save her own Imperial Tower, which had amassed close to a hundred of them.

Still, these guild leaders had brought relative peace and prosperity to Tierra for the last thirty years. Rafe, whose degree was in sociology, and Elfe explained to her that in effect, these guild masters had ended the long-standing traditions of kings or lords as sole ruling monarchs. In their own way, these guild masters had helped ensure Queen Isabella's concepts of democratic kingdoms survived. Still, the problem remained — most of the voters were illiterate, which the guild masters continued to point out to Queen Amy.

Nadja's school in Exchange City was doing wonders, graduating around twenty new students each year. Each had approximately eight years of education, hardly an Academy education, but they were bright and literate. Returning to their kingdoms, these young men and women sung the praises of an education. Already the demand for schools in all kingdoms was quite high, something that could not be met until effective means for printing the required texts was available on Tierra. Hence, Amy knew this spring's engineers simply had to succeed in getting the guilds to accept their new inventions, which would lead to the bulk production of paper and printing presses, however crude by Imperium standards. After that, so many other inventions could not help but raise the standard of living throughout all Tierra. Everything depended upon acceptance this spring.

However, even after thirty years, Queen Amy knew almost next to nothing about the guilds and their internal operations. True, the top leaders often met once a year with her, but that was just high-level business. What went on in secret? She had many questions that needed answering, if she was going to continue to be a competent leader. In another year or two, three at the outside, she would have perhaps five hundred to a thousand young men and women who were very well educated at the Imperium Academies. They would certainly begin to apply their skills to invent many new things to improve everyone's lives.

Outside, the snows were falling once more. Normal for this time of year, the accumulated depth was over fifteen feet. The only person that Amy knew who knew much about the guilds and their operations was Nita Valen Franks co-owner of Elegant Fashions Inc. She decided to have a chat with her, while putting off her choice for their new senator. After what had happened to Senator Franco Hermanes, she, like many other rulers, was hesitant to send another off to potential doom. Seeing Nita would give her an excuse to put that chore off a while longer.

She and Jan headed down the stairs to the long tunnel system that connected the dozen manor houses of the complex, as well as the basement of Elegant Fashions Inc. "I hate stairs," Amy growled. She couldn't see the steps over her bosom. Besides keeping her balance in her toe shoes was tricky enough on level ground. She activated her crystal and used her *mentales* gifts to lower herself down to the tunnel's floor. "That's more like it."

"Slow down dear, wait for your side kick," Jan teased her, as she made her nearly as precarious way down the steps. At least, she thought, I don't have to wear those dismal toe shoes. She caught up with Amy and put a loving, steadying arm around her. "One day, I wish we could just be normal people. Come on. I got you."

A billion tiny steps later, Amy reached the elevator in

the basement of the five story building. At least it seemed that many to her. They found Nita in her top floor office, waiting for them, a pot of hot, black tea freshly made. The overly long spoons lay beside the three cups. "Hi ya. Tea's ready. Sure is snowing a lot. So what's up this time?" Nita gaily chatted, as the two made their slow, careful way from the elevator to her office desk.

After sitting down and sampling a teaspoon of the tea, Amy dived in. "I need to know everything that you know about the guilds and how they operate. You know more than anyone else that I know."

"Well, it's not all that much. I do deal a lot with a number of guilds now, no question of that. Let's see. They do control nearly all the various craftsmen and women. They guarantee the workmanship of all products produced by the guild members. Money back guarantees. I can definitely say the quality is now uniform between various members. Take the Fabric Construction Guild. I make regular purchases of bolts of cotton, satin, wool, paca, and linen, among others. Before the guilds took over, I would have personally to inspect every person who came here to sell me their bolts. Some were of such low quality that I had to reject them. Now, I almost never inspect them, if they are a guild member."

Amy asked, "What happened to the small, local producers?"

"Oh, I've heard they either had to join a guild and learn to make quality products or find another line of work."

"That's interesting. So how do they join a guild?" Amy inquired.

"Well, I can only say what I've heard, you see," Nita replied, pausing to lift another spoon of tea between her giant lip plates, as did Jan for Amy. "You approach the guild you wish to join and meet with the local Guild Master. If he or she approves, you are then apprenticed to one of the guild members for a period of time during which you learn the proper way to make whatever you are supposed to be making. When you are ready, you take some kind of test, but I've never gotten anyone to tell me much about it. It's all super-secret, you see. If you pass, then you are accepted into the guild house and are allowed to open your own shop. Of course, after that, the guild master could well send other apprentices to you for training as well."

"Okay," Amy said slowly. "So how does one become one of the Guild Masters? What's their hierarchy anyway?"

"Well, there's the local Guild Master. He or she is very visible here in Exchange City. I've heard talk that there is a Central Midlands Guild Master, who oversees all of the guilds of one type around here, like the Fabric Construction Guild. There must be dozens and dozens of these middle men and women, one for each type of guild. Of course, you have met the Supreme Guild Masters, who I think must be above these regional ones. I find it curious that these middle leaders operate across kingdom boundaries. Curious," Nita explained and took another sip of tea.

She then added, "That's about all I know."

"Well, it's something to go on at least. It's not like the old days when we could spot the nobles a mile away and know that they wielded the power," Amy lamented.

"I know what you mean," Nita replied. "Still, isn't it just fascinating?"

"What's fascinating?" Amy asked, not grasping what Nita was talking about.

"The elegant fashions. Back in the pre-guild days, anyone who had power and wealth always wore the latest elegant fashions. Pipe corsets, fine gowns, expensive suits, lip plates, heels, even the huge earrings. The craftsmen and women wore simple, practical clothes, frowning on the extravagances of the nobles and wealthy," Nita explained.

"Why is this fascinating?" Amy asked, still not grasping Nita's point.

"Because it's what — thirty plus years later. Now, the merchants and the craftsmen and women have grown in wealth and are beginning to wear similar outfits. Why, only yesterday, I fixed up the local Miller's Guild Master and his wife. He purchased a pipe corset and lip plates for himself, along with three excellent suits, while his wife got the same modifications, along with the six inch heels that Jan and I wear, and six really fancy satin gowns like you and Jan always wear. You see, the Guild Masters are now looking much like the nobles, lords, and ladies do. I think Rafe and Elfe said it was a social status thing. Anyway, it's good for business."

"Interesting," Amy commented. She wasn't aware of this development.

"Indeed. Nowadays, if you walk the streets of Exchange City or any other large town in which we have a store, if you see an elegantly dressed man or woman, he or she could be merely a wealthy merchant or even a Guild Master or spouse, if not a noble or lord or lady. One can't tell the difference any longer," Nita advised.

"Curious. I wonder if those secret individuals higher in the organizations are also doing this?" Amy wondered.

Nita replied, "No way to tell. Could well be, but I'm sure they won't be admitting to being one of the secret leaders."

"No, I suppose not. Just how many non-nobles and lords have you outfitted?" Amy inquired.

"Have to check." She got up and found her laptop before returning and taking her seat. She brought up her sales records and programmed a simple database search. A minute later, she said, "Well, in just the Midlands, we sold fancy modifications and outfits to around three thousand men and women, none of whom are known nobles or lords. While I can't say for sure, these are likely guilds men and women or merchants. After all, it takes a bit of silver to purchase these outfits."

"Wow. I had no idea. You are making money still," Amy teased her.

"You bet. I simply supply what's demanded in fine clothing, as well as everyday outfits, but not so much the latter," Nita teased back. "So why all this interest in the guilds anyway, if you don't mind my asking?"

"Some of those who have been rescued are trying to put their Academy educations to work here on Tierra. They want to get approval from the guilds for some of their projects," Amy answered.

"Ah. Double whammy then," Nita replied, taking another spoonful.

"Huh?"

"Oh, I mean they are hermaphrodites to be technically correct. There is a lot of pent-up hostility against these people just because their bodies are so very different from everyone else. Silly really, but you know how superstitious and biased some people can be. They have to fight prejudice, as well as getting their plans accepted. Double whammy," Nita explained.

"I didn't know. How bad is it, do you think, this prejudice against us?" Amy asked.

"Don't really know, but it's growing, I think. If you want my opinion, I'd get them all doing some kind of valuable public works, so the average person can see they are really just another person, much like themselves."

"Good idea, Nita. I'll give that some thought and soon. Well, I best be going. Thanks for the tea and advice."

Later, Amy sat in her private study, pondering what she'd learned. That there was a growing distrust and dislike of the hermaphrodites bothered her. After all, her own group, including those of the spaceport numbered over fifty, ignoring all those victims she'd accepted here. Perhaps the visit by the Supreme Guild Masters was just the tip of the mountain. She now had two things with which to wrestle: the prejudice against "her kind" and learning the secret ways by which the guilds operated. Three: their plans for the future.

She decided that picking a new senator was an easier task. She focused and sent message to Venerado Henry Valen Franks. In turn, he had the Circles send out her message to the many rulers of the kingdoms. By now, everyone had heard what had happened to Senator Franco, though Amy kept his new identity as Sasha a secret. As she anticipated, to a kingdom, they all agreed with her suggestion to appoint someone from her large group. The ideal candidate was Ruthy Agahve-Jones, Zarita's eldest. She'd recently graduated the Academy on Winno-3 with a degree in political science. Unfortunately, her mate, Lela, wanted to teach history at Nadja's school. Amy decided Lela ought to be their ambassador. Worse still, each had a six year old daughter and were expecting their second daughters later this year.

An hour later, the two pregnant women came to meet

with her, along with their mothers, Zarita and Doctor Whitney. Amy quickly explained what she had in mind. Ruthy was clearly elated. "All right! I was so hoping I'd get a chance to follow in my parent's footsteps. Tierra's senator! Terrific. And Lela, you, our official ambassador."

Lela frowned. "True, but what about our kids? This is a dangerous assignment. So far, every senator we've sent to the Imperium Senate has met with disasters. I don't want to put them at risk if something happens to us." Amy knew her fears were well founded and didn't try to minimize the danger they would be facing.

Zarita spoke up. "Look kids, you can leave the children here with us. Yes, it's a dangerous job for any of us from Tierra, but Franco had no troubles for many years. He always was surrounded with the other senators from the Ataro Empire. As I understand it, they protected him, until the genocide attack."

Doctor Whitney added, "I agree with Zarita. We can look after our grandchildren. That's what grandparents often do. I know how badly Ruthy wants this appointment. Lela is a history buff. As our ambassador, she can get access to volumes of historical documents on the Imperium and many other worlds. All I ask is that she writes it all down in one of our language so we on Tierra can learn and avoid past mistakes of other worlds."

Queen Amy cautioned, "I agree, but I do need to caution you both. Right now, there are few people on Proxima Prime. You are going to be mostly on your own. I don't even know if some stores are even open. I've no idea what the medical facilities will be if you should have pregnancy issues. Still, with your own private transport, if you run into difficulties, you can get to Winno-3 in one day at top speed. Just always keep your transport fully fueled at all times."

Zarita added, "She's right. Plus, I'm giving each of you some of my special crystals that will greatly amplify your gifts." This really pleased both young women. "Besides, you can return here for two weeks every quarter and all summer. The Senate breaks for three months in the summer, so it's not like you are going to be gone for extended times."

The more they chatted the more comfortable everyone became with the two leaving Tierra for the heart of the galaxy. The young couple headed home to explain it to their six year olds and to begin packing. After they left, Doctor Whitney commented, "I take it this was easier to handle than the guilds?"

Amy chuckled. "How did you know about that?"

"Little birdies," she teased, and then added, "Jan. Seriously, you should have a chat with Maggie and Len Childa." Doctor Whitney didn't say more, leaving Amy curious enough to do just that with Katrina and Carla's youngest. The youngest, who were still attending the Academy on Winno-3, were home for just a few more days before heading back for the spring semester. She still had time.

With Jan's help as always, Amy paid a visit to the pair, who lived in one of the newer add-on manor houses of the extended Imperial Castle complex. When they entered the large commons room, they found Maggie and Len playing with their four year old children. Both were pregnant again, due later this summer, as were so many of the hermaphrodite children around the castle and spaceport.

Maggie looked up in surprise. "Well, this is a surprise, Amy. Something must be up. You could have just sent for us. We can walk lots better than you are able to. Come, sit down, and look out for the kid's toys." She hastily moved clutter off of their sofa, a bit embarrassed by Amy's sudden appearance. "Tea or something?"

With Jan's assistance as usual, Amy sat down. "No thanks. I came to chat with both of you. Doctor Whitney suggested it. I suppose I should explain, since I really don't know exactly why she said I ought to visit you two. It's this darn guild masters problem that I've been wrestling with off and on for neigh onto thirty years, except I keep getting sidetracked by Imperium events. You see, we know next to nothing about the secret guilds, how they operate, what their goals are, and their plans. They remain secret organizations, but I can see why they have done that. None of the noble or lords were ever able to directly attack them, let alone find them." Amy elaborated a bit more.

Maggie shot a look at Len. Amy acknowledged their right to private thoughts and didn't try to catch even their surface thoughts. Maggie adjusted her lip plates a little and then volunteered, "Amy, what about letting Len and me join two guilds and see what we can learn? We both really aren't very interested in more studies at the Academy. Len's not interested in all his mother's computer things, and I'm not like my mother either. I don't want to be a governor. You see, I really want to make fine tapestries that show our history, and Len's a good portrait painter. He could join the Painter's Guild, and I, the Weaver's Guild."

Len added, "But you'll have to help us break the news to our mothers. Both are so dead set on us graduating the Academy, just as they and our older siblings did. Frankly, we really want to pursue our passions. You help us, and we'll help you. Deal?" He was grinning, but of course, with their giant lip plates, it was invisible, except for his eyes.

Amy chuckled, and Jan laughed. Jan teased Amy, "They get the better deal this time, dear."

"Okay, I'll speak to your parents," Amy agreed. "I best do it now; you are supposed to be heading back tomorrow."

Two hours later, Amy breathed a sigh of relief. She'd gone over to the spaceport to meet with Katrina and Carla personally and outlined both her problem and what Maggie and Len wanted. She felt both women stiffen, as she explained that their youngest wanted to drop out of the Academy and join local guilds.

Finally, Katrina sighed. "I know Maggie's always been keenly interested in weaving tapestries. With our foot long fingernails, that was almost an impossible task for her when she was little. Then, when we were able to shorten them to six inches, she began to make them again, but it was still excessively hard for her. I was hoping she'd grow out of it. Obviously, she hasn't. As much as I want her to get her Academy degree, I really should allow her to do what she wants to do. After all, she's twenty-five and has her own family. It's her life to live. If she can get us inside information, then even I would be grateful for that. We know next to nothing about the internals of these guilds. I'll give her my blessings."

Carla grinned. "Men, they do pretty much what they want to do. Sure, I'm disappointed he isn't going to finish the Academy, but he's got talent as an artist, so I'll not stand in his way. Kat, we should speak to them right away. We can have Mary Beth and Bethi pack up their things there on Winno-3 and send them back later on. They are to leave tomorrow, so we best hop to it."

An hour later, both Maggie and Len hugged Amy. "Thank you, thank you," Maggie gushed.

"You're the best. We'll not let you down. You can count on us," Len insisted.

"Just don't do anything to cause troubles in the guilds. And be aware of the prejudice that many 'normal' people have against us," Amy both ordered and suggested.

"We won't," Maggie promised. "We know about the prejudice. We see it every time we go for a walk in Exchange City. We can handle it." Amy wasn't so sure it would be easily handled, but backed their youthful enthusiasm.

Chapter 17 Dealing with Divas

Ariceli de la Vegas knew where she was born, Bonito, and the year, 1250. She knew she was special, had known that since she was five and learned to hear her parents and other children's thoughts. By seven, she was already skilled at getting others to do what she wanted them to do, though she didn't have a name for her gift, until she was fourteen and briefly trained at Valen Tower. Dominate. Well, she'd used that gift all her life. The trouble for Ariceli was she didn't know the planet on which she was born, not until very recently. This was a life-long problem for her. Why? She was another kidnaped fourteen year old telepath. She also knew the ruling Emperor and Empress were being deposed, but admired them. Once, her father had taken her to visit Exchange City. There she'd met them and became fascinated by their lack of arms.

She'd been drugged during her sleep, taken off-world, and purchased as a slave telepath by Griswold Gring of Halcion-3. When she awoke, she was on a strange new world, unable to understand anyone, unless they wore their ULAT boxes. The fifty year old man, well-dressed, was the first sight that she saw when she awoke. "If you do as I say and assist me, I will see that you are very well treated and have all the finest gowns and jewelry money can buy." Terrified, she did as he asked, discovering he had not lied to her.

For two years, she looked for a way to escape his clutches, but found nothing practical. Still, she accumulated an expensive wardrobe and jewelry, as promised. When she was sixteen, an event occurred that forever changed her life. Griswold had a critical meeting on Proxima Prime, something to do with guns that his company was manufacturing. He took her with him.

To a "primitive" from Tierra, Proxima Prime seemed to her to be the culmination of everything. She'd called it Heaven. Giant skyscrapers, shuttles as thick as bees in a hive, and people — more people than she ever imagined existed. From the moment she landed on Proxima Prime, she knew this was the world for her!

After the successful meeting in which she used her "talents" as Griswold called them, he celebrated and took her to the Royal Imperium Ballet. The music sent shivers down her spine, almost continuously, but the dancers — walking on the tips of their toes — such grace, such beauty, such expressionism. She just *had* to become a ballet dancer! When the ballet ended, she jumped up and joined the crowd's enthusiastic standing ovation. Ariceli knew that she wanted to be down there accepting this volume of admiration for a stellar performance.

That night when they returned to their hotel, she made her plans. She had most of her clothes with her, three shipping crates. Since she would have been denied past customs unless she had a proper ID card, Griswold had one made for her. With it, she had access to her own bank account and could come and go on her own. She didn't need the old man any longer. As he slept, she entered his mind and worked her magic on him. Then, she rose, dressed again, summoned a man to carry her crates to the public shuttle bay, hired a shuttle to take her back to the Royal Imperium Ballet building.

As the performers, musicians, and hands began arriving in the morning, they found Ariceli and her crates at the main entrance. To each person that walked up, she said, "I want to be a ballet dancer. Who do I see about it?" Most shrugged her off, but one young woman her own age didn't.

"Hi, I'm Carys Brann. I'm learning too. You need to see Mr. Baggio. Come on. I'll introduce you to him. He's always looking for new talent. Have you danced before?" She was sixteen with long, wavy blonde hair, and pale, enchanting blue eyes. Coming from the Westerlings, Ariceli had very long, wavy, black hair and yellow eyes with brown speckles.

A bit later, an effeminate man walked up, well-dressed, immaculately so, Ariceli thought. Carys stopped him, "Mr. Baggio, this is Ariceli. She wants to be a ballet dancer too."

He looked her over from top to bottom, before speaking. "Have you had your basic dance training? Any en pointe work?"

"No sir. I saw the performance last night, and I just

have to be a ballerina too," she replied honestly. She sensed his mind. No basic training, no en pointe work, no job. Before he could vocalize his rejection of her, she focused and Dominated him.

"Oh! Well, you are hired. Come on in. You can begin with Carys' class. Carys, you show her where to dress, get her to Wardrobe, and outfitted properly." *Why did I hire her?* His mind felt strange. He shook his head and went on inside.

"Cool, Ariceli. Come on; the hands can bring your crates. You can stay with me. This way, we have to get into our tights and get our slippers from Wardrobe," Carys explained cheerfully.

By the end of their practice day, Ariceli's legs felt like mush. Her feet ached; even her arms were sore, but she felt elated. She was dancing and knew this was it! She moved into the small suite with Carys. Almost at once, the two became best friends, each helping the other master the next dance actions and moves. However, she noticed absolutely no one had yellow eyes, so she took Carys' advice and had them died a pale blue, similar to her girlfriend's.

Five years passed like a whirlwind for the two young dancers, both of whom excelled beyond the others in their classes. At twenty-one, the two finally had their first major roles in the ballet *George's Follies*. From the first thunderous applause, both women were entirely hooked.

During the next ten years, their skills peaked, and Ariceli continued to use her special skills to guarantee that she and Carys always had top billing in each performance. Of course, others began to harbor grudges and ill feelings towards these two, who always seemed to have the eye of the director, Mr. Aesop Lag. Then, for ten years after that period, the two continued to improve and ended up holding the respect of all the other dancers. They were the prima donnas.

To help them stay on the very peak of their game, both women had their feet done, joining about half of the other dancers who took this route to improve their performances. That is, the bones in their toes and feet were fused into the en pointe position. Their ankles still worked as normal, but their toes no longer moved. Nothing flexed below their ankles. With more training and exercise, this gave the dancers a more powerful lift or so all the dancers claimed, although no one has ever proved this procedure actually helped.

Once this was done, when doing normal walking, the two had to wear sturdy ballet shoes or boots, since their feet were otherwise rigid when flat on the floor. When merely walking in these shoes or boots, they had a sort of stick-walking gait. The soles of their shoes or boots only had about a square inch of surface area, but that was partially balanced by the tall, spiked, metal heels. When dancing, they swapped these shoes and boots for their pointe slippers. Obviously, most of their dancing was done en pointe, further wowing the audiences. The big drawback was handling stairs, which put stress on their knees and leg muscles, as one might expect. They, like the other dancers who had the procedure done on themselves, didn't complain, but reveled in the grand applause that always ended their performance, done almost entirely en pointe.

However, nearly every day during these years, Ariceli had to use her "gifts" on one of their fellow dancers or Mr. Aesop Lag. The former complained that Ariceli and Carys were hogging the diva performances, while the latter continually urged caution, and to give conservative performances. At the end of this period in their careers, they were forty-one, the age around which most dancers chose to retire from performance and perhaps move into the teaching arena.

By this time, Ariceli and Carys were rather wealthy. Neither wanted to retire. She decided to take matters in her own hands. To Carys, she declared, "Okay. I've had it with all this conservatism of Mr. Aesop Lag. He has to go! I can be a far better director of the Royal Imperium Ballet!"

"But he isn't about to retire. You know directors. He'll be here long after we retire, Ariceli. Besides, we're missing some of our leaps now. We're not as flexible as we were," Carys countered, recalling her embarrassment earlier during practice. "Perhaps, we should retire."

"I'll take care of us, Carys. And I'm going to be the new director! It's time that we give them a *real* ballet — a performance they will never forget! Tomorrow, Mr. Lag goes, one way or the other!"

"The hell I am retiring! Are you nuts? It's you who should retire. You missed a leap yesterday," Mr. Aesop Lag fumed, when she told him he ought to retire early the next morning.

Ariceli focused, her crystal activated. Mr. Lag threw his hands up to his head, fighting her domination of his mind. Accidentally, a blood vessel in his head burst. By the time the emergency crew arrived, he was dead, but Ariceli was already gone. At the time he was pronounced dead in his office, she was Dominating the Arts Committee members, who "chose" her to be the new director.

She returned to the building. By now, all the musicians and dancers had arrived for their practice session and were standing around discussing the untimely death of their director. "May I have everyone's attention?" Ariceli called out. "I'm now the new director of the Royal Imperium Ballet. I've just come from the Arts Committee, who has unanimously chosen me. My first action is to get anyone, who wants to continue dancing and needs it, a trip to the medical facilities and the Rejuvenation Machine. I'm personally paying for the rejuvenations, not the ballet company. It's on me. From now on, we're going to set entirely new and unprecedented standards in our performances! It's time that we really showed our fans just what we really can do!"

While this move cost her dearly, she now had the full backing of all the other dancers. She and Carys were twenty-one again. Once the many rejuvenations were completed, she set to work on revising their current ballet, *The Elegant Swan*. "Look fellows, we need a spectacular jump and catch. Something to wow and stun the audience, something they've never seen before. So when we get to the dual jump, Carys is to be thrown ten feet up over to you, while I'm going to arc over her at around twenty feet. You guys are fired if you let us fall."

"But that can't be done! No one can leap ten feet, let alone twenty. Besides, how can we possibly catch you if you are going that fast?" one young man protested. Many other dancers' heads nodded in agreement. *She must be out of her mind.* Ariceli picked up that unspoken though from several dancers.

"We can do this. Positions everyone. Maestro, the finale jump music scene please. Come on, Carys. To our positions," Ariceli ordered. Everyone quickly took their positions. Two male dancers put their arms around Carys and Ariceli; they were on opposite sides of the stage. As the music began, both women were en pointe, being twirled around several times before the great lift and toss. Ariceli focused. As the men tossed the two women, she used her gifts to lift Carys up to ten feet and herself to twenty. Those watching saw the two women traversing a huge arc, one above the other. As they came down, Ariceli began lifting them up, braking their momentum, allowing the men to catch them in a position horizontal to the stage, then pivoting them upright, while twirling them around three times. When they stopped, Ariceli saw all of the other dancers and musicians had stopped and were staring at them, their mouths wide open.

"My god! That was spectacular!" one dancer yelled. Then, they all broke into a loud applause. Ariceli knew she had them under her thumb now. A week later, the Royal Imperium Ballet held the first performance under their new director. As she expected, their grand finale jumps brought the house down. The applause was thunderous; many yelled and whistled. The reviews the next day were full of superlatives. "Never have we witnessed such jumps!" "Director Ariceli de la Vegas has outdone herself!" "A performance not to be missed!" "All previous ballets pale compared to this performance." "Royal Ballet sets new standards!" On and on went the accolades, which were not missed by the many dancers and musicians.

For the next twenty-three years, Ariceli continued to break all box office records for profits. At the turn of the century, once more, she paid for the Rejuvenation Machine for all those dancers who wished to continue dancing. As she and Carys chatted after becoming twenty-one once more, she said, "We need to break new ground. We need something entirely new, entirely awe inspiring, something that will bring even more to watch our performances, Carys. What haven't we done yet?"

They had already performed all the major ballet works. Finding new material was becoming more challenging. "Say," Carys had an idea. "There is an old ballet done only on Cadoc-3. It's a history allegory and very spiritual and uplifting. *Carwyn Ascending*. It's about a woman, who through travails of this world, maintains her faith and is rewarded by being uplifted into Heaven as an angel at the end. But I don't know if it'll be acceptable here on Proxima Prime, though."

"Cool. I like the sound of it. Can you get us the score and choreography?" Ariceli asked.

A week later, a large crate arrived from her home world of Cadoc-3. While Carys hummed the score, Ariceli read through the text and looked over the suggestions for the choreography and the scenery. "I like this. Carwyn loses her arms to a bear when she was a child. She grows up and deals with the hard travails of her life, inspiring others along the way. This is very timely, Carys. After all, there are so darn many of these terrorist attack victims who are facing a terrible life, just like her. We simply *must* do this one and in a spectacular way. All terrorist attack victims will be given free passes to the ballet. Wait, it would be even *more* dramatic if I, as Carwyn, didn't have arms either, just like the story."

"But you can't. How could you live like that?" Carys instantly reacted.

Ariceli ignored her protest. "I will certainly have to do an awful lot more practicing, just to get used to keeping my balance and jumps. Think of the image it would create! If we do this right, it'll give hope to the many terrorist victims. I simply must do this. Besides, think of how much more all the other ballets that we do after this one will be. You can be my arms when I need them, Carys. Okay? Good." She didn't give her dearest friend time to find more reasons not to do this extreme thing.

"Okay, but only if we test this first. We need a proof of concept before I agree, dear," Carys declared. Ariceli agreed. Always before, she insisted on a proof of concept from the others who gave her suggestions. She ought to follow her own rules.

An hour later, Carys had tied her arms securely behind

her back and then tied her hands to her waist. "Okay, try to move them," Carys ordered. Try as she might, Ariceli couldn't move her arms in the slightest, only her fingers, but those didn't matter. "Okay, now stand up on your own and see if you can even walk." Both were still wearing their normal walking ballet boots. Without her hands to assist her, Ariceli lunged up and got to her feet, wiggling significantly to get her balance.

"Not very graceful," she commented. "This is a bit scary, Carys, but I'm doing it." She walked around their room for a time, proving to herself that she could do it, more or less. Then, she sat back down, but had to toss her head to one side to get her quite long black hair out of the way. She'd allowed it to grow some and it fell just below her knees. This, she often utilized in her performances, allowing her partners to swing her around with her hair flowing outward, a spectacular effect. Carys allowed her blonde hair to be also the same length. It was common for both prima donnas to be twirled around with their hair flowing out behind them. Audiences seemed to love the effect. With her gifts, Ariceli always sensed the impact of a dancer's move had on their audiences. That was one reason she was the most successful director in the history of the Royal Imperium Ballet.

"Okay, put my slippers on and let's see if I can still manage to dance some," she ordered. A few minutes later, she again awkwardly got to her always en pointe position. Carys joined her. Together, they began some simple moves. "Well, I am doing it, but I'm going to have to practice a whole lot. I look more like a beginner again." She laughed a little.

"Now, I'm going to try a move. Twirl me when I am in position," she ordered. Cautiously, she leaned over while raising her right leg until her torso, head, and right leg were perfectly straight and parallel to the floor, perpendicular to her straight left leg standing en pointe. Once in the position, Carys touched her right toe and began to twirl her around in a circle, her hair flying out in a black wall. Once she let go, Ariceli nearly fell trying to recover with both feet on the ground. "Well, I did it; needs practice though. Look, I can do this, Carys. Think how incredibly beautify this ballet will be! It will knock the socks off everyone in the audience. We will raise the bar on quality ballet performances yet again."

"As long as I only have to feed you and dress you, I guess that won't be too much," Carys finally agreed, imagining the total effect with Ariceli in the appropriate costume on stage.

"Thanks, this is the perfect time to have this done. We're on the summer break for two months. After that, we have to begin rehearsing, building the sets, handling the music, casting the others. Tons to do. I best get this done right away and then spend the two months practicing to get back to where we're at now," Ariceli declared.

The next day, she and Carys made their careful walk into the medical center. In order to have the procedure done, she was again forced to use her Dominate gifts on the doctor. An hour later, he helped her sit up from the medical machine. She looked down at her empty shoulders. They were perfectly smooth, slightly hollow, but zero scarring. In fact, she could not tell that she'd even been born with arms. Carys helped her back into her blouse, which now looked strange on her, empty sleeves dangling. "I can see that we're going to need new costumes and clothes for me. Thanks, doctor." She carefully got to her feet, determined to walk out of the medical building on her own, just as she had entered, as if she were perfectly normal.

She got to the door ahead of Carys and realized she had no way to open it now. She hadn't thought of that detail. Walking down the long hallway filled with other people was more than a little scary for her. One bump and she'd go down like a log, especially walking on her toes in the ballet boots. Outside, the wind was blowing slightly, and she found she couldn't push errant hair from her face anymore. Small price, she thought. To get to their shuttle, they had to descend one set of stairs. When she got to them, she nearly panicked. She was used to holding onto the railings securely. Ariceli took a deep breath and very carefully descended them, unwilling to have Carys help her unless it was absolutely necessary. Getting into the shuttle turned out to be more than she could do by herself, as well as getting out of it. She had no hands or arms to brace or pull her body.

Thus, began two frightening months of adaption for Ariceli. She had no choice now but to go through with her grand plans. Carys hired a seamstress to alter all of Ariceli's many gowns, dresses, and blouses. For eight hours each day, Ariceli practiced her dancing, stopping only for restroom breaks and meals. At first, she found even her old simple moves extremely frightening. More than once, she attempted to break her fall or catch her balance using her arms, only to take an ugly fall. Undaunted, she struggled to get back onto her own feet without Carys' assistance. "Look, I have to be able to do this myself. It's enough that you are feeding me and dressing me. Practice, practice, practice. I have to get really good again. I just have to, Carys." She picked up her friend's thought: *I tried to tell her not to do this.*

At night, she and Carys poured over the new ballet, *Carwyn Ascending*, working out the myriad details. However, Ariceli now found she could no longer write anything. "Sorry, I guess from now on, you have to do the writing for me. On this performance, I'm making you acting director, since this one comes from your world, and you know best how it's to be done." That pleased Carys enormously.

When the cast, crews, dancers, and musicians reassembled after their summer break, everyone was shocked at what Ariceli had done to herself. However, she responded immediately. "Gang, we are about to break all box office records. We're doing a very special ballet from Carys' home world called *Carwyn Ascending*. I'm playing the lead, which is why I've had this done so I can be in persona properly. Carys is acting director on this one. Tell them about it, dear."

After Carys gave a long narrative, they began to see Ariceli's reasoning, but still thought she should never have done such a thing. Could she even dance now? That was the uppermost question in many minds. That notion soon dispelled. During the next hectic month, sets were built, music rehearsed, choreography worked out, and costumes made. Organized chaos. Well, all new productions fared little better. Day by day, it all began to come together.

Finally, opening night came. Ariceli was a little nervous. She had many, many fans out there in the audience. They would be utterly shocked when they first saw her appearance on the stage. She wore a light blue gown, heavily pleated below her waist. When she would raise and swing her leg, the folds of her gown would sweep around magnificently. From backstage, she gazed out at the absolutely packed hall. She felt a surge of pride. She and Carys had really put the Royal Ballet on the arts map, so to speak.

The lights dimmed for the third and last time. Now, it would begin, she told herself. Even the music was incredible. A long ancient instrument called a harpsichord began playing, the tingling sound of its quill-plucked strings echoing in the giant hall. The curtains rolled back, revealing the opening set, a rural farmstead. She took a deep breath, and en pointe took her tiny steps onto the stage, prepared to hear gasps from the audience. For some reason, she only heard a few. Later, she realized most people assumed this was an illusion, that she had her arms somehow tied inside her costume.

Two hours later, the final scene was at hand. Breathtaking was the only way to describe it. Surrounded by a host of angels, Ariceli executed ten of her famous giant leaps, thankful that none of the men dropped her. Then, amid an exciting trumpet fanfare, she took her final leap. Nearly invisible wires lifted her and six other angels up into the blue sky, while villagers looked on in awe. Slowly, the curtains closed. Even before the music hit the final resolving chord in D Major, the audience broke into a thunderous applause, nearly deafening, some dancers claimed afterwards.

One by one, the dancers moved on stage. When Carys and Ariceli came on last, again the applause was utterly deafening. For once, no one could whistle louder than the clapping. Ariceli bowed graciously, hoping she wouldn't take a fall before everyone. After three more cameos, they were forced to do an encore of the final scene once more. *Carwyn Ascending* became an overnight sensation to those who enjoyed ballet on Proxima Prime. The box office was soon sold out. In fact, they had to do four showings each week for nearly a year. After that first week, the only way anyone could get tickets was for nine months down the road. *Carwyn Ascending* became one of the longest running ballets ever hosted by the Royal Ballet.

As promised, Ariceli insisted that any of the terrorist attack victims who wanted to see the ballet got free front row seats. Many took advantage of this one time offer. The ballet company had never made so much profit in one nine month period in its entire history. Although known as a bossy prima donna who always got her way, she became highly respected by everyone in the company. As one Arts Committee member put it, "She can be as bossy and demanding as she wants to be. Look at the box office receipts."

In 1320, she, Carys, and many other dancers once more used the Rejuvenation Machine, becoming twenty-one once more. However, she continued to hire and utilize new, young dancers, giving them a chance, just as she had so long ago.

Five years later, although both women were really seventy-five, yet their bodies were a young twenty-six, disaster struck everyone on Proxima Prime, the time of the planetary genocide attack. Neither prima donna had married. There was no time in their lives for such things. They slept together and pleasured each other instead. Although unspoken, they loved each other. Even their own menstrual cycles were in synch with each other and had been for half a century. Ariceli also depended heavily on Carys for mundane things she was unable to do for herself, ever since she had her arms removed for the incredible ballet show. Yet, because of their fame and success, Carys didn't mind helping her in the least. If truth were told, she knew that she would never have risen to her stellar height without Ariceli beside her, guiding her, and leading her. Together, they were an unbeatable, unstoppable pair. That terrible night so much changed for the worst, as it did for hundreds of billions of others on Proxima Prime.

The two were in bed in their penthouse suite on the hundredth floor of the Performing Artists Skyscraper, within walking distance of the Royal Ballet complex and hall. Because of their usually long and hectic days, they had always had both a maid and a cook working for them. Their maid came once a week to clean and dust. Louise, their cook, came by twice each day, once in the early morning to prepare their breakfast and then in the evening to make their dinners. She also cleaned up the morning dishes each evening and the supper dishes in the mornings. Further, she handled the grocery shopping for the two women. Ariceli and Carys always had their pantry very well stocked. Often, they'd throw a celebration party for some of their close associates, their fellow dance partners. Hence, they insisted on having lots of food in stock.

This evening, the two had finished eating around seven, leaving the large pot of stew in the refrigerator and the dirty dishes on the table for Louise to handle in the morning. Evenings were particularly bothersome for Ariceli. Only when they came home each evening did she feel the real loss of her arms. First, she could only sit and allow Carys to feed her supper and hold her teacup up so she could sip her after-dinner, black tea. Afterwards, she would carefully rise on her own and walk to their bedroom, but after sitting down, Carys then had to undress her and draw their bath waters. They had an oversized tub and bathed together. Both had to slip on ballet mule heels in order to walk from their bedroom to the bath. Ariceli then had no choice but to allow her dearest friend to bathe her, and later help her out of the tub and dry her off. The final straw was having to sit and allow Carys to brush out her lush, long black wavy hair, and sit there watching while Carys did the same to her equally long, wavy blonde hair. That done, the two slipped naked beneath the blue satin sheets, though Carys always pulled up the covers for them.

Yes, each evening, Ariceli was bitterly reminded of just what she'd given up for the ballet and how dependent she really was on Carys. Yet, once in bed, she always did her very best to see that Carys was pleasured. That she could do and do well. Slipping into rapport with Carys was as easy for her now as breathing, so long had they been together. While in rapport, she knew just what Carys desired at any moment and did her best to fill that desire, much to Carys' immense pleasure. That fateful evening followed the same pattern as most all evenings had for countless years. As they drifted into a satisfied sleep, neither sensed nor knew that they were slipping into a coma that would last for three entire days.

Ariceli always slept on the left side of the bed so that if she needed to get up to use the bathroom, she could slip out of the bed and into her mule ballet shoes without disturbing Carys. She awoke very groggy. Her mind felt fuzzy for some reason, and she needed to go badly. Carefully, she slipped her legs over the side of the bed and used them more or less to pivot herself into a sitting position. Two large lip loops dropped down touching her upper chest, startling her awake. As she looked down at them and suddenly sensing these were her lips, she could no longer see her feet! Her perky breasts were gone. Two enormous basketballs had replaced them! As she was staring in complete disbelief, Carys stirred. Her awkward motions to sit up had roused her. Carys screamed, and Ariceli turned to look at her lover and gasped.

Calm. Calm. Tranquil waters. Ariceli slipped into rapport with Carys, and forcibly sent calming waves through the woman's body. Her screaming ceased. "What's happened to me?" Carys wailed, struggling mightily to sit up, but that only aroused even more panic in the woman.

"Use your feet like levers. Pull yourself over to the side and sit by me," Ariceli whispered. Fortunately, ever since they first met, they had always used Imperium Standard as their spoken language, bypassing the constantly need to wear the ULAT boxes. Further, IS was used all the time at the ballet, since dancers couldn't wear the ugly black boxes while performing. Hence, her whispers were understood. As Carys struggled wildly to get across the bed and into a sitting position on it edge, sheer, stark panic grew steadily. Her stomach knotted into a ball. It took all Ariceli's power to dampen some of it and keep her lover from freaking out entirely.

Finally, the two sat side by side on the edge of their bed and looked at each other, gasping at what they saw, and with Ariceli continuing to do all she could to restrain the ever growing panic in Carys. "Slow, steady breaths," she whispered, and watched as Carys tried to steady her panicked breathing.

"I — I can't hardly understand you," Carys whispered back. "What's happened to us? Our lips are gone; my arms are gone. Look at our breasts! They're bigger than our heads. I can't see over them! Oh god, Ariceli, we can't live like this!"

Ariceli didn't need to hear that and for a moment lost

her focus. Panic seeped into her own stomach. Her crystal grew brighter than it ever had, before she was able to calm her own terror and then slightly diminish that of Carys. However, no sooner has she gotten her own self a bit calmer and Carys a little less panicky, when Carys shrieked, "Oh god! Look down there! You've got a penis! Do I have one?"

Ariceli swallowed hard, looked over at Carys and nodded, unable to speak for fear of unleashing her own terror, as simultaneously, both women realized they too had become the victims of the same horrific bio terrorist attack, as had so many others during the past thirty-some years. Finally, Ariceli whispered, "Not our feet! Good god, not them!" Desperately, she swung her right foot up to her lap. Now she did shriek, her magnificent fused feet were malformed. Her toes wiggled and bent. Gone was her precious en pointe feet, her claim to fame, the sole thing that mattered the most to her. Worse, they were so badly malformed, she'd not be able to rise en pointe, even in her ballet slippers! While she might have been able to adjust to the other physical changes, the loss of her ballet-shaped feet was a crushing blow, dashing her entire career, and her reason for existence. Ariceli now screamed and lost it. Beside her, Carys also checked her own feet and soon screamed along with her lover. Both of their careers were destroyed. Neither could dance any longer! Utterly crushing.

Shrieking eventually gave way to sobbing grief, which yielded to urgent needs to use the bathroom. Tears of defeat streaming down their cheeks, both women attempted to slip on their mule ballet shoe, only to find their "warped" feet wouldn't remotely fit their shoes. Since their toes now worked, they attempted to stand up on them. Only their extensive ballet training allowed them to manage to stand and move slowly, though Carys wiggled and wobbled crazily, just as Ariceli had so many years before.

"You can do it. Balance, dear. Lean on me if you need too," Ariceli said, providing the only support that she could do, once more feeling the sting of the loss of her arms. *Don't be silly. Even if you hadn't done it back then, they'd still be gone now. This was a terrorist attack.* Still, chiding herself didn't help her any.

As they headed for their large bathroom, both finally noticed their hair. It had grown about two feet and had thickened considerably. Like all the other victims, their hair reached nearly to their ankles. "At least we can mostly walk," Ariceli attempted to console Carys, as she struggled to toss her hair out of the way so she could sit on the toilet.

"But this is impossible, Ariceli; we can't live like this. Our dancing is gone, utterly and completely gone. We lived to dance. What's the point of going on living, if we can't dance? None," she declared and broke into sobs once more. Ariceli had no reply.

Hunger then struck the pair, and they made their way to their spacious penthouse suite's kitchen. Again, Ariceli kept close to Carys, encouraging her, as she wiggled wildly, panic growing once more. Carys sat in the first chair she came to, while Ariceli continued on to the refrigerator. She found a use for her new massive bosom, pushing against the door's edge to open it. She spotted the leftover pot of stew from the night before — er, several nights before. How to get it out of the refrigerator became her next problem. Again, she was swamped with memories of all the times Carys had done similar things for her. Feelings of shame and regret swept over her for having leeched off her dearest friend for so many years.

She tried picking it up using her teeth and managed to get the pot over to the table. Using her teeth, she pulled the silverware drawer open and struggled to get hold of a clean spoon, as drool from her mouth dripped into the tray, compliments of her lip loops. Ariceli knew that somehow she had to feed Carys. If they could not manage to do this, they would likely starve to death. She tried to bite down on the spoon and use her head to scoop up a spoonful. That met with a dismal failure. The only way left was to use her feet and toes, even more awkward. However, she was able to both hold the spoon and dip it into the pot. Carys was so hungry that she assisted Ariceli by moving her open mouth to the spoon.

An hour later, both were full. "Well, we can at least feed each other; that's something," Ariceli commented. *Thank god for that much!* "We should see if we can call for help." They headed into their living room. In one corner was their entertainment-comm center. Using her nose and teeth, Ariceli managed to get it onto the emergency news channel. She made her way back to the plush, velvet-covered couch where Carys was sitting. Once more, she had to toss her head about to get her hair out of the way so she could sit down too, again feeling the loss of Carys' helping hands. Slowly, the amount she'd had to depend on Carys all these years hit her like a chunk of concrete. She felt even guiltier as she sat beside her lover.

The two women sat in a stunned silence, trying to cope with the news that everyone on Proxima Prime had been infected with the vicious genetic mutation. Everyone they had ever known was now as helpless as themselves. For hours, the two just stared at the large monitor, speechless. Their entire world was gone, swept away from them without their having the slightest say in it or foreknowledge of its happening. Hours later, Ariceli finally broke the silence. "We have a lot of food. We'll just have to wait until a rescue comes for us."

"Why?" a very depressed Carys whispered. "Why bother? There's nothing left for us, nothing at all. We're just shells, hollow, useless shells now."

Ariceli had no answer to that one. Carys was right; they were just mere shells of people. The day turned into night before they realized they were thirsty and hungry again. Once more, Ariceli took the lead, got them something from the refrigerator, and fed Carys, who then struggled mightily to reciprocate. Full, they mechanically headed for their bed. After mostly falling into bed, Ariceli rolled over onto her side and gave Carys a tender loving kiss. Soon, both found their new sexual organs were just as aroused as they were. An hour later, draped in masses of hair, the two highly satisfied women fell into a deep sleep.

During the ensuing days, Ariceli got Carys to practice walking just as she had many years ago. In time, Carys finally was able to walk fairly well on her own and was no longer terrified of walking. Later, while watching the non-news news, Carys commented, "Well, we now live for sexual gratification. At least we can do that very well." Both women laughed. They spent more time in bed than anything else.

Days drifted into weeks before their rescue came.

Neither had any knowledge that they were some of the very few who were still alive on Proxima Prime! "Bust the damned door down! Help! We're in the living room," Ariceli yelled as loudly as she could. Rescue had finally come for the two. A pair of soldiers entered the room.

"We are taking you to Halon-6," one soldier explained.

"Hey, we need to bring some things with us. We can't go without our ballet heels and slippers," Ariceli ordered. She had to use her Dominate gifts to get the men to pack up six crates of their things; many were ballet portfolios of the one's they had performed. In the back of her mind, she had not given up on somehow, someway getting back on the dance stage. "Hang our ID cards around our necks," she ordered, trying hard not to forget anything.

Unlike most of the rescued victims, the two soldiers found these two women could walk fairly well on their own, but they had no idea why they could. None of the others was able to walk without supporting hands. Still, they grumbled about having to carry so many shipping crates. A week later, they found themselves in an assisted living complex on a strange world. They shared a single bed, their six crates were piled up in one corner.

Now the problems began. The caretakers measured them and then got them properly dressed. "I'm sorry you can't breathe well. You know as well as I do that these pipe corsets are necessary to give you proper back support for your giant boobs. So shut up about them. No, you must wear these toe shoes. How else can you walk to the dining room. Everyone wears the lip plates. We can't have you accidentally ripping your lip loops on something. Now, shut up and behave or you'll get no supper," the aide griped, and left them alone, sitting on their bed.

Daily, arguments ensued. Ariceli yelled, "Don't you know who we are? I'm Ariceli de la Vegas, the best prima donna ballet dancer and director of the Royal Imperium Ballet!"

"Was lady! That's the key word, *was*. Now, you're just another pair of victims. I don't care if you are the President. Shut up and be quiet," the aide yelled back at her, turning off her ULAT box so she couldn't understand anything more that she said.

After weeks of complaining and using her Dominate more and more frequently, Ariceli got into yet another shouting match with the head aide. "Look, this is wholly intolerable. I don't give a damn about the Big Five worlds attacking and killing each other! I demand to see your boss, right now! Go get him!" She used her Dominate, certain this imbecile would bring the top man running through this dismal assisted living complex to her. The man stormed out of her small room.

By the time he reached the office of Mr. Dalag, he'd cooled down. "What's up, Joni?" he asked in a cool voice. Running this place with its massive over-crowding and so dismally shorthanded was taking its toll on him as well. Over budget, that was the last communication he'd received from the Office of Finance. *How the hell do I cut costs any lower than they are, when they keep on bringing in more victims?* He was not in a good mood.

"It's that damned diva, Ariceli and her mate, Carys, again, boss. Honestly, those two cause more trouble than all the others combined!"

"What's she belly-aching about this time?" he barked. He really didn't want to know.

"Better food and better clothes and to get their feet restored so they can dance again. I keep telling them they should be thankful for what they do have. She's demanding to see you, boss," the man replied.

"Oh, very well then," Dalag sighed. *At least, I can put aside the budget problem a spell.* He rose and headed off to find Room 659. At their door, he picked up their chart, glanced at it, and entered.

"It's about time!" Ariceli fumed. "We're fed slop, not real food. We are dancers. I demand you put us in a medical machine and fix our feet so we can at least dance again. In case you don't know it, we're the Imperium ballet's two finest prima donnas. I'm the director of the Royal Imperium Ballet as well. Now make this happen!"

"Was lady. Was. There is no more Royal Ballet. No

more Proxima Prime, for that matter. You are alive and here, and should be grateful we're taking care of you," he retorted. *Impossible women!*

"Then move us to another place, where they will treat us properly and repair our feet so we can dance again. Do it now!" Ariceli fumed, but focused and used her Dominate gifts once more. Dalag threw his hands up to his head, rubbing his temples. Talking with these victims had just given him a sudden headache.

"You realize you've been here two months and have filed nearly a thousand complaints? That's a thousand times more than anyone else! Oh very well. But no one can fix your damned feet! You are stuck here. What more can you freaks expect?" Dalag stormed out of the room, tossing their chart onto a chair as he passed it. *Damn women anyway!*

She yelled after him, punching her wishes into his mind. "Well, call someone and get us transferred to a place where they will fix up our feet so we can dance again!" He put both his hands on his head. *Infernal headache! Damn those women! They've given me a migraine!*

Hours later, his call was put through. "Legate Mary Smith here. To what do I owe the pleasure, Mr. Dalag? Over."

"Hello Legate Smith. Mr. Dalag. I'm the director of one of the assisted living complexes for the terrorist victims here on Halon-6. I have two victims here that are making demands and causing problems that simply cannot be handled. Before the attack, I believe they were rather wealthy and influential women. Both were ballet dancers, prima donnas, for the Royal Imperium Ballet on Proxima Prime. One claims to have been their director. They are demanding, among other things, to be sent to another world where they can get their feet fixed so that they can dance again. I've told them that's impossible, but they're creating an infernal mess here. A thousand complaints during the last couple of months. I hate to bother you with such trivial problems, but I have heard rumors that some geneticists somewhere have been able to do something about the malformed feet of these victims. If I am not mistaken, would it be possible to send these two there and have their feet handled? Over." *God, I hope she doesn't bawl me out for bothering her like this! Better yet, I hope she takes them off our hands. I don't think I can take much more of those two women!*

After a much longer than normal comm delay, the monitor activated again. "Yes, the geneticists on Ashford-5 have developed a partial cure. I've looked up their records. They are telling you the truth about their past. Put them on the next transport to Winno-3. From there, I'll have them sent on the next one to the rim. Tell them that they'll get their wishes. Over and out."

"Now this is more like it!" Ariceli declared. Mr. Dalag had just finished explaining about their transfer, very much relieved to be finally rid of these two troublemakers. "Thank you. When do we leave? Don't forget our crates."

"Tomorrow. I'll make sure they go with you. Good day," he turned and left them. *Thank god for small favors! Tomorrow, no more divas!*

Chapter 18 The Butterfly Effect

Albert Fresco was thirty-one and quite autistic. Unable to cope in the cities of Halon-6, he had spent most of his life since adolescence here in the assisted living home. A likeable fellow, he had free run of the place. It's just that his communication skills left nearly everything to be desired, and he was unable to care for his own needs. For example, unless you reminded him, he would forget to eat for days on end.

Shortly after Ariceli and Carys arrived at the assisted living home, Albert paid them a visit. "Hello. Albert, I. You who?" he said.

"Oh hi. I'm Ariceli de la Vegas, my mate Carys Brann. We are prima donna ballet dancers at the Royal Imperium Ballet," she replied. His surface thoughts were unlike any mind she'd ever touched before. Very strange.

"Chaos. Everywhere. I see it. You see it? Ballet what? Flowers good. You need flowers. Albert find them. No eat flowers," he added very seriously.

"No, we don't eat flowers," she answered, and then tried to explain ballet dancing. He looked confused.

"Walk on toes. Get it, I. Chaos there too. You see chaos? Go time now. Pills not help. Albert not walk on toes. Have ten though. Everyone have ten. Chaos there too. Chaos everywhere. Albert help."

An aide came in and said, "Oh don't mind Albert. He's our resident guest welcoming lad. He's not right in his head. Autistic. Don't pay him any mind." She turned to Albert and said, "Albert, I need to care for these women now. So you go visit someone else."

"Chaos everywhere. Albert sees. Albert go visit. Back later. Albert ten toes has." He turned and left.

Nearly every day, Albert paid a visit to the two divas. Once, he even remembered to bring them some flowers. Actually, they were weeds, but Ariceli didn't complain. At least once each visit he mentioned Chaos and never failed to ask them, "See Chaos you?"

Finally, Ariceli replied, "Yes, we see Chaos. It's everywhere now. Our whole lives have been wiped out by Chaos. Everything lies in ruins. Everything that we've ever worked for is now a chaotic ruin. Yes, we see Chaos, Albert."

"Knew I it. Yes, you see Chaos. Albert sees. Ariceli sees. Carys sees. No one else. Albert asks. No one." He then rambled on about something else entirely.

When Mr. Dalag told the two women that they would be leaving the next day, Albert was just on his way to see them. He overheard Mr. Dalag's instructions. After he left, Albert entered.

"Hello Ariceli. Hello Carys. Albert sees. Ariceli sees. Carys sees. Albert go too. Albert help. Bye now."

"Well, that was his quickest trip yet. Strange fellow, kindly though," Carys commented.

"True. Shame that he is being treated so badly around here. No one gives him any respect," Ariceli replied.

Around ten the next morning, Ariceli and Carys walked themselves out of the assisted living complex. Behind them, an aide pushed along a cart carrying their crates. They were lifted into a shuttle and flown to a spaceport, where they were lifted out of it and deposited in seats within an old cargo transport. There was a distinct, nasty odor, but Ariceli couldn't place it. Before long, they felt the ship lifting off. Only now did she relax, thankful she hadn't had to Dominate anyone. *Now, it's a matter of time until we can get our situation sorted out properly.*

For months, she and Carys were miserable. Neither could breathe well. They were forced to wear the pipe corsets. They hated the lip plates and were constantly drooling onto the tops of their dresses. Walking in the toe shoes was much more difficult than it had ever been for the two when they had to wear their ballet shoes or boots. The spiked heels on those were several inches back of their en pointe toes, giving them more support. In contrast, the heel of the toe shoes lay just behind the backs of their toes, virtually no support at all, but then, that was the shape of their malformed feet. Both women sat rigidly erect. There wasn't even a view port.

Presently, a bearded man wearing rather grubby work

clothes stepped into their compartment. "Just letting you know, we're on our way to Winno-3 now. Got your seven crates onboard. Be there tomorrow. Sorry, there aren't any staterooms on this ship. It's a cargo hauler. Guess you can sleep where you are sitting until we get there." He didn't wait for a reply, but turned and left them, wondering about food and the bathroom.

Ariceli carefully rose and moved to the door and peered out. She spotted their crates. "Funny, I thought we only had six crates."

"We did," Carys replied, unwilling to hazard walking about and taking a fall with no one to help her if she did.

Just then, one of the lids of the crates opened. "What the devil?" Ariceli exclaimed. Watching curiously, she saw the head of Albert appeared and then the rest of him rather unfolded, as he got his cramped body out of the shipping crate. "It's Albert! Albert, what are you doing here?"

"Hello Ariceli. Hello Carys. Ariceli sees Chaos. Carys sees Chaos. Albert sees Chaos. Chaos, go from. No flowers today. No time. Smell pig. Comes Albert too," he said by way of explanation, at least Ariceli thought.

"Okay, come back this way. You can help us when we need to eat or go to the bathroom. You can be our helper," she said.

"Albert helper," he replied, wandering into their smaller compartment, his black eyes darting from place to place. "Pig too here." He finally sat across from them. For some time, Ariceli attempted to get him to explain why he had stolen away and wanted to come with them. Unfortunately, she couldn't get much from him other than his usual Chaos lines.

An hour later, she guessed, the bearded man poked his head in once. He was startled to see Albert smiling at him. Quickly, Ariceli focused and Dominated him. "Oh yes. He's your assistant. Good. Where was I?" he looked confused for a moment. "Oh, I remember. I just heard on the news channel. You two are really lucky you left when you did. Someone bombed your assisted living center. Hundreds of victims were killed. Thought you might like to hear that. Later." Abruptly, he pivoted and left.

Albert merely said, "Chaos. Leave is good. Stay is bad. Ariceli is good. Carys is good. Albert is good." Both women began wondering if Albert had somehow known about the bombing ahead of time and fled because of that. She touched his mind, but found his thoughts mostly indecipherable and left it.

As a helper, Albert was a dismal failure. He had no idea what was wanted or needed, but clumsily was able to lift up their dresses so they could use the crude toilet in the back of the small room. It looked like it had not been cleaned in centuries. They limited their use of it as much as possible and prayed for a swift trip!

"Are we there so soon?" Carys asked. They felt the cargo transport setting down, definitely landing. "I thought he said it would be twenty-four hours." Ariceli shrugged her shoulders.

Within a minute, the bearded man stuck his head into their cramped compartment. "Stopping on Haffren-3 to unload some cargo. You can stick your heads out and get some fresh air if you like. Just don't stray far from the ship. Oh, and I'm not going to be lifting you either in or out of the ship." He turned and left. Shortly, they heard crates being moved.

"We can at least get a look. We don't have to go outside," Ariceli suggested, lunging to her feet, avoiding her hair and wobbling slightly to get her balance before taking small steps to the larger cargo compartment. Carys and Albert followed her. From here, they got a good look at the world of Haffren-3, at least at the spaceport.

This world had a reddish sun, but the air smelled of ozone. The tarmac was wet, but the ambiance was substantially better than their room in the ship. Both women breathed as deeply as their tight corsets would allow.

Albert watched one of the local men, who was unloading some of the crates. He was tall and thin. A patch on his blue uniform read Alun Arthmael. His skin tone was definitely brownish, rather an unusual color, Ariceli thought. His hair was black. He smiled at the two women. Just then, Albert spoke to him. "Albert see Chaos. Ariceli Chaos see. Carys Chaos see. Alun? See Chaos?"

The man looked up, as his ULAT box translated Albert's

Imperium Standard. "What's that you say? Chaos?"

"Albert Chaos see. Ariceli Chaos see. Carys Chaos see. Alun see Chaos here. To Ashford-5 go. No Chaos." Albert repeated himself, adding a little.

"He's a little autistic, but has a kind heart," Ariceli quickly advised Alun. "We're going to Ashford-5 to escape what Albert here calls Chaos; we think that's what he means. We're terrorist attack victims, and we're praying that we can get cured on this Ashford-5 world."

"Oh, I see," Alun responded. "I'm sorry for you both. Chaos? Interesting idea. I had not thought of that one. Thanks for the tip, Albert. Best get moving before they grumble about my not hurrying with these crates." He picked up another and headed out of the bay. From his surprised facial expressions, he must have had a bright idea, but she didn't eavesdrop on his thoughts. Instead, they headed back to their compartment and seats, since it appeared that they were just about done unloading. Ariceli didn't think they'd wait for them to get seated before taking off.

Twelve hours later, the three very hungry passengers were dropped off on Winno-3, Ataro Empire. The grubby man decided to lift the passengers down the ramp. Why? He saw Queen Altha and her group waiting on their arrival. Ariceli smiled, as she noticed his sudden change of heart, but was thankful that he had. She knew she'd not be able to walk down the sloping ramp without falling.

"Welcome to Winno-3, Ariceli de la Vegas, Carys Brann. I am Queen Altha. Your fame precedes you both. I once caught your performance of *Carwyn Ascending*, and I was both amazed and enchanted with both of you. Such leaps. Anyway, who is your young man? I didn't get any word about a third person."

Ariceli explained, "Albert. He's autistic, but kindhearted. He sensed that our assisted living complex was going to be bombed, and he stole away to come with us. He was right. Someone blew up the complex and killed a lot of us victims there. Albert, this is Queen Altha of Winno-3."

"Pretty flowers. Albert Chaos see. Ariceli Chaos see. Carys Chaos see. Oh no! Chaos see Altha? Go should we soon!

Chaos here! Albert Chaos see!" He seemed terribly anxious and ran back inside the transport.

"It's all right, Albert. That's the wrong ship. We have to get into another transport," Ariceli called out to him. Hesitatingly, Albert came back out, but began nervously looking in all directions.

"It's this way. Would you like to freshen up and perhaps dine with me?" Queen Altha asked. "Your transport isn't scheduled to leave for another two hours. Do you know what is bothering Albert?"

"Sure, we've not had anything to eat for a whole day. I've never seen him like this. He sure is nervous about something," Ariceli replied.

"Albert, come look at our flowers. We have many on Winno-3. We grow them for our sacred wasps," Queen Altha suggested.

"Albert come. See flowers. Ariceli like flowers." Albert tagged along with them, but continued looking all around him, as if scared of what might be lurking nearby.

As they walked, Queen Altha whispered something to her aide, who left them right away. She only commented, "Taking precautions. If you were here in the spring, the many colors of the irises are just incredibly beautiful." She chatted away.

Two hours later, with full stomachs and cleaned up some, the three were taken to their next transport. Thankfully, the women were helped aboard. This one was a passenger transport. At last, the three had good accommodations and assistance when they needed it during the two-day flight to Ashford-5.

The first of March 1326, their transport landed on Plateau Grado, Tierra. The dim orange-red sun was in the far western skies, casting its usual hues on the mountains and tarmac. Governor Katrina and Doctor Whitney were on hand to greet the new arrivals and watched the sliver ship slowly descending. "They were a couple of top ballerinas at the Royal Imperium Ballet on Proxima Prime," Katrina explained to Whitney, while the watched. "Apparently, at their previous assisted living homes, they caused no end of troubles. I guess we'll just have to see what's with them."

"Has Queen Amy been notified?" the doctor asked.

"Yes, she's already lining up Basic Therapy sessions for them, once they get handled by their medical staff. This time, you won't have to deal with them. I know you are busy as heck with all the arm regrowth procedures," Katrina explained.

"That's a relief. I'm here if they need emergency assistance, though. The bay door is opening," Doctor Whitney pointed out.

As Ariceli stepped carefully toward the exit ramp, she got her first smells and sights of Tierra or Ashford-5. Sixty year old memories came flooding into her mind, confusing her. Somehow, this world reminded her of her home planet she'd not seen or heard of for sixty-two years! *Could this be it? So familiar. The pine scents. The cold. The ruddy colors. Do I dare hope?* A crewman lifted her down, making sure she had her balance before doing the same for Carys. Albert stood on the ramp for a moment, inhaling deeply. He smiled and seemed satisfied, and then walked down following the two women.

"Welcome to Ashford-5 or Tierra as we locals call our world. I'm Governor Katrina Lutgard. Our base doctor, Whitney Jones."

"Tierra? Could it be? Please, is there a place called the Westerlings here and a port city of Bonito?" Ariceli gushed, ignoring the introductions.

"Why yes. All the lands west of the Goza Mountains here are called the Westerlings. Bonita is a large city on the far coast. Why? Have you studied our world?" Governor Katrina asked, growing curious. Meanwhile, the blonde woman was merely looking around, trying to grasp the nature of this strange looking world and its smells. The man was waiting patiently, but Ariceli's emotions were so strong that Katrina and Whitney could not help but sense them.

"Home! My god! After all these years, I am finally home! Carys, I was born here, before I was kidnaped and taken away. My god, I am really home!" Ariceli exclaimed.

"Oh my. Another one," Doctor Whitney exclaimed, suddenly paying Ariceli far more attention. She sensed another telepathic mind and spotted the germanium crystal resting between her enormous cleavage, just as her own did.

"I'm Carys Brann; she's my mate, Ariceli de la Vegas. He's our autistic friend, Albert," she hastily introduced them. Turning to Ariceli, she asked, "Dear, is this really your home world?"

"It must be. The smells, the colors — it just has to be!" Ariceli gushed.

"Welcome home. Why don't we go inside and have a cup of tea. I must have you tell me all about this," Governor Katrina insisted, taking control of this introduction. This wasn't quite what she'd expected. She sent a quick telepathic message to Amy, alerting her to Ariceli's claim.

Albert spoke up, "No Chaos. Albert Chaos see. Ariceli Chaos see. Carys Chaos see. No Chaos here. Is good now." Both Katrina and Whitney gave him a sideways glance, not quite comprehending what he was intending.

"No, it's all normal and quiet here, Albert. We like it that way," Katrina ventured. He nodded and followed them, quite contented.

An hour passed. While sipping tea, Ariceli eagerly told the two her life's story. Much of it, Carys didn't even know. Once she'd finished, Governor Katrina had two new ID cards made for them, giving them dual citizenship, adding Ashford-5 to their older cards. No longer would Ashford-5 be a Closed World for the two women. Then, they took them into the basement and helped them into an electric car. While driving down the tunnel, Katrina explained, "We're taking you to the Imperial Castle, where Queen Amy wants to meet you. She and her staff will be assisting you to recover and give you a place to stay for now."

"I remember hearing about the Imperial Castle, but I've never seen it," Ariceli replied. They chatted more, and Whitney explained about all of the other terrorist attack victims they were helping here, well over a thousand at this point in time. "Wow, this must be great in the winter. Lots of snow up here, right? I've never seen snow, mind you, just heard others talking about it. Bonito is sort of balmy in the winter. It's on the seacoast."

They parked the electric car near several others. Katrina advised, "We've got to climb some stairs, so we take it slow and easy. Whitney and I can't really see our feet either. Easy does it. Let us know if you need a steadying hand." Both gladly accepted their arms; all four went up mostly by feeling the next step with their toes.

"It's more like a maze now; she's added so much onto the castle," Katrina explained. They walked down a long hallway that had far too many side rooms to easily count. "Ah, here we are, her private study."

Ariceli didn't comment much, but wondered why Governor Katrina and Doctor Whitney still wore the same toe shoes as they, as well as the giant lip plates. Seeing Queen Amy who also looked like themselves, they were beginning to wonder if they really could get cured here. "Welcome Ariceli de la Vegas. Welcome home. I'm Queen Amy Valen Gervasi, my mate, Jan Bellweather. Come on in; have a seat."

After introductions, Amy told the three that she would provide room and board here at the castle for an indefinite time. She outlined their Basic Therapy, which she insisted both have as soon as possible. "Our doctors can cure up a few of the minor genetic modifications. Regrowing arms takes time, and they are limited on how many they can do at one time. There are about a thousand ahead of you, so be patient. They will get to you as soon as they can. Come, let's get you to see the doctors, and let them see what can be done for you both."

They followed Amy and Jan, who led them back out into the hallway. Before long, both women were lost. "It's so huge," Carys commented.

Jan replied, "No kidding. If you get lost, just ask the next person you meet. Ah, here are our medical facilities. We are lucky to have four genetic researchers and doctors, plus Doctor Whitney too. Excuse us; this is Doctors Ruth and Alex Hammil. Doctors Mindy and Andy Hammil are checking on patients right now. Docs, this is Ariceli de la Vegas, who was kidnaped from Bonito when she was fourteen, back in 1250. Her mate, Carys Brann, and friend Albert. They were top ballerinas at the Royal Imperium Ballet, and Ariceli was its director for many years. We'll leave them in your hands for a while."

The doctors were busily studying the genetic samples and notes that Andy had brought back, looking for clues about how the other geneticists had been able to reform malformed feet. Alex had the genes displayed on his big monitor, with the modifications that caused the bio genetic attack's mutations highlighted in red. He had no intention of just using their new methods to restore one foot back to normal, because the process also eliminated the entire left leg of the patient. He was trying to see where they had tapped into this original sample, turning it into one cured foot and one lost leg. However, everyone here had advanced warnings about these two prima donnas via Mr. Dalag of the assisted living home.

Doctor Ruth stopped her work and explained, "Hello Ariceli, Carys. You've come to the right place. We're on the leading edge of cures for this terrible genetic mutation. We're able to regrow your arms. But that's going to be a while; there's almost a thousand ahead of you. However, we can handle two more of the mutations yet today. We are now able to remove the pain neurons from your hair so that it can be cut in any style or length that you prefer. We also are able partially to restore your feet. The downside is that you'll still have to wear tall heels as Alex and I are wearing. How do these sound?"

Ariceli declared, "But we are ballerinas. We need our feet fused into the en pointe position or else back to normal feet. They can't just take away the only thing that matters in our lives, our ballet dancing. They just can't! We won't let them. I was the most spectacular dancer, after I had my arms removed for the special ballet we did, *Carwyn Ascending*. It was a blockbuster, broke all attendance records. Simply the Royal Ballet's finest performances ever. We just have to be able to dance again. Besides, I'm the Royal Imperium Ballet's director. I have to get the ballet going again, though we'll probably have to train a whole set of new dancers from the very beginning lessons. Still, we have to be able to dance again; we just have to. We've got lots of credits. That should be no problem. Carys has to have her arms back though. She selfishly took care of my needs all these years, but maybe I should as well. I've made her work so very hard helping me. I just didn't realize how much she had to, until now, you see. So you have to help us somehow. Fuse our feet somehow. I don't know, break them into little pieces and fuse them into the en pointe position if you have to. We just have to dance again."

She would have talked even more, but just then, Albert starting talking loudly. "Chaos there," he pointed to the DNA sequencing on the monitor. "Albert Chaos see. Ariceli Chaos see. Carys Chaos see. Chaos there. Albert Chaos fix!" While everyone stopped to try to understand what he meant, Albert sat down at Doctor Alex's computer terminal and began typing furiously. "Albert Chaos see. Albert Chaos fix. Albert fix. Now." Doctor Alex moved over to him, intent on stopping him or at least see what he was typing. Doctor Ruth moved to the man's other side, looking over his shoulder.

"Albert. You shouldn't mess with the doctor's computer. That's not polite," Ariceli cried. "I hope he isn't damaging anything. It's not like him. He's autistic, but really nice," she defended him.

"Wait," Doctor Alex held up his right hand behind him, still watching what Albert was doing. "He's writing a programming script. Wait, we've seen those formulas somewhere, Ruth, but where?"

"There. Albert Chaos see. Albert Chaos fix." He pressed a key and the big monitor responded to his script. Right before their eyes, some of the red genetic mutations vanished, replaced by the normal sequences.

"Oh no! He's altered your image," Ariceli cried out.

"Wait, I see! Albert, you're a genius! I see what you've done. Let's see how much that would undo. Move over son," Doctor Alex insisted.

"I know where we've seen those equations. They're non-linear. Chaos theory, Alex. He's applied Chaos Theory to our genetic mutation problem. Has he found a solution?" Doctor Ruth exclaimed, just as excited as her husband.

"I do believe that he may well have," Alex answered very animatedly. "Doctor Whitney, why don't you give them their checkups, while Ruth and I work on this discovery? Ruth, please let Doctors Mindy and Andy know about this. Have them come as soon as they can. Albert has put us onto another breakthrough. I'm sure of it!"

"Already did that, dear. We should break the components down; isolate just the extra changes beyond what we've already worked out," Doctor Ruth replied, lost in the research as much as her husband was.

"Albert hungry."

"You come with me, wonder man," Governor Katrina suggested, while Doctor Whitney led the two women to the next room. A pair of normal medical machines sat amid the chaos of the workroom of four scientists.

An hour later, Doctor Whitney finished giving them both thorough medical exams. "Two good things," she began relaying the results to them. "First, you were exposed to the same bio genetic mutation agent as most have been. That means, we do have some cures for some of the mutations. Second, you are both two months pregnant. Congratulations to the both of you."

"What? Pregnant? Us? Oh!" Ariceli exclaimed, taken by complete surprise.

"Oh, well, Ariceli, that explains why we both haven't felt like eating much of a morning for a while. It sure is a surprise. Oh," Carys blushed.

Doctor Whitney finished her thought in a professional manner. "Yes, the new organs actually are fully operational. In this case, I believe it's safe to say that you are each going to have a daughter. Now, we ought to talk about proper diets and exercise. Then, Amy wants to get you both into their special therapy session. Trust me; you won't regret getting Rafe's Basic Therapy. It's given most of us here a whole new lease on life." She continued disseminating her medical advice, after which Amy and Jan saw they were properly settled into a nice suite in her castle.

At dinnertime, the two new arrivals dined with several hundred others, many of which were victims like themselves. Nearly all were hermaphrodites like themselves; a few already had their arms regrown. Unlike the assisted living homes, here they were treated with respect. Friendliness abounded, so much so, that they found themselves doing more chatting than eating. When they were helped into bed that evening, both knew intuitively they'd come to the right place.

Meanwhile, the four doctors poured over Albert's solution. "Yes, it's definitely Chaos Theory being applied to these genetic mutations," Doctor Alex declared. "The science of order and disorder in nonlinear, deterministic systems — and this is definitely being applied to our situation. Look here," he pointed to some key elements of the script that Albert wrote, which nullified the mutations, some of them at least.

"He's on to something here, for sure, dad. Let's see if we can isolate these. We may well have more cures," Doctor Andy replied. Like the others, he was very excited about the possibilities, not only for himself and his family, but also for every terrorist attack victim. During the next two weeks, the four spent every waking hour developing this unexpected discovery into workable genetic therapies. Of course, they then had to actually test their solutions on humans, which was, of course, illegal.

"Tell that to the terrorists and those on the Big Five worlds. Oh, you can't, most are dead," Doctor Andy countered. The four were holding discussions on just how to test their proposed solutions. "Just inject me with them, will you?"

"Son, we dare not. Look, there are only four of us geneticists, five if you count Doctor Whitney who has been helping. If something goes wrong, we can't afford to lose you, son. We must approach this from a different perspective. It isn't testing or experimentation, per se, you see. We know it should work, scientifically that is, from all our studies. Hence, it is an experimental cure and not testing."

"Clever dear, clever," Doctor Ruth smirked. "Fine line, but I think we can sell it. I know just the two on which we can test it out: our two new arrivals, the ballerinas. They are still demanding cures so they can dance again. Let's test the solutions on them first. I'll get the women's permissions; you get it by Queen Amy and Governor Katrina."

By this time, both Ariceli and Carys' Basic Therapies were completed. Actually, Carys was finished in less than a week. As expected, her major trauma came from the terrorist attack. Other than stresses and strains, sore feet, and muscles from her extensive years dancing, she had suffered relatively little other trauma, but she was rather shocked to re-experience her birth. Ariceli, on the other hand, was a tough case. So much of her life had been twisted by having been kidnaped when she was fourteen. In many ways, that experience had helped formulate her strong "drive" in life. Trust no one. Only I can make it happen. I'm the only one who matters. Tell no one. Must get home, can't get home. Such were pivotal considerations that turned up as key, driving forces behind Ariceli's life. These had been greatly tempered in the advent of the attack. She realized at long last how much Carys meant to her, how much Carys had cared for her, and that she had, in fact, been in love with her for decades. Two long weeks of therapy finally paid off, Ariceli was free from all the trauma she'd endured for nearly three-quarters of a century.

Now, she was truly ready to have the discussion with the doctors about what body modifications she and Carys wanted to have done. Doctor Ruth explained, "Okay, here's where we stand. We have three proven cures. We can repair the genetic mutations to your hair. That will allow you to cut it to any length you desire. Yes, once repaired, it will be nowhere as thick and lush as it is now. Your hair will be back to what it was before the attack. Next, we can partially repair your feet, but your feet will still not lie flat on the floor. You'd have to wear stilettos like ours, but trust me, that's a whole lot better than the toe shoes. Third, as you know, we are able to regrow lost arms, but that's a lengthy process. We've over a thousand others who have been waiting patiently for months to have it done. It's not fair to move you two to the front of the line, but give us time, we'll get it done for you."

"Now, the really interesting thing is that thanks to Albert's solution, we have also perfected a way to restore your lips. No more giant lip plates. We also have a way to restore normal breast sizes. We suspect that the restored normal size will be Tierra-sized, however. I should explain about that. You see, for centuries, women on Tierra have always had much greater breast sizes than normal. We suspect this has to do with enhancing survival potentials for our babies. Expect a reduction from these monsters to perhaps an H cup size."

"Finally, and also as a result of Albert's solution, we believe that we will now be able to completely restore your feet to those of a normal person. If so, your feet would be perfectly normal once more."

"As yet, we have no hints of any solution for the hermaphrodite mutation, but if all else about our bodies get back to normal, we can live with the dual sex organs. We won't look like 'freaks' any longer. However, we have not yet tested the lip, feet, and breast solutions. We would like to try them on you first, with your permission. We believe these will allow you to be able to dance once more. Besides needing your permission, we also need to know just which of these genetic modifications you wish done. Note, if we do them now, they'll also modify the genetic structure of your babies. I'm afraid we'll have to restore their arms after they are born."

"This is wonderful news! Carys, we can be normal once more," Ariceli exclaimed, looking lovingly at her blonde-haired mate. "I think we want all the changes undone. Before, I thought we'd be better ballet dancers if we had our feet permanently fused into the en pointe position. I see now I felt driven to have to be the very best ballet dancer ever. It's not important now. Carys is my life. I want everything; how about you, dear?"

"Absolutely, everything!" Carys replied, just as enthusiastically. "We can be almost normal, and we can dance again. Please, what must we do?"

Two days later and with the approval from both Amy and Katrina, the two women were given the new genetic cures. A week later, the two women walked into the Great Hall for dinner. They now wore simple flats; their bosoms were normal sized for Tierra women. Both had their hair trimmed so that it fell to the small of their backs, perfect for flairs while doing dancing spins. Their lips looked normal, not even a scar line could be seen close up. To their slight embarrassment, hundreds cheered them when they made their grand appearance for dinner. Further, Lena and Drina sat beside them, showing them how to use their feet to feed themselves.

Spontaneously, cheers arouse when the four doctors joined the throng for supper. Doctor Alex spoke loudly, "Don't worry; we'll be getting to the rest of you as soon as possible. These changes only take a few days to do! Of course, you'll need a whole new wardrobe." That brought another round of laughter and cheers. Even Amy cheered, knowing her key new engineers would be handled before they were to make their presentations to the guild members. They would look far less like "freaks" and hopefully receive a better acceptance.

The only worry that Doctors Alex and Andy had was what would happen to male bosoms? If they vanished entirely, how could they feed their babies? Or would the process make men now infertile? Those questions had yet to be answered. The next morning, the five doctors began handling a dozen more, including the key engineers, who were putting the final touches on their presentations for the guild masters on May Day. Two days later, they had some answers. The men now had normal Tierra women's sized breasts. Still, once they got their clothes altered, they did look more like the average man of Tierra. Secretly, Queen Amy hoped this would go a long way towards their general acceptance by the guild masters and others.

By now, Amy, and Katrina had dismissed Albert's appearance and tremendous insight to their problems, as mere serendipity or fortunate happenstance. But no, Doctor Alex had weeks ago pronounced Albert's appearance as part of the well-known Butterfly Effect of Chaotic Systems, in which seemingly minuscule changes can produce tremendous effects in such systems. His timely departure had avoided the bombing of the assisted living complex. His arrival here had led to new genetic solutions within hours of his arrival. Then, there were the effects on Winno-3 just after his departure there, along with Ariceli and Carys, to say nothing of the changes on Haffren-3 caused by Alun Arthmael, after his brief exchange with Albert.

Later the very afternoon that Albert had landed on Tierra, Governor Katrina and Queen Amy received an emergency, but secure, call from Emperor Kino and Queen

Altha. After that discussion and with Albert's permission, he was sent back to Winno-3 and the Ataro Empire. Why?

Queen Altha was startled by Albert's seemingly incoherent and brief words. "Pretty flowers. Albert Chaos see. Ariceli Chaos see. Carys Chaos see. Oh no! Chaos see Altha? Go should we soon! Chaos here! Albert Chaos see!" He seemed terribly anxious and ran back inside the transport, but Ariceli had been able to get him calmed down. Just what had he meant by this Chaos, she wondered.

After she saw the three off on the last leg of their trip to Ashford-5, her thoughts continued to be haunted by Albert's words. Chaos was here on Winno-3. How could that be? She ran a tight ship, an honorable one. Her world was quite civilized and ordered. The only trouble they'd had on this world had been the murders of security men and two assistants, when Amy and Jan had been kidnaped. But that was years ago. She'd beefed up security since then, particularly so when any of Ashford-5's telepaths were present, like they were now. She was in the midst of the training of Linda and Rael.

With the genocide attacks on the Big Five worlds fresh in her mind, Queen Altha decided to act. She ordered a full-scale defensive action, sending every available ship in her fleet into orbit around Winno-3. Her orders were very specific. "Be alert for an incoming attack, possibly by drones. Shoot them down. Do not let any unauthorized ship into our atmosphere."

Two days after Albert left Winno-3 for Ashford-5, two deep space transport ships dropped out of hyperspace close to Winno-3. Each attempted to launch three unmanned drones. With a hundred cruisers, heavy cruisers, and a battleship armed to the teeth and with nearly double that in smaller ships serving as lookouts, the surprise attack was squelched before it had a chance to infect Winno-3 with the bio agent, the horrific genetic mutation agent.

Never had Queen Altha faced such an attack before. Someone had wanted to inflict planetary genocide on Winno-3! Hers was a peaceful world, never having attacked or even threatened any other world, not in over two millennia.

Unnerved, she placed an emergency call to Emperor Kino. After describing the attack, she also explained how she had received advance warning from Albert. "Yes, my generals are working now to trace where this attack originated, but there could well be more against our worlds," she argued. Emperor Kino then placed all thirty-eight worlds of the Ataro Empire on highest alert, following Queen Altha's methods.

He then established a secure, emergency communication connection to Governor Katrina and Queen Amy. Emperor Kino outlined what had just happened on Winno-3 and the role that Albert had played in giving Queen Altha the advanced warning she needed to prevent another instance of planetary genocide. "I would like this Albert fellow to return to the Ataro System. I want him to visit each of our worlds and check for Chaos there. His simple warning save billions of lives. Over."

Governor Katrina subsequently explained to Albert that his warning had been heeded by Queen Altha, and what had happened as a result. He seemed pleased, as far as she could tell. His autism made reading him very challenging. "Chaos gone. Good is. Altha Chaos sees. Got Chaos gone. Is good." When she told him that Emperor Kino wanted him to return and check on the other Ataro Empire worlds for threatening Chaos, he replied, "Albert helps." Hence, he found himself on the next transport back to Winno-3, with barely enough time to say goodbye to Ariceli and Carys.

Already, Legate Smith had been informed by Emperor Kino, and she'd responded, sending five battleships and ten heavy cruisers to the Ataro Systems to help him keep up a constant patrol around the densely populated inner planets of the empire. Still, it took her generals and their men several days to work out precisely who had launched the surprise attack on Winno-3. The destroyed drones were of Mal Dynamics origin, no surprise there. Debris from the destroyed transports was painstakingly collected from their high orbits around Winno-3. Then, the pieces were analyzed, looking for clues. The flights of the transports were not registered with Central Control, an action highly unusual and often indicative of clandestine, illegal activities. From the registry numbers on parts of the hulls that were recovered, they obtained some basic facts.

First, the transports were purchased by a governmental agency on Haffren-3, the Office of Defense. Second, they had been leased out to subsidiary company of the Mal Dynamics branch office on Haffren-3, Agrona Solutions. Third, curiously, Agrona Solutions filed a missing transport report with the local authorities, but two days after the attack. Armed with this information, Legate Smith headed there personally in her battleship command post, along with three other battleships and a host of cruisers. She promised Emperor Kino a full and thorough investigation.

While in transit, she reviewed the history of Haffren-3, especially their relationship with the Ataro Empire. Haffren-3 was located on the boundary of the hub with the spiral arm. A millennia ago, they'd filed a formal protest against being considered a mid-arm world and not a more prestigious hub world. Further, their senators were always at odds with those from the Ataro Empire, claiming that sooner or later the Ataro Empire would attempt to take over Haffren-3, adding it into its ever growing empire of planets. That Haffren-3 was actually quite distant from the Ataro worlds and that, until Ashford-5 had been added, the Ataro Empire had not added a new world for nearly one and a half millennia apparently didn't figure into their paranoia.

What bothered Legate Smith more was the anecdotal data concerning Haffren-3. It was an old world. It's four continents had evolved into many countries, fought many wars against each other, formed into a United Countries organization, converted all countries to a form of democratic rule, and had seen a slow decline from there into welfare states — all that before joining the Imperium, which bolstered their economy, as well as providing for the unification of all government organizations into a planet-wide rulership. In recent centuries, the utter dependence of the many on social welfare programs had led, according to much speculation, to a decline in moral standards. What so disturbed Legate Smith was that apparently, if it involved sex in some way, you could get it on Haffren-3! All reports indicated their society had degenerated into depths of all manner of sexual perversions. The only taboo still enforced was child pornography. Exploitation of children was not only illegal, but such laws were strictly enforced. However, once one reached the age of eighteen, all bets were off.

Quite why Haffren-3 should launch a surprise attack on Winno-3 in an attempt at planetary-genocide eluded her. Further, there apparently weren't any genetic research facilities on Haffren-3 nor had any of the bio agent cylinders been shipped to this world. As her battleship neared Haffren-3, she found the connection at long last. Penal colonies. Almost a half-century ago, Haffren-3 had accepted Imperium criminals into specially built assisted living homes for criminals. As a result, they'd been given the necessary bio agent cylinders with which to mutate the criminals sent to their facilities. "So they do have access to the bio agent!" she declared to her general, who smiled, relieved she'd found just such a connection. In his mind, it was obvious they'd misused their supplies. He didn't care why.

Weeks before the attack on Winno-3, President Arthfael Arwel, who liked to be called AA for short and rather proud of the abbreviation's several alternate meanings, was both a sociopath and a psychopath. Yet, he had a brilliant command of rhetoric and was considered one of the best social orators of the century. He had the uncanny knack of telling any block of voters just what they wanted to hear from him. He'd been elected by a landslide three times now. When Legate Smith's general had announced the genocide attacks on the Big Five worlds, President Arthfael summoned his top advisors and generals to a secure meeting.

Never had so many anti-scrying devices been in full operation in one room on Haffren-3. "Gentlemen, my noble generals, at long last, we have been given something of enormous value from the Imperium worlds. Yes, the Big Five have finally shown us the way, casting the light of brilliance upon us all! Such magnificence! Such superiority! Such ingenuity! Why, I have hardly the words with which to praise their efforts on our behalf!" Of course, none present had the slightest idea what he was talking about, but none dared make such a suggestion, not if they wanted to retain their posts and lives.

"You see, the Ataro Empire is once more expanding its suffocating tentacles ever outward, strangling more and more worlds, as its wasps suck the very life from those worlds, like it has always done. We, the proud, brilliant people of Haffren-3 have long known about this empire's true intentions. After all, we know from our own history books that it was the Ataro Empire, which created the Imperium two millennia ago, only because of Haffren-3's people along with so many other worlds united and worked together to stop the outward expansion of the Ataro Empire, confining it to thirty-six worlds."

"As you know, these wicked, evil worlds are once more devouring other worlds. Look at Ashford-5 and now Bailey-3! Ataro's gluttony is worse than ever before! Ashford-5 is far out on the outer rim of the galaxy, but Bailey-3 is within our own backyard! I ask you, how long do you think it will be before they attempt to devour us here on Haffren-3? Days, weeks? Months, if we are lucky!" he ranted.

"And now even as poor Bailey-3 succumbs to the genocide attacks from its neighbors, they have shown us the way to achieve our own salvation! Gentlemen, noble generals, we must strike a definitive blow to the Ataro Empire to protect our precious, gentle, peaceful world of Haffren-3!" He pounded the table, jarring the many water glasses. His rise of anger was replaced by a giddy, sickly laugh.

"We must emulate the wisdom just shown to us by Bailey-3. This is our finest, golden hour. We can and we must defend Haffren-3 from the strangling tentacles of the Ataro Empire. It's now or never, gentlemen, unless you wish to become a slave of the wasp-lovers." He paused to look at the smiling faces around him. He'd slept with five of his six aides, who all performed so very well in his bed. President Arthfael ignored that as the reason he'd chosen these aides, however. Hell, he'd long ago lost count of the number of sexual partners he'd consumed, both men and women. That was his right, no, his duty as their president — to spread his seed, his love, far and wide.

"Look," he lowered his voice, creating an air of mystery

and intrigue, "we have the means at our disposal. We have the bio agent cylinders that we use on the incoming Imperium criminals. Bailey-3 has shown us the means of delivery: drones. I ask you, who manufactures these drones?"

One aide ventured, "Mal Dynamics?"

"Precisely. Precisely. We need ten drones and two transports to deliver them and their cargo. Let's make this happen for the sake of our beloved Haffren-3!"

Many heads nodded in full agreement. To do otherwise was to risk being sent to one of the criminal assisted living complexes, but not until after undergoing their "special treatment." President Arthfael continued, "Of course, we need plausible deniability — that goes without saying. So how do we make this happen, my good generals, my brilliant planners?"

One general suggested, "Well, we can't just use our own transports. They could easily be traced back to us. But I know where we could get a pair with no questions asked. Agrona Solutions is always eager to assist us. We've used them on several other occasions. They can be counted upon to be discrete."

"Good. Have Agrona Solutions provide us with two transports," President Arthfael declared. "Now about the drones?"

"Say, let's have Agrona Solutions steal them from Mal Dynamics. Then, it can't be traced to us," an aide suggested with a wry grin. He saw the president taking note of him and knew that his suggestion would ensure he would be sharing the president's bed later this evening. He smiled appropriately to his boss.

"Excellent. Let's make it so. About the bio agent. From all reports I've received, a hundred cylinders ought to be enough to wipe out a planet. How do we get that many?" President Arthfael asked. In his mind, this was the only obstacle. Legate Smith's recent orders placed a stranglehold on these cylinders, even though they were being used on the criminals. No one spoke up. "Well, just as I expected. None of you has the brilliant mind that I have. Summon Warden General Dylan Eilian at once!"

An hour later, the portly, slightly effeminate, man

arrived, his puffing breath attracting attention his way. He wore a suit with a bright pink shirt and yellow tie. "You sent for me, President Arthfael? As always, I am your humble servant. How may I help you today?"

"Ah my good man. Correct me if I am wrong, but your Department of Prisons has our stock piles of the bio agent that is used on our incoming Imperium prisoners, right?"

"Absolutely. Kept under lock and key. All the more so since Legate Smith's recent orders that are costing me a fortune to implement, I might add," he replied, putting in a hint that his new budget would be reflecting a much higher cost to handle these Imperium criminals.

"Excellent, as it should be, Warden General Dylan. I've always said no one does a finer job than you do, right fellows?" he nodded to his aides and generals, who nodded agreeably, like puppets on a string, played and pulled by Arthfael. Perhaps, it was more like harps than puppets; these men made sweet music when plucked. Warden Dylan puffed up noticeably.

"Undoubtedly, you've heard about recent events on the Big Five worlds?" The warden nodded. "I have been giving some serious thought about these bio agent cylinders. I think it would be prudent if Haffren-3 had a secret, super-secure stockpile of the cylinders, just in case the Imperium steps in. After all, if we are to continue accepting Imperium criminals here, we simply must have a way to make them into handleable creatures." He wanted to say sexual toys, but thought better of it. They were all obviously being so used. It was one of the growing "industries" on Haffren-3. For a small fee, one could be "entertained" by these prisoners for an evening. It was a totally safe and secure experience. After all, what possible harm could these prisoners cause? They were helpless and could not speak or write. Anything done to them or with them was ex post facto confidential. Any and all STDs were cured right there at the assisted living compounds, long before the prisoners' services were utilized.

Of course, the assisted living compounds were making a windfall profit from this new industry, with five percent going directly into the coffers of the Warden General. "Oh I so do agree with you, President Arthfael! Yes, yes, by all means. We must be able to continue 'treating' our incoming Imperium criminals. How can I be of help?"

Once again, President Arthfael felt he'd played the warden absolutely adroitly. "We ought to have say a hundred twenty of these cylinders duplicated and sent to our top secret, secure facilities. Of course, there must be no conceivable record of such duplications."

"Ah, I can arrange that myself."

"Excellent. I'll have the generals prepare and guard the shipment while in transit. How soon can they be ready for shipment?"

"Ah, well let me think a moment. How about three days? I'll need some time to prepare that many and get them packaged up, as shall we say, garden produce?"

"Superb! Superb, Warden Governor. Generals, prepare for the delivery of some garden produce in three days," he ordered, though he need not have.

Well, what he doesn't know won't hurt him, thought Warden General Dylan. *My side business of selling these cylinders is incredibly profitable. I must have sold double that many already! So many Counts, Countesses, Dukes, and Duchesses so badly want to get their hands on the stuff these days.*

After the portly man waddled out of the room, President Arthfael then directed their conversation to their first target. "Look, if this works as planned, and how can it fail — six worlds have already been entirely wiped out — then we can slowly but surely reduce the Ataro Empire to zero planets!" They discussed the potential worlds and decided upon Winno-3, since it was the closest to Haffren-3, since it was on one edge of the Ataro System, and thus less heavily guarded.

A week later, they had acquired the cylinders, the transports, and the drones. However, more time was required to work out a proper delivery system in the drones. Finally, after a small flight test to make sure that the drones worked well, the generals ordered a set of pre-programmed flight orders for the drones, each of which would make ten passes around Winno-3, uniformly delivering its payload of the bio agent on each pass. That done and installed in the drones, President Arthfael ordered the execution of Project Freedom.

A day later, he received the terrible news. "How in Hell could Winno-3 know about our attack?" President Arthfael screamed at his aides and generals. "They knew we were coming. They destroyed our transports and the few drones that were released long before they could release their bio agents. How can this be?" He smashed his fist on the table, knocking several glasses of water over.

One general suggested, "We must have a spy in our midst. Someone here on Haffren-3 must have notified Winno-3 of our attack. We have a traitor in our midst!" Suddenly, every man began looking at the others.

President Arthfael smiled; that had been his own carefully deduced conclusion. A traitor on Haffren-3, but who? That was simple deduction. Only these men and the few soldiers who prepared the equipment had known. The transport pilots were already dead. President Arthfael already had his solution prepared when he'd sent for these men. While they stood there looking at each other, the doors burst open and a number of d-gun armed security forces barged in, arresting all the aides and generals.

"What's the meaning of this?" a general demanded.

"I will show leniency to you if you will write down the names of all personnel who assembled and programmed our drones and transports," President Arthfael explained. "Precautions. I need that list of all personnel who in any way knew of our plans," he reiterated. Hastily, the men complied. "Okay, I've a way to handle our traitor. Thank you. If you'll all go with these security guards for the moment, I'll find us our traitor in no time." Begrudgingly, the group of aides and generals obeyed. In fact, they had little choice. The guards had their d-guns drawn. If they tried to grab theirs, they'd be shot long before their gun cleared its holster.

They were marched into one room and the door shut. From outside, President Arthfael could hear them talking among themselves, trying to figure out which of their numbers had betrayed Haffren-3 to their enemy. "Now," President

Arthfael ordered. A guard pressed a button. Inside, the hissing sound of the entering knockout gas wasn't heard above the arguing. A minute later, all were unconscious. "Okay, strip them of their clothing and take them to the Imperium Incoming Prisoner Center." He watched, as one by one, they were stripped and carried out to a waiting shuttle. Ten minutes later, the shuttle took off for the center, followed by the Presidential One shuttle. He was taking no chances with these men. Meanwhile, the security guards headed off to round up the other men on the list.

As he watched a half hour later, each man was put into a medical machine, which quickly removed his voice box. That process took all of five minutes per man. Then, each was laid on a cot in a bio containment tent. Once the last man was finished, a bored attendant sealed the tent and released the bio agent. Finally satisfied, President Arthfael headed off in his shuttle to chat with the Warden General, explaining he'd just received a new shipment of Imperium criminals and had taken care of them.

"Yes, yes, no problem, President Arthfael. Our processing system is flawless. I assure you they'll be properly handled in no time. Of course, it'll be about five days before the process is completed. As usual at revival time, that is techno speak for when they wake from their comas mind you, they will be given a new woman's name and properly attired. That done, they'll be assigned to one of our many assisted living complexes and put to work, bringing in some income to help pay for their care. Yes, it is a perfect system. Criminals now pay for their constant care and upkeep, a far better system than we used to have and so very much cheaper. I can't fathom the excessive cost the Imperium paid to house them on that burning penal planet." He chatted away, convincing the president everything would be properly handled.

When he finally returned to his office, President Arthfael relaxed at last. Obviously, someone in the "know" had betrayed him. Now, that traitor would pay for his crime. That he'd sacrificed many innocent men didn't matter to him. He'd taken care of the traitor. "Besides, now no one can be questioned and toss the blame at my feet," he said to his walls.

"Not even the Warden Governor knew of my plan. My butt is secure, even if they come knocking on my door. I do need some new aides though, and I best promote some more generals soon."

Several days later, President Arthfael smiled. He'd just received word that Legate Mary Smith was coming to Haffren-3 with a large fleet to investigate the bio agent attack on Winno-3. He smiled, because he had already made certain that everyone directly involved and who had knowledge of his plan were now unable to answer to such charges. Only he knew the truth; hence, he was most confident. He recalled his reply to her message, "Oh how terrible. Yes by all means you have my full cooperation. The guilty simply must be flushed out and sentenced. I'll make my Presidential Guest Suite available for your use. If there is anything that I can do to assist you, just let me know. I'll make all at your disposal, Legate Smith." *Only I can be this incredibly smart and wise. The betrayers are gone. Nothing can point back to me. In time, I can try this attack once more, only next time I'll have far fewer men knowing about it. I erred by having too many in on the plan. One must have spilled the coffee grounds. Well, that won't happen again.*

He and his new aides met Legate Smith at the spaceport nearest the Presidential Offices. "Welcome Legate Smith. Your new look does you wonders," he admired her appearance, having forgotten the news that she too had become a terrorist attack victim. She grimaced a little, still getting used to wearing the restrictive pipe corset, lip plates, and toe shoes, depending heavily on Helene, her Personal Assistant, for most everything, except her voice-activated laptop. Additionally, a dozen investigators and security men came with her.

"I wish this were a courtesy call, but I'm afraid it isn't. As I said, we traced an aborted terrorist attack originating from here on Haffren-3. We must get to the bottom of this unfortunate incident as soon as possible. My investigators must interview the people at Agrona Solutions. Of course, we must interview you as well."

"But of course. I assure you no such attack came from Heffran-3, but perhaps your investigation will prove otherwise. If you will follow me, I'll take you to your quarters in the Presidential Guest Suite." He had decided to play innocent of any knowledge of an attack. He could have claimed he'd already discovered the plot among his generals and had them convicted and imprisoned. He'd chosen not to go that route, since it would raise questions of his own involvement. *Let her find any real facts first. If she does and comes after me, I can then explain it all away.*

After getting her settled into her new and plush suite, he suggested, "Of course, you will join me for a state dinner this evening?"

That was the last thing Legate Smith desired. Being seen in public looking as she did, and as helpless as she felt, was humiliating enough, but to have to attend a formal dinner was far worse. Unfortunately, as a Legate, she could not refuse his offer. "Yes, we will join you. Thank you for extending such hospitality to us. Now, if you will excuse me, I do have a lot of work to do, and I'm pretty darn slow these days."

"Yes of course. If you need anything, just use the intercom, or rather have your assistant do it," he replied, covertly hinting he knew that she was really quite helpless. Only having her voice separated her from the many convicts in the assisted living complexes.

At the formal dinner, Legate Smith attempted to remain calm and unperturbed, though she was still embarrassed. All eyes focused on her as she made her extremely slow walk into the banquet hall. They also covertly glanced her way, watching as Helene fastened her lip plates into their horizontal position, preparatory to dining. The stares continued as Helene fed her, further embarrassing her. Over an after-dinner coffee, President Arthfael and his advisors chatted with her. Later, one by one, they excused themselves and left.

When only she, Helene, and President Arthfael remained, he rose and said politely, "If there is any entertainment you might wish this evening or any evening, why just let me know. I can discretely arrange for a young man or woman of your choice to spend some private time with you in your bed."

Legate Smith flushed. That was about the last thing she

desired. "No thank you, that will not be necessary." She began to realize how depraved this world had become. It was now considered polite to offer sexual encounters to visiting dignitaries!

Once back in her suite, one of her investigators held up a paper. She read: Suite is bugged. Found five. Should we remove them? Disable them? Legate Smith thought for a moment then answered, "P Eight-one." He nodded. Protocol Eighty-one meant to leave them in place, but never to speak anything of a confidential or sensitive nature. Additionally, guards were posted both inside and outside of the suite. Thus began the investigation of the attack on Winno-3.

During the ensuing few days, Legate Smith conducted her normal business, via her laptop, but her many investigators began showing her written reports of what they were uncovering. Agrona Solutions began to yield substantial information. Bit by bit, her investigators began unraveling the plot against Winno-3. While the men at Agrona Solutions didn't know the intended target or why, they had stolen the drones and "borrowed" the two transports, providing the two pilots and two navigators. Their involvement didn't go beyond this point. The men didn't know that they were providing the means by which a planned bio agent attack could be carried out. Some suspected something akin to a sneak attack, but really had no proof. They were just following orders of some generals.

Further checking showed that these generals had mysteriously vanished a week ago. However, her investigators were thorough. Each general's quarters was searched extensively. Investigator Mark returned one afternoon. He showed Legate Smith a sign that read: Come with me. I have something that you must listen to. She nodded, and he and Helene helped her outside to his shuttle. Once inside, he played the recording for her. "Got it off of General Glyn. How do you want to proceed?"

Legate Smith thought for a moment. "Let's confront him with this evidence and see how he answers. He'll probably deny any role in it. We'll then insist he take a lie detector test and see how he responds. Of course, any such evidence isn't legal; people can fake such tests easily, but perhaps he lacks such skills. Have your men waiting with drawn guns. That will help rattle him and guarantee our security as well. We don't know how many others are involved. This may explain why all his aides and generals are new to their posts, because they are. Come on; this should be interesting."

A half hour later with her advance preparations made, Legate Smith confronted President Arthfael in his office. "Welcome Legate Smith. What can I do for you this afternoon?"

"Ah, you can answer some rather serious questions about your involvement in the attack on Winno-3. We've traced much of the equipment used back to Agrona Solutions. They in turn pointed to specific orders given to them from several of your generals, all of whom have recently vanished. However, we searched their quarters and found this recording that General Glyn made. Allow me to play it for you. Helene, if you would, please?"

As the recording played back, General Glyn outlined President Arthfael's grand plan in very explicit terms. While it played, she watched the man's reactions closely. His face gave him away. He was involved in some manner, of that she was convinced. Now came the tricky part.

"Alas, I cannot deny having uncovered most of this myself. I had nothing to do with this plot. Some of my closest generals misunderstood me. Unknown to me, they planned the whole thing. When I learned of the attack, I too launched an immediate investigation uncovering their plot. I had them all arrested and sent to the Imperium assisted living complex for the rest of their lives. So yes, I purged my government of all the guilty men. I was hoping to avoid the embarrassment of having this occur on my watch. It so undermines my credibility with the voters. Surely, you can appreciate my position, Legate Smith. Such news would not be taken kindly." He played his backup plan perfectly, as far as he could tell. "I do hope we don't have to go public with all this. I assure you the guilty men have been punished, as per Imperium laws."

"Ah, then our investigation is nearly complete, President Arthfael," Legate Smith replied. "What remains is for you to take a lie detector test to prove to me you are telling the truth, and that you had no knowledge of this plot nor did you instigate it. You see, as President, you commanded these men, and apparently had them arrested, tried, and sentenced. However, we've not been able to find the court records of their trial or conviction. For all we know, they are dead or in hiding somewhere. So you can understand my position. I have to have you undergo all of the psych men's testing to prove your veracity."

His perfect world began to crack. "But you can't do this to me. I'm the President of all Haffren-3! This is illegal!"

"No, Mr. President, planetary genocide is illegal. What I want to know is why you chose this time to attack Winno-3? They've never been your enemy. They've never attacked your world. They are innocent of any crimes against Haffren-3."

President Arthfael snapped. He began yelling, "Can't you see the Ataro Empire is once more expanding its suffocating tentacles ever outward, strangling more and more worlds, as its wasps suck the very life from those worlds, like it has always done. We, the proud, brilliant people of Haffren-3 have long known about this empire's true intentions. We know from our own history books that it was the Ataro Empire which created the Imperium two millennia ago, only because of Haffren-3's people along with so many other worlds united and worked together to stop the outward expansion of the Ataro Empire, confining it to thirty-six worlds. And even today, these wicked, evil worlds are once more devouring other worlds. Look at Ashford-5 and now Bailey-3! Their gluttony is worse than ever before! Ashford-5 is far out on the outer rim of the galaxy, but Bailey-3 is within our own backyard! I ask you, how long do you think it will be before they attempt to devour us here on Haffren-3? Days, weeks? Months, if we are lucky!" he ranted and raved. "We can, and we must defend Haffren-3 from the strangling tentacles of the Ataro Empire! It's now or never. We refuse to become a slave of the wasp-lovers!"

Legate Smith asked, "Helene, have you gotten all of this?" Her assistant nodded. "Okay then, President Arthfael Arwel, you are under arrest for attempted genocide of Winno-

3. Take this piece of trash from me before I vomit all over him!" At last, Legate Smith allowed her pent-up anger to surface.

A few days later, Arthfael joined the generals and aides at the assisted living complex. Thereafter, he was called Aderyn. Her name meant bird. Legate Smith's investigators then visited Warden General Dylan Eilian. He explained how President Arthfael had asked him to provide a backup set of the bio agent cylinders, in case some disaster struck their Incoming Imperium Prisoner's building. "You see, we would have a backup supply with which to restart the prison system. Why? What has he done with the cylinders," the portly man asked, sweating slightly.

At Legate Smith's insistence, he underwent a lie detection session and passed. She then cleared him of wrongdoing, but fined him for violating the Imperium orders on not allowing any of the bio agent outside the official Incoming Prisoner building. Her official report to Emperor Kino stated the attack was instigated by a psychopathic president. While Emperor Kino would have also preferred to have learned who had so convinced President Arthfael that the Ataro Empire was his enemy, he was satisfied with her findings. He did insist on more strict regulations on the bio agent cylinders officially permitted on Haffren-3, which she fully implemented.

Emperor Kino also kept Albert busy, going from world to world in the Ataro Empire checking on the state of Chaos on each. He considered Albert to be his early warning system, while he and Legate Smith attempted to get the Imperium functioning once more. Yet, another aspect of Albert's Butterfly Effect occurred at nearly this same time, wholly unrelated to the bio attacks.

Chapter 19 Sanity Versus Perversion Paradise

Alun Arthmael. Rather Chief Detective Inspector or CDI Alun Arthmael was on his own time. Had to be. His boss had officially marked the case Cold, ending all further ongoing investigation. He could not and would not cease his investigation into the disappearance of his fiancé, Miss Morwen Severn. He had proposed, and she accepted, making him the happiest man on Haffren-3, but that was now nearly six months ago. A week later, she simply vanished without a trace.

He still carried a portrait photo of her in his wallet. Her skin had the light brownish hue as did all natives of Haffren-3. Her lovely wavy black hair fell to her shoulders, but with bangs that draped down her forehead to her eyebrows. Her eyes, oh her eyes, the most intense blue eyes he'd ever seen. Her face was somewhat pentagonal and her lips always seemed to radiate her special smile.

Morwen was twenty-four and a grade school teacher, fourth grade to be precise. The day of her disappearance was just like any other school day. She taught her students, and at the end of the day, she walked out of the school building never to be seen again. Alun had jumped all over this case, naturally. No witnesses. No one heard or saw anything out of the ordinary, except one horse drawn carriage that was taking sight seers on a picturesque trip around the heart of old Cairn Glen.

Alun was a year older with jet-black hair and moustache to match, a handsome fellow or so Morwen always told him. He'd risen to CDI rapidly, solving numerous crimes during his seven years on the force. He'd joined up at eighteen with the intention of making a difference on Haffren-3 or here in Cairn Glen specifically. The son of a preacher, Alun was brought up indoctrinated with the beliefs of the Unification Church. Primary among their beliefs is that each of person is a Holy

Temple, and that each and every one is a god or goddess, and should strive to become one with all Nature, seeking a Holy Union with the Universe. These beliefs were now wholly in the minority on Haffren-3, where carnal lusts, sexual cravings, deprivations, and all manner of sexual perversions had become the norm, independent of societal position, but far more pronounced within in the higher echelons of society, where money could purchase anything one desired.

Alun had been on a crusade to clean up society, at least in the city of Cairn Glen. He had no idea why people had fallen into such debauchery, but whenever he found illegal activities going on, he stepped in to shut them down. Naturally, this had made him many enemies. For weeks, he thought that perhaps Morwen's kidnaping had been retribution for his self-righteous crusade. He'd exhausted all obvious avenues along those lines weeks ago. He had no leads at all. With the case marked Cold, he turned to working on it after hours, getting at most a few hours' sleep each day.

He had discussed what he should do with his aging father. Reverend Glaw replied, "Son, in this legalized Den of Iniquity of Haffren-3, you must not forsake her. Do not give up your search for Morwen. The few of us of the Faith who are left must set clear and unequivocal examples for the many that are following their own paths to self-destruction. Remain pure of heart, my son, just as Morwen must. Find her and consummate your shared vows. No matter the suffering the dear child has suffered, you must be strong and lift her back up from the fires that threaten to consume her very soul."

"But dad, what if she chose to run away? What if she didn't want to marry me and chose to disappear?" Alun countered, doubts seeping into his mind.

"That's not the Morwen that we both know. She was pure of heart, unlike the multitudes of human shells that inhabit our world, son. Doubt Morwen not. Find her and take her, lift her back into the Holy Grace of Our Lord."

"Thanks, dad. I needed that. I will not fail her," Alun breathed a sigh of relief. Hearing the encouraging words bolstered him, casting the lingering doubts from his mind. *I'll find her no matter how long it takes. I'll marry her, no matter what has befallen her. I'll raise her back into the Holy Grace, the Holy Light, once again.* Thus, steeled against all doubts, Alun redoubled his efforts.

He'd heard rumors women were sometimes smuggled out of the city at the spaceport. Hence, he'd taken a part-time job as a cargo handler, keeping his eyes open and making casual inquiries of his fellow workers. Until that fateful day, he'd learned next to nothing, and was about to quit and try another avenue. Then, that autistic lad in the company of two obvious terrorist attack victims said his magic words: "Albert Chaos see. Ariceli Chaos see. Carys Chaos see. Alun see Chaos here. To Ashford-5 go. No Chaos."

What had struck him like a hammer was the word Chaos. High society of Haffren-3 was dominated by numerous Counts, Countesses, Dukes, and Duchesses — a throwback into antiquity. At one time, Dukes ran what other worlds called countries, while Counts ran smaller states within countries and were vassals of their Duke. What had struck him like a thunderbolt was Chaos — namely Countess Morgana Twyrth, the Countess of Chaos Lynn. While these anachronistic titles no longer carried any real political significance, Chaos Lynn was the picturesque lake at the edge of Cairn Glen and squarely in the middle of her sprawling estate. Further, he knew she was a Purveyor of Elegant Women.

That is, she traded in female sexual slaves of only the finest quality. Only the very wealthiest could afford one of her highly trained women. *Could Morwen have been kidnaped by her thugs? Dear god, I hope not!* Those thoughts were what so startled him about Albert's simple statement.

The next day, he quietly researched what his office had on Countess Morgana Twyrth. To his dismay, there wasn't much to go on. Reputedly a hundred twenty years old, at last report, she didn't look a day over forty. Her children had filed a lawsuit claiming she ought to have given them the Chaos Lynn estate years ago. That the multi-million credit estate was to go to her eldest upon her death was in her will that was on file. It was just that she didn't die. Rejuvenation of course. Her son lost the legal battle. As part of the court proceedings, much of her "elegant female sexual slaves business" had been mentioned. That's where he'd heard about it. Not much to go on, but at least he had a clue.

Since the case was officially Cold, he couldn't pay her an official visit. Besides such dealings were perfectly legal, satisfying the needs of the very wealthy of Haffren-3. Hence, he decided to case the estate the next evening. He quit his temporary job at the spaceport and headed off to the southern edge of the sprawling city of Cairn Glen. From the last low hill, he could see the large estate with its central lake. A stone wall some eight feet high entirely surrounded the grounds. A single highly ornate entrance gate displayed Twyrth Estate in wrought iron. A security post was manned by a guard, even at seven p.m. He drove on by in his private electric car. Using back roads, he circumnavigated the outer walls, estimating that it was square, about a mile per side. The mansion or manor house was built from the same grey granite blocks as the wall and gave the illusion of an ancient castle wall and manor house. It rose three stories with prominent second and third story southern facing balconies overlooking the lake and the more distant countryside.

The manor house was extremely large, perhaps twenty rooms per floor. He didn't doubt that it also had an extensive basement. There was a horse racing track on the eastern side, but what appeared to be stables were not connected to the manor house per se, laying some two hundred feet further east. A hedge maze was located on the northern side of the home. The grounds consisted of immaculately cultured grass, as befitting a golf course on which he once played east of the city. Great trees lined the lake, and several shaded the grey manor house. Even as he circumnavigated the estate, he could see that it was well guarded. At least six security men were on duty at various locations, but considering its vastness, he knew there must be many other security features installed. He could not just walk in there and search the place for his fiancé.

No, that would require probable cause and a warrant, which he couldn't possibly obtain. Alun needed another way to get inside and have a look. As he drove back, he pondered this idea. He called in sick the next day and spent the day using binoculars casing the place from a concealed location along one wall, where the guards seldom strolled. They did have an electric golf-style cart, which they used periodically to traverse the inner side of the walls, once every hour on the hour. He couldn't quite see into the rooms, however. Great, thick curtains covered most of them, though through one, he caught glimpses of women inside, at least he thought they were female forms, somehow strange in appearance.

That evening while watching the newscast, which he seldom did, he heard mention that on the tenth of the month, Countess Morgana Twyrth was holding a formal ball for specially invited guests and their female companions, all of whom were "graduates" of her school for elegant sexual slaves. "Here's my way in there, my golden opportunity. How do I pull this one off?" he commented to his comm center.

The men who could afford her "products" had to be extremely wealthy. No doubt about that. Hence, he would need to fabricate just such a disguise. Alun was a master of disguises. He owed his tremendous success as a CDI to his uncanny ability to infiltrate, get the goods on the criminals, and then arrest them. He never used the same disguise twice. Now, he knew he had to fabricate the disguise of his life! He had to become a Count and decided on becoming Count Alun of Mared.

Next, he hocked everything he owned and created an account in his new name. Secretly, he also tied the account to the Police Department's Special Unit's funds, which were often used to handle enormous sums when dealing with the illicit drug trade. Thus, if anyone checked up on his available "funds," they would discover he apparently had access to nearly a billion in credits. That handled, he then visited the finest tailor in Cairn Glen and purchased the finest suit money could buy, wholly handmade and costing half his yearly salary. Taking a weeks' personal leave of absence from work, he dressed in his new suit and checked into the penthouse suite of the finest hotel in Cairn Glen as Count Alun of Mared.

Once there, he then composed a letter of introduction to Countess Morgana Twyrth of Chaos Lynn. After sending it, he called in many favors that others in the department owed him. "Meinir, I need a big favor. This account." He carefully read off the numbers, "I need it monitored for activity. Send me a text that says merely 'Hit' whenever anyone checks on its balance. Keep this on the QT. It's an undercover operation; off the books."

She replied, "Okay, I owe you. Is this about Morwen? Have you got a clue?"

"Yes, but I can't say more. Thank you. I owe you." He imagined her face as she smiled and hung up. *I can trust her. I saved her bacon in the Torrid Affair last year.*

Next, he fabricated a quick Count Alun of Mared web page and activated it. Within an hour, the Web Spiders would access it and index its pages into the massive search engines. Now, he could only wait and hope the Countess of Chaos Lynn would take the bait. If she didn't, he was out a rather large amount of credits. Alun paced the penthouse suite, but repeatedly had to turn down management's many offers of sexual favors. "No, I don't need an escort at this time. I'll contact you when I do." "No, I'm not in need of a massage at this time." "No, I don't need 'company' this evening. I'm not going out just yet. I'll let you know."

Everywhere in the Haffren-3 upper society, men and women were handed about as sexual toys, much like children's playing dolls. For the "toys," this was a well-respected and lucrative business. Alun knew this from police files. A gigolo of his own age could make triple his annual salary, ignoring all of the small "gifts" that were often bestowed on them. From his own childhood, after his mother passed away, he knew just how difficult it was for his father to find a maid and a gardener, who were actually not expected to be also providing sexual favors while cleaning or handling their lawn. His father had gone through four cooks before finding a "real" cook, who wanted nothing more than to prepare their meals.

Statistically, he also knew nearly a quarter of the population of Haffren-3 was involved in "being toys," a fact he found revolting and disgusting. Yet, these men and women made vastly more credits than he did. Perhaps more than anything else, Alun was shocked to learn one disturbing fact. The average birth rate had now fallen below one per family. He'd read about this during his police academy training, when he was just eighteen. Obviously, women carefully controlled just when they would have a child. In fact, when he looked into the numbers a bit further, he discovered the death rate exceeded the birth rate for Haffren-3 and had been so for nearly a century now.

On the other hand, all these things kept the children of the wealthy contented and satisfied, while their parents continued to use the Rejuvenation Machines, prolonging their lives. Many lawsuits had been filed by children attempting to get their hands on their parent's wealth. Thus far, the courts had sided with the parents, not their children, who were told they had to wait upon the deaths of their parents before they could inherit.

In the larger cities of Haffren-3, enormous casinos and luxury hotels accommodated the heavy volume of very wealthy Imperium tourists who sought out Haffren-3's many "pleasures." Alun also knew the men and women who worked that circuit were the highest paid "toys" on the planet. Everywhere he'd turned during his life, he saw this nearly frantic emphasis on sexual actions, yet with incredibly little actual creation of children. In today's world, three-quarters of the children eventually ended up in the trade, one way or another.

He considered himself one of the luckiest men on Haffren-3 to have found Morwen, who like him, despised the trade. She wanted to change things for the better and had begun to do so by teaching fourth graders to respect themselves. Now, she was gone, taken from him. By whom, he still didn't know.

Two days later, he received a text message that contained one word, "Hit." He smiled; she'd taken the bait, but would she respond? He kept his fingers crossed. She should have seen that Count Alun of Mared was worth many billions of credits. If money was a key factor with this Countess, she ought to send for him, but what if she had other criteria? What if she wanted breeding, lineages, good looks instead? He bit his lip and continued pacing around the luxurious suite. Later that afternoon, he received an invitation from the Countess Morgana Twyrth of Chaos Lynn. The light purple envelop smelled of perfume. He opened it and read.

My Dear Count Alun of Mared,

This Saturday night at six p.m., I'm holding a formal reception for some of my clients, who have purchased their fine women from me. For the women, this is a reunion party as well.

Your timing and credentials seem impeccable. If you are seriously interested in purchasing one of my women, please attend our party. You'll be able to see for yourself the absolute finest quality of the women whom I train.

I assure you, Count, there are no finer women available on Heffran-3 at any price. Whatever your desires, whatever your fantasies might be, whatever avenues your pleasures might take, I give you my personal guarantee that my women have been highly trained at fulfilling them exquisitely or I will refund your fee.

Hope to see you then,

Countess Morgana Twyrth

P.S. If you like what you see, plan to spend the night at my estate. Over breakfast, we can discuss the arrangements. I currently have four women in training from which to choose. However, none has quite finished their extensive training. I do hope this will not pose a barrier for us.

At the very bottom was a set of landing coordinates for a shuttle. "All right! She took the bait!" Alun danced around the suite for a moment. Taking a deep breath, he sat down and reread the note carefully. Then, he set about making his plans. He purchased two more shirts, so that he'd have a "change of clothes."

On the off chance that Morwen was actually one of these four women in training, he knew he just had to rescue her from the clutches of the Countess. If he left and attempted to get an arrest warrant filed and come back with a police raid, by then the Countess would already know about the warrant and probably dispose of Morwen and maybe the other three women. *No, I have to do this alone and be prepared for whatever I find. Wait! What if she's there and these other three have been kidnaped? I can't just leave them there! I'll have to get all four out of her clutches. That means I'll need to deal with the security guards. I'm going to need some equipment, that's for sure.*

He changed out of his unbelievably expensive suit, donning another one of his many disguises. Looking into the mirror, he smiled. He looked like a very seedy, disreputable character. Pocketing a wad of credits and his penthouse suite key, he checked the hall. Clear. He ducked out and took the service elevator down. An hour later, he'd purchased some "illegal" electronic equipment. Back in his suite, he changed personas once more, and then ordered an expensive shuttle for Saturday night and Sunday. That done, he set to work assembling his special devices. He did not intend to kill the guards, not if he could help it. After all, he was a CDI, and they were merely hired men for security. If he did find Morwen at the estate, he needed to rescue her and possibly the other women. The security men could not be allowed to interfere.

Another thought struck him. What if she had already been sold? His heart raced! This was a reunion party for the women. What if she now belonged to some wealthy man? What could he possibly do then? Once more, he paced the suite, a sickening feeling in his stomach. At last, he resolved to snatch her away from such a perverted man, who had no right to his precious Morwen. She was pure; she wanted to remain pure, free from the sexual perversion pervading this despicable world! *If I do that, with all his money, he can come after me in more ways than one! I'll have to flee Haffren-3 with Morwen!*

His resolve knew no bounds. Hastily, he made some travel arrangements. If he had to flee, he could not use commercial flights. They'd be on him in an instant. No, he'd have to hire his own private deep space transport. Using his new persona, he made the arrangements. A deep space transport would be standing by for his exclusive use, beginning Saturday night. If he didn't need it, he would only be out his deposit. If he did need to use it, he'd have to fork over substantially more funds. He sighed; he'd be almost broke if he had to go that far to rescue Morwen. *Well, I've given her my pledge, my word. Whatever else I am, I am true to my word.*

He spent the rest of the day going over contingency

plans. As a CDI, he knew how clandestine operations were run. This time, he found himself using these same methods and grinned. Finally, he could do no more and forced himself to relax and rest.

At five Saturday evening, he carried his equipment to his rented shuttle and installed them. He tested the contraption. It worked to his satisfaction. With all his preparations completed, he took a deep breath, entered the coordinates, and lifted off on the short flight to Chaos Lynn. As he allowed the autopilot to descend, he spotted two dozen other fancy shuttles already parked on the grassy knoll just west of the manor house proper. Party lights lined the portico of the grand entrance. Carrying his invitation, Count Alun of Mared walked across the manicured lawn to the ornate double doors, handing the well-dressed security man doubling as doorman his invitation. The man glanced at it and motioned him to the door. He pressed the doorbell.

He steeled himself, prepared for what might lie beyond these fancy doors. As CDI, he'd seen many unusual and downright strange and perverted things before, but even his background didn't prepare him for the sights that greeted his eyes as the doors opened for him.

Leaving her grade school, Morwen walked down the sidewalk. All the children had left. The street was quiet, just the way she preferred. Silently, an electric car came up behind her. Both side windows were down. From the backseat, a woman's voice called out, "Morwen Severn?" She stopped and turned to see who was calling her name. As she did so, the car stopped and a dart shot out from a blowgun, sticking in her neck. She felt drowsy. Vaguely, she saw a man step out before her eyes closed. He kept her from falling. Simultaneously, the woman in the backseat opened her door. The man lifted Morwen into the car, sitting her on the seat. After he shut the door, the woman pulled down a blind, hiding them from outside views. Shortly after that, the electric car sped silently off at the speed limit.

A half hour later, the car pulled into the attached garage behind the giant manor house. As two well-dressed women stepped out of the car, one spoke in a commanding, alto voice, "Take her to the operation room, and lay her on the medical machine, please." The driver nodded and carried out her orders. By the time the two women reached the room, he'd already deposited the unconscious Morwen on the machine.

"If you will be so kind, Megan, remove her clothing; we will see what we have here. By all reports, she should be workable material, but let's see for sure before I send our chauffeur away," Countess Morgana ordered.

Several minutes later, Megan had Morwen stripped naked, but still lying on the medical machine. The Countess carefully examined the young woman from head to toe. "Yes, a few blemishes, but those can be handled. Okay, she is another good candidate. Prepare her for the machine. I want her to have the usual whole works, dear Megan: voice, arms, breasts, hair, feet, eyelashes, lips, ribs, everything. Let's also get rid of that birthmark and those blemishes here and here. Signal me when she's finished, please." The Countess turned and made her elegant, but slow walk out of the room, leaving Morwen in the competent hands of her lifelong servant Megan.

A few hours later, while Morgana was taking tea, a buzzer sounded — Megan's signal. Carefully, she rose on her tall heels and made her way back to the operations room to inspect the final product. I say final product, but in reality, this wasn't the final, final product. Rather that would come many months from now, after Morwen learned to adapt to her new role and learned how to exquisitely satisfy any man or woman's sexual needs and fantasies, as well as perform some routine household chores. No, final product at this point merely meant her physical body was prepared for her potential new role.

Countess Morgana carefully inspected the modified Morwen, looking her over from head to toe. Satisfied, she said, "Excellent work, Megan, as always dearest. Now, let's get her properly dressed in her first training outfit." Carefully, they slipped a strapless chemise over her now very slender waist. Next, a very confining corset filled with more steel stays than heavy cotton or so it seemed, was fastened around her. While Morgana held the still unconscious woman up, Megan fastened the long cords to the corset-tightening machine and activated it. Relentlessly, the strings tightened it, leaving precisely an inch to go from being fully closed in the back. After another half hour, they would finish the tightening process, allowing her organs some time to adapt to the constriction. The two continued dressing her partially, slipping on seamed, black nylons, and then the knee high ballet boots with steel heels, impossible to break or bend. That done, the two carefully applied Morwen's new permanent makeup, most noticeably giving her cherry red lips and a light blue eye shadow. Megan brushed out her much longer and wavier black hair. At last, the waiting period was over, and she attached the machine once more. It quietly but efficiently finished the tightening of the corset. Megan then tied off the ends.

Next, the two slipped a silky black slip over Morwen, and then worked to get her into the extremely tight-fitting black satin gown, which hugged her curves down to the middle of her lower legs. Megan then applied the final touches, securely fastening a pair of very heavy, long earrings with red rubies in them to her ears and a matching necklace. Both women stood back and looked Morwen over once more. Megan looked at Morgana. "Yes, she's prefect. Okay, Megan, let's wake her up and introduce her to her new life. I find this to always be the most scintillating of times, positively stimulating!" Megan smiled and nodded, fetching the smelling salts, while Morgana moved the viewing mirror into position. She then stood just to one side of the mirror so she had a perfect view of Morwen when she awoke, saw her reflection, and heard her words.

An awful smell roused Morwen. She raised her hands to her face and nose to ward it off, but felt nothing at all. She opened her eyes and saw a reflection of some woman in black staring back at her, while another elegantly dressed, middle-aged woman stood beside the mirror. The alto voice spoke. "Welcome Morwen to the beginning of your new life, one guaranteed to please you. As you can see in the mirror, we've modified your body into that of an absolutely flawless, perfect woman, a magnificent sex toy if I do say so myself. As you can see, we've removed your arms. From now on, you have no need of them at all. Don't try to speak. Like Megan here, your voice box has been removed. A sex toy never has any need to speak, not ever. Besides, we like our quiet here."

"As you can also see, we've reduced your waist to a proper eleven inches. Of course, we needed to remove some of your ribs and re-arrange internal organs somewhat. You are wearing our specialty training corset that will force you always to have simply perfect posture at all times. You will be wearing it all the time, except when Megan here bathes you. I know; breathing is quite difficult. Take shallow breaths dear. In time, you'll get used to it. We all do."

"Your feet have been properly fused. Elegant women always walk on the tips of their toes. From now on, you can only walk if you are wearing these ballet shoes or boots. Initially and until you learn to walk in them, we'll keep you in the knee high style. Of course, once you've mastered them, you can then wear the vastly fancier ballet shoes, similar to mine and Megan's. They come in a wide variety of styles and colors, as you'll eventually see. So walking like a proper, elegant woman will be your first challenge, but I've devised ways to help you learn quickly."

"We've also enlarged your bosom to what's acceptable among our elite clientele. You have H cups now, quite exotic, don't you think? We've lengthened your hair some. As you can see, it drapes nicely over your shoulders to the middle of your back. Quite elegant. Your lips have been thickened. Men and women like their toys to have thick, sensuous lips, you see. We've lengthened your eyelashes considerably. Don't they just look fabulous, dear? When you blink, they really add to your ability to flirt with men and women. Oh yes, we've applied permanent makeup so you never have to worry about needing a freshening."

"Now then, Morwen, when you need to go to the bathroom, you lean your head to your left. Megan will assist you with that. Like all my women, you are about to undergo very extensive and demanding training, educating you to not only walk and act as a very elegant woman, but also to serve every sexual fantasy, whim, and perversion that men and women may have. Only when you pass my very rigid standards will I then sell you to your new master. In the meantime, I've opened a bank account in your name. As you progress in your training and master the actions required of you, I'll make substantial deposits into your account. When you have completed your rigorous training here and are purchased by an extremely wealthy man or woman, a portion of your sale price will also be deposited into your account, as you will have earned it. So you see, there are definite financial gains to be had by your mastering what is now required of you. On the other hand, I do not permit disobedience and failures. Such will be met with punishments suitable to the offense. Do I make myself clear? Nod if you understand this."

Morwen fought to breathe. The pressure was intense; she felt her head would explode if her chest didn't do so first. She tried to scream, but she only saw her mouth wide open with what little air she had coming out. Twice, she passed out only to be revived by that awful smelling tube Megan waved below her nose. Gasping, she tried to wake up from some hideous nightmare but couldn't. Crushed utterly, she began silently bawling.

The Countess Morgana was so excited by Morwen's wild reactions that she simply had to pleasure herself. "God, Morwen, you are really exciting me. I do so love to watch young women's first reactions to all of this. So utterly stimulating in so many ways. Oh!" She finished and sighed as deeply as her corset would allow. The Countess wore a normal corset, and her waist was only eighteen inches around, a far cry from what Morwen was having to endure.

"Okay, enough with the introductions, it's time that you met your fellow trainees and had some supper. I'm famished myself. Megan, help her to her feet. Just this once, Megan will support you as we head off to the dining room." The Countess carefully rose on her own ballet shoes and led the way out of the operation room. Poor Morwen froze when she was forced to her toes. She waved her arms wildly with no reaction; they weren't there any longer. Her satin gown was so tight fitting that she could only barely move one boot two inches in front of the other and that only if she swung her lower leg around in front of the other, more or less. No way could she remotely

398

keep her balance, even with her knees heavily bent. Without Megan's support, she would have fallen countless times on their long way to the dining hall.

She entered the fanciest dining room she'd ever seen. Golden fixtures illuminated the polished table. Tapestries adorned the wall. Everything about the room spoke of ultimate luxury. Three other women already sat at the table. All resembled Morwen, armless, large bosoms, unable to speak, sitting rigidly with perfect posture, and wearing fancy black patent, knee high ballet boots. The Countess spoke up as Megan led the wildly wobbling Morwen into the room. "Ladies, I would like you to meet our newest trainee, Morwen. Morwen, this is Rhonwen." She pointed to another raven haired young woman, who nodded sadly towards Morwen, her eyes exuding sympathy. "This is Siana." The woman was quite blonde, but her hairstyle was otherwise identical to Morwen's. "This is Terren." She had wavy brown hair. At least Morwen could recognize her fellow trainees by their hair color.

Megan helped her get seated. Then, she inserted a rubber plug into her mouth. It had a long straw sticking out of it. She fastened the leather straps behind her head for her. Megan moved on down the line of women, inserting similar plugs and fastening them securely. That done, while the Countess explained to Morwen, Megan left the room, returning with a tray containing four tall glasses filled with a strange looking, liquid mixture.

"You dine by using your straws to suck up your dinner. My chef has taken the liberty of pureeing your steak dinner for you, Morwen. You can't expect Megan here to feed all of you. Occasionally, when you deserve it, I'll allow Megan to feed you. Your new masters will always have that option available to them. That is, to allow you to feed yourselves or to feed you or to have someone else feed you. Usually, they simply expect you to feed yourselves. It is a very well balanced meal, Morwen. Eat up." She began daintily to cut up her juicy steak.

Megan soon sat down at the opposite end of the table, facing the Countess. She proceeded to cut hers, emulating the regal manner the Countess used. Morwen watched the other three and then attempted to emulate their motions. Using her head, she maneuvered her straw into the glass and began sucking up her diner. She was full long before the glass was empty. She couldn't speak; couldn't write. She had no way to communicate anything. Tears continued to stream down her face. Beside her Siana nodded her head sympathetically.

Later, coffee was served. While the other three drank some, Morwen could only swallow a small amount. She felt as if she was about to burst wide open. After that, Countess Morgana announced, "Okay, that was a fine dinner. Tonight, I believe I will sleep with Siana here and test how your training is progressing along, dear. First though, Megan and I will need to get Morwen to the dungeon and prepared for the night. Terren, Rhonwen, you may return to your rooms and prepare for bed. Megan will be by shortly. See you all in the morning. Pleasant dreams." She rose slowly as did Megan. Together, they forced Morwen to rise precariously to her feet.

After what seemed an eternity of endless halls, they arrived at the stone stairs leading downward. Morwen panicked. She couldn't possibly descend these stairs! The two women held on to her waist and forced her to make the attempt anyway. She nearly fell with each step. "Don't worry. When you've finished your dungeon training, you'll be able to manage these steps elegantly, Morwen. It takes time and practice. You'll soon see," the Countess explained as they slowly descended.

Again, there seemed to be an awful lot of rooms down here, all illuminated fairly dimly. They took her to a wall. Megan fastened a neck collar around her. It was fastened securely to the wall, holding her head tightly against the stone. Another steel collar was fastened around her tiny waist. It too held her back firmly against the walls. Yet another collar was secured just below her hips. "There. You cannot move a fraction of an inch. As you sleep, your legs and toes will become more accustomed to bearing your weight like this. Pleasant dreams, dear. Megan will return for you in the morning." The two women left her standing perfectly erect against the wall. Morwen's feet were aching, but she couldn't move any part of her feet except her ankles. The bones in her feet had been fused solidly together. Morwen silently sobbed herself to sleep, trying to will herself to die somehow.

The next morning, Megan helped her out of the device and led her to a nearby bathroom. That handled, she held a glass of liquid breakfast up for her to drink. At least Megan was patient with her. That finished, Megan led her into another room with a strange walking machine. She pressed a button and waited silently. After a time, the Countess entered, wearing a blue satin gown this morning. "Morning Morwen. Today, we begin your training. First, you must learn to walk well. To aid you, we have this walking machine, but first, we have to install the punishment for failure device." The two women inserted a pair of electronically activated plugs into her lower orifices. Next, they lifted her onto the walking machine. Metal collars fastened around her waist and neck. Long wires connected them to the ceiling.

"There we go. You are all fastened in, Morwen. When I start the machine, you have no choice but to walk. The wires will prevent you from falling, no matter what happens. However, if you do not walk, then you'll pull on the wires. That will throw a switch, which will activate the devices inside you. The result will not be pleasant by any means. Only when you begin walking again and reduce the tension on the wires will it stop. We'll give you a lunch and supper break. Happy walking. Got to get your toes and legs strengthened a whole lot. Bye." The Countess pressed a button, and the rubber floor began moving. Morwen had no choice but to begin to take her minuscule steps. The two women left her alone.

Soon, she tired and stumbled, pulling hard on the wires. At least, they kept her from falling. However, the electrical shocks in her privates caused her to shriek, but no sound came out. It took all she could do to get her feet moving again. She bawled nearly constantly for hours. By lunch, her legs were mush. By supper, when they unhooked her, her legs gave out completely, and she fainted as well. She awoke chained to the wall as before, tightly and vertically. She broke down and cried again until drifting into a miserable sleep.

One day of torture turned into another, seemingly endless. Then one day, Countess Morgana announced, "Perfect Morwen. You walked a whole day without tripping the wires.

Time to move onto your next round." She didn't realize the device recorded whether or not she tripped the wires when falling. This time, she was attached to a similar walking device, only this one was sloped. Part of the time, she was walking up hill and then partly downhill. Going up was drastically easier than going down. She felt her knees were ripping apart. Again, the unforgiving pain in her privates forced her to continue as much as possible.

Untold days later, she was able to handle this challenge. Next, she was placed into a different device. Before her were a set of stone stairs, six tall going up to a platform, and then six steps going down. At least they dressed her in a gown that would more easily permit her to take the step. Wires again held her up and pulled her forward, forcing her to climb the stairs, cross the platform, descend the stairs, turn around in place, and repeat the cycle, endlessly with only breaks for lunch and supper. Again, she endured far more rounds of the excruciating pain in her privates. Days passed by endlessly. She no longer wanted to will herself to die and didn't even wish for death. She was merely numb, completely numb, save for her aching legs, knees, and toes.

Somehow, she must have finally succeeded, because the Countess congratulated her and hooked her up to a circular walking machine next. Wires again held her to the steel boom over her head. The circle that she was forced to walk contained level areas, two up and down ramps, and one set of stairs. This time, the wires wouldn't hold her up entirely. When she fell, she was nearly on the ground, while the electronic pains shot through her lower insides, unrelenting until she struggled to her feet by any means possible.

Some days later, the Countess explained, "Okay, Morwen, you are ready for your dungeon test. If you pass, you will move ahead to other training actions. If not, more of the Circle Walk until you do pass. What you are to do for me is to walk the circle path there wholly on your own without falling down. Got it? Nod. Okay, let's see you walk."

Morwen heard the magic words: if you pass, you will move ahead! Anything to get out of this dungeon! She even surprised herself as she made the circuit without falling, though several times she very nearly did so. "Congratulations. You've passed Basic Dungeon. Come on; up the stairs. Time to work on your dexterity. See, your legs have become solid muscles now, dear. Beautifully done." The Countess lavished praise on Morwen, who for some reason seemed to relish in her words.

The next days were miserable ones for her. The next room contained a fifty foot long, wooden, two by four secured to the floor with the two inch wide side forming the top. All around, thick mats covered the floor. "Your task is to climb onto the plank and walk its length. If you take a fall, the mats will protect you somewhat. It will be your job to get back onto your feet and start over. You see, if an elegant woman should take a fall while accompanied by her master, he or she will be so annoyed with her lack of skill and balance that they'll insist you get yourself up without their help. You've disgraced them and yourself. So you get to practice getting up if you fall. You pass when you can cross it in a minute and not fall. Have at it, dear."

She carefully stepped onto the plank, wobbling wildly. As she tried to take her first step, she missed the top of the board slightly and fell. Morwen wildly swung her arms to break her fall, but they weren't there. She hit the mat hard, stunning her for a moment. Once more, she broke down and bawled for quite some time. Yet no one came. At last, she struggled mightily to get back onto her feet. It was anything but easy and graceful. Tossing her hair back out of her face, she tried again and made a few steps before falling again.

At least a night, they allowed her to sleep in a real bed, but her bruised body ached just the same. One day, she was actually able to accomplish this task, much to her own surprise. "Ah, good work, Morwen. Now, we move on to the rough surfaces. You see, your masters may well desire you to accompany them as they cross a lawn. So in this room, we have installed a well-manicured lawn. You pass when you can walk around the room ten times in succession without falling down and in under two minutes. You will have to walk fairly briskly to succeed. Your masters don't want to be delayed by you just because you are not walking on pavement. Go for it,

Morwen," the Countess ordered.

This was worse that the wooden two by four! The uneven ground caused her to wobble wildly with each hesitant step. Again, when she fell, the ground was far harder on her, and she was left to get herself onto her feet by herself, as before. An eternity of days later, she passed this one too.

"Excellent Morwen. You have passed all the basic walking skills. I've place ten thousand credits into your account as a reward. Now, we move on to teaching you how to satisfy the sexual pleasures that may be requested of you. First, we will deal with straight sex. In this room, you see a male mannequin lying on its back on the bed. You are to mount the bed and ride him. You must train your vagina muscles to contract in synch with your pulling motions. When you do it properly, the mannequin will simulate a male ejaculation. When you sense it, you can stop and relax some. You must fine tune all of your senses and bodily muscles in order to be able to provide the ultimate in sexual pleasure for your master, be they male or female. Today, we are beginning with the simplest male position often requested by my clientele."

A seemingly endless series of days passed by Morwen, who experienced dildos in every conceivable position and method of operation. At least this part was relatively easy, no more nasty falls that knocked her senseless. When she graduated from these, she was then permitted to share beds with the other women, alternating nights with each of the other three. Now, she was forced to practice what she'd learned on these women, who in turn reciprocated on her.

One sunny day, Countess Morgana felt in a particularly good mood. At breakfast, she announced, "Today ladies, we need to get outside and some fresh air. You will each be taking turns being the pony in a pony cart race. Morwen and Siana will be one pair and Terren and Rhonwen the other. A dish of ice cream goes to the winning pony and driver. Morwen had no idea what she was talking about. The other three did and shook their heads no, giving Morwen a sinking feeling.

Megan changed their gowns for a leather harness over their corsets, hose, and knee high ballet boots. Then, she inserted a horse's bit in Morwen's mouth and fastened the harness to her head securely, adding a fancy red feathered plumb to her head. She did the same to the others, but left the bits out of Siana and Terren's mouths. The six headed outside, walking across the grassy lawn. Now, Megan realized why she had been trained to walk on the uneven ground. It was treacherous going for the four "ponies," but Megan and the Countess held onto each other for support. Morwen's ire rose, they are cheating, she thought.

A bit later, she found herself harnessed to a small two wheeled pony cart. She was being the pony! Siana was helped into the driver's seat and given the reins to hold between her teeth. Once Rhonwen and Terren were similarly prepared, Megan led Morwen, while the Countess led Terren. They walked onto the small, dirt racetrack. "Here is the starting line. When I say go, you race around the track. The first pony to cross this line is the winner. On your marks, get set, go!"

Morwen tried to pull the cart, but with only her toes, it barely moved. She dug her toes into the dirt and strained. Now the cart began to roll along. Soon, she was panting heavily, extremely short of breath, gasping was more like it. She fainted as she finally pulled Siana over the finish line, collapsing onto the ground. A bit later, that awful smell roused her. She was sitting in the cart now, and Siana was hooked up as her pony. Megan put the reins into her mouth and she bit down on them. As she watched, Siana now had to pull her around the track. Morwen felt a huge surge of sympathy for Siana, her blonde hair blowing in the light breeze, straining hard to pull her along. When they crossed the line, Siana was gasping as hard as she had, but somehow managed not to faint.

The next day, the Countess announced, "Today, Morwen, it is time that you learned to perform the basic domestic duties an elegant woman must be able to perform for her masters. Don't worry; you won't be expected to cook. But there are a number of actions you can do, the first of which is dusting." Megan inserted the handle of a pole feather duster into her mouth, securing it there in a leather harness around her head. After spraying some polish on the feathered end, she was instructed to dust off the various objects in the room. Meanwhile, the other three were similarly attached to other devices held in their mouths. One had to scrub out the toilet. One had to use a whiskbroom to sweep up some dirt from the floor. And so it went for several days, until each woman was doing fairly well each of these tasks.

"Serving day, ladies. One very common duty you will have is to act as your master's server at the parties he or she gives. Megan will attach a tray to your waists, held horizontally by a pair of chains attached to a collar around your necks. She will then place typical party drinks on your trays. You are to bring them to me, wherever I'm located on this floor. Do not spill them. If you do, you'll be given a rag to mop up your spill and clean it with the mouth attachment scrub brush."

This proved challenging, since every wobble or wiggle to keep their balance resulted in the drinks slushing around, spilling over the sides of the cups or glasses. It was several days before all four finally passed this test, walking the drinks all around the entire first floor of the spacious mansion.

"Today, we are going to tackle perhaps the most difficult task of all, my wonderful ladies," the Countess announced over breakfast. "Every elegant woman simply must know her residence forward and backward, and be able to navigate it and handle whatever your master might need, even in the dark. Megan will place these inflatable black spheres over your heads. Make sure that the nose plugs are secure in each nostril. Without them, you will suffocate. She will blow them up with air, like a balloon. You won't be able to see anything and your hearing will be lowered, simulating a power failure or a nighttime action you might be called upon to do for your master, such as fetching them a drink, turning on the lights, answering the door. Such things are done at night and in the dark. You must be able to perform well in the dark."

Megan had Siana's sphere on her head and had it blown up. Morwen saw what looked like a woman with a black sphere in place of a head. She also saw Siana's body trembling and grew worried herself. Soon, it was her turn. Megan pulled the sphere over her head, making sure the nose pieces were in place, before blowing it up. It was pitch black! At least the four were seated. The voice of the Countess seemed quite distant.

"Stand up, ladies," the dampened alto voice registered in Morwen's mind. She tried, but unable to see anything, she wobbled wildly, and hit the floor rather hard. She heard similar bumps and realized the others were fairing as badly as she was. This was impossible. Unable to see and with only her toes on the floor, she didn't see how this was even possible at all. She heard the voice commanding them to get back onto their feet. She struggled mightily and finally managed that, standing precariously in one spot, terrified of moving and falling again. "Tiny, feeling steps." The dampened voice of the Countess registered again. She did her best, but this was more terrifying than anything else had been!

After several days of this new, diabolical torture, Morwen realized indeed she had to learn this skill! What if she had to use the restroom at night? She dare not wake everyone. The Countess had long ago drilled into their heads that their masters would not be helping them with anything they could not do for themselves. "Look, getting you dressed and your hair brushed is about all that they and their busy schedules have for you. You must be prepared to do as much for yourselves as you can." A tiny thought appeared in the back of Morwen's mind: then why did you remove our arms? Quickly, she squashed that thought; it only led down the path of utter despair.

"Okay, ladies. Come with me to the front doors," the Countess ordered. "Now notice this pressure plate here. When you put your foot on it, the doors automatically open. See?" she demonstrated. "Now, each of you try it." Each did. "Okay, now plant the location of the plate firmly in your minds. You have to be able to find it in the dark. Your masters will have similar automatic door opening mechanisms that you must be able to find in the dark. Okay, back to the chairs in the other room. Megan will put the opaque spheres on your heads now. Your task is to go from your chair in this room, open the doors, and then return to your chairs. Keep the layout of the rooms firmly in your minds so you don't get lost. It's probably very easy to get all turned around in these huge mansions. I assure you your new masters will have equally large and elegant mansions where you will be living. You must be able to navigate your way in the dark, that's rather obvious."

While none could find the door switch that first day, at least they didn't fall down, but wandered all over the mansion, rather like a blind man's walk. The second day, the Countess advised, "As you discovered yesterday, this is a most difficult action to perform, though absolutely vital. Today, I will make it easier. Your chairs are positioned here directly across the room from the doors. Let's see if you can get them open and find your chairs again." More torture followed, though some did get the doors opened. Few found their chairs, having been turned around in the process.

Days passed. Then, the Countess made an announcement. "Ladies, I am holding a reunion party for some two dozen of my past graduates and their masters here on Saturday night, starting around six at night. While I know none of you is quite finished with your training, you are all very close. You just need to master finding your way around the whole mansion including the stairs at night in total darkness, and you are finished. From your predecessors, that will take you about another two weeks. However, the party cannot be delayed that long. Hence, I'll have you acting as my serving hostesses, carrying drinks to everyone. Megan will play barkeeper, as she always does."

She continued, "Since this will be a very formal affair, we should allow you all some practice time wearing the large billowing ball gowns over your form-fitting under-gown. You won't be able to see your feet, making this more challenging than normal. So let's get cracking."

Megan got each woman into a giant hoop skirt and then the elegant outer skirt that covered it. Beneath the hoop skirt, they wore their usual pencil-tight gowns. Each outer gown was about ten feet across, as it approached the floor, adding to their already spectacular figures. Then, the serving trays were attached. Once more, the trays were filled with crystal goblets filled with water, though the night of the party they'd contain wine or Champaign. All found it far more difficult to walk, wholly unable to see their feet even remotely.

The day of the party, each was bathed and dressed up.

Each wore an identical ball gown, designed to look like a maid's outfit. A headband was affixed to their hair and then the serving trays were attached. They had four chairs positioned to the left of the temporary bar that Megan set up at one corner of the ballroom, adjacent to the left to the front doors. Here, they waited patiently for the partygoers to arrive. Finally, the Countess made her appearance, dressed in a stunning light green ball gown with many layers of ribbons attached to her gown. She'd done up her hair and looked quite stunning for a forty year old woman.

"One last thing. A potential client will be here among the guests, looking to purchase one of my graduates. I've told him none of you is quite ready to graduate just yet. So be on your best behavior. Make good impressions, because in a few weeks, one of you may well be selected. He's quite a wealthy Count." She then sampled the Champaign, pronouncing it perfect.

The doorbell rang, and the first of the guests began arriving. At first, the four paid close attention to the masters and their women, who looked just like themselves, for the most part. The masters, as they'd been told, were both males and females alike. The men wore very expensive suits; the women masters wore elegant ball gowns, very similar to the one worn by the Countess.

However, the armless "sexual toys" also wore similar elegant gowns as the other female masters. Their faces with their permanent makeup were full of smiles, bowing to Countess Morgana when she approached them. As far as the four could tell, the toys were contented and happy with their lives, at least from what little they could see. All of them were able to walk well and hovered around their masters. Now, the four had to work.

Megan filled the crystal goblets and placed them on Morwen's tray. When Megan nodded to her, she carefully turned around and headed out into the ballroom, pausing before each guest, allowing the master to retrieve two goblets. She saw that most of the masters had brought along a straw for their toy to use to drink from the goblets. At least the masters held the goblets for their toys.

Before long, the ballroom was filled with two dozen masters and their two dozen "companions." The four were kept busy bringing the drinks to the guests. Just then, the door opened once more, and Count Alun of Mared entered.

He stood just inside the doors, getting his bearings, and trying hard not to react to the incredible sights all around him. "Ah, here at last," the Countess called out. "This is Count Alun of Mared." Many eyes turned to face him, and he bowed respectfully.

Morwen heard the name and a tiny part of her mind reacted. Alun? She turned carefully to look at the new arrival. Her heart fluttered. *No, it can't be my Alun. He's not a Count. But he looks like him. Oh dear god! He'll see me like this!* Morwen felt a rise of panic coming over her and fought it hard. If she lost it, she'd take a nasty fall and disgrace everyone here! She froze temporarily, unable to dare even to move. Meanwhile, Siana moved over to him with her tray of goblets. He took one and thanked her. She smiled, and moved slowly and carefully along to another couple.

Countess Morgana moved over to Count Alun. "Welcome Count Alun. We meet at last. My, you are a handsome devil." She held out her hand, and he gently kissed it. "Just a word of advice, all the armless women are my graduates. The four carrying the drinks around to the others are my four new trainees, but like I said, they are not yet ready to graduate. They need about another two weeks of training. You may have your choice of the four."

She continued, "My women are the prettiest and most elegant women on Haffren-3. Their voices have been removed so there are never any arguments or such things. They will always behave like perfect ladies, but they are all guaranteed to be able to satisfy any of your sexual fantasies or desires. However, you must see they are dressed and undressed or have a servant to do this for them. Also, if your chef purees their meals, they can feed themselves with straws, much as the women here are doing with their wine or Champaign. They are also trained for some light housekeeping duties, such as dusting."

She continued, "With your purchase, each will come

with a complete starting wardrobe and all of their usual mouth-held tools of their trade. I back all of my sales with my guarantee of your complete satisfaction or I will replace her or return your credits. Oh, one more minor detail, when they need assistance with the bathroom, they are trained to nod their head to the left. That's the signal."

Just then, a soft waltz began. "Ah, my music has started. Regrettably, you will not be able to dance with them. They are acting as my servants for the party tonight. Tomorrow, you can meet each one and make your selection. Then, we can work out the financial arrangements. Would you care to dance with me, Count Alun? Later, I'm sure others would like to dance with you as well. Remember, we all are standing on our toes, so it's small steps, especially for the toys."

Count Alun said, "Excellent, Countess. They already vastly exceed my wildest expectations! Best guide me a little on the dance floor. I've never danced with a charming woman wearing such heels." She grinned and did so.

Before long, several other female masters wanted to cut in on her. "Oh, you simply cannot possibly go wrong with one of the Countess' toys. They are just fabulous in all ways!" one woman explained, as she danced with him. "Say, would you like to dance with my charming toy?"

"It would be my great pleasure to do so, Countess," Alun replied. She led him over to her woman, who rose quite carefully, moving up close to him as instructed by her master. She smiled, batting her overly long eyelashes at him, as he slipped his arms around her incredibly tiny waist, just beneath her long brown, wavy hair. Again, he marveled at how well she managed to dance with him.

During the evening, many of the two dozen couples took turns dancing with him. Count Alun was somewhat embarrassed to dance with some of the men, however. Nevertheless, they also had nothing but praise for their "toys."

Around nine, the music ended. Countess Morgana then gave a short speech to her graduates. "Thank you all for coming. I am so very pleased to see each and every one of you once more. You have given me a great honor by living up to and exceeding all my expectations. I love each and every one of you women. Continue with your excellent work. Let's do this again next year, shall we? It has meant so very much to me." The masters gave her a polite round of applause, while her graduates smiled broadly. One by one, the couples came up to her, thanking her for everything, before heading for the doors.

After the last guest had left, the Countess said, "Count Alun, if you will follow me, I'll take you to the guest bedroom. My assistant, Megan, will be tied up handling the four trainees for a time. If I might make a suggestion for this evening, Count?"

"Oh, please do. I am utterly overwhelmed with what I've seen here tonight. Where do you find all of these incredible young women? I've not words to express how delighted I've been this evening," he replied, quite sincerely, though for entirely different reasons. He'd found Morwen!

"Well, if you are interested, I'd like you to sample one of the four trainees so that you can see just what I mean about their fabulous skills in bed. What do you think?"

"Delighted. Wonderful, beyond all my expectations! I don't know their names, though. I guess I can just point one out," he replied. While he wanted to wait for such things to happen on their wedding night, he needed to get her alerted to the coming rescue.

"Ah, see the raven haired beauty glancing our way? She's Morwen. The blonde behind her is Siana. The other raven haired woman is Rhonwen. The brown beauty is Terren. Which one entices you the most?"

"The one called Morwen," Alun replied, trying to keep his voice calm.

"Excellent choice. After Megan has her prepared for the evening, I will send her to your room. Just keep your door open so she can enter easily." She flashed him a broad grin and added, "If I were you, I would allow her to be on top. She can then give you the experience of a lifetime. Of course, you will then be hooked like a fish!"

"But I am already hooked," Alun jested. She laughed coyly, and left him to prepare for the evening, confident she'd made another sale.

A few minutes, she entered Morwen's room. "Morwen, dear, you get a very special treat tonight. Our client, Count Alun has requested that you sleep with him and show him just how fabulously you can serve him. If you do your very best, I'm sure he'll purchase you as soon as your training is finished. Here, I'll help you prepare." She deftly began removing the ball gown, hoop skirt, and then her form-fitting normal gown. When she was down to her corset, hose, and ballet shoes, Countess Morgana took an unusual step. She brushed out Morwen's wavy, long hair for her. "There you go. You look just fabulous, dear. He is in the guest room and is expecting you. Go now and enjoy yourself. I've suggested he allow you to be on top tonight. Do your very best, and we both will win handsomely."

Nervously, Morwen headed slowly down the long hallway. *Is it really him? What will he think of me now? How can he ever want me when I am like this? He'll never want me now. Maybe the Countess is right. He might if I do my job really well. But why would he want me now? I'm reduced to being nothing more than a sex toy, just like she says. I wouldn't even want me. Oh god! What's happening to me? Why didn't I just die? I'm so confused!*

She reached his door and peered into the dimly lit room. Her nervous stomach almost caused her to take a tumble right before him! She managed to take another step entering the room. He rose and came over to her, slipping his arms around her incredibly tiny waist. He leaned into her and whispered into her ear, "Morwen! It's me, Alun. I've found you at long last! I love you. I've come to rescue you and the others too, I think. But we best play along with the Countess for tonight. I know you can't talk any more, but I love you, no matter what terrible things she's done to you. Come on; let's lie down." Morwen did as asked, but began crying. Alun couldn't tell why. "You still love me?" he whispered, trying to guess why.

She nodded. "Is it okay for you to sleep with me?" he whispered. Again, she nodded more vigorously. "Are you crying because you are happy and relieved that I found you?" he tried another approach. She nodded once more, and he pulled her close and gave her a passionate kiss. She responded, but thought, *I have to please him so that he will continue to want me. I must. I must.* As the Countess suggested, he allowed her to be on top of him. Morwen smiled and set to work. Later, two exhausted bodies lay contented beside each other. "Morwen, I so love you. That was incredible. Tomorrow, we're escaping. Sleep now, my dearest."

She laid her head on his shoulders and fell asleep, contented, and happy for the first time in many months. Alun lay awake thinking and planning. At the crack of dawn, Alun slipped out of bed and dressed quickly. He then pressed the small button in his pocket, activating his special device outside in his shuttle. Next, he prepared his hand-held stunner, disguised as a ring. He rotated it to the inside of his hand and left the room.

He followed his nose towards the cooking breakfast. He found Megan cooking their breakfast, while the Countess sat sipping coffee and reading the morning paper on her laptop. "Good morning, Count Alun. I trust all went beyond your expectations last night?"

"Yes, Countess, far beyond them in fact." He leaned over as if to plant a social kiss on her cheek. Instead, he pressed his stunner to the side of her neck, and she slumped over in her chair. Megan looked up with a frightened look on her face.

"Megan, I'm with the police force. You have nothing to fear from me. Has the Countess here kidnaped these other women?" he asked. Megan nodded her head rather vigorously, confirming his suspicions. "Okay then, I'm rescuing them this morning." She shook her head no and moved slowly over to the table where she found her pad and pen. She wrote: security guards!

"I've already taken care of them. They are all stunned and will be out for many hours. I need the women all dressed and their things gathered to take with them. Can you do that?" She nodded and wrote out: They all have clothes, shoes, tools, and bank accounts. Need help with all that. Can you watch breakfast? Hurry? "Yes, hurry. I'll help you pack later. I'll finish the cooking."

She nodded and headed off to wake the others and dress them. When she returned leading the four, he had their breakfast ready, but Megan shook her head no. She took three quarters of it and dumped it into the blender. Then, she poured the mixture out into four glasses setting them before the four women. Each then leaned over and picked up their straws, maneuvered them into their mouths, and began to suck up their breakfasts. Meanwhile, Alun paid close attention, while he and Megan ate normally.

As he watched the nearly helpless women, he had an idea. "Megan, do you know how the Countess turns women into these?" he pointed to Siana. Megan nodded and hastily wrote out: I do all of the body modifications. She never does them. Only me.

"Excellent. Let's get her into her own modification machine. I want you to give her the complete works. Turn her into a woman just like these four. Can you do that?" Megan sported the largest grin imaginable! As the other four grasped what he was suggesting, they too grinned and nodded their heads strenuously in total agreement.

"Good. Megan, once that's done, can you deal with 'training' the Countess?" Again, Megan smiled and vigorously nodded. "Excellent. Show me where to bring her body and let's do this immediately." A few minutes later, he laid the unconscious Countess on her own operation table. Megan began undressing her, and Alun quickly joined in to help her. Then, he sat back and watched her as she closed the medical machine over her boss and set the program. After pressing the Activate Program button, she looked up, and both smiled and nodded.

"Okay. Will this take long?" She held up four fingers. He guessed hours, and she nodded. "Good. Let's get the women's things gathered up. Show me what to do." Each woman eventually had six large shipping crates of clothing and one that contained their "domestic tools." Next, Megan led him to her office. She handed him a lengthy document that outlined the care and needs of the women, and how best to fulfill them, including dressing instructions, in case a single man purchased one of her toys. She wrote out each woman's name and her bank account number for him. She then showed him where the Countess kept her grav-lifter.

He piled some of the crates onto it and activated its controls. Hovering just off the ground, he pushed it outside and across the lawn, past the unconscious security guards. After four trips, he had all their things safely stowed, but he kept her grav-lifter in the shuttle, figuring he would need it at the spaceport. Back inside, Megan wrote him a note asking him to help get the Countess properly dressed. Figuring this would be good experience for him, he readily agreed. A half hour later, Countess Morgana Twyrth was jogged awake by Megan waving the vile of smelling salts below her nose, while Alun held her in a sitting position, facing the mirror. Alun had to grin. Megan had done him one better. She'd Rejuvenated her back to her early twenties so she would have far more years as a sexual toy herself!

The shocked expression on the Countess' face when she came too and discovered that she was now one of her own helpless toys was priceless! Like her many other victims, she couldn't breathe, and was so shocked that she passed out three times. Naturally, Megan took enormous pleasure reviving her each time. Megan then wrote: Help me get her into the basement, please.

He did so, but didn't stick around to see what Megan would do to her down there. Instead, one by one, he led each woman out to the shuttle, beginning with Morwen, who was very glad she'd learned how mostly to walk on the uneven grass. *I can't fall down. I just can't. I don't want Alun to see me disgrace myself and himself. He might just change his mind and leave me here.*

A half hour later, he had all four women on the shuttle. Looking back at the doors, he spotted Megan there, smiling and waving goodbye. He returned her wave, and closed the door. Presently, the shuttle lifted off, ending the continuous stunning beams that had dropped all security men who approached within five hundred feet of the manor house doors.

Ten minutes later, he landed the shuttle next to his rented deep space transport ship. He turned to the four women. "We've got to hurry here. So I am going to carry each of you over to the transport. Okay?" The four nodded. This was the really dangerous part of his plan. At any moment, spaceport security personnel could wander over and spot him with the women. Too many questions would be asked. None of which he wanted to answer at the moment. He moved as quickly as he could. Once the women were carried over, he used the grav-lifter to move their many crates. Only when he closed the bay doors did he start to relax even a little.

He raced to the pilot's seat and punched in his preprogrammed flight, then activated it. Shortly, he received confirmation from the control tower and pressed the Execute button. At that instant, a substantially large number of credits were withdrawn from his account, payment for the ship's use. The transport lifted off, dropping shortly into hyperspace. He hastily cleared the destination and effectively parked the transport in hyperspace. Only now was he totally safe. His huge problem was where to go now?

He'd broken countless laws getting this far. Where to go now? He decided to chat with the women. After all, some of them might have husbands or boyfriends who were as frantically worried about them as he was for Morwen. "Okay ladies. Let's see if I have your names right. Terren? Siana? Rhonwen?" The three nodded. "All right then. I am or was CDI Alun Arthmael. Morwen and I were engaged to be married when she was kidnaped by the Countess. I've been searching for her ever since. At long last, I found her. Were all of you also kidnaped?" The three nodded yes.

"Okay. Well, at least the Countess now is getting a taste of just what she's done to you four and the many others before you." All four heads vigorously nodded, and they smiled.

"The question now is what do I do with each of you? Do you have a husband at home or perhaps a fiancé?" All three shook their heads no. A bit dismayed, he asked, "Do you have somewhere I could take you where you would be safe and could live?" Once more, the three shook their heads no. Siana began sobbing silently. Soon, the other two began crying as well. In desperation, he asked, "Do you want to come along with Morwen and me?" All three raised their heads, nodded yes quite vigorously. Their crying abated a little. "Okay then. You are coming with us. I promise you I'll do my best to care for you always." They smiled and nodded once more. He was greatly relieved to see that their crying ceased.

"All right. Here's our problem. I don't know where we can go just yet. For sure, we can't return to Haffren-3. I'll soon be classified as a criminal there. I need to somehow get you healed up as much as possible. Let me think this through. Back in a bit." He left them, returning to the pilot's seat. Just looking at them distracted him greatly. They were utterly dependent upon him, and he simply had to do right by them somehow, someway.

"Think, man, think!" He knew he needed political sanctuary. He was after all rescuing the women from the clutches of the most despicable men and women he'd ever seen. His mind wandered to the many terrorist attack victims. Why? Because the four's physical condition so closely resembled what he'd seen on the newscasts. Then, he recalled hearing about the incredible research being done on a rim planet. He tried to recall its name. When he stopped trying to recall it, the name popped into his head: Ashford-5. "Ah, that's one of the new planets in the Ataro Empire. Okay, I shall go there and beg for political asylum or sanctuary. Then, I'll do whatever it takes to get them to undo what can be done for the four. Sounds like a plan. Enough fuel? Nope. Ah, I can stop off in the Ataro System and refuel. Great." After looking up the coordinates of the first planet in the listing, he entered the coordinates of Winno-3, and activated the autopilot. A distinct lurch announced that fact the transport had responded to the new heading. Only now did he fully relax.

A few minutes later, he contacted the control tower on Winno-3 asking for permission to land to pick up additional fuel. "Please dock at these coordinates and await further instructions," a voice responded. He did as told, unaware of the sudden flurry of actions going on below him on Winno-3.

Paranoia ran high in the aftermath of the failed genocide attack from Haffren-3. Here was another transport coming to Winno-3 from that world. The manager of the control tower contacted navigation control back on Haffren-3 and discovered this was a rental transport. While everything appeared to be nothing more than a rental, the heightened security surrounding the attack did not allow ground personnel to take any chances. They had the transport land in a remote section of the spaceport, hoping to contain or limit any terrorist attack.

Once he landed, Alun suspected something was going on. His ship was quite some distance from the main terminals and the refueling station. Soon, he received orders to open his bay doors and prepare to be searched. As he headed to the bay, he spoke hastily to the four women in the small staterooms. "I don't know what's happening here, but if anything goes wrong, I'll try to protect you with my life." He moved to the cargo bay, opened the doors, and stared in disbelief.

Six men wearing the red bio containment suits and with drawn d-guns pointing at him stared back at him. "Hello. Alun Arthmael of Haffren-3, Cairn Glen. My papers?"

"Stand back. Prepare to be boarded and searched," a muffled voice replied from within the suits. He did as ordered, while watching two of the men waving sensor around the bay area. Several poked into the crates, only to discover women's clothing. They walked through the narrow hallway, poking their heads into the various rooms, but saw only the silent women. After fifteen anxious minutes, the same man spoke. "All clear. No bio weapons." He looked at Alun. "A tanker is on its way to refuel your ship. Sorry about the inconvenience."

"That's okay. What's going on? Are we under some kind of attack? I thought Winno-3 was a safe world," Alun asked.

"Aye, but you should be watching the newscasts. Seems your government launched a genocide attack on us a short while ago. We're naturally suspicious of any transport coming from Haffren-3. Here comes your tanker." He nodded and the men left, but took off their helmets, as they walked back to their electric car. Refueling took only a few minutes. He'd used up only a small amount making the hop from Cairn Glen, but that was just enough to fall short of making Ashford-5. An hour after landing, he was cleared for takeoff once more, which he did the second he was cleared.

Once in hyperspace and on his way to Ashford-5, Alun

breathed a huge sigh of relief. That was close. Obviously, his raid on Countess Morgana Twyrth had not yet been discovered. The anticipated hue and cry hadn't happened yet. He poked his head into Morwen's cabin, but the other cabins were nearby so all could hear. "Okay everyone, we can relax now. I've enough fuel to get us to our destination. I'm going to see if we can get political asylum or sanctuary on Ashford-5. It's a world on the far outer rim. I'm going there because they seem to have the only doctors who have been able to find some partial cures for all of the terrorist attack victims. I know you've not been exposed to that awful genetic mutation stuff, but I'm hoping that somehow they can help the four of you. Anyone need to use the bathroom? Anyone hungry?"

He spent the next half hour helping the four use the bathroom facilities. "I think I need to really read the document Megan gave me on how to care for you." Morwen appeared to be laughing, but he heard no sounds. He smiled and did just that before preparing them a meal.

"Sorry, I don't have a blender onboard, so I'm just going to have to feed you like normal people. Hope you don't mind," he chatted. The five were crowded into the tiny galley, but with them all so close, his task was easier. From their eyes, he sensed how grateful they felt. "I don't want to run low on fuel, gang, so we're going at a conservative speed. I think we'll be there in about four days. Time enough for me to digest all these instructions on your care. I don't think they are specific enough for me. It says to brush out your hair before bed. How? I've never brushed any woman's hair." Siana appeared to be silently giggling or possibly laughing, he couldn't tell which.

However, Morwen felt really bad. She knew he didn't have any idea just how much care she and the others were going to need, let alone how to do it. Would he give up in frustration and abandon them all when they landed? He ought to, she concluded. Her life was completely worthless now.

The dinner finished, he decided they all needed a good night's sleep. After seeing each woman safely back to her bunk, he went to Morwen and began to undress her. "Do you all sleep like you were when you came to me last night?"

She nodded, but thought otherwise. *Well, we don't. But*

420

it's going to be too hard for him to take our shoes and hose off of us, let alone put them back on in the morning.

While she sat totally erect on the side of the narrow bed, he struggled to figure out how to brush out her hair, but slowly got the hang of it. "You wait here while I do the others, my love. I'll be back," he whispered.

A short while later, he had Siana prepared and was about to lower her into the bunk when she leaned over and gave him a loving kiss. She mouthed "Thank you." He whispered the words back, and she nodded and smiled. He tucked her in and gave her a goodnight kiss, bringing a smile to the blonde's face. To his amazement, both Terren and Rhonwen acted similarly, giving him a kiss and attempting to thank him.

When he returned to Morwen, he was smiling. "I think they said 'thank you' to me, dear." She smiled and mouthed it as well, then nodded. He grinned. "I got it. See, we can communicate a little bit. Somehow, dear, we'll get through this. I promise. Now let me look at you. You seem prettier than ever." She smiled a little.

"What I don't understand is your shoes. Can you even walk in them?" Images swept over her mind of her hellish days in the dungeon, but she nodded she could. "Okay, then I won't worry about having to carry you everywhere. Time for sleep." He crawled in beside her and pulled her head onto his shoulder, holding her tightly.

Please don't ever let me go, she thought.

With four days' worth of practice helping the four women with nearly everything, Alun learned quickly what they could and could not do, while cooped up on the ship. If he got them their straws, they were able to drink by themselves, for example. The time passed quickly for the five. At last the transport dropped out of hyperspace above Ashford-5.

Chapter 20 Salvaging Lives

"This is the Control Tower on Ashford-5. This is a Closed Word, Transport 459674 from Haffren-3. Unauthorized landings are not allowed. You can be refueled while in orbit. Over."

"Well, that didn't work," Alun exclaimed. He'd tried the direct approach of requesting permission to land and refuel. He flipped the switch and said, "Okay. I would like to land and meet with the governor of Ashford-5, please. It's important I speak personally with the governor, please. Over."

"Nature of the meeting with Governor Katrina Lutgard? Over."

Ah, he didn't reject that one out of hand. Emboldened, he replied, "We wish to discuss the possibility of seeking political asylum or sanctuary here. Please, it's important I speak to the governor. Over." He kept his fingers crossed. The reply didn't come for several minutes, which he took as even more hopeful.

"Okay, Transport 459674. Here are your landing coordinates. The Governor will meet with you upon landing. Over and out."

Alun punched his hand into the air. "Now we're getting somewhere." He entered the coordinates and yelled loudly for the women to hear, "They're letting us land, and the governor will meet with me. Keep your fingers crossed." As soon as he said that, he regretted it. They didn't have any fingers to cross. He couldn't have said toes either. He'd already examined Morwen's feet and toes. They were fused solid, wholly immobile. Only her ankles were normal.

A half hour later, the ship touched down. As he looked out of the window, he saw he was close to the twenty story admin building, nearly identical to the layout of all spaceport admin buildings, compliments of Imperium standards. Now he faced the real crisis. Somehow, he had to get this governor to allow him to stay here on this Closed World, as well as see the doctors.

One by one, he lined the four up near the bay doors and opened them, lowering the walk ramp. "Are you going to be able to walk down the ramp without help?" Alun asked. All four looked at it, fighting memories of similar ramp tortures, but they nodded they could. He added, "We have to walk inside yonder Admin Building to meet with this governor. Can you all walk that far?" Again, they nodded. He took a deep breath, and stepped down the ramp. He turned around, making sure the four could make it.

Morwen took it slow and very carefully. *I must not fall and disgrace him. I mustn't. I just mustn't.* In turn, as Siana, Terren, and Rhonwen faced the declining ramp, they too fought against their memories of their ordeals and had very similar thoughts. None of the five had any idea they were wildly broadcasting their thoughts, and that Governor Katrina and Carla were picking them up. The two came walking out of the building just as the ship touched down and were a hundred feet from them, as the five descended the ramp.

Alun put his arm around Morwen and also Siana. "Okay, Terren, Rhonwen, you walk beside us. This way, I can keep my eye on you in case you have trouble. The tarmac is pretty smooth, if that helps. I think those two women ahead are going to lead us to the governor." He was rather surprised at how well the four walked on the level concrete. His worries lessened a little. As they neared, Alun added in alarm, "Darn, I forgot to get us ULAT boxes!"

"Welcome to Ashford-5 or Tierra, as we locals call our world. I'm Governor Katrina Lutgard. My Computer Technician, Carla Childa. You must be Alun Arthmael. Who are your beautiful companions?" To all five's great relief, she spoke in Imperium Standard, though she was a little hard to understand with her giant lip plates.

"Yes, I'm Alun. This is my fiancé, Miss Morwen Severn. These are three others who I've rescued and promised to care for. Sorry, I don't know their last names. Siana, Terren, and Rhonwen. They've all been kidnaped, tortured, mutilated, and cannot speak. Please, is there somewhere we can talk? I beg you to hear our story and give us sanctuary here. I'll do anything, pay anything to get proper medical help for the women, please, I beg you." His face echoed his sympathetic voice tones.

"Of course, this way. However, since Ashford-5 is part of the Ataro Empire, and Queen Amy Valen Gervasi is the ultimate authority here. She is on her way to meet with us. I figure you would prefer to explain everything only once. Are the four women in need of emergency medical attention? If so, we should handle that first," Katrina asked, speaking slowly, making sure the five understood her.

"No, they are healed. Thank you," Alun answered. The seven continued their slow walk to the main doors. Alun and the four women could not help noticing the enormous breasts of the two women and Katrina's giant lip plates. They presumed correctly that the two were victims of one of the many terrorist bio agent attacks that had been widely covered on the Imperium newscasts.

Katrina led them into the first floor meeting room. She carefully observed how Alun handled the women in his care. He quickly pulled out a chair for Morwen and Siana, helping them get seated, while Carla and Katrina did the same for Terren and Rhonwen. "Queen Amy should be here soon. Can I get you anything to drink? Tea, water, coffee?" she asked.

Alun looked at Morwen on his right and Siana on his left. "You prefer tea, dear. Would you like some? Siana?" To Katrina, he added, "They would have to have some straws."

Oh god! I would look so weird in front of these important women! Morwen thought, shaking her head no. Catching Morwen's head motion, Siana also indicated no. *I simply can't embarrass them or Alun. We should have just died! This's so horrible.*

"Ah, here's Amy now," Governor Katrina broke the rather awkward moment. Just then, Jan opened the door for Amy and followed her inside, helping her mate sit gracefully. Once more, the four women could not help noticing she also must have been a terrorist attack victim. That both Amy and Katrina wore toe shoes and were almost as hobbled as they were didn't go unnoticed by the four women.

"This is Queen Amy Valen Gervasi and her mate, Jan Bellweather. Amy, Jan, this is Alun Arthmael, his fiancé,

Morwen Severn, and three others, Siana, right?" she asked the long haired blonde, who nodded. "Terren and Rhonwen?" Both also nodded. "They are unable to speak. Alun has come from Haffren-3 and is seeking asylum here. Okay, Alun, why not tell us your story in detail? That way, we'll have all the information we need to come to a judgment in your case."

"Of course. Of course. Thank you both at least for hearing me. I admit right here at the start, this's mostly a wild notion that I've had, but I'm at my wits end with this one. Okay, I'm or used to be a Chief Detective Inspector of the Cairn Glen police force on Haffren-3. I joined the force six years ago and have been very good at solving crimes. About six months ago, I proposed to Miss Morwen Severn, and she accepted. She is or was a fourth grade school teacher. My father is a preacher. He instilled a strong sense of morals and ethics in me, and I was so elated to meet Morwen here, because she too shares my feelings. I hope I'm not boring you, but this is important."

"Oh no, please continue," Amy insisted. "The more data we have, the better we'll be able to understand your situation."

"Okay, you see, for centuries our world, Heffren-3, has been going downhill. Sexual perversion is running rampant in our society. Nothing is verboten, especially with those in power and the wealthy. Do you realize a quarter of our people work in the sex trade? They make four times my yearly salary, and it's all legal. I can do nothing to stop or slow it. Anyway, some months ago, shortly after Morwen here accepted my proposal, she was kidnaped, as she was leaving her school."

"Naturally, I conducted a full investigation, but honestly, it was so well done, that there were simply no clues left for me to follow. That didn't stop me; I spent weeks on it, day and night. Nothing. Nada. A few weeks ago, my boss filed the case as Cold. That meant I could not spend any more of my time working on it. I was furious, but he was unrelenting. The only thing I have that's truly mine is my word, and I gave Morwen my word. I simply could not abandon her, not when she needed me the most. So I continued my investigations at night. I took several odd jobs around town, infiltrating various groups, seeking hints, clues, any word of the kidnaping. I learned that sometimes, women are taken off-world as sex slaves, so I worked for a time loading cargo at our spaceport, but learned nothing at all."

"That's when chance gave me my first real hint. A transport landed with some cargo to unload. While I was doing that, a very strange man, I think they said he was autistic, said something to me. I can't remember his exact words. They were so strangely phrased, but something like Alun sees Chaos or Chaos is here. Very strange. But that reminded me of Chaos Lynn, a lake and giant walled estate of Countess Morgana Twyrth. She is a known purveyor of sex slaves. I got to thinking perhaps she had abducted my Morwen."

"I did a lot of background checking on her. She is extremely wealthy and sells her elegant slaves only to the very wealthy of Haffren-3. I cased the place. Her business is legal, mind you, so I had no way to simply walk in and see if Morwen was there. Then, I got lucky. I spotted a notice that she was having a reunion party for two dozen of her former graduate sex slaves and their masters. That's when I made my plans."

"I sold everything I owned and set up a disguise as Count Alun of Mared. I also illegally tied my new bank account to the Police Station's Special Fund, figuring the Countess would investigate me. I even created a fake Web page for Count Alun. I bought myself this suit, the finest handmade suit in Cairn Glen, and took the penthouse suit in our best hotel. Then, I sent the Countess a letter, asking if she still had any of her elegant women for sale — that I was single and looking to purchase one."

"She sent me back an invitation to her special party, saying that I should spend the night and look over her current trainees. She said they would not be ready to graduate for another couple of weeks, though. I decided if Morwen was there, then I would rescue her from the Countess' clutches. Then, I reasoned, if this Countess had kidnaped Morwen, she probably also kidnaped the other three trainees as well. I also know how corrupt our system is. This is important, Queen Amy, Governor Katrina. You see, if I spotted Morwen there, and then left and took the time to get a warrant to go back and raid her place, the Countess would already know about the warrant the instant the judge granted it. The wealthy control nearly everything in our government. By the time I could raid the estate, she'd have gotten rid of Morwen and the others. I'd come up empty and lose Morwen again."

He sighed, "So I took matters into my own hands. I figured that if I needed to rescue four women, I'd need a way off Haffren-3. The Countess would surely put out the hue and cry for us. So I rented yonder deep space transport and had it standing by at the spaceport. I went to the party in a rented shuttle, but with some of my own little inventions. She had many security guards around the estate. I didn't want to harm them, so I setup a stun system. Once I activated it, anyone coming within five hundred feet would be stunned, but not seriously injured."

"When I entered the manor house, I was frankly stunned! I couldn't believe what I was seeing. It took all my inner strength to keep my composure and not give myself away. All the evil Countess' graduates and sex slaves were just like my Morwen here, and Siana, Terren, and Rhonwen! This wicked woman had cut off their arms, cut out their voice boxes, and fused their feet. I'm not sure what they did to get their waists to unbelievably tiny. She did something to her breasts too; they were never as large as they are now. Honestly, I really don't know what all this vile woman did to the women, but it had to be horrific. They can't talk now or write, so they can't tell me either. Horrible, just horrible."

"Anyway, I promised Morwen I would rescue her and the others too, and I swore to them I would always look after them. I gave them my word, and I swear to you both now that I'll never abandon them, not ever. Where was I? Oh, I also learned that the Countess had an assistant called Megan, who can't talk either and has crippled feet and a tiny waist too, but she still has her arms. Apparently, poor Megan was made to help the Countess' tortured women. When Megan learned I was about to rescue the four, she wanted to help. Honestly, Megan has been wonderful. She wrote notes to me, giving me their bank account number, instructions on the care of the women, and helped me pack their things and more."

"After I stunned the Countess unconscious, I realized

this woman needed to be brought to justice. Look what she's done to these four women. I'd just seen what she'd done to two dozen other women the night before. Worse, with our pathetic justice system, the Countess would merely donate a pile of credits to the judge hearing her case, and she'd walk out totally innocent. I need to obtain some justice for these women. So I broke the law. I took justice into my own hands with Megan's very willing and enthusiastic assistance."

"Megan put her into the same machine the Countess used to make all the modifications to her sex slaves. A few hours later, the Countess Morgana was turned physically into one of her own creations. She looks just like these four and the other two dozen I saw at the party. Further, Megan wanted to put her through the same training the Countess always put her victims. Honestly, I have no idea what that entails, but it can't be good. I've no way to find out what all Megan, Siana, Terren, and Rhonwen suffered through or the other women, but it can't be good. So the Countess is getting a taste of her own medicine, and I am guilty of making that happen."

"Anyway, I got them to the transport, along with their few possessions and things they need. Where to go was the last problem to solve. When I planned the rescue, I had no idea of the terrible physical shape the women would be in. I can't imagine how perverted this Countess must be to have done these things to all the women. Anyway, after a lot of thought, I remembered from the newscasts that Ashford-5 had a lot of famous doctors who were working miracle cures for many of the terrorist attack victims and decided that here they stood the best chance of getting somehow helped. So I brought us all here. We can't go back to Haffren-3. They would only be sold into the sex trades."

"So I am asking and begging you to grant us political asylum or sanctuary here on this world. I'm a trained police detective. I'm willing to do any kind of work to support these four women. They supposedly have some credits in their bank accounts, and I hope that will be enough to pay for their medical treatments. I don't have any idea what can be done for them, but if anything can, somehow I simply must find a way to make that happen. I've given all four my sworn word, and

I'd rather die than break it. Please, you must help us. If not for me, then do it for these four innocent victims. They are so helpless now, please, I beg you." He finished his long explanation, prepared for whatever the outcome might be.

"Incredible, Alun," Queen Amy spoke first. "Ladies, nod yes or no. Were you all kidnaped by this Countess?" They nodded yes. "I'm sorry for that. Were your bodies modified by this woman as well? Your arms, voices, and so on?" Four heads agreed with her. "Were you also tortured by her?" Again complete agreement. "And are you all willing to have Alun Arthmael here look after you?" Once more, they didn't hesitate, but Amy suspected that in their present condition, they dare not say otherwise.

"Okay then. Here's what we'll do. First, I want Doctor Whitney to give each of the women a checkup. She'll be able to ascertain what medical remedies are in fact possible for you. Meanwhile, Katrina and I will discuss how to proceed. Rest assured, if what Alun has told us is true, we'll not be turning you over to the authorities on Haffren-3. No way. You've all suffered enormously. Jan, will you and Alun escort them to Doctor Whitney, please. Katrina and I will discuss what we can do."

"Thank you. Thank you. On behalf of the women, thank you as well. I know they want to but haven't any way to tell you," Alun replied in a rather propitiative manner. He and Jan led the four out of the room and down the long hall to the medical wing.

"Carla, see if you can contact the police headquarters in Cairn Glen, Haffren-3. We need to check on his story a little," Katrina asked. While she was off doing this, Katrina said, "Did you sense those poor women's minds?"

"Hard to ignore. They are still squarely in the middle of a giant traumatic incident. They don't dare do anything to disgrace Alun. They are, quite frankly, extremely desperate at the moment," Amy replied. "Kind of hard to miss. Unless he's lying, we should allow them to stay. Certainly, we need to get those four into therapy right away. Crap, they can't speak or write. We'll have to use telepathic communications and that will be revealing a bit much to these arrivals."

"Quite true. We should wait for Whitney's report on them before making any serious decisions. If she can't restore their voices, should we consider giving them the *mentales* gifts?" Katrina asked.

"Possibly. Without it, their futures are grim indeed, even if their arms can be eventually regrown," Amy agreed.

Katrina then pointed out, "The one legal technicality with granting political asylum or even with sanctuary is the person must be able to support themselves or have a spouse who will be the primary supporter. I can certainly marry Alun and Morwen, since they are already engaged. But what do I do for Siana, Terren, and Rhonwen?"

"Sorry, you have me there on those legal issues," Amy admitted. "That does pose a problem. Couldn't they be classed as terrorist victims and thus given sanctuary?"

"No, they were the victims of crime, not a terrorist bio attack. Subtle legal difference."

"Well, there's always the Easterlings approach," Amy suggested.

Katrina laughed. "One mate is more than enough for me!" Amy laughed as well, thinking of her and Jan's ever growing clan. She added, "That certainly would get around the legal angle, but Amy, we can't force them to marry him or he, them."

"I know, we'd have to get into telepathic contact with them and sort it out, I suppose. Best wait on the two reports. I hope Carla has good news for us. We could use a good detective around here. Exchange City is growing by leaps and bounds and so is the crime level."

"True, I'll hire him as Chief Detective Inspector for Exchange City, if it works out," Amy volunteered.

"Dual citizenship. Then, he can also work for me," Katrina teased Amy, who laughed again.

Laughed again was precisely what was happening back at the Chaos Lynn estate and manor. While Morgana was quite accomplished in walking in her ballet boots and shoes and had been wearing them constantly for years, she'd always had the use of her arms. Now without them and mercilessly constricted by the eleven inch pipe corset, she continually lost her balance, which activated the electrical jolts in her privates. She cried out loudly, but no sounds came out. She bawled, just as had her many victims over the years, all to no avail. Megan only checked on her and smiled.

However, by the time Morgana finally managed to progress to attempting to walk along the fifty foot two by four, her eldest son, Emlyn, came by, the one who had filed and lost the law suit against Morgana. "So where is the old biddy, Megan? I've gotten reports from a security guard that she's vanished. Is this true? Is the estate finally mine? I've waited too damned long for this."

Megan wrote: She is being trained to be an elegant sex toy herself. She's in the dungeon training. Are you now my boss?

"What?" the forty year old man exclaimed. He never anticipated this aspect. "This I have to see. Show me." She did, and he roared with laughter, humiliating Morgana even more. She was hooked into the training machine and had fallen off the two by fours. She couldn't get to her feet and had to endure the relentless electrical charge in her privates, while being utterly humiliated by her own son.

He was married to Ceri. Their children were adults and had long ago moved out on their own. Both had already once used the Rejuvenation Machine themselves. He had rich black hair and moustache; she had wavy blonde hair. After seeing Morgana's fate, he and Megan returned to the Business Office room. "Okay, Megan, show me the financial records and the account, please." She did, and he exclaimed, "Even richer than I ever imagined."

Megan fixed them a coffee. As he sat down beside her, he asked, "You know. Mom has run a very profitable business with her elegant sex toys. By any chance, do you know how it is done? How she did it all?"

She wrote: Yes, I did all the real work. She just always gave me orders. So are we still going to run the business?

"Brilliant, Megan. Yes, we should. I'll have to see about getting some more lovely young women to join mom in the dungeon. First, though, Ceri and I are going to move in here."

Ceri tossed her long, blonde hair back. She was growing annoyed with Emlyn. He had a long track record of being unfaithful to her. Whenever they went to any social occasion, Emlyn could be counted upon to get into the pants of any young flower in attendance.

They had moved in to the mansion only two days before he was at it again. He kidnaped two young blondes, Brynne and Lin, and had Megan modify their bodies and begin their training. She found him continually watching the helpless women struggling mightily just to stand up and walk on the flat walking machine. She'd had enough!

Over tea with Megan, she asked, "So Emlyn tells me you know all there is to know about running the toy business. Is he right? You can do everything yourself?"

Megan wrote: Yes, but I need some help lifting them up, getting them dressed, and into the machines or down the stairs for the first time. Why?

"You know, I've had it with Emlyn. He flirts with any young woman and beds nearly anyone. What say you to expanding our line?" Megan gave her a quizzical look. "Let's add men to our mix."

Megan wrote: But we only have women's apparel.

"That's fine. They can look elegant in such clothes too." Megan grinned along with Ceri.

The next morning while Megan was serving Emlyn his breakfast, Ceri came into the dining room, leaned over to give him a kiss and then some. She injected the knockout drug, and he slumped over the table, spilling his morning coffee. The two women dragged him into the Operations Room, stripped him, and put him onto the medical machine. "Give him the works, Megan."

She wrote: Breast too? Lips? Long hair? Eyelashes? Permanent makeup?

Ceri laughed loudly. "You bet! The works, Megan, the works. And can you make him twenty-one again? He should have many years to enjoy being a sex toy for someone." Megan laughed silently to herself and proceeded to follow orders.

Hours later, when Megan roused him with her smelling salts, he was sitting up on the machine, facing the mirror. Ceri was standing beside the mirror ready to watch his reactions. She more than got her revenge. He awoke to find he looked more like a young woman; he couldn't breathe; had no arms now; his feet were fused, and he had no voice. He fainted five times before Megan and Ceri had him stabilized from his utter shock and panic.

Ceri gloated and said, "Don't worry so, Emlyn. Your manhood is still intact down there somewhere. Now, you can join the pretty women that you were getting off on so much these past few days. We have to train you to be an elegant sex toy, just like the others. So up you go, time to start your training, dear." They forced him to stand, and he wobbled so wildly that they could barely keep him upright. "Dear, you really do need to be trained. Come on; take a step." She pushed him forward, and he had no choice but to try to walk. An hour later, he was hooked up to the same flat walking machine as the two young women that he'd kidnaped and had been watching the last two days.

Later on, Ceri had Megan write out just how Morgana acquired more of her trainees. "We will have to get some more, but we best wait until these three progress beyond the initial walking machine, don't you think?" Megan nodded.

However, after only a few more days, Morgana's youngest son, Ffloyd dropped by to see what the situation was like, now that Emlyn and Ceri had moved in. He was just as shocked as Emlyn had been to see Morgana as one of her sex toys down in the dungeon, having just as hard a time as all her previous victims. Yet, he roared with laughter at how his womanizing older brother looked. "Emlyn, we're going to have to call you Linn now or perhaps you'd prefer Gwenith?" He could see Emlyn's face turning beet red. He stumbled and fell, pulling on the wires, resulting in the electrical shock to his privates. Ffloyd roared even louder with laughter. "Ceri, you've outdone yourself this time. Well done indeed."

Over coffee, Ceri explained how the business was run and that Megan actually did all the real work with the trainees. She was so happy that she agreed to Ffloyd's proposal that he and his wife, Dilys, move into the manor house to help Ceri manage everything. Ceri agreed, having found it terribly difficult lifting her husband onto the medical machine and later handling him in the dungeon at night. "Yes, we could use a pair of strong arms around here, Ffloyd. Move in as soon as you wish." He and Dilys moved in the next day.

A couple of days later, Dilys whispered to her husband, "Look, we don't need Ceri telling us what to do. You are the man around here. You should get rid of her. She's not a real Twyrth, is she?" At breakfast, he slipped the knockout drug into Ceri's coffee.

They chatted over breakfast, and Ffloyd allowed her to explain her grand ideas for expanding the business. "Look, one can never have too much money," Ceri explained, finally sipping her coffee.

"Oh, I couldn't agree more, Ceri. You are right, as always. We should expand our business," Ffloyd agreed with her wholeheartedly.

Sitting beside her husband, Dilys smiled. *They are both right about the money. Ah, Ceri is going down. My, this drug is sure fast working! From what I saw in the records, Morgana kept refusing to make male trainees. I surely don't know why.*

Hours later, a shocked Ceri awoke to find herself now a sex toy trainee, just as helpless as her husband, Morgana, Lin, and Brynne. Try as she might, she could do nothing about her new state, no matter how badly she wanted to kill Ffloyd! It took all three of them to get Ceri safely down the stairs, hooked up to the first walking machine, and going. As always, Megan had him read the instructions to Ceri, just as Ceri had read the diabolical instructions to Emlyn, and as he had read them to poor Lin and Brynne.

Some days later, Morgan's daughter, Eirwen dropped by to see what was going on with her mother and brothers. Unlike her mother, she had wavy blonde hair, but had her good looks. Her brothers had always teased her about probably having had a different father. To this day, she'd resented them for this. She had recently used the Rejuvenation Machine and looked an attractive twenty-two.

"I must say I am glad I dropped by. Emlyn was always an embarrassment to the family, what with his being unable to keep his thing in his pants," Eirwen commented.

Ffloyd laughed. "How true, sis, how very true. After he gets trained, he can use it all he wants." All three laughed.

"So how does all this work? Mom only told me a portion of how she ran the business," Eirwen asked. She got an earful.

Ffloyd was so pleased with everything that he suggested, "Sis, you are still single. We could use another woman's touch around here, what with all these new trainees to handle. I'm sure that you'd enjoy seeing Emlyn more." Both chuckled, and she accepted very readily.

Eirwen was like her mother in many ways. That ought to have been rather obvious to her brother, since she was still unmarried after all these years. She loved to party, but usually in the friendly company of other women. Men, she considered, were nothing but overpowering brutes with no tastes or refinements. Wham, bang, thank you ma'am. That succinctly summed up her experiences with men. This attitude of hers completely eluded her older brothers.

After a few days in the elegant manor house, Eirwen decided that her brother didn't deserve to have all this wealth. He was a man, after all. *Hell,* she thought, *he'll just go around screwing all these trainees. He and Emlyn ought to learn to hold their climax off until their partner has had hers. Mom, I'm doing this for you!*

The next morning at breakfast, she arrived early and slipped the drug into both Ffloyd and Dilys' coffee. An hour later, both were unconscious at the table. Eirwen rose and said, "Okay Megan, that's justice for mom. I'm taking over mom's business. We'll run it just as she did. Let's get these two into the Operations Room. I'm making you a full partner, Megan. I wish mom hadn't removed your voice. Still, we'll make do, partner." Megan flashed her a huge grin.

Barely a month after Alun had turned the tables on Morgana Twyrth, her youngest child, Eirwen, took over her business, with the full assistance of Megan. She had no other heirs, only grandchildren, but they were pretty much out of the picture by this time. Megan and Eirwen found the extensive work on their part just to train the seven superbly well was rather exhausting work. They were not fully satisfied with them for another four months. Finally, when the two men were able to control themselves well, Eirwen opened the bids for five of them, her relations, that is. She never would forget the looks of horror on their faces, when each one left with their new "masters!"

By mutual consent, Eirwen retained Lin as her personal pet, while Megan had Brynne as hers. After that, the two closed the business. They had a huge fortune amassed, and decided to sit back and enjoy life with their well-trained partners. Thus ended the long running business that Morgana had begun some seventy years ago.

In the midst of all this, the Cairn police checked up on the estate, but found nothing amiss. They didn't bother checking the dungeon and reported that any illegal activities at the manor had ended. Hence, they were able to report to Carla that no more criminal activities were taking place at Chaos Lynn. They also verified that Alun had been a top CDI before he had resigned. In addition, they confirmed that the sex trade was legal on Haffren-3, inviting her to come for a visit and experience real sex. She declined the offer and reported to Katrina. She added, "Honestly, I can't believe I was hit on over the comm link and by a policeman to boot!"

"Well, that settles it; we have to find a legal way for us to give them Tierra citizenship," Katrina declared. "No way am I sending anyone back to that planet of perversions!"

Several hours later, Doctor Whitney presented her findings to Amy, Katrina, and Carla. After giving them their exams, she'd also taken the group to the cafeteria and gotten them a good, nourishing meal. She stated, "Alun is feeding them right now. I want them chewing and eating real food, not sucking up liquefied food. Too much liquids and not enough nutrients. Okay, onto the findings. All five are perfectly healthy. The women's feet are completely fused solid. There's not even a trace of their previous joints left. I'm afraid that nothing can be done about their feet."

"However, their legs are extremely well-muscled now, compensating for their feet. I believe they do well in those boots and shoes. I couldn't help noticing some of their mental traumatic incidents, where they were being trained to walk well in them. Anyway, they sure as heck need Basic Therapy quickly. Their arms can be regrown. They were simply amputated by a medical machine. I also told them we have over a thousand others who need theirs regrown as well, and that they would have to wait for a year or more before it could be done. I must say, they were very happy that it could even be done."

"As far as their shocking waists are concerned, two pairs of ribs were removed in order to squeeze their waistlines so darn small. Very unhealthy. I advised them to begin to wear far less restrictive and tight corsets. Their back muscles are very weak, so they can't just stop wearing them. I think I can work up a gradual procedure to allow them to be corset-free in a few months, but right now, none of the four was interested in that — something about having to please Alun and everyone else."

She went on, "Their breasts were greatly enlarged, but as I explained it to the five, if they stay here on Tierra, within six months, their breasts would have grown to the size that they are now. I also told them this was to better nurse their babies, and they seemed to accept that explanation."

"Now the nasty part. Their voice boxes have been removed. Sorry, there's nothing I can do to restore their ability to speak. I did suggest that all five take a crash course in lip reading. Of course, that will be useless with those of us with the lip plates. However, I made tentative appointments for all five to return to the med lab for such training, of course depending what you all decide. I sure wish I could do more for them, but regrowing arms is about all. They've basically been butchered," Doctor Whitney lamented. She added an afterthought, "You know, perhaps Ariceli and Carys could use the four in their ballet company. The four certainly are adept at walking en pointe."

Amy smiled invisibly. "Great idea. Okay, let's get them back, and see if we can get around the legal issues first." A few minutes later, Carla and Whitney led the five back into the meeting room. Katrina and Amy both sensed great apprehension coming from the five. Three of the women were terrified of being left out, while two were more afraid they'd be sent back to Haffren-3.

Once seated, Governor Katrina began, "Okay, you've no health problems that would interfere with staying here on Tierra or Ashford-5. We've checked on your story, Alun, and have verified that you were a CDI and highly thought of before you resigned a few days ago. The police also reported all illegal activities at the Chaos Lynn had ceased, but between us, I sincerely doubt the veracity of that statement. So there remains only one legal issue that poses any problems with granting you all citizenship here."

She went on, noticing that the five were literally clinging to her every word. "The legal issue is that anyone granted sanctuary here must be able to support themselves or be supported by their spouse. In the case of Alun and Morwen, if I marry them, that legal issue is solved, but what about Siana, Rhonwen, and Terren?" Five faces fell.

"Don't lose hope just yet. There is another possibility. You see here on Tierra, there are three distinct cultures, the Westerlings, the Midlands, and the Easterlings. Our location here is on the border between the Westerlings to the west and the Midlands to the east. I mention all this because, in the Easterlings culture, a man is permitted and *expected* to have multiple wives, as many as he can reasonably support. I'm not aware of your religious beliefs as such. But if Alun would marry all four of you, then there would be no reason for me not to grant all five of you Ashford-5 or Tierra citizenship."

Alun looked at Morwen first. "I gave my word to them. I'll do this, if they will have me. Siana, Rhonwen, Terren, will you also marry me? Then, I can take good care of all of you as I have promised to do." The three nodded yes, but Katrina and Amy also knew the poor women had little choice but to marry him.

"Okay then. Here's the grand plan, Alun, ladies," Governor Katrina explained. "First, I'll marry you in proper Easterlings fashion. That done, I'll grant you dual citizenship, that is, you are already citizens of Haffren-3, but now you'll also be citizens of Ashford-5 or Tierra. Carla will make you new ID cards, and setup your local bank accounts. I would request Alun not use the funds of Siana, Rhonwen, and Terren just yet, unless absolutely necessary."

"Why? Because as soon as we get these formalities handled, I want to get all of you what we call Basic Therapy. It's the most remarkable technology of the mind. It'll erase completely all the trauma you've undergone, giving you a new lease on life. Trust me; you'll never, ever regret it. Once that is completed, the five of you can then better evaluate whether or not you wish to remain married. Siana, Rhonwen, Terren, if at that time you do not wish to remain married to Alun here, I can arrange a legal divorce, but that will then not impact your own citizenship. You will still be able to live here on Tierra, and hopefully find another young man to fall in love with. Alun, that's why I would like you not to touch their funds unless necessary. If they later wish to go their own way, they'll have their own substantial funds."

Katrina continued, "I might add that you four women's bank accounts are extremely substantial for life here on Tierra. Here, you would be considered extremely wealthy women. So how does all this sound to you? Nod, if you are in total agreement."

While the four women nodded, Alun said, "Thank you, Governor Katrina, thank you from the bottom of my heart. I promise I'll treat them as angels."

"Okay then," Katrina went on, "Doctor Whitney wants you five to attend lip reading classes. This way, Alun and you women can mouth words and be understood by each other. We need you also to learn the three languages spoken here, as well as the version that those of us with these giant lip plates speak. Queen Amy has more than ample room in her Imperial Castle and Manors to house you. She's got quite a few other terrorist attack victims staying with her as well. Besides, there will be lots of help available too."

"Alun, both Amy and I want to offer you a job with us as a Chief Detective Inspector for Exchange City. Once we get the therapy sessions done and your situation worked out, we'll get you hatted on your new job. Additionally, there might even be some employment opportunities for you four women, but Amy has some checking to do on that detail before we dare promise anything. So are we ready to proceed?" They nodded.

"First, let me explain a bit about the Easterlings marital customs. They number their wives in the order that they marry them. Always the Number One wife is handled or cared for first. Then, Number Two is handled, and so on down the line. It is a hard and fast pecking order. It works for them, as each wife knows her order in daily life. Since this is to be an Easterlings marriage, Alun, you'll need to define their order. I assume Morwen will be your Number One wife."

"Of course. This is so strange. I don't want to insult the other three," Alun replied. "But I have to decide, don't I?" Katrina nodded. "Okay, then I'll have Siana as Number Two, Terren as Number Three, and Rhonwen as Number Four. Ladies, I hope I'm not insulting you by this," All four shook their heads no. As if they really had any choice, thought Katrina.

Governor Katrina delivered a very short ceremony, marrying them. "You may now kiss your brides. Remember to go in the proper order. Wives, remember to insist he obeys the proper order too." Alun did so, feeling very happy and greatly relieved. During the ceremony, Carla dashed off to prepare their new ID cards for them. Once she delivered them, Governor Katrina declared, "I hereby grant all five of you sanctuary on Ashford-5 and citizenship. You are free to travel anywhere on Tierra and to live your lives freely. Of course, you have a lot of culture shock to deal with, new languages, foods, customs, history, all that and more. Give yourselves time to absorb it. Make lip reading and the language tapes top priority. Most everyone around the Imperial Castle speaks IS, but beyond there, the locals do not, as a rule."

Amy then rose, "All right, let's get you to the castle and manor, and find you a nice suite. Follow Jan and me, we've got electric cars to take us there. My castle is just on the southeastern corner of the spaceport, right at the western edge of Exchange City."

Alun asked, "Why is it called Exchange City? And are you one of those official Ataro queens?"

"Yes, I am a queen. Trained on Winno-3 by Queen Altha. It's called that because the aliens, that is the Imperium, delivers its yearly spaceport lease payments of iron ore and gold there. The city sprang up as a place where goods are traded between our world and the Imperium."

"I've got a whole lot to learn!" Alun commented, as he followed her into the elevator.

In the basement where the tunnel began, several electric cars were waiting for them. Alun, Jan, and Amy were quite surprised to see the four women had no trouble going up the short steps into the cars on their own. Amy began to relax; they were not wholly helpless after all.

As they began to drive the two cars with Jan and Alun at the controls, Amy turned around and explained another key detail. "One more thing all of you. Tierra has a rather large number of telepaths. Whenever you see anyone with yellow eyes, you know for sure they are a telepath. However, don't worry. No one will ever pry into your thoughts. We call that mental rape, and it's highly illegal. Those, who will be giving your wives their therapy, will be using telepathy to receive their thoughts. Pretty cool, eh?"

Alun laughed, "I certainly picked the right planet to bring them to. Ladies, I think there is real hope here for us all." Amy smiled invisibly, *You can say that again!* He then asked, "Queen Amy, I should pay you something for our food and lodging."

"It's all covered until your wives are finished with their Basic Therapy, and we all work out what's next. It comes out of my budget to help others. I hope you don't mind being around hundreds of hermaphrodites. Most are terrorist attack victims that are here recovering their lives, similar to you. Don't be shocked by all you see."

"Here's the really hard part," Amy called out. They'd arrived and parked the cars. She reached the stone stairs leading up into the castle proper. "I always get a little nervous taking these stairs without Jan's arms around me. Ladies, if you need help, nod, and we can get some help real fast." They didn't nod. In fact, Morwen nodded Alun away from her. The four women took the stairs in stride, amazing the other three.

"I didn't think you all could do that!" Alun praised his wives, who were smiling when they reached the top.

"Amazing. You do far better than I do in these toe

shoes," Amy complimented them as well. "Okay, this way. There are hundreds of rooms around here. So I'm going to keep it as simple for you as possible. I've got a suite that's close to the Great Dining Hall where we take our meals. You'll find all your crates have been brought here already. I took the liberty of returning your rental transport and covered some of its cost. So you still have some funds left, Alun. Tomorrow, we can go over all your finances. Ah here we are. Number 101 is your temporary new home. I hope you like it. Castle staff will come by periodically, stoke the fireplace, and clean out the ashes. When you hear a gong sounding, that's the dinner signal. Just head on down that way, and you'll run into the giant hall where we all eat. Sit anywhere. I'll let you all get settled in and worry about everything else after dinner tonight. Okay?"

Alun opened the door and allowed his wives to enter, following them. Alone at last, the five stared at their new surroundings. Their many crates were piled into a nice stack just inside the door. The walls were grey stone. A crackling pine log fire provided the heat. Oil lanterns gave their living room a warm, yellowish glow. Several tapestries adorned the walls. Several couches and small tables and chairs were strategically located around the room. Two bedrooms opened off this room. One had a king sized bed and several walk-in wardrobes, dressers, along with a pair of commodes. The other was smaller but was similarly equipped. Thick quilts covered the beds.

"I think we are stepping back in time, sort of," Alun commented. They nodded yes. "Well, unless you have any objections, why don't we all sleep in the big bedroom. I think the bed will hold us all. What do you all think? Damn, this is so hard with you being unable to tell me a thing." The four fought hard to keep from breaking down; they were acutely aware of this. "Okay, keep it simple, Alun. Is it okay if we sleep in one bed?" They all nodded yes.

"Okay, I best get your things unpacked. I don't know whose things are whose, so you are going to have to help me with the unpacking. Plus, I'm not even sure what a lot of these things are."

While he opened a crate and asked whose these things belonged to, Morwen looked around the room. She spotted a stack of paper and pencils. An idea formed. She pushed the chair out a little and sat down. With some effort and maneuvering of her nearly rigid body, she got her teeth onto the pencil. More wiggling followed. Then, leaning over as best she could, she used her head to write. When she finished, she grinned, got up, and walked over to Alun, bumping him with her hips. Then, nodding with her head and moving back towards the table, she got him to look at what she'd done. Naturally curious, the other three followed him. In crude, wiggly letters, he read: love u. Alun picked her up and swung her around. She'd found a way to communicate at least a little bit. After that, Alun made sure there was always a supply around their suite.

Things began looking up for the five. The next day, five women from the Underground arrived to deliver their needed therapy sessions. Rafe had to have telepaths handling these four women, plus she wanted those giving them the therapy sessions to have a wider reality than just the world of Tierra. Hence, she chose the Underground members. Rafaela, Andres, Fred, Lana, and Annie came to deliver it for Rafe, who wanted to oversee all five cases, rather like a supervisor. Once more, she needed to ensure that her technology actually worked on "aliens."

As expected, Alun's trauma was handled in just a few days, leaving him feeling more alive than he had felt in ages — his words. He then got into a lengthy discussion with Rafe, concerning the decline and fall of morality on his own world. On the other hand, the four women proved an enormous challenge. While the givers could verbally give the women the commands, they had to maintain a constant telepathic connection with them and attempt to sort out the woman's answers from the actual mental images they were seeing. It was grim, tough going, primarily because in many ways, the trauma was ongoing. Adapting to a real life, constrained as they were, led to nearly a continuous trauma-like situation, replete with constant upsets.

One day in frustration, Rafaela commented to Rafe, "I

wish we could just bring Drina in on these and have her just zap the images with her *mentales* gift!" She sighed, "I know, but then they wouldn't have gained the knowledge that they are more powerful than their upsets and traumas. Still, I can't help wishing for a magic mental cure."

"I know, I know," Rafe replied. "I'd like to get my hands on that Countess woman, tie her down, and drill her with 'What have you done?' Over and over and over until she comes entirely clean. I wonder if something like that would actually work?"

"Hey, also ask: What haven't you revealed? You know sometimes, they just try to hide their bad actions," Rafaela added. Rafe left her, pondering this new idea of hers. Would such a thing work?

Early June 1326, the four women finally completed their Basic Therapy. All traces of the nearly half a year of trauma had been wiped out, along with other incidents including their births. Two even had encountered a few past lifetime incidents as well. They were bright and cheerful, but still confined to nearly helpless bodies. At least by this time, Alun was fairly competent at lip reading, as were the women themselves. That and their mouth writings allowed them some basic personal communication. On the positive side, their extremely strong leg muscles and untold hours of practice in the dungeon and elsewhere allowed them to get around very well, unlike so many others who had to wear toe shoes.

As promised, just as soon as they finished their Basic Therapy, Katrina checked with Siana, Terren, and Rhonwen to see if they still wished to remain married to Alun. They all did; it was working out very well for them. Hence, Amy then introduced them formally to Ariceli and Carys. She explained, "I think that these four might have ballet skills that you could develop." Both women were rather pregnant at this time, but were quick to see the potential of the four.

Ariceli and Carys took the four under their wings right away. Carys chatted, "We're like nearly last on the long list to get our arms regrown, but I guess you are even behind us. No matter; we can still dance. Well, not well until we have our babies, but we can teach you. We can form a real ballet company here on Tierra. They don't have any such thing on this world, so we are bringing culture to them."

"We are going to have to have a crash course in lip reading," Ariceli added. "Then, we'll be able to understand you. This is going to be great!"

At the same time, Alun became a CDI for Exchange City. During the many weeks his wives were getting their therapy, he was "educated" on the culture of Tierra and the city in particular. Now, he needed a true home for his large family. However, Amy suggested, "You know, I think it would be best for your wives to continue to live right where they are until their arms get regrown, don't you think?"

"They do love it here, but I should begin paying you rent at least," Alun countered.

"Agreed. Ten silvers per week is more than ample."

"But it ought to be several hundred credits," Alun protested.

"This isn't Haffren-3, Alun. Here, for perhaps a hundred Imperium credits you could purchase your own house. Don't worry, you'll get used to it in time."

Time. As June came, the baby months began, as most all of this large clan had their babies during the next three months. Thirty new grandchildren were born, keeping everyone hopping for the three months and afterwards for the next six with late night-early morning feedings. One morning in early August, Jan complained to Amy, "We're now running a nursery!" Both laughed. On the brighter side, all of the many terrorist victims now had the benefit of the latest genetic "undo" processes. A few like Amy and Katrina kept their lip plates, but none kept their monster breasts, which pleased Elegant Fashions Inc. Business became quite brisk once more. Only Amy and Katrina kept their toe shoes. Amy had to in order to remain an Ataro queen; Katrina did so to maintain affinity with the many rulers and now guild members. The only remaining genetic modifications were the dual sexual organs. They remained hermaphrodites still.

Time was also running out on Haffren-3, though none

there was even aware of it. Emperor Kino and Legate Smith, on the other hand, were. "I don't like the situation on Haffren-3," he explained. She'd dropped by to consult him on other matters. The Senate was about to officially reconvene. That meant at last there would be a new temporary President and Senate President, and she could lift Martial Law. Thus far, it had been a long haul getting the worlds to send new senators and bureaucrats in sufficient quantity. Plus, the salvage rights had become a nightmare of overlapping conflicts.

"How so?" she replied.

"Look, you and I both know that the only truly stable system in the Imperium right now is the Ataro Empire. Undoubtedly, other worlds also see this. I've received about fifty requests or feelers about the possibility of joining the Ataro Empire, especially since the additions of Ashford-5 and Bailey-3. While I would like nothing better than to allow more worlds into our domain, doing so will only further antagonize other worlds, such as Haffren-3, who see this only as a power grab by me, which has just enough truth in it to make it believable. In truth, the more that I add, the more secure we all become. I've had to temper the two opposing forces for now."

He went on, "On Haffren-3, their societal decay has become truly awful. Do you realize that one in every four people there is involved in the sex trade, one way or another? Those in the industry are making many times more money than the normal worker. Worse, with all their over emphasis on sexual pleasures, bordering on a certain franticness, their actual birthrate has plummeted far below their death rate. Meaning their population is slowly dying off."

"Perhaps that is a good thing, considering their attack on Winno-3 earlier this year," Legate Smith countered.

"Point taken, but we can expect more trouble from that world, but probably no more attacks on other worlds. We should keep alert to conditions there." He sighed, "I'm getting too old to try to keep this darn Imperium together. So many worlds are on the verge of seceding. Yet, if I sit back and do nothing, chaos and anarchy will follow. Maybe even the Federation of Planets will sweep in and gobble some up."

"Hang in there a bit longer, sir. The Senate will be meeting in a few weeks. Hopefully, that will be just the spark that things need to settle down," Legate Smith advised.

Part III The Return of Order

Chapter 21 Sparks Fly

Sparks. That was just what was happening on Haffren-3. Societal polarization had peaked with the widespread news that their President and generals had ordered a sneak bio agent terrorist attack on the Ataro Empire. About an eighth of the world's population felt completely isolated and disenfranchised, forced to condone the abysmal sexual perversion now so wide spread across the planet. True, the "tourist" industry was still booming. "You can get whatever you desire on Haffren-3" read the many advertisements scattered in seedier locations on many, many other worlds.

July warmth from their red dwarf sun brought very balmy days for Countess Eirwen and her companion Megan, whom Eirwen anointed as Duchess Megan Mabon, much to the silent woman's pleasure. They spent the early days of the month sunning themselves on the third floor balcony, with their sex toys in attendance, Lin and Brynne. Now that they had closed the family "business," the two were quite calm and relaxed, though Lin and Brynne certainly weren't. The initial sparks quickly changed that mood.

A shuttle landed on the grounds. "Damn, who can that be?" Eirwen swore. She was about to send Lin down to see who it was when she remembered that Lin couldn't talk. Grumbling, she rose, slipped on a silk robe covering her bikini-clad form and headed down to greet the arrival. As she stepped out of her wide front doors, she inhaled involuntarily. There was her mother and the wealthy man who had purchased her. Morgana looked very distraught, struggling to keep from falling on the soft grass, as she determinedly headed for the doors. Her master mostly ignored her struggling steps. Behind them, a servant was unloading a number of crates.

"Countess Eirwen, alas, I must return my fabulous toy. I've just been elected to be our new President. As the head of our world, I no longer have the luxury of handling my toy's needs," he spoke solemnly.

"Can't you hire a servant to deal with her?" Eirwen

449

countered.

He flushed. "I can't be seen with — well you must appreciate my new, high status, Countess. I'm not asking for my fee to be refunded. Heavens no. I've already gotten my money's worth from this charming creature. No, I simply will not have time to spend with her. I thought it best to return her and allow you to pass her on to another master in need."

"How kind of you. Thanks," Eirwen replied somewhat coldly and distantly. He bowed, turned, and left. At least the master's servant left the dozen crates stacked just inside the doors. As the shuttle lifted off, Morgana finally reached the flagstones below the portico and relaxed, here the going was much easier for her.

"Well, hello mother. So I have you back. I can't seem to get you out of my life. What am I to do with you?" Eirwen addressed her silent mother, who stopped and stood, her shallow panting announcing just how short of breath she was in her eleven inch pipe corset. She glared back at Eirwen.

"Well, let's put you into a room for now. This way, mother, no, you are not getting your old room back. That's my bedroom now. You get a toy's room, since you are still a toy, albeit a used one. I do hope you've been enjoying yourself with that master."

If eyes could kill, Morgana's would have done so! Unfortunately, when Eirwen gave her a push in the right direction, she couldn't do anything except take a step. Begrudgingly, Eirwen had to carry the many crates into her mother's new room and unpack them. Later rejoining Megan, she relayed the news. Duchess Megan smiled and laughed silently.

The next day, Eirwen and Megan stuck the ends of the feather dusters into the mouths of Lin, Brynne, and Morgana and secured their leather head harnesses. "Okay, the whole place is dusty. Today, your job is to dust everything. Get going," Eirwen declared. Morgana gave her a pleading look, which she ignored. The two headed off to sun bathe on the second floor balcony.

They no more than laid back on the lawn chairs when two more shuttles landed. "Oh hell, what is this? Return week?" Eirwen cursed. This time, both women headed down to meet the arrivals. Both cringed slightly. They saw Emlyn and Ceri being lifted down from separate shuttles. Their two masters walked up.

"Returning your toys?" Countess Eirwen asked coldly.

"Right. You've heard the news then. I've become our new senator. I'm off to Proxima Prime tomorrow. Unfortunately, I'm unable to take my toy with me," the woman explained.

The man piped up, "And I'm our new ambassador. I leave tomorrow as well. Honestly, we tried to bring our super toys with us, but we simply could not get them through customs on Proxima Prime. So regrettably, we're returning them to you in hopes you can find some others who'll be able to make use of their simply incredible skills."

"Thanks. Have a good trip to Proxima Prime," Eirwen replied, through slightly clenched teeth. The two turned and left without exchanging further words. Wobbling a good deal, the pair came up to the flagstones and stopped, panting from their exertion. "Well hello big brother. Ceri. You've come back to me. How unfortunate. Well, get yourselves inside. It's cleaning day. We'll just have to put you to work. You have to earn your keep somehow."

Emlyn's mouth formed many words, but only silence came out. Taunting him, Eirwen said, "Oh dear brother. You're trying to tell me how happy you are to be back with us, and how much you want to help keep the manor cleaned up. Well, I'll certainly let you do just that." He glared at her, but was helpless to do anything about it. Ceri simply cried silently.

Once inside, Eirwen pointed out, "Look, you remember mother, don't you? She's back too. Well, since you two are still married, I guess I'll put you into the same bedroom. This way Ceri, Emlyn." Ceri looked at Emlyn and smiled. Eirwen was at least showing them some kindness, she thought. A bit later, the two holding dusters between their teeth were sent out to join the other three.

At the same time as this was happening, just a few miles north in Cairn Glen proper, several men met in secret. One said, "That damned fool Afon just got himself elected

President. Everyone knows he's a sexual pervert. Even has one of those fancy sex dolls. It's the last straw!"

Another countered, "No, they elected that bitch Aerona as our senator! Hell, she's the biggest pervert in Cairn Glen, if not the whole damn continent! Someone has to put a stop to all this heathen works. I got me a plan. Listen up. It's up to us good guys to put an end to the insanity that's devouring our world."

"No kidding, the Devil's Work. That's what the preachers keep telling us. What'cha got in mind? I'm all ears," the other replied.

"Teach them a lesson. That's what."

"Yeh, but it's got to be a big lesson. One they won't forget. Besides, they got all the money."

"What I have in mind, all the damned money in the world won't help 'em none. Listen. How many others do you reckon we can find to help us?"

"Plenty, but what's the plan?" he asked.

Around noon, Senator Aerona was packing the last of her things at her fancy penthouse suite in downtown Cairn Glen. Halfway across the continent in the capital city of Angharad, President Afon was doing the same thing, preparing for his move into the Presidential Suites. Timed to the minute, several loud explosions rocked both cities. "What the hell was that?" President Afon yelled.

The explosions were perfectly placed at two very key locations where the bio agent cylinders were stored. These were the supplies being used to "treat" incoming prisoners before they were sent to the assisted living complexes in both cities. While the highly dangerous cylinders were kept in super secure locations where theft was nearly impossible, no one had thought of what now happened. Several lowly paid janitors knew the precise layouts of the buildings. They were among the one eighth of the population, who bore the brunt of the labor needed to sustain the wealthy and their enormous sex trade. They'd had enough, and many chose this moment to lash out in the only way that they saw remaining to them. None had any voice in the government whatsoever, such was controlled by the perverted wealthy class.

Two well-placed bombs blew giant holes in the walls surrounding the secure rooms. Secondary charges followed, disintegrating the bio agent cylinders. Giant clouds of the toxin mixed with the explosion's debris rose high, engulfing a large percentage of the two cities. Worse, because of the design of most buildings, the deadly agent was sucked into their air intake lines, spreading uniformly throughout the skyscrapers.

True, several thousand died with the initial explosions and subsequent collapse of some structures. Rescue personnel quickly responded. President Afon was on the comm network almost at once, trying to find out what had happened and what was needed. Senator Aerona shrugged it off and continued her packing, but did turn on the news channel to stay in touch with what was happening. Nothing was going to prevent her from taking her new power post as one of their three senators.

By the time that the emergency responders ascertained what exactly was happening, it was too late. Half of Cairn Glen was engulfed in the toxic cloud. A third of the capital city was as well, except there the impact was on the very wealthy who had their business offices located in the heart of the large city. As soon as the newscasts reported the exact nature of the situation, chaos and panic erupted in both cities.

Having seen the explosions from their balcony, Eirwen and Megan headed inside to their comm center. They tuned to the emergency channel and sat down to watch the situation unfold. An hour after the explosion, the head of the ERT, the Emergency Response Team, stood before a wall of cameras and microphones. "It has now been confirmed. The explosion has ruptured a number of the extremely deadly bio agent cylinders. The gas has been released into the air of Cairn Glen. You may have seen it, a slightly yellowish color. This is the bio agent that is used to treat the criminals when they arrive. Yes, it is also the same bio agent that the terrorists have used on Proxima Prime and the Big Five worlds."

The newscaster continued, "If you live inside the cloud, you have been exposed to the genetic mutation agent. At once, remove your clothes and shoes. Find a place to lie down. Before long, you will fall unconscious and remain in a coma for three to four days. When you wake up, rescue personnel will be by to assist you into temporary rescue tents. If you live outside the affected area, my advice for you is to flee the city immediately. The cloud is expanding. At this time, we cannot tell just how much of Cairn Glen will ultimately be affected by the bio agent. If you've been infected, do not attempt to flee. You'll be going unconscious and could well be killed long before someone finds you. Here are the current boundaries of the outer edges of the impacted areas." He rattled off a number of streets, while a map of the city highlighted the affected areas, close to half of the city, its heart.

After repeating the message twice, the channel broke to cover the unfolding story in the capital city. By then, widespread panic had already set in. Every available shuttle shot out of the city. Massive electric car traffic jams followed. With the only way out then being on foot, thousands died by being trampled by the mobs, frantic to flee before becoming infected. Quite a few of those who were infected attempted to flee as well, adding to the utter confusion and chaos.

At Cairn Glen, people fled in all directions. Unfortunately for those on foot or those who took too long to flee, the prevailing light summer winds blew the cloud over the northeastern portion of the city, affecting many who were on foot, running away. Most kept on running anyway, at least until they dropped. From there, the cloud continued both expanding and rolling along the surface of the planet. The bio agent was slightly heavier than the air. This kept it from rising significantly. The prevailing winds continued to push the cloud northeast. Though slowly diluting by virtue of its cone-shaped expansion, still the concentration was quite deadly.

A week later, although now covering a vast percentage of the planet, the bio agent had finally become too diluted to have any effect on the remaining population. Still the damage had been done. Three-quarters of the population of the world either had been outright killed during the bombings and riots or were now in comas, as their bodies responded to the genetic mutation agents within their bodies. Looting and chaos had spread widely before the expanding cones of the deadly bio agents. The disenfranchised attempted to gain material goods while fleeing the clouds. During that ill-fated week, chaos and anarchy ran rampant over Haffren-3.

Eirwen and Megan watched the news that first day. That afternoon, when the reports of the bio agent gas first appeared on their local news channel, Eirwen cried out, "My god! Megan, look at that! We have to protect ourselves! I know, into the dungeon!" While Megan slowly headed to the stairs, Eirwen ran into the other rooms to warn the five toys. "Mom, everyone, it's a bio agent attack! Get into the dungeon as fast as you can!" She verified that all were complying, looks of fear on their faces.

Then, she thought a moment. If the cloud of gas reached the mansion, the air circulating system would suck it in. She ran to the master power box and opened it. Rapidly, her eyes scanned down the labeled switches. Finding the right one, she threw it, shutting down the air system. She then found a small, portable comm system, battery operated. Carrying it, she too raced for the stairs.

When she got there, the others had just reached them, and together, they began making their extremely careful way down them. Seeing how pathetically slow they were, Eirwen began helping each one, beginning with her mother. Afterwards, she realized she'd just shown them kindness for the first time. Megan motioned everyone into the deepest corner off the dungeon where the two by four walk was located. Once everyone was in and sitting on the mats, Eirwen closed the door, sliding a mat over to help block the crack between the door and stone floor. She too sat down. "Now we wait it out," she said nervously and turned on the set. The others watched the small screen intently.

Meanwhile, the newscasts continued. More information kept coming out, particularly concerning the widespread panic that was occurring in both cities. Then, the reporters finally identified the group that was taking responsibility for the bombings. "This just in. The SAISTH or Society for the Abolishment of the Insanity and Sex Trade of Haffren-3 has claimed responsibility for the two bombings. According to the document they've just released, and I quote, 'If Haffren-3 does not immediately outlaw the sex trade industry and eliminate the insanity in government, expect more bombings until the government does.' Until today, no one seems to have heard of this SAISTH organization, but government officials are looking into it."

"In other related news, our new President Afon and Senator Aerona are both in the impacted areas. No word on their conditions at this time. Vice-president Alis has taken temporary control of the government. We are anticipating a news conference in about an hour. Stay tuned, as more details of today's twin bombings come in."

Two hours later, Vice-president Alis declared Martial Law in the two impacted cities and mobilized the entire armed forces of Haffren-3. Unfortunately, many of the low paid grunts were also polarized against the wealthy purveyors of sensual delights. Besides, none wanted to go anywhere near these infected areas, rightly so. Thus, with soldiers now covertly giving access to explosives of all types and with so many now sympathetic to the aims of the SAISTH as outlined on the news, more and more explosives fell into the hands of dedicated members, who made good use of them.

By the second day, more explosions rocked other cities. By the end of the week, nearly every large city on the planet had been struck by one or more very destructive attacks. Rioting and looting were rampant. The soldiers themselves often contributed to the looting. Anarchy had indeed broken out across Haffren-3.

The six huddled in the partially sealed room. All were frightened, but only Eirwen could vocalize her fears. "If we fall into a coma, our bodies will mutate. Megan, we'd best get all of us undressed as much as possible, just in case." She didn't need to see Megan writing her response; her eyes radiated the fear that the speechless woman felt. Together, they undressed everyone and waited.

As she sat beside Megan and her mother, Eirwen realized if they did become infected and their bodies mutated, they would all likely die down here in the dungeon. She knew none of the "toys" were even able to open the doors and hence leave the dungeon on their own free will. They'd be trapped in this room. Yet, while she wanted to leave all the doors open just in case, she dare not. The gas could well seep down and infect them.

By the third day, Eirwen also began to realize she alone was now responsible for the lives of Morgana, Ceri, Emlyn, Lin, and Brynne. Even Megan was dependent upon her to some degree as well. She alone had normal feet and could speak. Hence, she decided to open the door and see about getting water and food for everyone. At least they had been able to use the attached restroom. Each of these dungeon rooms had its own bathroom, since the toys-in-training spent several months down here learning to walk well in their ballet boots. If she were infected, at least the six would have one last meal. She owed them that much.

Several hours later, the six had full bellies for the first time in three days. "Well, I'm not unconscious yet," Eirwen commented to Megan, who smiled and nodded. "We wait it out."

Of course, what they would do when the all clear sounded remained wholly unknown to Eirwen. She estimated they had enough food to get by for a couple of weeks, if they rationed it. Still, after that was gone, where would they be able to get more? If the world was as destroyed as the newscasts suggested before they too went off the air, then obtaining food would be a major problem.

Perhaps this SAISTH had a point, she thought. Haffren-3 society had plummeted to new depths. Surely, the perversions sitting beside her on the mats were testimony to that. Her mother had made a fortune in the sex trade. Worse, she'd kidnaped the women. Lin and Brynne had no choice in becoming sex toys. Now, that they were toys, they were utterly dependent upon her and Megan for their very lives. With the bio agent wiping out lives along with the bombing and all the rest, she alone stood between their life and death. The necessity of dealing with the crisis hit home to Eirwen, rather heavily.

A week after the bombing, a newscaster finally gave the all-clear message. The bio agent cloud was no longer toxic. Slowly, the six emerged from their dungeon, only this time, Eirwen and Megan kept their arms around the four others, making sure that they could handle the stairs. After turning on the power, Megan set about preparing a good, hot meal for everyone, while Eirwen checked on the rest of the mansion. She headed to the top balcony to survey the estate and city to the north. Smoke curls rose above Cairn Glen, not a good sign.

Just then, someone rang her gate bell. She looked towards the gate and saw a man standing there. All her security guards were long gone, having fled the day of the initial bombing. Her heart fluttered. She waved and headed down the stairs. A few minutes later, she walked up to the gates and opened them. A smartly dressed man introduced himself. "Hello. I am Police Commissioner Cadfael Wynn. I am looking for Countess Twyrth."

"Hi, I'm Countess Eirwen Twyrth. Pleased to meet you. We've just come out of our basement where we've managed to avoid becoming infected. Would you like to come in?" she replied politely.

"Thank you, Countess. I'm here in a formal capacity. I've taken over running Cairn Glen for the moment. We've got quite a mess on our hands, I'm afraid." He began walking beside her back to the mansion doors. "Bombings, looting, dead bodies everywhere. Most all services are gone, as are the people. Don't know if they will be back either. Our whole world has been turned upside down this past week."

"So how can I help?" Eirwen asked. They reached the doors and entered. The five toys and Megan were standing near the entrance, curious about who was coming. For a second, Eirwen flinched. Here was the police commissioner and apparent new leader of Cairn Glen staring at the exotic "toys!"

As he watched the six, Eirwen introduced them. "My dear friend, Megan, who helps me run the manor. My mother, brother, his wife, and two friends, Lin and Brynne. This is Cairn Glen's new leader, Police Commissioner Cadfael Wynn. He's come to ask our help. Oh, they can't speak, Commissioner Cadfael," she added hastily. "Would you like some coffee or tea? We still have some, though I don't know how long our supplies will hold out or where or when we can get more."

"Please, thank you," he replied politely. Megan led the group through the manor to the kitchen, but Cadfael watched how well the six managed to walk in their ballet shoes. He noted none needed any help getting themselves seated. Nor did they need assistance a few minutes later when Megan served everyone tea. The five used their straws.

Finally, Cadfael got down to business. "Countess, I'd heard that there were women such as these five here on your estate. Further, they seem to be able to walk quite well. I expected them to be completely helpless in all things. Tell me, just how independent are they? Don't they need steadying arms when they walk? I'm rather impressed with their adaptations."

"Sorry, I can't take any credit for their skills. It is all mom's doing. She invented their entire training regimens. Yes, they are able to walk very well and not just here inside. They are adapt at walking on just about any surface, including the lawn. They use straws to drink and sometimes to eat. Megan often purees their meals so they can feed themselves. They are also able to pull carts and do light housework. They could do more, if we could work out ways and means for them to carry things," Eirwen explained.

"Amazing, simply amazing, ladies. Impressive. You see, Countess Eirwen, they could well be the answer I'm looking for. You see, we have a very big problem. Three quarters of our world's population either is dead or have become victims of that bio agent. Here in Cairn Glen, we've lost ninety percent of our population. At the moment, we've maybe twenty thousand left. Worse, three out of four of those who are here have been genetically modified and are utterly helpless at the moment."

"My god! It's that bad?" Eirwen gasped. "I've been looking after these six, we've only surfaced now since the news said it was finally safe."

"Yes, it's that bad. I've been racking my brain to figure out how we, who are unaffected, can possibly handle or deal with so many helpless men, women, and children. I was told about your mother's 'sexual toys.' Mind you, I don't approve of such things. I know, I'm in the distinct minority on Haffren-3, but maybe not any longer. Anyway, I got to thinking and recalled hearing about them. I came here today to see if what I heard some time ago was true. I must say I'm truly impressed with how much they are able to accomplish on their own. Somehow, I need to get thousands of the armless victims able to function as well as your mother is doing. That would go a long way to helping the few of us who are still able-bodied to get our city on the mend somehow."

He continued, "None of the victims can walk on their own without support. Their feet are so malformed, you see. I've gotten two Fabrication Machines working on making clothing and shoes for the victims, but their toe shoes, as they are called, don't help them walk better much at all. Yet, your mother and the others are doing phenomenally well with their even stranger boots or shoes."

"Yes, from what little I have seen, the ballet boots give them more support and balance," Eirwen commented.

"I can see that it does. By chance, do you have any way to modify a victim's feet so they could wear such shoes or boots?" he asked.

"Yes, we have a medical machine that can do it. Why?" she replied, curious about his intentions. "It's a very harsh training regimen that they have to handle. It takes them several months to build up their strength, balance, and skills. It's a rather harsh regimen that they must endure, but the end product. . ."

He interrupted her, "The end product is they are able to be vastly more independent than the ordinary terrorist victims, who end up being confined into assisted living dorms, where they have pretty much constant assistance. Here in Cairn Glen, the few of us who are still normal simply cannot afford to give them that kind of constant help. Instead, we must focus on rebuilding our world. Countess, are you and Megan willing to lend me hand in this project?"

"Of course, Commissioner Winn," Eirwen answered without hesitation. "During this past week, I've realized I really am responsible for my mother and everyone here. They haven't any choice but to depend on me. If I don't step up, they die. Pretty simple, really. I can't imagine why I never saw that before, but I didn't. How can I help, Commissioner Winn?"

"Please, just Cadfael. Thank you, Countess. Yes, you are quite right. Today, our responsibilities are positively huge. I'm truly impressed with your generosity and compassion. When I came to your gates today, I was expecting to have to give a big lecture on our responsibilities. I was told that Chaos Lake was just another den of iniquity, like so many others. I'm very happy that I was misinformed."

Eirwen laughed. "You were not misinformed, Cadfael. When the estate was in mother's hands and then in my brother's hands, it was just that, a den of iniquity. I admit Megan and I wrapped it up and ended it. We closed it down, you see, but then some who had purchased the sex toys kindly returned mom, my brother, and his wife, when they could no longer keep them. So now, Megan and I are looking after them. We just couldn't sell Lin and Brynne here to such people, but we've no way to undo what mom and the others did to them. I do believe all three have learned their lessons from their experiences as sex toys and are now willing to do their part to help us. Oh, just call me Eirwen, please, Cadfael. So what can we do to help?"

He smiled and said, "Okay then. I'm putting the able bodied men to work on the heavier work. My biggest problem is with the many helpless victims. I have two doctors back in the city now. As more victims are discovered, they are being brought to them. They are able to stitch their lips back together, more or less, but that's about all. They also use the Fabrication Machine to get them properly clothed. However, in those toe shoes, most of the time, they simply can't walk independently without assistance."

"What I would like to propose is to bring them here, and have you and Megan alter their feet like theirs, equipping them with those fancy ballet type boots, and then fully train them. If you can, get them as independent as your mother and the others are. We can then put them to work in ways that they can help the rest of us rebuild our world. If they can walk, pull carts, feed themselves, and other light duties, that alone will be of immense help to the rest of us."

She replied, "Okay, we can do that, but the training is pretty demanding. I believe that is one reason why mother always removed her victim's voices so that they couldn't scream and make a fuss during the many weeks of their training. We could house at least a hundred here at one time, but Megan and I'll need some help dealing with that many. Besides, we don't have enough food on hand to feed them. We'll need a supply of the boots too and more of the apparatus that mom had built for their training."

"I can get you about a dozen other women to help out. I can have a Fabrication Machine brought here. You can use it to make more of what it is that you need. I'll see that you won't be lacking food supplies. As far as the victims go, I'll see that they are fully informed. If they complete your training program, become somewhat independent, and willing to help the rest of us, then they'll be taken care of and have their arms regrown in the future, when we get that operation up and running. If they fail, give you too much trouble, or don't want to help, then we'll just leave them where we found them — they can get by on their own. Of course, that's a death sentence, but as hard as these times are, that's a blessing. Everyone has to pitch in or we're all doomed," he sighed.

"No, we could just kill all of these new victims and eliminate the problem," Eirwen countered, "but that would be inhumane. In the past, I suspect our leaders would have done just that, but we can't do such a thing. That's genocide. As much as I detest what my family has done in the past, I just can't outright kill them or leave them to die. Neither can I devote my life to caring solely to their needs. They have to carry their own weight as much as is possible," she explained.

He smiled broadly. "I couldn't agree more. By the way, if some of these victims give you too much trouble, then go ahead and remove their voices too, but only as a last resort. If even that doesn't help, then let me know, and I'll have them returned to their homes, and they can fend for themselves."

"Agreed. How soon do we start?" she asked.

"How soon can we get things ready? I can fill the manor today, but I know you'll need time to get things prepared first," he answered. Eirwen sensed his great relief and smiled.

An hour later, two dozen men and women arrived at her manor. A Fabrication Machine, along with a rack of samples, was setup in one corner of her giant ballroom. Others helped convert many unused rooms into bedrooms, installing some bare necessities, while several women stocked her pantry. Meanwhile, Eirwen and several men checked out the dungeon level, that is, the basement. Only a third of the basement rooms were in use. Hence, the men used the Fabrication Machine to make more of the training equipment. They added two more of the fifty foot long, two by four walks in the mat room and then duplicated it, providing space for six trainees at one time.

When they finished, she could handle fifty people at one time on the flat surface walking machines, forty on the slopes machines, thirty on the up and down stairs machines, ten on the circular walk with many obstacles, and six on the final circle walking machines. The rest of their training could be done upstairs and not in the dungeon.

At the end of the very busy day, Cadfael himself dropped by to inspect everything. "I hope they built it all to your specifications, Countess Eirwen."

"Yes, they were very cooperative. Would you like a tour?" she asked. "It'll seem rather grim. I've asked mom and the others to give you a demonstration of how the equipment is used." Her mother flashed her a frown, but knew she hadn't any real choice. All five had heard Commissioner Cadfael's previous discussion with Eirwen, and knew that if they didn't "pull" their own weight, he'd have them removed from the mansion and left to their own devices — a death sentence.

He followed them all down the stone stairs into the basement dungeon. However, he watched the five carefully, noting they all managed the stairs very well without any assistance, wholly unlike the many victims he had gathered up already. While Megan hooked Morgana up to the flat surface walking machine, Eirwen explained its operation. "This is the first one. The wire supports them so they cannot fall down. They spend the day walking. As you can see, the machine makes them walk. When they stumble and would fall, except for the wires which prevents that, it activates an electrical stimulus to their privates, which encourages them to regain their feet and continue walking. They pass when their legs and knees have strengthened enough so they can walk on the flat surface all day without falling."

"Now here," she led him to the second room where her brother was hooked up to the next machine, "the flat surface is now an up and down ramp. Again, they pass when they can walk all day without falling down. A bit later, Ceri demonstrated the next phase. "Here, they are forced to climb the stairs and descend them, over and over until they can do it all day without falling."

"Impressive. No wonder they can walk so well," he replied.

"Now here, Lin is demonstrating one of the more difficult ones. She's attached to a circular arm that forces her to walk that circle of obstacles, with some ramps and some stairs. Again, passing is to be able to do this all day without falling down."

A few minutes later, Brynne demonstrated the next one. "This one is perhaps the most difficult of all these training regimens. She has to walk down that board without falling and in less than a minute. Dexterity and balance are critical. The mats protect them from their many falls. Megan says they get an awful lot of bruises before they master this one."

Cadfael laughed, "Countess, I doubt I could walk that beam in my shoes! No wonder they are so adept on their feet. Well done, Brynne," he complimented the young woman, who smiled.

"Finally, this room has artificial grass in it. Here they learn to walk on rougher surfaces, such as the lawn outside. Once they've passed all these tests, they can get around well on their own," Eirwen explained. "Then, Megan takes them back upstairs where they learn to do light housekeeping duties, pull a riding cart, and most importantly, be able to navigate around the place while blindfolded. You see, at night when it's quite dark, they have to be able to move around, perhaps turning on lights or finding the bathroom. That's a very important safety precaution, but," she chuckled, "they don't see it that way when the blindfolds are first put on them."

"Amazing, simply amazing. Yes, I can see why this is such a rough regimen, but the final product is well worth the effort. Well done, all of you," he praised the five who had been through this whole procedure when they had been turned into sex toys. "Tomorrow, I'll bring the first fifty here to begin on the flat walking machines. I'll give them a preparatory speech first, impressing upon them that they must complete this training or be left on their own to fend for themselves. Again, if they give you too much trouble and nothing else works, you can remove their voices. If that doesn't do it, then let me know, and I'll remove them from the program at once."

"Excellent. Would you care for some coffee or tea?" she asked. Somehow, she didn't want this handsome man to depart just yet. He smiled and nodded.

Over tea, he asked, "Do you mind if I drop by each day to check on their progress?"

"Not at all, please do," she replied, wondering if that was all he wanted to see. Her stomach fluttered in unusual ways.

The next morning, he arrived, along with twenty women helpers and the first fifty men, women, and children to be trained. After getting them all seated in the ballroom, Police Commissioner Cadfael gave them all a lengthy speech, outlining what was going to happen to them. He ended with, "So you see, there is really no choice. You have to learn to become semi-independent, just as these five are. You have to be able to help us rebuild our world in ways that you can. Everyone must work together. This training regimen is extremely tough, but as these five here bear witness, it can be done. When you complete the Countess' program, you'll be given work that you can do to help us rebuild and survive and the assistance in other things that you need. Plus, you'll be put on the list for arm regrowth, once we are able to resume that process. If you fail or opt out or quit or give the Countess here too much trouble, then you'll be removed from the program and sent to your home, there to fend for yourself in all things, with no one to assist you. I know, that's tantamount to a death sentence, but we all must step up and assume responsibility for the state of our world. We, as a people, simply will not survive, unless we all lend what assistance we can, you included."

He finished, "Yes, the Countess and I realized that it would be far simpler to just kill all of you victims right now.

Perhaps, the several hundred thousand of us who escaped the destruction and mutations could rebuild our world by ourselves, but we aren't following that path. As far as I know at this time, that would involve killing ninety percent of what remains of our population here on Haffren-3. We don't want any part in such genocide. So we are accepting the responsibility of saving you, giving you a way to become somewhat productive members of society once more. It'll be up to you to assume some responsibility yourselves and get through this training regimen. It'll be tough on you; I won't pretend otherwise. I've also authorized the Countess to remove your voices if you scream, protest, or give them too much trouble. Others will gladly take your place. So good luck, work hard, and we'll all win."

"Questions?" Seeing none, he asked, "Does anyone want out before we begin?" Again, silence. "Okay, Countess, you may get their feet prepared and get them started."

That evening at dusk, Cadfael dropped by to see how the day had gone. Secretly, he'd kept his fingers crossed. So much depended upon getting these victims somewhat independent. He knew the few survivors, like him and the countess, simply could not care for ninety percent of the world's population. If the multitudes were going to survive, they'd have to become at least marginally productive members of society. If not, he had no other choice but to allow them to die.

"Well, how did it go?" he asked, after entering the manor where Eirwen met him with a smile on her face.

"Extremely well, all things considered. I'm amazed with the children. They took to it right away. Some of the adults haven't, but I've taken another approach. Instead of constantly telling them to stop yelling and complaining, which we tried and which didn't work, one of my new helpers simply duct taped their mouths shut. That beats permanently removing their voices. Honestly, these first few days are going to be rough on them," she answered honestly.

His visibly tense muscles relaxed all at once. "That's music to my ears, Countess. I was hoping and praying this would work. Honestly, one of us with arms cannot take care of nine who are helpless in all things and still do anything to rebuild our world. Food production is going to be our major concern for the next few years. I took a survey of the surrounding zones, and it's pretty grim out there. So much has been destroyed."

"Surely, the automated farms are still operational," she countered, trying hard to remember what little she knew about food production on her world. She seldom, if ever, paid attention to such things. She simply used her computer to order her week's worth of groceries, and a deliveryman brought them. "I guess I can't just order food and have them deliver it any longer."

Cadfael laughed, "You're right about that one. No deliverymen. No stores. The whole supply line has been disrupted. We're living off warehouse stockpiles at the moment. The real question is just what can these people actually do to help, once they've finished their training?"

"Perhaps there is something we can do to find the answer, Cadfael," Eirwen answered, trying hard to be helpful.

"I've given that some thought. Would you mind loaning me your five tomorrow? I'd like to conduct some experiments with their permission, of course. I've assembled ten men and women who have a bent for inventing things. Between us, I'd like to see just what might be possible with them. You say they can pull a cart?"

"Yes, a one person pony cart. Mom had them doing such a thing — pulling their masters around on a pony cart. Pretty debased, if you ask me, but they can do that," she replied.

"Hum, perhaps they could pull supplies instead of a person. That would help. I wouldn't have to take able bodied men off of other activities just to make routine deliveries, such as more food supplies here, for instance," he theorized.

Eirwen sighed, "You know, it's almost as if we're going to have to rework our whole society, somehow making it drastically easier for all these victims to survive and help out. Take doors, for example. You probably haven't noticed, but mom has an automatic door opener installed on the main doors. It's a footplate. One steps on it, and it opens the doors."

"You and I think alike, Eirwen. Amazing," he smiled broadly at her. "I agree; we're going to need to rework, rethink everything. Somehow, someway, we need to rebuild our world so the ninety percent of us can get by and contribute, and not simply be leeches as they have been in the previous assisted living complexes."

"True, but won't things change if they can at least have their arms back?" Eirwen asked.

Cadfael sighed, "In an ideal world, yes. Here, the sheer number of victims who need it is mind boggling, Eirwen. Mind you, we haven't gotten accurate figures yet, but there are around a hundred thousand just here in Cairn Glen alone, but only ten thousand of us who have arms. As I understand the procedure, it takes about three months per person. We've one machine here locally that can do this. If we can't speed things up, we're talking about twenty-five thousand years to get to everyone."

"Good god! I had no idea! I see where you are heading now. We simply have to find ways to integrate them as they are into our new world. It's either that or let them die off, isn't it?" she replied, quite shocked with the monumental magnitude of the process.

"Precisely so. It's either integrate them somehow, someway, or let them die. Cruel and harsh, but what other choice do we have? The other worlds in the Imperium are already overloaded on terrorist victims. They've had to let the vast majority of the terrorist victims on the densely populated Big Five worlds and even Proxima Prime die. Besides being unable to get to billions of affected people in time, there are only a limited numbers of assisted living homes. Already Juno-3, the retirement planet, is hopelessly swamped with victims and their children."

Taking another sip of tea, he continued, "I for one don't wish to see genocide here on Haffren-3. I'll admit last year, I was more than willing to allow all the sexual deviants to die off — let those multitudes in the sex trade perish. Now that it's almost a reality, I've changed my mind. They're human beings still."

Eirwen replied, "I know. I felt the same way. Funny how

things change. She's my mother, after all. In spite of what all she's done, she's still mom. Plus, I think she's changed, learned from her experiences of being a sex toy. I certainly hope so. I know my brother has changed from what he's been through. He was a womanizer, and now he treats his wife quite well, very loving. As far as I can tell, he's a changed man, though he looks more like a woman now."

Cadfael chuckled, "So do all of the male victims — they look like women as well. He's got plenty of company. Say, perhaps you'd like to come along with them tomorrow and toss out any ideas you have to the inventors."

She grinned, "Sure thing. We have an immense challenge ahead of us, if we are to remake our world in ways that mom and the others can be truly independent, living on their own. We have to try, don't we?"

He smiled back, "Yes, we have to give it our best shot. Still, we must also be willing to accept failure, and allow those who can't adapt to die. We can't sacrifice those of us who are still normal. That's the biggest beef so many others now have. I admit. I'm walking a fine line here. So many of those who survived believe we should just let the helpless victims die off. If we can somehow pull this off, we all win, but we must also be prepared to deal with failure as well, harsh as that sounds."

"Practicality. I agree. It's all Megan and I can do to care for the five. I'd like a life too," she hinted.

Cadfael grinned back. "Same here. But we can't, unless we solve this mess."

The next day, Cadfael and Eirwen drove two electric cars into Cairn Glen proper, bringing Morgana, Emlyn, Ceri, Lin, and Brynne with them. They went into a huge warehouse near the southern edge of the city where the team of "inventors" were waiting for them. Already, they had worked out various foot operated, automatic door openers, using footplates similar to those that Morgana had long ago had installed in her mansion. Additionally, Eirwen brought along one of the pony carts.

Soon, Emlyn and Morgana were demonstrating for the men and women. He pulled the cart, and she drove it, holding the reins in her teeth, and moving her head to either side, causing him to turn. This evoked many "bright ideas." Instead of a passenger, one man suggested a simple basket system so the person could pull cargo instead. They hooked both Ceri and Emlyn up to a pull-test machine to determine just how heavy a cargo a team of two could pull. Then, they hooked all five up as a team.

Finally, one explained, "Eureka! With a team of five, they could pull a plow and till the soil. With a team of two, they could transport cargo. Even one could pull a load of groceries from the warehouse to their destination building. Such things would take some of the pressure off of us normals."

"Yes, but someone will have to harness them up, load and unload the carts," another countered. "Wait, that could be their full-time job, deliverymen. They could be hooked up in the morning and undone at the end of the day, minimizing intervention on our part."

Another commented, "I'm truly amazed at just how well they are able to walk on their own! No one continually has to lend them a supporting arm. That alone is going to help us tremendously." The five did smile at the compliment, noticed by both Cadfael and Eirwen.

Thus, began the restructuring of Haffren-3 society. It started in Cairn Glen and slowly expanded outward, encompassing the whole planet by year's end. Ideas followed ideas, with many building off previous ones. One of the first changes was the removal of the highly restrictive corsets. Now almost no one fainted from lack of breath, but they had to endure the back pains from their monstrous bosoms. In time, they found their backs strengthened sufficiently to support the extra weight.

Yoke carrying baskets were invented, allowing them to carry all manner of things in a pair of weight-balanced baskets. Jobs were plentiful for the new transporters and deliverymen. Additionally, teams of five began to be used to work the land, producing organically grown vegetables. This freed a number of normal men and women to run the giant machines that farmed vast tracts of land, producing their staple crops.

They repackaged foods into formats that the victims

could manage to handle. Pre-cooked steaks, for example, were pureed and poured into bottles that had nipples that could be easily bitten off, thereby opening the sealed bottle. Via a straw, the person could then eat their liquefied steak. Plus, by using their noses to push the buttons, the victims were able to use a microwave to warm things up.

Still, the victims had to be housed in large groups, where a normal person, usually a woman, would dress them in the mornings and undress them at night. The problem of dressing and tying up their ankle-length hair remained unsolved as yet. Men and women all wore very short dresses so that they would go to the bathroom without help, in most cases. It wasn't perfected yet, but for sure, life was becoming more bearable for the many victims, who felt some pride in that they were finding ways to contribute to the survival of everyone.

Thus, the situation on Haffren-3 changed dramatically, some claim for the better. Certainly, the many centuries of sex trade had completely ended. Others claimed that necessity lay behind the changes. None can seriously doubt the role that necessity played. This marked the first time that planetary genocide was avoided, for the most part.

Vic Broquard

Chapter 22 The Juno-3 Solution

Necessity. That's how President Fishwaters II presented his solution to the almost unconfrontable problem on Juno-3, a bluish planet just barely in the outer rim of the Imperium Arm of the galaxy. It was an ocean planet with only two large landmasses, one located in the north temperate hemisphere, one located on the opposite side in the south temperate hemisphere — North Juno and South Juno respectively. He resided in the capital city of North Waters, North Juno.

Because of its mild climate nearly everywhere on the land masses, Juno-3 had long been the retirement planet of choice. It was a magnet for retirement-aged couples, who flocked to this nearly perfect-weather planet. Before the invasion of the terrorist victims, these older men and women accounted for one quarter of their normal population, who supplied nearly a third of the Gross Income of Juno-3! But that was before, not the present.

Juno-3 had developed extensive assisted living complexes scattered across both hemispheres. These facilities used to provide stable employment for a flotilla of CNAs, that is, Certified Nurse's Assistants, who cared for the needs of these wealthy elderly. Then, they had accepted many terrorist victims, usually wealthy and who could pay well for their intensive care while they recovered from the attack, in so much as was possible. Then came the bad with the good; they had to accept three thousand criminals as well, who were kept in assisted living homes on South Juno.

Freaks. That was the common designation, although derogatory, the locals used for these many terrorist victims. Why? Because they had mutated into being hermaphrodites! Quickly, they had many children, with a birth rate more than double the normal inhabitants of Juno-3. Their genetic mutations carried over to their children and their children's children, each of which was wholly dependent on nearly constant care. By 1326, Juno-3 had nearly three million of these freaks to care for in their facilities.

472

This was the massive problem facing President Fishwaters II. Vast, vast over population of freaks. In order to care for the nearly constant needs of nearly three million helpless people, nearly that many CNAs were needed, not to mention the flotilla of doctors and nurses. Even the support staff was enormous. So many mouths to feed, beds to change, laundry to do — mind boggling. Plus, the millions of babies and small infants, who required loving attention, gave rise to a new industry of Baby Care Givers, the cadre of BCGs.

At this date, all large buildings in South Juno had been turned into makeshift assisted living centers. Workers had been transferred from all types of jobs and hastily pressed into service in some form to assist the freaks. Finding a doctor on North Juno was darn near impossible, except for dire emergencies, when one would be flown up from South Juno. Most all commerce had come to a near standstill. Only food production continued, but at an escalating rate. The quiet, laid-back population had finally had enough. Last year, riots and protests had broken out all over North Juno. Some were actually calling for North Juno to secede from the government and form their own country, abandoning South Juno to its fate. While that had not happened yet, talk about doing just that was now rampant. At least the mad bombers had now eliminated all of the criminals who were being housed in South Juno assisted living complexes.

President Fishwaters II finally hit upon a workable plan and by early 1326, it was beginning to work and work well. One problem faced on all worlds was that of finding babies and young children to be adopted. Always, there were families, who for one reason or another, needed to adopt children. In fact, baby adoption was a big business, though one which few ever discussed, openly at least. The going rate for a normal, healthy baby was close to sixty thousand credits.

His plan was the essence of simplicity: sell mutant babies at a very low cost of a thousand credits. This way, families, who could not afford the exorbitantly priced normal babies, could easily afford a child. At least, he ensured that each baby sold had as many cheap genetic cures applied as possible. That is, their hair would not contain the terrible pain neurons, their bosoms would not become basketball-sized when they matured, their lips were repaired, and their feet partially repaired so that they could wear normal six inch heels and not the debilitating toe shoes when they grew up.

By 1326, the baby business was booming, particularly so because little was done in the way of "background checks" of the prospective parents. At only a grand per child, why waste good money on such things? Here in January, nearly sixty thousand babies had been placed in new homes, all off-world — that being the only stipulation behind the adoptions. His solution looked very promising, even more so with the meeting he was about to attend.

A dozen adoption agencies from ten other worlds had requested an official meeting with him and he'd consented. They entered his spacious meeting room, very business-like, depositing their briefcases on the floor and setting up their laptops. President Fishwaters II was terrible with names. Afterwards, he couldn't recall who was who at the meeting. Instead, he always labeled them Man A, Man B, Woman C, and so on.

Woman A opened the meeting. "President, your idea of making readily affordable babies for adoption is groundbreaking. So many families, who were priced out of the market, can now afford to adopt. That's why we are here."

"Yes," the president replied, "it gives the babies a loving home, something we cannot provide here. Honestly, assisted living homes are not conducive to child rearing. Babies need a loving family." He continued to spout his selling points, now well memorized.

"Indeed," Man B spoke up. "That's why we have requested this meeting. I believe we may be able to assist in this adoption process of yours, rather significantly."

"How so?" he asked.

Man C replied, "We represent some of the larger adoption agencies of the Imperium. It's our business to place babies with loving families."

"Precisely so," Woman D broke in. "We would like to act as your go-between, streamlining both of our operations. You sell the babies to our agencies, and we then handle getting them proper homes." She didn't specify what a proper home was, however, and the president didn't inquire.

"Yes, that would save you considerably. Your people would not have to deal with all the paperwork, the finding, and delivery of the babies to their new parents. That's our job," Man A added.

President Fishwaters II asked, "So how would this work? How many babies are we talking about? We have quite a lot here."

Woman A answered, though looking briefly at the other eleven. "Each of us are prepared to accept batches of a hundred babies each month, if you have that many. We pay you nine hundred credits per child; that way, we can charge the one thousand credits, recouping our expenses as well. You can save that much by not having to do all the work that we do. You simply sell them to us, and we resell them to loving families."

While he was terrible with names, he was good at arithmetic. Twelve hundred babies per month substantially exceeded the numbers that his people were selling. Besides, this amounted to over fourteen thousand babies sold per year. Their current rate was barely five thousand sold per year, ignoring all of the Imperium red tape that was involved.

"Yes, that sounds like a most workable plan, but what about the older children, say in the ages of two years to six?" he asked, hoping to make an even better deal.

Man B replied, "Well, we could accept some of those as well, perhaps say fifty per month? As you probably know, older children are in far less a demand, though there is some."

Woman E added, "But of course, it goes without saying that all of them must have their basic genetic cures. If not, we'd have to pay significantly less per child to cover giving them such treatments."

"Yes, yes, of course," President Fishwaters II replied hastily. "I believe that we have a deal, ladies, gentlemen. How soon can we implement this?"

"Yet today," Woman A replied, a coy smile appearing on her cherry red lips.

"Excellent, excellent. Let's get this done!" President

Fishwaters II effused.

By the end of 1326, over thirty thousand babies had left Juno-3. Other adoption agencies wanted in on the deal. Further, nearly that many older children left for new homes as well. That first year, his grand plan had reduced the freak population by a whopping four percent. In fact, that rate would continue yearly for several more years, until only the older freaks remained, numbering approximately a million. As far as he was concerned, the massive overpopulation problem was solved, especially as some of the older freaks died off. He was quite pleased with his solution. He never once followed up to see how the children fared in their new homes with their new parents. It was none of his concern, or so he told himself.

In actual fact, these agencies also didn't follow up on these cheap babies, either. While they did so for those that sold for sixty thousand credits, a child sold for a grand wasn't worth the expense of a follow up. While some of these children did end up in loving families scattered throughout the inhabited planets of the vast Imperium, many did not.

Some of the adopting parents decided the constant care and needs of their special child was just too much or too expensive for them to handle. Their children subsequently perished from a variety of causes; a nasty fall was the most common cause of death. Others ended up in the illegal sex trade market, resold to unscrupulous men and women. Even worse, some were forced into the illegal stem cell market. Here, they were kept continually pregnant and harvested for stem cells, before the fetus was destroyed and the process repeated until the person died. With all the arm regrowing that was needed, the market for pure stem cells from embryos was enormous. Vast fortunes were made during these ensuing years.

Before the year ended, many other worlds, that had a similar problem of excessive numbers of terrorist victims and their children, followed the lead of Juno-3. This was allowed to happen primarily because the Imperium simply wasn't functioning much at all just yet. There were just too many problems inherent in repopulating Proxima Prime and reestablishing the ruling bodies, to say nothing of providing the necessary support personnel for these leaders.

On many of the hub worlds, the various religious groups began singing the same song. They considered these hermaphrodite terrorist victims to now be either evil or somehow in league with the devil or the negative afterlife. For sure, they were seen as being somehow "not human" any longer. While they stopped short of inciting their members to murder the freaks, they began to preach the notion of sending all the freaks to their own world, where they could live their own lives, segregated from normal human beings. Many rulers were forced to consider such notions, but considering they were nearly helpless people, they did not act on this suggestion. Besides, just as soon as the Senate and the Legates were back in operation, they anticipated each victim would be receiving a huge monetary compensation from the assets of the destroyed worlds of Aquila Prime, Proxima Prime, and the Big Five worlds.

However, on Juno-3, an inventor, fifty year old Professor Arnold Baxby, began to have his own ideas about these helpless victims. He liked the notion his church was suggesting, namely sending these hermaphrodite freaks off to their own world. He reasoned that in order for this to occur, machines would have to be constructed that they could operate in some manner to compensate for their lack of arms and for their poor walking abilities. "What they need is a personal robot assistant to help them with their many needs," he explained to his pet cat. She only meowed. "Look, we have several ideal worlds now where they could just be moved to, complete with all the needed infrastructure, like Zelan-3 or Beta Carnae-4. Now, if they had a mechanical assistant, they'd be able to survive just fine." Meow.

Already most all factories had robots working in them, albeit they were primitive and more like robotic arms, wholly immobile. If they could be given propulsion methods and better programming, he reasoned the project was doable. He spent most of the latter months of 1326 developing a crude prototype. In January, he was able to obtain a meeting with

President Fishwaters II.

After making his presentation, he added, "You see, it is entirely feasible. If I'm given sufficient funds, time, materials, and help, why, we can make robots smart enough to handle the needs of the victims. We could establish a hermaphrodite world on say the vacated Zelan-3, where everything they need to thrive is already in existence."

"Brilliant Professor Baxby, positively brilliant!" the President exclaimed. "This is the best idea yet. We must make it happen and as swiftly as possible. This is the answer that I've long sought. We're expecting to begin receiving vast funds from all the settlements, just as soon as the Senate and Legates work out the accounting. Anything you need to make this happen will be yours!"

True to his word, President Fishwaters II set up Professor Baxby in the best laboratory on North Juno. His funds seemed unlimited, or so the professor imagined. Within a week, he had dozens of design engineers and computer programmers in his employ. For a month, ideas flew back and forth among these fifty bright minds, all guided by the professor.

A gyroscope in the chest of the robot was used to keep the robot oriented to its environment at all times. Their greatest challenge was providing for legs that emulated those of a human. Their arms were already a solved problem; they simply scaled down the robotic arms used in factories. They would be powered by rechargeable batteries that could be plugged into any power outlet found anywhere on an Imperium planet.

The biggest challenge was programming the robots to deal with what the victims would be needing in the way of assistance. This broke down into first working out just what those actions would be. They brought in some of the CNAs to explain in detail what all they had to do for the victims. Dressing, undressing, feeding, bathing, and dealing with their long hair were at the top of their list. That was followed by mundane actions, such as meal preparation and cleanup, changing beds, and washing clothes. Following that, rooms had to be vacuumed and dusted. Food supplies had to be purchased, as well as replacement clothing and shoes from time to time.

Then, they realized other actions were needed. Doors had to be opened. Arms had to steady the people when they walked. Comm centers needed to be controlled. All manner of equipment had to be controlled, from the giant farming machines, to the food preparation and packaging machines, to the delivery methods. What started out as a simple idea or notion quickly turned into a nightmare of complexity.

That's when Professor Baxby had his brilliant insight. "Look, we need to create specialized robots. All of the robots must be voice activated. We have personal hygiene robots. Food preparation robots that cook, serve the meals, and then clean up when it's done. We have a special robot to dress and undress the person. We have a special robot that handles controlling the farming machines. We can have a special robot that merely opens and closes doors." His idea mushroomed at once. Only the walking robots, the ones that supported the victims while they walked, needed the complex legs. The others could move around by more appropriate means.

Considering that those who they were to be assisting were mostly completely helpless, the computer programmers decided to install a hierarchy of rules that each robot would have to follow, the most fundamental rules. First, a robot was forbidden to ever harm a human. Second, a robot was always to obey a human's orders, subject to the first rule. Third, a robot was never to allow harm to come to itself, subject to the first two rules. These seemed like a most sensible set of underlying rules that would safeguard both the helpless humans and subsequently the machines themselves.

In March of 1237, the reconstituted Imperium Senate finally had a quorum and met. Shortly after this, President Fishwaters II and Professor Arnold Baxby appeared before the full Senate and presented their grand plan for establishing a hermaphrodite world on Zelan-3. Quickly, the Senate decided to make use of Aquila Prime and not Zelan-3, because Zelan-3 had tremendous mineral resources that many companies wanted to mine.

Because so many worlds had the same problem of

overpopulation of these victims and their offspring, the Senate approved the plan, but made one further stipulation. They had to include medical facilities to regrow their arms. While everyone knew such a process would take a very long time to handle everyone, they knew the victims would never agree to the project unless this was promised to them. Further, it solved the latest problem of parents complaining bitterly about having their young children taken away from them and put up for adoption. Families would no longer be broken up. However, the Senate insisted no hermaphrodite be sent to this world unless they chose to go there of their own free will.

With the modifications, the Senate passed the proposal unanimously. No one heeded Ashford-5's new Senator Ruthy Agahve-Jones, who cautioned them all, "We should beware that the solution to today's problem will become tomorrow's problem." Footnote: her mate, Ambassador Lela, was already exploring the historical archives, amassing volumes of information towards her goal of providing a book on the history of the Imperium.

With the infusion of the Senate's vast appropriations for the project along with nearly unlimited physical resources, Professor Baxby's project became a reality within a year. All of the worlds, which had accepted terrorist victims and criminals, had a stake in lending their full support behind the project. Admittedly, the first generation of the robots were pretty crude, but they did fulfill their missions.

On Juno-3, the first phase involved getting the initial one thousand migrating victims used to commanding the robots that would be providing their means of survival. Commands had to be spoken in IS, slowly and clearly. At the first session where the men, women, and children were being paired with their own personal dressing-undressing robots, Professor Baxby explained, "In time, your personal robots will learn to understand your speech better and better. Think of it as a stranger, who over time, gets to know you. Commit these commands to memory and say them slowly to the robots. Okay, let's try it again." As he watched the awkward contortions of both humans and machines, the professor was pleased that at least the process worked. The victims were being undressed and then properly dressed.

A month later, the first of the new inhabitants of Aquila Prime and their robots arrived at their ghost city, now renamed New Hope. Once home to nearly ten million, New Hope now housed the first one thousand terrorist victims and their many robots. Simultaneously, a ground crew accompanied them, setting up the farming robots and later the production robots. Within another month, crops were growing, and the food preparation robots and machinery were in full operation. This allowed the second one thousand to arrive. So it went. By the end of 1328, Juno-3 no longer had any terrorist victims or criminals living in any of their assisted living complexes! New Hope, Aquila Prime, now had around two million inhabitants, who depended utterly upon their many new robots. Only a tiny minority of them had already had their arms regrown.

Meanwhile, the other hub worlds, which had vast numbers of the victims in their assisted living facilities, followed Juno-3's lead. New Life, Second Chance, New Haven, Sanctuary, and Retreat were christened and rapidly populated with their terrorist victims and newly constructed robots. By 1330, the estimated population of Aquila Prime was twelve million. Only a few wealthy or nobles who had been terrorist victims remained on their home worlds. Countless assisted living facilities on the major hub worlds finally returned to handling the aged, for which they had been originally founded.

In 1330, the Imperium Senate formally recognized Aquila Prime's first senator, giving the world their place in the governing body of the vast Imperium. Finally, the dissensions and ill-will evaporated from the many hub worlds, and some semblance of stability finally returned to the Imperium. Still, the Imperium was on a very shaky footing.

Chapter 23 The Return of the COG

Late summer of 1326 and just as the many baby births had ended, Bishop Hector Smith decided to make his move. He paid a visit to Rafe, that is, Rafaela Gervasi-Jones. She and Rupert had just given birth to their new daughters, Adora and Aleta, both of whom were now three months old. "I'll watch the babies, dear," Rupert volunteered and carried the pair into their children's bedroom, leaving the two to the comforts of their spacious living room here in the Imperial Castle.

"Have a seat, Bishop Hector," Rafe said politely, sizing up this Church of God leader. He was in his mid-thirties and spoke with the Midlands dialect. Rafe knew that centuries ago, the COG had been responsible for the persecution of the witches and had played a role with the initial Rigel-3 spaceport personnel, a role that had ended in the massive explosion which had forever altered the climate of Tierra. Civilization had been close to extinction, but with the beginnings of the *mentales* gifts that followed, total disaster had been averted. The Great Climate Change had turned their verdant jungle country and spiritual center of their church into an uninhabitable desert. After that disaster, the COG lost nearly all of its power, existing down through the ensuing centuries as merely priests who were authorized to marry couples. Their churches were all quite tiny with very few parishioners. Hence, she was somewhat curious about the purpose of Exchange City's bishop. She also knew that thanks to the archaeological work of Elfe, an original copy of their Holy Book had been found. Recently, Nadja had published a translation of the work, primarily for historical reasons.

"Thank you for seeing me, Rafe. I wanted to talk to you about religion and this Basic Therapy of yours, if you don't mind," Bishop Hector began, somewhat unsure of just how to proceed. He had no *mentales* gifts, but knew from her eyes that she did. That also added to his discomfort. "I've been doing some extensive research. I have already thanked Nadja and Elfe profusely for having found and preserved our original

Holy Book, which has been lost to us for centuries."

"Yes, that was quite a find. What is the nature of your research, if I may be so bold to ask?" Rafe asked politely. While she could just probe his mind, her sense of ethics prohibited such. He seemed honest and sincere enough; she didn't anticipate or sense any hostility towards her.

"Spiritual beings. You see, these past few years, I've been interviewing many here in Exchange City and up in Brom — men and women who have had your Basic Therapy. So many have discovered their basic nature as spiritual beings. They refer to such things as past lives that they've lived here on Tierra. I find that they are most sincere in their belief of their immortality as a spiritual being," he explained carefully. "Mind you, I've not had this Basic Therapy, but I've kept an open mind while doing my researches, you see. I doubt them not. Indeed, that we are all immortal spiritual beings is a fundamental belief of our church."

"Yes, many do discover their basic natures while in therapy sessions," Rafe replied, in a rather non-committal manner. What did he want?

"I've also spent my life researching the ancient penta-pantheon of gods on Tierra. Perhaps you have heard of them? There were five all told. Lysandra was the Goddess of Life and of Death, Ariana was the Goddess of Fertility."

"Yes, I am very familiar with them," she admitted.

"Ah, good. I'm quite convinced that at some points in our history, they were and are today quite real. I believe they are spiritual beings, like ourselves, but somehow far more powerful, capable of operating without the need of our fleshly bodies. Further, I believe they are our Guardian Angels sent by our Creator, God, to watch over us."

"I see. That makes sense," she replied, wondering where all this was headed.

"You see, everything is falling into place. The COG believes that we are all immortal spiritual beings. Our goals are to help everyone realize this fundamental truth and to help guide them on the path that leads them towards becoming worthy of God and his Holy Grace. Indeed, I must say the majority of our few local parishioners have all come to the

COG after having had your Basic Therapy. They come in search of ways to live better lives. That's what sparked my researches some years ago."

He continued, "In the recent past, our priests were only able to provide guidance in the form of the Holy Commandments, the tenants of our faith. I hesitate to use the terms good and evil, for I truly believe those terms are relative ones, based upon the society in which one lives. Rather, I would speak of guidelines, such as these. Do not kill other humans. Honor your parents. Treat others, as you would have them treat you. I've been working hard to put these ancient commandments into modern words, easily communicated to the parishioners. I've tried to keep the 'do not's' balance with the 'do's.' In this way, those, who have not had this Basic Therapy, can understand the proper conduct that will help keep them from straying afield."

"Yes, those would be ideal codes of conduct," she replied, still in mystery about his purpose.

"Yet, times are changing, as are the attitudes of many. Here in Exchange City, we now have a rather large number of strange, new body forms, the hermaphrodites. Please, I mean you no offense. I see these as merely another form of physical body for us spiritual beings to inhabit. Perhaps, it is God's will that men learn to share the gift of bringing forth new life unto the world. However, not everyone believes as I and the COG does. Hostilities are growing out beyond our city. Then, there is this incredible rise of the merchants and guilds. They've become the wealthiest men and women on Tierra and are running our kingdoms. All too often, I am seeing greed and envy taking root in some of their minds, overpowering their good sense. I fear if something doesn't help guide them on the proper path, soon, they will become tyrants, just as the ancient lords and kings and even our ancient COG bishops became centuries ago."

"Now, we are also seeing the revolutionary development of many fine inventions. Nadja's school has become the launching pad, I believe. Plus, so many of you have gone off-world and received an Imperium education that I can only wonder about. Changes, major changes are coming to our world. Already, the guilds are building these new river-powered sawmills and paper manufacturing plants. Soon, I've heard, a machine cheaply and rapidly to manufacture books will be made — all to allow rapid expansion of education to the children of Tierra. Change and innovation are upon us now. Yet, there is no one to provide proper guidance so we can remain firmly rooted to our spiritual natures."

"I know that you've been out there among the vast Imperium. Might I ask you, on those worlds, do they have great religions that provide for proper guidance so their people continue on paths of spiritual enlightenment?"

"The honest answer, Bishop Hector, is no. There are some religious institutions among the many worlds, but while some perhaps mean well, many are just as corrupt as everyone else is. It's sad," Rafe answered honestly.

"Then, it's as I feared. As Tierra becomes more and more modernized, our people will soon lose sight of their spiritual natures and become obsessed with material goods, just as the merchants and guilds are doing now." He sighed and took a deep breath.

Okay, I must do this, as the Goddess Lysandra has shown me. Bishop Hector prayed for a moment, and then looked up, looking Rafe squarely in her eyes. "I have come to suggest the COG, you, and your Basic Therapy givers join forces. Together, we can spread the word of God and deliver the therapy that will open their eyes to their true nature, and thus save our world and our people from going down the wrong path."

Rafe was not expecting anything like this! For a moment, she was speechless. Before she could even formulate any coherent reply, a yellowish glow began forming in the room. Rafe recognized it at once. "You didn't? Did you? Lysandra? Pray to her?" she gushed, but she already knew the answer. He had done just that. The shimmering form of Lysandra appeared before them both.

Although she seemed to speak, no words were physically spoken; the thoughts appeared in their minds. "Good to speak with you once again, Raffaella. Yes, Bishop Hector Smith has prayed long and hard to me for guidance.

Before I responded, and as you know it's rare indeed for me to respond to a male, I took a very close look at events unfolding here on Tierra. Bishop Hector is quite right to be so worried about the future direction events are leading the beings on our world. His proposal to unite the Church of God and your Basic Therapy has great merits. His visions of establishing great cathedrals across Tierra and using them to forward your Basic Therapy to large numbers of common people can happen. We are at a junction of many paths, all of which can be aligned towards this worthy purpose. I've come to you, Rafe, to ask that you consider his proposal. I truly believe this may be the route we've all been seeking for centuries."

"I have got a basic group of nearly five hundred therapy givers ready to go now," Rafe replied. "But you probably already know that. They are young, bright, and more than willing. I've just been unable to work out the best way to proceed. I'll consider his offer, Lysandra, but what is the price of this visit?"

Lysandra laughed, "For you, Rafe, none. Bishop Hector is willing to pay the price to make this happen. He is strong of faith and will, but he lacks the subjective reality that only Basic Therapy can give him."

"I'll see he gets his Basic Therapy at once," Rafe replied. "But what price is he to pay?" *You shouldn't have done this, Bishop. You could just as easily come to me.*

Once more Lysandra laughed. "Rafe, that was just what I was going to ask you to do. Give him his subjective reality on Basic Therapy immediately. His price is to get a subjective reality on the hermaphrodites so he can know both sides. Yet, I'll be merciful; he needs to be able to fulfill his role in this endeavor. Hence, he will be as your husband is. You'll need to help him once I'm gone. I give you both my blessing in this venture. Both Ariana and I hope it succeeds, and that is saying something. Goodbye Rafe. Keep up the excellent work. Oh, I nearly forgot. Rafe, Ariana wanted me to tell you to, and I quote, 'examine seeing something as it really is.'"

Her form slowly dissolved, leaving behind a yellowish afterglow, which then too faded away. Rafe stared at Bishop Hector, watching his body rapidly transform into that of a

486

hermaphrodite. "Oh my!" he exclaimed, awed by this visit by Lysandra, the second time he'd seen her. "Thank you, Rafe. Now, I've gone and done it this time. I've got to get out of these clothes fast!" His face turned beet red, but his rapidly swelling bosom and expanding hips left him little choice but to undress as rapidly as he could.

"Let me help, bishop," Rafe advised. Wisely, she left his underpants on, though they were now quite stretched. "You could have just come to me and discussed this."

"But I had to make sure you would truly consider my proposal. Centuries ago, the COG did despicable deeds and nearly destroyed our world," he explained.

Rafe sighed, "You are probably right, bishop. I would've had to think long and hard about this merger. Okay, let me get Rupert out here. He can help you with this."

"Thank you, Rafe. I would feel less embarrassed around another man, though as I understand it, there is now very little physical difference between you and Rupert."

Rafe smiled, "Yes, that's quite true. Rupert's a doctor. I'm going to have him also give you a checkup just to make sure all is well." She rose and headed into their children's bedroom. After quickly explaining to him what had happened, she took over watching the two infants, while Rupert joined Bishop Hector. She purposely didn't attempt to spy on them.

A few minutes later, Rupert called out, "Dear, I'm taking Bishop Hector over to Elegant Fashions Inc. Back in a while." She smiled. At least, the bishop was being spared the worst of what the many terrorist victims had endured and were enduring. While his body was now that of a hermaphrodite and had the usual massive size bosom, his feet, arms, and hair were unchanged. Regrowing arms would have caused a serious problem, because so many were still waiting patiently for that to happen. Further, she didn't have to bother the doctors with undoing the other smaller genetic changes.

An hour later, Bishop Hector and Rupert returned. He wore one of the new men's style suits, but with a priest's black shirt and white collar. However, there was no disguising his bosom, tiny waist, and wide hips. Still, she though, it could have been far worse for him. "Well, you look quite good,

Bishop Hector," she complimented the man. He had black hair. His face was rather square and plain, but his eyes were still as penetrating as they had been.

"Well, I feel very different, but yes, it could well have been far worse. Still, I'm elated that you are going to give my proposal serious consideration. I believe we can and must make a huge difference here on Tierra. I'll meet with one of your educated architects and see about getting the design of our first new Church of God done," he replied.

"First things first, Bishop Hector. We need to get you your Basic Therapy. The only requirements are that you've had enough sleep and nourishing food. I've asked Andres to deliver yours just as soon as you are ready," she countered.

Rupert took him off to the dining room, while Rafe waited for Andres to arrive. "Hi, is our patient ready?" Andres asked, walking into her living room. Both he and his wife Raffella had previously their arms regrown and now their feet finally fully repaired. Thus, he, too, looked more like a normal man once more. Hastily, Rafe explained what had just happened and what was needed.

"Lysandra again? So she thinks you should join forces with the COG? After all the damage that they did centuries ago?" he asked.

"She does, and I'm inclined to agree with her. This could well prove a very beneficial move, but I want to think on it more. Hector might be a tough case. Good luck with it," she responded.

Andres grinned, "Love a tough case."

An hour later and in a quiet, private room in the Imperial Castle, Andres began Hector's Basic Therapy. "But I've not got any real trauma, Andres. I've not even broken an arm. I admit having my body suddenly changed is a bit, shall we say, unnerving, but I've known this would be happening since I originally prayed to Lysandra, and she appeared to me. Maybe this isn't going to work."

Andres smiled, "That's good you haven't broken anything. How about strange feelings that you may have had?"

"Strange feelings?" Hector asked. "Well, come to think of it, I've always had this feeling I was immune to the cold and to fire. It's so silly, but when the snows come, I keep thinking I could walk out in it stark naked and not feel the cold. Silly, isn't it?"

"Good. Close your eyes. Okay. Now let's return to the last time you felt that way," Andres commanded. Hector was off and running. After running through several dozen, earlier and earlier such times he felt he could walk naked in the snow, Andres and Hector hit the crux of the matter. Andres had just asked him once more if there was something similar and earlier in time.

"Oh, I see white snow, a blue sky, and caverns. High in the Goza. Oh! Oh! My god! I was Brother Sheridan Abrams, the founder of Skylar Abbey! I got the *mentales* gift. I can control my body's reaction to both heat and cold! Archbishop Mata Hatta decreed we were all devil's spawn and had to be burned at the stake! I try to help others with their gifts. There I'm, tied to a stake, and they're tossing a torch into the kindling. The flames rise up, burning away my clothes and the ropes that are binding me! I walk away unharmed in the slightest. I see their shocked faces. I'm leading another fifty men out of the town. We go to the northern, desolate Goza and build Skylar Abbey. Oh god! I took no women with us. I'm responsible for the deaths of all my followers!"

Andres spoke softly, "I understand. Continue, please."

He went over the incident several times before realizing, "Well, that was a stupid thing to do! We're being persecuted and my solution is to simply retreat from the world! I took fifty others with me. We all died in total isolation, but at peace. Still, what a stupid thing to do. I should've done what Father Shane was suggesting, go down and convince Mata Hatta to change his decree. No wonder I feel like I can walk in the snow. Oh! Oh! I've lived before! I'm an immortal spiritual being! I really am! I really am. We all are. Oh my! This is so utterly real to me! Wow!"

"Very good. We're going to stop for today. Shall we resume first thing in the morning?" Andres said softly.

Hector was laughing, but he managed to agree. "I've truly lived before! Amazing. No wonder I'm so involved with getting the COG off onto the right foot these days. I've been trying to make amends for what I did centuries ago! Isn't that something, Andres? Thank you, thank you."

The next day, Hector ran out his birth and some prenatal traumas. Then, he ran into another lifetime where he's been one of the priestesses of Madiera, providing sanctuary for women in need at their hidden tower, not far from Adelmira Tower in Alba. "So that's how I knew all about the Goddess Lysandra! No wonder I knew I could call on her. Oh! No wonder she appeared to me and granted my wishes. She knew who I had been, one of her priestesses. Incredible, just incredible, Andres!"

The following day, Hector discovered just why he was so against wars and killing. He'd been a young man who had been conscripted by Damiano. He'd been forced to fight for the mad conqueror, but had died when the very earth had opened up and swallowed him and thousands of others, there on the plains near Wye. Once that was handled, Andres and Hector could find nothing else to handle, and Andres pronounced his Basic Therapy complete.

Next, Hector met with Backus Acronis, the civil engineer, and his wife, Aria, the Imperium historian. "I need a spectacular Church of God designed, one that uplifts all who enter it. It must be made from stone and positively huge. I want it to soar over all other buildings in Exchange City, calling everyone's attention to it, and to come to hear the Holy Word of God and get their Basic Therapy."

The two used their laptops to bring up many examples of modern churches within the Imperium. None satisfied him. Then, Aria brought up some ancient churches. "That's it! That's it!" Bishop Hector exclaimed. "Yes, the hundred foot tall vaulted ceilings. Wow! Yes, that's more like it."

Aria smiled, "How unusual. That's a very ancient type of Church found on a few rim worlds. It is called a Gothic Cathedral, but no one knows where that style originated from or even when. It's rather like an anomaly."

"It's perfect. The nave is fantastic," Bishop Hector exclaimed. The columns rise up towards the heavens, exploding in the six-part vaults. Ah, it has two aisles. Ah, the clerestory must have the stained glass windows, but the triforium should have plain windows to allow in as much light as possible. The choir needs to be well lighted. I want musicians and singers to perform for services."

"With so many windows and so little stone walls and columns that have to support the weight of the stone vaults, buckling will be a major problem," Backus countered.

"So how do we fix that?" the bishop asked.

"With buttresses on the outside."

"Make it so. And the apse should be rounded and filled with stained glass windows," the bishop declared, growing more and more enthused with this design. "The front facade should be equally impressive, say with two tall towers on either side, a giant set of doors for the entrance to the nave and two smaller sets for the aisle entrances. Let's have enormous bells in each tower to call everyone to the services. Now, we also need an attached rectory building with many small, private rooms where Basic Therapy can be delivered and with living quarters for the therapy givers, the pastors, and staff to live."

"This is going to be quite a project," Backus replied, a broad grin on his face.

"Indeed. We'll call this first church Saint Shane's," Bishop Hector pronounced with some finality. "Get me the designs, and I'll get the stone workers going on it. Once we have this church finished, I'll need many more designed for all the other large cities on Tierra. I think I'm going to keep you very busy, Backus."

"Busy on something truly worthwhile," Backus replied, catching the bishop's enthusiasm for the project. It took him until spring to get the detailed plans drawn up to his satisfaction. Once the snows melted, many guilds around Exchange City donated their *mentales* gifted to handle the construction, along with the Imperial Tower's many Circles. Rafe was quite impressed with how well Bishop Hector was able to get the many guilds to cooperate on this enormous project. With all the concentrated workforce, Saint Shane's was completed in late 1328. The massive amount of interior decoration would take another five years to complete.

The day the last part of the flat top roof was installed

covering the stone vaults, Bishop Hector led Rafe into the church through the massive nave doors for the first time. While she'd taken peeks before, now she walked in as though she was seeing it for the first time. The sheer height of the six sided vaults a hundred feet overhead took her breath away. *My god, I'm moving out of my body!* Indeed, Rafe was literally pulled out of it by the enormous space of the new cathedral. This alone will help others know their true spiritual nature, she thought.

"Bishop, where did all the money come from to build this magnificent cathedral?" Rafe asked, still in awe with its splendor.

"Ah, I've sold various niches and walls to the many guilds. They, in turn, will be providing the decoration for their areas in any manner of their choosing. Each one will be trying to outdo the other, unless I'm terribly mistaken. Everyone wants a part of the action on this church. However, you and I will deal with just how the High Altar and the apse should be decorated. The Musician's Guild has been preparing both vocal and instrumental music to be performed from the choirs," he replied.

Then, he added, "I hope you have your fifty therapy givers and their families ready to move in. The rectory is done and ready for occupancy. Our first service will be on Sunday. The Wood Workers Guild has promised me the many pews will be ready by then. I have invited Queen Amy and Governor Katrina, and asked them to bring any and all they know who want to come. We may have a full house on Sunday; it can hold a thousand at one time, at least in the pews. Standing room only, after that," he added.

"Say, what's going onto those tall niches on either side of the apse entrance?" Rafe asked.

Bishop Hector grinned, "I've commissioned five bronze statues, one of each of our five angels. The Goddess Lysandra will have the most prominent location there, just above the High Altar. After all, she inspired all this and made it come about. I've worked with an artist to draw up a likeness of her. I wish I knew what the others look like."

"Well, I think Queen Amy can give you a description of

Ariana. Don't know about the others, though."

"She can? Great! I'll go bother her yet today," he gushed.

Sunday morning was quite an experience for a great many, particularly so for many who had finished their Basic Therapy. Queen Amy and Governor Katrina led their very large group into the nave. Musicians were playing high above them and from both sides of the choir loft. The echoes and acoustics were indescribable. Combined with the enormous sweep of space above them, Amy felt a flood of emotions and slipped out of her body, just as many who had had Basic Therapy did when they entered this enormous cathedral. Somehow, this space, this design inspired a rush of spirituality or holiness, as many claimed.

A large number of guild masters were already seated in the front rows of the pews, the seats of highest honor. Rightly so, Rafe thought, for they'd helped finance and build this incredible building. No one spoke. Even if Amy had wanted to say something, her voice simply didn't work. She sensed the many other beings around her, all in utter awe. She and Jan took seats in the front of the nave, just behind the elegantly dressed guild masters. Even Jan sensed the sheer number of others filing in behind them, as well as on both smaller aisles to their right and left.

Many eyes gazed up and around at the incredible sights. As Bishop Hector walked slowly to the high altar, Katrina noted that every seat was taken and hundreds more were standing. Now the special music ended. High above them in the right side choir loft, a lone high soprano began singing another piece written especially for this dedication ceremony. Never had she heard such a sound, and her eyes watered. Goose bumps traveled up and down her body. Perhaps, the reaction was due to the incredible lighting that filled the enormous space, orange-red. Perhaps, it was the incredible beauty of the giant sets of stained glass windows behind the High Altar.

The stained glass held images of the new Holy Symbol of the Church of God: an orange-red sun shining down upon a field of men and women, each of which had a yellow circle around their body's head. That this was representing the immortal spiritual beings inhabiting the physical bodies was plainly evident. Nevertheless, the image communicated the concept with a high level of aesthetics.

When the solo soprano finished, Bishop Hector Smith began to speak. His bass voice carried throughout the entire church without any need for mechanical amplification or shouting. "Welcome one and all to the Dedication Service for Saint Shane's Basilica, the finest Church of God on Tierra and the new home of Basic Therapy. Thank you all for coming and sharing this monumental occasion with each of us present today. If you have not yet had your Basic Therapy, there is a sign-up sheet at the doors. Fifty volunteers are waiting to deliver it to you."

"We are here today to celebrate and rejoice in the immortal spiritual nature of all God's creatures. We, all we human beings, are more than these fleshly bodies with which we use in our day to day activities of life. Man as we know him is composed of three separate and distinct parts. We here have these physical bodies that age and will one day die. Often, too many of us see no farther than this, focusing our efforts and striving towards the body's comforts and accumulated wealth. Yet, man has two other parts, both of which are far, far more important. Man has a mind, a mind unlike all other creatures. With our minds, we can think; we can design and create such things as this magnificent church. Yet, also our minds record the traumas that we suffer, incidents and events that can thereafter adversely impact our thinking processes."

"Yet the most important part of man is ourselves, the personality, the I, the person who uses the mind and runs the physical body. We are immortal. We are spiritual beings and are not made of physical universe matter like our bodies are. Often I am asked who created us and the vast universe out there? The answer is simple. God. Lord God created the universe and our physical bodies. It is said that God created us in his image. Hence, we are like God, immortal beings. We are all basically good. Yet, the traumas we've endured sometimes force us down a path that some would call evil. Know this: it is the trauma that is causing the evil. Basic Therapy can wipe out that trauma and evil, allowing you to become free and good once more."

"For many months, I've heard others speak in hushed voices of the freaks that have come to Tierra in hopes of salvaging their lives. That they are abominations and should be killed or worse. They, like everyone else, are immortal spiritual beings inhabiting fleshly bodies, only their bodies are slightly different from what we are used to seeing. Worse, so many of them are terrorist attack victims themselves. Through no choice of their own, their bodies were mutated into what they are today. Condemn not those whose bodies are different from yours. It's just the fleshly form that is different. Minds and spirits are the same as yours; perhaps they are even stronger than you are, considering what they've endured and are yet still here."

"Some have said the aliens are not true people, that they are somehow inherently different than us, that they are evil and have goals to destroy us all. Again, that is pure folly. We've seen Tierra men who have very nearly destroyed us all, such men as Damiano the Conqueror. In any society, Tierra or Imperium, there are good men and evil men. Yet, we know the evil men are only acting that way because of severe trauma they've endured in their past. If that trauma can be faced, confronted, the good returns, and the evil is forever destroyed."

"So what must each and every one of us do? What must we strive for in our everyday lives? Oh, I can stand up here and give you long lists of things to do and things to avoid doing. I know in the past, I have done just that. But no more. Just as we are dedicating this new church, I too am following a new path. I'm not going to tell you what is right, what is wrong. Rather, I'll give you a rule you can apply to your everyday lives. I know in the past, I too have been guilty of doing just that, spouting rules such as thou shalt not kill your fellow man. I've grown up, spiritually. I now see how wrong I was in spouting such platitudes, useless sayings that cannot be followed."

"Consider the mass murder, this Damiano, the conqueror. His actions, his orders directly killed untold thousands of men, women, and children throughout the

Easterlings and central Midlands as well. He had to be stopped. If he had not been killed, our whole world would have likely perished. So you will hear no more of these platitudes from me."

"My own Basic Therapy has shown me what I knew instinctively, but had never put into words before. All men, be they of Tierra or aliens or even the hermaphrodites, all men are trying to survive, to flourish and prosper. Yet, this survival is directed down a number of different avenues. First, we're all striving to survive and do well for our own selves. Second, we're all striving to survive and prosper through our marital partners and our children. Third, we're surviving as various groups, such as the Stone Mason's Guild and the Dressmaker's Guild. Fourth, we wish to survive as a human species and not succumb to the Montaña Beasts, for example. Fifth, we need the plants and animals of the world to flourish and prosper as well, for if they do not, so do we then perish, for we are dependent upon them. Sixth, we need the physical universe around us to continue to survive well. We still suffer from the Great Climate Change that happened centuries ago, which should serve as a wake-up call to us all. Seventh, we're all immortal spiritual beings, and as such, we need to continue to survive and become free and self-determined."

"What has all this to do with us? Simple. The rule that I wish to leave you with today is this. Do those actions, which benefit and aid more of these seven avenues, and which harms the least of them. Use this as your measure of right and wrong conduct." He then gave a series of examples, beginning with that of Damiano, the Conqueror. He pointed out how cheating on your marital partner harmed more of the avenues than it helped and was thus a wrong action to do. In particular, Governor Katrina noted he spoke in ordinary ways, quite unlike the often archaic language other religious leaders used on other worlds within the Imperium. He talks to the ordinary man, she thought.

After these examples, he continued, "Now why is this so important? Why is it we must strive to do the optimum actions in our lives? Our own spiritual freedom is what's at stake. Long ago, we were made in God's Holy Image, free spiritual beings able to live life without the remotest need for these physical shells, these short-lived bodies of ours. Then, we did things we should not have done. Since we are all God's Children, we are inherently good. Seeing we've just done wrong actions, we restrain ourselves from doing such things again. Action by action, we limited our ability to act, to do, out of distrust of our own selves. Down, down, down, we spiraled, until now we can only do and act by using a physical body. Yet still, we continue to do actions that we should not do, and we find ourselves, having forgotten who and what we really are. We believe we are this body, having forgotten that we once were just using it, as a child might use a doll. Thus, we are doomed to continue this seemingly endless cycle of living one lifetime as a body, only upon its death, to grab the next baby body we can find. Over and over and over."

"It is long past time we reverse this deadly spiral. By applying this rule to your lives, you will be helping yourself stop this downward spiral and begin to reverse your decline. With Basic Therapy and much hard work, you can be free once more to operate as you once did, free from the need to have a physical body, just as our Guardian Angels are doing yet today."

"Guardian Angels, you ask? Yes, they have been here for all our history. Yet, in these times, so very few of us have ever even detected their presence. I speak of the ancient Penta-pantheon. The Goddesses Lysandra and Ariana, of Wystan, Calder, and Alleric. Yes, they have always been around us, caring for us, and helping us survive. Some of you among us have had contact with one or more of them. They are very real, if only you open your senses. No, they are not to be worshiped, for they are not God himself, but like us, they are also God's Children, Children who have not fallen as low as we have."

"These five niches here to my sides will one day be filled with statues representing the created forms these five angels have taken when they appear to us. Only one is completed at this time. Here is the image of the Goddess Lysandra, as she recently appeared to me. She is very real and has shown me the powers that I once had, but have lost because of my own evil deeds, done over many, many lifetimes. Through my own

Basic Therapy, I have begun to undo them, regaining some of what I've lost. You can too. Follow that rule."

"So our goal is one that is worthy of us, we Holy Children. Strive in all ways to become a free spiritual being, as we all once were. There can be no loftier goal in this universe. This is what this new church, this Saint Shane's Basilica, stands for and works for. In time, we'll have new churches like ours in every large town across all Tierra. We will become free once more. We will rise to join the Penta-pantheon, once more taking our places as God's Children. Thank you."

As he spoke, Amy, Jan, and Katrina sensed the unseen presence of Lysandra and Ariana. As he spoke his last words, a bright, yellow glow appeared surrounding the giant bronze statue of Lysandra. The glow contrasted sharply with the soft, orange-red illumination from Ashford, whose rays entered from the giant, tall windows around the massive ceiling vaults. Gasps echoed throughout the church. Even Bishop Hector was humbled. Amy sensed that Lysandra was giving them all a sign that she approved of what was being done and said here today. She was lending a push in the right direction, she thought. Slowly, the glow diminished and then vanished.

As if this was an unspoken cue, the musicians began playing once more. Everyone rose and began inspecting the church while they slowly filed out. An hour later and finally outside, Amy saw that a huge crowd had gathered; they'd not been able to get inside. Bishop Hector had them lined up to attend a second service, just as soon as the original attendees had finished filing out.

Rafe was impressed with the entire experience. That no one was talking and that everyone seemed to be extremely serene as they left the church was not missed by her. Everyone who attended had been spiritually uplifted, no question of that. Later, she discovered that many had had the same experience as she had — having moved out of her body, rising some distance above the body's head — a further demonstration that each was an immortal spiritual being and not just a physical body. It was a most moving and convincing experience. *To be reminded each Sunday of just what we are is quite a powerful, moving, and important thing!*

Later, as the large group met in the Imperial Castle's Great Dining Hall for lunch, Governor Katrina told Rafe, "You know, that was humbling. I was out of my head almost from the moment I walked into the nave! Incredible. Perhaps the music had something to do with it."

"Was that really Lysandra there, making her statue glowing?" asked Doctor Whitney.

"Yes, I sensed Lysandra and Ariana both," Rafe answered. "I think they are sending me a very clear signal that we're on the right path." The table talk all centered on the incredible experience that most had just had.

Later in her bedroom while nursing her new daughter, Rafe began to ponder the message from Lysandra — to observe and see things just as they are. After burping Adora and then gently placing the sleeping baby into her crib, she sat down and laid the slightly messy, milk-stained rag on her table. She focused her full attention onto the rag, observing it in detail. Rupert joined her, having done the same with his daughter, Aleta. Silently, he studied his wife, not interrupting her.

The rag seemed to dissolve into a multitude of woof and warp threads, and then each of those into tiny particles strung together. Suddenly, the entire rag vanished from the table, rather startling Rafe. She looked up, "Rupert! The burp rag! It's vanished!" He looked, and for an instant, he didn't see it there either. Just as suddenly, the rag reappeared. "Oh! It's back," Rafe exclaimed. "How very interesting! Did you?"

"Yes, dear. For a moment, it was gone, but it's back now. What happened?" he asked, keenly interested in the most unusual phenomenon.

Rafe explained what she was doing and then tried it again. After some time, the rag vanished for her once more, and shortly after that, it disappeared for Rupert as well. Then, it reappeared. "How very interesting, Rupert! I think I know how my Basic Therapy actually works! By having the person repeatedly re-experiencing the trauma, they finally are able to see it exactly as it was or is. When they finally duplicate it, and that's the key word, Rupert, duplicate it exactly as it is, the trauma erases and become mundane memories with no further ability to harm the person. When I duplicate the rag exactly as it truly is, the rag vanishes, just as the traumatic incidents do. Amazing. This is extremely important, Rupert! This is the answer I've been searching for all this time — *why* it works. This opens up a whole new arena of therapy possibilities! Get the person to actually duplicate what he or she has done, and it will vanish."

"Hey, that would be a powerful thing to be able to do, love. I wonder if you can make burp stains go away without washing the rag. Now that would be useful. Aleta got me good this time," he chuckled.

"I wonder if that's possible. Let's see," Rafe replied, caught up in her own discovery. A half hour later, both looked closely at Adora's rag. The milk stains had indeed vanished without a trace. "Incredible. This, Rupert, is how Lysandra and Ariana do things, only they are so vastly more powerful than I am. I can only vanquish a milk stain, but we've seen what they can do. We are truly on the right path now! I've got vast amounts of work to do now, dear. This opens up a whole new avenue for Advanced Therapy!"

At suppertime, Maggie rushed up to her mother, Katrina, and gushed, "Mom! Guess what? I get to help make one of the giant new tapestries for the new church! Our whole guild has the commission to make five. I get to help!"

At the same time, her husband, Len, came up to his mother, Carla. "Mom, I get to help make some of the painting for our new church! The Painter's Guild is going all out on this project. I'm in the big leagues now, mom!"

Katrina and Carla looked at each other and then their two offspring. Both proud parents responded by heaping praises on their children. Their news was bandied around the giant dining hall. Queen Amy sat back and began to think that perhaps a renaissance had finally come to Tierra. For once, the future looked incredibly hopeful.

Chapter 24 Changes Come

In March of 1327, the Imperium Senate finally had a quorum and met officially for the first time since the massive round of terrorist attacks. True, Proxima Prime was a mere shell of what it once had been, but daily more and more people were arriving, filling the millions of positions available. Legate Mary Smith walked onto the center platform to conduct their first meeting. As usual, she wore a white silk blouse, a black skirt, with matching nylons and the necessary tall heels. Her assistant walked beside her, ready to be her hands as needed. Already, the other Legates had returned, their bodies repaired, as much as was currently possible. However, they had decided to allow Legate Mary to officiate, because she alone had held things together all this time since the attack on Proxima Prime.

As she walked out before the fifteen hundred new senators, they rose and gave her a standing ovation for her selfish and tireless work. "Thank you. Thank you," Legate Mary repeated a number of times, before they ended their applause.

"Thank you. Okay, it's time for serious business. First, you must elect a new temporary President. Then, you must elect a new Senate President. Once that's done, I will turn the Senate over to your new Senate President. At that time, the other Legates are prepared to present many details for your considerations. So following protocol, the floor is open for your nominations for our new temporary President," she explained quite formally. *One more day and I can retire for a time!* Already, she had a deep space transport fueled and ready to take her to Ashford-5, where she would be able to get her own arms regrown, finally putting an end to her nearly continuous nightmare.

Someone quickly spoke up, "I nominate Legate Mary Smith." Another quickly seconded it.

Mary flushed. This, she was not expecting, but quickly saw the hands of H-cubed behind the move. Broon-5's senator made the nomination! Legate Helyeon H. Hoon obviously wanted her in this position, but why? Her mind raced, but she forced herself to reply, "Please, are there other nominations?" To her dismay, there wasn't and another senator called for a vote. She was elected unanimously, much to her consternation. This was not at all what she had envisioned for this day.

"Well, thank you all. I will endeavor to do my best. As I understand it, new Presidential Elections will be held during 1332. Okay then, I'll have to change my plans. Now, you must elect your new Senate President. At least, you can't elect me to that post," she jested, bringing numerous chuckles from the gallery of senators. Again, they had probably already worked this out in advance, she thought, because once more they nominated only one person and then voted him in. President Mary Smith then formally announced, "I give you Senate President Becktold Arnold of Bangor-3. Senate President, the floor is yours. The other Legates await your summons to present their extensive reports. Thank you all." She bowed and headed off the platform, shaking slightly.

Once in the long corridors heading for the exit, she whispered to Helene, "This is not at all how I expected this day would go. I guess my long awaited trip to Ashford-5 is going to have to wait even longer. Damn."

"I know. I'll cancel the transport for now, Madam President. It has a nice ring to it, doesn't it?" Helene replied.

As they reached the exit, a dozen armed Security Guards appeared. "Madam President, we're your escort now. You don't go anywhere without us. Your safety is our prime concern. To the Presidential Office?" he asked. She nodded, fighting from breaking down. She'd so hoped to have time off to actually recover from her own trauma, and at least get her arms back.

An hour later, she sat behind her new desk on the top floor. Sighing, she had Helene place a secure call to Emperor Kino. He had to hear this news at once. After outlining what had happened, Emperor Kino responded, "Congratulations, President Mary Smith. Actually, I do believe this is quite opportune to have you as our President just now. I'll provide you with all the support and aid possible. I'll have someone from Ashford-5 come to you to give you your Basic Therapy. Expect them within a few days. Perhaps, you'll be able to have someone on Proxima Prime restore your arms. Over."

Later, she thought long and hard about her first and most important duty. She had to find a replacement for herself, the Legate in charge of the entire ID Division. Her first thoughts were for Commander Torres, who had run the Bops here on Proxima Prime. However, she decided against her because the devastating attack on Proxima Prime had occurred on Torres' watch. She'd missed this one, and the Imperium very nearly collapsed as a result. She also realized the Imperium was still here primarily because of her own work, combined with Emperor Kino's.

This is a critical posting. I may well want to resume my Legate's job once my term is up. Yet, I must have someone on whom I can depend. Someone I can trust, but who? She pondered this long and hard. At last, she chose her second in command here in the Hub Sector, Martina Wells, a forty year old ID veteran. She summoned Martina to her office.

The next morning, Hub Sector ID Minister Martina Wells arrived at the Presidential Skyscraper. She'd taken a transport from her battleship to answer the summons. Her stilettos clicked on the steel floor as she entered and went to the bathroom. There, she touched up her minimal makeup, re-fluffed her long, wavy blonde hair, smoothed her black skirt. Satisfied, she headed out and for the elevators.

While she hated her new appearance, she was more than thankful that her home world of Descartes-3 had seen fit to rush her arm regrowth process. She too had been one of the Proxima Prime terrorist victims. While she had been able to take advantage of most all of the genetic cures currently available, from her point of view, she still had an overly large bosom and was still forced to wear the dismal lip plates. At least her feet had been partially restored, but she didn't like having to wear these impossibly tall stilettos. She marched as best she could manage into the Presidential Office.

"Hub Sector ID Minister Martina Wells, reporting as requested, Madam President," she said as clearly as possible in

IS, knowing well that her speech was hard to understand because of the lip plates. She was not surprised at the President's appearance, however. She saw an attractive woman in her thirties, dressed much as she. She also knew Mary had not yet had any time off to get her arms regrown or many of the other genetic cures. Martina respected Mary for this, rather immensely so, since Mary had worked tirelessly on behalf of the entire Imperium, holding it together all these months. That had helped her be able to take the time off to get her own arms regrown and to recover from the attack. However, as she saw her fellow Descartes-3 woman, her new hermaphrodite organ rose on its own. She was quite attracted to Mary, much to her instant embarrassment.

Mary saw the blonde woman, who looked much like herself. Once more, she too felt a strong attraction to the woman, but fortunately was sitting down at the moment, for which she was grateful. "Welcome ID Minister Martina. Thanks for coming on such short notice. Please, have a seat. You are looking very well."

"Thanks, Madam President. You look very good yourself. It's a shame that you've not been able to get your arms regrown yet. I know that you must be terribly disappointed. I know you've had to cancel your long planned trip to Ashford-5. The Senate ought to have given you time off to recover. I'm extremely grateful for all that you've done for us and the Imperium. Thanks to you, I was able to get myself recovered back home."

"Indeed, it came as a shock, but then I ought to have suspected H-cubed would have played a strong role in getting a new President installed," Mary replied, honestly. "This is my Personal Assistant, Helene. As you know, I'd be lost completely without my voice-activated laptop. Anyway, please, just call me Mary."

"H-cubed always does seem to have his hands in nearly everything," she jested. "Please, call me Martina."

"Okay, Martina. I need to fill my old Legate position. I want you to be our new Legate and Minister of ID. What say you?" Mary asked. "I need someone in this position on whom I can depend completely."

"What? Me? A Legate?" Martina exclaimed, quite shocked by Mary's announcement. "Surely, there are others more qualified than I am. Look, I had no advance warning about the terrible attack here on Proxima Prime. As Hub Sector ID Minister, I failed completely." She didn't add that billions died as a result.

"It's not your fault. The attack came from some disenfranchised locals. No one could have predicted they would have committed genocide. Besides, Martina, there is no other person in the ID divisions who I can trust fully. Right now, I need someone to watch my back. What say you? Are you up for the challenge?" Mary asked.

"Yes, I'm flattered and honored, Mary. I promise you that I'll do my very best to fill your shoes," Martina replied.

"Good. Then, I'll make your appointment official. Please, I would like you to make your office on the floor below mine. Let's stay in close contact. I'll feel like I'm naked, if I don't have instant access to all the incoming Intel. I've grown old surrounded by such."

Martina laughed, "I know what you mean. Little goes on around here without the ID Division hearing about it. Thanks for having confidence in me. I'll be your arms too when you need them, like Helene. It's the least I can do for you, Mary. Honestly, they ought to have allowed you time to recover, but I know, it takes three months, but even now my arms are still quite weak."

Is she giving me a subtle hint? "I'd like that, Martina. Say, I'm supposed to move into the Presidential Compound, but all that's there are tons of Security Guards. I'd feel a lot safer if you would move in there with me." *There, if she was hinting, maybe she'll notice this one. Why is my thing swelling up so? I'm sure glad she can't see the bulge.*

Is she hinting to me? "I'd love to, Mary. I'll have my things moved there today. I can cook, you know. How long has it been since you've had one of our native dishes?" *At least I'm sitting now, and she can't see my arousal. This's so utterly weird.*

Mary sighed. "Far, far too many years. I've not been to Descartes-3 in over two scores. You can cook every night, if you like. That would be wonderful, Martina. I'll see you around five. Perhaps, we can share a flight to the compound. Save a bit on Imperium expenses that way."

"Great. Yes, it'll save some expenses if we share. It's the very least I can do for you, Mary. Wonderful. Thanks for the promotion. I won't let you down."

"I know that you won't. Okay, I best get on with things here. See you at five." Martina rose and turned around hastily, trying hard to disguise her own arousal.

Turning to Helene, President Mary said, "Well, now I need to appoint some Presidential aides. Can you bring up the list of those who are applying?"

That evening, Martina fixed them a traditional Descartes meal, much to the delight of Mary. "That was indescribably delicious. How I've missed such meals," Mary exclaimed, quite stuffed. Helene was now spooning her coffee for her, but was interrupted by a knock on the door. Whomever it was, President Mary knew they had already gotten clearance from the Security Guards. Hence, she called out, "Come on in. I can't operate the doors."

To her surprise, in walked Senator Ruthy Agahve-Jones and her mate, Ambassador Lela. "Hello, come on it. Join us for some coffee? Have you eaten?" Mary asked. She didn't try to get up; that was difficult for her.

"Thanks. We've eaten, but we'll take coffee. Can't get it much at all on Ashford-5," Ruthy replied, pulling out a seat for Lela, helping her get seated, before sitting herself. Helene brought two more cups out and filled them.

"Hope you don't mind the blend; it's from our world, Descartes-3," Martina volunteered.

"Wow, it has an unusual taste. Like nuts?" Lela asked.

"Good observation. Yes, it has nuts added for flavor," Mary replied. "Martina is now my replacement. She's a Legate, Minister of the ID Division. I owe all this to her. She's somehow brought it from home. So what brings you to the Presidential Compound?"

"Ah, Emperor Kino, actually, kind of roundabout. You need your Basic Therapy. I know how disappointing it is for you. We had it all planned for you, back home. Still, I think we made the best possible choice for President right now. Anyway, rather than wasting time transporting a therapy giver from Ashford-5, Rafe called us up. She wants us to give you your therapy sessions right away. In the meantime, mom is sending along very detailed instructions on how to reprogram the medical machines to repair genetically more of the modifications. We should be able to help you get rid of the lip plates, reduce your breasts to our sizes, fix your hair, and even your feet. Say, Martina, you could use some of those too."

"Indeed. You can repair our lips and feet now? Amazing what your doctors are discovering on Ashford-5," Martina replied. "That would be wonderful. I hate these plates. But what is this Basic Therapy thing that everyone is so insistent Mary here have?"

Since they were already well fed and not really tired, the two began their therapy sessions that evening. While they would have preferred to work their magic all day long, they were constrained to evenings and weekends. It took nearly three weeks before Mary was finally pronounced complete on her Basic Therapy, though Martina finished many days before. She'd not had to suppress so much of her grief and had gotten her genetic repairs shortly after the attack.

"I feel so incredibly alive! So full of life! How can I ever thank you both?" Mary exclaimed, enthusiastically.

"Like I said, this is miracle therapy," Martina added once again. "I'm a new person, fresh and clean, and wholly alive."

"Just keep things going on an even keel," Senator Ruthy answered. "We're only too pleased to be able to give you the therapy similar to what was given to us. We win as much as you both win too, you know. Can't you see our smiles?" she teased them.

She added, "Tomorrow, we'll get the minor genetic changes done. Lela and I have gotten a medical machine reprogrammed, following mom's instructions. I hope it works okay."

It did. The next evening, both women's lips were repaired fully, as well as their feet. Further, Mary's monster bosom was reduced to the size of the others, and her hair was fully repaired. Finally, she could have it cut to whatever length she desired.

"Thank you, thank you. I feel wonderful now, and look so darn much better there's hardly words for it," Mary explained. "Say, can I ask you some really personal questions, about our reproductive systems?" she ventured. Martina looked on with keen interest.

"Sure. We've both had two children now," Ruthy replied.

"This is so embarrassing, but I'll ask anyway," Mary began, her face rather hot. "Before, I occasionally was aroused by a handsome man, though I never acted upon such things. No time for that. I'm always professional, you see. But now, I'm attracted to women too. It's so embarrassing. It seems to have a mind of its own." She hoped the two would catch her meaning without being more explicit.

Ruthy laughed. "Tell us about it! At least, we have an appreciation for the men's point of view now. Easy to rose, but so hard to get a woman to satisfy the need. Seriously, give it time, and you'll get used to it. Honestly, Lela and I get really turned on with each other. Being a hermaphrodite has its benefits. We have a wider field from which to find a mate. Besides, now the sex of our mate makes very little difference. But I will say that it's been a whole lot easier for us women to adjust to the change than the fellows. They're really having a very hard time adapting to being able to have babies. In their defense, I ought to add that they work very hard at being a good 'mother' to their babies. It's getting late; we best be going. How about we all get together for a card game or something on the weekend?"

That evening, the ice broke between Martina and Mary. Both were used to being the person in control of everything, and had been most all of their lives. Still, Martina was quite enchanted with Mary and made the first move. One passionate kiss was all that it took. Both women's new organs responded. "We've got to come to an agreement here," Mary insisted, as they headed for her bedroom. "I've got to be on top at least half of the time."

"So do I, dear," Martina replied with a wry smile.

In May 1327, Cadfael Wynn and his new wife, Countess Eirwen, nervously awaited in the wings for their appearance before the Imperium Senate. He held their prepared script in his hands. At last, they saw Senate President Becktold Arnold motioning to them. As they walked out before the mass of senators, Becktold announced, "Today, we are honored to have the new rulers of Haffren-3 paying us a visit. President Cadfael wishes to address the full Senate at this time. President," he motioned to the pair.

"Senators, I am President Cadfael Wynn, my wife, Countess Eirwen. We are here today representing our world of Haffren-3. As you probably know, our world has also seen an enormous upheaval, death, and destruction. Yet, we've managed to avoid the mass genocide that has attended other such worlds." He outlined their current situation, painting it in grim statistics.

He then got to their purpose. "We've come here today to obtain Senate permission to be allowed to join the Ataro Empire. As a world, we no longer able to maintain any security, let alone any effective commerce. We need quite a lot of assistance getting back on our feet. Emperor Kino Sango has kindly volunteered to assume this enormous responsibility to help Haffren-3, even though our demented rulers attempted to commit genocide on one of his worlds. We've asked several other worlds for help, but have been turned down. We are truly desperate. We also know our request to join his empire can be viewed as a power grab by other worlds, but we are here to assure you that is not the case here. We are desperate for assistance. Ninety percent of our population is terrorist attack victims. We few normals left simply cannot handle everything by ourselves. We need help, and Emperor Kino has agreed to provide it. Since we don't even have a senator here anymore, I've come to you directly to ask for your permission to join the Ataro Empire. What do I need to do now?" He fumbled, uncertain of just what he should next do or say.

President Becktold walked back before the senators and took over. "We have heard this motion from Haffren-3. Is there any debate before us?" There wasn't. None of the major worlds wanted anything to do with Haffren-3, not since their Great Upheaval. He then called for a vote and it passed. "Officially, President Wynn, you have the Imperium Senate's approval to join the Ataro Empire. Good luck with that." The two took that as a sign of dismissal and headed off stage. Once out of sight, Cadfael punched his hand in the air, a sign of victory.

Later that week, Haffren-3 became the thirty-eighth world in the Ataro Empire. Queen Calandra was sent there as their official queen. She took up residence in some first floor rooms of Chaos Manor, compliments of the Wynn's.

A year later, the thirty-ninth world was added to the Ataro Empire. Aquila Prime, home to millions of victims whose survival depended utterly on their many new robots, petitioned to join as well. True, Emperor Kino desperately wanted to monitor the robot-controlled world and lobbied hard for their admission. Why? He didn't trust the robots. Compassion for the millions of helpless men, women, and children also played a significant role in his decision to send Queen Maya there. If anything went wrong with the robots, millions would die rather rapidly. While the other worlds were quite willing to disown all these helpless victims, he was not.

The Senate also made another safety ruling. From this point onward, all Imperium criminals who were to be sentenced to undergoing the genetic mutations would be sent to Proxima Prime. Here at one secure location, they would be exposed to the bio agent. Once modified, they would then be transported to Aquila Prime. Thus, the Senate ordered all outstanding samples of the bio agent, its cylinders, and crates to be delivered to the authorities on Proxima Prime. Their reasoning was this would remove this horrific bio agent from all the other worlds. Hopefully, it could be tightly controlled on Proxima Prime, removing the possibilities of further bio agent terrorist attacks.

This was H-cubed's special project, and he used all of his political pull to get the senators to approve this measure, despite their vested interests in keeping a sample of the agent. He'd also gained the backing of Emperor Kino, sealing the deal. No one wanted this bio agent destroyed or contained more than the Ataro leader. Still, even Emperor Kino suspected that bio agent cylinders were still out there among the many worlds of the Imperium. He hoped that everyone had learned their lessons about this hideous agent and would think twice before using it. Still, he could not argue with the benefits it had brought to the criminal justice system. The cost savings had been and still were huge, especially just now, when the Imperium was held together on a silken thread.

With President Mary's help, he'd somehow managed to keep the Imperium intact, despite everything that had happened. Yet, could it continue to hold together? Could it truly rebuild? This, he doubted very much, which was why he continued his program to create many more queens. If the collapse came, he anticipated many other nearby, mid-arm worlds would beg to join the Ataro Empire. Here in middle of the spiral arm, the Ataro System was the single major force. If the collapse came, could he and his system withstand the pressures from the vastly more populace hub worlds?

He needed to lay the groundwork in advance. Hence, in 1328, he dispatched his newly created thirty queens to key, neighboring worlds, acting as goodwill ambassadors. If nothing else, they would be laying some foundations upon which he could build, if things continued to disintegrate in the hub of the galaxy. Now, the queens' assignment was to help develop mutual defense pacts. If he could get them established, he would have a protective ring around the heart of the Ataro System, a buffer against future trouble.

Chapter 25 Discoveries

Ambassador Lela Agahve-Jones found little to do as Ashford-5's official ambassador, but this she didn't mind in the slightest. She had her own mission, her own agenda: compiling a history of the Imperium. Soon, that subtly began to change in focus. She'd amassed a giant listing of all known Imperium worlds. From here, she began collecting world histories, including respective images of its native inhabitants.

One entire room of their senatorial suite was covered in world labels and representative photographs. She'd used up many color-ink cartridges printing all of them. One evening, as she was staring at her enormous collection that would one day grace her history book, she noticed a very peculiar aspect to all of these sample people. "Honey, come here. Take a look at this, will you?" she called out to Ruthy, who wandered in, munching on an apple-pear. "Thanks. Look at these people, will you. What do you see?"

"People. Lots of people. Why?" Ruthy answered.

"Yes, but look at them. Can you see the differences?" Lela asked.

"Well sure. This man has brown hair, and his skin looks slightly brownish, while that woman there is blonde with slightly yellowish skin. Now that woman over there is a knock-out!"

Lela gave Ruthy a teasing slap on her butt. "No, seriously. What is it that we are not seeing with all these people?"

"I don't know. They're just ordinary people, I suppose."

"Here, let me go at this from another angle. Look, here's Lena Squire's world. Here are some of their native animals. Do they look anything like the animals on our world? Then, here are Broon-5's native creatures. Here are Descartes-3's animals. Here are Hron-3's animals. Here are Carac-4's creatures."

"Wow, they are all so very different, but surely there are cows, horses, chickens, and pigs there too," Ruthy replied, mystified by whatever Lela was getting at with all this.

"Those animals, we know, were all imported to the worlds and were not natively found there when the worlds were settled. Now that you've seen the vast differences in animals, look again at the people, dear," Lela insisted.

"Well, they all look pretty much the same. There's the dark skinned group, as Lena's, but most are quite similar really. A slight difference in skin tones, hair colors, but little more. Why?"

"Don't you see? That's just it. The humans of the Imperium worlds are all basically very, very similar in appearance, and yet, the native animals of these worlds are vastly different," Lela pointed out.

She continued, "Look, from all the records, we know the hub worlds were settled first. From there, they expanded outward into the middle of the spiral arm, and only relatively recently have reached out to the rim where we are located. All of the Imperium people are descended from the original settlers who colonized the hub worlds. Each of the worlds had their own unique biological evolution of species. Each is different, yet the people are not."

"This flies into the commonly held notions the newly discovered planets that have native humans on them, like us a couple centuries ago, developed and evolved on their own. They could not have or we'd expected vast differences in how the people look. Instead, everywhere, people look pretty much the same. True, there are culture differences, particularly on those worlds that are classified as more primitive, like Ashford-5 is. There have even been some virus-caused alterations, as seen on Karlson-3, where Nadja and Konrad worked. Remember, the virus altered their women. Something about recessive genes. Other than those types of changes, humans are quite similar from world to world. That should not be if the human species developed and evolved on each world, separate from all the other worlds. Yet, that misconception is rampant in the Imperium history books. It just can't be."

Lela added, "So, what we really have here are settlers moving ever outward from the hub. I bet in the distant past, some exploring ship crashed on a new world and lost contact with their home world, stranding the explorers on that new world. Somehow, they survived and eventually thrived, but without the technology of their original worlds, they would ultimately have to revert to far more primitive methods, such as those on Karlson-3. You know, hunter-gatherers and such."

"I think you are on to something here," Ruthy finally saw what Lela had uncovered. "I bet that these worlds send out thousands of deep space exploration ships each year. Some of them undoubtedly get stranded on strange, new worlds. It makes sense, but what's the big deal about all this?"

"Where did those original settlers come from? That's what I want to know. Also, did one of those ancient exploring ships crash on Ashford-5, and the survivors begat all of us?" Lela asked. "Just who were our ancestors? Where did they come from? What were they like? I've got a million questions."

Ruthy laughed. "Keep on working, love. I'm sure you will find more answers."

Back on Tierra, finding more answers was just what Elfe and her son, Lelos, were after. She had finally completed her intensive GPMS mapping of the entire continent. Her fancy Ground Penetrating and Mapping System had worked to perfection. She and Lelos marked out known ancient locations, such as the ruins of the old Oakham Tower. Even the ancient Skylar Abbey, where she very nearly died during her first three weeks on Tierra, was plainly visible. Already, she'd explored the ancient ruins of Valcia, the original location of the old Church of God and its Archbishop Mata Hatta.

The GPMS was so sensitive it also displayed the locations where the Underground members had used the Earth Elementals to open up giant fissures to swallow up invading armies, both in the Goza Foothills and then out on the plains southeast of Wye. Those were quite visible and duly logged for future reference. One by one, Elfe and Lelos consulted with everyone they could to help identify the discovered underground anomalies. Although the secret Madiera Tower of Lysandra was also located on her survey, she purposely kept that one unidentified. Besides, it was so enchanted by Lysandra that no man could ever actually see it, even if they stood at its very door.

In May of 1328, Elfe and Lelos noticed another anomaly near the fork of the Brockton River and the great Wyndl River, just north of Madya and before it hit the small, marshy delta around the large city and port. "Look at this spot, Lelos. What a strange shape."

"Mom, it looks kind of like a bent cigar, doesn't it. And those dots. Post holes perhaps?" Lelos suggested.

"Indeed, they could be. I wonder what used to be there? We best check with everyone again," Elfe replied. During the next week, they did just that, along with bringing up some detailed geo-sat images of the location. No one had any suggestions about what could be located there. There had never been any town, tower, or fortress here that anyone knew. The two even took a quick trip to Madya to ask their city leaders about it. It was at this point that the two became far more interested in this potential site.

Via Queen Amy and the Madya leaders, who were part of the City-States Alliance, they received permission to excavate the site. However, the stipulation was that, if they found anything, Queen Amy would have to build a masonry museum in Madya, and house the all the discovered artifacts there. Elfe and Lelos readily agreed to this stipulation.

Mid-May, the two loaded a transport ship with their archaeological equipment and supplies, and headed down there to thoroughly study the site. Both were extremely pleased the doctors had been able to work their genetic, magical cures on them. "Last time that I tried doing field work, I could barely walk or even see the ground over my boobs. Now, we can wear sturdy boots and deal with this without physical handicaps," Elfe declared, as she and Lelos began unloading their equipment and setting up their base camp.

Armed with precise printouts and coordinates, the two first flagged the zones to be searched. There were three, including the bent cigar formation. The terrain was low, grass covered hills. Just a few miles further west of their location, the grasses began to give way to the beginnings of the vast desert, which had once been a lush jungle before the Great Climate Change centuries ago.

Their first major action was to use their GPR system,

Ground Penetrating Radar, to map out the site fully. As the radar images indicated something of interest below the hard packed soil, they placed identifying flags there. Three days later, that task was finished, and the two took photos of the flag layout, documenting their initial work. Now, they had to decide where to begin their excavations first.

"Mom, the bent cigar has to come first. What the devil is it?" Lelos declared.

Elfe chuckled, "I know. That has me baffled too. Agreed, we dig that location first. Let's get out the digging equipment." The object would have been about a thousand feet long, when straightened out, but a third of it was bent at a forty degree angle to the remainder. It was two hundred feet wide at its greatest width. Currently, one end, the southwestern portion, was around three feet below the surface, while the bent end was closer to twenty feet down. They began at the shallower location.

Rough excavation was done using Elfe's GRS, Ground Removal System. This clever device used radar mapping to control its digging process. Ground was removed and neatly deposited some twenty feet to the south of the machine, but the digging was controlled by its onboard radar system, ensuring it didn't hit any object larger than an inch in size. Further, the fine dirt that came out the rear of the GRS was put through a filter, catching any smaller objects.

While they were mostly small pebbles, Lelos constantly kept watch on them, while Elfe handled the machine's frontal digging. It made perfect cuts and also laid out a precise three-dimensional grid upon which any findings were mapped to within a fraction of an inch of their location. As Elfe neared the bottom edge of the object, she eventually had to turn off the machine. "Okay, now it's time to get our hands dirty, son. From here on, it's trowels and toothbrush time." By that, she meant that they had to go the last few inches by hand so that whatever this object was, there would be no chance to damage it, in case it was quite fragile.

Late that afternoon, Elfe and Lelos used small whiskbrooms to brush away the last fragments, giving them their first look at a tiny portion of the object. "Mom, it's metallic!" Lelos exclaimed. What the heck is this?"

"Can't say, but keep working," she replied, growing more excited by the minute, as more and more of the metal was revealed. Soon a three-foot section lay exposed to the orange-red sun. "What is this?" she asked.

Lelos tapped on it. "Mom! It's hollow! There's something inside."

"Could this be a spaceship?" Elfe wondered aloud. By the end of the next day, they were convinced they were unearthing some kind of spaceship.

A month later, the two had exposed the entire top length of the ship, leaving a few feet of its bottom still untouched. At this time, nearly half of everyone at the spaceport and Imperial Castle just had to come to see this startling discovery. Already, Elfe had brought Nadja here to translate the markings or writings they found on one side of the ship.

"It's an ancient language quite similar to the Westerlings dialect, only more archaic. Roughly translated, I believe it says El Salvador, the Savior. It must be the ship's christened name," Nadja explained. "How soon can we get a look inside and see if there are any logs — anything with more writings?" She was quite excited as well.

Amy, supported by Jan, and Katrina, supported by Dr. Whitney, gazed at the excavation, along with hundreds of others. Jan suggested, "It looks like a spaceship, but it has obviously crash landed. Its front, if that's its front, hit first, digging itself into the ground, but it hit that rock formation, which bent the whole front of the ship."

"Yes, that is our viewpoint as well," Elfe agreed with her. "The ship sustained major damage, and it's obvious it could not be repaired. So whoever landed here and survived must have been marooned here for some time. Lelos is working on a draft of it, hoping to reconstruct what the ship must have looked like before it crashed. We've also found nearby other bits and pieces that fell off as it crashed. Show them your sketch, son," she asked.

Proudly, Lelos held up his reconstructed sketch, his best guess as to how the ship must have appeared prior to the crash. Katrina spoke up, "That doesn't look like any Imperium ship I've ever seen. If you don't mind, I'll take a copy of your sketch back with me and run a full historical ship search. Based on Nadja's translation of its name, perhaps, we can discover who these people were and the story behind this crash. What an interesting find, Elfe, Lelos."

"Indeed. Lelos is going to handle the rest of the ship's excavation, while I am going after the second site over there by those flags. There are signs of more metal beneath the surface and possibly postholes. So far, we haven't found anything we can date. However, Katrina, I'd like to send a tiny metal sample back with you, and have your geologists determine its composition. That may give us some clues. Whatever the metal is, I believe it contains a relatively high amount of aluminum. It's pretty light in weight, and it appears to be oxidizing like aluminum does," Elfe explained. Many asked other questions, most of which were either obvious or which had no answer as yet.

By the end of August, the two had far more results to display. Lelos had finished his excavation of the ship itself. Inside, he found that it had indeed sustained heavy structural damage in the crash. Most everything useful had been stripped and carried away by the survivors. He was rather disappointed that he could find nothing particularly useful. Katrina had been wholly unable to identify the ship, based on his reconstructed sketch. There never had been a ship remotely similar to this one anywhere within the Imperium's historical records. However, that alone wasn't sufficient to rule it out. Many world's more ancient records were not computerized and available.

Elfe, on the other hand, had her hands full of work. She uncovered a primitive shelter or habitat. What she suspected were post holes were in fact the remains of a wooden long building, added on to a crude shelter complex built from salvaged bits of metal from the ship itself. She was able to get a carbon-14 dating of the post remains. The date found was between eight hundred twenty to eight hundred thirty years ago, making the date of the construction and presumably, the crash landing to around the year 500, as Tierra now reckoned their years.

Besides finding all manner of strange objects and possibly tools, she discovered some ancient writings sketched onto a piece of metal, clearly a hastily written log of some kind. Unable to translate it accurately, she again sent for Nadja, who became extremely excited over this find.

"It's fragmentary because it's too hard to write much by etching or scratching onto the metal. Roughly, it says the following, Elfe, Lelos," Nadja began translating, speaking into her voice recorder:

> EU Colonizing Consortium left Earth 2154 — caught in worm hole — lost — out of fuel — crash landed on first habitable planet — Nueve Tierra — 600 survived — established base — salvaged equipment — discord among settlers — agreement reached — split into three groups — Adrian going far west — Alfredo going far east — Cliff going just north to the mountains — logs and records going with Cliff — God help us all.

"Wow! This is an incredible find," Nadja exclaimed. "These must have been our original ancestors! Their first names are illustrative, but I wish I had more. It's written in an archaic form of Midlands, and Cliff is a common Midlands name. Likewise, Adrian is indicative of Westerlings, while Alfredo is a typically found Easterlings name. What a find, Elfe!"

"Yes, but what about the logs and records? Does it say anything more about them?" Elfe asked. "Those would be invaluable."

"Duh, no kidding. What I would give to get my hands on those, Elfe. You have to continue your searches," Nadja exclaimed, very much excited over this find.

A week later, working together, Elfe and Lelos uncovered some of the third sight, revealing a cemetery. They exposed ten remains before ending their dig. With Doctor Whitney's assistance, they studied the skeletons. These ten, Dr. Whitney concluded, died during the crash. Broken bones predominated, along with skull fractures. The obvious conclusion was the survivors buried here those who died on impact or shortly afterwards. The study done, the two respectfully re-buried the remains.

Living up to their agreement, Queen Amy met with the leaders of Madya and got their agreement to have the museum build around the three sites. Much of the find was simply too delicate to be moved. Besides, left in situ, the site could be preserved for the ages. Thus, construction began on a simple set of stone buildings, encompassing the three locations.

During the winter, Elfe and Lelos paid a visit to Alpha and Beta on their buried spaceship. After showing them his sketch and relating what they'd found, Lelos asked, "Have you ever seen a ship like this before? Any mention of El Salvador?"

"On it," Beta said in his non-human voice.

Alpha replied, "The design does look familiar. It is similar to many Earth ships of a century before ours was built. EU could represent the European Union, though this is mere speculation. If this ship was from Earth, then that would explain the close similarities between your languages here and that spoken by the women we brought here."

"Yes, Nadja believes they are very closely related and probably are the same languages," Elfe agreed.

"Confirmation," Beta spoke up. "In 2154, the El Salvador was built by the European Union. It was a colonizing ship bound for Alpha Centauri C, carrying six hundred colonists and their equipment. The ship was lost six months after its launching and never heard from again. How very interesting. The ship was blown halfway across the galaxy. I wonder what happened to cause that?"

"Amazing. Thank you, Beta, Alpha. This is tremendous news indeed!" Elfe gushed. An hour later, she spread the word far and wide. Nadja smiled, her old theories based on her linguistic studies had just been confirmed. She decided to write another linguistic paper, outlining her original theories and how they'd been confirmed by the archaeological discoveries.

The following spring, Bernardo and Lena accompanied the pair as their protectors, while they began a thorough search of the very southern region of the Goza Mountains, which ended some seventy miles from the ocean. While they searched diligently, alas, they were unable to locate this new site. Undaunted, the two archaeologists continued to survey and study Tierra, looking for further indications where the three groups had settled down. Obviously, they had to have made some kind of permanent settlements. From these, everyone on Tierra had ultimately descended. These were exciting years for the two archaeologists, who anticipated more finds would be appearing. At least, some of the mysteries surrounding the initial inhabitants of Tierra had been answered at long last.

However, as Queen Amy pointed out, "This means we're more closely related to the people of the Federation of Planets than we are to those of the Imperium. I wonder what that may mean?"

The End.

Other Books by Vic Broquard

Without Warning (fantasy)

The Trident Series: (fantasy)
    Volume 1 The Trident and the Book
    Volume 3 The Trident and the Scepter
    Volume3 The Trident and the Resurrection

The Adventures of Elizabeth Stanton Series: (science fiction)
    Volume 1 The Evolution of the Path
    Volume 2 The Great Messiah
    Volume 3 Of Kings and Queens and Troubadours
    Volume 4 Chaos in the Aftermath
    Volume 5 Power Plays
    Volume 6 Age of Exploration
    Volume 7 Abducted
    Volume 8 The Emperor and Empress
    Volume 9 A Job Worth Doing
    Volume 10 Degradation
    Volume 11 The Second Crusade
    Volume 12 When Worlds Collide
    Volume 13 Dark Ages

The Lindsey Barron Series: (fantasy)
    Volume 1 The Rod of the Apocalypse
    Volume 2 The Board of Governors
    Volume 3 The Crown of Moses
    Volume 4 Dominus for President
    Volume 5 The National Health Care Program
    Volume 6 States Justice
    Volume 7 Cross and Double-cross

Zoran Chronicles Series: (fantasy)
    Volume 1 A Dragon in Our Town
    Volume 2 Dragons, Power, Courts, and War

Planet of the Orange-red Sun Series: (science fiction)
    Volume 1 When Kingdoms Fall
    Volume 2 Dark Ages
    Volume 3 Age of the Towers
    Volume 4 Difficillis Exitus
    Volume 5 Age of the Lords
    Volume 6 The Renegade Tower
    Volume 7 Rebellions
    Volume 8 The Aliens Return
    Volume 9 Power Struggles
    Volume 10 Guilds, Genetics, and Gods
    Volume 11 Magi, Witches, Swords, and Superstitions
    Volume 12 The Voyage of the Eagle's Seed
    Volume 13 Justifications
    Volume 14 Responsibilities

The Return of the Wizards: Twelve Companions – The Making of Wizards (fantasy)

www.ingramcontent.com/pod-product-compliance
Lightning Source LLC
Chambersburg PA
CBHW050840030726
47503CB00007BA/2252